P9-DOH-146

ALSO BY ALISON WEIR

Britain's Royal Families: The Complete Genealogy

The Six Wives of Henry VIII

The Princes in the Tower

The Wars of the Roses

The Children of Henry VIII

The Life of Elizabeth I

Eleanor of Aquitaine

Henry VIII: The King and His Court

Mary, Queen of Scots, and the Murder of Lord Darnley

Queen Isabella

Innocent Traitor: A Novel of Lady Jane Grey

THE LADY ELIZABETH

THE

LADY ELIZABETH

A NOVEL

Alison Weir

BALLANTINE BOOKS

New York

The Lady Elizabeth is a work of historical fiction. Apart from the
well-known actual people, events, and locales that figure in the narrative,
all names, characters, places, and incidents are the products of the author's
imagination or are used fictitiously. Any resemblance to current
events or locales, or to living persons, is entirely coincidental.

Copyright © 2008 by Alison Weir

All rights reserved.

Published in the United States by Ballantine Books,
an imprint of The Random House Publishing Group,
a division of Random House, Inc., New York.

Originally published by Hutchinson, a division of
Random House Group Limited, London, in 2008.

BALLANTINE and colophon are registered trademarks
of Random House, Inc.

ISBN 978-0-345-49535-8

Printed in the United States of America

Book design by Dana Leigh Blanchette

To my dear friends
Tracy Borman,
Sarah Gristwood,
Kate Williams,
Martha Whittome,
Ann Morrice,
and
Siobhan Clarke
for all their help and support,
with much love.

THE TUDORS

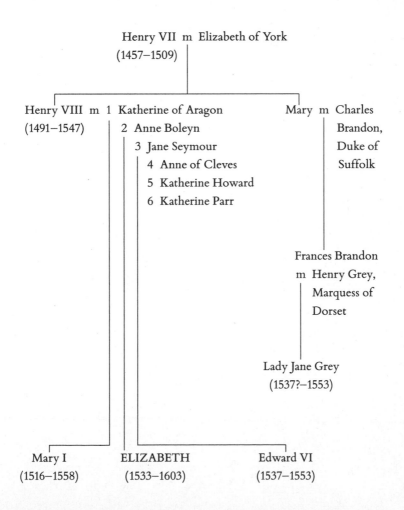

Henry VII m Elizabeth of York
(1457–1509)

Henry VIII m 1 Katherine of Aragon
(1491–1547)   2 Anne Boleyn
                       3 Jane Seymour
                          4 Anne of Cleves
                          5 Katherine Howard
                          6 Katherine Parr

Mary m Charles
            Brandon,
            Duke of
            Suffolk

Frances Brandon
m Henry Grey,
     Marquess of
     Dorset

Lady Jane Grey
(1537?–1553)

Mary I
(1516–1558)

ELIZABETH
(1533–1603)

Edward VI
(1537–1553)

PART ONE

THE KING'S DAUGHTER

On a hot, still morning in July, the Lady Mary, daughter to King Henry the Eighth, arrived at the great country palace of Hatfield, trotting into the courtyard on a white palfrey followed by four gentlemen, two ladies-in-waiting, and a female fool.

As soon as she had dismounted, she stooped to kiss the small girl who was waiting to greet her, whose nurse had just reminded her to sketch a wobbly curtsy to the older sister she had not seen for many months. The child was solemn-faced, fair-skinned, and freckled, with long tendrils of burnished red hair escaping from the embroidered white coif that was tied beneath her chin.

"My, you have grown, sweeting!" Mary exclaimed in her gruff voice, stroking Elizabeth's hair and straightening her silver pendant. "You're nearly three now, aren't you?" Elizabeth stared back, unsure of this richly dressed lady with the sad face and skinny body. Mary was not beautiful like Elizabeth's mother: Mary had a snub nose and a downturned mouth, and although her hair was red like Elizabeth's and their father's, it was thin and frizzy. And of course, Mary was very old—all of twenty years, she had been told.

"I have brought you gifts, Sister," Mary said, smiling and beckoning to a lady-in-waiting, who brought over a wooden box. Inside, wrapped in velvet, was a rosary of amber beads and a jeweled crucifix.

"For your chapel," Mary said, pointing to the latter.

"Pretty," said Elizabeth, gently fingering the beads.

"How does my sister, Lady Bryan?" Mary rose to her feet and greeted the governess with a kiss. "And you yourself? It is good to see you again, but I would it were in happier circumstances."

"I too, my Lady Mary. We are well enough, both of us, I thank you," the woman answered.

Elizabeth, watching them, was slightly discomfited by their words and curious at seeing a pained expression fleetingly shadow Mary's plain features.

"I will speak with her presently," her sister said. Lady Bryan nodded.

"I am grateful, Your Grace," she said. "I pray you eat first, for it is nigh to eleven o'clock and dinner is almost ready." Elizabeth was no longer listening; her attention had now focused on her new beads.

"I have brought my fool, to afford a diversion later, if need be," Mary said, and Elizabeth's ears pricked up. She liked fools. They were funny.

While the roast goose and hot salad were being served with appropriate ceremony to Mary in the great hall, Elizabeth was sent to the nursery to have her dinner.

"I hope Your Grace will excuse us," the nurse said to the Lady Mary. "The Lady Elizabeth's Grace is too young as yet to eat with the grownups." After being pressed into another curtsy, the child was led away by the hand.

As soon as she had gone, Mary laid down her knife and shook her head sadly.

"I hardly know how I am going to tell her, Margaret," she said miserably, looking to her former governess for support.

Lady Bryan rested a comforting hand on hers.

"I wouldn't be too explicit if I were you, Madam."

"Oh, no," agreed Mary fervently. "Does she often speak of her mother? Do you think she will be much discomforted? After all, she cannot have seen much of her."

"I'm afraid she did. Her Grace—I mean the lady her mother—kept the child with her, more than was seemly for a queen. If you remember, she even refused to have a wet nurse," Lady Bryan recalled with a sniff of disapproval.

Mary looked at her with mounting anxiety. She was dreading the coming confrontation.

"Do you think she will understand?" she asked.

"There is much she understands," Lady Bryan replied. "My lady is more than ordinarily precocious. As sharp as nails, that child, and clever with it."

"But a child for all that," Mary said, "so I will break it to her as gently as I can, and may our Holy Mother and all the saints help me."

Seeing her so distressed, Lady Bryan sought to steer the conversation away from the subject, but while she and Sir John chattered on about household matters and the state of the weather, and while all of them toyed with their food, having little appetite for it, Mary, her heart swelling with love and compassion for her little sister, could only think of the heavy task that lay ahead of her.

Why should she feel this way? she asked herself. Why had she agreed to come here and perform this dreadful errand? Elizabeth's very existence had caused her untold pain and suffering, and it was because of Elizabeth's mother, that great whore, Anne Boleyn, that Mary had lost all that she held dear in life: her own mother, the late sainted Queen Katherine, her rank, her prospects of a throne and marriage, and the love of her father the King. Yet Mary had found nothing to resent in an innocent child, had in fact lavished all the love of which she was capable on the engaging little creature, and now, when the perilous twists of cruel fate had reversed Elizabeth's fortunes too, she could only grieve for the little girl.

As soon as the meal was finished, Elizabeth was brought back to her sister, and together they walked in the sun-browned park, away from the palace, their attendants following a short distance behind. The daystar was blazing down, there was barely the stir of a breeze, and the sisters were sweltering in their long-sleeved silk gowns; Elizabeth was glad of her wide-brimmed straw hat, which protected her face from the sunshine and the glare, while Mary, wearing a smart French hood with a band under the chin, was suffering decorously. Her lips were pursed, and she looked unhappy, Elizabeth noticed.

"You have been much in my thoughts, Sister," Mary said. "I had to come and see you, to satisfy myself that all was well with you, and . . ." Her voice trailed away.

"Thank you, Sister," Elizabeth replied. Again, Mary caressed the long red curls that fanned out beneath the sun hat; again, she looked unutterably sad. Young as she was, the child could sense her misery.

"What's wrong?" Elizabeth asked. "Why are you unhappy?"

"Oh, my dear Sister," Mary cried, sinking to her knees on the grass and embracing Elizabeth tightly. Elizabeth struggled free. She did not like to be squeezed like that; she was a self-contained child. Yet Mary did not notice, for she was weeping. Elizabeth could see Lady Bryan watching them intently, standing a little way off with Mary's ladies and the nursemaids, and she was puzzled as to why her governess did not hasten to her rescue.

"Come, Sister," Mary was saying, sniffing and dabbing her eyes with a white kerchief. "Let us sit here." She drew Elizabeth to a stone seat that had been placed in the shade of an oak tree to afford those who rested there a grand view of the red-brick palace spread out beyond the formal gardens, and lifted the child onto it.

"I am charged by our father to tell you something that will make you very sad," Mary said. "You must be a brave girl . . . as I too have had to be brave in my time."

"I am brave," Elizabeth assured her, none too confidently, wondering fearfully what this was all about.

Nothing had changed outwardly—her daily routine had remained the same, and the people in her household still curtsied to her and treated her with deference. If it hadn't been for something her governor had said, she would not have realized there was anything untoward. But she was a sharp child, and the change of title did not go unnoticed.

"Why, governor," she had asked Sir John Shelton, in her clear, well-modulated voice, "why is it that yesterday you called me Lady Princess, and today just Lady Elizabeth?"

Caught off guard, Sir John Shelton had pulled at his luxuriant chestnut beard, frowned, and hesitated, while Elizabeth stood before him, her steely gaze imperiously demanding a response. Not for the first time, he was struck by this regal quality in her, which in his opinion was unsuited to the female condition but would have been admirable in a prince, the prince that England so desperately needed.

"The King your father has ordered it," he said carefully.

"Why?" asked the child, her dark eyes narrowing.

"The King's orders must always be obeyed," he declared.

The little face clouded, the lips pouting, the brows furrowing. Sir John had sidestepped the question, but Elizabeth was determined not to let him off so easily. At that moment, mercifully for him, Lady Bryan entered the room. Always immaculate in her dark velvet gowns, with never a hair nor any detail of dress out of place, she had been ruling her army of nursemaids, servants, and household officers with quiet authority since her royal charge had been given her own establishment at the age of three months.

Lady Bryan was carrying a pile of freshly laundered linen strewn with herbs, heading for the carved chest that stood at the foot of Elizabeth's bed. Seeing Sir John, who had overall charge of the household, she dipped a neat curtsy without in any way sacrificing her dignity, then bent to her task. But Elizabeth was tugging at her skirts. Surely her governess, who knew everything, would tell her the answer to her question.

"My lady," she pleaded, "I have asked Sir John why he called me Lady Princess yesterday, and Lady Elizabeth today. Why is that?"

Elizabeth was stunned to see tears well up in her governess's eyes. Lady Bryan, who was always so calm, so composed, so in control—was she really about to cry? She, who was always instructing Elizabeth that a lady never betrayed her feelings, never laughed too loudly or gave way to tears. It was unimaginable, and thus shocking. But perhaps she had imagined it, for when she looked again, Lady Bryan was perfectly in command of herself.

"You have a new title, my Lady Elizabeth," she said, in a voice that was clearly meant to reassure. "The King's Highness has decreed it."

"But why?" persisted the child. She had a sense of things hidden from her . . .

"I'm sure the King has very good reasons," answered Lady Bryan in a tone that forbade further discussion. "Now, where are those dolls you were playing with earlier?"

"I put them to bed," said Elizabeth, plainly not interested.

"In the morning? The very idea!" exclaimed her governess. "Look, I've got some pretty silks in my basket, and some scraps of Holland cloth. Go and fetch your best doll, and I'll help you to make a cap for her."

Elizabeth toddled reluctantly to the miniature cradle by her bed. It was clear that the answers to her questions would not be forthcoming.

Elizabeth often sat with her governess, being taught the things that all well-brought-up little girls needed to know. They might look at the vivid pictures in one of the beautifully illuminated books that the King had provided, or sort through embroidery silks, Lady Bryan allowing the child to pick the colors herself. Then she would teach Elizabeth how to make rows of different stitches. Elizabeth learned this quickly, as she learned everything. Already, she knew her alphabet, and her numbers up to one hundred, and in chapel she was already striving to understand the Latin rubric of the Mass.

"What is Father Matthew saying?" she would pipe up, ever inquisitive, and Lady Bryan would put a finger to her lips and explain patiently, murmuring in a low voice. Afterward, Elizabeth would pester the chaplain, urging him to teach her the words and phrases that so intrigued her.

"I do declare that my Lady Princess has the gift of languages," he told Sir John Shelton and Lady Bryan, and indeed he appeared to be right, for Elizabeth had just to hear a thing said once and she had it by heart.

When the embroidering palled—after all, Elizabeth was only in her third year, and her quick, darting mind was always flitting on to the next thing—Lady Bryan would see to it that her day was filled with distractions: a walk in the great wide park of Hatfield, a visit to the stables to see her dappled pony, or a spell in the kitchens to watch the cook making marchpane, which she was allowed to sample after it had cooled; the child had an inordinately sweet tooth. Then a story—nothing too somber, but perhaps that old tale of Master Chaucer's about Chanticleer the cock, which always made Elizabeth laugh out loud; and after this, a light supper of pottage and bread, then prayers and bedtime.

Once Elizabeth was settled in her comfortable bed, with its feather mattress, crisp heavy linen, rich velvet counterpane and curtains, and the arms of England embroidered on its tester, Lady Bryan would sign the cross on her forehead then leave her to go to sleep, settling herself with a book in a high-backed chair by the fire, a candle flickering at her side. The room would be warm, and soon she herself would be slumbering, her book abandoned on her lap.

Elizabeth, however, would lie wide awake, her fertile mind active, puzzling over the mysteries and marvels of her life . . .

Her earliest memories were of her father. Her big, magnificent father, King Harry the Eighth, the most wonderful being in the world. It was Elizabeth's greatest grief that she did not see him very often. The rare occasions on which he visited her at Hatfield were the most exciting days of all. God-like in his rich velvets and furs, his jewels and chains, he would chuck her under the chin, then swing her up in the air and whirl her around, she shrieking with delight, her beribboned cap askew and her long red tresses flying.

"How does my little Bessy?" he would inquire. "Are they keeping you hard at your books and your prayers, or do they let you out to play as often as they should?" And he would wink conspiratorially, so that Elizabeth could know that it was all right to say yes, she did spend a lot of time playing, and that she loved the latest doll or toy he had sent her.

"But I do learn my letters, sir, and my catechism," she would tell him.

"Well and good, well and good," he would say, pulling her onto his wide lap and sitting her on strong muscular thighs, with her cheek against the brilliant rough surface of his doublet, which was encrusted with gems and goldsmiths' work. She would breathe in the wholesome smell of him, a smell of herbs, musky perfume, and the great outdoors, and nestle against him, enjoying the sensation of his bristly red beard tickling the top of her forehead.

"I will tell you something, Bessy," he said once. "When I was a young king, I did not wish to be at my prayers or attending to state affairs; I wanted to enjoy life. So can you guess what I did? I would sneak out of the palace by a back stair and go hunting, and my councillors would never know I had gone."

"Didn't you get into trouble?" Elizabeth posited, wide-eyed.

"Hah!" roared her father. "I am the King. They would never have dared!"

"Can you do what you like when you are king?" she asked, a whole new vista of freedom opening up in her mind.

"Of course I can," her father replied. "People have to do my will." There was an edge to his voice that, young as she was, she missed.

"Then," she told him, "I am going to be king when I grow up."

She had not understood at the time why this angered him. Suddenly, he was no longer her loving father, but a man of steel, cold of visage, and inexplicably cross. Without a word, he put her from him, setting her none too gently on the floor, and drew himself up to his towering height, a big bulk of a man, powerful and daunting.

"You can never be a king," he told her in a voice as quiet as it was menacing. "Until you have a brother, you are my heir, but it is against Nature and the law of God for a woman to rule, so enough of such foolishness, for I *will* have a son to succeed me!" Then he was gone, his broad figure disappearing through the oak door of the nursery. But he had been back to visit her since, as cheery and as boisterous as if nothing had upset him. She had understood by that that his rages were but passing storms.

Whenever her father came, her quiet, ordered world would explode into color, gaiety, and noise. He was always surrounded by brilliantly dressed gentlemen and ladies—who made much of her—and attended by hordes of ministers, officers, and servants, many of whom, she was told, were very important people. She watched them all flattering and fawning upon her father, and was impressed when they always did exactly as he ordered. It was marvelous to be the daughter of such a king.

She was a great lady; her father had often said it. All must bow to her, and none scant their respect to her, for she too was important. That was why she lived away from the court in her own household, with her own servants. She was the Princess of England, and—Lady Bryan had revealed—one day, if God did not see fit to send her a brother, she would be its queen, despite what her father had said to her that time. Something called Parliament had decreed it, and no one could gainsay that.

These were more recent memories. The first thing she could remember was her father carrying her in his arms about the court, that glittering world where he lived, and showing her off to all the lords and ladies. Both he and she had been wearing yellow, and she had been aware that it was a special occasion, although she wasn't sure why. Her father kept saying how pleased he was that some old harridan was dead, but Elizabeth had no idea of whom he spoke, and only the vaguest notion of what *dead* meant.

Her mother, also wearing yellow, had been there on that night—she remembered this too. Her beautiful, slender mother, with the raven hair, the vibrant, inviting eyes, and the witty smile. But she had been talking to other people as the King paraded Elizabeth around the room, bidding his courtiers to admire her. It was strange, but Elizabeth had very few memories of her mother and father being together. Usually, they had come separately to see her at Hatfield, and she had understood that her father was so often occupied with ruling the kingdom that he could only rarely get away. Her mother, Queen Anne, visited more often, bringing her beloved dogs, and gifts for Elizabeth too, most of them beautifully made clothes—an orange satin gown, a russet velvet kirtle, a pair of crimson taffeta sleeves, a pearl-embroidered cap, or some tooled leather leading reins. Her mother did not play with her as boisterously as her father, but would sit with her in the walled garden, looking at the colorful pictures in the Queen's exquisite Book of Hours, or strumming a lute— even at this young age, Elizabeth was already showing aptitude as a musician, a skill she had inherited from both her parents. Anne was more patient with her than Henry, and never seemed to grow bored in her daughter's company. To Elizabeth, her mother was the ideal queen, beautiful, poised, and kind, and her love for her was tinged with reverence and awe.

Lying in her bed, with the firelight flickering on the wall, it had occurred to Elizabeth that it was a long time since her mother had been to Hatfield. The last time she had seen her was when the court was at Greenwich, a few weeks back; but that occasion had left Elizabeth disturbed and fearful. For the first time in her short life, she had sensed unhappiness and danger, for her mother and father had been angry with each other, very angry, and then her mother had grown tearful and distracted, which frightened the child. She could not understand why they were at odds, nor why, later, her mother had picked her up urgently and hastened to seek out the King once more. He had been standing by an open window, looking down on the courtyard below, when she approached him, and his anger was a tangible thing that left his daughter shrinking in her mother's arms. Harsh words were exchanged, words that Elizabeth did not want to remember. She hated hearing her father calling her mother a witch, among other unkind names. Witches did bad things, things she could never associate with her mother. And what, she wondered, was a whore? And why should her mother have been so upset just because she had found the King with a wench called Seymour on his knee? There was nothing wrong with that, was there? Elizabeth herself had sat on his knee many times.

She could not recall how it had ended. The last thing she remembered of the encounter was her mother lifting her up, willing her father to take her in his arms.

"She is your true daughter!" Anne had wept. "You have named her your heir, and Parliament has approved it. She is yours—you have only to look at her." Her father was frowning darkly, his face flushed with anger. He would not take her. Elizabeth had wriggled around and buried her face in her mother's silken shoulder, full of fear. Then the Queen was almost running with her, hastening through one lavishly decorated apartment after another, until she reached a small wood-paneled closet hung with bright blue cloth. A young man was there, a priest by his garments, and when Elizabeth's mother set her on the floor and sank to her knees on the prayer desk before the little altar, he laid a comforting hand on her shoulder.

"Tell me, Daughter," he said.

"I may not have much time," her mother whispered, mysteriously— and alarmingly. "Dr. Parker, I want you to promise me something. Swear you will do so."

"I will do whatever is in my power, madam," he answered. There was great kindness in his blunt features. Then Queen Anne rose and began breathlessly murmuring in his ear, her words indistinct, so that Elizabeth could not hear them. Dr. Parker's face grew grave.

"If aught happens to me," the Queen concluded, more audibly, "I must charge you with the welfare of my poor child here. Promise me you will look after her interests."

The kind man had not hesitated to promise, and Elizabeth began to hope that he would speak to her father the King and tell him not to be nasty to her mother anymore. She had been horrified to witness the father she idolized behaving in such a harsh manner toward her mother, and appalled to see Anne's distress. It was all far beyond her infant comprehension, and all she wanted was to retreat into the safe little world she had hitherto inhabited, with her parents in harmony with each other, and she happy and secure in their love.

Soon after that, Elizabeth had been sent back to Hatfield, a new doll in her arms—a parting gift from her mother. When she went, clutching Lady Bryan's hand, to bid her father farewell, he had been his usual genial self, patting her on the head and smacking a kiss on her cheek. Once more she was his Bessy, which left her feeling greatly reassured, and by and by, as the daily routine of the nursery asserted itself, she began to forget the nastiness at Greenwich, and to believe that all was now well in her small world.

Until Sir John Shelton had called her my Lady Elizabeth.

Looking down on her little half sister, who was far too young to understand fully what she was about to say, Mary was filled with all the old conflicting feelings. She loved the child dearly, knowing that she was an innocent whom it would be unfair to hold responsible for the wrongs that her mother had done Mary and her own mother, Queen Katherine. Yet she could never forget that Elizabeth was Anne Boleyn's child, and Mary had hated Anne Boleyn more than any other mortal on earth.

She should forgive, she told herself; her faith demanded it. But it was hard, nay, impossible, for the hurts had cut too deeply. Were it not for Anne Boleyn, her father would not have wickedly broken with the Pope in Rome, her mother would not have died abandoned and alone, and she herself would never have been declared a bastard—she, who had been the King's true heir and successor to the throne—nor made to act as maidservant to the baby Elizabeth. But her father—and here again, there was that conflict of emotions, and loyalties, for she loved him too, for all her fear of him—had fallen in love, bewitched by the black eyes and cunning charms of that whore, Anne Boleyn; and after that, twenty years of chaste and loving wedlock to Queen Katherine had counted for nothing, and Mary's world had crashed in ruins about her.

Her sainted mother had borne rejection, harassment, exile, and mortal illness with great patience and fortitude, insisting all along that she was the King's true wife, and believing through the weary, bitter years that he would one day come to his senses—even after he had set her aside and married Anne, even in the face of Anne's threats to have Katherine and Mary executed for their refusal to acknowledge that marriage, which, Mary knew, was no true marriage.

On her knees, Mary had prayed that she might be granted that same patience, that fortitude. But she had been young, bitterly miserable, and deeply resentful, and she missed her mother desperately. How she had longed to be with her: Her yearning for the comfort that only Katherine could give had been constant, and not even five years of enforced separation could diminish it. And nor, she had found, could death, for Katherine had been dead these six months, poisoned, Mary was convinced, on the orders of *that woman*. She had been ailing for some time, and when they had cut her body open for the autopsy, they had found her heart to be black and putrid. What else could that betoken but poison? And then her father and the whore, wearing yellow for the mourning, they said, parading Elizabeth around the court, gloating in their triumph.

Anne had not gloated for long. On the very day of Katherine's funeral, she had miscarried of the son the King so desperately wanted, had failed him in the same way that Katherine had failed him. He had been King of England for twenty-seven years, and still had no son to succeed him. Just two daughters, both now declared bastards.

Which brought Mary back to the matter at hand, the dread task from which she shrank. Elizabeth's pointed little face was looking up at her, her black eyes inquiring. Apart from her coloring, she was entirely Anne Boleyn's child—even her long-fingered hands were Anne's. Anne, Mary remembered, had had a sixth finger—a devil's mark, some people were saying, knowing that it was at last safe openly to revile her. But her detractors were not so many now, for astonishingly, in the wake of what had happened recently, there were an increasing number who expressed sympathy . . .

Yes, Elizabeth was her mother's child, in her appearance and her quick wits, her mercurial temperament and her vanity: Already, she held herself with poise, delighting in fine gowns and peering into mirrors to admire herself. But was she King Harry's? This thought had tortured Mary ever since she had heard the accusations against the lute player Mark Smeaton. Mary had never seen him herself, she had not been at court for many years, but some of her friends there were of the opinion that Elizabeth had a look of him, although of course they could not be certain, since they had never thought to pay him that much attention during the years before he had won notoriety. It worried Mary, though, because no one else, even the King, appeared to entertain the suspicion that Mark was Elizabeth's father, and it would continue to vex her: Every time she saw Elizabeth, she was consciously or subconsciously scrutinizing the child, hoping to see in her some trace of the King.

Resolutely, she pushed the thought aside. Whoever her father was, and whatever Anne Boleyn had been, Elizabeth was a helpless little child who had to be told that her mother was dead. Mary resolved to be gentle with her, and her innate kindness asserted itself.

Elizabeth was swinging her legs restlessly, wondering when Mary was going to say something. Something in the way her sister was regarding her, at once mournful and questioning, made her feel uncomfortable. Then Mary laid a hand on hers.

"Elizabeth, sweeting, do you know what treason is?" Mary had been agonizing for days as to how she would broach this painful subject. She had even thought of beginning by saying that Anne had gone to live with God in Paradise, but Mary did not believe this herself—the witch was surely in Hell—and her inborn honesty demanded that she speak the truth.

"No," said Elizabeth doubtfully, her innocent eyes wide and perplexed.

"It is when someone does something bad against the King. Hurts him in some way, or plots wickedness. Do you understand?"

Elizabeth nodded. Plotting wickedness featured largely in the stories Lady Bryan told her, like the naughty fox in Chanticleer. She was in familiar territory here.

"People who commit treason get punished. They are put to death," Mary went on.

Death. Elizabeth now knew what that was. The chaplain had explained it to her. It meant your body going to sleep forever and ever, and your soul—although she still wasn't quite sure what that was—going to Heaven to live with God and all the saints and angels—if you were good. If you had been bad, you went to a terrible place called Hell where devils were horrid to you all the time and hurt you with their sharp pitchforks.

Elizabeth had once seen a painting of Hell in a church, and had had to hide her eyes because it was so frightening. Ever since then, she had tried to be good—but it was very difficult, for there were so many pitfalls into which a headstrong little girl such as herself might stumble.

"Do you understand, Elizabeth?" Mary was saying. "People who commit treason are put to death. Treason is the worst crime of all, worse than murder or stealing, because it is against the King's Majesty, who is God's Anointed on earth."

Elizabeth nodded.

"Sweetheart, there is no easy way to say this"—Mary's words were coming in a rush now—"but your mother committed treason against the King our father, and she has suffered the punishment. She has been put to death."

Elizabeth looked as if she hadn't heard. She was staring into the distance toward the palace that basked in the sunshine, her face a passive blank.

"Do you understand?" Mary asked again, squeezing the little hand beneath hers. Elizabeth drew it away. Suffered the punishment . . . put to death . . . suffered the punishment . . . put to death . . . Mary's words were beating over and over in her head; she was trying to make sense of them. What did Mary mean? Put to death . . . put to death . . .

Lady Bryan was walking toward them.

"My lady, have you told her?" she inquired gently. Suddenly, Elizabeth slid off the bench and ran to her governess, burying her face in her skirts and bursting into violent tears.

"Mother! My mother! Mother! Where is she? I want her!" she wailed piteously, her small body trembling in fear. "I want her! Get her!"

Both Lady Bryan and the Lady Mary knelt down, doing their best to comfort the stricken child, but she would not be consoled.

"Where is my mother?" she wailed.

"She is dead, my lamb," wept Lady Bryan. "She is with God."

At this, Elizabeth began to scream. "I want her! I want her!"

"You must pray for her," faltered Mary.

But Elizabeth was beyond speech, howling her heart out.

They were all very kind to her in the days that followed. Lady Bryan found her special tasks to do in the house, the cook served her favorite foods, her sister's female fool made merry jests and capered before her at mealtimes, brandishing her jingling bells, but it was Mary whom she wanted, Mary who was kindest of all, who spent hours playing with her and rescued her from the tedium of the well-meaning Sir John's dull stories.

"What shall it be tonight, my lady? *Patient Grizelda* or *Theseus and the Minotaur?*" he had asked.

"I had *Theseus* yesterday, *again*," declared Elizabeth, sighing. "Read *Patient Grizelda*."

"Listen carefully," he said, opening the book. "This is a fitting tale for a little girl such as yourself, who might profit by its example of an obedient wife."

"The Lady Mary reads stories much better than you do," his audience pronounced, fidgeting, before he had completed the first page.

"Allow me," smiled Mary, taking the book. Sir John withdrew gratefully, but not a little disgruntled at the criticism.

Later that evening, Mary joined him and Lady Bryan for a cup of wine before bedtime.

"Did the Lady Elizabeth enjoy her story?" he asked.

"No," said Mary. "She was very definite on the subject of how *she* would have treated Grizelda's husband."

"Oh, dear," frowned Sir John ruefully. He knew his charge well. "I hope it diverted her, at least."

"I think so," said Mary. "It took her mind off things for a time."

There were no further storms of tears. With the resilience of childhood, Elizabeth allowed herself to be further diverted and, although subdued, responded to the comfort afforded her by others. Praised be God, Lady Bryan said to herself, the worst moment is surely over.

"I have something to tell you," Mary said, fanning herself with her kerchief as they sat in the shade in the flower garden. It was still hot, and the scent of roses and honeysuckle hung heavy on the air.

Elizabeth looked at her suspiciously.

"Nothing bad. Good news in fact. We have a new stepmother."

"I don't want a stepmother," said Elizabeth through pursed lips. "I want you!"

Mary smiled, touched by this, and patted the child's cheek.

"Sister, you should rejoice. She is a kind lady. She has been so good to me, and she is ready to be a mother to you too."

Elizabeth thought about this.

"What is her name?" she asked.

"Queen Jane," Mary answered. "Jane Seymour that was."

Seymour. Where had Elizabeth heard that name before?

"The Queen has made me most welcome at court, and she wants you to visit her there also," Mary continued, then paused. Of the price of her return to court, and being received back into her father's favor, she could not bear to think.

"Sign!" Master Secretary Cromwell had urged. "Submit to your father, as is your duty. Admit that your mother's marriage was incestuous and unlawful, and that you were wrong to defy His Majesty. Then all will go well for you."

If she signed, as they were hounding her to do, nothing would ever be well again: She had known that for a certainty. How could she be cowardly and give in when her mother had held fast and stood firm on these very issues for so many years, and in the face of great adversity?

But Mary also knew that her submission would win back her father's love, so she had written, begging for permission to come to him, had even offered to prostrate herself at his feet and ask his pardon for any offenses she had committed against him; but he had not answered. All he was interested in was her written submission to his demands: He must see with his own eyes her unequivocal acknowledgment of the rightness of his decision to set aside her mother.

She could not bring herself to give it. She was ill, with the megrims and monthly aches from which she had suffered these many years, and she could bear no more pain.

"Sign!" insisted the Emperor's ambassador, Chapuys, sent by his master to champion the cause of the late Queen Katherine and her daughter. The Emperor was Katherine's nephew and Mary's cousin, and Chapuys assured Mary that he had her best interests at heart.

"Sign," he said again. "His Holiness the Pope will absolve you from all moral responsibility, for an oath given under duress is void."

So Mary had signed. Not only did she accede that her mother's marriage had been incestuous and unlawful, and that she herself was therefore a bastard, but she also acknowledged her father the King to be the

Supreme Head of the Church of England under Christ. In one stroke, she had admitted herself baseborn, repudiated the authority of the Pope, and abandoned all the principles and loyalties she and her mother had held most dear, and although the promised absolution was in due course forthcoming, she knew she would never, ever forgive herself.

Elizabeth was watching her sister. Mary had withdrawn into one of her brooding reveries and seemed to have forgotten her presence.

"This Queen Jane," she said, making Mary start, "is she beautiful?"

"Not really," replied Mary, "although some call her fair. She *is* very fair—so pale, actually, that her skin looks quite white."

"My mother was beautiful," Elizabeth said in a small voice.

Mary did not answer. She had not thought the whore beautiful, with her coarse black hair and sallow skin, but she could not say that to Elizabeth, not in the present circumstances. And in any case, she was holding her breath, because this was the first time that Elizabeth had mentioned Anne Boleyn since that dreadful day in the park.

The child looked up at her, regarding her with eyes that seemed old in that young face.

"What did my mother do that was bad?" she asked, voicing the question that had been in her head for some time now. Night after night she had wondered about this, burning to know the truth. Mary, she had decided, was the only person who might tell her.

"She was unfaithful to the King," Mary said, picking her words with care. "And she plotted to kill him." She looked anxiously at her sister, waiting for the storm to break. It didn't. Elizabeth was in command of herself this time. She had learned, in one bitter lesson, that tears could not alter things, and anyway, it was babyish to cry. But inside, she was raging. How could her lovely, kind mother have plotted to kill her father? She could not believe it. Of course, if Mary said it, it must be true, but it was a hard thing to stomach, and she felt a little sick. She struggled to control it.

"How was she put to death?" she asked, staring at her feet in their soft kid, square-toed shoes.

"With a sword," Mary replied firmly, as though there was an end to the matter. That was surely as much as a young child could bear to hear. The details were too horrific, even for someone of Mary's age, to endure, and because of this she could not triumph in the death of her enemy, for Anne had more than paid the price for her sins. Nor was it for Mary to judge her now: Anne had been summoned before a higher tribunal.

"A sword?" Elizabeth's eyes widened.

Mary swallowed.

"It was very quick, and she did not suffer. They say she was extremely brave." She had had spirit, the witch, you could say that for her. "You must pray for her, Sister, pray for the repose of her soul."

Mary got up and held out her hand to Elizabeth. The child took it, her face pale. She was imagining the sword descending, slicing, like a knife through an apple.

"Let us go and see if we can get these flagons refilled," Mary said, leading her toward the kitchens. "It is so hot again today."

A short while later they were sitting in the cool schoolroom, enjoying the breeze from the open windows.

"Shall you like to go to court and see our father and our new stepmother?" Mary ventured, seeing that Elizabeth was very quiet, and hoping to divert her.

"I want my mother," Elizabeth said simply, her voice breaking. "They shouldn't have killed her with a sword." Her control had vanished: The tears were streaming down her face. But she was bearing her grief quietly. Mary drew her into her arms and cuddled her.

"I am so sorry, sweeting," she said. "So sorry . . . Believe me, I do understand. I too have lost my mother, so we are both in the same case. And we are both bastards now, as our father will have it."

Elizabeth ceased crying.

"What's a bastard?" she asked. She had heard that word before, had caught it on the tongue of Sir John Shelton when she surprised him talking confidentially to Lady Bryan recently; seeing her suddenly appear in the doorway, both of them had looked up from their talk in startled fashion, and stuttered their greetings. But of course, the word had meant nothing to her then.

Mary looked as if she were about to weep herself.

"A bastard is an unfortunate person who is not born in true wedlock," she explained. "When a man and woman are married, any children they may have are trueborn. But if they are not lawfully married, then their children are bastards. I don't expect you to understand that, Sister—you are far too young to be troubled with such matters—but suffice it to say that our father the King came to believe he was not lawfully married to either of our mothers, so he put them both away, one after the other, and declared you and me, in our turn, bastards. That means we cannot inherit the throne or rule England after him."

"You mean I really am not a princess anymore?" Elizabeth asked miserably.

"No, Sister, you are not, and neither am I," Mary answered, her tone bitter. "We are to be honored by all as the King's daughters, but in law we are bastards. And because we are girls, no one bothers too much, for women are not meant to rule kingdoms. What our father needs now, so very urgently, is a son to be king after him. We must pray that Queen Jane is able to give him one. Will you do that, Elizabeth?"

"Yes," agreed Elizabeth doubtfully. "But I do wish I was still a princess."

"Good-bye, sweet Sister," said the Lady Mary, stooping to kiss Elizabeth before mounting her horse. "I will tell our father that you are in good health and that your accomplishments are such that he will have cause to be proud of you in time to come. I shall next see you at court, when you are summoned to greet our new stepmother."

Elizabeth did not have long to wait for that summons, which arrived at Hatfield a week later in the saddlebag of a messenger wearing the green-and-white Tudor livery.

"Elizabeth, the King's Highness has commanded you to Hampton Court," Lady Bryan told her, looking pleased. "We must start packing at once." There followed a flurry of activity as a pile of small garments—chemises, gowns, kirtles, sleeves, hoods, and stockings—were dragged from the chest or from their pegs on the wall and packed away in a large trunk. On the top of the pile went Elizabeth's lute, and the horn book from which she was learning her letters. Her doll was to travel in the chariot with her.

It was a long journey down the bumpy Great North Road into London, and not a comfortable one, for despite the plump cushions lining the horse-drawn chariot in which Elizabeth traveled with Lady Bryan, the vehicle was unsprung. It swayed and jolted on the bumpy roads, making her feel a little sick, but she was happy to snuggle back into the cushions and ignore the discomforts because she was going to court, to meet her new stepmother! Near Whitehall Palace, however, their progress became easier, because there they could join the private royal road, recently built by the King, that led through Chelsea and then all the way to Hampton Court.

Looking out of the window, Elizabeth saw the ramshackle dwellings of the poorer people clustered around Westminster Abbey, the solid timber houses of prosperous merchants, the churches with their ringing bells, and the townsfolk bustling here and there. She drew away, wrinkling her nose, from the city stink of sewage, rotting food, and unwashed bodies, or the sight of a beggar in rags, his stump scabrous with sores, but peeped out again, emboldened by the broad grin of a rosy-cheeked goodwife, who boldly offered her an apple from her basket. Suddenly, there was a thud, as a well-aimed egg splattered against the painted side of the litter, and an indignant Lady Bryan shook her fist at the impudent apprentice who cheekily bit his thumb before disappearing into an alley.

All along the wayside, clusters of people were gathering to stare in awe at Elizabeth's fine carriage with its royal crest, and wave to its small occupant. It gave her a good feeling to be accounted so important, and looking at the plain, homespun garments of the common folk, she felt a certain satisfaction that she did not have to live as they did in their humble cottages, but was housed in a great palace and clothed in rich fabrics.

If Elizabeth had thought Hatfield grand, she was struck by awe when she saw the massive rose-brick palace nestling by the River Thames at Hampton. Mighty and sprawling it lay, its myriad windows reflecting the twinkling sunlight, its tall chimneys silhouetted against the sky. It looked, thought Elizabeth, like a fairy-tale palace of legend. As the Yeomen of the Guard at the gatehouse raised their pikes to let the chariot through, her eyes were wide, taking in the spacious ranges of courtier lodgings that lined the base court, the press of people hastening to and fro, most of them servants or household officials on errands, with here and there a handsomely attired lord or lady, or a black-robed cleric. What drew her attention most, as the chariot pulled to a halt just inside the inner court, was the massive great hall towering above her, almost touching the sky. If she had been here before, she had no memory of it, which she surely would have done, for the splendor of the place was breathtaking. And she hadn't even seen inside yet.

Escorted by the Chamberlain of the Household, who had come to greet them, Lady Bryan took Elizabeth by the hand and led her through the inner gateway and up the imposing processional stair that led to the great hall. Elizabeth gasped as she entered it, her eyes drinking in the brilliantly colored tapestries that lined the walls, the jeweled glass in the high windows, and the massive hammerbeam roof far above them. The wooden trestles were being set up for dinner, and she was fascinated to see hundreds of trenchers and beakers being laid out on the cloths. Then she was tripping in the wake of Lady Bryan across the green-and-white-tiled floor to a door to the left of the dais. Here, in a narrow passage, servants were folding napery and polishing ewers. The Chamberlain led his visitors to a small room nearby where refreshments were set out on a table.

"You may make ready in here, Lady Bryan," he said kindly. The governess took one of the brushes that had been set out and began removing the dust of the journey from her own clothes and Elizabeth's, and put their hair and hoods to rights. Then she made Elizabeth twirl around in front of her. The child looked very pretty in her orange satin gown: its tight, square-necked bodice and full skirts became her slender little figure. It was one of the last garments Queen Anne had bought for her daughter.

"Let me just brush your hair, and then we can go in," the governess said briskly. Elizabeth was squirming with impatience.

Another door, more pikes raised, and they entered a huge chamber where the Yeomen of the Guard stood to attention along all four walls, watching all those who entered or departed. Here, there was a great throng of people, mostly courtiers by the look of them, and their eyes were all fixed expectantly on a massive door in the far corner, the door toward which Elizabeth and Lady Bryan were now being steered.

"Make way for my Lady Elizabeth's Grace!" cried the Lord Chamberlain, and the ranks of avid, envious people obediently parted to let them through. As they neared it, the big door swung open and the Chamberlain called, in an important voice, "The Lady Elizabeth's Grace approaches!"

At his words, the luxuriously gowned ladies and gentlemen standing in the inner chamber bowed or made obeisances as Elizabeth entered the room. How marvelous it was to know that these important grown-ups were doing this for her!

"Curtsy now!" whispered Lady Bryan. Elizabeth dipped gracefully, then ventured to raise her eyes to where the canopy of estate dominated the far end of the room. Beneath this, on his velvet throne on the carpeted dais, sat her father the King, majestic and imposing, and beside him, in a smaller chair, a lady in a golden dress with long blond hair. Elizabeth realized at once that this was Queen Jane. She recognized her by her marble-like skin, which was just as white as Mary had described.

Three steps forward, and another curtsy; three more steps, then she and Lady Bryan fell to their knees, heads bent. The King rose, aware that all eyes were upon him, waiting to see what reception he would accord Anne Boleyn's daughter.

"Rise, Lady Bryan," he commanded in his high, imperious voice, and as he spoke, he descended from the dais and scooped Elizabeth up in his arms.

"Welcome, my little Lady Bessy." He smiled and planted a smacking kiss on her cheek.

"Good day, sir," she piped up, a little overwhelmed by it all, and looking around her at the curious, speculative faces, some of which were now smiling.

"I trust your journey was not too difficult," the King inquired.

"Oh, no, sir, but it was very long!" Elizabeth replied. "And I was very bored."

The King could not suppress a grin.

"Come and meet your new stepmother, Bessy. Let me present you to Queen Jane." He set the child down.

The lady seated on the dais was rather plump, Elizabeth thought; her nose was long, her blue eyes a little wary, her small mouth tightly pursed. But when she smiled—and she was smiling now—her face was transformed. Elizabeth started to curtsy, but when the Queen held out her arms, she abandoned the effort and went into them, finding herself enveloped in gold brocade and soft flesh, for her stepmother's gown was cut very low.

"Welcome to court, my Lady Elizabeth," she said, and there was compassion in her voice. A few courtiers ventured to applaud the touching scene; others continued to watch, smilingly or inquisitively. Elizabeth was just happy to be back with her father. She only wished it could have been her mother beside him; her mother had been so much more beautiful than Queen Jane. Oh, how she missed her.

Dinner had been delayed so that the King could receive his daughter, but it was now past eleven o'clock with the sun high in the sky, and everyone was hungry. Henry had decided to dine in public this day, so that all could witness this happy domestic reunion, and presently a table was set upon the dais and a damask cloth embroidered with flowers unfolded and spread in the most precise fashion. Elizabeth was utterly intrigued by the ritual involved in setting the royal table, a ritual far more intricate than any ever employed at Hatfield. Napkins were laid on the cloth, which was sprinkled with sweet-smelling herbs, then gold plate and cutlery, goblets of Venetian glass, finger bowls, white manchet loaves, and chased ewers of wine. The crowning glory was a great golden saltcellar fashioned in the form of a ship, which was placed before the King.

Other tables were being set up at right angles to the dais, and by and by, the lords and ladies took their places, remaining standing until the King and Queen were ready to eat. Elizabeth and Lady Bryan were seated at the top end of the table nearest the King. For the young child, it was a great and grown-up privilege to be allowed to eat formally with the lords and ladies in her royal father's presence, and she took care to remember her table manners. She must lay her napkin over her left shoulder—Lady Bryan helped her to do this—and wash her hands in the finger bowl provided. On no account was she to rest her elbows or her fists on the table, and she was to hold her knife in one hand and use the other to carry the food to her mouth. A gentleman sitting opposite kindly cut up her meat with his dagger, since she had none of her own. Wine was served, neat—not watered, as it was at Hatfield—and it went straight to her head, leaving her sleepy and a little giggly. As soon as the meal ended, at a nod from the King, Lady Bryan carried Elizabeth to the apartment that had been made ready for her, and left her to slumber the afternoon away.

There followed three days filled mostly with feasting and merriment. The King continued to make much of Elizabeth, and the gentle Queen Jane went out of her way to show affection to this child whose mother she had supplanted. Then Mary arrived at court, and there was more jollity, and it seemed to Elizabeth that she was now very much part of a warm, united family. If only her mother could be a part of it . . .

All too soon, she was on her way home again, with Lady Bryan, for the King and Queen were about to depart on a visit to Kent. Elizabeth was disappointed at having to say good-bye to her father, but very grateful to receive an affectionate farewell. When she was brought to him in the presence chamber, which was packed with the usual throng of courtiers, Henry picked her up, tickled her under the chin, and kissed her lovingly.

"A charming child, Your Majesty," observed the French ambassador obsequiously. The King beamed.

"Yes, it grieves us to part with her," he said, to Elizabeth's delight. "She's a true Tudor, there's no mistaking that, eh? Bright as a button, and witty too!"

He set her down.

"Go, Daughter, and God be with you. You shall come and see us again soon."

As she sat in the jolting litter, sad to be leaving the excitement and pleasures of the court for the placid routine of the nursery at Hatfield, and even more desolate at being gone from her father and her dear sister Mary, she thought about her new stepmother. Kind as Jane had been, Elizabeth knew she would not miss her very much. The memory of her mother was still too vivid, and the new Queen could not hope to live up to that.

Several months passed, and there was always a reason why Elizabeth could not go to court, nor her father visit her.

"His Majesty is away hunting," said Sir John Shelton.

"His Majesty is much occupied with plans for the Queen's coronation."

"There is plague abroad. The coronation has been postponed, and no one is allowed to visit the court for fear of the pestilence."

Then Sir John had even more alarming news, although Elizabeth did not fully understand what he was talking about.

"There is a great rebellion in the North. They are calling it the Pilgrimage of Grace. The Catholics are determined to halt the King's religious reforms."

Lady Bryan looked grave, but Elizabeth was more interested in the hobbyhorse that the Queen had sent for her third birthday in September. Up and down the gallery she rode on it, progressing from a walk to a trot to a canter and then a gallop. Careering along in this fashion, she heard very little of the conversation between her elders, and thus never found out that her father had come perilously near to losing his throne. In fact, the rebellion meant nothing to her until she was allowed to participate in the celebrations to mark its suppression in December.

"And we are to go to Whitehall, and then to Greenwich for Christmas!" beamed Lady Bryan, holding Elizabeth's hand as they watched the bonfire that had been lit in honor of the occasion. The villagers of Hatfield were capering around it, hands linked, and the ale was flowing freely. The child's eyes shone, and she jumped for joy in her excitement. The horror of her mother's death was now fading, and Lady Bryan marveled, and not for the first time, at the ability of the very young to live for the moment.

Again, they took the Great North Road south to London. It was bitterly cold, and the governess saw to it that Elizabeth was swathed in furs for the journey. For the child, the snow was something to be marveled at, and Lady Bryan stood shivering as her charge busied herself throwing snowballs when she was supposed to be availing herself of the privy at an inn at which they stopped briefly on the way.

In London, there were further marvels, for the Thames had frozen over. The talk at Whitehall Palace, which overlooked the river, was of little else, for such a thing had not been seen for a very long time. Elizabeth wasn't sure which excited her most: the marvel of the ice on the river, or the joy of being reunited with her father. And then there was her sister Mary, standing beside his throne. After being greeted affectionately by the King, a delighted Elizabeth ran to hug her.

"Why, Sister, you are forgetting your duty to the Queen!" cried Mary, but Jane Seymour was laughing.

"Welcome, my Lady Elizabeth!" she said. "We are pleased to have your company. Although I fear we might not be able to get to Greenwich, for the ice on the river."

"Fear not, darling," the King said. "We will ride there. Wait and see!"

The next morning, Lady Bryan roused Elizabeth early and dressed her in a warm gown, sable-lined cloak, and fur bonnet.

"Quickly, say your prayers and break your fast with this," she instructed, laying on the table a warm loaf, some slices of beef on a platter, and a beaker of ale.

"Why?" inquired an intrigued Elizabeth.

"The King's orders!" replied the governess mysteriously.

Elizabeth was never to forget the day that followed. The King and Queen, attended by the small group of courtiers that Henry called his riding household, led Mary and Elizabeth to the gateway of the royal apartments of Whitehall, where fine horses were saddled and waiting. They all mounted, and Elizabeth was swung up in front of the King. It was rather a tight fit, because he was a big man and they both were muffled in furs, but she loved it; up here on horseback, she could survey the world around her from an unusually high vantage point, and what was even more exciting was being in close proximity to her father, against whose bulky belly she was reassuringly pressed. It was thrilling and strange, and she thought she was in Paradise as they trotted out of the palace and made their way through its precincts to Charing Cross and the Strand. Elizabeth had never been abroad in London before, and she marveled at the great houses that lined the streets, the beautiful churches with their chiming bells, and the roar of the people who came racing to line the thoroughfare to see their sovereign.

"God save King Harry!" they cried. "God keep Your Majesty!"

Her father was doffing his bonnet and bowing from left to right, smiling broadly. How wonderful he was! The common touch came effortlessly to him; he loved the adulation. Elizabeth loved it too, and began waving herself, much to everyone's amusement; and on that day, there was born in her a craving to be thus acclaimed, to be such a person as her father was, to bask in the people's love and approval. No matter that there were a few discordant voices in the crowd daring to yell out abuse at their king; they were in the minority and did not count, at least as far as Elizabeth was concerned. Henry ignored them, and so did she, for there was so much else to cheer and amaze her. She had never known such excitement!

Beside them on one side rode the Queen, sedately sitting sidesaddle and nodding stiffly at the crowds. Born a mere knight's daughter, she was always too much on her dignity as the King's consort, and her natural modesty proved a drawback on these public occasions. But even she was soon affected by the festive mood, and ventured to smile shyly at the crowds from time to time.

On the King's other side, the Lady Mary, an accomplished horse-woman, rode astride, joying in her little sister's pleasure, marveling at the way Elizabeth was instinctively responding to the crowds, and grateful to be herself acknowledging the delighted acclaim of the people after being in exile from the court for so long. However badly she felt in her con-science about it, her submission had brought manifold benefits, she had to admit. And then, being Mary, there came into her head the disloyal and shocking thought that, had her mother not stood out defiantly against her father, her own life might have been so much happier. Yet no sooner had the notion come into her head than she rejected it, horrified; her sainted mother had been right, absolutely right, to stand up for her prin-ciples.

Elizabeth, waving madly at the press of people on either side and all but dancing up and down in the King's saddle, briefly noticed that her sis-ter was frowning, then lost interest as they rode through Temple Bar and entered the City of London itself. Here, the Lord Mayor was waiting, bowing low before his sovereign, and offering his civic sword and the keys of the City. The King touched them with his gloved hand, then nod-ded courteously to the Lord Mayor and his brethren, and the little proces-sion rode on through Fleet Street and up Ludgate Hill, at the top of which, straight ahead of them, rose the magnificent Gothic edifice of St. Paul's Cathedral, its tall spire reaching, it seemed, right up to Heaven it-self. Elizabeth was so overawed at the massive church before her that she ceased bouncing, and she was quiet and well behaved when she walked in stately procession through its portals with Mary holding her hand, be-hind the King and Queen.

Inside, the cathedral was dark and cold, despite the many candles that had been lit to cheer it; stone vaulting and imposing tombs and monu-ments could be seen in the gloom. Elizabeth shivered all through the Christmas Eve Mass, partly through cold, but mostly from uneasiness at being in such a shadowy place, and she was glad when the service had ended and the royal party emerged into the weak noontide daylight, waved to the people, and remounted their horses.

Then the fun began. Instead of returning to Whitehall, the King led them past Bridewell Palace and out onto the River Thames, which was a solid sheet of ice. Elizabeth shrieked as she realized that they were actually trotting along on the frozen river itself, and to begin with she felt not a little fearful that the ice might crack, but her father, her sister, and the Queen were laughing, invigorated with the novelty of it all, so she was soon reassured.

"I said we would go downriver to Greenwich," the King shouted, "and not even the weather dare gainsay me!"

The snow on the riverbanks was sparkling in the wintry rays of the sun; the air was clear and sharp. Their fingertips and noses grew sore with cold as they rode on along the frozen Thames, but no one was complaining. Once or twice, the horses skidded or slid on the ice, although when reined in sharply, they managed to recover their balance; when this happened, Elizabeth squealed, but her father held her even tighter, which felt marvelous.

"Sit up tall, Bessy!" he commanded. "Never slouch on a horse. Chin up, there's a good girl!"

Elizabeth straightened her back, tilting her head proudly.

"Look at me, sir!" she cried. The King chuckled with pleasure to see her so spirited.

Here and there, they passed booths that had been set up on the frozen Thames, where those who had donned skates and ventured to test their skills could buy hot chestnuts or mulled ale to warm themselves. The King waved genially at the skaters, who could not believe their eyes when they saw his liveried attendants and realized who he was; one man attempted a bow but fell flat on his face, which made Elizabeth giggle and Henry's lips twitch in mirth.

"My own jester couldn't have done it better!" he murmured in her ear.

All too soon, the fantastical ride was over, and they arrived at Greenwich, where the King's favorite palace, the place where he had been born, fronted the riverside. Here, all was hustle and bustle as great preparations were made for the coming twelve days of Christmas. In the great hall, the mighty yule log was already crackling merrily on the hearth, and the palace had been adorned throughout with boughs of ivy and bay. Elizabeth was wide-eyed as Lady Bryan led her to the nursery suite to make ready for the evening's entertainment, doubting that she would ever get the child to sleep that night, with all this excitement.

"Oh, it was a lovely day!" Elizabeth cried, clapping her hands and dancing around the room. "I can't wait for the revels to begin."

Lady Bryan smiled, shaking her head in mock despair as she placed a plate of fish, some bread, and an apple on the table.

"You are far too excited, child. Calm down and eat your supper. It's plain fare tonight, for on Christmas Eve we fast, before we feast tomorrow."

But the festivities themselves were to start that evening, and at last, wrapped up warmly again, Elizabeth was taken down to the inner courtyard where the King and Queen and their court, with the members of their households, had assembled. There, by torchlight, they all watched a company of mummers perform a play about St. George, England's patron saint, defeating the dragon. St. George was tall, dashing, and handsome on his white charger, and the dragon satisfyingly realistic, with coals from a brazier glowing in its mouth. It roared terrifyingly, so that Elizabeth hid her face in her governess's skirts, convinced it was coming for her, but then she heard the crowd laughing reassuringly and looked again to see St. George drive his lance into the monster's breast, whereupon it rolled over, kicking all four legs in the air, sobbing comically and expiring melodramatically. The best bit, as far as Elizabeth was concerned, was when the saint rescued the princess and knelt to kiss her hand. The princess—the child did not realize it was a youth playing the part—looked very beautiful, with red lips and golden hair, and the gown she was wearing was covered in golden spangles. Wild applause greeted the conclusion of the performance, and then there was a rush to the kitchen hatches for refreshments. Elizabeth was allowed briefly to join the King and his party in the privy chamber, where, to her joy, she was served candied fruits and spiced wine. Glutted with these sugary confections, she was asleep when Lady Bryan finally laid her in her bed.

The twelve days of Christmas passed in a whirl of worshipping, feasting, and merrymaking. Young as she was, Elizabeth thrilled to the soaring harmonies of the choir of the Chapel Royal, gasped at the sight of a roast peacock being borne in all its glorious plumage to the royal table, shrieked with laughter at the naughty disports of the Lord of Misrule, and itched to join in with the gorgeously attired lords and ladies as they danced merrily to the ancient carols. And at Twelfth Night, she was bursting with excitement when the King's gifts, and the Queen's, were distributed: Elizabeth received an exquisite little silver cup with a lid, and a string of pearls tied with red silk ribbon. The pearls were so beautiful, so perfect, and late though it was when she retired to bed, having been allowed to stay up to watch the disguisings in the presence chamber, she insisted that Lady Bryan put them on her, and twirled around happily before the mirror admiring the effect.

"To bed, you vain girl!" admonished the governess, and Elizabeth scampered, giggling. In truth, she could not remember ever being so happy, and she wished it could go on for ever and ever, that she could stay here, in this glittering, enchanting palace, and never go back to the quiet of Hatfield. If life could always be like this, she might even begin to forget her mother and the tragedy that had overtaken her.

CHAPTER 2

1537

Wake up, my Lady Elizabeth, we have just received the most wonderful tidings!" exclaimed Lady Bryan, shaking her charge by the shoulder. Elizabeth rubbed her eyes, then opened them to see her governess beaming happily.

"England has a prince!" she cried. "Queen Jane has borne the King a son! A baby brother for you, child! Oh, this is a great day, for the King's Majesty and for us all!"

"A baby brother," echoed Elizabeth, wide awake now. At last, she would have someone to play with! He could come and live at Hatfield, this new brother, and . . .

"His name is Edward," Lady Bryan told her, "and he was born two days ago on the twelfth of October, the eve of Saint Edward the Confessor, a most auspicious day. Now we must make haste, my little lady, because we are summoned to court without delay. The King wishes you to play your part at the christening."

"Ohh!" Elizabeth was scrambling out of bed, bursting with elation. "What will I be doing?"

"You are to take part in the procession."

"Is that an important part?" asked the child.

"Very important, I believe," said Lady Bryan firmly, suppressing a smile. "Now we must get you ready quickly!"

Once more, they found themselves in a litter trundling down the Great North Road. It had been ten months since Elizabeth had made her last journey to London for that magical Christmas, and that all seemed like an enchanted dream now. Life had quickly fallen back into the familiar pattern of lessons, meals, walks, rides, and prayers, enlivened from time to time by letters and gifts from her father and her sister.

As they neared the City of London, they could hear a mighty pealing of joyful bells from all the churches. The Tower cannons were booming a salute in the distance, and the people were out in the streets in their thousands, dancing around bonfires, feasting and toasting the new Prince. It seemed to Elizabeth that all England rejoiced in his birth, for along the road that led south to Hampton Court, there were celebrations in each village, with garlands and painted cloths hung from windows and much jollity everywhere.

"God be praised, we are free from all threat of war!" Elizabeth heard a man cry.

"Why does he say that?" she inquired.

"Because the King now has a son to succeed him, and no man can challenge his right," Lady Bryan explained.

"You mean the Prince will be king one day?" Elizabeth asked. She was beginning to realize that her new brother would be more than just a playmate.

"When God calls your royal father to Himself, which we must pray will not be for a long time."

"I do pray for that," Elizabeth said devoutly.

"And we must pray that God spares the Prince to us," Lady Bryan added.

"If He doesn't," said Elizabeth, considering, "might I be queen?"

"Oh, no, sweeting, that could not be," cut in the governess hastily. "You and your sister are barred from the throne, and in any case, women do not rule kingdoms or men. Such a thing would be unnatural."

"I could learn," insisted Elizabeth. "I should like to sit on a throne and order people about."

"The very idea!" Lady Bryan laughed, for she could imagine Elizabeth doing just that. "We have a prince now, and more to follow, if God wills. I've no doubt that the King will in time find you a good husband, and that you shall be a godly wife and mother and not bother your head with ruling kingdoms!"

Elizabeth pulled a face. It would be much more fun to be queen, she felt.

At Hampton Court, she was taken to pay her respects to her father. The presence chamber was packed with courtiers and ambassadors, all eager to offer their congratulations, and in the midst of it was the King, beaming broadly and slapping well-wishers heartily on the back.

"My Lady Elizabeth!" he cried, noticing his four-year-old daughter and swinging her into the air, to her evident delight. "God's blessings on you, child!"

"Can I see the Prince, sir?" she begged.

"You shall, but you must be very quiet. Excuse us, ladies, gentlemen. We will be back anon. I must introduce this little maid to her brother."

Big, broad, and imposing in his red velvet and furs, and smiling jovially, he led Elizabeth through his privy apartments to a secret door that opened onto the Queen's bedchamber. At his appearance there, her women ceased their tasks and sank into billowing curtsies before disappearing into the shadows.

It was very dark in the room because tapestries had been hung across the windows, and it was also stuffy and uncomfortably warm, thanks to the fire that roared and crackled in the grate. In the candlelight, Elizabeth could see Queen Jane propped up against fine white pillows beneath a tester embroidered with the arms of England. The Queen was eating some candied fruits, but seeing her visitors, she set them aside, wiped her fingers on a napkin, and smiled. She looks tired, Elizabeth thought. She is even whiter than at Christmas!

"Sir, this is a pleasant surprise," she said. "And my Lady Elizabeth too."

"I am so happy that Your Grace has had a prince," Elizabeth said, remembering what Lady Bryan had told her to say. The Queen smiled again. Her eyes were dark-ringed and a little bloodshot.

"Elizabeth wishes to greet her new brother," the King said, taking the

Queen's hand and kissing it, tears of gratitude sparkling in his eyes. Elizabeth looked from her father and stepmother to the massive gold cradle by the bed, from which came funny little snuffling sounds.

"Edward," beamed her father. "Prince Edward."

Elizabeth peered at the tiny scrap of humanity lying in the cradle, tightly swaddled in a rich crimson cloth so that only the crumpled face with its rosebud mouth and pointed chin could be seen. He was so sweet and comely, this little brother of hers, and she hoped he would grow up very quickly, so that she could have him for a playmate.

"May I pick him up, sir?" she asked her father.

"Not now, you must let him sleep," he told her. Elizabeth ventured to caress the infant's cheek very gently—it felt like velvet, and so soft.

"He is so beautiful," she whispered.

"He is indeed," agreed the King proudly, wiping his eye. "He is the most beautiful boy in the world." The Queen continued to smile complacently. Duty done, she was feeling very pleased with herself, and mightily relieved. Never again would she have nightmares about being set aside for another, or worse. She knew herself to be invincible now, the mother of the future king, the Queen who had triumphed where her predecessors had failed. She could not wait to enjoy the public acclaim that must be hers once she emerged from seclusion.

Mary too had seen the little Prince and said all the right words of congratulation, but alone in her chamber afterward, listening to the shouts and flurry outside that betokened hasty preparations for the christening, she felt like weeping. Her half brother's birth had finally put paid to her long-cherished, albeit remote, hopes of succeeding her father.

All my life, she thought, I shall remain nothing but the Lady Mary, I who was a princess but who am now a bastard without prospects. What can I look for in the future?

She got up and walked unheeding to the window, looking down on the merry bustle outside. What man of rank would want her now, disinherited and debased as she was? It seemed that the husband and children for which she longed were to be forever denied her. Oh, the King had made various noises about betrothing her to this prince or that, but it never came to anything, and likely never would.

She pulled herself up. One must be grateful for the consolations that

God did send, she told herself severely. She had the love of her father, which had been restored to her, a good friend in her stepmother, and a child to care for in the person of her little sister, the most toward and engaging child one could wish for. And now there was this new baby to love. She must be contented with these things that God had vouchsafed her, and not look for more.

It was late evening, and the air chilly. The palace was lit by hundreds of torches set in sconces on the walls. Hordes of people were gathering in the Base Court, each with a part to play in the christening of the Prince, be it in the procession or the ceremony itself. There were knights, squires, ushers, and members of the royal households; bishops, abbots, clerics, and choristers from the Chapel Royal; the King's councillors, the ambassadors from foreign lands, and a chattering throng of great lords and ladies richly dressed in their peacock finery.

Lady Bryan held on tightly to Elizabeth's hand as she searched for the Queen's brother, Edward Seymour, Earl of Hertford, among the crowd. He was to escort Elizabeth in the procession.

Elizabeth was wide-eyed, taking in all that was going on around her, and very conscious of being dressed in her best gown, the orange satin one. It was a little tight now around the bodice and sleeves, and Lady Bryan had had the hem let down, but with its gay green underskirt and matching French hood, it looked very fine, Elizabeth thought, and it showed off her red hair to advantage. Holding herself as a princess should, chin in the air, back straight, she followed her governess, nodding left and right at the courtiers, as she had seen her father do. Not a few of them smiled and bowed in return.

My lord of Hertford was very grand, as was often the case with many new-made lords, and swept a flourishing obeisance to Elizabeth, doffing his lavishly feathered bonnet. With him was one of the Queen's ladies-in-waiting, reverently holding a tiny, richly embroidered garment, neatly folded, and a golden vial.

"These you must bear to the Chapel Royal, my Lady Elizabeth," the Earl explained. "They are the Prince's baptismal robe and the chrism oil for his anointing. Do you think you can manage to carry them?"

"Yes, my lord," said Elizabeth solemnly, aware of the importance of her task.

The lady-in-waiting carefully laid the robe across Elizabeth's outstretched hands, then placed the vial on top.

"She has no hand free to manage her train," pointed out Lady Bryan.

"Then I will carry her," said Edward Seymour, bending to lift a delighted Elizabeth in his arms. He walked with her, she clutching her precious burdens, to the waiting line of dignitaries, and took his place at the rear, behind the peers.

"His Highness the Prince approaches!" someone said, and the cry was taken up. Elizabeth twisted her head around to see the royal infant being borne toward them in the arms of the Marchioness of Exeter; a golden canopy supported by four lords was above their heads, and the long train of the Prince's velvet mantle was carried by his nurse, Mistress Penn, who followed behind. After her came the Lady Mary with a great company of ladies. As the little procession approached, everyone present sank to their knees on the ground, then rose and took up their places in the procession, which was now about to enter the palace.

Elizabeth felt very important indeed as she was borne along by Lord Hertford just ahead of the Prince, and she played her part well in the chapel, delivering a rather crumpled robe to Mistress Penn and offering the vial to the splendidly vested Archbishop of Canterbury, but by the time the long ceremony had ended, and a jubilant *Te Deum* had been sung, it was well after midnight and she was fighting a losing battle with sleep. As the procession made its way to the Queen's apartments, where the royal parents were waiting to receive their newly baptized son, the Lady Mary gripped her somnolent little sister's hand and kept her on her feet until such time as she could hand her back to Lady Bryan. The last thing Elizabeth remembered of that marvelous night, before she could keep her eyes open no longer, was her father weeping with joy as he cradled her brother.

Queen Jane had looked radiant and well as she sat on her state bed receiving her guests, so Elizabeth was shocked to hear, two days later, that she was ill.

"Her Highness has a fever," Lady Bryan told her. "They say she has eaten too many rich foods."

The anxious concern in her governess's face alarmed Elizabeth. She noticed that there was an ominous pall over the court: People were conversing in hushed voices, and no one was making merry anymore. This frightened her. She liked Queen Jane, who had been kind to her, and she knew that her father loved the Queen very much. She prayed to God that her stepmother would get better soon.

But one evening, several days later, her sister Mary came to her.

"The Queen our good mother is very poorly," she said sadly. "Her confessor is with her, and our father the King." Elizabeth's spirits fell. She feared for the Queen, for her father, for herself, and for that poor little baby lying in his massive cradle. Was yet another royal child to be deprived of its mother?

"Will she die?" she whispered.

"We must pray she will not," Mary replied, putting an arm around Elizabeth. "We must ask God to spare her life."

Elizabeth went immediately to her prayer desk and knelt down.

"I'm going to ask Him now," she said, and closing her eyes and putting her hands together, she began praying fervently.

Behind her, Mary pressed a hand to her cheek. "Ooh, this tooth is giving me misery," she groaned.

"Cloves, madam, that'll help," said Lady Bryan.

"I've tried that," Mary said, clearly in pain. "Nothing works. I must bear it as well as I may. As my sainted mother used to say, we never come to the kingdom of Heaven but by troubles."

"A hot brick wrapped in flannel, held to the spot, will ease it," Lady Bryan persisted, rising to her feet. "As for you, my Lady Elizabeth, it is time you were in bed. I will attend you presently, when you have finished your prayers."

Elizabeth woke to the sound of quiet sobbing. The dawn was just breaking as she slid out of bed and put on her nightgown. Holding her breath, she quietly opened the door to the antechamber. No one was there. The weeping seemed to be coming from beyond the farther door. Elizabeth lifted the latch.

The Lady Mary and Lady Bryan, both already fully dressed, rose to their feet at once. Elizabeth looked from one tearstained face to another and guessed that something dreadful had happened. Mary came swiftly to her.

"Sister, if we accept good things from God, then we must also endure the trials He sends us," she said, holding Elizabeth close. "Alas, the good Queen has been taken from us."

"She has surely gone to Heaven, child, for she did many good deeds," Lady Bryan assured her, dabbing her eyes.

Elizabeth said nothing. She had lost control when her mother died, and she doubted that anything would ever hurt her as badly again, so she was trying not to cry. She was a big girl now, and must accept God's will, difficult as it was.

"The Queen made a good end. She died in her sleep, after receiving the last rites," Mary told her. "We have that consolation."

"I am so sorry she is dead," whispered Elizabeth. "She was very kind to me. I will miss her." Tears were threatening, but she would not give in to them.

"We will all miss her," echoed Mary, "especially our poor father."

"Where is he?" Elizabeth asked. Suddenly, she wanted the comfort of his strong arms, his powerful presence, his reassuring confidence.

"He has gone from here," Mary said. "He left for Windsor before sunrise. He would see no one, and wants to bear his grief alone."

Elizabeth felt doubly bereft. Two mothers had she lost, both in a short space of time, and her father had ridden away without even attempting to console her.

Clutching Mary's hand, Elizabeth entered the Chapel Royal. There before them, on a black-draped bier, lay the still body of Queen Jane, dressed in robes of state with her crown on her head and jewels at her throat and breast. Her hands lay crossed on her bosom; her eyes were shut forever.

The sisters were wearing somber black mourning gowns and white hoods.

"The white hoods signify that the Queen died in childbed," Mary had explained.

They knelt together through the solemn Mass, then when the priest and choristers had departed, they approached the bier. A faint odor of spices, masking something less pleasant, emanated from the body of the Queen, which had now been lying here three days; and when Elizabeth, lifted by her sister, kissed the dead woman's white forehead, she found it as cold as the marble it resembled. Yet Jane Seymour looked as if she were merely sweetly sleeping. If only, Elizabeth thought desperately, if only she would wake up, then everyone would be happy again, and the King would come back. But she knew that the Queen would never wake up, that her soul had fled, and that, in some mysterious way, having the Prince had killed her.

Appalled by the sweet scent of death, and realizing with dread that there were more perils in the world than she had ever imagined, Elizabeth buried her face in her hands to shut out the sight of the white, waxen face and tried very hard to pray.

"How does the King?" Lady Bryan looked up as Sir John Shelton joined her by the roaring fire. It was November, and Sir John had returned to Hatfield as soon as the Queen had been laid to rest at Windsor. Elizabeth was lying on her belly near the hearth, pretending to be learning the letters inscribed on her horn book.

"I fear he is in low spirits," said the governor, "but by all reports, he has framed his mind patiently to bearing his loss. It is said he has also framed his mind to . . ." He leaned forward and murmured something in the governess's ear. Elizabeth, straining to hear, caught the words "fourth time."

"And the Queen not yet cold in her grave!" Lady Bryan exclaimed. Oh, but she *was* cold, she had been very cold, before they ever laid her in it, thought Elizabeth, remembering with a shudder that marble body.

"Master Secretary Cromwell was saying that it is his tender zeal toward his subjects that has overcome his sad disposition," said Sir John. "He was referring to the matter of the succession. The life of the Prince is all that stands between stability and chaos in this realm, and you well know how many children die young. For the sake of all our futures, the King needs other sons—he himself has clearly recognized this. And, of course, there are advantages to be gained through a new marriage alliance."

Elizabeth wasn't interested in marriage alliances. She was more concerned about her dear little brother, that sweet babe, who—like herself—now had no mother to love him. Was Sir John hinting that he was like to die? Please God, no—that would be more than she could bear.

Her fears were immediately allayed.

"At least the Prince is in good health, praised be God—a lusty child, I hear," said Sir John. "And so he should be, for the King guards his health rigorously."

"Poor little lamb," Lady Bryan murmured.

"His Majesty has commanded that the walls, floors, and ceilings of the Prince's chamber be washed down thrice daily, and that none who has been in contact with any infection may approach His Highness," Sir John told her. "You can hardly blame him, in the circumstances."

"So who is His Majesty to marry?" Lady Bryan asked softly, returning to the topic of the moment and glancing at Elizabeth to see if she was listening. The child appeared to be absorbed with her ABCs.

"Well, it was to have been a French princess, I heard, but the French weren't of a mind to it. Apparently, His Majesty had told their ambassador that the thing touched him too near, and that he needed to see the lady before any contract was signed." Sir John again leaned closer to the governess, so that Elizabeth had to hold her breath in order to hear what he said next. "He asked that suitable French ladies be brought to Calais so that he could meet them and get to know them a little before choosing. Well, the ambassador was furious. He said that the great ladies of France were not to be paraded like prize animals in a market. And then he dared to suggest"— Sir John was almost whispering—"that His Majesty might like to mount them one after the other, and keep the one he found most agreeable."

Lady Bryan gasped and clapped her hands to her cheeks, which had gone rosy pink.

"Aye, you may well blush, my lady," said Sir John, "and the King did too. I've never seen him so embarrassed. As you can imagine, he has somewhat gone off the idea of a French alliance. He is looking to Cleves . . ."

Elizabeth was bored by this talk of alliances. Besides, she was puzzled. Why had Lady Bryan been so shocked? And why would her father want to mount the French ladies? That was what you did to horses—you mounted them. It was all very strange and beyond her comprehension. She stared at her horn book. The italic letters carved delicately into the wood danced before her eyes, unseen by their owner. She was too busy striving to imagine her father riding the French ladies, much as she would ride her hobbyhorse, round and round Calais. The images this conjured up made her giggle under her breath. Adults did the silliest things.

CHAPTER 3

1538

Elizabeth hurried down the stairs to the great hall at Hatfield, wondering why she had been summoned there by Lady Bryan. As she neared the bottom, she saw her governess standing at the door, greeting a fashionably dressed middle-aged woman with dark hair and kind, doe-like eyes.

"I had not expected you so soon," Lady Bryan was saying. "Please bear with me." Looking a little flustered, she reeled around to her charge.

"My Lady Elizabeth, allow me to present Mistress Katherine Champernowne," she said. The visitor executed a graceful curtsy, which Elizabeth returned in kind.

"You are welcome, Mistress Champernowne," she said politely.

"I am honored, my lady," replied the dark-haired woman. She had a gentle Devon accent, rounded cheeks, a slightly turned-up nose, and a hint of mischief in her face, while about her there was an air of refinement. Is she a friend of Lady Bryan? Elizabeth wondered, expecting to be dismissed now that the greetings had been exchanged. But that did not happen.

"Refreshments will be brought to you," Lady Bryan told the visitor, still sounding a bit nonplussed. "Please sit down and make yourself comfortable. My Lady Elizabeth, you come with me. We will be back presently." Briskly, she led the way back up to Elizabeth's chamber. The child was mildly curious, and completely unprepared for what came next.

"I must tell you that Mistress Champernowne is to be your new governess," announced Lady Bryan.

"My new governess?" Elizabeth was startled. "But I have a governess. You are my governess."

Lady Bryan took a deep breath. "Not anymore, dear child, I'm afraid. I am to be governess to the Prince and rule over his new household. That is why Mistress Champernowne has been sent here."

Elizabeth could not quite take it in. For as long as she could remember, Lady Bryan had looked after her. In all but blood, she had been a mother to her, the person who had cared for her, nurtured her, comforted her, and disciplined her. All her life, Lady Bryan had been there, and now—it appeared—she would be there no more. It was unthinkable.

"Has my father commanded it?" she asked.

"He has, child," Lady Bryan said gently.

"It must be a mistake," declared Elizabeth. "Send that lady away. *She* can look after the Prince. You stay here."

There was a short silence.

"The Prince needs an experienced lady of rank to be his governess," Lady Bryan said. "Long before you were born, I had care of your sister, the Lady Mary. Then you. Now I am commanded to Hampton Court to look after the Prince himself."

There was pride in her voice as she said it, and suddenly Elizabeth knew that this was not just the King's doing but Lady Bryan's own wish. Her brother was more important than she was—she was old enough to know it—and for Lady Bryan, this was promotion, and a great honor at that. Young as Elizabeth was, she realized that it would be futile to protest further; she must accept the situation. But it hurt, oh it hurt, for she was not only aware that her small world would never, ever be the same, but also shocked at the realization that Lady Bryan's devotion to herself had not been entirely lacking in self-interest. Once again, the universe had shifted, as it had done violently when she had learned of the awful fate of her mother, and less so when Queen Jane had died.

She was a big girl: She was four years old, and she would not make a fuss. She allowed Lady Bryan to take her hand and lead her downstairs to greet Katherine Champernowne; she bowed regally when the new governess sketched another curtsy, and even returned her smile.

"You are welcome, Mistress Champernowne," she said.

"It will be an honor to serve you, my Lady Elizabeth," said the governess.

Lady Bryan beamed. She had no idea of the pain and resentment that burned in Elizabeth's breast, or of the tears that threatened to spill, two days later, as her charge waved her good-bye, standing in the doorway of the great hall.

I am alone, Elizabeth thought. There is no one but a stranger to care for me now. She stiffened her young shoulders and resolved that she would bear life with this newcomer as best she could.

As soon as Lady Bryan's litter had disappeared down the London road in a cloud of dust, Mistress Champernowne turned to Elizabeth and smiled kindly.

"Let's walk in the gardens," she said brightly. "It's such a fine day. Why don't you fetch a ball. We can play some games, if it pleases you, my lady."

Elizabeth looked at her in wonder. Lady Bryan had never suggested such a thing; of course, she was much older than Mistress Champernowne, and imagining that stately lady, skirts and sleeves flying, throwing or kicking a ball was so hilarious that she could not suppress a giggle as she ran to her chamber. And the game was so much fun, with the two of them laughing and panting as they raced across the greensward, chucking the ball at each other and failing, more often than not, to catch it. The new governess had so much energy for one of her years; she was not even above crawling through the rosebushes to retrieve the prize, much to Elizabeth's astonishment and admiration.

Out of breath and still in high spirits, they sank onto a bench in a sunny arbor.

"My Lady Elizabeth," said Mistress Champernowne, "will you do me the honor of calling me Kat? It's so much shorter and friendlier than Mistress Champernowne, and Kat is the name by which I am usually known in my family."

"Kat," repeated Elizabeth, "Yes, I should like to call you Kat—Kat!" She giggled again. "That's a funny name, Champernowne."

"It's an old Devon name," said Kat, "and an old family. Did you know that we are cousins, related by marriage, my Lady Elizabeth?"

"Are we?" asked Elizabeth, delighted. "How?"

"Through your lady mother's family," Kat said carefully.

Elizabeth was pleasantly astonished, but she said nothing. For a long time now, she had preferred never to mention Anne Boleyn. It was easier for her to forget that she had ever had a mother, and therefore not to wonder about how she had come to her terrible end, and the gruesome details of that end. Nor had Lady Bryan and the other members of her household spoken of Anne since that dreadful day when Elizabeth had been told she had been put to death.

But Kat knew nothing of that, although she was of course aware that the subject was a highly sensitive one; and she had her own strong views about Anne Boleyn, her kinswoman, *and* about the man who had sent her to her death. Not that she could voice them to his daughter, of course, or to *anyone* for that matter, but she was determined that, one day, Elizabeth should find out the truth. And if that was to happen, Anne Boleyn's must not be a forbidden name.

For the present, however, that could wait.

"Come," Kat said, "it will soon be dinnertime. I'll explain how we are related when we sit down."

Elizabeth was charmed. Already she was feeling a sense of affinity with her new governess, and a dawning affection—much to her surprise. There was something warm and reliable about Kat Champernowne. Dared she hope that this kinswoman was someone who would truly love her, and not leave her?

Almost immediately, Elizabeth received a summons to Hunsdon, a dozen miles away, to visit her sister Mary.

"Since Lady Bryan has left, I felt it meet that the Lady Elizabeth should be with someone she knows and trusts for a time," Mary told Kat Champernowne soon after their arrival, unaware of the rapport that Elizabeth had instantly struck up with her new governess.

"That was most kind of Your Grace," Kat said, thinking how generous Mary was in her consideration for Anne Boleyn's child. It cannot be easy for her, she thought.

But Elizabeth found life at Hunsdon stultifyingly boring. Although she loved her sister, there was little there for a four-year-old girl to enjoy. Mary did play with her, but she also required her to attend frequent interminable services in the chapel, and expected her to spend long hours at her private devotions. Elizabeth would fidget with impatience as the devout Mary knelt, a still, rapt figure, at her side, and Kat would frantically press a finger to her lips to keep the child quiet.

As they processed out of the chapel after Mass one day, Elizabeth asked, "Why do they ring those bells?" Mary looked shocked.

"Have you not been taught, Sister?" she asked, frowning. "The bells signal the elevation of the Host."

"Father Parker says that it's wrong to have bells at Mass," Elizabeth said, quite innocently.

Mary looked fretful. She knew of Father Parker slightly by repute, for he had been Anne Boleyn's chaplain, and she suspected he was one of those dreadful Reformists.

"It is very wicked of him to say such things," she said firmly. "The bells signify the holiest moment in the Mass. Come with me."

Taking the child's hand, she led her back into the empty chapel, to the altar rails.

"When the priest holds up the bread and the wine before the people," she explained, "he does it to show that a miracle has taken place, for during Mass, as Our Lord promised at the Last Supper, the gifts of bread and wine become His very body and blood, given for us for the redemption of our sins."

Elizabeth looked doubtfully at the altar, bare now except for its white damask cloth, rich frontal and golden crucifix.

"But how can that be?" she asked. "They are still bread and wine. I have tasted them."

Mary was appalled. What *had* they been teaching the child?

"But that is the miracle!" she exclaimed. "When they are consecrated, they still look like bread and wine, but they become the real body and blood of Jesus Christ. I'm surprised that Father Parker has not explained this to you. It is our Faith."

Elizabeth forbore to say that Father Parker had said something rather different: She guessed that Mary would be cross if she did. She was more concerned about drinking wine that was really blood, and eating bread that was supposed to be flesh. It didn't sound very nice, nor did it make sense to her. But then a lot of things didn't make sense, like wicked witches weaving magic spells, King Perceforest being turned into a bear, and his Princess Zellandine sleeping for a hundred years. Elizabeth was beginning to suspect that such stories might be made up. But with the Mass it was different, for if Mary and nearly everyone else she knew—people who were quite old enough to know—said that a miracle took place during the Mass, they must be right, and she, Elizabeth, must believe it.

Mary went straight to Kat Champernowne.

"I am horrified that the child is so ignorant," she reproved. "Were you not aware? As for Father Parker, he appears to have failed signally in his duty. Pray assure me that Elizabeth at least knows her catechism and the Lord's Prayer."

"She does, madam," Kat said. "And I am sorry if I have been remiss, truly sorry. I genuinely believed the chaplain had instructed her fully."

"Not fully enough, I fear," Mary rejoined. "You must speak to him urgently upon your return. In the meantime, my own chaplain will school her rigorously in what she should know. She has no mother, and I feel responsible. I am determined to see that she is guided in the right way. For now, I suggest you keep her at her prayers awhile, for the good of her soul."

"Yes, madam," said Kat meekly, dipping a curtsy.

But when Mary had left Elizabeth's chamber, Kat, believing that there were more ways than one to God, and having something very important in mind that morning, kept Elizabeth at her devotions for only a short time, summoning her restless charge from her prayer desk after just a quarter hour.

"I think we will have a story," she said, "a story about a saint, as it is Sunday. I will tell you the one about Saint Ursula, because it is a special one for you. You see, you were born in the Virgins' Chamber at Greenwich, which is hung with tapestries telling the story of Saint Ursula and her eleven thousand virgins."

Elizabeth settled at Kat's feet. She loved stories.

Kat had chosen this one for a purpose.

"Saint Ursula was a British princess, and her father arranged a marriage for her," she began, "but she wished to remain a virgin, so he and her betrothed agreed to allow her three years of grace in which to enjoy her virgin state."

"What's a virgin?" Elizabeth asked.

"A lady who is unmarried, pure, and virtuous," Kat told her. "So Saint Ursula spent that time sailing the seven seas with ten other noble virgins, and each of them had with them a thousand maidens."

"It must have been a very crowded ship!" observed Elizabeth.

Kat smiled. "Indeed it must. But after making a pilgrimage to Rome and having lots of adventures, their vessel was blown by strong winds up the Rhine River to Cologne in Germany, where in those days the people were wicked pagans and did not believe in God. Seeing that Saint Ursula and the eleven thousand virgins with her were Christians, they tried to make them give up their faith, and when they did not, they put them all to death."

Elizabeth was quiet for a moment, recalling that she had heard those words before.

"All of them?" she asked, after a few moments when her thoughts had been elsewhere.

"All." Kat paused. "Hundreds of years later, their bones were found, and all were made saints by Holy Church."

"How . . . ," faltered Elizabeth, "how were they put to death?"

Kat had been building up to this moment. It was better, she had reasoned, that Elizabeth learn this from her than from someone who believed in Anne Boleyn's guilt.

"Their heads were cut off with a sword as, one by one, they were made to kneel."

"That's horrible," said the child.

"Ah, but I expect they didn't feel a thing. It would have been very quick," Kat reassured her.

Elizabeth turned a tragic face upward to look at her governess. Kat stroked her hair and gazed into the girl's dark eyes.

"Is that—is that what they did to my mother?" Elizabeth asked.

"It was, child," Kat said, still stroking her hair. "Poor soul, she died very bravely. And she could have suffered no pain, for it was all over in a trice."

Elizabeth was silent again.

"She did bad things," she muttered in a low voice.

"No, she did not!" Kat said firmly. "It was said that she had been un-faithful to the King, and that she had plotted to kill him. But I am sure those accusations were made up by her enemies in order to get rid of her, and that they made such a clever case against her that your father the King believed it."

"Who were *they*?" Elizabeth asked.

She's wise as an owl, thought Kat. "Some that were about the King at the time." Kat was not going to mention the name of Master Secretary Cromwell, for Cromwell was still the King's chief adviser and already, she feared, she had said too much.

"And were they telling the truth?" Elizabeth had already had drummed into her, mainly by Lady Bryan and the Lady Mary, the impor-tance of telling the truth.

Kat knew she had to be very careful: What she said next would be cru-cial to Elizabeth's future well-being and peace of mind, but it must be said in such a way as to invite no criticism were the child ever to repeat it.

"A grand jury thought they were," she said, "and the peers of the realm found Queen Anne guilty. But there were many who said that it was all just an excuse to get rid of her." That much was true, and no one could dispute it.

Elizabeth, however, was unsatisfied.

"So *you* don't think my mother did those things?" she persisted.

"So help me God, I do not," Kat whispered. "But I would get into ter-rible trouble for saying that, so you must never repeat my words. My lady, your mother was innocent, of that I am convinced. Never forget it."

"I will never forget it," Elizabeth declared solemnly. "But it was wrong to put her to death when she was innocent."

"Sometimes, child, innocent people have to die. And kings, who have the power of life and death, have to make harsh choices. I am sure that His Grace your father felt he was doing the right thing at the time. You must not blame him."

"I wish I could tell him he was wrong," said Elizabeth with passion, but then, seeing the look of fear on Kat's face, she hastened to reassure her. "I promise I will not, truly I do."

"Bless you, child," Kat breathed. "Come now, let's go and play ball. I'm sure we've allowed long enough for your prayers!"

—

"Your Majesty," declared Chapuys, the Imperial ambassador, suave and black-browed with a pointed beard, "the Lady Elizabeth, she is so very pretty. A credit to Your Majesty."

"Hmm," grunted the King, distracted by the pain in his leg; the abscess was getting worse, and he knew he would soon need to have it lanced. It was so frustrating for a man such as he, who had shone in the lists and excelled at every sport, to be confined indoors through increasing infirmity, and it made his temper vicious. He was rapidly running to fat also, which was slowing him down; ever since that witch had cuckolded him, and impugned his manhood, he had overindulged at table—and would have done the same in the bedchamber, had he been capable of it. Then too, he was still smarting at being rejected as a suitor by the young Duchess of Milan, whose seductive portrait had spurred him to cast off his mourning garments and ask for her hand.

"Tell His Majesty," the impudent young minx had said, "that if I had two heads, one would be at his disposal." How dare she! Was he not the greatest match to be had in all Europe? But no matter. There were other princesses. Perhaps he should consider the one in Cleves—what was her name . . . ?

"I have never seen a child so forward," Chapuys was saying. Henry looked across the presence chamber to where his younger daughter was gracefully pirouetting and dipping in a *ronde,* and realized the truth of the ambassador's words. Elizabeth *was* growing up to be very pretty, and spirited as well; she was not his daughter for nothing, nor Anne's too, he grudgingly conceded. She had her mother's vanity and flirtatiousness, and her capacity to charm, even at this young age; and those black eyes . . . He could never forget those inviting black eyes, was damned never to forget them . . .

Someday, he thought resolutely, he must find Elizabeth a husband. For all her bastard status, there would be suitors aplenty ready to forge an alliance with her father. Until then, she could be dangled as a carrot—a very pretty carrot, who would, he guessed, prove in due course to be quite a handful for any man.

The matter was shelved, though, for Henry was too preoccupied with his marriage negotiations and the discovery of another nest of traitors. After the Easter celebrations were over, Elizabeth went back to Hunsdon with Mary, and there she was once more constrained by her half sister to behave decorously and attend to her devotions. She chafed at the strict regime imposed on her, for she seemed to be constantly on her knees or plying her needle. How she hated sewing! The tedium of it!

Kat reined in her rebellious spirit, but also spoiled her, smuggling sugary comfits into the schoolroom, reading her the most fascinating stories, giggling with her at silly jests and pompous officials, yet all the while imposing her own gentle forms of discipline.

Kat's lessons fascinated her. Elizabeth soon discovered that she loved learning, and proved an eager pupil. Each day she would be up bright and early, racing through her prayers and her breakfast so that she could hasten to the schoolroom and learn more about the enticing wide world that was opening up before her.

Kat taught her numbers using an abacus, and set her little problems to solve.

"If I have five cherries and eat two, how many have I left?"

Elizabeth counted on her fingers.

"Three!" she said quickly.

"Good," smiled Kat, impressed at the child's ability.

Kat taught her to form letters, having her trace rows and rows of them in a copy book. Soon, Elizabeth was able to write her name, and after that it was only a matter of time before she was scribing simple sentences.

Kat told her stories of the kings and queens who had been her forebears; she particularly loved to hear about William the Conqueror winning the Battle of Hastings, and Queen Philippa successfully pleading for the Burghers of Calais, but best of all was the tale of how Elizabeth's grandfather, Henry the Seventh, had vanquished the wicked Richard Crookback at the Battle of Bosworth and thus become the first Tudor King. Elizabeth shuddered to hear how Richard had murdered his little nephews, the Princes in the Tower, and was of the opinion that he had met the fate he richly deserved. How she admired her victorious grandfather!

One day, Kat unrolled a map.

"This shows the British Isles," she said. "This part here is England, this is Wales, and this is Ireland. Your father the King rules all three."

"And what is this part?" asked Elizabeth, pointing to the top of the map. She was always anticipating the next part of the lesson.

"That is Scotland, and it is ruled by your cousin, King James the Fifth. Now, across the sea—see here, the English Channel—is France, and your father is King of France too, by right of blood."

"My father is a mighty prince!" enthused Elizabeth.

The next chart Kat produced showed the heavens, with the planets revolving around the earth. There was another too, with gaily colored signs of the Zodiac.

"See, here is yours, my Lady Elizabeth," Kat said. "You are a Virgo. Clever but modest, and virtuous of course."

"Virgo," repeated Elizabeth. "Does that mean I'm a virgin, like Saint Ursula?"

"Bless you, child, it does for now, until you marry," Kat replied, smiling.

"You mean I can't be a Virgo after I marry?" The child was puzzled.

"You will always be a Virgo, because you were born under that sign. But a girl ceases to be a virgin when she marries."

"Why?" Elizabeth persisted.

"Because her virginity is something she must surrender to her husband," answered Kat, not wishing to be too specific.

Elizabeth, recalling that dreadful tale of Patient Grizelda, didn't like the idea of surrendering anything to a husband. She had already decided that, when she grew up, she was going to do whatever she pleased and not let anyone order her about.

Elizabeth was at her happiest in her dancing lessons. She had learned with ease the courtly steps of the *ronde,* the *salterello,* the *allemagne,* and the *basse* dance, could move slowly and with dignity in the stately *pavane,* and threw all her energy into rumbustious brawls and jigs, executing competent kick steps, leaps, and whirling turns.

"Bravo!" the dancing master would cry, and Kat would clap, admiring Elizabeth's gracefulness while reminding herself to curb the child's vanity, for Elizabeth loved nothing more than to show off her skills. But Kat never quite succeeded, because already she was in thrall to the little girl's vibrant charm, and anyway—she told herself as Elizabeth ignored yet another weak admonition to stop admiring herself in the mirror—a king's daughter should have a certain air of confidence about her, especially one who bore the disadvantage of having been declared a bastard.

Riding was another skill at which Elizabeth excelled. She quickly mastered her first pony and progressed to a docile palfrey. With grooms following and Kat at her side, she rode out every day, around the parks at Hunsdon, Hatfield, Hertford, Enfield, Elsynge, and Ashridge, the nursery palaces in which she spent her spacious childhood, lodging at each in turn, and vacating a house when it needed cleansing. She also liked to accompany Kat on long early-morning walks in the fresh air, whatever the weather, trying to match her stride to the governess's when it was cold and they had to maintain a brisk pace to keep warm.

The afternoons were usually given up to the learning of tongues.

"It is important for a king's daughter to know different languages so that she can converse with foreign princes and ambassadors," Kat said. She blessed her own progressively minded father for having tutored her in French, Italian, Spanish, and Dutch, so that she was able to impart the rudiments of these to her very able pupil. Elizabeth learned fast—she had the gift—and soon they were able to hold simple conversations in those tongues.

One day, Elizabeth came upon one of her nursery attendants singing a song in a strange and lilting speech as she tidied the schoolroom.

"What's that you're singing?" she asked the singer, a woman with fair, straw-like hair and cornflower-blue eyes, who was hastily dipping a curtsy.

"It is an old Welsh ballad, my lady," she answered in a beguiling, musical voice. "It is called 'Carol Llygoden yn y Felin'—the mouse in the mill."

"It's a merry song," Elizabeth said. "Will you teach it to me?"

"Oh, I don't know, my lady," the woman faltered. "I have my work to do."

"You must obey me," said Elizabeth imperiously. "I am the King's daughter."

"Yes, my lady, of course, my lady," mumbled the other. "I'm sure it's all right."

"Of course it is!" said Elizabeth. "It's Blanche, isn't it?"

"Blanche Parry, if you please, my lady."

"Let us sit here." Elizabeth drew Blanche to a window seat, and, hesitantly at first, then with mounting confidence, Blanche taught Elizabeth her song, line by line, until the child had it word-perfect.

"I shall go and sing it to Kat!" Elizabeth cried, and hastened to show off her perfect rendering of the Welsh tongue to Kat.

"I have learned a new song," she announced. "I will sing it for you."

Kat seated herself on the settle, laying aside her hemming.

"Now listen," instructed the child. And she sang the Welsh carol, without faltering once, in a clear, true voice. Kat clapped in admiration when it ended.

"Where did you learn that?" she asked, astonished.

"From Blanche Parry," said Elizabeth. "I want her to teach me more Welsh."

"That would be most fitting," Kat pronounced. "Your grandfather, King Henry the Seventh, was half Welsh and descended from the ancient princes of Wales. He was born in Wales, at Pembroke, and the name Tudor, the name of your House, is Welsh. I will see that Blanche is granted an hour or two each week to teach you the Welsh language."

And that was what happened. Blanche was not the greatest of educators, but she was able to teach Elizabeth songs and poems, and their meanings. And during those hours spent together, Blanche conceived a great devotion for her vivacious young mistress, who was so interested in the history and traditions of a conquered people, and who was so friendly and kind.

On the day Elizabeth gave her a red ribbon, which she thought would look pretty in Blanche's hair, the woman was overcome and barely able to speak, and when she recovered her tongue, she fell to her knees.

"I would serve you forever, my lady, so God spare me," she declared fervently. Elizabeth smiled; Blanche's response was so gratifying.

"I will see to it!" she said. "You must stay with me."

"I will, I promise!" cried the Welshwoman.

CHAPTER 4

Whitehall Palace was thronged with people when the six-year-old Elizabeth and her small train arrived for the Christmas season. An air of happy anticipation filled the air, and it was not inspired solely by the coming festivities.

"I cannot wait to meet my new stepmother," Elizabeth declared as they followed the Lord Chamberlain to the apartment that had been made ready for her, one that overlooked the broad Thames meandering downstream to London.

"Well, my lady, you will have to be patient because, from what I've heard, she is still in Calais waiting for a fair wind," said Kat, opening a traveling chest.

"There are so many ladies at court!" Elizabeth had marveled at their rich gowns, their bejeweled hoods, their air of sophistication.

"The King your father will have invited them in honor of the new Queen," Kat explained, unpacking chemises and nightgowns. "I'll warrant he has already appointed some of them to her household."

"They say she is very beautiful," Elizabeth said. "And I hope she is kind too."

"I'm sure she will be." Kat smiled.

The King, when he received his younger daughter in the presence chamber, was in high spirits.

"Greetings, my Lady Bessy! Your sister Mary is already here, and your brother the Prince arrives tomorrow."

"I am very glad of that, sir," Elizabeth said, delighted to be with her father again. "I cannot wait for him to come. I do not see him often, but I think of him a lot. And I have made him another shirt." She pulled a wry face.

King Henry smiled. "I am sure he will look well in it, however begrudging the effort to make it!"

"Oh, but sir——" Elizabeth protested.

"No matter. I recall that, when I was a boy, I chafed at being made to sit indoors scribing when I could have been practicing in the tiltyard or shooting at the butts. It was the same when I became King and found myself burdened with state business; all I wanted to do was go hunting——"

He broke off, remembering those heady early days when he had been a young god in the saddle and in the bedchamber, when the world had seemed full of promise, and Kate and he had loved each other. That was before the Great Matter had blighted his life. Now Kate had been dead these four years, Anne too, God damn her, then Jane . . . and he was a fat, aging man who was contemplating marrying a fourth wife to provide more heirs for his kingdom, and hoping to find love just one more time before eternity claimed him.

"We are two of a kind, Bessy," he said ruefully. "We do our duty against our greater desires." Elizabeth thrilled to hear him say that.

"I try to be like you, sir," she said eagerly.

Henry considered her, this fiery little flame-haired child, who had been born of his desperate lust for her mother, and conceived before their marriage.

"You *are* like me," he said. Indeed, she was so like him there could be no disputing that she was his daughter, although there were those who had cast doubts on that, in view of what had been proved against Anne later. But Elizabeth had much of him in her—and much of her mother too, he conceded, or rather, the best of her mother: It was becoming more apparent every time he saw her. She had Anne's wit, her sense of humor, her strength of character, her inviting eyes . . . How they had bewitched him! Had she really betrayed him with all those men? He had to believe it. Yet doubts tortured him still. Would he never be free of Anne Boleyn?

But Anne was no more. It was her daughter who stood before him, a daughter whom he had deprived of a mother. With justification, of course; he had been right to act as he had, entirely right. And now that lack would be rectified.

"Will you be pleased to welcome your stepmother?" he asked.

"Oh, yes, sir. I hear she is very beautiful."

"That is so, they tell me. Master Cromwell says she excels both the sun and the moon. And Master Holbein has painted her likeness for me." He took from his bosom a tiny circular box of white ivory, carved like a rose just coming into bloom, and lifted the lid to show the child what lay therein. It was the picture of a lady with delicately lidded eyes, a faint blush on her creamy cheeks, and the hint of a smile on her red lips.

"She *is* beautiful!" Elizabeth cried, thinking how gentle and kind the Princess looked.

Henry gazed at the miniature.

"Anna," he breathed. "Anna of Cleves. God speed her coming!"

The next day, the Lady Mary took Elizabeth to see their brother, Prince Edward, a solemn two-year-old whom they found seated on the floor of his opulent nursery, surrounded by building blocks, a miniature wooden dagger and shield, a gold rattle, a spinning top, a hobbyhorse, and a pretty white poodle, which, Elizabeth remembered, had once belonged to his mother, Queen Jane. His nurse, Mistress Penn, a homely woman with a white apron over her dove-gray gown, rose as the King's daughters entered, and bobbed.

Elizabeth curtsied low before the Prince, who looked up and fixed his ice-blue gaze on her. Beneath his wide-brimmed feathered hat and bonnet, his straight fringe was very fair, his round cheeks rosy, his mouth cherry red, and his chin tapering to a determined point. Mistress Penn lifted him onto her lap.

"Say welcome to your sisters, my Lady Mary and my Lady Elizabeth," she instructed.

"Welcome, Lady Mary, Lady Lisbeth," lisped the infant. He did not smile.

"I have a gift for you, Brother," said Elizabeth, holding out the finely stitched cambric shirt. Edward stretched out a fat hand to take it from her, studied it for a moment, lost interest, and handed it to his nurse.

"I am sure he will look very fine in it, my lady," smiled Mistress Penn.

"May I hold him?" Elizabeth asked, seating herself beside the nurse and making a lap. The nurse lifted the infant carefully, and he settled contentedly into Elizabeth's arms.

"My Lord Prince is heavy," the child said, relishing the warm closeness of the little body snuggled against her. "Aren't you, Brother?"

He raised steely blue eyes to her. Their father looked out of them.

"Aren't you going to smile for me?" prompted Elizabeth, pulling a face. There was a faint reaction, no more.

"He'll soon find his tongue, my lady," predicted the nurse.

Gently, Elizabeth tickled the Prince's sides. He jumped in her arms and chuckled.

"You've done well with him, my lady," Mistress Penn remarked. "He's a solemn boy and rarely smiles."

Edward was now beaming at Elizabeth. She beamed back and bent to rub noses with him.

"May I hold him now?" asked Mary. The nurse passed Edward to her, and Mary seated him on her knee, crooning to him, caressing him, and hugging him tightly to her. The child bore this for a few moments before struggling to get down, much to her evident disappointment. He toddled over to his playthings and picked up the hobbyhorse; soon he was careering around the room on it, chasing an imaginary quarry.

"When the Queen arrives," Elizabeth said, "I hope we will all be able to live together at court."

Mary looked doubtful.

"We must wait on the will of our father and our new stepmother," she said.

Just then, Edward drew to a halt in front of them.

"Bow!" he piped imperiously. His sisters looked at him in surprise, hesitating.

"Bow!" he repeated. "I'm going to be king, like my father!"

Mary and Elizabeth rose, suppressing their smiles, and swept deep curtsies before him.

"Rise," he ordered them, in perfect imitation of King Henry. The sisters obeyed.

"Now you may go," Edward said. Mrs. Penn was shaking her head at his forwardness.

As they left, Elizabeth took a rather sticky piece of marchpane from her pocket and pressed it into the nurse's hand.

"Give this to the Prince," she whispered.

Christmas had passed in a whirl of festivities, with everyone eagerly anticipating the coming of the new Queen. Now the New Year's Eve revels were in full swing: The great hall at Whitehall was packed with people; candles flickered, the fire roared in the great hearth, dogs scavenged for scraps, and servants with ewers were passing about the room, topping up goblets. Elizabeth was enjoying herself hugely. The Lord of Misrule had demanded a forfeit of her, and she was commanded to kiss the ten most handsome gentlemen in the room. Everyone, her father included, roared with mirth as she selected first this man, then that, and, with eyes screwed shut, offered a puckered-up mouth to each. In the end, she was so helpless with laughter that she had to abandon the play for a space, holding her aching sides till she got her breath back.

"What of me?" cried the King with mock indignation. "Am I not the handsomest man in the room?" Elizabeth, still breathless, ran to him and planted a big kiss on his lips. The courtiers clapped and cheered.

"Of course you are, sir!" she panted.

It was at that point that a messenger in the King's livery entered and whispered in her father's ear. Henry smiled broadly, drew himself to his majestic height, and raised his hand for silence.

"Great news, my lords and ladies! The Princess Anna of Cleves is arrived safely in this kingdom and is even now at Rochester. What say you? Shall we await her formal reception before we behold our bride, or shall we ride to Rochester now, in the guise of an ardent suitor, to nourish love?"

The company, flushed with wine, shouted their approval of the latter plan, and soon Elizabeth was standing at the front of the throng gathered in the palace courtyard to wave good-bye to the King and the eight gentlemen who were to accompany him.

"The furs, Sir Anthony! My gift to the Princess! Did you remember them?" Henry cried as, swathed in sables, he hauled himself into the saddle.

"I have them here, Sire," smiled Sir Anthony Browne.

The King grinned, clapped his bonnet down firmly on his head, and waved to his watching courtiers.

"We will see you, one and all, very soon, then we will repair to Greenwich for the wedding. Farewell!"

"God speed Your Grace!" the gentlemen and ladies cried. "Go to it, old goat!" Elizabeth heard someone mutter.

"Can I come?" she cried impulsively as the King wheeled his horse around.

"Not tonight, Bessy! I go to nourish love, and little girls might get in the way!" her father replied jovially, then he was gone, clattering through the palace gateway at the head of his train.

CHAPTER 5

No one knew when the King would return, so the Lord Chamberlain announced that the New Year's Day revels would proceed as planned without him. Elizabeth spent much of the day in her chamber with Kat, both of them kneeling before the fire and labeling the gifts they would distribute that night.

It was late in the afternoon, already dark outside, when Elizabeth clapped her hand to her mouth.

"I forgot! I promised the Lady Mary I would join her in chapel for Vespers," she exclaimed.

"Don't worry," said Kat, looking at the hourglass. "If we hasten now, we won't be late."

She fetched Elizabeth's cloak and gloves, helped her to put them on, then escorted her down the spiral stair to the courtyard. The chapel lay opposite, and the glow of candles could be seen through its stained-glass windows. Mary would already be at her devotions.

Elizabeth could hear hooves pounding on the hard ground, coming closer and closer. She and Kat stood back to give the approaching riders a wide berth. Through the gate they rode, trotting now, and Elizabeth was thrilled to see her father the King, back in time after all for the evening's frolics. Thrilled, and then perturbed, because he did not look like a happy bridegroom. Indeed, his face was rigid with what appeared to be anger, and he seemed completely unaware that she was there. Glowering, he dismounted heavily, then stumped off toward his apartments, his long-faced gentlemen following at a safe distance as stable lads hastened to take the horses.

Elizabeth and Kat looked at each other, stupefied.

"Why does my father look so cross?" Elizabeth asked.

"I cannot think," replied Kat. "Hurry, my lady, we will be late for chapel."

Mary, on her knees, glanced up briefly in reproof as they hurried in, then quietly returned to her prayers. Elizabeth found it hard to concentrate and made the responses mechanically. Why had her father looked so fearfully angry?

She felt a chill of apprehension. She had learned by now that when her father was angered, bad things happened. His wrath was far more frightening than most men's, for it held the power of life and death. People had even died . . . She moved closer to Kat and clutched her hand.

Henry frowned as he took his place on the dais for the feast. He sat there, enormous in his jeweled doublet, a feathered hat perched on his balding, graying head, obviously fuming, as his narrow eyes raked over his courtiers. The presence chamber was quiet; instead of the usual hum of conversation, he could hear muffled coughs, the odd sniff, and stifled whispers. He espied his daughters, regarding him with anxious eyes from their places at the end of the high table. They, like he, had been let down. They had been expecting a stepmother, he a wife he could love. He felt like exploding.

Where was that villain Cromwell? He should be here! And here he was, all smiles and affability, entering the room late, after his sovereign. But discourtesy was the least of it, Henry thought.

Cromwell's eyes met those of the King, and his smile faltered and died. The court collectively held its breath, looking from one to the other. Elizabeth, who missed little, realized at once that Master Cromwell had in some way offended her father. So *that* was why the King was in a bad mood. Things were beginning to make sense.

"We missed you on our return, Master Secretary," Henry said ominously, his voice tight.

"I crave Your Majesty's pardon," answered Cromwell smoothly. "I was dressing for the feast. I was unaware until an hour ago that Your Majesty *had* returned."

"We returned, Master Secretary, because there was nothing to stay in Rochester for." The King's voice was icy.

"Is Your Majesty saying that the Princess Anna was not there?" asked Cromwell. The courtiers were devouring every word.

"Oh, she was there, Master Secretary, she was there."

"That is a relief, Sire," babbled Cromwell. "And how does Your Majesty like the Queen?"

The King leaned forward menacingly.

"I like her not. I like her not!" The last words were spat out staccato. "She is nothing so well as she was spoken of, by you and others. And if I had known as much before as I know now, she would never have come into this realm!"

He sat back in his chair, looking like a lion about to pounce on its prey.

"What remedy, Master Cromwell? What remedy?"

Cromwell looked like a man who had just been punched.

"Sire, the contract has been signed and agreed. There might be difficulties . . ." Looking at his master's face, he added quickly, "But I will look at it carefully and see if there is a way out."

"You had better find one," said the King. "You got me into this pass, and you are going to get me out of it!"

When Cromwell had scuttled off like a whipped cur, Henry nodded at the minstrels. They began to play, and the courtiers thankfully resumed their conversations in a subdued fashion. Elizabeth felt uncomfortable. This was not the happy New Year's Day revelry she had anticipated, and she now feared she might not be getting a new stepmother after all. Nor could she understand why, for the Princess Anna had looked so lovely in her picture. What did her father not like about her?

She realized that the King was grumbling to the Duke of Norfolk, who sat at his left.

"Poor men can marry the woman of their choice," Henry was saying plaintively, "but princes must take as is brought them by others. Whom can men trust?"

"Your Majesty is ill served," observed the Duke, shaking his head in sympathy. "No doubt about it."

"Indeed I am," agreed Henry sadly. "But must I needs put my neck in the yoke? What remedy is there?"

"We must hope that Master Cromwell will find one, Sire," soothed the Duke. Elizabeth was surprised to see his thin lips curl in a furtive smile.

The next day, the court moved to Greenwich, regardless of the fact that no one now knew whether or not the royal wedding would be taking place there. The King had left the feast early on the previous evening, and no one had seen him since, while Master Secretary Cromwell had gone to ground somewhere.

Before they departed, Elizabeth paid a farewell visit to her brother Edward, who was to leave shortly for Hertford Castle. She had seen him several times over the past days, and he now knew her and greeted her enthusiastically.

"Lisbeth!" he shrieked as she entered the room, and he ran with arms outstretched to embrace her. Imperious he might be on occasions, but he was also an adorable toddler, and her heart swelled with love for him.

His attendant, a woman, curtsied. Elizabeth stopped. It was Lady Bryan.

"My Lady Elizabeth, you are most welcome," she said composedly.

"I thank you." Elizabeth nodded stiffly. She still felt the pain of her former governess's desertion. "I came to see my lord the Prince."

Lady Bryan recognized the snub.

"I will send Mistress Penn in," she said, and withdrew.

"I am going to Greenwich," Elizabeth told Edward, cradling him on her lap. "I came to say farewell. I must hurry. God grant that we shall meet again soon, sweet Brother. And God keep you until then."

A kiss, a curtsy, and she was gone. She did not see the tear run down the little boy's cheek as the door closed behind her.

"The King's wedding *is* going ahead tomorrow," Kat said excitedly, coming into Elizabeth's chamber. "I heard some courtiers talking."

"Will I be going?" asked Elizabeth, looking up from her book. "I could wear my new blue gown."

"I'm not sure, my lady," Kat replied uncertainly. "You must wait to be summoned."

"I hope I am," the child said. "It's Twelfth Night tomorrow. There will be feasting and revels. I do so want to be there!"

She waited, fretting. The hours passed. Nothing happened. The King did not send for her.

Elizabeth was bitterly disappointed to discover, late the next morning, that the wedding had already taken place, in a private ceremony in the chapel.

"Never mind," said Kat, "the good news is that you are to attend His Majesty in his presence chamber this evening. There will be a masque and dancing and the usual revelry for Twelfth Night."

Elizabeth clapped her hands in glee. This was what she loved best . . .

"The blue gown, I think," said Kat, smiling.

The King, flushed with fine wine, sat glowering at the masquers, who were nervously performing a piece in which Hymen, the God of Marriage, was blessing the wedding of Orpheus and Eurydice and encouraging them to be fruitful. Young girls of good family in flowing white robes were trilling in praise of nuptial bliss while weaving in and out in an intricate dance.

Elizabeth thought the players were enchanting and the singing beautiful, but she was equally interested in the new Queen, who sat stiffly beside the King, her angular face set in a smile that did not reach her heavy-lidded eyes. She was not much like her picture, Elizabeth thought, and her outlandish German gown was frightfully unflattering, and lacked the long train that was de rigueur at court. Worse still, worse than the deep, guttural voice with which Anna had greeted her on her presentation the previous day, was the unsavory odor of unwashed linen and stale fish that the Princess carried everywhere with her. Yet she was amiable enough, and seemed well disposed toward her new stepdaughters, so Elizabeth steeled herself to overlook that, wondering only what her father, that most fastidious of men, would have to say about it.

He certainly did not appear very pleased with his new bride, and that unfortunate lady now looked plainly terrified, as well she might, for Henry's good manners—stretched to the limit these past days—had finally failed him, and no one could be in any doubt that he was in a very bad temper indeed. Contrary to his normal fashion, he had not applauded the masquers once, and consequently they had played to a silent court.

Hymen was now addressing His Majesty, reminding him of the joys to be had in the marriage bed. Elizabeth couldn't understand much of what he said, but her father didn't seem very pleased by it; in fact, he looked anything but joyful.

After the masque had ended and the relieved players had fled the chamber, the King's jester, Will Somers, tried to raise a smile by telling some jokes, but Henry still sat with a face like thunder, eyes narrowed. Somers rashly decided to take advantage of his fool's immunity and plunged on.

"Are we keeping you from your sport, Harry? Go to it, man, delay no longer! Take your sweet bride to bed and swive her lustily!"

The King banged his fist on the table, and everyone jumped.

"Enough!" he snarled. "Hold your tongue, Fool. Remember, the Queen and the ladies are present."

He waved Somers away and signaled to the musicians once more.

"Play!" he commanded.

The music began, a lilting melody with a lively drumbeat. Henry surveyed his courtiers with a jaundiced eye.

"What ails you all?" he barked. "Up, up, dance!"

Several gentlemen rose hastily, bowed to their ladies, and led them onto the floor. Elizabeth was tapping her foot in time to the music, praying that someone would ask her to dance, when she saw the King turn to the Queen, a malicious twinkle in his eye.

"Will you do me the honor, madam?" he asked.

Queen Anna looked perplexed and turned to her interpreter, the stately German matron standing at her elbow, for enlightenment.

"Madam, the King wishes you to dance," frowned the matron disapprovingly, as if this were a most outlandish and immoral request. Henry glared at her.

Anna's face fell, and she spoke in a low voice to the interpreter.

"Your Majesty, the Queen does not dance," announced that lady virtuously. "We do not have dancing in Cleves."

"By God, she will dance!" Elizabeth heard her father say irately. "Get that dragon out of my sight!" As the woman was escorted, protesting, away, he turned to Anna.

"Up!" he commanded, rising. There was no mistaking what he meant.

The Queen rose and allowed herself to be led out. It was true, she could not dance, and the courtiers held their breath as she stumbled, fell in and out of step, and trod heavily on the King's toe. He winced but said nothing as he lumbered heavily across the floor. At last, the dance drew to its embarrassing close, and the King handed his red-faced bride back to her seat.

"We will retire now," he announced, and the whole court rose to its feet. Anna's ladies followed her out, and the King and his gentlemen went after. As he left, Elizabeth heard him muttering to the Duke of Norfolk, "I tell you, my lord, if it were not to satisfy the world and my realm, I would not do what I must this night for any earthly thing!" And he stumped out of the chamber.

After that, Kat hurried a sleepy Elizabeth away to bed, fearing she might overhear more bawdy talk and speculation among the courtiers.

Elizabeth had seen lots of letters written by grown-ups, so she knew what to write. She dipped her quill in the ink and scribed slowly and laboriously in her clear, childish script.

> *Permit me to show, by this letter, the zeal with which I respect you as Queen, and my entire obedience to you as my mother. I am too young and feeble to have power to do more than send you my felicitations at the start of your good marriage. I hope that Your Majesty will have as much goodwill for me as I have zeal for your service.*

That sounded well, she thought, and it might move Queen Anna to invite her back to court. She was enjoying her sojourn at Hertford, that pleasant red-brick palace nestling on the banks of the River Lea, as well as the company of her little brother, for it was rare that they were lodged in one place together, but she had had a prolonged taste of court life and she was desperate to return there.

Kat entered the schoolroom.

"What's that you're writing, my lady?" she inquired.

"A letter to the Queen," Elizabeth replied imperiously.

"To the Queen?" Kat was astonished. "Let me see." She read the letter carefully, twice.

"I'm not sure that you should send this," she said.

Elizabeth looked crestfallen.

"But I *so* want to go to court," she said plaintively. "*Please, Kat.*"

Kat thought for a moment.

"Very well," she said reluctantly. "I suppose there's nothing in it that could give offense. Seal it and I'll have it sent."

Elizabeth spent the next few days excitedly anticipating her return to court. She looked forward to the feasts, the revels, the chance to wear her fine clothes, and the lords and ladies praising and complimenting her. She resolved to win the love of Queen Anna, unpleasant odors or not, who would surely use her influence with the King so that Elizabeth could be given her own apartments at court. That would be wonderful!

What happened next therefore came as a shock.

"You have received a letter from Master Secretary Cromwell," announced Kat, entering her chamber. Elizabeth jumped up excitedly, then checked herself, for Kat's face was grave.

"What does it say?" she cried.

"I hardly know how to tell you, child," Kat said, her voice sounding unusually emotional. "He writes, *I am commanded by the King to say that he will not hear of your coming to court to attend upon the Queen. I am to tell you that you had a mother so different from this woman that you ought not to wish to see her.*"

Elizabeth burst without warning into noisy tears, shocking to Kat, for this child was usually so composed, so contained.

"What does he mean?" she sobbed.

"I would not take it too seriously," Kat soothed. "This is a difficult time for His Majesty. By all reports, he is not happy with the Queen."

"But what does he mean, I had a mother so different from this woman that I ought not to want to see her?" Elizabeth had ceased crying now, but her face was tragic and perplexed.

Kat sat down at the table next to her and pushed away the copy book. She took the child's hands in hers and held them tightly.

"Elizabeth, your mother was a charming lady. She was not beautiful, but men found her very attractive. Your father the King pursued her for seven years, which must give you some idea of how fascinating she was. Accomplished too. Everything she did, she did gracefully—she could dance, sing, embroider, write poetry, play the lute and virginals, and as for intelligence and wit—well, she shone. She was slim and poised and always elegantly dressed, for she had a way with clothes and could make much from a little. You are very like her in many ways. Already I can see that."

Elizabeth smiled weakly, avidly drinking in this information about her mother. She had not known these details, and yet in some strange way, they were familiar to her. She could just remember a gorgeously attired lady, smelling of rosewater, running with her through a corridor or tying a pearly bonnet under her chin. There were other vague, less comforting, images, too, but they lay just beyond her recall now, no matter how hard she tried to summon them up. They were all she had of her mother, those memories, but now she could flesh them out from Kat's revelations.

"The King is right," Kat went on, "Queen Anna *is* so different from your mother. In no way could she hope to conform to his ideals of womanhood, God help her. So my impression is that the King is feeling very sorry for himself, having married such a lady. He would never admit it, but he is probably remembering how much he was captivated by your mother, and who knows, he may even regret putting her to death. I do not believe he will ever love another as much as he loved her."

She patted Elizabeth's hand.

"So that is almost certainly why he says you should not wish to see the Queen. Calling her 'this woman' is not complimentary, and it appears he would rather you did not associate with her."

"But he *could* mean that Queen Anna is good, and my mother was bad, and that is why he doesn't want me to see her, because I am not worthy."

"I hardly think so, having read this," Kat said. "Sweeting, I knew that letter would hurt you, but I think it reflects your father's own unhappiness. Do not set any store by it. Come, I have something to show you."

Kat rose and led an intrigued Elizabeth up the stair that led off her chamber and spiraled up to the attics above. Here there were dusty, unused rooms leading one into another. The first two that they entered were bare, but the third was filled with the detritus of past occupants of Hertford Castle. On an old settle lay two fraying cushions embroidered with designs of monkeys and butterflies, their colors faded with age. A threadbare tapestry and a scorched carpet lay rolled up on the floor. There were ancient chests, broken stools, bits of dented armor, and a curious horned headdress festooned with cobwebs hanging on a peg. Elizabeth reached out for it. She could see that the material had once been very fine.

"Don't touch," warned Kat. "It's filthy, and it will probably crumble to pieces if you do."

"I've never seen a headdress like that," Elizabeth said.

"It's very old," Kat said. "Long before our time. I've seen similar ones on effigies in churches. Many of your ancestors lived here in the past, so it may have belonged to one of them. In fact, most of these things were probably royal possessions at one time or other."

She looked about her. "I can't think why someone doesn't clear this place out. I've only been up here once before, when Sir John wanted something stored away. I suppose I shouldn't have, but I poked about, and it was then that I found something very interesting." She picked her way over to where a stack of framed pictures lay propped against a wall. Elizabeth followed, bursting with curiosity, while Kat began looking through the paintings. The first was a likeness of a man in armor, dulled with time; the second a portrait of a pretty young woman in a brown velvet gown and hood with a rich collar around her neck; she had golden hair, a round face, and a demure expression.

"Who is that?" Elizabeth asked.

"That is the late Queen Katherine, the Lady Mary's mother. It must have been done when she was a girl, before her looks faded and she put on weight."

Elizabeth could not help feeling sorry for that pretty girl. She knew how her father had put away his first wife and banished her from court for her stubbornness. Of course, he had been absolutely right to do so, but all the same, it was poignant to see this picture of a young lady who must have been so thrilled to be his Queen, and whose life had turned out to be so sad.

"That isn't what I came to show you," said Kat, lifting out of the stack an unframed wooden panel. "This is. It's your mother, Queen Anne."

She held up a half-length portrait of a dark-haired lady with merry, captivating eyes, high cheekbones, and a smiling mouth. She had on a low-necked black gown trimmed with pearls, braid, and fur. There were pearls edging her French hood and a rope of them around her slender neck. She also wore a jeweled pendant in the form of a B. On the chipped dark green background were painted, in gold, the Latin words ANNA BOLINA UXOR HENRI OCTA.

Elizabeth stared, marveling. So *this* was her mother. She had never seen a picture of her, had only the dimmest memory, and had often wondered what she looked like.

"It's a good likeness," said Kat. "I saw her several times."

Elizabeth was struck by the sitter's resemblance to herself. The black eyes, the cheekbones, the pointed chin, the mouth. She was nearly all Anne Boleyn, she realized. Only her red hair marked her as a Tudor. And Kat had said she was like her mother in other ways. She could dance well, like Anne, and she had already mastered the lute and the virginals; her music master had told her she had a talent for it. Anne had been good at needlework too, and she had loved fine clothes and carried herself well. She had been clever, and Elizabeth knew herself to be clever too. Gazing at the portrait, she felt that she at last knew who she was.

"Can I have this to keep?" she asked.

"Oh, I don't know," said Kat, who was beginning to wonder if she had been wise to divulge so much.

"Why not? No one else wants it."

Kat pondered anxiously for a minute.

"Well, if you keep it well hidden, I suppose you may take it," she said. "But no one must ever see it."

Elizabeth grabbed a grubby old painted cloth and wrapped it around the portrait. Then she hurriedly followed Kat down the stairs to her bedchamber, where she stashed the picture behind her bed.

"No one will find it there," she said.

"They won't," Kat agreed. "That bed hasn't been moved in years. It was probably built in this room."

Every night, for some time afterward, Elizabeth would get out of bed and look at her mother's picture, and soon she had the features by heart.

"That pendant my mother was wearing in her portrait," she said to Kat one day. "Do you know what happened to it?"

"No," answered Kat. "All her belongings disappeared. After she was found guilty of treason, they were forfeited to the King. I don't know what he did with them."

Elizabeth felt sad. She would have liked to have just one item that had been owned by her mother. If only for a keepsake, just to touch something that had once been Anne's.

Lessons over, Elizabeth grabbed her straw hat and ran out into the August sunshine.

The great park at Hertford lay before her, green and golden in the heat, and she strode forth, a determined little figure in her cream-colored summer gown. Kat watched her from the schoolroom window, marveling at how fast her charge was growing.

"Nearly seven years old," she mused, ". . . going on twenty!"

As she turned back to the table and began piling up the books, Sir John Shelton entered. He was clearly in some haste.

"There's a royal messenger below in the courtyard. They're just taking his horse. We should go down." Kat hurriedly popped the quills into a pot, smoothed her gown, and followed the governor.

Elizabeth had just seated herself in the shade of her favorite oak tree and taken the first bite of her apple when she espied Kat running toward her and beckoning frantically.

"Come, my lady! There is important news from court!"

Elizabeth sprang to her feet, nearly choking on the piece of apple in her mouth, and ran toward the house.

"What is it?" she called.

"There is much to tell!" Kat said, putting an arm around her shoulders and hurrying her through the open doors of the great hall. There stood Sir John, handing a cup of ale to the messenger.

Sir John bowed. The child looked at him breathlessly.

"My Lady Elizabeth, we have received important tidings. First, the King's marriage to the Princess Anna of Cleves has been dissolved upon the discovery that she was previously promised to another, and therefore not free to wed."

"Oh, the poor lady!" cried Elizabeth in some distress, but Sir John shook his head.

"There is no need for pity, I assure you," he said. "His Majesty has made a very generous settlement on the Princess. He has given her a handsome allowance, as well as Richmond Palace, Hever Castle, and Bletchingly Manor, and she is henceforth to be known as the King's dearest sister."

"From what we hear, she is very happy with the settlement," Kat put in, "so there is no cause for concern."

The messenger said, "By all accounts, the King wasn't at all flattered by her eagerness to accept what he offered." He grinned.

"That will do," said Sir John sharply. "You may go. There's further refreshment to be had in the kitchens. *I* will convey the rest of the news to the Lady Elizabeth."

The man doffed his bonnet and left.

Elizabeth was looking visibly relieved, but her ears had pricked up at Sir John's words.

"What other news, governor?" she asked.

Sir John nodded at Kat.

"We are to tell you that your father the King has taken another wife," she said. "You have a new stepmother."

"*Another* wife?" echoed Elizabeth, doing some rapid counting. "That makes *five* wives that my father has had!"

"Ahem, I'm sure His Majesty would take issue on that, my lady," reproved Sir John. "The new Queen Katherine is his second lawful wife, after Queen Jane. You would do well to remember that."

"Are you not pleased to have a new stepmother—a proper stepmother?" put in Kat, seeing Elizabeth's chastened look.

"Who is my new stepmother?" asked the child.

"Katherine Howard that was," said Kat. "A niece to the Duke of Norfolk, and therefore your cousin, since her father was brother to your grand-dam on your mother's side. She is said to be very pretty. She is certainly very young."

"When will I meet her?" Elizabeth wanted to know. "Are we to go to court?"

"Not as yet," Sir John told her. "But that brings me to the last piece of news. The Princess Anna has shown an interest in you; she has asked the King if you may visit her, and he has agreed. She has gone to view her new properties, and is even now lodging at Hever Castle in Kent. You are to travel there tomorrow for a few days' stay. Kat here will go with you."

"How kind of the Princess!" Elizabeth exclaimed, surprised and delighted. Hever Castle might not be the court, but it would at least provide a welcome change of scene. There might be dancing and revels . . .

Sir John beamed at Elizabeth. "Go and make ready," he said.

Elizabeth scampered off, planning her wardrobe for Hever. She had never been there, nor even heard of the place, but she was sure that the Princess Anna would keep a fine court in the castle.

Sir John did not realize that she was still within earshot when he turned to Kat and asked, "Is it wise to let her go there?"

"She knows nothing of the place, Sir John," she heard Kat replying. "And why should she not go there? She must know of the lady her mother sometime."

Sir John grunted and said no more, but Elizabeth was left feeling strangely thrilled to be going to a house that was connected in some way to her mother. It made the prospect of the visit even more exciting.

As the little cavalcade crested the hill, the castle came into view, a mellow stone pile nestling in its lush green valley. Elizabeth spurred on her palfrey, eager to embark on the joys of her stay, conscious that she was an honored guest, bestowing the favor of her presence on her hostess.

"What do I call the Princess Anna now that she is not queen?" she asked Kat.

"Your Highness, I should imagine," said Kat, reflecting that it was becoming a new pastime, this thinking up titles for ex-queens. The first Queen Katherine had become the Princess Dowager, and Elizabeth's mother had been stripped of her royal rank and had gone to the scaffold as plain Lady Anne Boleyn.

With two men-at-arms riding behind, and three waiting women in attendance, Elizabeth and her governess clattered over the drawbridge and into the castle courtyard. There, before the open doorway, stood the Princess of Cleves, her household drawn up behind her. At Elizabeth's approach, she swept a deep curtsy. Elizabeth noticed that she was wearing a green gown in the English fashion, and when she had dismounted and raised her former stepmother, she was relieved to find that the only odor that clung to her was a faint hint of roses mingled with that of cloves. A hint had perhaps been taken!

"Welcome, Lady Elizabeth!" Anna smiled. "It is most kind of His Majesty to allow you to come here to me." She spoke haltingly, but clearly she had been spending much of her time learning English.

Elizabeth inclined her head regally and allowed the Princess to lead her into the castle. Here, on trestles in the hall, were laid out cold meats, raised pies and custard tarts, and a selection of candied fruits that made the little girl's mouth water.

"We have also a dish from Cleves!" Anna announced proudly later as they seated themselves at the high table, with Elizabeth in the place of honor. At Anna's nod, two servants came forward. One poured wine; the other carried a platter piled high with what looked like a greenish white mess.

"What is it?" Elizabeth was curious.

"It is sauerkraut," Anna said. "Cabbage with salt, with wine and juniper." Another nod, and the servant spooned a generous amount onto Elizabeth's plate. Elizabeth tasted it.

"Very good!" she pronounced, enjoying the pickled taste.

The Princess beamed. Kat, watching, was delighted that the visit had gotten off to a promising start.

As they entered the long gallery, Elizabeth saw the portrait.

"It's my mother!" she cried impulsively, then clapped her hand over her mouth, realizing what she had said. She had long ago understood that her mother's name was never to be mentioned publicly. But there in front of her was a portrait very similar to the one she herself had hidden away, only in this one, Queen Anne was holding a rose, had a gold filet across her forehead, and looked younger and more beautiful than in the other picture.

The Princess looked dismayed.

"I should have remembered!" she cried. "I had mean to have it replaced. I have been so busy make ready . . ."

Kat came to her rescue.

"No matter, Your Highness. The Lady Elizabeth has seen pictures of her mother. I think it is important that she knows something of her."

"Oh, yes," said the Princess with feeling. "The poor child. And that poor woman." She shuddered. "That is why I do something for the Lady Elizabeth. I cannot be a mother to her now—but a friend."

"Your Highness's kindness is deeply appreciated," said Kat. The two women exchanged sympathetic looks.

Elizabeth was gazing at the picture, barely aware of their words. She was wishing that she could have it for her own.

"She looks so beautiful," she said.

"It's a fair likeness," said Kat.

"I was pleased to find it here," Anna said. "No one would talk about her at court."

"They are too afraid of the King," Kat said quietly.

The Princess tactfully took Elizabeth's hand.

"Come. I have something else to show you." She led the child along the gallery to a bedchamber. There stood a magnificent oaken bed, with the arms of England carved into its intricate design.

"They tell me that this was your mother's bed," she said.

Elizabeth's heart leapt.

"Why is it kept here?" she asked.

"This was her home," revealed Kat. "She spent her childhood here, and your father came here to pay court to her. Not that she would have him then: She kept him guessing for many years."

"But he was the King!" Elizabeth was shocked, but impressed even so.

"Yes he was, yet in asking your mother to be his chosen lady, he was placing her above him, to be worshipped like an image on a pedestal, so to speak. She was the mistress of his heart, the one who held his happiness in her hands. It was ever so, in the game of love," Kat said.

"In Cleves it was not," the Princess put in tartly. "There, the young ladies have always been made to marry the men their fathers chose for them."

"And here too, that is the custom," said Kat. "But the King was already married. He could not ask the lady to be his wife. So he asked her to be his mistress."

"His mistress?" Elizabeth asked, running her fingers over the carvings. Her mother's head must once have rested against them.

"The one who ruled his heart," Kat said, telling only half the truth. "As I am your mistress and rule you."

"And she refused? She was, how you say, a brave woman!" Anna declared.

Elizabeth marveled also. Her mother must have been a remarkable woman; what power she had enjoyed! What daring!

"Did my father love her very much, all that time?" she asked.

Kat was silent for a moment, considering her answer.

"He did. He thought of no one else. He made himself Head of the Church of England so that he could marry her, and in the end he won her."

After that, of course, things had gone badly wrong, so Kat resolved to divert Elizabeth from further questions.

"Let's find your bedchamber, shall we?" she said.

"Ach, yes. Come this way." Anna quickly took the hint.

"Can't I sleep here?" Elizabeth asked. She knew she would feel nearer to her mother if she slept in her bed.

"I think this is the Princess Anna's room," Kat said doubtfully.

"That is all right," the Princess said amiably. "The Lady Elizabeth may sleep here. I will order it." She beamed down at the little girl, who looked at her gratefully.

"Now I want to show you the beautiful gardens!" Anna declared.

Wherever Elizabeth went at Hever, there were reminders of her mother. Her memory was there in every room, every garden walk, every shady arbor. Many of the Boleyn family's possessions had been removed by the King's officers, but a few items had been left, such as the bedstead and the portrait, for—Kat thought—who would want such reminders of a fallen queen? Yet, even with the castle stripped of Anne's belongings, it was easy to imagine her at Hever.

"Did you ever come here when . . . when she was here?" Elizabeth asked Kat as they strolled through the glorious gardens that first afternoon.

"Once," Kat recalled. "It was very splendid then. I remember attending a great feast to celebrate the ennobling of your grandfather, Sir Thomas Boleyn, when the King made him Lord Rochford. There were dances and disguisings, and your mother was the center of attention. The young men were openly vying for her favors."

Elizabeth thrilled to hear this. How wonderful to be so popular, and to have people admire you.

"Did she look very beautiful? Tell me what she was like," she urged.

"She was wearing a gown of dark blue silk, with pearls at her throat, and her hair was loose. It was very long and very dark, and I remember that there were little gems glittering in it. And she was laughing a lot . . ." Kat shook her head sadly, remembering that Anne had had very little cause to laugh in later years.

"When I grow up, I am going to be like her!" Elizabeth announced. "I'm going to be beautiful, and wear silk gowns and have jewels in my hair!"

Kat smiled. She was growing so fond of this vain charge of hers with her vivacious character and determined little face.

Elizabeth had stooped to gather wildflowers. The sky glowed golden and hazy in the late-afternoon sunshine, and there was a fair breeze. Kat stood for a moment relishing the peace and beauty of the place.

"Come, young lady," she said at length. "The Princess Anna will be arising from her nap, and we must tidy ourselves for supper."

Elizabeth was lying in her mother's bed. The curtains had been drawn, and the candle blown out. The room was dark, but in the dimness she could make out the shapes of the chairs, the prayer desk, and the clothes chest that lined the walls; and there, on a peg, hung her cream gown, brushed ready for the morning. In the distance, the hoot of an owl broke the silence.

The child could not sleep. The unfamiliar room, the strange house, the exciting discoveries and revelations of the day—all had unsettled her, and no matter how tightly she shut her eyes, or mentally recited her prayers, it was an age before she finally drifted off, and then she slept fitfully, or so it seemed.

She wasn't sure what awoke her. Probably the cold, for she came to her senses shivering. Then she became aware that she was not alone. There was a dark shape standing at the end of her bed.

"Kat?" she whispered. But the figure did not answer or move. Its face was in shadow, indeed, the whole of its body was shrouded in the gloom, but it looked like a woman, and she felt, with the first stirrings of unease, that it was watching her. A pang of alarm gripped her.

"Kat?" She spoke the name more insistently now, huddling the bed-clothes around her, peering over the sheet with frightened eyes. The dark figure was still there, but it was too slender to be Kat, Elizabeth realized. She was beginning to wonder if it was a trick of the darkness or the shadow cast by a piece of furniture or the bed itself, when suddenly it held out its arms toward her. In that poignant gesture, there was supplication, yearning, and something else, something that was not frightening at all, but surprisingly comforting.

Astonished, Elizabeth rubbed the sleep from her eyes. When she opened them again, the shape had gone. The room was empty.

Her heart was pounding fearfully. Had she dreamed it? Or had it

really been there? Of course it had, she had felt the cold, had woken up
noticing the cold before she noticed the figure. It was strange, but she was
no longer cold. The room was now temperate: it was August, after all.

Elizabeth lay there wondering.

"Mother?" she whispered, trying out the sweet, unfamiliar word on her
tongue. The irresistible conclusion, the only one she wanted to believe, was
that Anne Boleyn's shade had come to her. But there was no answer.

Elizabeth did not mention her experience to Kat or to the Princess. In the
cold light of day, it all seemed like a dream anyway; or perhaps she had
imagined it. Even if it had been her mother's ghost, which she now
doubted, it had surely come to convey how much Anne had loved her in
life, and probably still did love her in the hereafter. The figure did not appear again, and nothing untoward happened during the rest of her stay at
Hever, which tended to confirm those conclusions. The days flew by, she
slept well, and all too soon she was curtsying farewell to the Princess Anna.

"You must come again," that lady told her. "Your visit has given me
great pleasure. I hope you will think of me as your friend."

"I will," declared Elizabeth fervently, extending her hand. But Anna
ignored it. Bending, she drew the child into a warm embrace and kissed
her.

"Come back soon!" she said.

Elizabeth did not see Anna of Cleves again until the New Year of 1541,
when both were invited to Hampton Court to participate in the festivities.

"At last, I am going to meet my new stepmother!" Elizabeth cried,
dancing around her bedchamber with excitement. "I must have a new
gown! Please can I have a new gown, Kat?"

The tailor was sent for.

"My, you have grown, my Lady Elizabeth," he said, taking her meas-
urements.

"I am seven now," Elizabeth told him. "Am I not tall for my age?"

"Indeed you are," he said, suppressing a smile. "And very pretty, if I
may say so."

"You may," she told him regally. "I am going to court, so you must
make me a very fine gown."

"My lady, when I have finished it, you will outshine all the other ladies!" he told her, summoning his assistants. Elizabeth gaped in awe at the bolts of sumptuous fabrics being unraveled before her.

"We must have an eye to cost," said Kat, anxiously. "I am permitted a certain allowance . . . not always forthcoming in the past." She grimaced, recalling what she had heard of Lady Bryan's heroic efforts to make ends meet in the weeks after Anne Boleyn's fall, when the King appeared to have forgotten his younger daughter. Since then, though, he had been fairly generous.

The tailor bowed. He was aware of Elizabeth's uncertain status.

"How about this, Mistress Champernowne?" He showed her a dark green taffeta shot through with gold thread. The price he named was reasonable.

"It will look ravishing against my Lady Elizabeth's red hair," he said.

"It's gorgeous!" cried Elizabeth, looking pleadingly at Kat.

"Very well," said Kat. "It *is* a special occasion."

And so it was that Elizabeth arrived at Hampton Court with the glorious gown packed in her luggage, along with gifts she had painstakingly—and reluctantly—embroidered for her father, her sister, her brother, and her new stepmother.

No sooner had she arrived in the apartment assigned to her than the Lady Mary came to see her.

"Welcome, Sister!" She smiled, noticing that Elizabeth had grown up somewhat since their last meeting, and shed her infant chubbiness. The girl who was curtsying before her carried herself very gracefully indeed, and there was a new pride in her. Yet she was, after all, still very young, Mary reminded herself, and would be in need of moral protection now that she had come to court.

While Kat unpacked and organized Elizabeth's gear, Mary sat on the window seat and listened to her sister's news, which was mostly concerned with lessons, puppies, and what sounded like servants' gossip.

"And I went to visit Anna of Cleves at Hever," Elizabeth said.

"At Hever?" echoed Mary, startled. She looked at Kat.

"The Princess was lodging there, madam, and it seemed most convenient."

Mary said no more, but pursed her thin lips. Sometimes, she doubted Kat's wisdom. The less Elizabeth was told about her deplorable mother, the better.

"Have you met our new stepmother, Sister?" Elizabeth asked.

"I have," said Mary carefully. "Her Majesty is looking forward to making your acquaintance."

"Is she beautiful?" Elizabeth wanted to know.

"She is pretty," said Mary. "I will take you to see her later. She has promised to send for us. In the meantime, you must change, and then we can go to the Chapel Royal for Vespers."

Prayers again, Elizabeth thought. Mary was always at her prayers. Elizabeth had said hers that morning and saw no need to say them again. But she dutifully suffered Kat to dress her in her second best gown, the crimson damask, and Mary to lead her along the interminable corridors that led to the chapel.

The Queen's chamber was brilliantly lit by myriad candles set in many-branched sconces, and a fire was crackling on the hearth. Musicians were playing softly in a corner. As Elizabeth and Mary made their obeisances, a diminutive figure detached itself from the bevy of ladies that thronged the room and came toward them.

"Rise, my Lady Mary, my Lady Elizabeth," said a childish voice.

Elizabeth saw standing before her a plump little person, a very young lady, lavishly gowned and dripping with jewels. The new Queen had chestnut hair, haughty, heavy-lidded eyes, a generous, pouting mouth, and the sweetest puppy in her arms.

"You are welcome," she said, extending her hand to be kissed, and almost dropping the puppy in the process.

"My Lady Elizabeth is eager to meet you, madam," said Mary. Short as she was, she was taller than Katherine Howard and looked, Elizabeth thought, so much older. How strange to be older than your stepmother!

"You are very pretty, Elizabeth," said the Queen. She saw the child eyeing the puppy.

"Would you like to hold her?" she asked, and lifted the warm, furry body into Elizabeth's arms. Elizabeth espied the Princess Anna smiling at them.

"We are about to practice our dance steps," Katherine said. "You may both join in. Ladies, if you please! *La Mourisque!*"

Elizabeth hastily put the puppy down. The women formed two circles, and the musicians struck up a rousing tune. Someone shoved a pair of castanets into Elizabeth's hand, and suddenly she found herself in the midst of the dance, skipping first this way and then that, and meeting a different partner each time. It was at these points that she had to twirl about and click her castanets. It was all enormous fun, and she could not understand why, whenever she glimpsed Mary in the melee, her sister looked so disapproving. The little Queen was laughing happily, galloping about with gusto, and the ladies enjoying themselves hugely, when the doors were flung open and the King was announced.

The dancers sank into deep curtsies, skirts fanning over the floor, as he limped into the room, a bulky great figure in a vast furred coat, leaning heavily on a stick. Elizabeth was alarmed to see him looking so old and ill, her mighty father who had always appeared invincible. Yet he was in ebullient spirits.

"Rise, ladies!" he said, waving his hand in an upward motion and heading for the Queen.

"How does my sweet Kate today?" he inquired, bending and kissing her full on the mouth. His eyes were devouring her.

"I am well, sir," she replied, "but happier for seeing you."

Elizabeth, waiting for her father to notice her, thought that the Queen's words did not quite ring true. And she caught Mary looking at Katherine with ill-concealed disapproval.

Henry, his arm possessively around his young wife, was leading her toward the two chairs of estate on the dais. Elizabeth watched as they seated themselves, then saw her father reach out and caress the Queen, his fingers lingering on her cheek, her throat, her ample breast, which the low-cut bodice exposed almost to the nipple . . . Beside her, Mary stiffened.

Katherine bent toward the King and murmured something. He smiled at her and chucked her under the chin, making her giggle. Suddenly, noticing his daughters standing waiting, he removed his hand from the Queen's breast and beckoned. Mary moved to the center of the room and made a deep reverence, and Elizabeth followed suit.

"God's blessing on you both, my Daughters," Henry said. "You are very welcome to court. We have great revels planned for this evening, which I am sure you will enjoy. And the Queen here"—he smiled intimately at Katherine—"is looking forward to getting to know you better, Elizabeth."

Katherine simpered, but it was clear that she was impatient to focus her attentions elsewhere. Elizabeth was fast realizing that her new stepmother was not really interested in her at all. And she suspected that Mary felt that too.

But Mary would not be drawn. As they sat playing chess in Mary's chamber the next day, Elizabeth ventured to voice her opinion.

"I don't think our stepmother cares very much for us," she stated.

"She is very young," said Mary. "She has much to learn about being queen."

"She didn't seek me out once last night," said Elizabeth. "I tried to catch her eye, but she never looked my way. She only wanted to dance and show off."

"There were many people demanding her attention," Mary said.

"But I am the King's daughter!" Elizabeth pointed out. "I *am* quite important, and she should not have ignored me."

"You may be quite important, but you need to learn some humility," Mary reproved. "Sister, I am sure the Queen *will* send for us and spend some time with us."

"You don't like her, do you?" Elizabeth persisted.

"I did not say that, Sister," Mary said sharply. "I hardly know her. And she *is* from a good Catholic family. I would rather have her as queen than one set up by the religious reformers, like the Princess Anna."

"But I like the Princess Anna!" Elizabeth said. "She sat with me for a long time last night. And she brought me a lovely present." She lifted the jeweled pomander that hung from her girdle and admired it afresh. "And I enjoyed watching her dance with the Queen. I think our father should have stayed married to her."

"Hush!" hissed Mary. "You must not say such things. You will get into trouble. And if you move that queen there, you will lose it! Concentrate!"

CHAPTER 6

1541–42

I wish we could have gone to court for Christmas," Elizabeth grumbled, spearing a slice of roasted boar and staring at the mummers with scant attention. "We've hardly been there at all this year."

It was not possible, my lady," Sir John Shelton said. Elizabeth did not miss the glance that passed between him and Kat. Something was afoot, and she was determined to find out what it was. At least that would liven up the proceedings. Watching a lot of rustics cavorting in the courtyard at Hatfield had nowhere near the appeal of the magnificent revels at court, and she had been crushed by disappointment when the anticipated summons had failed to arrive. It was now Christmas Eve, and she knew she could look for it no longer.

"My father is ill, isn't he?" she asked Kat suddenly. The governess, her homely face rosy in the torchlight, looked perturbed.

"No, my lady, he is well, I believe," she said. "We have not heard anything to the contrary."

"But something *is* wrong," Elizabeth persisted, her sense of foreboding strong. "Why am I not to go to court this Christmas, when I went last year? Have I offended the King in some way?"

"Not at all," said Kat. "This has nothing to do with you, child."

"So there *is* something amiss," Elizabeth insisted.

Kat turned to Sir John.

"I am going to have to tell her," she murmured.

"Wait," he urged. "We have had no instructions."

"No," said Kat, low. "The King has other things on his mind."

"What?" asked Elizabeth, who was listening avidly.

"Come with me," said Kat.

Sir John shook his head. "Is this wise?" he asked.

Kat frowned at him and steered Elizabeth firmly toward the open doorway of the palace. Sometimes, you had to take matters into your own hands. If you waited on orders from court, you might wait forever.

Kat sat Elizabeth down on a bench in the deserted great hall. Everyone was outside enjoying the tomfoolery and the spit roast. The flames from the bonfire cast leaping lights on the tall, mullioned windows.

Kat seated herself next to her charge.

"You are right, Elizabeth," she said, "something has happened, and when I tell you what it is, you will understand why you cannot go to court just now."

Elizabeth tensed. She had known it, her father *was* ill, or hurt, or even dying. She braced herself for bad news, and was surprised, therefore, when Kat said, "It is the Queen."

"The Queen? Is she ill?"

"No, child, she is in disgrace. Worse than that, in fact. She is under house arrest at Syon Abbey. She has behaved very wickedly."

"What has she done?" Elizabeth could vaguely recall echoes of a similar conversation to this, many moons ago, its details misted by time.

"She has been unfaithful to the King with two gentlemen. Well, hardly gentlemen, by their behavior. Do you understand what I mean?"

"She—she let them kiss her?" Elizabeth asked uncertainly, remembering her father kissing and caressing his young wife.

"No, more than that," Kat said. "There can be *much* more than that between a man and a maid, more than you can ever have dreamed of, innocent and sheltered as you are, child." Her voice sounded a touch wistful, as well as sad.

"Men," Kat went on, choosing her words with care, "are born crested, women cloven. You know, down there." Elizabeth caught her meaning and blushed. Kat continued steadily, "To make a child, the crest must go into the cloven part, but such a thing is only sanctified within marriage. But the Queen, they say, has done it outside of her marriage, and has betrayed your father the King, to whom she should have been faithful."

"How *could* she?" Elizabeth's mouth gaped, her eyes widened. It was bad enough imagining men and women doing such a peculiar thing when they were wed, still less wanting to do it with other people. As for her father doing it with the Queen, well, the very notion was shocking! Of course, Elizabeth had only the vaguest idea of what Kat had meant, but it sounded quite frightful and very immodest.

"And she did this with *two* gentlemen?" the child asked.

"I fear so," Kat said.

"At the same time?" Elizabeth wanted to know.

"Bless me, no!" cried Kat. "It is a private thing. Always!"

"And she is under house arrest for it?" Elizabeth asked fearfully. "What does that mean?"

"It means that she is not in jail but being held prisoner in her lodgings," Kat explained.

"Will she have to stay there for a long time?"

"Until the King decides what is to be done with her," Kat said slowly.

"You mean—they won't cut off her head, will they?" Elizabeth asked in a small voice. She was trembling.

"In faith, I do not know," Kat told her truthfully. "We must pray for her."

Elizabeth's quick mind was moving on rapidly.

"These things the Queen has done wrong," she said after a moment. "Were they the kind of things that my mother did, to deserve death?"

"That's what was alleged against her, yes," Kat replied slowly. "But I do not believe it, and neither should you. I am convinced she was innocent."

"But my father believed it," Elizabeth said.

"Oh, they made a convincing case against her, never fear. A lot of people believed the charges were true. But she defended herself stoutly at her trial, and as I told you, even her enemies ended up saying that an excuse had been made to get rid of her. But your father the King was not behind it, that I firmly believe. It was Master Cromwell, God rest him, who plotted to remove her and all her faction, since they stood in his way."

"He was an evil man!" Elizabeth burst out. She had been glad to hear, after the breaking of the Cleves marriage, that Master Secretary had gone to the block, accused of heresy.

"Aye, but he paid the price," Kat said. "He made a fatal blunder in bringing the Princess Anna to England, and thereby laid himself open to the malice of his enemies."

"He got what he deserved," said the child severely. "He killed my mother."

"Do not dwell on it," said Kat kindly. "It will do you no good. Pray for the Queen when you can, and for the repose of your mother's soul. And for Thomas Cromwell, for it is your Christian duty to do so. In the meantime, let us enjoy Christmas. Life's too short for moping!"

"I fear I must break to you some grave news, Elizabeth," Kat said suddenly. It was a freezing February morning and they had dragged the schoolroom table nearer to the fire; Elizabeth was now seated there, practicing forming italics with her quill pen. She had thought Kat somewhat subdued during the past hour, but had supposed that the governess was concentrating hard on marking her sums.

Elizabeth looked up. Her pointed little face was questioning, apprehensive, and Kat braced herself.

"The Queen was beheaded yesterday morning," she said quietly. "She had been found guilty of treason by Act of Parliament, and sentenced to death."

Elizabeth could not speak. She was struggling to accept the fact that that plump, pretty young woman, who had giggled as the King stroked her breast, was no more; that her pert head had been brutally parted from her neck. There would have been pain, quick and sharp, and blood, lots of it. She could imagine the young Queen's fear, her shrinking steps as she approached the block, her terror as she knelt down and waited for the ax to strike. Elizabeth shuddered. It was as if her mother, Anne Boleyn, had been beheaded all over again.

She felt the vomit rise in her throat. She stood up suddenly, covered her mouth with her hands and fled to the privy, where, retching horribly, she voided her breakfast down the stone chute. Then she stood trembling, trying to compose herself; and that was how a concerned Kat found her.

"Hush, hinny," she soothed, folding her distressed charge in a warm embrace. Elizabeth tried to push her away, not wishing Kat to see her lose control, but the grief and horror were overwhelming, and, forgetting that she was a big girl of eight who was too old to cry like a baby, she sought refuge on her governess's shoulder and howled. And as she held the sobbing, shaking child, Kat could feel her unbearable pain, and a tear slid down her own cheek.

After that, Katherine Howard's name was never mentioned again. Neither Kat nor Elizabeth wished to risk a recurrence of that painful scene. Aware of how deeply the knowledge of the late Queen's fate must have affected her charge, Kat sought to divert Elizabeth from morbid thoughts of death with merry stories, games of hide-and-seek, and even a snowball fight when the weather was sufficiently severe. They toasted muffins by the fire, played skittles in the gallery, and sang songs, with Elizabeth picking out the tunes on her lute or her virginals.

"You are getting so good at your playing," Kat complimented her. "In fact, you have proved such an apt pupil in every way that I fear I can teach you little more. I think, child, that the time has come for you to have a tutor."

"But I like you teaching me," Elizabeth protested.

"And I like teaching you," said Kat, "but I have exhausted my poor supply of knowledge. I should tell you that I have written to His Majesty to ask if you may share the Prince's lessons."

"You have?" Elizabeth was delighted. She had an unquenchable thirst for learning, and also a great desire to spend more time with her brother, whom she saw all too infrequently. "Will I go to court?"

Kat smiled. "No, my little lady, you will ride over to Ashridge or Enfield, whenever the Prince is in residence. He is about to begin some elementary lessons, and it would be enjoyable for you both if you were sometimes to be taught together."

Elizabeth was considerably cheered by this, and spent the next weeks in a fever of expectancy, longing for her father to respond to Kat's request.

"Why is he taking so long to agree?" she grizzled.

"I expect he has a lot on his mind just now," Kat answered. She did not repeat what her sister Joan had written to her: Joan was married to one of the gentlemen of the King's privy chamber, Sir Anthony Denny, and she had confided to Kat that His Majesty was sunk in a deep depression, and painfully troubled by his bad leg. Kat knew, therefore, that she could not expect a speedy answer. It was, indeed, May before the letter came.

"Good news! You are to go to Ashridge next week to begin lessons," a happy Kat told an ecstatic Elizabeth. "There is a condition. You are to be careful with whom you come into contact before visiting the Prince, and if you have been exposed to any contagion, you must stay at home."

"Yes, yes, of course," agreed Elizabeth, barely listening. "My father must think I am very important to merit learning with the Prince."

"Of course he thinks you are important!" Kat laughed. "You are his daughter."

"And I must have new gowns!" trilled Elizabeth, executing a lithe, joyous dance step.

"Hold on a moment!" chuckled Kat. "You're going to lessons, not revels!"

"But I should look my best," the girl insisted, admiring her slender hands.

"I do declare, the man who marries you is going to have to be mighty rich!" Kat jested.

"*I* shall be rich," said Elizabeth. "I'm the King's daughter. And I'm not going to get married."

"Of course you are," Kat said, shaking her head. "All noble girls marry. It is a woman's duty to marry and have children. It is what God created us for."

"Then why aren't you married, Kat?" Elizabeth asked impishly.

"I had a suitor once," the governess said, a touch wistfully. "My father chose him for me. He was a nice boy, but he died. Now my father is too old and infirm to find me a husband, and I do not have much opportunity to meet one here, but still I hope one day to be married."

"If you do, you must never leave me," Elizabeth declared. "Your husband must come and live here."

"I'll tell him," smiled Kat. "When I meet him."

Elizabeth lay in her bed, wide awake, staring at the dying embers of the fire. She couldn't understand why all Kat's talk of marrying disturbed her so much. She supposed it had something to do with that naughty thing Kat had told her about some weeks back, the thing that married people did, and that Katherine Howard had done with those wicked gentlemen. The thing that people had accused her mother of doing with a man not her husband.

She tried to imagine what Kat had meant by men being born crested, but all she could think of was that curious tiny appendage she had glimpsed when her little brother had had his clouts changed in babyhood. Was it that which a man had to put into that unmentionable place down there, to make a child? That was silly, it was far too small, and anyway, Elizabeth was absolutely certain that she didn't want any man ever doing such a rude thing to her. The remedy, of course, was never to marry. But what if her father chose a husband for her, like Kat's had? Would she dare gainsay the King?

She would, she told herself defiantly. For it was not just the unseemly aspects of the business that repelled her. There was something more, something darker and more sinister, something all bound up with the horror of Queen Katherine's beheading and her mother's. They had both died for doing that naughty thing. And there was another reason to fear too, for had not Queen Jane died bearing a child? Having a child was also the consequence of having a man put his crested bit inside you. So if you let a man do that to you, or—worse still—if he forced you, you might die, one way or another. It did not bear thinking about.

No, resolved Elizabeth, turning over and shutting her eyes firmly, "I will never marry."

Elizabeth was amazed by the change in her brother the Prince. Gone was the chubby infant she had last seen—when was it?—eighteen months before, and in his place stood a slim, five-year-old boy, not yet breeched, but bearing himself in very manly fashion in his long-skirted velvet doublet.

"You are welcome, Sister," he said solemnly, inclining his head precociously as Elizabeth swept a deep curtsy. "May I present Dr. Coxe, our tutor."

A lean, middle-aged man wearing an owlish look and a black clerical gown and bonnet stepped forward, bowing.

"My Lady Elizabeth, this is a privilege," he said. "I have heard exceptional reports of your learning, and I make no doubt that you will exercise a beneficial influence on your brother the Prince."

They seated themselves at a table laden with books, parchments, pens, and inkwells.

"I think you will find you have little to fear from me," said Dr. Coxe. "Learning should be a pleasure, and beating it into my pupils is not my way, although I know that many tutors hold by it, especially in our grammar schools. No, Your Graces, I prefer the carrot to the stick. We shall embark on a splendid adventure together."

Elizabeth enjoyed the lessons, for they were longer and harder than those that Kat had set her, and she relished the challenge. Dr. Coxe was a good linguist, and under his guidance, her grasp of foreign tongues improved. Soon, she was reading simple Latin texts and translating short French poems. But it was the religious instruction that really fascinated her, for Dr. Coxe had an inspired zeal for this subject.

"We attain Heaven through our faith in Jesus Christ," he declared. "That is all that is needed for salvation. You must love Him with all your heart and believe in Him as your Savior."

Edward nodded, his heart-shaped face serious.

"My governess says we must do good deeds in order to get to Heaven," Elizabeth said. "Like giving alms to the poor, or visiting the sick."

"Most edifying," said the tutor, "but not necessary for our salvation. We may be justified through faith alone."

Elizabeth wasn't quite sure what he meant by that, and she was certain that Edward didn't know either, as he sat there looking rather lost, and Dr. Coxe was so carried away by the force of his arguments that he failed to notice. But after that, she tried very hard to love God more and more. It was difficult, though, because really she loved her father the best, and Kat.

On another occasion, Dr. Coxe opened a large, exquisitely bound book that he had brought to the lesson.

"This is the Holy Bible, lawfully in English for the first time, and there, on the title page, you see your father the King, presenting the Word of God to the clergy and the people."

The children looked at it in awe.

Dr. Coxe reverently turned a few pages and read aloud the tale of Adam and Eve.

"And that," he concluded, "is the story of the Fall of Man."

"What did the serpent look like?" Edward asked fearfully.

"Like a big green snake!" Elizabeth said, her eyes full of mischief.

"Your Graces, the serpent was the devil himself, sent in disguise to tempt the woman. She chose to disobey the Lord out of her own free will, and because of her weakness, she and Adam were cast out of the garden."

"I would not have disobeyed," said Elizabeth spiritedly.

"No, my lady," said Dr. Coxe, "but you are an unusual example of your sex, for it is well known that women are generally weak and frail creatures, who, like Eve, can lead men into sin."

"*I* am not weak and frail!" Elizabeth declared, a little indignant.

"I would never presume to say so, my lady," blustered Dr. Coxe. "But there are generally good reasons why God has set men above women, to hold dominion over them. And that is because of the sin of our mother Eve."

Katherine Howard had been weak, Elizabeth thought. But other women she knew of had had strong characters. What of Cleopatra? Brave St. Katherine, who had stood up to the heathen Emperor and risked a cruel death? And Isabella of Castile, who had led armies into battle and conquered the heathen Moors? There were many more alive today, she suspected, who would prove as indomitable, given the chance, and it occurred to her to wonder why it was that God had ordained that men should be the superior sex. Was it just because Eve had led Adam into sin?

"That's probably a made-up story," she said, shocking herself and Dr. Coxe.

"Heavens, child, do you question the Scriptures?" he exclaimed. "That is a wicked thing to do! Of course it is not made up."

"But how can God make a woman out of a rib?" Elizabeth asked, determined to argue her case.

"God can do anything He pleases," frowned the tutor. "And you would do well to pay heed to wiser and more experienced heads than yours. God made woman in all her imperfection to serve and obey man. That is the way of the world. Now let us read the story of the Flood."

"Girls are silly," said Edward smugly. Without hesitation, Elizabeth stuck her tongue out.

"Enough!" thundered Dr. Coxe. "That is no way for royal children to behave."

"No, it is not, Sister," said the boy severely. "I am the Prince, remember."

"Then you should be wise enough to know that girls are not silly," retorted Elizabeth. Edward made a face.

"The Flood, if you please," Dr. Coxe reminded them.

"I feel sorry for my brother," Elizabeth told Kat as she prepared for bed. "He's so serious. He has no sense of fun. Do you know, he hardly ever smiles."

"Poor little boy, I fear he is already overburdened with the knowledge that he will one day be King," Kat observed.

"You are right," said Elizabeth.

"I am sure that Lady Bryan and Mistress Penn do their best for him," Kat soothed.

"That is true, but he is surrounded by ceremony, and he has little freedom. Those about him are always telling him he must follow our father in greatness." Elizabeth was mentally contrasting the relative liberty that she herself enjoyed with the strict protocol surrounding her brother, and the easy affection that lay between her and Kat with the formality and deference with which Edward's attendants treated him.

"The King has his reasons, of course, but that poor child is overprotected," Kat opined.

"He does have friends to play with and share lessons with. There are several boys of good family in his household. Including Barnaby Fitz-Patrick, who is his whipping boy. Barnaby's nice."

Elizabeth was very fond of the young Irish lad. He was older than his master, and full of the charm of his race, and Elizabeth enjoyed sitting beside him at lessons and showing off her talents. Barnaby would tickle her under the table when Dr. Coxe was not looking, his smile impish beneath the unruly dark curls. Edward, she noticed, rarely joined in any horseplay, but gravely and diligently gave his full attention to his studies, frowning when his companions got up to mischief.

"Come and play, Brother," Elizabeth invited him one day when the tutor had dismissed them for the afternoon.

"I wish to read my book," he said. He had learned to read early, and was very advanced for his age, she had noticed.

"You can read your book anytime," she wheedled. "It's warm outside and we could run races in the park."

"Good idea, my lady!" smiled Barnaby. "How about me teaching you to fence, sir?"

Edward shook his fair head.

"My father the King would not allow it," he said sadly. "It would be too dangerous. I might get hurt, or killed, and then he would have no heir."

"Every gentleman must learn swordsmanship," Barnaby said.

"You could teach *me,*" suggested Elizabeth, her eyes twinkling.

Barnaby chuckled.

"You, a girl? My apologies, my lady, but it would not be seemly."

"Seemly be damned!" retorted Elizabeth wickedly. "Come, we shall fence!"

They raced to the park, Edward's nurses following at a discreet distance. Barnaby produced two blunted swords and taught Elizabeth the correct stance, feet turned outward, one hand on hip, the other holding forth her weapon. Then he demonstrated thrusting, parrying, and feinting. Elizabeth found it exciting and exhilarating, and performed very creditably. Edward watched with longing eyes.

"I wish I could have a go," he said wistfully.

"You can, sir!" said Barnaby.

"Why don't we go behind those trees over there?" Elizabeth suggested. "They won't be able to see us then." She nodded briefly in the direction of the nurses, who were watching anxiously from a distance.

"Yes!" agreed Edward, with more animation than she had yet seen in him.

Once shielded from view, Barnaby went over the drill again, this time with the Prince as his pupil.

"*Garde!*" the little boy cried as Barnaby diplomatically let him take the initiative, and the contest commenced.

"Bravo!" cried Elizabeth, clapping her hands. Edward's fair face was flushed with pleasure. He danced across the grass, thrusting and slashing the air as he went. They were all enjoying themselves so much that they did not notice Mistress Penn and her acolytes approaching.

"Stop!" that lady roared. "What are you thinking of? You'll have us all in the Tower."

The three children froze.

"I am so sorry, mistress," drawled Barnaby. "I meant no harm. It was just a bit of fun."

"My brother the Prince *should* be learning to fence," Elizabeth said defiantly.

Edward said nothing but fixed a glacial stare on his nurse, which she ignored.

"All in God's good time, and the King's," said Mistress Penn. "His Highness here is not even breeched. And, my Lord Prince, you know very well that you are not allowed to take risks. When the time comes for you to learn to fence, you will be taught by an expert swordsman, who will ensure your safety."

Elizabeth frowned. Barnaby's mouth opened in protest, but he was quickly silenced by the nurse's next words, which were addressed to a scowling Edward. "You have been disobedient, sir, and I fear that Barnaby here must pay for it."

Barnaby groaned.

CHAPTER 7

The green court gown was heavy with its elaborate sleeves and long train, and the pearl-encrusted border of its wide square neckline was cutting uncomfortably into the skin on Elizabeth's slender shoulders, but she was determined to ignore these things, for today she was one of the chief guests of honor at her father's wedding.

Beside her in the gilded splendor of the Holyday Closet of the Chapel Royal at Hampton Court, the Lady Mary stood solemnly watching the ceremony. Her gown was of tawny damask with rich crimson velvet oversleeves; like her, the score of lords and ladies here today were all magnificently dressed, and all—following the King's lead—were in a jovial, holiday mood.

Elizabeth watched as Archbishop Cranmer placed the bride's fine-boned hand in her father's giant paw and pronounced them man and wife. She had met Katherine Parr only a few times, but she liked her enormously and was glad she would be having her for her latest stepmother.

The King turned to face the congregation, happiness and jubilation plain to see in his face, and led his new wife through the bowing line of courtiers to the gallery beyond, and thence through the state apartments to the privy chamber, the guests following, laughing and jesting. The processional route was lined with members of the court and household, all jostling for a view of the new Queen.

She was not pretty as such, Elizabeth reflected, as she watched a smiling Katherine nodding regally to the left and right, but she had a comely face framed with auburn hair, and her manner was gentle and dignified.

"She is very well learned," Kat had said on learning that the King was to marry Katherine.

"I feel sorry for her," Elizabeth had opined. "Married to two old husbands, one after the other—I should have hated it."

"I heard she was not so much a wife to them as a nurse," Kat observed. *And I suspect,* she thought, *that the King knew something of this and foresaw her playing a similar role in future.* For Henry's health had declined steadily since Katherine Howard's execution. Even in his wedding finery, one could see his bandaged, ulcerous legs beneath the fine white hose, notice the fleeting wince of pain as he limped around the room, leaning heavily on his cane, and count the white hairs in his red beard. He had grown fat too; at court, there were covert jokes that three men could fit inside his doublet.

Elizabeth hated hearing such things, could not bear to think of her father as being mortal. He was Great Harry, Emperor in his own realm, Supreme Head of the Church and Defender of the Faith, and England needed him. *She* needed him. He *would* get better soon, he must.

Queen Katherine would help him, she was sure. Katherine was a good woman, a kind woman—he could not have chosen better.

"At least she is no giddy girl like the last one," Mary had said on her recent visit to Hatfield. "Although I fear she harbors suspect views on religion."

"That lady is a true lover of the Gospel," Dr. Coxe had declared in the schoolroom at Hertford. "She will be a friend to all who wish to see the Church reformed from within."

"The ladies she has chosen for her household are all of that persuasion," Mary had sniffed. "Be very wary, Elizabeth. You must not become infected with such ideas."

"You could do no better than follow her example," Dr. Coxe had told Elizabeth. "She will guide you in sound principles."

Elizabeth had decided she would make up her own mind. Already, Katherine Parr had shown a motherly interest in her, summoning her to court as soon as the forthcoming wedding had been announced. It had been long months since Elizabeth had been there, and she was highly excited when she arrived and was brought to her future stepmother.

"My Lady Elizabeth!" the widowed Lady Latimer—as she had then been—exclaimed, making a respectful curtsy and then holding out both hands, clasping Elizabeth's, and kissing her unaffectedly.

"Welcome to court!" she said warmly. "It is an honor to meet you, my Lady Elizabeth."

She smiled at the Lady Mary, who had been sitting with her when Elizabeth entered the chamber. Elizabeth noticed that the room was filled with the heady scent of summer flowers, which were arranged in pots and bowls all around the apartment. Clearly, Lady Latimer loved flowers. She noticed too Katherine's beautiful velvet shoes, embroidered with gold, peeping out from beneath her scarlet silk skirt.

Mary, hitherto disapproving of Katherine, was—to Elizabeth's surprise—smiling at her with overt friendliness.

"Lady Latimer has just been reminding me that her mother once served mine," she said.

"She was devoted to Queen Katherine," Lady Latimer said. "But that was long years ago, my Lady Elizabeth, and you and my Lady Mary here have suffered great misfortunes in your lives. It is my sincere hope that you will both come to regard me as a loving stepmother who is willing to do you all the service that she can."

Elizabeth was amazed to see Mary's eyes fill with tears and her sister suddenly lean forward and hug Katherine.

"I am sure we will become loving friends," Mary declared.

"And you, Elizabeth," said Katherine, holding out her arm. "You are a child still and need a mother's love and guidance. I know you have the excellent Katherine Champernowne as your governess, but I hope you will think of me as your mother, and come to me if you need any help or advice. It will be my pleasure rather than my duty to assist you."

"I will, madam," Elizabeth said fervently. Her eyes were shining.

A light banquet was being served as the guests mingled, and Elizabeth took care to help herself to as many sweetmeats and comfits as she could eat, for the grown-ups were too preoccupied with their wine and their talk to notice a greedy girl overstuffing herself.

The King and his new Queen were circulating, greeting their guests in turn.

"My congratulations, Sire," Lord Hertford was saying. "Your Majesty is a very lucky man." He bowed courteously to Katherine.

Elizabeth looked with interest at the King's former brother-in-law, a sober-looking man with a thin face, large nose, and thick russet beard, who, after the death of his sister, Queen Jane, had managed to stay close to the throne by virtue of being the young Prince's uncle and a man of some political astuteness.

"We are indeed, my lord!" Henry clapped him on the back, winking at Katherine. "It's about time I took myself a wife again, for the sake of my realm, and to be a comfort in my old age."

"You're hardly in your dotage yet, sir." Katherine smiled. As the King beamed broadly, she went on, "How does the Prince, my Lord Hertford?"

"My nephew is in good health, madam, and excelling at his studies. It is a comfort to know he now has a caring stepmother at last."

"I wish he could come to court," she said. "Sir, could we not have him with us? After all, his sisters are here."

The King shook his head.

"There is little I would deny you, Kate," he told her, "but the Prince's health must be my priority. The court can be a hotbed of contagion, as you know, and if he were to be exposed to that . . . The prospect is too terrible to think on, for his life is all that stands between mine and civil war."

"Of course, sir, I would not press you," she agreed hastily.

"But if, in due course, *we* have a son, Kate," Henry went on, his eyes narrowing lustfully, "then I would not need to be so protective of Edward's safety."

"I shall pray for it, my lord," Katherine assured him calmly without a trace of a blush.

"Pray on," muttered John Dudley, Viscount Lisle, who was standing nearby, to Henry's niece, Lady Margaret Douglas; Elizabeth, stealing another candied plum behind them, could hear every word. "She'll need nothing more than a miracle to achieve that!"

Anna of Cleves, invited to the wedding as the King's dear sister, joined the little group.

"Lady Margaret, my Lord Lisle," she greeted them, then cast a glance toward the newlyweds.

"A fine burden madam has taken upon herself," she murmured.

"From what I heard," said Lady Margaret in a low voice, "our new queen would have preferred to wed elsewhere."

"Hertford's little brother, Sir Thomas Seymour," Dudley supplied.

"Really? Well, he *is* very handsome," observed Anna. Elizabeth could agree with that; she had seen him often about the court.

"He's a rogue," smiled the Lady Margaret, "and by all reports she was in love with him. But the King, my good uncle, sent him packing. I hear he has gone to Brussels."

"A convenient diplomatic mission," Dudley added. "We'll not see him back for some time, I'll warrant."

"Well, I heard," whispered Anna, "that when the King proposed marriage to the lady, she said she would rather be his mistress than his wife."

"Can you blame her?" asked Margaret Douglas. "Remember Anne Boleyn and Katherine Howard! And what he did to me. I was twice in the Tower, and just because I fell in love with men he didn't approve of."

Elizabeth, listening unashamedly to this fascinating conversation, felt some alarm on hearing that the new Queen had been in love with another man. She wanted desperately to warn Katherine to take care, for terrible things could happen to a lady who was married to the King but loved someone else, or was merely accused of loving someone else. Elizabeth herself, more than most people, had good reason to know that.

Then too, having heard of the punishments meted out to Margaret Douglas, she was beginning to realize to her dismay that, if and when the time came, she might not be so successful after all in defying her father over the matter of her marrying. That was a worrying thought.

"Why, it is the Lady Elizabeth!" cried the Princess of Cleves, noticing who was standing nearby, and Elizabeth found herself enveloped in a hearty embrace, which made her feel just a little better. Dudley shot a wary look at the Lady Margaret, and the little group dispersed, the Princess leading the child back to the laden table. But somehow the sweetmeats that Anna pressed on her seemed to have lost their appeal.

Later, as Kat was helping her to disrobe, Elizabeth repeated what she had overheard.

"It's a good thing the King didn't hear them," Kat observed with an anxious look on her face, "otherwise the Lady Margaret might have found herself in the Tower a third time!"

"Do you think it's true, that the Queen was in love with Thomas Seymour before my father asked her to marry him?" Elizabeth asked, sitting down so that Kat could brush her hair.

"There was some talk of that," Kat replied, "but it may just be court gossip. Things get garbled. By all accounts, she is very fond of your father."

"Well, I'm glad he has married her," Elizabeth said. "I think she will be a very good queen. And a kind and loving stepmother. I have always dreamed of having such a stepmother."

Kat could not help feeling a dart of jealousy. To all intents and purposes, *she* had been a mother to Elizabeth, and virtually the center of her world for many years now. She had thought her position invincible. True, she was glad that the new queen was so well disposed toward her charge, but she was also inwardly fearful that Katherine Parr might prove a rival for Elizabeth's devotion. The German Princess and that giddy girl, Katherine Howard, had neither of them seemed to pose so much of a threat to Kat's position as did this charming widow with her very genuine concern for the girl's welfare, and the power to do all manner of good things for her.

But Kat was determined to ensure that no one should ever usurp her place in Elizabeth's life—not even the Queen of England.

"I have something to tell you that I think will please you, Elizabeth," the Queen said. "I have approached the King, and he has agreed that you should now have permanent lodgings at court, like the Lady Mary. And he has consented to both of you being appointed my chief ladies-in-waiting."

"Oh, madam!" cried Elizabeth ecstatically. She was already greatly fond of her new stepmother, and now she had so much more for which to be beholden to her. "I am so grateful! I am sure I do not deserve such kindness."

"Nonsense! I knew you would be pleased." Katherine beamed, and herself insisted on showing Elizabeth to her new apartments.

"They are right next to mine, overlooking the river," she told her, leading the way along the gallery, "as they will be at Whitehall too. I have sent orders there."

"Your Majesty is so kind to me," Elizabeth exclaimed, almost skipping with joy. "I could not wait to come here, to be with you—I have long sighed for such happiness. And these rooms, they are *so* beautiful." Her admiring gaze took in the vivid tapestries, the Turkish carpets, the polished, carved furniture and bright curtains. All for her!

"I asked for your table to be set in the window embrasure," the Queen said, "so that you get the best light for your studies."

"I cannot thank you enough, madam." Kat, already installed and unpacking clothes, felt the resentful tears prick as Elizabeth, never a child to show much affection, ran to her stepmother and spontaneously hugged and kissed her.

"I promise," the child vowed, "that you will never have cause to complain of me, and that I will be diligent in showing you obedience and respect."

"I have no doubt of that." The Queen smiled. "Now you will assist in tidying away your belongings, and then attend me after dinner in my privy chamber." She kissed her stepdaughter on both cheeks; then, with a kindly nod at Kat, she was gone.

"Come and sit by me," Katherine invited, and Elizabeth knelt at her feet.

"Leave us, please, Mistress Champernowne," the Queen commanded, and Kat went stiffly away.

"You really are very pretty, you know, with that striking coloring," Elizabeth's stepmother said. "We will have to order you some new gowns, seeing you are now living at court."

"Oh, that would be wonderful!" the child breathed.

"We'll do that tomorrow," Katherine said. "For now, I want to talk about your education. The King and I have marked that you are a wise and intelligent girl. You must therefore be aware that Mistress Champernowne, learned as she is, can teach you very little more. The King tells me you have been sharing some of your brother's lessons, but now that you are growing up, and lodging at court, it is meet and seemly that you have your own tutor. Your father, in his great wisdom, wants you to have every opportunity to become an example of virtuous womanhood and an ornament to the House of Tudor, and with this in mind, he entrusted me with making inquiries as to someone suitable to instruct you. I'm happy to tell you I have found such a man. His name is William Grindal, and he is a famous Greek scholar."

"Greek? You mean I am to be taught Greek, madam?" Elizabeth cried.

"And many other things besides," the Queen told her, patting her head.

"I am all impatience!" the child declared eagerly. "I cannot wait to begin."

The grizzly-haired William Grindal was no longer young, but he was very learned, and he had a quiet, tranquil way with him. On the first day, he produced a timetable of lessons and handed it to his pupil.

"If it please Your Grace, we will study languages in the mornings, when the mind is at its most retentive," he began, in his calm, authoritative voice. "You already know some Latin, French, Italian, and Spanish, I understand."

"And some Welsh, sir," Elizabeth interrupted.

"Indeed. That is interesting. Very good. Well, you will of course continue with those languages, and you will also learn Greek, for Greek is essential for the study of the New Testament, and such works of the ancients as Sophocles' tragedies and Isocrates' orations. Thus you will acquire the skills to become a great orator yourself."

"I hope I will not disappoint you, sir," Elizabeth said humbly. This was all she had hoped for, and more, and she could not cease blessing her father and stepmother for making it possible.

"For three hours each afternoon, we will read history," Master Grindal continued. "That is a good habit to establish. Through the study of history we learn more about our own civilization. Then we will look at philosophies ancient and modern. And, of course, you must practice your calligraphy and your needlework with Mistress Champernowne. The accomplished Master Battista Castiglione will attend twice a week to instruct you in Italian, and I understand that the Queen has engaged not only a new music master to further your skill on the lute, the virginals, and the viol, but also"—he sighed—"a dancing master, such is the vanity of this world; yet if you are to adorn princely courts, then you must know how to comport yourself. Her Majesty wishes you take the air each day, and walk and ride regularly, which she tells me you enjoy. Oh, and the King has specifically requested that you be given some instruction in using a crossbow. He thought that you might like to try your hand at shooting, seeing you are so good at fencing." This was accompanied by a wry smile. "It is not for me to question His Majesty's wisdom," Grindal added.

"I should like that very much!" Elizabeth told him excitedly.

Kat had received the news of Master Grindal's appointment equably enough, but inside she was boiling. So she was being relegated to teaching just calligraphy and needlework, was she? Clearly, her role as governess was being usurped, and there was nothing she could do about it. An honest woman, she admitted to herself that, no, there was not a lot more that she could teach Elizabeth; yet still she felt slighted and hurt.

Of course, she knew whom she had to blame. This was one more notch in the tally against her rival for Elizabeth's affection.

When Elizabeth arrived at Ashridge on Edward's sixth birthday, she was impressed to see him out of long skirts and breeched.

"That's a fine suit of manly clothes you have, Brother!" she complimented the little boy as he stood, feet apart, one hand on his hip, the other clasping the hilt of his dagger, looking for all the world like a miniature imitation of their father. He doffed his feathered bonnet in acknowledgment of her curtsy.

"I thank you, sweet Sister," he replied. "It was high time I left off those silly skirts."

Dr. Coxe came forward to greet Elizabeth.

"His Highness looks every inch the prince now," he declared, smiling.

"Dr. Coxe is now my governor," Edward explained proudly. "From today, I will no longer be under the governance of women. Lady Bryan and Mistress Penn have already left."

He spoke dispassionately, as if this were as inconsequential a matter as the weather. Elizabeth tried to imagine how she would feel if her beloved Kat left her. Her brother's coolness disconcerted her.

"Are you not sad?" she asked. "Those ladies have looked after you from birth. You will miss them sorely."

"It is not fitting that the heir to the throne be subject to petticoat rule," Edward said haughtily, obviously reciting words he must have heard several times in recent days, and dismissing the subject. "Come and meet the young gentlemen whom our father has appointed to share my education and be my playfellows."

He turned to a waiting line of more than a dozen young boys, all aristocrats by birth, and presented each in turn to Elizabeth.

"Henry Brandon, son to the Duke of Suffolk . . . Henry, Lord Hastings . . ." Each boy bowed low in turn as Elizabeth progressed along the line.

"Robert Dudley, son to the Viscount Lisle."

Elizabeth's eyes met the saucy fellow's bold gaze and recognized a kindred spirit. Robert Dudley was about her age, she guessed; he looked like a gypsy or satyr with his dark, Italianate coloring and foxy face, and he had a mischievous glint in his eyes. The bow he swept was almost insultingly exaggerated, and certainly designed to draw attention to himself. I shall have to watch this one, thought Elizabeth. *And* I should like to teach him some manners . . .

As it was Edward's birthday, there would be no lessons today. Instead, the Prince's long-cherished wish was to be granted. The King had agreed that he should start his formal instruction in fencing and horsemanship. The boys were chattering excitedly about these activities as they divested themselves of their doublets and tested the points of their blunted foils.

"My Lady Elizabeth, pray be seated," invited Dr. Coxe, indicating a high carved chair on the dais and pulling a stool up beside her. "We will have a good view of the sport from here."

"Am I only to watch?" Elizabeth asked, a little indignant. "Barnaby here knows I can handle a foil as well as any boy. He taught me."

Barnaby FitzPatrick, hearing her words, grinned.

"That is very true, sir. The Lady Elizabeth might put all of us to shame."

"A girl, fencing?" Robert Dudley asked, raising a sardonic eyebrow.

"You are impudent, sir," Elizabeth told him haughtily. "I will show you. Fencing Master, may I be this gentleman's partner?"

Robert's jaw dropped. She smiled at him sweetly.

"We shall play to decide which is the better, boy or girl," she declared.

"But Your Grace cannot fence in those long skirts," Barnaby pointed out. "Master Robert will have the advantage."

"Then let him!" Elizabeth laughed. Robert's cheeks were flushed with annoyance.

"Must I, sir?" he appealed to Dr. Coxe.

"We cannot gainsay a lady, especially a King's daughter," the tutor told him with a satisfied grin. It would be good for this proud boy to suffer a little humiliation.

The other young gentlemen having been paired off, the master demonstrated the correct stance and a few expert thrusts. "There are two kinds of swordsman. The duelist will rely on his skill with a rapier," he explained, "while the athlete will achieve victory through his footwork. You must decide which you will be, gentlemen—and my lady!"

"I will be a duelist," Elizabeth stated, her eyes gleaming.

"Then I must be also," Robert muttered reluctantly.

"*Garde!*" she cried and lunged forward, parrying thrust for thrust. Taken unawares, for he had not really believed in her boasts, Robert was unprepared for the determination of her assault, and found himself stepping backward and bumping inelegantly into the young Lord Hastings.

"Parry!" he cried, recovering himself, but Elizabeth stood her ground determinedly. After some minutes of this, the master, seeing that the match was becoming dangerously competitive, called a halt.

"A good first effort, Your Grace!" he cried, beaming at the Prince, who had also been giving a good account of himself.

As they withdrew reluctantly to the dais, Robert, freed from the fear of being vanquished by a mere girl, said gallantly, "You were good, my lady."

Glancing sideways at the dark-haired boy, Elizabeth was surprised to read admiration in his expression.

"I had a worthy opponent, sir," she answered. Having proved her point, she could afford to be generous.

She saw a lot of Robert Dudley during the week of her visit, for she was allowed to join the Prince and his noble companions for lessons. Robert did not shine in the schoolroom.

"Why should I learn Greek?" he grumbled, taking advantage of Dr. Coxe's temporary absence to lay down his pen.

"So that you can be a Humanist and study the works of the ancients," Edward told him.

"I'd rather be out riding," Robert said. He had a passion for horses.

"I can understand that, for I also love riding," said Elizabeth, "but I love learning too, especially history and languages."

"It's all right for you, my lady, you are a girl and are not obliged to learn the things that a young gentleman needs to learn," Robert said, a touch patronizingly.

"I assure you, Master Robert, that I study the same things as you do!" Elizabeth retorted hotly.

"What, geography, statecraft, and classics?" Robert asked.

"Those things and more," she told him proudly. "And I love every minute of it."

"How can you?" he groaned.

"Shhh," Henry Brandon hissed. "Dr. Coxe will hear us."

"He's gone for a piss," smirked Hastings. "Saving your pardon, my lady."

Elizabeth smiled. She liked hearing the boys' earthy chat.

"But Sister, you are not going to be king of England," Edward pointed out. "Why should you learn such things when all you will do when you grow up is just get married and have babies, like all girls."

"I will not!" cried Elizabeth hotly. "I will never marry!"

"Oh, yes you will," the Prince said placidly.

"Wait and see!" she challenged him.

"If our father commands it, you will have to obey," he told her smugly.

"We'll see about that!" she said spiritedly.

"I'd like to see you try to defy him," Robert said. The boys laughed.

"He'd cut off your head!" yelled young Henry Brandon, then wondered why a hush had suddenly descended. Fifteen wary pairs of eyes looked uncomfortably at the red-haired girl sitting frowning at the end of the long table.

"It's all right," said Elizabeth, quickly recovering herself. "Hadn't we better get back to work? I think I can hear Dr. Coxe coming."

"Did you mean it, my Lady Elizabeth?" asked Robert Dudley, falling into step with Elizabeth as she set out on a brisk early-morning walk through the woods at Ashridge with Blanche Parry in tow. It was cold, and their breath was misty in the air. It was the last day of her visit.

"Mean what, Master Robert?" Elizabeth asked.

"What you said yesterday, about never marrying." His eyes were unexpectedly sympathetic. "Would you really disobey the King if he ordered you to?"

"I do mean it," she said. "I *would* refuse. My father loves me. He would not force me."

Robert looked doubtful. "He might wish to marry you to a great prince or lord, for some good advantage to himself. You could not refuse then."

"I would, even if I were promised to the Emperor himself," she answered vehemently. "I should hate to be married."

"My father says it is our duty to marry," Robert told her. "He said he is arranging all our marriages for policy or profit."

"All?" Elizabeth inquired.

"I have lots of brothers and sisters, some older than me," Robert explained. "I suppose I too will have to marry someday. But not for ages yet—I am but ten."

"Me too," said Elizabeth.

"Well, in two years' time," he warned her, "you can be married."

"Not if I can help it," she replied stoutly.

"Why are you so afraid?" Robert asked.

"I'm not telling you," she replied.

"I noticed you were upset when that stupid Henry Brandon joked about the King cutting your head off," he ventured. "I can guess why. My grandfather was beheaded. My father says all the best families have a traitor among their forebears."

"My mother, Queen Anne, was no traitor," Elizabeth said.

"Neither was my grandfather," Robert countered. "But he had made himself unpopular by raising heavy taxes for King Henry the Seventh, and when your father came to the throne, he wanted the people to love him, so he had my grandfather executed. Oh, don't worry," he added, seeing her face, "I don't hold it against you or the King."

"I should hope not," she retorted, and they walked on in silence for a space.

"It seems we have something in common, then," Elizabeth said at length.

"More than that." Robert smiled. "You like riding."

"I love it," she replied.

"Shall we ride out together?" he invited.

"Yes!" she cried gleefully. "Let's go now!" And she wheeled around and raced back toward the stables, with Robert in close pursuit.

CHAPTER 8

1544

Life at court was as wonderful and exciting as Elizabeth had dreamed it would be. It was colorful, busy, and noisy, all the things that life in the nursery palaces was not, and most marvelous of all was the privilege of being close to her father. He was the center not only of her universe but of everybody else's too, massive, powerful, and magnificent. Everything revolved around him, and from him flowed an endless tide of patronage and favor. Elizabeth became used to seeing the hordes of petitioners who were constantly crowding the galleries and state apartments, all of them seeking place or preferment, or just the chance of a word or nod from the King at his daily coming forth in procession to chapel.

As his daughter, she was herself courted and flattered. The courtiers curried favor with her, bowing and scraping as she passed. She reveled in the heady sense of importance that this gave her, she who, despite her bastard status, had always clung to the belief that she was still an important personage. Yet she was old enough now to sense the darker side of life at court, the insincerity, the vicious intrigues, the backbiting, the tensions and jealousies. And fear too . . . that was often palpable. How could it not be, when the King's displeasure could mean imprisonment, ruin, or even death?

But Elizabeth preferred not to dwell on those aspects, for they unsettled her too greatly. Fortunately, there were many splendid distractions, such as Katherine's first Christmas as queen, which had been as wonderful as Elizabeth had anticipated, with lavish festivities at Hampton Court and the revels she so enjoyed; and her stepmother had been delighted with the linen coif that Elizabeth had painstakingly embroidered for her.

In the New Year of 1544, however, the King's bad leg laid him low.

"Can I see my father?" she asked Katherine Parr. "I am worrying about his health."

"Not just now," the Queen said distractedly, arranging and rearranging her beloved flowers. "He is not well enough to receive visitors."

"Will he get better?" the child inquired anxiously. Katherine recovered herself with an effort.

"Yes, of course he will," she replied briskly, displaying more confidence than she felt. "Wait a day or so, and then perhaps you may see him."

Katherine was as good as her word, but when, a week later, Elizabeth was at last admitted to the King's chamber, she was horrified to see him looking so gray and drawn with pain, with his heavily bandaged leg propped up on a footstool. His appearance brought home to her forcefully the possibility of his dying, but she shied away from that unthinkable thought, unwilling even to imagine a world without her father in it. Surely day and night would cease following each other without him here to order everything! He could not die, he must not die! It was impossible.

Trying not to wrinkle her nose at the sweet stink in the room, she sank into her deepest curtsy.

"Up, Daughter," the King said. "I am sorry I have kept you from me. I did not wish you to see me laid so low."

He shifted painfully in his chair, wincing as the agony speared through his calf.

"The bone worked its way through," he told her, grimacing. "It's troubled me mightily since I had the cursed misfortune to fall from my horse all those years ago. And to make things worse, those wretched doctors are nagging me to restrict myself to a plain diet. They say I am grown too fat. Would you say that, Bessy?"

"Never, Sire," she said. "I would never presume so far."

"That's what I told the knaves, that they presume too far! Hah! You're a chip off the old block, eh, Bessy!"

Elizabeth smiled. She loved it when her father called her Bessy and laughed with her. Then she felt sure of his love and filled with a blessed sense of happiness and security.

"You are not to worry," he told her. "In a few days I'll be up and about again, sound as a bell. Now sit on that stool there and tell me what you have been learning lately."

"I've been studying Cicero," Elizabeth said proudly.

"*Appetitus rationi pareat*—can you translate that?" asked the King.

"Yes, sir. Let desire be ruled by reason."

"It is a good maxim," he told her, thinking it was one he could with profit have applied to himself in the days when he was pursuing her mother without thought for the consequences of his reckless passion. Oh, but he had been younger then, strong and virile, and had thought himself invincible. Now, he thought sadly, I am a wreck of a man, old before my time. May God preserve me until my little son is grown.

"*Saepe ne utile quidem est scire quid futurum sic,*" he recited sadly. Elizabeth looked at him uncertainly.

"Shall I translate that too, sir?" she ventured.

"Yes, yes," he said, managing a smile.

"Often," she said, choosing her words with care, "it is not advantageous to know what will be."

"Another truism," the King observed, "and sadly apt too. He had a sound understanding, did Cicero."

"There is a saying of his that I especially like," Elizabeth told him. "It is *Semper eadem,* always the same. I hope I shall always be that, unvarying in my love and duty to you, Sir, and to the Queen, and to my brother the Prince."

"I am glad to see you are such a dutiful child," Henry said, reaching out his heavily beringed hand and patting her shoulder. "I was very impressed by your gift to the Queen. One day, you must make me a nightcap like it." His eyes twinkled wickedly.

"Oh, sir, I did not mean to neglect you!" Elizabeth protested in a fluster. "I merely wished to show my devotion to Her Majesty, who has been so kind to me."

"I but jested, Bessy!" Henry was grinning; his narrow blue eyes, sunk in creases of fat, were twinkling. "Of course you did, and I applaud that, for I know how much you hate needlework!"

There was a tap at the door.

"Come in, Kate!" the King called.

The door opened and the Queen entered, carrying a covered silver bowl.

"Some aleberry, sir, to tempt you," she said, placing it on the little table by the King's chair and handing him a small apostle spoon.

"You are a good wife, Kate." He smiled, avidly sampling the pudding.

"What's that, sir?" Elizabeth asked. The smell was mouthwatering.

"Have you never had aleberry, Bessy?" the King asked, extending the spoon. "It's a bread pudding of sorts, with fruit. Try some, here."

"It's delicious," his daughter said, thrilled to be sharing food in such a homely fashion with her father, who usually ate with great ceremony.

"Have another spoonful," the King offered.

"You should be eating that yourself, sir, to build up your strength," Katherine said, moving gracefully to the other side of the room, where she smoothed the coverlet on the bed and plumped the pillows.

"You see how I am ordered about, Bessy," Henry said ruefully. "Your good stepmother has forgotten who I am."

"Oh, but, sir, I never intended . . . ," Katherine cried.

"I know, Kate," he grinned. "Calm yourself, I but jested. Now help me up, I would lie down for a space. Elizabeth, you may finish that pudding." He handed her the bowl and tried to lever himself out of the chair, gripping the arms to steady himself.

"It's no good," he wheezed, sinking back into it, "I haven't the strength."

"Shall I call your gentlemen, Sire?" the Queen asked, concern in her face.

"No, Kate, do not trouble them. I will stay here rather than have them see me so weak. Elizabeth, you may go. Press on with Cicero—he will reward you manifoldly."

Elizabeth swallowed the last of the aleberry, made her obeisance, and slipped out of the room.

"I think we will have cause to be proud of that young lady," Henry told Katherine as the door closed. "We'll make a doctor of her yet!"

Katherine smiled and handed him a goblet of wine.

"And Mary," he went on, "she's conformable enough these days. You've done well with her, Kate."

"If I may venture to say so, sir, what Mary needs is a husband. If you could ever see your way to finding one for her . . . She is twenty-eight now, and so longing for marriage and children."

Henry frowned.

"I have been meaning to. There have been discussions, negotiations . . . I fear that her bastard status is a barrier to a royal match, yet there is no courtier I would favor with her hand at present. But I will bear it in mind."

"Your Majesty is, as ever, most careful for your children," Katherine observed, seating herself on the stool beside him and taking up her needle and thread.

"I wanted to speak privately with you, Kate," he said gruffly, and with uncustomary hesitation. "There is to be a new Act of Succession, to take account of our marriage and other things. My councillors thought it advisable." He did not tell her that they had urged him to make provision for the succession out of fear that the Prince would succumb to a childhood illness, as many children did. They think I will not live long, he thought, although they dare not voice that concern, since predicting the King's death was now high treason.

Henry took a deep breath. What he had to say to Kate was humiliating in the extreme for one such as himself to admit to, but it had to be said.

"The act refers to the possibility of our union being blessed with offspring," he said. "I wanted to assure you that you need not fear my having any such expectations. I have not been much of a husband to you, and I doubt I will be again."

Katherine's eyes filled with tears. She could easily guess what it had cost him to say that.

"Of course you will, sir," she hastened to reassure him. "You are ill and not yourself at all. And if your recovery takes longer than anticipated, well then, I am truly happy and contented as we are."

The King smiled sadly at her and patted her hand.

"I have never had a wife more agreeable to my heart than you, Kate," he said quietly. "You are the light of my eyes, the staff of my old age. I and my children have much for which to be grateful to you. And you will doubtless be pleased to hear that, when this new act becomes law, Mary and Elizabeth will be reinstated in the succession after Edward."

The Queen's amiable features lit up with joy.

"Oh, sir, you can surely understand what this will mean to them both."

Henry, basking virtuously in her approval, went on, "I intend the throne to descend to the heirs of my body, and not to the Queen of Scots, my sister Margaret's granddaughter. Her I mean to marry to Edward, and not all the Scots from Jedburgh to Inverness will stop me. Scotland will be mine, and the Crowns will be united."

"Will that not mean war?" Katherine asked.

"It may," said Henry grimly. "But let us face that in due course. In the meantime, I intend that my daughters will have the right to succeed me, in turn, after Edward, and after them, the heirs of my sister Mary, the Brandons and the Greys. But it will never come to that. Edward will marry and have children, and I may even find a husband for Mary."

He smiled at his wife. "And Elizabeth too, if God spares me that long."

"Elizabeth is telling anyone who will listen that she will never marry," Katherine confided.

Henry chuckled.

"Maidenly modesty, eh? Most fitting. She'll change her mind in a few years when the itch comes upon her!"

"Sire!" exclaimed his wife, reddening. "For shame! Seriously, my lord, I think she is resolved on the matter."

"Well I'll unresolve her," laughed the King. "She's far too young to make up her mind on such a matter. We'll give her time to grow out of it. Marriage is a woman's natural state. Just wait until she sees a lusty man she fancies!"

The Queen smiled.

"Regarding Your Majesty's daughters," she said, "does restoring them to the succession mean that they are to be legitimated?"

Henry frowned.

"Nay, Kate. That would open up a nest of vipers, to be sure. They are both the fruit of unlawful unions, and I will not undo what I have already done. Yet I am the King, and if I wanted to put my bonnet on a pole and name it my next heir, I could do it. Thus I can place my bastard daughters in the line of succession."

"Your Majesty's wisdom is, as ever, faultless," Katherine flattered him.

Henry leaned back in his chair, satisfied that he had chosen the best possible course.

"I am to be restored to the succession?" Elizabeth was so speechless with astonishment and delight that she forgot respectfully to address her father by his due title. He had taken the opportunity of breaking the good news to her and Mary at a private supper in the privy chamber, with only the Queen and Archbishop Cranmer present. The tablecloth had been removed, the servants had withdrawn, and they were all partaking of sweet wafers washed down with the spiced wine known as hippocras.

Mary's eyes were brimming with tears. Looking at the two sisters, Queen Katherine felt like crying with joy herself.

"Yes," the King replied magnanimously, "but only after Edward and his heirs. Then, Mary, it will be you and your heirs, and after you, it will be Elizabeth."

"And my heirs, Sire?" Elizabeth asked.

"Naturally. But rumor has it, young Bessy, that you do not intend to take a husband, so in all likelihood you will have no heirs." The King winked at her.

"That is so, sir," Elizabeth said in all seriousness. She had thought a lot more about marriage lately, now that she was within eighteen months of reaching marriageable age, and even more about its rather alarming crested and cloven aspect, and it still seemed to her that the state of matrimony had no advantages at all, and indeed, much to be said against it.

"Hmm," Henry murmured, pulling his beard. "We will see about that in time to come."

He was thinking that someday, and that day not too far distant, Elizabeth's budding charms would wreak havoc among men. She already knew well how to play the coquette, as Anne had, God curse her. Anne . . . He had been young then, young and in the vigor of his manhood. And she had spurned it. All those wasted years of longing . . . He pulled himself up. He was married to Kate now, and must forget Anne. He had been trying to forget Anne for years. His good mood dissipated.

The Queen and the Archbishop were endeavoring to hide their smiles. Mary was preoccupied, trying to digest the momentous news and hardly daring to ask the question that was burning in her mind.

"Sire," she began nervously, her voice coming out as a croak. "Does this mean that Your Majesty intends to declare us trueborn?"

"Alas, I cannot do that, Daughter," the King answered, "for I was never truly married to your mother, nor to Elizabeth's, as His Grace of Canterbury here will confirm."

Cranmer rose quickly to the occasion.

"Indeed, Your Highnesses. The marriage to the late Princess Dowager was expressly forbidden by Scripture—Leviticus, chapter eighteen, verse—"

"Yes, yes, we know all that," interrupted the King.

"And as for the Lady Elizabeth's mother," Cranmer hurried on, "there was of course the consanguinity caused by Your Majesty's previous, er, um, relations with her sister."

"Indeed," cut in Henry, embarrassed. "So, my Daughters, you understand the position."

"Yes, Sire," said the sisters in unison, both looking uncomfortable and unhappy, although in Elizabeth's eye there was a question.

"Pardon me, sir," she said, innocently enough, "I thought I had been declared a bastard because my mother, Queen Anne, was executed for treason."

As Mary stifled a gasp, Katherine's face registered dismay, and Cranmer looked as if he would rather be anywhere else. No one, these eight long years, had ever dared mention Anne Boleyn's name, still less her beheading, to the King.

Henry rested his steely gaze on his younger daughter.

"Did you indeed, Elizabeth? Did no one ever explain otherwise to you?"

"No, sir."

"Well, someone has been greatly remiss," he observed darkly. "You should know that my union with your mother was no true marriage. It was dissolved before her death. *That* is why you were declared baseborn."

"But if my mother had not committed treason, sir, surely you would have stayed married to her?" Elizabeth inquired with precocious insight. She knew she was venturing into a quagmire, but for the sake of her mother's memory, and the injustice that she was sure had been done her, she felt compelled to pursue the matter. And her father had answered her question, after his fashion.

"Enough!" Henry banged his fist on the table and everyone jumped.

"Your mother was a traitor," he snarled. "She betrayed me with five men, one her own brother, do you hear me? And she plotted my death! Would you still have had me stay married to her?"

"Sir," ventured the Queen nervously, clutching his sleeve, "the child is distressed . . ." Shocked tears were spurting from Elizabeth's eyes.

"As well she might be," he roared, "having a mother like that!"

"She was not like that!" cried Elizabeth, goaded beyond circumspection.

Henry stopped raging and stared at her. Mary got up suddenly, curtsied, and ran softly from the room, almost weeping. The Archbishop's hands were clasped as if in prayer, his head bent. Katherine looked at Elizabeth in distress. The girl's face was white, her cheeks wet.

"What did you say?" the King asked quietly. His tone was menacing.

"Sir, I know my mother was innocent," Elizabeth faltered.

"And who told you that?"

"I heard it from several people . . . servants . . . ladies," Elizabeth lied, hoping fervently that her father would not guess it had been Kat.

"Then you heard wrongly," the King barked decisively. His blue eyes were ice-cold, but Elizabeth pressed dangerously on.

"I've heard it said that Master Cromwell took occasion to get rid of her, sir, and that he made such a good case that you had to believe it." At least that sounded diplomatic.

"This is arrant nonsense," Henry growled. "Was I a puppet, to be manipulated by others? That woman was as guilty as sin. I knew her well, never forget it."

"I cannot believe it! She was innocent!" Elizabeth wailed, bursting afresh into noisy tears. Katherine made to go to her, but the King's firm hand on her shoulder kept her in her place.

"Then you must have leisure in which to think on the matter," he decreed ominously. "You will be banished from court for your impudence. You will go to Hatfield tomorrow, with Mistress Champernowne, and you will not be allowed to return until you have arrived at proper regard for the truth. Do you understand?"

Elizabeth was weeping copiously, her body racked with shuddering sobs.

"Do you hear me?" her father thundered.

"Yes, sir," she mumbled.

"Now go!" he commanded. She fled from the chamber.

"My lord," Katherine ventured later that night, when they were alone and seated before the fire in their bedchamber. "Forgive me for interfering, but might I speak up for the Lady Elizabeth?"

Henry grunted, glowering. He was still angry, and had called a halt to the supper party as soon as Elizabeth had left. The Archbishop had made his grateful farewells, and the Queen had then steadied her nerves by drinking a large goblet of Rhenish. The King was sipping his in silence, staring broodingly at the leaping flames.

"I cannot think what you can say in her defense, Kate," he huffed. "She dared to contradict me, and to question my justice."

"Sire, may I be candid with you?" Katherine pleaded.

"Well?" the King asked petulantly. "Speak; out with it."

Katherine took a deep breath. "She is a child, Sire, and it must be difficult for her, coming to terms with what happened to her mother, however just it was. She has listened to servants' gossip and taken it for the truth. You cannot blame her for wanting to believe the best of her mother."

"Ah, but Kate, if she believes the best of her mother, then she has to believe the worst of me, her father. Believe me, I was justified—"

"Of course you were, Sire, the whole world knows that. Yet she wants to think that you were misled, but that you acted in good faith."

Henry regarded his wife through narrowed eyes.

"Are you saying she believes me a fool, Kate?"

"Nay, Sire, Heaven forbid. As you said, you knew her mother well. Obviously, the charges were entirely credible."

"Now *you* go too far, Kate," the King accused her, scowling. "A sorry thing it is when my daughter and my wife accuse me of sending an innocent woman to the block. I tell you, she was guilty. And yet you dare to question my justice!"

"Never, Sire!" cried Katherine. "I did not say *I* believed her innocent, only that a ten-year-old child believes it. And I pray you to consider her youth, and the fact that it is her mother of whom we speak."

"Nevertheless, she must learn her lesson," stated the King harshly. "And there's an end to the matter."

Katherine looked crestfallen. She sank into her chair and toyed with her empty goblet, thinking she might do well to refill it.

"You mean to be kind, Kate." Henry's voice was gentler now. "But you meddle in matters that do not concern you. Oh, come," he said wearily, seeing her face, "you are a kind and gentle soul, darling, I know that. Ever the peacemaker. I tell you, it will not harm Elizabeth to cool her heels at Hatfield for a space and reflect upon her outrageous behavior. I may be her father, but she must learn how to address her sovereign, and never to gainsay or question him."

"Yes, Sire." Katherine smiled weakly and reached for the decanter.

Elizabeth was being jolted along the frosty road that led to Hatfield, a mournful Kat at her side.

"I do wish the King had given us more time to prepare for this," Kat had moaned as she bustled about Elizabeth's apartment, chivvying the maids to pack and look sharp about it. "I've all your gear to pack, the house won't have been aired, and I'll wager it'll be freezing, as the fires can't have been lit for weeks."

Elizabeth was too sunk in misery to care. Banished from court, banished . . . The dread words were beating a pattern in her head. She barely noticed the freezing draft that flapped the leather curtains of the litter. She could not forget what the King had said, and not only his harsh words banishing her from court. He had been adamant about her mother's guilt, and worse still, he had accused Anne of betraying him with *five* men—and one of them, shockingly, her own brother. She had not known about that, had in fact assumed that Anne had had only one alleged partner in crime. But her own brother? Could it be true? She felt sick at the thought. Surely it was very, very wrong to do that act with one's brother? It was bad enough doing it with four other men. *Had* Anne been that wicked? Her father had been adamant about her guilt.

It seemed as if her carefully nurtured image of her wronged mother was about to crumple like a house of cards. That was more than she could bear, and suddenly, she found she could contain herself no longer.

"Kat," she said, turning a tragic face to her governess. "The King—he said my mother betrayed him with five men, and that one was her own brother." Her voice trailed off . . . She could say no more, or she would lose control of herself.

Kat could see the despair and misery in Elizabeth's eyes. All she had known up till now was that her charge had offended the King and been ordered to Hatfield in disgrace; a regretful Lord Hertford had been sent to confirm it. More than this Kat had been unable to extract from a tight-lipped Elizabeth, and there had been no time to seek out the Queen, even if she had wanted to.

But now things were beginning to be clearer. She curled a consoling arm around the girl's thin shoulders.

"Comfort yourself, child. That is what was *alleged* against your mother. But as I have told you, I firmly believe that was not the truth of it."

"Which is what I told my father," Elizabeth cried.

"You did what?" Kat was horrified.

"I said she was innocent," Elizabeth explained. "I did not say you had told me. He asked where I had heard it, and I said I'd heard the servants gossiping."

Kat slumped in her seat. Her heart was pounding fit to burst, and her whole body was atremble.

"Dear Lord, I would get into terrible trouble if the King found out I had told you your mother was innocent," she gasped.

"I know that," Elizabeth protested. "I took care to protect you. He did not press me further, so I am sure you are safe. But I *must* know what happened, Kat. I must."

"Very well, but you must *never* repeat what I am about to say," Kat warned. "Unless you want a new governess, that is." She was not jesting.

"I promise I will not," Elizabeth vowed.

Kat relaxed a little.

"Your mother was accused with five men, so much is true," she began, "and one was her brother, Lord Rochford. It was his own wife who laid evidence against him. He had never loved her, and she was vilely jealous of his natural affection for his sister. My belief is that she did it out of spite, after Master Cromwell offered her a bribe. Certainly, she was looked after very generously when it was all over. All the other accused men except one were gentlemen of the King's Privy Chamber; the fifth man was Mark Smeaton, a musician of the court. *That* caused a huge scandal, I can tell you. People were wondering how the Queen could have stooped so low, but of course, she hardly knew him, and anyway, she was too proud to have thus demeaned herself. Believe me, I spoke to those who knew her."

"So you think Lady Rochford lied?" Elizabeth asked, praying there would be no room for doubt.

"Indeed I do," said Kat grimly. "A nasty woman she was. She abetted Katherine Howard in her crimes, and was executed for her pains."

"Executed?" echoed a startled Elizabeth.

"Aye, just after her poor young mistress. Lady Rochford had gone mad under questioning, and so the King had to pass a special Act of Parliament allowing him to execute lunatics. But they say she was sane enough when she went to the scaffold. I say she got what she richly deserved for having borne false witness against her poor husband and your mother."

"Was there not a great scandal about that too?" Elizabeth wanted to know. "I mean, the thing that Lady Rochford accused my mother of." She could not bring herself to describe it.

"Well, some people pretended to be shocked, but I think most just found it hard to believe. It was as if Master Cromwell was grasping at anything he could think of to get rid of Queen Anne. As for that charge of plotting to kill the King, well, that was utter nonsense. She was—how do I say this?—not popular, and without the King to protect her, her enemies at court would have tried to bring her down. So why should she wish to do away with her protector? It would have been folly, and she was no fool."

"So you think she was innocent of *all* the accusations?" Elizabeth urged.

"I do, my lady, I do," Kat declared. "Four of the accused men protested her innocence, and theirs, to the end. Only Mark Smeaton confessed, but that was under torture, I'm sure."

"Torture?" Elizabeth exclaimed, with a shudder. She knew what torture was.

Kat paused. Elizabeth was still quite young. Was she ready to hear the brutal details of what was believed to have happened in Master Cromwell's house?

"Master Cromwell had him put to the torture," she said carefully. "They say the pain was so great that he would have said anything to stop it."

"What did they do?" Elizabeth was wide-eyed with horror.

"They tied a knotted rope around his eyes and kept twisting it," Kat told her, hoping that this would not prove too much for her charge to stomach.

"Oh, the poor wretch," Elizabeth said, feeling a little sick. "No wonder he talked. I would have talked."

"Your mother herself declared her innocence before God at her trial," Kat went on. "What more can I say? They just made an occasion to get rid of her. Master Cromwell had his reasons, I suppose. But little of it made sense to me. Elizabeth, you must never doubt that your mother was a good woman, nor that she loved you very much. Cherish her memory, child, but learn to dissemble. To speak of her as you did to the King was rash and dangerous, and we are paying the price of it now. But our punishment could have been far worse, remember that."

"I will, dear Kat, I promise," Elizabeth said, feeling greatly cheered. "I will never mention my mother's name to anyone but you again."

"My lady, a messenger has come! He has something for you!"

When the Queen's missive arrived, it was high summer and the King, ignoring his infirmity and his bad legs, had gone to Boulogne to fight the French. Elizabeth had been watching out for a messenger for days, and when one cantered into the courtyard at Hatfield and she heard Kat calling her, she pattered down the stairs as fast as she could and grabbed the rolled parchment he handed her with scant ceremony.

For several long months now, she had languished in exile. Kat had sent good reports of her to the Queen, and had stressed her dutifulness, and Katherine had spoken up for her, but there had come no word from the King, no reprieve.

Elizabeth felt as if she were pining away; her banishment was becoming unbearable. Without her father's favor, she could not live.

I have tried my best, she told herself. I have worked hard at my lessons—Master Grindal told me he's known no finer scholar—and I've tried to behave impeccably. Why is there no word from my father? Does he not love me anymore? Have I forfeited his love forever?

Her life in the shadow of his displeasure was arid, devoid of comfort. It was like being deprived of the sun.

Kat had come upon her moping, sitting dejectedly on a window seat and drumming her heels against the wooden paneling.

"Come now," she said briskly. "Stop wasting your time. If you've nothing to do, find a book."

Elizabeth raised plaintive, tragic eyes to her.

"Don't look at *me*!" Kat cried in exasperation. "You brought this on yourself, child. Perhaps it will teach you never to be so rash again as to speak your mind in front of the King. Wiser fools than you have done so and not gotten off so lightly, so be grateful we're both safe here, instead of in the Tower."

"Shouldn't I write to my father and beg his forgiveness?" Elizabeth asked. "Then perchance he will summon me and all will be well. I do so want all to be well."

"Bide your time," Kat counseled. "Your father is in France and busy with the war. Wait until he returns. He may be in a different frame of mind then, especially if God grants him great victories."

But Elizabeth was too sunk in misery to heed such comfort. At length, unable to bear it any longer, she had sat down at her desk and composed a letter to her stepmother, explaining that she dared not write directly to her father, and entreating Katherine to speak once more for her.

My exile is most painful to me, she wrote. *I thank you for all your intercessions on my behalf, and beg you to pray just one more time for His Majesty's sweet benediction on his humble daughter.* She read this over, then added, *And tell him I beseech God to send him a good victory over his enemies, and soon, so that Your Highness and I may rejoice in his happy return.*

Now, days later, her fingers were trembling as she unrolled the scrolled parchment that she had received in reply. It bore the Queen's seal. With Kat at her elbow, Elizabeth scanned the page quickly, hardly daring to hope.

"He has relented!" she cried ecstatically. "My father has relented, and he has said I may go to Hampton Court to keep the Queen company. I knew the Queen would be my friend. It is she whom I must thank for this, I'm sure of it! Oh, I am so relieved and happy!"

Kat embraced her, concealing her dismay as best she could. For these few months, fraught as they were, Elizabeth had been entirely hers again. Now, once more, she must share her with that interloper, the Queen—

for thus did she regard Katherine Parr. Then again, she could not but rejoice that Elizabeth had been restored to her father's favor, and that the anxious weeks of exile were over.

Elizabeth's return to court was not as joyful as she had anticipated. Katherine greeted her warmly enough with outstretched hands, but her hazel eyes were shadowed with worry. The King had entrusted her with the government of the realm during his absence, and she now found herself faced with a more deadly peril than the French forces that he was confronting.

"There is plague in London," she said fearfully. "We must leave Hampton for Enfield, and take the Prince with us, as a matter of urgency."

Enfield was a palace Elizabeth knew well, for she had stayed there on several occasions. At least this time she would be in residence with the court.

While she and Kat were making ready, the Lady Mary came to her chamber. Elizabeth noticed that Mary was holding herself unusually stiff and aloof. After long weeks of separation, she saw subtle changes in her sister that she had not been aware of before. Mary looked older; there were fine lines about her eyes, and she appeared a little faded in her bright finery.

The sisters embraced.

"I am pleased to see you back at court," Mary said. "I trust your banishment has taught you discretion and wisdom." Her manner was faintly disapproving.

Elizabeth did not want to discuss the reason for her exile. That matter was best left alone.

"I hope so, Sister," she said quietly.

As Kat left the room, her arms laden with chemises and stockings, Mary seated herself in the only chair. There were things she felt she had to say.

"I have not been able to forget what you said to the King our father," she began.

Elizabeth looked at her, startled.

"It's not true that your mother was innocent," Mary said vehemently, the words tumbling out. "I have no doubt whatsoever that she was guilty as charged. She was a ruthless woman who injured many, myself and my sainted mother included. She was quite capable of playing the King false, I promise you. My advice to you, Sister, is to forget you ever had a mother like that."

Elizabeth caught the note of obsessive grievance in Mary's voice. She knew instinctively that it would be unwise to provoke her further by arguing with her.

"Forgive me, Sister, but I had heard otherwise," she said simply.

"Then you heard wrongly," Mary retorted. Her voice grew shrill. "She was evil, that woman. She urged the King, again and again, to send me and my mother to the block. She had me sent to wait upon you when you were a baby, and she told those that had charge of me to beat me for the little bastard that I had become. How could you think such a one innocent?"

"I am very sorry for your afflictions, Sister," Elizabeth whispered, aware more of the need to be diplomatic than of the desire to defend her mother. "They were not of my making, nor my desire."

"How could you think her innocent?" Mary persisted. Her thin lips were pursed with resentment. Elizabeth had never seen her like this, so fervent, so driven.

"I heard things," she answered, then grew a touch defiant. "The whole world does not think my mother guilty."

"Who said these things to you?" Mary demanded to know.

"I forget," Elizabeth said firmly.

"Oh, you are clever," Mary cried. "You are like her, you can twist words. But she was not so discreet. The whole world knew of her malice; she did not trouble to hide it."

"Sister, *I* bear you no malice," Elizabeth hastened to reassure her. "I am ever mindful of your kindness to me."

"I daresay, but you are *her* daughter," Mary said.

Elizabeth dared not trust herself to answer. Instead, she moved to the window and stood there looking out, her back to Mary. Suddenly, she realized her sister was sobbing, and when she turned, she saw that Mary had buried her face in her hands.

"Forgive me, Sister!" the older girl cried. "It is unkind of me to visit my hurts on you. You are but a child and have yet to learn from your indiscretions."

Elizabeth hastened over and hugged her weeping sister. Her new-found happiness had been too dearly won to be jeopardized by them falling out.

"It's all right, Mary," she soothed. "I forgive you. And believe me, I have learned from my indiscretions. I intended nothing unkind against you, I promise."

"We will speak no more of our mothers," Mary said. "It would be better to let the subject alone, if we are to stay friends. And believe me, I *am* your friend, and I hope you will be guided by me." In a rush of affection, she embraced Elizabeth again.

Kat, returning, stared as she saw them thus. Mary hastily dabbed at her eyes with her kerchief and bade them good day, not wishing to be seen crying by an inferior person. Hurrying toward the sanctuary of her own apartments, she found her mind in turmoil. How could she have been so thoughtlessly cruel to an innocent child? She should not have made Elizabeth the butt of her own inner miseries and frustrations. But was her sister such an innocent as she seemed? Was that disarming candor genuine or feigned? Anne Boleyn, after all, had been a great dissembler, so why should Elizabeth not take after her? And who else might she take after? Was that face, glimpsed in profile as she bent to embrace Mary, similar in feature to both Anne's and the King's? Or was it the very image of Mark Smeaton? In Mary's fevered imagination, stoked over so many bitter years, it was a question unanswerable.

He was home! Their father was home, in England, to the joyful acclaim of his subjects, for he came in victory, having captured Boulogne.

"God willing, the days of this kingdom's greatness are returned, and this triumph will be the first of many," the Queen said fervently as they waited for the King at Leeds Castle, a short ride from Dover. She well knew what this vanquishment of his ancient rival must mean to the aging King.

"Amen to that," Mary replied. "God must surely be smiling upon us, for the plague has safely abated too, which gives us further cause for rejoicing."

Dressed in their finest clothes, the King's daughters were standing behind the Queen and the young Prince beneath the gatehouse arch, watching the colorful cavalcade with its fluttering banners approach. Although he was meant to be on his dignity, in his plumed bonnet and crimson satin robes, Edward, at nearly seven, was practically jumping up and down with excitement, while the Queen, smiling, forbore to restrain him.

Elizabeth knew that she had Queen Katherine to thank for the fact that she was here at all on this joyful day. What a difference that sweet lady had made to all their lives. But despite her stepmother's calm and reassuring presence, her heart was fluttering wildly. How would her father receive her?

And there the King was, dismounting heavily, large and magnificent in his gorgeous clothes, swaggering with success, and enfolding his wife in a bear-like hug.

"You have done so well, sir!" she cried.

"I have missed you, Darling!" he muttered thickly, kissing her heartily on the lips. "And you, my children . . . How well you all look."

Edward bowed and Mary and Elizabeth curtsied as their father addressed them.

"I am delighted to see Your Majesty in such good health," Mary told him as he raised her. He kissed her on the forehead.

"You look very well yourself, Daughter," he told her.

Then it was Elizabeth's turn. The moment she had longed for and dreaded had come, and she bent her head low as she knelt before the King. He put one finger under her chin and tilted it upward.

"And you, Bessy, are you pleased to see your father?" he asked. His expression was unreadable.

"More than I can ever say, sir," she answered wholeheartedly. "I am so proud of having such a father. It was a marvelous victory."

The King smiled; it was gratifying to bask in the praise of his womenfolk, especially this fiery girl who was so like him. But he was not letting Elizabeth off the hook quite yet. His face resumed its impassive expression.

"I trust you are now come to your senses," he murmured.

"Oh, yes, sir," she said fervently. "I am so deeply sorry to have offended Your Majesty."

"Then we will say no more about it," he declared magnanimously, and raised and kissed her lovingly. Elizabeth felt a heady sense of relief. He had accepted her back into his special favor, and her cup of happiness was full.

—

"My Lady Mary, how enchanting," smiled Sir Thomas Seymour as they came face-to-face in a gallery. He sketched an elaborate bow and smiled dazzlingly, revealing very white teeth.

Mary saw his flattery for what it was, but was nonetheless moved by it. He really was so handsome: the dark, mocking eyes, the full lips, the trim beard, the chiseled cheekbones. A very proper man, she thought, tall and muscular. For one dizzying moment, she tried to imagine what it would be like to have such a man make love to her, and failed abysmally, her heart pounding.

"It is a pleasure to see you back at court, sir," she replied; to her embarrassment, her cheeks felt hot. The blush did not escape Sir Thomas's notice. Here's a virgin ripe for the taking, he thought to himself. Outwardly, he continued to observe the courtesy due to her.

"I trust Your Grace is in good health," he continued.

"I am very well, sir, thank you," she said, and forced herself to move on. She dared not be seen passing any more than brief pleasantries with this man who had the reputation of being such a rogue with the ladies.

"How could the Queen ever have loved him?" she asked herself primly, but in her heart, and her stirring body, she knew the answer.

"Sir Thomas Seymour is returned to court," Henry said, apparently carelessly, watching for Katherine's reaction.

"I trust his tour of duty was successful," she said, betraying neither by look or gesture that the news meant anything to her. Inside, however, her heart was beating just that little bit faster. She must not think of this man. He was forever forbidden to her. She must love her husband: that was her bounden duty. And she did love Henry, she could say that with truth. It was just that she was not *in love* with him.

"He has done well," the King said, still watching her. "Now we have a fresh task for him. He is to be made Lord High Admiral."

Another duty that will keep him away from court, thought Katherine. And from me.

"I make no doubt he will live up to Your Majesty's good expectations," she said aloud.

Henry nodded, apparently satisfied.

———

Sir Thomas Seymour bowed low before the King and Queen, having just received the news of his promotion. It struck Katherine that he looked more dashing than ever.

"I am greatly honored, Sire," he declared.

"Serve us as well on the high seas as you have in the embassy, and you will give us cause to bestow further honors upon you," Henry said, extending his hand to be kissed and thus intimating that the audience was at an end.

Now it was Katherine's turn. The fleeting brush of Thomas's lips upon her hand was electrifying, but she kept her gaze steady and inclined her head as regally as she could, all too aware of the scrutiny of her husband enthroned by her side.

"Good luck, Sir Thomas," she said, wanting to drink him in with her eyes but not daring to look on his beloved face for too long.

"Your Majesties!" He bowed again, then paced backward from the dais and was gone. In Katherine's breast, relief mingled with longing. She had thought herself over her lovesickness; now she knew differently, yet she was resolved once more to suppress it and do her duty. And Henry needed her. Since his return from France, he had become an old man; he had attempted too much, and was now paying the price, with his bad legs worse than ever. They stank dreadfully when she replaced the bandages, yet she took care never to recoil or reveal her distaste. Infirmity alone was humiliating enough to Henry, whose prowess in jousting and sports had once been legendary. But that was hard to believe, looking at him now. Constant pain made him difficult, even dangerous, yet she told herself that his life had not been easy, and reminded herself that he had ever been a kind and loving husband to her. She had not wanted to marry him, had wanted Tom, madly, passionately, but there had been unexpected compensations. Love came in many guises— so much had surprised her. She could never betray Henry, she knew that.

"This," said a smiling Master Grindal one day, entering the schoolroom with a pleasant-faced man of about thirty, "is Master Roger Ascham, my former mentor and our greatest Greek scholar."

"Oh, Master Ascham! I have heard of your fame," Elizabeth exclaimed, rising to acknowledge his bow. "You are more than welcome."

Roger Ascham looked at her with admiration. So this tall, elegant young lady, with the flame-red hair and earnest, heart-shaped face, was the Princess whose erudition was already highly renowned and celebrated among academics throughout the land and even in the universities.

"It is truly an honor to meet you, my lady," he said.

"Master Ascham has joined the Prince's teaching staff, to assist Dr. Coxe and Dr. Cheke," Grindal explained.

"I have the honor of teaching that noble imp calligraphy," Ascham added, "but I really came here to see for myself this wondrous paragon of learning. If you would allow me the privilege of looking at some of your excellent work, my lady, it would make me the happiest man alive!"

Elizabeth found herself basking delightedly in his admiration, and willingly she showed him her Greek and Latin translations, her commentaries on Scripture and the classics, the historical works she was reading, and even samples of her embroidery. Ascham devoured them all with his eyes, appraised them to the minutest detail, quizzed her on her knowledge, then pronounced her the best scholar he had ever met.

"And may I ask how old you are, my lady?" he inquired.

"I am eleven," Elizabeth told him.

"Then, madam, without reserve, I do declare that you have a formidable—yes, formidable—intelligence way beyond your years. Your mind, it is so—so *acute*. I have never known a lady with a quicker apprehension or a more retentive memory. You have a masculine power of application. Continue as you have begun, and you will become the equal of men in learning."

Elizabeth was ecstatic to hear such praise. She had no false modesty and knew she was a good scholar; Dr. Coxe and Master Grindal had often told her so. But to learn that she was considered to be brilliant, and from someone as celebrated as Master Ascham, fired her with such elation that she could have kissed him.

CHAPTER 9

1545

The painter was Flemish; Elizabeth had not caught his outlandish name. He had set up his easel in the presence chamber, and she was watching him setting out his charcoal and chalks. Today, he was to draw the Prince's likeness. The King was present too, come to satisfy himself that his son's pose was sufficiently regal. He had seated himself on the throne beneath the canopy of estate; behind him, the arms of England were emblazoned on a richly embroidered backdrop.

"Edward, come and stand by me," Henry commanded. "Here." He positioned the seven-year-old boy at his right hand, and himself ruffled up the plumes on his son's bonnet. "Your hand on your dagger like so," he instructed.

"Yes, sir," Edward replied obediently in his cold, formal way. This was a big day for him, and he was conscious of the need to emulate his august sire in his stance and his royal manner.

"Now stay like that," the King ordered, then heaved himself out of his chair and departed to his privy apartments. His son remained very still, gazing straight ahead, as the artist sketched his portrait.

Mary had explained to Elizabeth and Edward that, when all the like-nesses had been taken, the painter would incorporate them into one big picture.

"It is to be an official state portrait of our father and his heirs," she announced proudly, "and it will hang in the gallery at Hampton Court." Elizabeth was thrilled that she herself was to be included—it was now her right, no less, of course—and was looking admiringly at herself in the burnished silver mirror. The new cloth of gold damask looked very well, she thought. Thus attired, no one could doubt her importance, or her royal status. And the red velvet hood and sleeves set it off very nicely . . .

"Sister!" Mary sounded exasperated. "Cease your daydreaming. The Queen bade me ask you to attend her briefly before your sitting. You will find her in her privy chamber."

Elizabeth sped off as fast as her long court train would permit. She found Katherine seated at a table with a painted wooden jewelry casket open before her.

"Elizabeth!" She smiled. "I wanted to see you all dressed up for the painter." She regarded her stepdaughter admiringly. "You look very fine," she declared as Elizabeth preened. Then Katherine hesitated.

"There's another reason for my summoning you," she said. "I wanted you to have this."

She held out a delicate gold chain with something hanging from it. Taking it, Elizabeth saw that it was a finely wrought A.

"It was your mother's," the Queen said. "It is fitting that you should wear it."

"But my father the King—"

"This is between ourselves," Katherine interrupted firmly. "I found it among the jewels I inherited from my predecessors. I can never wear it, and rightly it ought to go to you."

"Madam, I thank you from the bottom of my heart," Elizabeth said, kissing her stepmother. It was what she had always wanted, a proper keepsake of her mother.

She clasped the chain around her neck, aware that the last flesh that it had probably touched was Anne's. So absorbed was she in the gift that it took a while to dawn on her that the Queen was not wearing her court finery, just a simple green silk gown with a stand-up collar and jeweled girdle.

"Is that what you will be wearing in the picture, madam?" she asked in surprise.

"I am not to be in the picture," Katherine told her.

"Not to be in it?" echoed an astonished Elizabeth.

"No," the Queen said equably. "It is to be a picture of the Tudor dynasty, with the very likeness of Queen Jane, who bore the King his heir."

"But you must be in it!" Elizabeth insisted with passion. "It is unthinkable that you are being left out."

"Rest assured, I am content," Katherine said truthfully. "The King has assured me that no slight is intended, nor would I have imagined any. And that excellent artist, Master John, painted my portrait last year, so there is no need for another one just yet."

Elizabeth left the room thinking how strange it would be to see the late Jane Seymour occupying the Queen's place in the picture, as if she were still alive and had survived to see her son grow up. What power her father had! It was almost as if he were resurrecting his late wife from her grave, and could play tricks with time like a magician or a god!

Yet when the finished painting was finally displayed, it was not just the image of Jane Seymour that disconcerted Elizabeth and her sister Mary.

Of course, the King himself dominated the composition, gazing majestically from his throne, one hand on the shoulder of his son, who stood at his knee. Beside them, looking demure on her stool, sat Queen Jane, eerily large as life.

Edward, unnaturally composed for a child of his years, was looking up at her image. Elizabeth wondered what he made of it. He never spoke of his mother; of course he had never known her, and now he gave no sign of being moved at being brought face-to-face with her picture.

Mary, however, was frowning. In the painting, the canopy of estate, the throne on its rich Turkey carpet, and the three central figures were placed between two sets of richly ornamented pillars. Beyond the pillars, on either side, stood the King's daughters. Mary suspected that their father had had them both positioned beyond the pillars to set them apart from the legitimate heir, who occupied the place of honor beside their father, and to remind everyone who looked on the picture that, although the King had restored his daughters to the succession, he still regarded both as base-born: Positioning them outside the magical inner circle proclaimed to the world their bastard status and set them apart from the King and his trueborn heir. To Mary, the symbolism was hurtful and demeaning. Yet to Elizabeth, marveling at the rich detail and the faithful representation of herself in this, the first portrait ever painted of her, it was simply a wonderful picture.

The King was peering at the panel, well satisfied with the work he had commissioned. Here, at last, was the Tudor dynasty captured for posterity. Then he leaned forward, scrutinizing the figures, until they came to rest on that of his younger daughter. His eyes narrowed.

Elizabeth held her breath. He had noticed. She had prayed he would not, had hoped that the detail would escape him. She knew she shouldn't have worn the pendant, but she had felt that doing so would proclaim to the world that she was proud to be Anne Boleyn's daughter. So she had daringly put it on for the sitting. Afterward, she had immediately regretted the impulse, and had tried to seek out the painter and ask him to alter his sketch. But he had gone away, she knew not where.

She had seen immediately, to her relief, that the A was not very clearly delineated in the finished picture. Pray God her father would not notice it. She began to tremble.

But Henry turned and smiled at her.

"It's a good likeness, Bessy!" he pronounced.

Behind him, Queen Katherine's eyes met hers.

"His Majesty's sight is not what it was," she whispered. "Be grateful for that, you foolish girl!"

That summer, Elizabeth, who was now nearing twelve and becoming more aware of the interplay between the sexes, began noticing that her beloved governess was spending more and more time with John Astley, a gentleman of the court. She gave it little thought to begin with, but then she realized that Kat's step was sprightlier, her cheeks rosier, and her manner more lighthearted on the days when Master Astley came upon them in the gardens, almost as if by chance. These meetings grew more frequent, until Elizabeth began to suspect that he was trailing them on purpose.

But why? Why should he seek out Kat, who was quite content and getting rather plump? Perhaps it was because they were related, and both cousins to the Boleyns. That would explain it.

Elizabeth liked John Astley. A warm, hearty man, he always had a very kind word for her, and it was nothing to do with her being the King's daughter, for she had noticed that he was the same with all children.

"Hello, my little gillyflower!" he would cry whenever they met, his familiarity belied by a sweeping bow. And with Kat, he was consideration personified.

"Is it too hot for you here?" he would ask anxiously, should the sun be beating down relentlessly on their chosen bench. "Let me carry those books," he would insist. "Allow me to get you some cordial; it would be my pleasure," he might declare.

Kat basked in all this attention, although she always pretended that Master Astley was really being a bit of a nuisance.

"It's him again," she would say, sighing, as they watched the fellow approaching, predictable as the dawn.

"Are you in love with Master Astley?" Elizabeth asked when she was alone with Kat. Surely it was not possible—Kat was far too old for such things. Heavens, she was forty-five!

"The very idea!" cried Kat, blushing furiously. "I like him well, that's all. And he is going to join your household, to help Master Parry with his accounts." Thomas Parry, a distant relation of Blanche Parry, was Elizabeth's cofferer, a rotund, amiable fellow who loved nothing more than exchanging the latest gossip with Kat.

John Astley had been working with Thomas Parry for no more than a fortnight when Kat sat Elizabeth down in the schoolroom one afternoon and said she had something important to tell her.

"Although it shouldn't affect you too much, my lady," she said. "You see, Master Astley and I are going to be married."

"Married?" exclaimed Elizabeth. "But . . ."

"I know, you don't have to say it, my lady—you think I'm too old. Let me tell you, child, no one is ever too old to find happiness. No one ever paid court to me like this when I was young, and now that I have the chance to know true wedded bliss at last, I'm going to seize it with both hands!"

There was no mistaking the joy in her eyes and her voice. Maybe forty-five wasn't so old to wed after all, Elizabeth reflected . . . But then she felt a stab of alarm.

"I hope this will not mean your ever leaving me," she said sharply. "I could not countenance it if you were to go away."

"Fret not," Kat soothed, taking her hand. "Master Astley is to assist me and Master Parry in the running of your household."

"Oh, I am so relieved!" Elizabeth exclaimed.

"You know I could never leave you," Kat declared fervently. "Not even if the King himself were to ask for my hand!"

That brought on a fit of the giggles in Elizabeth.

"That is very naughty!" she gasped. "The very idea!"

Kat chuckled.

"The King has consented to us marrying in the Chapel Royal, and the chaplain has agreed," she went on excitedly. "All that remains is for your ladyship to give us your blessing."

Elizabeth preened. She liked being reminded of her own importance. And she also liked people being grateful to her.

"As long as you promise to stay with me, Kat, I will give it," she said graciously. "And as long as I can be your bride-maid!"

"Of course!" cried Kat, ebullient with happiness.

"I shall have to have a new gown," Elizabeth reminded her.

"Naturally!" Kat enthused. "And I too—I am the bride after all!"

They laughed again.

And that was how Elizabeth, wearing a cream gown sprigged with crimson and green flowers, came to follow Kat to her marriage, to the sound of pipes and shawms merrily announcing the arrival of the bride.

CHAPTER 10

1546

The time for laughter did not much outlast the New Year of 1546.

Elizabeth, excitedly looking forward to the festivities at court, had fortunately remembered to make a special present for her father, for which, afterward, she was to be very glad.

Henry looked at her elegant translations, into Latin, French, and Italian, of the Queen's soon-to-be-published devotional book, *Prayers and Lamentations of a Sinner,* and was visibly moved. His daughter had gone to all this trouble for him; she must have spent hours and hours working on this gift.

"I thank you, Bessy," he said, his voice thick with emotion, as he raised his faded-blue brimming eyes to hers. Dammit, he was becoming sentimental in his old age, was too easily moved to tears. But then, he was not a well man, he thought peevishly, and was becoming increasingly prone to moments of weakness.

"Would Your Majesty like to play a game of Primero?" Elizabeth was suggesting eagerly. Her father had aged a lot lately, and looked ill; she hated to see it, and was anxious to cozen him out of his melancholy mood.

"It lasts a long time," Mary, standing nearby, said doubtfully, "and might tire our father."

"I am tired all the time," confessed Henry sadly. "I waste so much time sleeping. And time is of all losses the most irrecuperable, for it can never be redeemed. I tell you what, my daughters, I will sleep a little now, and later you shall join me for a game of backgammon."

A few days later, the King shut himself up in his rooms, and even the Queen was forbidden to enter.

"I am glad you are to share lessons with me again, Sister," Edward said.

"It's only for a short time, while Messire Belmaine is in England," Elizabeth said, seating herself decorously at the table in the schoolroom at Ashridge.

She was surprised to discover that she was happy to be back at this familiar nursery palace and away from the court. With her father's health so precarious, the court had become a dreary and threatening place. She had become aware of bad undercurrents, of the various factions jostling for power, eager for the King to make his will and die, like vultures waiting for rich pickings from a corpse. She could not bear to dwell on their ill-suppressed anticipation.

Edward watched her with interest. He was genuinely pleased to see her; she was lively company, not like their sister Mary, who was forever telling her beads or adjuring him to virtue. As if he needed telling! With vigilant tutors like his, he had no choice but to be virtuous.

"I hear you correspond with Master Ascham," Edward said enviously as they waited for the new French tutor to arrive.

"He has been my mentor for nearly a year now," Elizabeth told him. "He writes the liveliest letters from Cambridge. When I come again, I will bring some to show you."

"It is good to have you here at Ashridge," Edward said. "How long will you be staying?"

"Three months," said Elizabeth, concerned as to what might happen while she was away from the court for so long. But there was no time to dwell on that, for here was Messire Belmaine, bustling into the schoolroom, looking for all the world like a crow in his austere black robes. He greeted them respectfully, then began arranging his books and pens on the table.

"It was once a monastery, eh, zis house?" the little man asked, looking about him.

"It was before my father the King dissolved it," Edward told him.

"Ah, he is a great man, King Henry," Belmaine enthused.

Edward's tutor, Dr. John Cheke, appeared.

"Do you have everything you need?" he asked the Frenchman.

"I could not have asked for a warmer welcome," Belmaine told him.

"You must tell the Prince about your travels in Switzerland," Cheke said. Elizabeth noticed the two men exchanging what appeared to be significant looks.

"It will be my pleasure," said Belmaine.

"You admire my father, then?" Edward asked him after Cheke had departed.

"Indeed, my Lord Prince. He is a great reformer of the Church."

"Master Cheke is hoping that my father will sanction further reforms," Edward said.

"We are all praying for it," Belmaine said fervently.

"Tell us about Switzerland, sir," Elizabeth put in, determined not to be ignored any longer.

"Ah, Switzerland." Belmaine sighed. "It is the cradle of true faith."

"Indeed?"

"I met many of God's elect there, and learned many wise doctrines," Belmaine went on.

"Who are God's elect?" Edward wanted to know.

"Those whom He has chosen to save."

"Surely, if we believe sincerely and follow His word, then we will all be saved," Elizabeth said. That was what she had been taught and what she firmly believed.

"Forgive me, madame, but only those souls to whom God extends His mercy can become His elect."

"So some people are destined for salvation whatever they do?" she persisted. "That does not make sense to me."

"The ways of God are inscrutable," Belmaine observed.

"How do you know if you are one of the elect?" Edward asked.

The tutor thought for a moment.

"You would perhaps become aware that God was making special efforts to rescue you from the spiritual apathy to which we are all inclined," he explained.

"I know God has rescued me," Edward announced.

"Brother, how can you know?" Elizabeth asked sharply. "How can any of us know in this life if we will attain Heaven?"

"I *must* be one of God's elect," Edward persisted, "if I am to succeed my father and lead the English Church."

"The English Church is a Catholic Church," Elizabeth pointed out, "and if I am not mistaken, Messire Belmaine, these doctrines that you preach are those of Jean Calvin of Geneva, are they not?"

"You know of Master Calvin?" Belmaine asked, impressed.

"My tutor has told me something of his teachings," Elizabeth revealed. "But I should warn you, sir, that they are considered heresy in this kingdom, and I therefore counsel you to beware your tongue."

"Sweet Sister, neither you nor I would report this gentleman for heresy," Edward protested. "I was enjoying our debate. These ideas have an appeal for me."

"I too found the debate interesting," said Elizabeth, "but it would be wiser to leave the matter alone. This is not Switzerland."

"I thank you for your wisdom, madame," Belmaine said smoothly. "Now shall we proceed to the lesson? I am come to improve your French, and I think we should begin with a little conversation—about the weather, as that is what you like to talk about in England, other subjects being, er, forbidden, eh?" His smile was mischievous.

The summer months passed quickly, bringing with them no ominous tidings, and soon it was time for Elizabeth to return to court and Edward to move to Hertford. Kat, who had enjoyed their peaceful stay at Ashridge, was downcast as she packed their gear. She did not want to go back to court. During the three years since the King had married Katherine Parr, Kat's jealousy of the Queen had not abated.

Edward was downcast too; he had grown used to his sister's company and enjoyed the healthy competitiveness between them. When she came face-to-face with him at the great doorway on the morning of her departure, he looked so mournful that, abandoning protocol, she bent down and kissed his cheek.

Struggling to control the tears that he would rather die than let fall, Edward took her hand.

"I hate leaving this house where we have been so happy, dearest Sister," he told her. "Write to me, please. Nothing could be more pleasing to me than a letter from you. And my Chamberlain tells me that, if this land remains free from plague, I may visit you at court."

"That would be wonderful," Elizabeth said. "And I will write, I promise. Farewell, dear Brother. God keep you."

When Elizabeth arrived at Whitehall Palace, she was received at once by the Queen, who looked pale and drawn, she thought. And there was a subdued atmosphere in Katherine Parr's apartments, as if her ladies were treading carefully, afraid to make a noise.

"I have so missed you, madam," Elizabeth said as she rose from her curtsy.

"Believe me, I have missed you too, Elizabeth," Katherine said. Her hazel eyes were weary, as if she had not slept, and she had lost weight: The crimson damask gown hung loosely. "I cannot tell you how glad I am to see you."

Something was wrong, Elizabeth guessed.

"Are you well, madam?" she inquired.

"Very well," replied Katherine firmly, though her voice had a brittle edge to it. Clearly, she was not going to enlarge, but Elizabeth was determined to find out the truth.

She sought out her cousin, Lady Jane Grey, who was being educated at court under the Queen's auspices. Jane, a plain child with red hair and freckles, was only eight, and being therefore much younger than herself, would not normally have merited much of Elizabeth's attention, but she was a formidably bright and observant little girl and might well know what had been going on.

Elizabeth came upon Jane in the privy garden, where the Queen's ladies were taking the air.

"Come walk with me, Cousin," she commanded. Jane fell obediently into step, for she was greatly in awe of Elizabeth, and soon they were out of earshot. Their talk, to begin with, was of lessons and family matters, but Elizabeth soon came to the point.

"Is the Queen unwell?" she asked. "She does not look herself."

Jane looked furtively about her. Her solemn little face was troubled.

"Bad things have been happening here, but all is better now," she said mysteriously.

"What has happened?" Elizabeth asked.

"Did you hear of the burning of the Protestant heretic, Anne Askew?" Jane asked in a low voice.

Elizabeth nodded, shuddering.

"Well, the Queen's enemies tried to accuse her of heresy too, and say that she and her ladies had been friends to Mistress Askew."

Jane looked about her fearfully. No one was nearby: the women were laughing and strumming their lutes some way off.

"Please don't repeat this, my Lady Elizabeth. You see, the Queen had offended the King—she argued with him about religion. I was there, and I heard it. She told him what his duty was . . ."

Elizabeth's eyebrows shot up. She could not imagine anyone daring to instruct her father in religion, still less getting away with it.

"Yes, it was foolish of her," Jane said, registering her cousin's expression. "But I think she got carried away by her opinions. And Bishop Gardiner heard her. He complained about her to the King. The next thing we knew, the soldiers came and searched her apartments."

"Searched for what?" Elizabeth asked.

"Books," Jane murmured, looking fearful. "Forbidden books."

"Oh, no! I trust they did not find anything?" Elizabeth was horrified. That anyone could have suspected dear Queen Katherine of heresy was unthinkable . . . The consequences might have been horrific. Her world rocked.

"They found nothing." Jane took a deep breath. "I think she *had* had some books, but she'd gotten rid of them when Anne Askew was put in the Tower. They tortured Anne Askew, you know, to make her talk. My mother said they wanted her to name the Queen."

"They?"

"Lord Chancellor Wriothesley and Sir Richard Rich."

Elizabeth knew them both. They were of the Catholic party with

Bishop Gardiner. And she had heard how the Lord Chancellor himself had turned the rack after the hangman had said enough was enough.

"But she did not betray the Queen," Jane was saying.

"Was there anything to betray?" Elizabeth asked sharply.

Jane looked at her and nodded, barely perceptibly.

"I think so," she whispered. "Promise you will never tell, but I think the Queen is a secret Protestant!"

Elizabeth was only faintly surprised. Katherine, normally so discreet, had given herself away by a word here, a hint there.

"So they couldn't prove anything against her," Jane went on, "but they persuaded the King to sign a warrant for her arrest anyway."

Elizabeth was shocked. They had tried to bring down the Queen! She had been unaware that she had come perilously near to losing yet another stepmother, and in the most dreadful manner: The penalty for heresy was death by burning.

Jane suddenly became animated.

"But then, one of the King's councillors dropped the arrest warrant in a corridor, and *I* found it!" she said triumphantly.

"*You* found it?"

"Yes. Wasn't that lucky? I didn't know what to do with it, so I took it to the Queen."

"And what happened?" Elizabeth was desperate to know.

Jane shivered at the memory.

"She just started crying and screaming! We were all terrified, as she wouldn't stop. You could have heard her all over the palace. The King heard her, and he came and asked what was wrong."

"What did he say?" Elizabeth interrupted.

"Well, the Queen said she feared she had displeased him by arguing with him. She said she had done it to take his mind off the pain from his bad leg, and because she had hoped to profit by his wisdom. And he said, 'Is that so, Sweetheart? Then we are perfect friends again.' "

Elizabeth was living the moment with her cousin, imagining Katherine's terror and fear, and her relief at being happily reunited with the King.

"The next day," Jane went on, "the Queen was feeling much better, and the King invited us all to sit with him in the garden. There we were very merry, as if nothing had happened, and then the Lord Chancellor suddenly appeared, with a lot of soldiers. We all thought that the Queen was going to be arrested after all, and I was so frightened. But the King got up and shouted at the Lord Chancellor, calling him a beast and a fool. The Chancellor just ran away, and the soldiers ran after him. We all ended up laughing, but it wasn't really very funny, not to begin with."

"My father himself must have signed the arrest warrant," Elizabeth reflected, almost to herself. "But surely he would never have gone so far as to have the Queen arraigned for heresy. He loves her. I've heard him say he has never had a wife more agreeable to his heart. But she was lucky, being able to see him and plead her case." Unlike poor Katherine Howard, she thought, or her own mother. If they had been allowed to defend themselves to the King, would they have been alive today? She pushed the thought away.

"I am sure my father loves the Queen too well to let her die a horrible death," Elizabeth continued, with more confidence than she felt; after all, the King had beheaded two wives already. "I'm sure he did it to test her. I cannot believe he meant to destroy her."

"I thank God she is still here," said Jane fervently. "She has been most kind to me."

"And to me too," said Elizabeth. "I am grateful to you for telling me this. I promise I will repeat it to no one. And now we should join the others."

Elizabeth and Katherine Parr were strolling through the privy garden that sloped down to the banks of the Thames. Behind them, the great red-brick palace of Hampton Court glowed in the mellow light of the late-afternoon sun. Their attendants trailed some way behind them, throwing balls to their little dogs amid much laughter.

"The King is too ill to take the air today," Katherine confided. "He is resting in his chamber. The reception for the French Admiral was too much for him, I'm afraid."

"Is my father going to die?" Elizabeth asked suddenly, her eyes full of fear.

"We are all going to die someday," the Queen said, "and you know we may not predict the King's death. But I am very worried about his health, and I know he is too, for he has talked about the councillors he will appoint to rule in the event of a minority, as the Prince is only a child—but keep that to yourself, I beg of you. They are all new men, men he has raised up: Edward Seymour, Lord Hertford; Archbishop Cranmer; John Dudley, Viscount Lisle . . ." She reeled off a list.

"None of them are of the Catholic faction," Elizabeth observed, surprised.

"You are perceptive for your years," the Queen said approvingly. "Indeed, they are all men who wish to see the Church of England reformed. Some"—she hesitated—"would go farther . . ."

"You mean they would have us all turn Protestant?" Elizabeth asked, in some amazement.

"I wonder, would that be such a bad thing?" Katherine murmured, lowering her voice. "It may even be that His Majesty, in his wisdom, foresees it happening one day."

"But he has burned Protestant heretics!" Elizabeth exclaimed.

"And he has burned Catholics too, for acknowledging the Pope," her stepmother reminded her. "Bishop Gardiner's Catholic party is out of favor now, and the Reformists at court, led by Lord Hertford, have the King's ear. Hence his choice of men for the Regency Council."

The Queen led the way along the paved walk by the bowling alley. "For many people, I suspect, the new religion has become the path to salvation," she said quietly. "Is it right that men should worship the graven idols of saints, or need intercessors to reach the ear of Our Lord? And is it credible that, in the Mass, a miracle takes place? We must be justified, and achieve salvation, through faith alone."

"That is what Master Grindal says, and Master Ascham," Elizabeth said slowly. "I believe it myself, and I am not very surprised to hear *you* say it too, madam. But I have known for some time that such opinions are heretical, so I have kept mine to myself. I often wonder why it is that there are so many disputes over how mankind can achieve salvation. Surely each person should discover that for himself, through reading the Scriptures."

"Ah, Elizabeth, you are just thirteen and an innocent," the Queen observed. "In this world, you must be one thing or the other; you cannot pick and choose each tenet of your faith."

"Ah, but how do we know which is the right path?" Elizabeth cried. "Maybe my father, in his wisdom, can see which way the tide is turning, or can envisage a golden age in which each must be free to abide by his conscience."

Katherine shook her head.

"Such tolerance would endanger our immortal souls," she said gravely. "There can be only one right path to salvation."

"But we all worship the same God!" Elizabeth declared, whirling around to face her stepmother. "Does it matter how? So long as we live godly lives and keep the commandments, the details are immaterial."

"So immaterial that men and women are prepared to burn for them," Katherine murmured drily. "Never forget it. *Tolerance* is not a word in their vocabulary, nor indeed in mine, nor in any right-thinking Christian's. Elizabeth, heed me: The saving of your soul must be the central issue of your life. Do not allow yourself to fall into error in the name of tolerance. There can be only one way to Christ. Think about it."

"I will, madam," Elizabeth declared, slipping her arm through the Queen's. "I am happy to be guided by you. But let us talk further when we are in private, for I hear the others catching up." She bent, picked up a ball, and threw it.

Elizabeth, dressed in her riding habit, was seated on her palfrey next to Mary, watching their father attempt to mount his horse. Even with the riding block raised, it was a wearisome and painful business for him.

"God's blood!" he roared. "Once upon a time I could leap into the saddle. Now it's all I can do to get my foot in the stirrup." He gritted his teeth and tried again. His daughters looked at each other anxiously. The Queen, already mounted and trying to calm her restive steed, looked distressed.

"He should never have attempted this hunting progress," Mary whispered. "He is not well."

"He dare not give up," Elizabeth observed.

Mary was struck by her insight. "No, you speak truth. I suppose he fears that if he gives in to his infirmity, he might as well take to his bed and never rise from it again."

"Don't say that," said Elizabeth sharply. Mary pursed her mouth. She too was afraid; what would the world be like when their father was no more?

The King was at last seated in the saddle, and his small riding household were themselves mounting their horses. Then the cavalcade set off, leaving behind the cozy little manor house at Chobham for Guildford, where they were to lodge the next night in the former Dominican friary, which the King had recently had converted into a handsome royal lodging.

But their progress was slow, and riding behind her father, Elizabeth could see why, for it was obvious that every jolt of his steed was agony to him. She was not surprised, therefore, when on their arrival at Guildford, Mary came to her and told her that the progress was being abandoned.

"We are to retire to Windsor Castle," she said, "so that our father can rest. They are saying he has a cold, but I don't believe it."

"Can I see him?" Elizabeth asked anxiously.

"No one is allowed near him," Mary told her. "I begged the Queen, but even she has been barred from his chamber by the doctors."

Elizabeth stared at her.

"Then he must be very ill," she whispered.

"We must pray for him," Mary replied. "Come, Sister, come with me to the chapel."

Together, they knelt at the altar rails, where once the Black Friars had celebrated Mass. Mary raised her eyes in rapturous beseeching to the impassive image of the Virgin that adorned the altar, and Elizabeth tried hard to pray as devoutly as her sister, but disturbing images kept intruding. She kept thinking of her magnificent father, now ill, in pain and helpless in his bed and at the mercy of the royal physicians, whose cures were often revolting and painful, and rarely successful. She thought too of the waiting nobles, the ambitious Reformists, hungry for power, men who would rejoice in the King's demise. The notion brought hot tears to her eyes, and she buried her face in her hands to conceal the fact that she was weeping.

Henry knew very well, although no one had dared tell him, that his days were numbered. No fool, he was aware that the remedies his physicians prescribed were useless, and that they could no longer do anything to delay the inevitable. He was not afraid, in fact he was content to go: So much that had been pleasurable in his life was now beyond his capacity, and that he could not bear. What mattered was that Edward's succession should be a smooth one, and that the wily Hertford should not set himself above the other members appointed by the King to the regency council. Power, he was determined, must be shared among them. As for their religious persuasions, again, he was no fool. He knew which way the tide of opinion was flowing. Well, let them have their heads, these reformers. He would not be here to see it.

There was a soft knock. The Queen put her head around the door.

"How are you feeling, my lord? Can I get you anything?"

He managed a weak smile. She was a good woman, and he had not been much of a husband to her. Doubtless after he had left this world she would marry Tom Seymour. Well, good luck to her. She deserved a proper man in her bed: He himself could not have had a more devoted wife or nurse, but that had been—mostly—all that had been between them. Although he was damned if he was going to allow that rogue Seymour to be anywhere near the regency council.

"A cup of wine, if you please, Kate," he said, content just to watch her moving about the room, doing his bidding. She looked very trim in her crimson gown. She thought he knew nothing of her secret conversion to the Lutheran faith, he reflected. Well, let her be. Let them all be. Kate, Hertford, Archbishop Cranmer, John Dudley, Coxe, Cheke, Ascham . . . heretics all. They would do well under the new regime. But not yet . . . not yet.

"It's going to be a sorry Christmas, Kate," he said, taking the cup from her. "There'll not be many disports for you and my children, with me lying here and everyone tiptoeing around as if I've died already."

Katherine winced.

"Nay, Sweetheart, I but jested," Henry assured her, then sighed. "I've a mind to close the court to visitors. There'll be no revelry this year."

"I will keep you company, my Husband," she said, patting his hand. "We'll have some quiet revelry in private. You can beat me at cards, as usual—"

"No, Katherine," Henry cut in. "Tomorrow, you, Mary, and Elizabeth will go to Greenwich and keep Christmas there in proper fashion. Edward can travel to Ashridge. I don't want him mingling with lots of people. He might catch something, with all these winter chills that are going about."

"But my lord," the Queen protested, "I would stay with you."

"It's only for the festive season," he told her. "No, no arguments! It is my will, and you are bound to obey me. Now go, make ready. I would sleep a little. I will see my children before they leave."

They stood before him, two slim girls and a child. The fruits, he reflected, of his six marriages. For a moment, it was as if Katherine, Anne, and Jane were in their places: pious Katherine, with her unshakable, irritating devotion; the witch, with her mocking, alluring smile; and sweet, pale Jane, who had given her all to provide him with his heir.

The images faded. He was wandering in his mind, he knew. Sometimes it seemed as if the past and the present were one. He opened his eyes again, saw Mary, with that same needy and pathetic expression her mother had worn, inscrutable Elizabeth, watching him warily, and the fair, pale boy, his son. He suddenly realized he might never see any of them again.

"Come here, Edward," the King commanded. The child stepped forward, reluctant to go too near the bed. He had never seen his father laid low like this, and he was clearly appalled at the sight—and the smell.

"You are to go to Ashridge for Christmas," Henry told him. "I daresay Dr. Coxe and Dr. Cheke will devise some seasonal games for you. Be a good boy, and make merry—it is my wish."

"Yes, sir," said Edward meekly. His woeful expression was anything but merry.

Henry beckoned to his daughters, who drew nearer.

"You will both go with the Queen to Greenwich," he croaked.

"No!" Elizabeth cried before she could stop herself.

"Please, sir," Mary faltered, "let us stay with you."

Her father shook his head.

"This is no place for you, my daughters, and besides, I need to rest. I have not been well, as you know. I will summon you back when I am recovered, never fear."

Elizabeth did fear. She realized that her father was very ill and might never recover; there was a good chance she might never see him again. But she could not say as much, for it was treason to predict the death of the King. Instead, she knelt with her brother and sister to receive his blessing.

"May God have you all in His keeping," Henry intoned. "Follow

God's word, and set a virtuous example to all. Now farewell, and I wish you a safe journey."

Edward bowed formally. Mary bent her head as she curtsied, praying Henry would not notice her weeping. But Elizabeth stepped boldly forward, leaned over the diseased body lying in the bed, and kissed her father tenderly on his forehead.

"It will be my constant prayer that God will soon restore you to health, sir," she said.

Henry looked up at her. There were tears in his blue eyes.

"Look after your little brother," he murmured, "and your good stepmother."

Then he waved them all away.

CHAPTER 11

1547

Elizabeth gazed through the tall, latticed windows at the boats on the Thames and the distant spires of London, looking like stark gray fingers pointing up to the leaden January sky. She then turned back to her book while surreptitiously nibbling on a piece of gilded marchpane left over from Twelfth Night. When Master Grindal entered, she swallowed it quickly.

"Madam, you are to leave for Enfield at once," he told her.

"Enfield?" Elizabeth echoed. "Why?"

"No reason was given," the tutor said. "But I imagine that you are summoned once more to share the Prince's lessons. Mistress Astley is already gathering your things."

Elizabeth's heart began to thud. Why the urgency? Could this mean that her father was better and that life was reverting to normal? Surely the King would not send her away if he were dying?

Throughout the long, cold journey, she puzzled and fretted. Kat, seated beside her in the chariot, sensed her inner tension and knew better than to probe, instead keeping their conversation light.

"I shall be glad of a good fire when we get there," she said. "I like Enfield. It might be a small house, but it's warm and so beautifully decorated. We shall be comfortable there."

Elizabeth smiled weakly.

When they arrived, it was late afternoon and already nearly dark.
Torches, flickering wildly in the wind, lit their progress into the house,
and Elizabeth had hardly entered the great hall when, to her surprise, the
Prince's Chamberlain appeared out of the dimness and requested her immediate repair to the presence chamber.

"Is His Highness my brother here already?" she asked, suspecting that
her being summoned here had nothing to do with lessons.

"He arrived earlier today, madam," the Chamberlain informed her.

Elizabeth's sense of foreboding increased, and she found herself trembling. Resolutely, she constrained herself to calmness, and divesting herself of her cloak, she straightened her hood, smoothed her skirts, and
proceeded with measured steps into the presence chamber, chin held
high.

There, standing beside the empty throne on the dais, stood the Prince,
looking as perturbed as she herself felt, and with him was his uncle the
Lord Hertford. Two other gentlemen—privy councillors, she guessed—
were in the room, as well as several household officers and servants.

As Elizabeth made her obeisance to the Prince, Lord Hertford and the
two gentlemen bowed to her.

"You are welcome, my Lady Elizabeth," Hertford said quietly.

As she walked toward the dais, Elizabeth, thoroughly frightened now,
braced herself for the worst.

The Earl swallowed and cleared his throat.

"It is my heavy duty to announce to you both the death of the late
King your father," he said, his face a mask of sorrow.

Then he fell to his knees.

"Sire, allow me to be the first to render homage and fealty to his successor, King Edward the Sixth. The King is dead—long live the King!"
So saying, he took Edward's hand and kissed it.

For answer, the boy burst into sobs. Elizabeth, stunned into silence by
the terrible news, could hardly take it in, but her brother's distress was all
too visible, and impulsively she folded her arms around him and then
found herself crying helplessly. At the sight of the weeping children,

even the servants began sniffing and dabbing their eyes, while Lord Hertford gulped and blinked rapidly.

She would never see her father again, Elizabeth realized, nevermore
hear that high, imperious voice or thrill to him calling her Bessy. The
world would never be the same. It was too much to bear. The shoulder of
Edward's surcoat was soaked with her tears; they seemed to flow from a
bottomless well, and she could not stop them. She was motherless, father-
less, an orphan. She wanted her father, as long ago she had wanted her
mother . . . She felt her heart breaking.

Edward was weeping piteously, and more copiously than at any other
time in his life. Hertford, watching him and his sister, became concerned.

"Calm yourselves, Sire, madam," he urged, then, when they heeded
him not, ventured to enfold both heaving bodies in his arms, and held
them there until they were still.

At length, Edward broke away and stepped toward the empty throne.
He regarded it solemnly for a moment, the tears still wet on his cheeks,
then slowly sat down on it with a dignity far beyond his nine years. Elizabeth, blowing her nose into her kerchief, watched him for a moment,
then collected her thoughts. Her brother was now King of England. She
must not forget to pay the honor due to him. Shuddering still from the
onslaught of her misery, she sank into a deep curtsy.

And suddenly, it occurred to her that another, more subtle, change
had taken place in her life. Edward was the King now, she the subject.
Never again would their lives be the same.

PART TWO

The King's Sister

With Henry's passing, Elizabeth sensed that her childhood was over and that she must begin to look out for herself in this strange and threatening adult world. She knew that without Henry to safeguard her interests, she was very much on her own, for she guessed she would have little part to play in the schemes of the Seymours, and suspected that she and her sister Mary would soon be marginalized in the rush to seize control of the young King and the government.

She could not rely on the Queen, she realized. Katherine had borne no sons to the late monarch, and so could wield no further influence in public affairs. And anyway, Katherine would be grieving, and should not be expected to concern herself with Elizabeth's troubles. No, she must depend on herself and use her wits to survive.

Thus resolved, she strove for that inner tranquillity that facilitated prayer. Her father, she realized, with an insight born of burgeoning maturity, would have need of her prayers.

After the lords of the council had sworn fealty to King Edward, Lord Hertford, who had ignored his dead master's wishes and set himself up as head of that council, wasted no time in preparing to depart for London so that plans could be made for the late King's funeral and the new King's coronation.

"Am I not to go too, my lord?" Elizabeth asked him. Hertford shook his head.

"I regret, my lady, that his late Majesty expressly asked that none of his children attend his obsequies. And as the King is unmarried, the presence of ladies at the coronation would not be appropriate. I am sorry."

Elizabeth felt her anger rising. Who was this man, with his upstart Seymour blood, to order all in her father's place?

"Then what am I to do, sir?" she inquired.

"Remain here for the time being, with Mrs. Astley. I will send word after the King has been crowned."

Frustration welled up in Elizabeth, and she clenched her fists. Not even to attend her father's funeral? The ever-ready tears sprang to her eyes. The Earl cast her a sympathetic look and gratefully produced a parchment from which dangled the Great Seal of England.

"This is your father's will, my lady," he told her, "and in it you have been left three thousand pounds. That makes you a woman of substance, and as rich as any great lord. I am to tell you that, when you marry, you will receive a final payment of ten thousand pounds. I feel I should warn you, however, that if you marry without the council's approval and consent, then you will be struck out of the succession as if you were dead. The same applies to your sister, the Lady Mary."

"I have no wish to marry," stated Elizabeth, who appeared unmoved by her good fortune. "I should like to accompany my brother to court, though."

"That will not be possible, I'm afraid," the Earl informed her. "At least, not until the King marries. You will continue to live at Hatfield, Ashridge, and your other accustomed residences."

"But the Queen is still at court," Elizabeth pointed out.

"Not for long. She is in mourning at the moment, of course, but already she has let it be known that she intends to retire to one of her dower properties. The King left her well provided for too."

Elizabeth turned away. The consequences of her father's death were even worse than she had envisaged. She was now wealthy, it was true, but what good were riches if she was barred from the court and left to rot here at Enfield? She could not even say a proper farewell to her father at his burial.

She fixed Hertford with a regal glare and was gratified to see him wilt slightly under her gaze. Thus she had seen her father do, and it cheered her a little to know that she had inherited something of his formidable will and presence. This was what it was to be royal, she reflected, this mysterious power that could make others tremble; it was something that might prove useful in the future. But what use was the semblance of power without the substance? For when it came down to it, King's daughter or no, she was just a helpless young orphan, with no choice but to do as she was told.

"What is there for me?" she cried, with only Kat to hear her. "I am the third lady in the land, and they expect me to become a hermit!"

"Why not speak to the King?" Kat suggested. "He has ever been very fond of you, and his word might carry some weight."

Elizabeth thought about this.

"You might be right, Kat," she said. "I will. I'll go and talk to him now."

"My Lady Elizabeth, this is not really convenient," said Lord Hertford, looming large at the door to the royal apartments.

"I wish to see my brother the King," she told him coolly, her tone brooking no argument. There was no mistaking the fact that she was her father's daughter, the Earl reflected; it would be easier to give way. He was married to the most domineering termagant in the land, and had long since learned that, where women were concerned, giving way made for a quieter life.

Elizabeth found her brother, resplendent in his jet-encrusted mourning gown, seated at his desk and carefully applying his signature—a spidery EDWARD R.—to a pile of official-looking documents. He looked up and nodded at her as she sank to her knees.

"You may stand, Sister," he told her magnanimously.

"I trust I find Your Majesty in better spirits," she said.

"I am, I thank you," he replied. "And you, my dear Sister—I am sure there is little need for me to console you, because from your learning and piety, you know how to accept God's will. I can see that, like me, you can already think of our father's death with a calm mind."

"I am trying hard to achieve that calmness, Sire," Elizabeth answered. "I remind myself that I am proud to be his daughter."

"One thing must console us," the boy replied, with a sanctimoniousness beyond his years, "that he is now in Heaven, and that he has gone out of this miserable world into happy and everlasting blessedness."

At his words, Elizabeth felt tears prick her eyelids once more, but Edward's face remained impassive.

"Was there something you wanted, Sister?" he asked. "Or did you just come to offer words of comfort?"

"Your Majesty, I beg of you, let me come to court!" Elizabeth pleaded. "Do not let them leave me here, cut off from the life that matters to me."

Edward frowned.

"Of course you must come to court," he said. "But not yet. Wait until after I am crowned, then I will send for you. I shall not forget you. You have ever been dear to me."

The coronation came and went, and Elizabeth waited hopefully at Enfield, but the promised summonses, from the King and Lord Hertford, never came. What did arrive was a letter from Katherine Parr.

"It's from the Queen!" Elizabeth cried, breaking the seal and eagerly scanning the elegant italic script. "She has asked me to go and live with her at Chelsea! And she says the council has agreed! Oh, Kat!"

Elizabeth's eyes were shining for the first time in weeks, and Kat could not but rejoice to see it. Inwardly, though, her heart was sinking. For her, this news could hardly have been worse, for she had thought to have seen the last of her rival. But she had been mistaken, grievously mistaken, and as a result, the prospect of removing to the Queen's new establishment was unwelcome to her. Still, she forced her face into a smile.

"I am delighted for you," she said.

"Her Grace has especially commanded that *you* head my household," Elizabeth went on excitedly. "And Master Grindal may come with us—and Master Astley, of course!"

"I'm flattered," Kat said, with only a trace of irony.

"Oh, I am so pleased!" Elizabeth sang. "It will cheer me no end to be with the Queen. She has been like a mother to me, has she not?"

Kat swallowed.

"I make no doubt she will be a support to you at this time," she said begrudgingly. Her charge was too preoccupied to detect her resentment.

"In truth, I have longed to see her," Elizabeth confessed, sitting down on the settle and spreading her slender fingers across the wide black skirt of her mourning gown, absentmindedly admiring the effect.

"Does the Queen say when we are to join her?" Kat asked.

"She expects to take up residence at Chelsea in March, and will send word then. Oh, I feel better already at the thought, dear Kat! And the Queen's removal to Chelsea explains why I cannot live at court."

"Oh, no," said her governess, "that would not be fitting. There will be no ladies living at court until the King marries, and that won't be for a few years yet, I'll warrant."

"We must make ready!" Elizabeth said excitedly. Her face set, Kat summoned a porter and bade him fetch the Lady Elizabeth's traveling chests from the attic.

The Admiral was back. No sooner had news of King Henry's death reached him than he had hastened home to England to seize his share of the power and rich pickings that would now be up for grabs by enterprising men.

The Queen, still in the seclusion that marked the early days of royal widowhood, heard of his return and found her heart leaping with joy and heady anticipation. He had wasted no time, but had come back to claim her! As soon as the first month of mourning was up, he would send word to her, she knew it!

Lord Hertford, busily asserting his dominance over the council, groaned when his brother turned up at Whitehall, swaggering into the council chamber as if he owned the place.

"Ned!" Tom cried in his booming, penetrating voice, clapping the Earl on the shoulder. "It is good to be home. I came as soon as I could."

"Welcome, Tom," Hertford replied, trying to feign pleasure while extricating himself from that bear hug. "I did not expect you . . ."

"D'you think I'd stay away when I'm needed here?" Tom asked him. "They told me there's to be a regency council, and I've come to take my seat."

Hertford was nonplussed. If Anne, his wife, were here, she'd put Tom firmly in his place on this matter, but Anne was not here, and he himself hated confrontations or unpleasantness.

"I regret to say that the late king did not nominate you to the council, Tom," he said unwillingly.

"What?" roared Tom. "I'm the new king's uncle, just as you are, and I have a right to be on it."

"I'm afraid all the lords are appointed and the councillors sworn," Hertford said, arranging his features into an expression of regret.

"I'll not take no for an answer!" Tom exploded. "You have no right to exclude me."

"The council's decision is final, Brother, and I cannot change it," Hertford explained, reining in his own temper.

Tom clenched his fists and thrust his face close to his brother's.

"You think to keep me from power," he hissed. "This stems from *you,* for you have ever been jealous of me. Don't delude yourself, I know who is behind my exclusion. But I warn you, I will have my rightful share in the governing of this kingdom, if I have to resort to murder or treason to do it."

"Such vain and misguided threats do your cause no good," Hertford pointed out, edging backward. "In forming the council, we but followed the wishes of the late King. Blame him for not naming you."

"Oh, you are clever, hiding behind Old Harry's skirts," spat his brother, grinning nastily. "But you will regret your scheming. I will have the power that is rightfully mine in this land, more than you could ever dream of, and when I do, then beware, Brother. Yours will be the first head to topple."

"You are upset, Tom, that's the only excuse I can make for you," Hertford said. "In the name of charity, I will forget what you have just said; but I am beginning to see that his late Majesty showed great wisdom in not nominating you to the council. This kingdom needs cooler heads than yours. Think on it."

"Oh, you have given me much to think on!" retorted the Admiral.

"My uncle Thomas is back?" the young King repeated.

"Yes, Sire, he craves an audience," Lord Hertford said, "but I have told him you are busy with state affairs."

"Let him come in," the boy commanded.

"Your Majesty, that would not be wise," his uncle warned. "He is a foolish fellow, and you do not have time to waste on him."

"Am I not the king, Uncle?" Edward piped up resentfully. "May I not decide for myself whom I should receive?"

"In the fullness of time, Sire," Hertford said smoothly. "For the moment, Your Majesty, although wise beyond your years, is a child, and reliant on the counsel of those wiser and more experienced than yourself."

"I am the king!" snapped Edward, spiritedly.

"And I, Sire, am at the head of the council appointed by Your Majesty's late lamented father, King Henry, to govern this realm during your minority. Your father would have wished you to defer to my judgment. I'm afraid I must insist on your cooperation."

Edward sulked. Being king wasn't anywhere near as enjoyable as he had anticipated. He had expected to be such a one as his father, feared and obeyed by all, but now found himself hemmed about with all sorts of rules and restrictions. He must attend to his lessons even more diligently than before; he must not neglect his devotions, but must demonstrate the virtue and piety expected of someone who had been hailed by his subjects as the new David or Samuel; he must hold himself aloof from even his friends and remember who he was; he must not risk his life jousting, since the stability of the kingdom depended on his survival. He must always keep in his mind the image of his august sire, and seek to be like him in every way. Now, it seemed, he could not even grant an audience unless he first obtained the council's, or rather his Uncle Hertford's, permission.

"I will leave you to your books, Sire," that uncle said now, bowing obsequiously and backing out of the royal presence. Edward scowled.

The Admiral was angry, but his fertile mind grew busy with plans. Ambition was festering in him, and if he could not make his fortune from court offices or royal patronage, then he was determined to do so by contracting an advantageous marriage. He was well aware that the King's two unmarried sisters were the most eligible ladies in the land. Marriage to the King's sister would bring him prestige, power, and wealth, and it would be a smack in the face for that weaselly brother of his.

But which sister to choose? He didn't need even to think about it. Mary might be the next heir, but the unlikely prospect of a crown could not compensate for her being a dried-up spinster who was probably desperate to get a man in her bed, and was probably of little use to him there anyway.

No, it would have to be Elizabeth. She was thirteen now, of marriageable age, and reportedly spirited and pretty, although he hadn't seen her about the court for some time. He would marry Elizabeth. The prospect of bed sport with such a young bride, the daughter of King Harry by that provocative flirt Anne Boleyn, made his loins quiver.

But how to approach the matter? Perhaps a letter to the young lady herself, who would surely be flattered by the attentions of so experienced a man? Perhaps he should send it, unsealed, to her governess, with a covering note. That would be more appropriate.

Kat stared at the letter. Fortunately, she was alone in the chamber she shared with her husband, tidying away their clothes, when the messenger brought it to her.

She read it again. *I beg you to let me know,* the Admiral had written to Elizabeth, *whether I am to be the most happy or the most miserable of men.* The cheek of the man! How dare he presume so far? And what of his onetime pursuit of the Queen, who would be free to marry him once a decent year of mourning had elapsed?

Yet when you thought about it, the Admiral was a fine specimen of a man, bold, dashing, charming, and daring. Most women would be overjoyed to have him as a husband, even allowing for his vanity and impulsiveness. But Elizabeth was not most women. She was a king's daughter and her marriage would be a matter of state, sanctioned by the council. Moreover, she had often said she had no wish to marry.

But he *was* a most desirable match. Together, he and Elizabeth would make a handsome, spirited pair. He was just the kind of man Kat wanted for Elizabeth. Truth to tell, Kat was a little in love with him herself, had been for a long time. John Astley was a good, kindly husband, there was no denying that, but he had not the power to make Kat's heart flutter as Sir Thomas did. Of course, Sir Thomas would never look at Kat in that way, she was far too old, but it would be exciting to live in close proximity to such a man. And married to my Lady Elizabeth, he *would* be living in close proximity, and Kat could worship him from afar, happy in the knowledge that her beloved Elizabeth was enjoying him in reality. Oh, it would be the most desirable match!

Sighing, Kat sat on her bed, debating whether to show the letter to Elizabeth, or whether to reply herself. In the end, prudence won, and she sat down at her table, pen in hand, and informed the Admiral that, if he wished to press his suit to the Lady Elizabeth, he must first obtain the council's permission.

"No," said Lord Hertford immediately.

"But why?" blustered the Admiral, surveying the hostile faces of the councillors.

"Because the Lady Elizabeth is one of the best matches in Europe, as well as a valuable political asset," his brother explained. "One day, in the not-too-distant future, we will wish to arrange an advantageous marriage for her."

"She is of the blood royal and cannot be wasted on a mere knight," John Dudley, a big bull of a fellow, pointed out, dark brows furrowed. "Even if he is the King's uncle. You must see that, man."

"Forget her, Sir Thomas," Archbishop Cranmer said smoothly. "There must be many young ladies whose families would be glad of an alliance with the Seymours. You may have your pick, I am sure."

The Admiral shot them a withering look and, gathering the remnants of his dignity, bowed and flounced out of the room.

Elizabeth unsealed the letter that Kat had handed her, read it, and stared at the words, torn between outrage at the fellow's boldness and nervous excitement.

The messenger, handing over the letter, had told Kat that his master had taken her advice and done as she asked. He did not say whether the council had agreed to the match, but surely, Kat reasoned, Sir Thomas would not be so rash as to approach Elizabeth without that sanction?

"The Admiral craves my hand in marriage," Elizabeth said.

Kat's heart leapt, yet she forced herself to be cautious.

"Does he say that the council has approved his suit?" she asked.

Elizabeth scanned the page again.

"No."

"So are we to assume that it does?" Kat wondered.

"We may assume what we like," Elizabeth said, "yet I will not marry him. Neither my age nor my inclination allows me to think of marriage."

"But you are thirteen," Kat pointed out. "Girls younger than you have been happily wed. And the Admiral is such a fine figure of a man, and one of great courage. Will you let this chance slip by?"

"Yes," said Elizabeth dogmatically. "I have resolved never to marry. But I will write him a kind letter and put him off by saying that I need at least two years to mourn the death of my father before contemplating marriage. He will not wait that long for me."

"My lady, forgive me, but you are a fool!" protested Kat.

"I would rather be a single fool than a wedded traitor," Elizabeth retorted. "We have no proof that my lord has obtained the council's blessing on this match. And anyway, I enjoy my virgin state and intend to keep it."

Kat shook her head in frustration.

"It's unnatural, this not wanting to marry. All girls want a husband, so why should not you? And if it's the marriage bed you fear, why, I can assure you, too much fuss is made about that. There's nothing to worry about."

"I have said I do not wish to marry!" Elizabeth flared, her dark eyes blazing with anger. In a temper, she was her father to the life. "Why won't you believe me? Don't you think I know my own mind?"

"You are very young," Kat rejoined, "and your opinions will change, believe me! Listen to someone who is older and wiser. Marry the Admiral—you will hardly find a more desirable husband."

"No," said Elizabeth, through gritted teeth. This unsettling business had reawakened all her old fears of marriage. She did not think she could ever submit to that state. She did not know why, but the idea filled her with a kind of horror . . .

Permit me, my Lord Admiral, to tell you frankly that, though I decline the happiness of becoming your wife at this present time, I shall never cease to interest myself in all that can crown your merit with glory, and shall ever feel the greatest pleasure in being your servant and good friend.

"God's blood!" the Admiral roared, crushing the letter into a tight ball. "Am I doomed always to be frustrated in my desires?"

"What is the matter, my son?" asked old Lady Seymour, come to see what all the shouting betokened.

"She's refused me!" her son muttered. "The frigid little minx has refused me."

"Which frigid little minx, dear?" his mother inquired.

"The Lady Elizabeth," he growled.

"Well, my son, you should not have looked to have her in the first place," a surprised Lady Seymour reproved. "She is not for you, and you might have known that she would turn you down. She is a very prudent young lady."

She sighed.

"You were ever the rash one, Tom. Just think things through before you act impulsively. Find yourself a nice noble wife, dear, one with a good dowry, and then settle down. Marriage with a good, steady woman is what you need. And not before time either."

"Yes, my Lady Mother," the Admiral said, sighing and rolling his eyes.

The servant, a fellow called John Fowler, came to take the King's plate away.

"A gift from the Admiral, Sire," he muttered, pressing a purse of coins into Edward's hand while keeping an eye on Dr. Cheke, who was seated at the far end of the room marking the boy's translations. Edward looked up gratefully.

"That is most kind of my uncle," he said. "Would that I could do him some service in return."

Fowler pretended to think.

"Sire, I am sure you could," he said, repeating the words he had rehearsed. "The Lord Admiral says he has heard men marveling that he is not yet married. He himself wishes to marry, as I myself have heard him say many times, but he has not yet found a suitable bride. Would Your Majesty be content for him to marry?"

"Yes, very well content," replied the King.

"Would Your Grace like to suggest a lady?" Fowler asked.

Flattered at being approached regarding so adult a matter, Edward thought about it for some minutes.

"How about my Lady Anna of Cleves?" he said at length. "No, wait—I would that the Admiral marry my sister Mary, to change her opinions. It is my wish that she embrace the true Protestant faith, as all loyal subjects are being required to do."

"I will convey Your Grace's recommendation to my master," Fowler replied, bowing. "He will be grateful for Your Grace's advice."

Edward nodded, feeling magnanimous.

———

"No again," said Hertford, "and for the same reason. Look, Brother, neither of us was born to be a king, nor to marry a king's daughter. We should both thank God and be satisfied with what we have, and not presume to advance ourselves further. I know for a fact that the Lady Mary herself would never consent to such a marriage."

"How do you know?" the Admiral retorted. "Look, all I seek is the council's approval for this marriage, and then I'll win her in my own fashion."

"Have I not said no?" Hertford almost shouted. "I warn you, do not pursue the matter further."

"I see you are no friend to me, *Brother,*" sneered Tom, "and that you are determined to thwart me at every turn. Well, I'll see you in Hell before I give in to your malice!"

"Your Majesty, I have told the Admiral of your wise suggestions as to whom he should marry," Fowler said carefully, surreptitiously placing another purse of gold coins beside the King's charger. "But he has said that there is one whom he loves more than the Lady Anna and the Lady Mary. What would Your Majesty say to a marriage between him and the Queen?"

"I should approve of it," declared the boy without hesitation. "In time, of course. My dear stepmother is but newly made a widow." His impassive face betrayed no grief at the memory of his own recent loss.

"I will tell the Admiral, Sire," Fowler promised.

Queen Katherine stood with arms outstretched in the great entrance porch of Chelsea Palace. For all that she was a widow of just six weeks in a somber mourning gown and hood of black satin banded with purple velvet, she looked cheerful enough, and was clearly thrilled to be greeting her stepdaughter.

"My Lady Elizabeth! How I have missed you!" she cried, enveloping the girl in a soft, sweet-smelling embrace. "And Mrs. Astley, you are most welcome. Do come within."

She led the way into the airy red-brick house, through a high-beamed hall with tall oriel windows, and up a grand processional stair to the private apartments, where she showed Elizabeth into a luxuriously appointed suite of rooms adorned with precious tapestries, costly carpets, and fine furniture. Bowls of daffodils stood on the oak tables and chests, and there were bright green velvet curtains at the latticed windows.

"Mr. and Mrs. Astley are to have the chambers below," the Queen said. "There is a connecting spiral staircase." Kat tried to look grateful, but so sick was she with jealousy that she could hardly bear to look at Katherine.

"Madam, I am so bounden to you for the care you have taken, and for these beautiful rooms," Elizabeth said delightedly, kissing her stepmother.

"It is my pleasure," Katherine told her warmly. "Now I will leave you to settle in."

Alone with her governess in the beautiful apartment, Elizabeth danced for joy.

"Are we not lucky, Kat? Oh, I feel happy again!" she cried. "Happier than I have been for a long time."

Kat struggled to stifle her own feelings.

"I pray you will stay happy," she said brightly, resolving to suppress her animosity toward Katherine Parr once and for all.

Later, at dinner, which was served in the Queen's privy chamber with only Elizabeth and Lady Herbert, Katherine's sister, at table, they ate fish in a piquant sauce, followed by Elizabeth's favorites, candied fruits and custards, and discussed the latest news from court. Elizabeth was thrilled to find herself being treated as a grown-up, allowed to join in the adults' conversation and offer her opinions.

"I hear that Lord Hertford has been named Lord Protector," the Queen said.

"Or rather, he has made himself Lord Protector," Lady Herbert put in, helping herself to some salt. "But of course, we should not be referring to him as Lord Hertford now, should we?"

"I beg your pardon. He has been created Duke of Somerset," the Queen explained to a puzzled Elizabeth. "Many have been advanced in rank to mark the King's coronation. John Dudley is now Earl of Warwick, and Sir Thomas Seymour is become Lord Seymour of Sudeley."

Her smile wavered momentarily. He had not tried to see her, nor sent any message. She could not suppress her disappointment. But of course, it was early days yet—he would not wish to intrude on her mourning, nor compromise her honor; he was an upright man, clearly capable of great sensitivity. But if she could just set eyes on him again . . . or receive one word . . . Her heart was filled with yearning. She had waited so long for him.

"It is marvelous to see the reformed faith openly embraced at last," Lady Herbert said. "Do you remember how we hid our English Bible and went in fear of discovery?"

"Do not remind me." Katherine shuddered. "I nearly died for it. Elizabeth, are you happy that England is now a Protestant kingdom?"

"I am happy, madam." Elizabeth's smile was genuine. "For me, it is the true road to salvation, the way in which I, all unwittingly to begin with, was brought up. But I fear the outlawing of the Catholic Mass will cause great grief to my sister Mary." She was thinking that it had been long since she had seen Mary.

"The Lady Mary must conform like everyone else," said Lady Herbert sharply. "She cannot gainsay the King's will."

"She is very devout," Elizabeth pointed out.

"But misguided," the Queen added, folding her napkin. "In truth, I feel sorry for her, even though I know she must be made to see that she is in error."

"The council might let her alone," Elizabeth wondered. "After all, she can do little harm by practicing her faith in private."

"Never underestimate her," Katherine warned. "She has the friendship of the Emperor, her cousin, and he is the champion of the Catholic faith in Europe. He is a mighty prince, and if he so wished, he could lead an army into England and force us to accept the Roman faith. Fortunately, he is much occupied with driving back the Turks from his dominions."

"I do not think my sister would wish to invite any foreign invader into this kingdom," Elizabeth said. "She is too loyal to the King our brother, and loves him very much. And anyway, all she really wants is a husband and children. She is not interested in politics."

"She may have to be," Lady Herbert said. "I doubt they will let her continue to have her Mass. After all, it will soon be illegal."

"We must pray for her," Katherine said. "And now, since we are all finished, perhaps a little music before we retire. Elizabeth, will you play your lute for us?"

It was a Friday evening in May, and after an unusually cold spring, Elizabeth and Kat were basking in the first warm weather of the year, sitting under a cherry tree and sunning themselves in the beautiful gardens that swept down to the Thames. Elizabeth had laid aside her book, Sir Thomas Elyot's *A Defence of Good Women,* which, for all its appeal, made for rather dry reading on such a glorious day. Her hood lay beside her on the grass, and she was wondering whether to waken the softly snoring Kat when she espied the Queen leaving the house and hurrying in the opposite direction between the railed flower beds before disappearing behind one of the lush privet hedges that bisected the gardens. There was that in Katherine's determined step which told Elizabeth that she was embarked upon something rather important.

She thought no more of it until three nights later when, having undressed for bed and doused her candle, she stood gazing out of her window at the night sky, recalling things her father had told her, long ago, about the stars. There were many of them visible tonight, and the moon was almost full. Elizabeth opened the casement and sniffed the fresh, scented air, breathing it in sensuously.

Then suddenly, there was the Queen, below her on the path, walking purposefully in the same direction she had taken three days earlier. Even more startling was the fact that Katherine had put off her mourning gown and was wearing a becoming one of a lighter shade—indeterminate in the moonlight—with a very low, square neckline.

Within seconds, she had disappeared from sight, but Elizabeth stayed at her window, watching. Her vigilance was soon rewarded, for the Queen did not tarry wherever she had gone, but quickly emerged from the trees in company with what was unmistakably a man. A tall man with a confident gait. They were talking in lowered tones, and even laughing in a hushed way as they approached the house. Elizabeth, astonished, recognized Thomas Seymour, the new Lord Sudeley, the man who had so recently proposed marriage to herself, and she was quite shocked to see him put an arm around Katherine's shoulders and pull her to him; then he bent and kissed her full on the mouth.

Something stirred in Elizabeth at that moment, something that was not altogether related to the shock of witnessing an entirely unexpected and also very intimate gesture. She could not see Katherine's face, but in the moonlight she could make out the way in which she was pressing her body against the Admiral's in an attitude of willing surrender. Maybe it was that, or perhaps it was the masterful way in which he had stolen the kiss, but suddenly Elizabeth knew what it was to desire a man; and with this knowledge came a bleak sense of loss, for this could have been hers, had she had the sense to heed Kat's advice.

The unexpected, unfamiliar heat in the pit of her stomach and her female parts was overpowering. Her budding breasts tingled. Young as she was, she recognized her body's response as desire. She found she was breathless and shaking, and there was a strange wetness between her legs. When she looked down, there was blood dripping on the floor.

Although the sight of it shocked her, she knew it for what it was, had been expecting her monthly courses ever since Kat had told her about them last year. Yet all the same she was a little horrified, and her tired mind was playing tricks. Desire . . . and blood. The two were inextricably linked in her consciousness, for by some strange coincidence, the one had come with the other.

Yet there was more to it than that: There were memories too, unhappy memories. A man and a woman might desire each other, but the result was often a baby, born in a gush of bloody fluid—she knew this because she had heard women talking about it. And some women died of it. Her own grandmother Elizabeth of York, and her stepmother Jane Seymour—both had perished in childbed. And desire might lead also to another kind of death. Her father had desired her mother, and her mother had met a bloody end, as had Katherine Howard, another victim of desire, illicit in her case. And now, like all women, she, Elizabeth, must bleed every month, and when she came to satisfy her own desires—Kat had been most explicit—there would be more blood, and pain, at least on the first occasion. These thoughts chilled her intensely.

But she had resolved never to marry, hadn't she? If she did not marry, she could avoid facing a bloody penetration or a bloody childbed, or worse. But then she would also have to forsake any chance of knowing that sweet melting tenderness she had just witnessed between the Queen and the Admiral, and which she herself, in her innocence, could only imagine. It was, perhaps, a small price to pay to feel safe, she reasoned, once the fleeting moment of arousal had gone and no longer had the power to sway her thoughts. Restored to sanity, she could only marvel at how easily she had forgotten herself. Now she must attend to more pressing practical matters.

They had gone, those two below her window, and the garden was empty. An owl hooted. She would forget what she had seen; she would not betray the woman who had been her kind benefactress, and she would not dwell on what might have been. Stuffing her chemise between her legs, she hastened barefoot to the chest in her bedchamber to find the linen clouts that Kat had laid there in readiness.

On subsequent nights, Elizabeth saw the lovers again, usually around the same time, making their way toward the house. A discreet investigation of the gardens suggested that the Queen admitted the Admiral by a little wicket gate in the wall. Occasionally, Elizabeth heard him leave in the small hours of the morning. On these occasions, he would be alone, hastening toward that gate.

She told no one. It was, she thought, fiercely protective of Katherine, no one's business but theirs.

But Kat, too, had also been looking out of the window, and—more worldly-wise than Elizabeth—had drawn her own conclusions. Surely the Queen should be more mindful of her honor! How could she indulge in such light behavior so soon after King Henry's death, and with a man so far below her in rank? And how dare she presume to dally with Sir Thomas Seymour, whom Kat had earmarked for Elizabeth? Was this just a flirtation? Or was it something of far greater import? In either case, it could have serious consequences for all concerned, and that would surely put paid to Kat's plans for her charge.

Kat's good resolutions immediately went out of the window. Sick with jealousy, she imagined herself confronting the Queen with what she knew, or denouncing her to Elizabeth for what she was, or even reporting her shameful goings-on to the council. But of course, she reasoned, this affair could not remain secret for long. Already, Kat had heard servants gossiping—it was impossible to keep anything secret in a great

household. Exposure would come soon enough, that was certain. Kat
need do nothing. It was better that way.

Two days later, making her way to the linen store, Kat caught the tail end
of a murmured conversation between two of the Queen's chamber
women, and was shocked at what she heard.

"Mark my words, they have been wed this past week!" one said. "I've
made the bed, and seen evidence of it."

"You don't say!" gasped the other.

"Who has been wed?" Kat, advancing into the closet, demanded to
know.

"Um, no one you know, Mrs. Astley," the first woman faltered,
clearly dismayed. She and her companion picked up their bundles and
hurriedly left.

Kat's heart was racing. Surely they had been talking about the Queen?
She was convinced of it. Married? To Lord Sudeley? How had they
dared, with the old king not in his grave four months? Oh, there was
going to be an epic scandal about this! And she, Kat, would make the
most of it.

Kat had taken to making occasional expeditions into London to buy
books for Elizabeth in St. Paul's Churchyard and to gaze at the jewelry on
sale at the fine goldsmiths' shops in Cheapside. Sometimes she would go
by chariot, at other times she walked, following the curving course of the
river. On one of the latter occasions, she was returning through St.
James's Park when she by chance encountered the Admiral.

"Well, if it isn't the gatekeeper!" he greeted her mischievously, but his
eyes were regarding her shiftily, she felt. She alone had been privy to his
secret ambitions regarding her young lady; did he guess that she had
lately heard gossip about him and the Queen?

"Good day, my Lord Admiral," she said, ignoring the jibe and resting
her basket on a bench.

"A very fine day, Mrs. Astley," he said. "I am just come from the
palace." He indicated the red-brick pile of St. James's behind them. "I
needed some air. My Lord Protector's apartments are a little heated!"

He smiled ruefully. Kat decided she would make him feel even hotter.

"I have looked to see you at Chelsea, sir," she said. "I thought you would be pursuing your suit to the Lady Elizabeth."

"Ah, that," he said, looking uncomfortable.

"I had heard it said by many that you would have my Lady Elizabeth to wife," she went on, her tone tart. She had heard nothing of the sort.

"Nay," he replied sheepishly. "I will not lose my life for a wife. I did speak to the council, but it cannot be." He lowered his voice. "I will let you into a secret—I am promised to the Queen."

Kat could barely contain her anger.

"From other rumors I hear, you are past promising, and married already!" she retorted.

The Admiral smiled, but his eyes were still wary.

"Do not heed idle gossip, Mrs. Astley," he said, then bowed and walked off, striding back in the direction of the palace.

Kat stood staring after him, simmering, painfully aware that all her hopes for Elizabeth were about to be dashed.

Elizabeth, summoned to the Queen's privy chamber, was surprised to find the Admiral standing behind Katherine, who rose from her chair and greeted her stepdaughter with a kiss on the cheek.

"I have something to confess to you," she said, without further preamble. "I have married the Admiral."

"Married the Admiral?" gasped Elizabeth.

"Yes, my dear," Katherine said evenly, reaching for her new husband's hand and looking up at him devotedly. He smiled back, revealing white teeth beneath his full lips. He really is very handsome, Elizabeth thought. I cannot blame him if he has looked elsewhere for a wife. I did refuse him . . .

"When I visited the King yesterday, I told him all, and begged his forgiveness for having remarried without seeking his permission," Katherine went on. "He has taken it very kindly, and promised publicly to give us his blessing."

"Not so my brother the Protector," said the Admiral, grimacing. "He is furious with us. Or rather, his good lady is. She has just realized she will have to yield precedence to the wife of her despised brother-in-law, and she is much offended and put out." He grinned.

"I do hope that you will be as kind to us as your brother the King has been, Elizabeth," the Queen said, a note of pleading in her voice.

"In faith, I know not what to say, save I am glad for your happiness," Elizabeth replied. It was true, she *was* glad, for by the glint in Katherine's eyes and the soft flush on her cheeks, she could tell that her stepmother was indeed happy, but it was too soon, this marriage, almost indecently soon. Was not the Queen newly widowed and supposed to be mourning the late king?

"I fear we have caused a terrible scandal, marrying so soon after your father's passing," Katherine said, her cheeks flushed. "There were many looking askance at me at court, I assure you. It was not a pleasant experience. It was pointed out to me, rather brutally, by the Lord Protector that, if I had proved to be with child so soon after the King's death, none could be sure whose child it was, and the lawful succession—and the King's title—would thereby be impugned. But we did not marry until the beginning of May, so his calculations are born of malice, not logic."

"I thought that widows had to wait a year before they could marry again, madam," Elizabeth said, unable to stop herself. "It would perhaps have been better to defer marrying until then."

"If I had had time to wait that long, believe me I would have done so," Katherine avowed passionately. "But I am no longer young, I am thirty-five, Elizabeth, and I yearn to have a child while I still can. I would not have you think that this marriage proceeds from any sudden passion. For as truly as God is God, my mind was fully bent to it when I was at liberty to marry that other time . . . before I was overruled by a higher power. And I mean no disrespect to your father, child. He was a good lord to me. But I have seized this chance of happiness, and all I can say is—well, God is a marvelous man!"

Her face was radiant, her joy tangible. Elizabeth smiled. She would not, for the world, spoil the Queen's happiness. She bent and kissed Katherine again.

"You have my blessing too, madam—and my lord."

Watching her, Tom thought how much like her mother she was becoming. Save for that red hair and Old Harry's nose, she was Anne Boleyn to the life. Give her a year or two, and she'd have men slavering over her.

He looked down fondly at Katherine. There were faint lines beneath her eyes. She had spoken the truth: She was indeed no longer young. But she was still comely, she was his wife for better or worse, and he loved her. He did truly love her.

Elizabeth thought the scandal had blown over until she received Mary's letter.

> *You must come to me at once and lodge here at Hunsdon,* her sister commanded, *and you must understand the urgent necessity to remove yourself from that household without delay. I am outraged to learn that the scarcely cold body of the King our father has been so shamelessly dishonored. However, as I do not wish to offend the Queen, who has been kind to me, you must use much tact in this matter of your removal, so as not to appear ungrateful. But you must not allow yourself to be exposed further to such wickedness, nor be seen to condone it.*

"What am I to do, Kat?" Elizabeth wept. "I do not want to leave. I am very happy here. I love the Queen, who has shown me so much affection, and I like the Admiral. How could I abandon them?"

"I think you would do well to heed the Lady Mary," Kat urged her, grateful for an unexpected ally. "I must confess, I had misgivings when you told me you had given this marriage your blessing. Elizabeth, your father the King was but lately dead; you must see that it was ill timed, to say the least."

Elizabeth looked uncertain.

"Yes, it was too soon," she agreed. "I did think so. But apart from the fact that they did not wait a decent interval, the Queen and the Admiral are lawfully wed. It's not as if they are living in sin. And I have been so happy here that I will not say anything against their marriage. Truly, I wish them well, and I will stand up to my sister and tell her. Tactfully, of course."

"Is that wise?" Kat asked. "I am only considering your reputation, you understand. I make no judgment against the Queen and the Admiral."

"Dear Kat." Elizabeth smiled, curling an arm around her. "You are ever thoughtful on my behalf. I do understand your concern, but I tell you it is needless. I will write to my sister tonight. I will dissemble and tell her that all is well with me here, that things are not quite as she perceives them, and that I will wait to see how matters turn out. Is that not the best course? After all, neither Mary nor myself has any power to change what has happened. We must make the best of what we cannot remedy."

"Very well," said Kat, knowing herself defeated, and trying to still a small sense of dread.

"Since the Admiral came to live here, this has been a much happier house," Elizabeth observed to the Queen. She had feared to begin with that it would be as if a serpent had invaded Eden, but after two weeks spent getting to know her new stepfather, and experiencing the positive impact he was making on all their lives, her worries had been dispelled. "Life is more exciting, we laugh a lot—"

"And we are full of joy!" finished Katherine. "In faith, we have not stopped making merry. Every day has seemed like a holiday. And I will never weary of it."

"Everyone speaks highly of the Admiral, madam," Elizabeth said. "He is affable to all, and not one whit condescending, even to the least of the servants. They all love him."

The Queen smiled. They were sitting companionably at a table under a peach tree on the lawn overlooking the river, enjoying a picnic. Picnics, Katherine had declared, were her favorite way of dining, and she had ordered a veritable feast: The table was laden with silver plates of chicken, game, pasties, peas, and fish, with Elizabeth's favorite candied fruits to follow. Beneath the trees, at a discreet distance, a musician sat softly strumming a lute. A gentle breeze stirred the air, which was heady with the scent from two hundred damask rosebushes. Elizabeth was consumed with a sense of well-being. Life was good, and already she understood that to be aware of happiness when you were actually feeling it, and not just in retrospect, was to be happy indeed.

Marriage suited Katherine well: There was a radiance about her, and she delighted in talking about her handsome husband.

"I told him," she was saying, "that if he must devise new pleasures and pastimes every day, then he would see other things slide." But she did not look too worried about this. "What matter, eh? This life is short, and we must make the best of it. I admit my lord is rather a naughty man, and not perhaps as devout as he might be. Strangely, he always has some urgent matter of business to attend to when it's time for morning service in the chapel on Sundays, but he is a law unto himself, I have found." She grimaced ruefully, yet her eyes were dancing.

"And it is good for you to have a father figure in your life, Elizabeth," she went on, reaching over and patting the girl's hand. "A proper guardian who can look to your interests."

"I am glad of it," Elizabeth told her, and suddenly there he was, that guardian, striding along the path from the house, his smile dazzling in the sunlight.

"Good day, Your Grace, ladies!" he cried, sweeping an exaggerated bow. "Can you spare a chicken wing for a starving man?"

"I think we've eaten everything," Katherine said mischievously.

"For shame!" he told her. "You will all get very fat!"

"Here, sir," Elizabeth said, passing the dish. "Her Grace but jests."

"Are you enjoying yourself, my Lady Elizabeth?" the Admiral asked, turning the full force of his intense eyes and brilliant smile on her. Her heart began to beat faster, and there was that strange sinking feeling low in her belly once more. He really was the most attractive fellow . . .

She pulled herself together.

"I cannot believe my good fortune, my lord," she replied. "I should be mourning my poor father, yet Her Grace here enjoins me to be happy, and you and she have made this place a very paradise for me."

Thomas regarded her for a minute, admiring her regal bearing and the way she held her head, and noticing also the budding breasts beneath the tight bodice.

"I am glad," he answered, then turned to his wife. "I go to court again tomorrow, Kate, to take my brother to task for giving the Queen's jewels to his grasping wife."

"They are mine by right, until the King marries," Katherine said. "I pray you be forceful. We cannot let them get away with it."

Thomas bent and kissed her full on the mouth. Elizabeth looked away, not understanding why seeing them thus caused her to feel such a pang.

By and by, Elizabeth realized that she was taking more and more notice of the Admiral. She was becoming increasingly aware of his presence, in the house, at table, in the gardens, or at chapel—on the rare occasions he was there. She would find herself surreptitiously sneaking a glance at him, noting his finely boned features, the dark, wicked eyes, straight nose, and bushy dark beard. She could not get her fill of looking at him.

There were plenty of opportunities to indulge this fancy, for although the Admiral often haunted the court by day, his barge would bring him back to Chelsea in the evenings, in time to eat supper with his new family. His manner toward Elizabeth was always exaggeratedly chivalrous, and he was fond of teasing her—for she always rose to the bait. Yet never once, in these early weeks, did he appear to remember that he had proposed marriage to her.

As the time passed, she found herself longing for him to appear. His sheer physicality appealed to her, as did his flamboyant personality. One morning, waking early, she looked out her window and saw him making his way back to the house from the tennis court, clad only in breeches and hose, a white towel around his bare shoulders. His hair was damp with sweat, so he must have been playing with some ferocity. One glance at his broad muscular chest, lightly covered in dark hair, and Elizabeth was lost. She had never seen anyone as pleasing to the eye, with all his limbs and features so well put together. What a proper man he was!

She knew of course that men were differently formed from women, and why, and she could not but surmise what wonders that well-stuffed codpiece concealed, although she had only the vaguest idea of how a naked man might appear, for the only male she had ever seen undressed was her brother as a baby. But alongside the delicious infatuation and fevered imaginings, she felt guilt too, for this was the Queen's husband, and she loved the Queen and had no wish to hurt her. Yet there was no harm in daydreaming, surely?

A new portrait of the Admiral had been hung in the great hall—a very good likeness. Kat came upon Elizabeth staring entranced at it one day, and summed up the situation at once.

"A fine man, isn't he?" she said. Elizabeth jumped.

"Indeed he is," she agreed, somewhat breathlessly.

"The Queen is a lucky lady," Kat went on. "But never forget that you were his first choice. And if I'm not mistaken, you're a little bit moonstruck on him, aren't you?"

She smiled questioningly at her charge.

Elizabeth blushed and said nothing, all the time gazing wistfully at the portrait. The artist had caught the Admiral to the life.

"Ah, Kat, I do not understand myself," she said at length. "You know that for a long time I was resolved never to marry. And you were right— now I am not so sure. It seems to me that love between a man and a woman is a thing that perhaps ought not to be denied. I should have listened to you, for I know now that marriage with a man such as the Admiral would surely have swayed my opinions."

"Well, it is too late now," Kat said flatly. "You cannot guess how bitterly I regret that it did not come about, for you and he would have made a handsome couple; and I'll warrant you'd go a long way to find so dashing a bridegroom. But he is married to the Queen now, and you must not think of him in that way."

"He is so handsome and charming, I cannot help but think of him," Elizabeth whispered.

"You will get over it," Kat said brusquely. "Young maids often develop a fancy for an older man, especially one as good-looking as the Admiral. Such an infatuation is harmless, and of no consequence, although I know it seems of great import to you. But he is forbidden fruit, child, so put him out of your mind."

But Elizabeth could not. He was with her everywhere she went. Even the unworldly Master Grindal noticed that she was not as attentive to her studies as before. Into her mind, unbidden, came tantalizing but uninformed images of herself and the Admiral in bed together, of him performing that intimate act which Kat, red-faced, had described to her in such embarrassing detail. And when she tried to imagine how it would feel to have such a man love her in that way, her heart would pound and her palms sweat.

She could not stop thinking about him.

Kat climbed into bed beside her husband and doused the candle. As usual, John Astley leant over and kissed her before lying back on the feather pillows. Kat relaxed. She would not have to pay the marriage debt tonight. What men got out of it she could not imagine. For her, it was an uncomfortable, messy business, and quite unnecessary anyway, since she was past the age for childbearing. Still, she loved her husband, who was a good and kind man in many ways.

"Kat," John said in the darkness, "something is worrying me. It concerns the Lady Elizabeth."

Kat was startled. "Whatever are you talking about?"

"I've been watching her," John explained, "and I've noticed that, whenever the Admiral is mentioned, she becomes very attentive and stops whatever she is doing to listen. When the Queen praises him, she is immoderately pleased, and today, when someone spoke his name, I saw her blush. I think you should take heed, for I fear that she bears some hidden affection for him."

"Nonsense!" said Kat tartly, jolted into defensiveness by his perspicacity. "He's an attractive man, and she's at an age when she notices such things. It's entirely innocent, and even if she *is* harboring romantic feelings for him, she would never do anything to hurt the Queen."

"*She* might not, but what about him?" John sounded agitated. "Think about it, Kat. I've seen him looking at her, and that look didn't seem innocent to me. You must speak to her, warn her. Just think, if there were ever any impropriety between the Admiral and the Lady Elizabeth, both would be guilty of high treason. *High treason,* mark me!"

"He wouldn't be such a fool," Kat opined.

"Many men have been made fools by pretty young girls," John interrupted. "And may I remind you of the penalty for high treason. For him, hanging, drawing, and quartering, although because of his rank they'd probably just chop off his head. And for her, it's beheading or burning."

"They'd never dare—she's the King's sister," Kat retorted, aghast.

"Two queens have already been beheaded, and not that long ago," John reminded her. "Her own mother was one of them."

"I tell you, there's nothing in it," Kat insisted, after a pause. "It's an innocent infatuation, nothing more."

"I hope to God you're right," John said with a sigh. "But just in case you're not, keep your eyes open, and if you see anything that troubles you, anything at all, put a stop to it."

"The Admiral would never take advantage of her," Kat said angrily. "He's an honorable man, *and* her guardian while she is under his roof. I cannot believe he would stoop to such evil conduct."

"Charmed you as well, has he?" John asked sourly.

"Oh, stuff and nonsense!" Kat was having none of it.

"In faith, Wife, you are too trusting of others," John observed, then turned over to face her, his eyes troubled. "As your husband, I command you to be watchful. Otherwise we could all end up in the Tower."

Kat said nothing. She did not believe it could ever come to that.

Elizabeth had just finished dressing one morning when the door opened and there stood the Admiral, elegant in a dark green suit.

"My lord!" cried a flustered Kat. "I beg you, please knock before you enter. My lady might not have been ready to receive you."

"Good morrow, Elizabeth," smiled Thomas, ignoring the governess and patting her nonplussed charge on the shoulder.

"Good morrow, my lord," Elizabeth answered, her cheeks flushed with the pleasure of seeing him.

"Are your attendants awake?" he asked, nodding in the direction of the maidens' chamber. "If not, I will go and rouse them! We cannot have tardiness in this household."

"They are awake, my lord," Kat said hastily. "I heard them moving about a few minutes ago. May I ask why you are here?"

"Why, I came to bid good morning to the Lady Elizabeth," he said, grinning. "May not a man pay such a courtesy to his own stepdaughter?"

Kat looked unhappy.

"Good morrow, my lord," Elizabeth said, coolly enough, although her cheeks were flaming.

"I trust you are well, my lady?" he smiled, nodding. "Do you always arise this early?"

"I do, sir," she told him.

"Well. So do I! Every morning!" Something in his tone, and the twinkle in his eye, made Kat blush. The naughty man! Fortunately, Elizabeth was too innocent to have understood his meaning.

"I am glad to see you well, and I bid you good day, ladies," he said, bowing, and departed.

"Well!" Kat breathed. "That was most irregular!"

"I think he came for a jest," Elizabeth said, her heart racing.

"He had better not come again," Kat retorted, agitated, although it did her heart good to see her charge looking so radiantly happy.

"I'm sure he will not," Elizabeth replied, but it was hard not to hope that he would.

Two days later, the Admiral returned, bursting into the bedchamber just as Elizabeth was putting on her French hood. He had timed his entrance well, for Kat had just gone in search of a laundress.

"Good morrow, my lady," he beamed, slapping Elizabeth lightly on the bottom. "How does my stepdaughter today?"

At the touch of his palm, felt through the thickness of her heavy damask skirt, Elizabeth had begun to tingle, and she was struggling to control the sensation. The tingling had started in the pit of her stomach, then spread downward, where it had metamorphosed into the now familiar aching feeling between her legs. Had that been his intention, to arouse her?

"I am well, sir," she said, her voice barely steady. "Forgive me, I must go to the schoolroom. Master Grindal is waiting."

"Good, good," beamed the Admiral. "I am pleased to see you so eager to be at your studies."

"I love learning, as you know," Elizabeth told him. "Now, if you will excuse me." And she more or less fled out the door.

Elizabeth stretched out between the sheets. Through a chink in the bed curtains she could see that it was still dull in the room. Dawn had not yet broken fully, so she could indulge in a few extra minutes in bed. Sleepily, she turned over.

Suddenly, the curtains were pulled apart and there was the Admiral, devastatingly handsome, smiling down at her.

"Still abed?" he cried. "Good morrow, my lady—time to arise!"

"Sir, you should not be here!" she reproved him, alarmed. "Mrs. Astley is not yet up."

"Then she is neglectful of her duty!" he retorted, grinning. "Come, get up!"

And he yanked the bedclothes off her, leaving her slim body exposed in its thin lawn chemise. Elizabeth gasped.

"Shall I tickle you?" he cried, wiggling his fingers and making as if he would come at her.

"You must leave, sir!" she told him, shrinking back farther in the bed.

"I will leave when I see you get up," he replied. "Come on! Do not dally!"

Reluctantly, Elizabeth gathered the skirts of her chemise about her legs, for modesty, and slid off the bed on the opposite side. Then she peered out from behind the bed curtains, aware that his behavior was most improper, and conscious that she must put a stop to it.

"I am up, my lord. Please leave."

Kat, entering at that moment, a vision of sleepiness in her voluminous nightgown and beribboned bonnet, took in the scene with a horrified glance.

"My lord! You should not be here!" she exclaimed.

"On the contrary, the Queen asked me to say good morrow to the Lady Elizabeth before I leave for court," the Admiral said smoothly.

"But she is not dressed; it is not seemly!" Kat protested.

"Of course it is seemly. She is just a child, Mrs. Astley; I am her step-father, and I was but jesting with her." His level gaze dared her to disagree.

"Very well, sir," Kat said doubtfully. "But in future, I should be grateful if you would wait until my Lady Elizabeth is dressed."

The Admiral ignored her.

"Good day, Elizabeth," he said, bowing. "I will look forward to seeing you this evening. Now I must go. My barge awaits, but the tide will not."

Elizabeth's cheeks were bright pink.

As soon as he had gone, she ran to her mirror and scrutinized her reflection in its polished silver surface. Fortunately the light in the bed-chamber was dim, yet she could still make out the dark peak of a nipple under the filmy fabric of her chemise, and was that a hint of pubic hair? How much of her body had he espied? She was trembling, torn between embarrassment and excitement. He had called her a child, but he would probably have seen all too clearly that she was a child no longer.

As she was pulling on her tawny velvet nightgown, Kat came in.

"If he comes again, you must call me at once!" she ordered. "What would people say if it became known that the Admiral visits you in your bedchamber, and you in a state of undress?"

"He thinks me a child. It is just his idea of a romp," Elizabeth said, only half believing it, and yet perversely hoping that he did not think of her as a child.

"A romp indeed!" Kat frowned. "There's more than one kind of romp! You just call me if he comes again."

That evening, Elizabeth saw to it that her nightgown was laid on a chair within reach of the bed, just in case the Admiral burst in on her the next morning. And Kat, torn between suspicion and anticipation, had promised to get up earlier and be in her chamber before dawn. Just in case.

But he did not come the next morning, or the one after that. Elizabeth began to relax, yet she was also inexplicably disappointed. The thought of the Admiral in her bedchamber, and she half clothed, was an arousing one, and she could not help feeling the stirring of desire. But this was wrong; she knew it was wrong. He was the Queen's husband, and she must never forget that.

"Awake, my lady! Up! Up!"

"Sir, I beg of you!" Kat's voice, pleading.

"Stop griping, woman. I am but come to see that my stepdaughter gets up in time for her lessons. The Queen knows I am here."

"My lady is never late, sir, there is no need. I really must insist—"

The curtains were flung back. The handsome face loomed down at Elizabeth, who instinctively huddled beneath the covers. Dare she make a grab for the nightgown? The chair seemed a long way away.

"And how does my lady today?" Thomas inquired. "Don't you think it's time you made ready? It's nigh on five o'clock."

Elizabeth was just about to answer when he suddenly hauled the bed-clothes off her, leaned forward, and slapped her on the buttocks. Her body responded treacherously, and neither her tormentor nor her nurse missed the shudder that coursed through her, or the fleeting gasp of ecstasy.

Kat moved quickly.

"Your robe, my lady," she said, snatching up the nightgown and handing it to Elizabeth. "Now, my lord, if you would kindly leave us, so that my Lady Elizabeth can have some privacy."

The Admiral looked as if he was about to protest, but evidently thought better of it. Without a word, he bowed and left the room.

"Tonight, we are locking the door!" Kat declared firmly. This was getting beyond a joke.

A key rattled in the lock.

"Whatever . . . ," Kat began, bewildered.

The door swung open and there was the Admiral, once again. This time, Elizabeth was sitting on the edge of the bed, pulling up her cloth stockings, and her slender thighs were exposed to his gaze. Quickly, she pulled down her chemise.

"My lord!" Kat cried, determined to put a stop to these morning visits. "The door was locked!"

"Indeed it was," he responded cheerfully. "But you see, Mrs. Astley, I have had keys made for all the rooms in the house, for my own use, and as I am master here, don't you agree that none should gainsay me entry?"

"We are not gainsaying you, sir, just asking, yet again, that you delay your arrival until my Lady Elizabeth is dressed. Surely that is not too much to ask."

"Calm yourself, Mrs. Astley. I have just come, as usual, to bid my stepdaughter good morrow. I mean no harm. Elizabeth knows that, don't you, my lady?"

Elizabeth was praying he could not see through the thicker linen chemise that she had deemed it safer to wear in bed.

"Yes, my lord," she said distractedly. "But I should prefer it if you came later."

"Indeed?" he asked quizzically, his eyes twinkling with mischief. "Naturally, I shall do what I know Your Grace to prefer."

Elizabeth felt the heat rising to her face. This was no innocent game. He knew, she realized; he knew how she felt about him, and he was taking full advantage of it. But why? she asked herself. He loved the Queen, didn't he?

Or had he loved her, Elizabeth, all along? Her heart leapt at the thought.

Later that day, Elizabeth received a note from the Admiral. It was brief but it made her tremble.

If you are still abed when I come to you in the mornings, I will bend you over a chair and give you the beating you deserve! he had written. Then underneath, he had added, *Of course, I but jest, but a father ought from time to time to remind his daughter of her duty.*

Kat had received a note too.

"Ooh, the very brazenness of the man!" she cried.

"What does it say?" Elizabeth asked, her heart still racing.

"He asks—oh, for shame, the naughty man—if my great buttocks, as he puts it, have grown any less or no!"

"That is so rude!" Elizabeth exclaimed. "What a strange thing to write."

"I know why he wrote it," Kat said. "The other day I was saying to the Queen that I should restrict my diet, as I have put on weight around my hips, and he overheard me and made some remark about liking women with big buttocks. Her Grace just laughed, but I told him off, saying he should not speak thus before ladies. This"—she waved the note—"is his revenge. Oh, the wicked knave!"

Elizabeth had crumpled her own note, which was now concealed in her sweating hand.

"Did you get a letter too?" Kat asked.

"No," she lied. She could not face Kat's reaction, or risk her showing such a note to the Queen.

It was at Seymour Place, the Admiral's fine London town house, whither they had removed so that Chelsea Palace could be cleansed, that Kat began to be really alarmed by his behavior.

The morning visits had seemingly ceased, much to her relief.

"Thank goodness the Admiral has put a stop to that nonsense," she said to Elizabeth.

Elizabeth said nothing.

Then suddenly, one morning, Thomas burst into her bedchamber, wearing just his nightgown, beneath which he was bare-legged in his slippers. Elizabeth, already up and dressed, raised startled eyes from her book, astonished to see him there. Immediately, her face reddened, for the nightgown was only loosely tied, and it was gaping slightly open. Hastily, she lowered her eyes.

Kat, seeing what Elizabeth had seen, swooped down on the Admiral like an avenging angel.

"For shame, sir! It is unseemly to come to a maiden's chamber so improperly dressed!"

The Admiral wrapped his nightgown more tightly about himself. His face registered anger at Kat's outburst.

"I must insist you leave at once, sir!" she went on, undeterred. "I have my Lady Elizabeth's reputation to consider."

Without a word, the Admiral left the room, slamming the door behind him. He did not appear in his nightgown again.

Yet he would not desist. Back at Chelsea, he came again and again, every morning.

"How much earlier will he come?" cried Elizabeth, who had taken to getting up well before dawn so as to be dressed and ready when he arrived. "I may as well stay up all night at this rate!"

By now, though, the maidens had talked and the other household servants were beginning to notice what was going on; Kat had already heard some bawdy gossip in the kitchens, and a couple of the Queen's ladies had made very pointed remarks about Kat's failure to put a stop to the Admiral's antics. That hurt, because she had tried, many times, to do just that, even though it had been in vain. He was the master of the house and he just would not listen. Nothing deterred him.

Then came the morning when Elizabeth awoke to see him bending over her, grinning purposefully.

"A kiss, my fair maiden!" he demanded, puckering his lips in anticipation.

"No!" cried Kat, emerging from the inner door and advancing on the bed. "I beg you, sir, go away, for shame!"

"Go away?" he growled in mock rage. "Nay! I will claim a kiss from my stepdaughter, my good woman, and *then* I will go away."

Kat stood her ground.

"Forgive me, sir, but I have my lady's reputation to protect," she insisted. "You should know that because of these morning visits, the servants are saying evil things about her—and about you too, my lord!"

The Admiral frowned.

"Are they? By God's precious soul, I will teach them not to gossip. They shall hear from me! I mean no evil, so I will not leave off. On the contrary, I will report to my brother the Protector how I am slandered. And then there will be some merry repercussions, I'll warrant."

After he was gone, slamming the door in his anger, Kat stood there shaking. It had all gone too far, and she knew herself to have been in some way to blame. Yet she *had* tried to put a stop to the morning romps, *had* tried to rein in the Admiral's boisterousness. Deep within herself, though, she was aware she had not tried hard enough; that she had obtained a vicarious pleasure from the interplay between him and Elizabeth. She had been thrilled to see the pleasure on Elizabeth's face, to observe her flushed responses to my lord's horseplay, and to feast her eyes on the handsome rogue as he plied his charms. And so she, Kat, had tacitly encouraged the Admiral, pretending to herself that her inferior rank rendered her powerless to resist his intrusions.

Well, she must delude herself no longer. It had to stop, or Elizabeth's reputation would be lost, her very life endangered even. Her dear little lady was being dreadfully compromised, and the spreading gossip was changing something that was essentially harmless into something awful. People might even think that Elizabeth was encouraging the Admiral . . .

Well, there *was* something Kat could do: She could tell the Queen.

CHAPTER 13

1547

Why, Mrs. Astley, this is a pleasant surprise."

Queen Katherine looked up from the letter she had been writing and smiled. She was well aware of the governess's jealousy, but knew it to be unfounded. In fact, she felt sorry for the poor woman.

"Your Grace, I would speak with you on a matter of some delicacy," Kat said.

Katherine laid down her pen and rose.

"Do sit down, please," she said, taking a seat on the settle and indicating that Kat should join her. Kat sat down stiffly.

"Now," said Katherine, looking concerned. "What is the matter?"

"Your Grace, forgive me, it's my Lord Admiral," Kat began hesitantly. "It's all innocent, of course, and he means no harm, I know that, but he *will* come of a morning to my Lady Elizabeth's chamber to bid her good morrow, and sometimes he comes when she is still abed and tickles or smacks her in play, as one would a child. But, madam, she is no longer a child, and the servants are talking. I have tried to tell him that it is unseemly, disporting himself thus with a great girl of fourteen, but he will not listen. Instead, he gets angry and threatens to complain to the Lord Protector that he is being slandered."

Katherine quickly collected her wits. Kat's words had plunged her into turmoil. Was it all as innocent as Kat claimed? Of course it was, it was merely Tom being his larger-than-life self. She must believe that, and not doubt his motives. Truly, she had no other cause to doubt him: He was as attentive and loving as ever, if not more so. A faint flush warmed her cheeks as she remembered last night's lovemaking.

"Fret not, Mrs. Astley," she said calmly. "I make no matter of this, and neither should you. I know my lord means well, even if he goes about things a little clumsily, and that he would do nothing to compromise my Lady Elizabeth's reputation."

"I hear what you say, madam, but however innocent, these visits cannot be allowed to continue," Kat protested. "People are talking."

"Well, I think I know how to put a stop to that," Katherine smiled. "I myself will accompany the Admiral whenever he visits the Lady Elizabeth's chamber of a morning. Will that set your mind at rest?"

"I am most grateful, madam," Kat told her, irate with herself for responding to Katherine's charm. Nevertheless, she felt relieved. As long as the Queen was present, there could be no suspicion of anything improper. Her little lady was safe.

They had come to Hanworth, one of the Queen's dower properties, for a change of scene. Elizabeth was delighted to discover that it had once belonged to her mother.

"All those terracotta roundels that you see were put in place for her," the Queen said as they strolled around the beautiful gardens, pausing to admire the birds in the aviary or pick a strawberry from the lush beds near the orchard.

"I love the antick style," Elizabeth enthused.

"The steward told me that your father remodeled the house in that style to please your mother," Katherine told her. The girl's eyes were shining.

"It is a lovely place," she breathed. "I can tell *you* this, madam—I feel close to my mother here. I wish I had known her better. I can hardly remember her. Did you ever meet her?"

"Not personally, for I was rarely at court before I married the King, but I saw her at her coronation, which I attended with my second husband, Lord Latimer," Katherine recalled. "She was pregnant with you then, and she looked very fine in her rich white gown. I remember that she had very long hair—so long, she could sit on it." Katherine refrained from mentioning the scurrilous jibes of observers, who had thought it scandalous that a woman so great with child should have appeared in public in the white robes and flowing hair that betokened virginity. Nor did she tell Elizabeth that there had been few to cheer Anne Boleyn, who had never been popular.

"I wish I could have seen her," Elizabeth said wistfully. "Alas, it is so sad to be an orphan, and have neither mother nor father."

"Neither of them would have wanted you to be sad," Katherine said. "Life goes on, you know, and there are compensations to be found. We cannot keep harking back to the past."

"I fear I have been guilty of that," Elizabeth confessed with a wry smile.

"Don't you think that you have worn mourning for long enough?" the Queen asked gently, eyeing Elizabeth's black gown. "Court mourning ended weeks ago. It is six months now since the King died."

"I am his daughter," Elizabeth said. "I but wish to honor his memory."

"Then you must think ill of me," Katherine replied ruefully, looking down at her own yellow dress.

"I could never think ill of you, dear madam!" Elizabeth protested. "I am happy for you. But I wish to wear my mourning for a little longer."

"I respect your wishes," her stepmother assured her, "but you are young and pretty, and youth should not be constrained to somber colors. No one will blame you if you put off your weeds."

"I will think on it," Elizabeth promised.

Since the Queen had insisted on accompanying him, the Admiral's morning excursions to see his stepdaughter had become less frequent. At Hanworth, however, they arrived together one day, in a mischievous mood, and found Elizabeth still abed.

"Let's tickle her!" the Admiral cried. Katherine bent and, giggling, lightly tickled the slender white foot that was protruding from the bed-clothes. But Thomas was bolder and made for his victim's armpits and ribs.

"Your Grace! My lord! I pray you desist!" cried Kat, as Elizabeth lay there in helpless spasms, clutching her sides.

"Calm yourself, Mrs. Astley, it is but sport!" cried the Admiral. "Look at her, she's enjoying it!"

"I think she's had enough," Katherine said, still laughing breathlessly. "Do as Mrs. Astley says, Tom, and desist!"

Tom ceased tormenting Elizabeth, but bent and gave her a parting tap on the bottom. Katherine frowned but said nothing.

"I think we will take a picnic in the gardens today," the Admiral announced. "My Lady Elizabeth, I trust you will join us?"

Elizabeth sat up in the bed, her long red tresses streaming about her shoulders.

"Aye, my lord, if you promise not to tickle me again," she challenged, her reddened face a mask of mock fury.

"Granted!" Thomas chuckled. "And wear that black gown you had on yesterday. It becomes you so."

"Tom!" murmured the Queen reprovingly. Kat caught the glance that passed between them. Was the Admiral up to something?

"Come, my love," he said to the Queen, "we will see the Lady Elizabeth after her lessons have finished." And with that, they departed.

The game pie had been excellent, Elizabeth thought, dabbing her napkin to her mouth. Before her, the remains of the picnic lay spread out on the table, and above her the trees sighed gently in the breeze. The servants had been dismissed, and there were just the three of them in the garden, herself, the Queen, and the Admiral.

"Some Rhenish, my lady?" the Admiral offered.

"Thank you, my lord," she replied.

The Queen leaned back in her chair, savoring the warmth of the sun on her face, and looked dreamily across at her husband as he refilled her goblet.

"Don't go to sleep!" he commanded, his eyes alive with mischief. "I thought we could all play tag to work off that very rich food your cooks prepared."

"Tag?" repeated Katherine. "It's too hot for that. Later."

"Nonsense!" retorted Thomas.

"Oh, yes, please!" cried Elizabeth. There was little she loved more than vigorous exercise in the open air. "Can I be It?"

"Naturally, my lady. Your wish is my command!" the Admiral said with a flourish. "Come, Kate, don't be lazy! Up you get! This is to be a special game, remember?"

"Oh, very well." The Queen smiled, rising. "But don't let it get too out of hand."

Elizabeth went and hid in a little arbor ringed by trees. After she had counted slowly to twenty, she emerged and looked about her. Was that a patch of scarlet she could see through the privet hedge? Both the Queen and the Admiral were wearing scarlet. On tiptoe, she padded toward it.

"Got you!" cried Thomas, coming up from behind and pinioning her by the arms. "Kate! I've got her!"

The Queen, giggling, appeared from behind a fountain.

"But I'm supposed to catch you!" Elizabeth protested, struggling.

"Ah, but this is a new version of the game, which I myself devised," the Admiral informed her. "You see, my Lady Elizabeth, I am weary of looking at you in that dreary black gown, and Her Grace here agrees with me that it is time for you to wear something more becoming to a young lady of your age and station."

"My lord, that is none of your business," Elizabeth said as firmly as she could, a little outraged at his boldness, yet trembling at the shock of feeling his body against hers. There was a strange hardness pressing against her lower back.

"It *is* my business, since I am your guardian," he told her, his breath hot on her neck. "Now, Kate, hold her fast, while I make sure that she is never seen in this monstrosity again."

The Queen, still laughing, caught Elizabeth by the hands and held her tightly as the Admiral produced a large pair of scissors and proceeded to cut and slash at her gown. At first, she tried to resist and struggle, but she was fearful that the blades might jab or injure her, so she let him do as he would as she stood there, torn between laughter and tears, and giggling helplessly, as was the Queen. Soon, her skirt, or what was left of it, was hanging in tatters, her sleeves were ripped to pieces, and the seams of her bodice were left hanging by threads. She realized she was out in public wearing not much more than a chemise, petticoat, and corset.

Embarrassment made her giggle. Her tormentors were shaking with mirth.

"This is a fine game!" cried the Admiral. His fingers were dangerously near her left breast as he made further inroads upon her bodice. The Queen, seeing this, suddenly ceased laughing.

"I think she's had enough," she declared breathlessly. "Stop now, my lord! The poor child is all but naked! I didn't think you would be *this* enthusiastic." She let go of Elizabeth's hands and pushed her husband away, only half playfully.

"You must forgive my lord's boisterousness," she told Elizabeth, "and take this in good part, child, for we both felt it was high time you put off your mourning. We but thought to make it easier for you by turning it into a game, and we are quite private here, so no one can see. Tell Mrs. Astley that I will replace the gown with another, finer one, and that petticoat too—it's torn."

Elizabeth nodded, aware that the Admiral's eyes were straying to the low neckline of her chemise.

"I thank you, madam," she said unsteadily, then turned and walked away with as much dignity as she could muster. Behind her, on the gravel, lay jagged strips of black cloth.

"Your Grace, I must protest!"

An outraged Mrs. Astley stood quivering with anger before the Queen.

"That gown had been cut into a hundred pieces and more! And my Lady Elizabeth was left to walk back to the house in just her underclothing. In truth, madam, the cutting of the dress by my lord was bad enough, but Elizabeth tells me that you were a party to it by holding her fast. Really, madam, I know not what to say to you . . ."

"It was but a harmless frolic, Mrs. Astley," the Queen soothed. "Maybe we went a little further than we had intended, and if so I am sorry for it. I have offered to replace the gown."

"It was a mourning gown," Kat said aggrievedly, looking perilously near to tears. "Worn in memory of the late king, your husband."

Katherine did not like the tone of Kat's voice as she said that. It was meant as a rebuke, she was sure. And perhaps, she thought wearily, she deserved it.

"My lord and I felt that the child had gone on wearing mourning much longer than was necessary," she felt obliged to explain. "It was precisely because it was a mourning gown that my lord devised the prank. He desired to show my Lady Elizabeth that life goes on and that she need not waste her youth in somber clothing. That is all. If we have offended her, and you, I am truly sorry."

Kat sniffed. *She* was not deceived, even if the Queen was.

"These romps must stop, madam," she said firmly.

"I promise you I will see to it," Katherine assured her. She now had the uncomfortable feeling that it had been inappropriate to behave as she had, even though Tom had made it seem harmless enough at the time. In short, she was ashamed of herself. She must beware of his unruliness, and seek to curb it, not abet it, for in so doing she had willingly been led to abandon all sense of decorum. In fact, the whole episode had left her feeling distinctly uneasy . . .

"My Lady Elizabeth, your cousin Lady Jane Grey is here," the Queen said, her arm around the richly dressed child whose red hair was so like Elizabeth's own. But whereas the adolescent Elizabeth was tall, slender, clear-skinned, and confident, the nine-year-old Jane was small and thin with a mass of freckles and a wary expression.

"Cousin, you are welcome," Elizabeth greeted the younger girl, extending a hand then impulsively kissing her on both cheeks.

"Lady Jane is going to live with us, as the Admiral has made her his ward," Katherine explained. "Jane is of course too young to share lessons with you, so she will have her own tutors."

She turned to the child and caressed her cheek.

"I hope you will be very happy here, Jane," she said warmly. Jane looked up at her with puppy-like devotion.

"Perhaps you would care to show Jane around the house, Elizabeth," Katherine suggested.

"Of course. Come, Jane. No wait, first I will show you this." Elizabeth picked up the book she had been reading. It was a volume of Italian poetry that Master Ascham had sent her.

"Master Ascham corresponds with me regularly," she said proudly.

"The famous Master Ascham?" Jane echoed. She too, Elizabeth knew well, was an avid scholar. "I do envy you, Cousin."

"Perchance you will meet him someday," said Elizabeth generously, basking in Jane's admiration. As she led her from room to room, she took great pleasure in displaying her own knowledge and did her best to impress her young acolyte.

"Why did the Admiral make you his ward?" she asked Jane.

"He has promised my father he will make a great marriage for me," Jane told her.

"With whom?" Elizabeth wanted to know.

"They have not yet told me," Jane said, "and I really do not care too much. I am just so happy to be living under the Queen's roof."

Elizabeth had heard Queen Katherine say that Jane's parents were unkind to her. She felt sorry for her, and understood why she was grateful to have been made the Admiral's ward.

"I wonder whom the Admiral has in mind," she said aloud. "A great match! It might be to one of the Lord Protector's sons."

"I should prefer not to marry at all," Jane said. "I should like to be left in peace with my books and my tutors."

"I felt like that once," Elizabeth confided, thinking about the Admiral and feeling the familiar thrill of excitement. "But now I am not so sure, and it seems to me that there is much to be said for the love of a good man. You may find, little Cousin, that you too change your mind as you grow older."

"Whether I change it or not, I must do as my parents command in the matter," Jane said sadly.

"Well, it is a long way off," Elizabeth consoled her. "Anything can happen in the next few years. Let us make the most of our time in the Queen's household."

Jane was entranced by Elizabeth, and took to trailing her like a devoted hound. Elizabeth enjoyed showing off to the younger girl, being as worldly-wise as she dared, and when they were alone together, she would swear great oaths just for the pleasure of seeing Jane's reaction; that made her feel very daring and grown-up. Jane would giggle in horror and hide her face in her hands.

"You would be beaten for that if anyone hears you," she warned.

"God's blood, they would never be so bold!" Elizabeth swore again. "No one gets beaten in this house. Everything is devoted to happiness and pleasure."

"In truth, I think I am in Heaven," Jane said. "I was beaten often at home. My parents are very strict."

"Well, you won't be beaten here," Elizabeth reiterated. "Now, would you like to come and see my fine gowns? The Queen has just bought me a new one."

"It grows dark in here," Master Grindal observed. "I think I will light another candle."

Elizabeth gazed out the study window at the November twilight. The evenings were drawing in fast now, and even the crackling fire in the brazier could not banish the chill in the air. She bent her head again to the passage from Tacitus that she was translating into French.

"I think we should finish now," Grindal said. "Supper will be ready soon."

"I will just complete this paragraph," Elizabeth told him, not looking up as he left the room. Minutes later, she laid her quill down.

She was glad to be alone with her thoughts. They had been in turmoil all day. For many weeks, in fact since Kat had complained about the dress incident, the Admiral and the Queen had desisted from visiting her in the mornings. Instead, she had exchanged greetings with them at table as they broke their fast after morning prayers. That was right and proper, Kat had told her.

In truth, she had missed the excitement of the Admiral's appearances in her chamber, the anticipation of his coming, and the heady feelings generated by his obvious admiration for her. She still looked to see him wherever she was in the house, and loved nothing more than to feast her eyes on his debonair features or delight in his vibrant personality. It was the sweetest of torments to be with him and be constrained by the bounds of courtesy and social convention.

Was this love? she asked herself. The love of which the poets wrote? She did not know. The Admiral did not act the ardent suitor with her, adoring her from afar and lamenting the fact that she was far above him and would therefore never condescend to love him. That was how lovers were expected to behave, at least in the romances she had read. No, he proceeded boldly, and overfamiliarly, and that—if she spoke the truth— was what she admired about him. In fact, his directness thrilled her. But did it betoken love?

She had often caught his eye upon her, often felt his hand on her arm or her waist, casually, as it were, during the everyday course of life. Naturally she had doubted there would ever be more between them, for he was happily married to the Queen.

Or so she had thought. Until today.

Wrapped in her thick cloak, she had been taking her usual lone morning walk in the gardens, striding briskly in the misty chill along frost-rimed paths shaded by skeletal trees. And there he had been, coming toward her, his eyes wicked with intent. Had he known she would be there? she wondered afterward. It was no secret that she liked to take the air before lessons began.

He bowed, observing protocol, as ever, and doffed his ridiculously large plumed bonnet.

"My Lady Elizabeth! I do declare, the cold has lent your cheeks a becoming hue!"

"It is exertion, my lord," she answered guardedly, refusing to acknowledge his courtly speech and thinking that Kat would have a fit if she knew they were alone together with no one else in sight. "A healthy long walk each day is good for you."

"*You* are good for me," he said, to her mingled horror and joy, and without preamble he stepped forward, clasped his arms about her waist, and drew her to him. "In faith, I have never been so stirred by a woman. I cannot bear this charade any longer."

"My lord!" Elizabeth broke away, striving to resist the treacherous responses of her body and her feelings. "You must not say such things, and I must not hear them. You are a married man, and I have my reputation to consider. What you are thinking is madness."

"Such a sweet madness!" Thomas breathed, holding his hands out in a helpless attitude. "My lady, I am consumed by my desire for you. I can think of nothing but you."

"Be quiet, sir!" Elizabeth commanded desperately. "This is wrong." She was saying it to convince herself as much as him.

"To deny it would be wrong," he replied, gripping her shoulders and gazing intensely into her eyes. "I love you," he said. "Don't pretend you haven't been aware of that. You may be a child in years, but I can sense you are as old as the hills in wisdom when it comes to bewitching the opposite sex."

"I beg of you, sir," Elizabeth pleaded desperately, putting his hands from her. "Remember that you have a wife, the kindest lady there could be. I would not hurt her for the world, and you are sworn to faithfulness."

"She need not know." The Admiral smiled. "We can be discreet. Don't pretend you don't want me. I can see it in your eyes, as plain as day."

"What I want is of no consequence!" Elizabeth cried, feeling the tears welling and turning to go. But he grasped her wrist and twisted her around to face him again.

"I *will* have you," he said, his eyes dark and determined, "I will have you, if I have to go to Hell for it and burn for all eternity. And then you will learn that what lies between us is of the greatest consequence."

"No, sir, you will not!" Elizabeth said, with far more firmness than she was feeling.

"We will see, my fine princess," the Admiral retorted, letting her go. "Who was it said she wanted to live and die a virgin? I think not!"

"Oh, you are hateful, my lord!" she flung at him, then ran back to the house, leaving the sound of his laughter behind her.

From an upper window, the Queen stared, her heart faltering. She had witnessed the whole scene from afar off, watching her husband and her stepdaughter, like tiny puppets, moving together then apart, then together again, their gestures implying desire on his part and conflict on hers. Then the girl had, quite clearly, fled.

Katherine sat down on the bed. She had had her suspicions, but had loyally suppressed them. Mrs. Astley had been suspicious too, but she herself had dismissed that as groundless, God forgive her. Now she knew.

The knowledge lay as heavy as a stone, crushing all that was precious in her life. She wanted to weep, to scream, but she found she was in the grip of a terrifying inertia, and unable even to raise her head. What to do? What could she do? What dare she do?

The habit, acquired over long years, of putting the needs of others first came to her rescue now. Her duty lay clear. She must protect the royal child who had been entrusted to her care.

She must confront her husband.

—

Tom strode in, throwing his cloak and bonnet across a bench. He noticed his wife, sitting unusually still on the bed. Something in her countenance alarmed him.

"Are you feeling all right, Kate?" he asked concernedly.

"I am well in body, I think," she replied slowly, raising sad, reproachful eyes to him. "In heart, I fear I am not so sure. What was your business in the garden with my Lady Elizabeth?"

"My Lady Elizabeth?" Tom repeated, playing for time and striving to think up a credible explanation. Katherine was watching his face intently.

"Why, Sweetheart," he said, sitting down beside her and taking her hand, "there is no need to vex yourself. When I met the Lady Elizabeth, she was in great distress and I got her to confide her worries to me. That was all. Would you not have had me offer a little fatherly comfort?"

Katherine's shoulders were poised to sag with relief. Dare she believe him? She badly needed to. She might have gravely misjudged him, after all, thinking him faithless when he had probably been trying to be kind. He *was* a tactile person, after all.

"Why was she so distressed?" she asked. "She seemed in good heart last night."

"It is a man, I fear," the Admiral told her, thinking rapidly.

"A man? Who dares presume so far?" Katherine cried angrily.

"Alas, I know not, for she would not say," Tom replied. "But I have seen him for myself. I have seen them together."

"When?" Katherine demanded of him. She was deeply shocked.

"You know that little window that overlooks the long gallery? I espied them from there. They were embracing; I fear she had her arms about his neck."

"Embracing? And you never told me?" She was aghast. "Tom, I am her guardian."

"Ah, Kate, but I did not then know it was Elizabeth. At first I thought it might be, but I could not see the girl's face, only her red hair, and she was wearing a dark cloak. Then I remembered that red-haired wench in your chamber, and I just assumed it was her. But just now, Elizabeth confessed to me that it had indeed been she."

He could not be making this up, Katherine thought. He would not dare. The matter was too serious.

"This is appalling," she said. "Has she told you who the man is?"

"She would not, I fear," Tom said, breathing easier now. "I tried all manner of ways to get her to confess, but she steadfastly refused."

"And just how far has this relationship progressed?" Katherine wanted to know.

"No further, she has assured me. In fact, the gentleman has withdrawn his affections from her. That was why she was so distressed."

"I must send for Mrs. Astley," the Queen said, rising.

The governess's face registered shock.

"In faith, Your Grace, I knew nothing of this," she declared unhappily.

"It seems we neither of us have been vigilant enough," Katherine said. "But that it should come to this! I pray the girl has spoken truth, and that she has indeed emerged as unscathed as she claims."

"I will talk to her, madam, at once."

"Please do. And please say that I insist she divulges the name of this unspeakable knave."

"Oh, I will, never fear, madam." Kat was almost beside herself. "Yet who could it have been? There comes no man near this house save the servants, and surely she would not have stooped so low? That leaves just Master Grindal, and he's a dried-up old stick of a man if ever there was one. I cannot imagine him entertaining a single lustful thought."

"He's a man," observed the Queen tartly, "and therefore we cannot rule him out. But it's unlikely, I agree."

"Let me talk to her, madam," Kat said. "I'll go and find her now."

After she had gone, Katherine still felt agitated. Whatever had gone on in the garden, it did not bode well for any of them. Yet if Elizabeth did deny having any dealings with this mysterious suitor, and something really had gone on between her and Tom, then learning that she, Katherine, was aware of what had happened in that garden might well jolt the girl into a belated awareness that it must cease.

In truth, Katherine did not know which possibility appalled her the most: the thought that Elizabeth had been compromised by a member of her own household, with all the implications that that threatened; or the prospect of Tom having lied to her, to cover up his own wicked pursuit of the girl.

—

"My lady," Kat said, appearing at the study door.

Elizabeth and her tutor looked up from their books. Grindal wondered why the governess was giving him such an odd look.

"Begging your pardon, Master Grindal, but could you spare my Lady Elizabeth for a moment?"

"Of course, Mrs. Astley," he replied, hoping for enlightenment but receiving none.

Elizabeth rose, puzzled, and followed Kat to her bedchamber. Whatever was wrong? Kat rarely interrupted lessons—Elizabeth couldn't recall the last occasion that had happened. Then she remembered the scene in the garden with the Admiral, and her heart plummeted. They had been discovered!

Shutting the door, Kat turned steely eyes on her.

"I have just seen the Queen," she said. "She told me something that has greatly disturbed me."

Elizabeth groaned inwardly. This was proving to be even worse than she had expected.

"What did she say?" she asked, feigning an innocent expression.

"That you told the Lord Admiral you have been seeing a man."

"I?" Elizabeth was stunned. "I never said any such thing to him." She looked genuinely amazed.

"The Queen said you were seen with him, embracing in the gallery. It was the Admiral himself who saw you."

A spark of understanding began to flicker.

"I deny that, for it is not true!" Elizabeth declared hotly. "When am I supposed to have told the Admiral about this man?"

"This morning, in the garden, Her Grace said. She had seen you out of the window, telling the Admiral about it. He said you had been very upset because the man had lost interest in you."

"I see," said Elizabeth. Yes, she did see: It was all making sense now. There rose in her a bitter fury against the Admiral, who had put her in the wrong, and caused her all this trouble, to save his own skin. It was craven, callous . . . and more than she could bear. She burst into bitter tears.

"Elizabeth, tell me the truth," Kat demanded. "Was there any such man?"

"No," sobbed the girl. "Never."

"But you did meet my lord in the garden?"

"Yes. He came upon me as I was walking there. I did not plan to meet him."

She sniffed and felt in her pocket for her kerchief.

Now it was Kat's turn to see the light.

"And am I right in thinking that his conduct toward you was not that of a careful guardian?" Kat asked gently.

"He caught hold of me. I fended him off, but he was insistent. He said he loved me." The whole sorry tale came out, punctuated by gulps and sobs. Kat sat in increasing turmoil, trying to grasp the situation.

"It seems to me," she said at length, when Elizabeth had subsided into a tearful silence, "that the Queen knows the truth, and that she herself made up this tale about a secret lover so that *I* might be more vigilant where my lord is concerned."

"You think the *Queen* made it up, and not the Admiral?" Elizabeth asked, astounded, wanting to believe it.

"Yes. I don't think she confronted him at all, now I think about it. She's probably scared she'll hear something she doesn't want to hear."

"What are you going to tell her?" Elizabeth asked. "If you tell her there was no man, then she will guess the truth, and that will hurt her greatly."

"I will say you misjudged the situation. You thought, mistakenly of course, that the Admiral was about to make an advance to you, and you made the tale up to deflect him. It's weak, but no weaker than the other nonsense. I'll say you are mortified at having misjudged him, and deeply sorry."

"Very well," said Elizabeth. "If it spares the Queen any hurt, I will go along with that."

"Look at me, Elizabeth," said Katherine. Elizabeth raised her eyes.

"Is this true, what Mrs. Astley is telling me?"

"Yes, madam," Elizabeth said in a low voice. "I am sorry for having so misjudged my lord. I swear there was no man. Ask my women if I speak truth: I have no opportunity for such dalliance, for I am hardly ever alone, and they see all I do. The only men with whom I come into contact are the servants, Master Grindal, and my Lord Admiral."

Katherine was still not convinced: The explanation sounded too contrived, and she was unable to suppress her own suspicions. Because of her inner dread, though, she dared not press the matter further.

"I'm afraid I have wronged you and the Admiral," Elizabeth was saying.

"You have nothing to fear," the Queen replied, striving to be fair, "either from me or from my lord. All is forgiven and forgotten. And I have some good news for you: You are to go to court for Christmas. Your brother the King has commanded it."

Elizabeth's features relaxed into a relieved smile. The furtive look had gone.

"That is indeed marvelous news, madam! And are you and the Admiral to go too?"

"Alas, no," Katherine said stiffly. "After the Lord Protector's wife appropriated the jewels that were rightfully mine, and uttered insulting words about me, I vowed never to go there again. But do not fear, we shall make merry at Chelsea. And you will have your sister Mary for company."

"I am glad to hear it," Elizabeth said. "I have not seen her since our father died. Or my brother either." She paused and looked at her stepmother.

"You really have forgiven me, madam, haven't you?" she asked. She could not enjoy going to court if she went there under the cloud of Katherine's displeasure.

"I have." The Queen smiled tautly.

When Elizabeth had gone, Katherine, still inwardly agitated, sent for Mrs. Astley again.

"All is resolved," the Queen told her, "but—oh, this is probably nonsense—there is a foolish notion in my mind that my lord was not entirely innocent in this matter. Men being what they are, you know . . ." She broke off in embarrassment.

Kat said nothing, and Katherine began to wonder if the governess knew more than she was saying.

"This must go no further," she went on. "I'm sure I am giving way to some silly fancy, and that there is no basis for my concern. But Elizabeth is my responsibility, Mrs. Astley, and I must be careful. I want you to take heed and be, as it were, watchful betwixt the Lady Elizabeth and my Lord

Admiral." She smiled self-consciously. "You know what my lord is like—he enjoys a harmless flirtation, like all men do. I would not wish it to be misinterpreted."

"Naturally, madam," Kat said, rather enjoying the Queen's embarrassment. "I will be most vigilant, you may count on it."

Hampton Court was as grand and as crowded as ever, but Elizabeth was dismayed to find that the court had changed dramatically since King Henry's day. It looked shabbier, less well organized—if she was to judge by the stained livery of the groom who led away their horses, and the kitchen servants who were lounging about in the courtyard, eating their noon-pieces. And, as she was to discover, there were no ladies at court, just men who were preoccupied with the cares of state.

She was greeted by the Lord Protector at the gateway at the foot of the processional stair; he looked older, graver, and far less handsome than his brother, but then, she supposed, he was much burdened with the responsibilities of his office. He lacked too the Admiral's charm: Instead of paying her compliments, he wasted no time in subjecting her to a long lecture on the protocols upon which His Majesty insisted. How she would ever remember it all she did not know.

Pulling herself up, she remembered that she was the King's sister and second in line to the throne. She would not be intimidated by these new-fangled formalities! This was her little brother whom she was about to greet, and she was his sweet sister Temperance, as he liked to call her.

Somerset was leading her through the magnificent great hall, where servants were setting up the trestles for dinner, and then to a tiny chamber where a fire had been lit and a table laid with refreshments. She had been here before, long ago, she recalled, visiting her father at court. Pages stepped forward to take her traveling cloak, and Kat and her women fussed around her, smoothing her skirts, fanning out her long court train, and straightening her French hood.

Now she was ready. The Duke was waiting to escort her into the great watching chamber, which was thronged with courtiers and petitioners, and lined with Yeomen of the Guard and Gentlemen Pensioners on sentry duty. The crowd parted for them as they advanced toward the farther door, which led—she remembered it well—to the presence chamber itself.

"His Majesty is in the privy chamber," Somerset explained. "He awaits Your Grace's company at dinner."

"I look forward to seeing His Majesty," Elizabeth told him. "I will be honored to dine with him."

She was aware of the envious stares of the finely dressed lords in the presence chamber as she sailed through the door to the inner sanctum of the private apartments beyond—and then abruptly halted.

The King was seated enthroned behind a laden table that had been set up on the dais. Above his head, the royal arms of England glittered with gold thread on the rich canopy of estate. Farther along the table, beyond the canopy, sat the Lady Mary, who smiled graciously as Elizabeth entered.

Edward was watching Elizabeth impassively. As she had been instructed, she went down on one knee and bowed her head, then rose, took three steps, and again fell on one knee, bowing. She repeated this obeisance three more times before she found herself standing before the dais, wondering what had happened to put this terrible distance between herself and her brother.

"Welcome, dearest Sister," Edward piped up in his high, haughty voice. "Pray be seated." He indicated a place set beyond the canopy at the opposite end of the board from Mary. There was no chair, just a bench with a cushion.

Elizabeth raised her eyebrows. Things *had* changed since her father's day; his court had never been so formal, nor the King's important guests so humbled. It was as if Edward wished to underline her own and Mary's bastard status.

Doing her best to ignore the slight, and wondering if it was the Protector's doing, so that she should be reminded just who it was that held the reins of power, she seated herself with all the dignity she could muster.

"I trust you are in good health, sweet sister Temperance," Edward inquired.

"Never better, Your Majesty," she told him.

"I rejoice to see you looking so well," Mary told her, almost shouting to make herself heard along the length of the table.

"And I rejoice just to see you again, Sister, after so long a time," Elizabeth called back, smiling warmly. "How are you yourself keeping?"

"In truth, not well." Mary sighed. "I've suffered much ill health, and it's worse in the winter months." Poor Mary. Elizabeth had already noticed how much she had aged since they had last met. Of course, Mary must be over thirty now, so that would account in part for her looking rather faded, but Queen Katherine had said that Mary was plagued with many ailments and suffered purgatory with her monthly courses.

"I have prayed to the Blessed Virgin to intercede for me," Mary was saying, looking at the King a touch defiantly.

Edward scowled, looking a lot like their father in a bad mood.

"I wonder you waste your time with that popish nonsense, Sister," he piped up disapprovingly.

"Sire, this matter of religion is one I *must* raise with you," Mary said.

Edward stiffened. His lips pursed mutinously.

"Our father, God rest him, left this realm in good order and quietness," Mary went on, undeterred, "yet I fear that the Lord Protector and his government are now doing their best to promote heresy and disorder by introducing these newfangled Protestant forms of worship. I hear that English has replaced Latin in church services, that we are no longer supposed to venerate images and relics, that the heresy laws have been repealed, and there is a shocking rumor that the Mass itself has been abolished. Sire, I feel compelled to protest. These things cannot be allowed to happen."

Edward turned cold eyes on her.

"I am astonished at your concerns, Sister," he said. "It was *my* will that these changes were made, and most of my subjects—my *loyal* subjects—approve."

"Sire," Mary cried, passionate, "with respect, you are but a child, and a child is incapable of making mature judgments in religious matters. Listen to those who are older and wiser, I beg you. What of those of us who have faithfully followed the true faith for years, and must go to Mass to satisfy their consciences? The Catholic faith has endured since Our Lord himself walked this Earth; it was founded on His authority. Who are you to dare subvert it?"

She had gone too far. The young King's expression was glacial.

"You must not challenge my authority," he commanded. "That would be treason. Be warned, Sister. I do not wish to persecute you, and I will leave you alone to practice your religion in peace, but you must not question my lawful decrees. Make no mistake, I am resolved to do away with popish doctrine."

There was an uncomfortable silence as Mary bowed her head, struggling to hold her tongue. Elizabeth found herself wishing that her brother and sister could each, in their own way, be a little less unbending. Why could they not let each other worship God in their own way and have done? What was the point of all this meddling with the souls of others? They would never convince each other . . .

Edward had turned his severe gaze on Elizabeth.

"And you, dearest Sister, where do you stand on matters of religion?" he demanded to know.

"I follow God's word and the King's commandment," she replied meekly, and sincerely.

Edward nodded, satisfied. But seeing Mary regarding her with undisguised dismay in her eyes, Elizabeth looked down at her plate and speared a piece of beef with her fork. It was time to change the subject.

"Are there to be revels over the holiday, Sire?" she asked her brother.

There were, but they were disappointing. There was a masque portraying the Pope as a lecherous villain—much to Mary's barely concealed distress—and a display by some acrobats. Otherwise, the courtiers disported themselves in overeating, drinking, and gambling, while the boy King sat watching them from his high place.

Elizabeth found herself wishing she could go home.

"What has happened to the court?" she asked Mary as they passed through the long gallery one evening. Elizabeth had just extricated herself from the amorous embrace of a drunken baron, who had been too intoxicated to recognize her. "There is a corruption about it that was not apparent when our father was alive. And the revels were poor."

"Indeed they were," muttered Mary, remembering with a shudder the sacrilegious portrayal of the Pope cavorting with nuns. "There is no queen, and therefore there are no women for whom men must normally curb their excesses. And there is no money. The war with France left the treasury empty. This realm is all but bankrupt!"

"In truth, I am looking forward to leaving," Elizabeth confessed. "Me! And I always longed to come to court."

"It is not so much the state of the court that troubles me as the dangerous nonsense with which they have infected our poor brother," Mary
murmured. "I beg of you, Sister, look to your soul. Do not be swayed by
these heretics."

Elizabeth bent her head demurely but kept her counsel. She had no
wish to offend her sister.

"I thank you for your concern, Mary," she said. "Never fear, I will follow God's word."

Mary's look was chilling.

"I wonder, Sister, how you interpret God's word," she retorted.

"I follow Jesus Christ, as all good Christians should do," Elizabeth said
quietly. Mary looked exasperated.

"As I have had reason to observe in the past, you are clever," she said
tartly. "You dissemble well. But God knows a true heart: He is not deceived."

They were now at the door to Mary's chamber. She opened it and disappeared inside without another word.

"Good night, Sister," Elizabeth said to the empty air.

CHAPTER 14

1548

Elizabeth was relieved to be returning to Chelsea, and to see her step-mother waiting to greet her, but as she alighted from her litter onto the snow-covered ground, she saw that the Queen's face was grave.

"I have some sad news," Katherine said after embracing and kissing her stepdaughter. "Grindal is dead. He went to his sister's for Christmas, as usual, but there was plague in the district. He caught it and was gone within hours."

The gentle, kind tutor, that good, learned man, was no more; gathered to his forefathers with scant warning. Elizabeth felt tears prick her eyes.

"I am deeply sorry for it," she said quietly.

"Come inside," the Queen said gently. "We shall get warm. The Admiral is waiting in the privy chamber. He has said how much he is looking forward to seeing you. How was the King's Grace?"

They were kind to her, the Queen and the Admiral. They made her sit down by the fire and gave her some steaming hippocras and wafers. Elizabeth was struck anew by the Admiral's debonair charm, but in her sorrow, she felt distanced from it, and he was playing the devoted husband anyway. Her mind was preoccupied with memories of poor Grindal, whom she would never see again.

Who would teach her now? she wondered, as she fell asleep that night.

"My Lady Elizabeth, there is a letter for you," Kat said, bustling into the bedchamber where her charge had been lying indisposed for the past couple of days. Elizabeth raised herself from her pillows, laid down her book, and broke the seal.

"It is from Master Ascham!" she said, looking instantly better. "He wishes to visit me. This was written two days ago—Kat, he will be here at any time!"

She bounded out of the bed, ignoring Kat's protests, wobbled on her feet for a few moments, then began rummaging in the chest for some clothes.

"My lady, take it easily!" Kat cried.

"I'm all right, I'm better," Elizabeth told her. "Just fetch my green gown, will you? The furred one."

Later that day, as she had anticipated, Roger Ascham arrived, and Elizabeth welcomed him with outstretched hands.

"The Queen and the Admiral are in London, Master Ascham, so you will have to make do with me as your hostess!" she told him gaily.

"I could not imagine a more delightful honor, madam," he replied warmly in his homely Yorkshire accent.

After Kat had served wine, they sat together in the winter parlor, where a great fire burned in the grate, and discussed Ascham's recently published book on archery and then the subjects that Elizabeth had been studying.

"But enough of me," she said at length. "You did not come to talk of my modest studies, Master Ascham. What brings you to Chelsea?"

The scholar's rugged face creased in a rueful smile.

"I had heard that you were without a tutor, madam, and am come to offer my poor services."

Elizabeth was delighted.

"That would be to my utmost pleasure," she declared.

"It would be an honor to instruct one who is so renowned for her learning," Ascham said. Elizabeth knew him to be sincere, and that this was not just idle flattery.

"It would be an honor for me to have such an eminent tutor," she responded, "and I am sure the Queen will approve. I will write to her today and tell her that I am minded to have you, Master Ascham, and no one else."

"Naturally, you must submit to your guardian's judgment," Ascham conceded.

"I have every intention of doing so, provided she agrees with my choice!" Elizabeth replied, laughing. "I will go to London myself and persuade her, if need be! And you, Master Ascham, will you go back to the university at Cambridge and ask for leave of absence to join the Queen's household?"

"Are you that certain of success, my lady?" Ascham asked, bemused.

"Never doubt it!" Elizabeth told him.

"That's a lot of work," observed Kat doubtfully, regarding the piles of books on the study table. Roger Ascham smiled.

"Not at all, madam," he replied. "Those will keep us busy for a long time. You will learn that I am no believer in cramming. If you pour too much drink into a goblet, the most part will run over the sides."

Kat nodded, satisfied.

Lessons with Master Ascham, for Elizabeth, were a joy. She was delighted to discover that his favorite Latin author was Cicero. She loved to read the letters Ascham received from the wide circle of European intellectuals with whom he corresponded. She thrilled to his praise for her command of Latin and Greek and her knowledge of the classics.

"You read more Greek in a day than most doctors of the Church do in a week!" he told her.

The mornings were spent in the company of Sophocles and Isocrates, the afternoons fencing with Livy and Cicero, or studying theology. When lessons were over, tutor and pupil often indulged in their shared passion for riding and hunting, cantering out into the fields beyond the palace, come sunshine, rain, or snow. In the evenings, Elizabeth would practice on her lute or her virginals—Katherine Parr had presented her with a beautifully crafted set that had belonged to her mother and bore Anne's device of a white falcon. They were among Elizabeth's most prized possessions, along with the portrait of Anne that now hung openly in her bedchamber, and the initial pendant in her jewel coffer.

Elizabeth was quick to notice that Master Ascham often appeared to be scrutinizing her clothes.

"What are you looking at, sir?" she asked one day, seeing a slight frown appear on his brow as he regarded her damask rose silk gown and costly gold chains, the latter a gift from the Queen.

"May I speak freely, my lady?" he asked.

"Of course," she agreed.

"Godly Protestant maidens usually wear simple apparel," he said.

Elizabeth looked down at her dress. It suddenly seemed rather extravagant, with its silver undersleeves, bejeweled girdle, and pearl trim around the neckline. And the five rings on her slender fingers . . . She found that she was embarrassed. It occurred to her that pious little Jane Grey invariably favored black clothing uncluttered by much jewelry, even though she came from a wealthy background. And Queen Katherine too—she had lately taken to wearing more sober colors, even though the fabrics were rich, and fewer pieces of jewelry. What must Master Ascham be thinking of her, Elizabeth, still got up in her gaudy finery? She cared very much for his good opinion.

"Wait!" she said impulsively, and sped away to her bedchamber.

"Where's my black velvet gown?" she asked an astonished Kat.

"Why, my lady, has somebody died?" the governess cried in alarm.

"Nay. I am but come to my senses, thanks to Master Ascham. Ladies who follow God's word must dress themselves simply and modestly." She was ripping off her necklace and rings.

Kat shook her head. The young were prone to fads and odd ideas, she knew. It just wasn't worth arguing with Elizabeth when she was in one of her determined moods. Better to indulge her fancy than provoke a tantrum. Bemused, she lifted the black gown off its peg in the closet, helped Elizabeth to change, and stood lacing it up at the back.

When Elizabeth presented herself again in the study, Master Ascham was gratified to see the change in her—and not a little disturbed. In the severe but elegant black gown, with its low, unadorned square neckline, tight bodice, and full skirts, and with her red hair loose about her shoulders, Elizabeth looked the epitome of a godly Protestant maiden—and unsettlingly seductive.

She espied him looking intently at her.

"Do I look godly enough now, Master Ascham?" she asked.

"Indeed you do, my lady," he replied. "The epitome of virtue."

"Yes," she said, reflecting with some shame on how, of late, she had been tempted to stray from the path of virtue. One could not look the part and be something quite other underneath. She meant it when she added, "Not only am I determined to dress soberly from now on but also to lead a sober life, and control whatever ungodly emotions and desires may come upon me."

She did not realize how soon this new resolve would be tested.

"Why, my Lady Elizabeth," the Admiral said, encountering her on the stairs, "you are a vision of perfection!" His eyes raked her partly exposed bosom.

"Thank you, my lord," she replied, basking in his naked admiration, yet willing him to let her pass, knowing that she dared not trust herself to be alone with him for long lest she betray her inner turmoil. For the madness—it could not be sanity to feel thus, she told herself—was still within her, feeding on regular contact with the beloved one, feasting on the sight of him and the sound of his voice. Since their near-catastrophic meeting in the garden, the Admiral had kept his distance, had no longer come to her chamber in the mornings. Yet despite his playing the devoted husband to the Queen, Elizabeth was aware, from the smoldering looks he gave her, that he still burned for her—as, despite her resolve, she still did for him, God help her.

Thomas raised his hand and gently touched her hair. His touch was like a shock to her senses, and instinctively she clutched that hand and put it away from her.

He was staring at her longingly, saying nothing—not needing to—and she knew she must break that gaze and proceed on her way. But she could not; she stayed there, rooted to the step, just that little bit too long.

Katherine Parr, hastening down the stairs in her soft shoes on some urgent errand, came upon them thus, standing staring wordlessly at each other, and her appearance abruptly broke the spell.

"Hello, Kate," stuttered the Admiral, recovering himself.

"Is everything well?" the Queen asked sharply.

"Yes, madam," whispered Elizabeth. She curtsied and fled upstairs.

"Of course everything is well," Tom said evenly.

Katherine looked long and hard at her husband, then went on her way.

—

Elizabeth began to notice, by and by, that the Queen was no longer so warm toward her. Katherine did not seek out her company as often as she once had, and when they were together at table, or during her regular visits to the schoolroom to inspect Elizabeth's work, she was civil, even pleasant, but these days her smile did not reach her eyes, which always seemed to be regarding her stepdaughter warily. And Katherine looked tired and drawn, too, her joyous spirit no longer much in evidence.

Thomas Parry, Elizabeth's cofferer, said as much one day in March when he joined Kat and Elizabeth for a nightcap one evening in the winter parlor. Elizabeth liked this rotund Welshman: He was a bit of a fusspot, but kindly and avuncular, and utterly devoted to her.

"I must confess I am concerned about the Queen," he said. "She doesn't look at all well."

Elizabeth, seated at the table, looked up from her book.

"So I have noticed," Kat said.

"She seems distant and preoccupied," Parry went on, "and she spoke very sharply to the Admiral this morning in the stables. She seemed very vexed with him for some reason."

Elizabeth could not help herself. She had to say something. If she did not, she would burst. She could no longer shoulder this burden alone.

"I think I know why," she said.

They both turned to look at her.

"I fear it is because the Admiral loves me too well, and has done for a long time," she confessed, "and the Queen is jealous of us both."

"I do not believe it," exclaimed Parry, shocked.

"How do you know this, Elizabeth?" Kat asked, looking at her charge closely.

"The Admiral told me he loved me. That day in the garden. I think the Queen knows of it." Her cheeks were flaming.

"He told you?" echoed Kat.

"Yes. In faith, Kat, I did nothing to encourage him. I got away from him as fast as I could."

"Did he touch you in any way?" Kat demanded to know.

"He has tried once or twice, but each time I pushed him away," Elizabeth told her. That was the truth, wasn't it?

"Then you have done nothing worthy of reproach," Kat said, relieved.

Oh, but I have, Elizabeth thought. I have wanted him. I have sinned with him in my thoughts . . . and might do so in very deed, given the chance. She knew in her heart that her much-vaunted resolve to remain a virgin might easily crumble in the face of his seductive charm.

"Well, you do amaze me!" commented Master Parry. "I would never have believed it of the Admiral."

"He has been after my Lady Elizabeth for a long time," Kat revealed. "He even asked for her hand after King Henry died. The council put a stop to that, so he married the Queen instead."

"And you think the Queen knows of his interest in you, my lady?" Parry asked Elizabeth.

"I fear so," she said, shaking her head. "I would it were otherwise. But what can I do?"

"Nothing, except be watchful of your conduct, and give the Admiral no encouragement whatsoever," Kat warned her, worried in case the situation was escalating beyond her control; the Admiral might be an attractive man—there was no denying that—but her responsibility was to protect the Lady Elizabeth from harm, and she had the uncomfortable feeling that she herself was in part to blame for what was happening because of her earlier laxness.

"I would do nothing to hurt the Queen, or injure myself," Elizabeth assured her.

The Admiral had arisen at first light and gone to attend to a bitch of his that had whelped the previous day. He had promised Elizabeth one of the puppies, and by God, he would see she got the best one. Of course, Katherine could have one too—they promised to be a fine litter.

There was a chill in the air, so presently he returned to the privy chamber to don a warmer doublet. He thought he would look in on his wife—she had not been well of late. Some vague malady, of the kind to which women seemed all too susceptible—he hadn't troubled to inquire too closely. Whatever it was, rest and hearty fare would cure it, of that he was sure.

But as he entered their bedchamber, he heard the sound of choking. Alarmed, he found Katherine, still in her night robe, retching into a basin.

"My love!" he cried. "I had no idea . . ." He held her heaving shoulders and stroked back the damp tendrils of hair from her forehead.

When the spasms had passed, Katherine wiped her mouth on a towel and sank down on the bed. Tom sat beside her, his face a picture of concern.

"It is nothing," she said, smiling weakly. "I am all right."

"We must summon a physician," he insisted.

"No, Tom, I do not need a physician. You see, I have been sick every morning for a week now, and my courses have stopped. You *must* know what that betokens. I am going to have a child."

"Oh, my love!" Tom exclaimed, and hugged her. "That is the most marvelous news. A child—a son and heir, hopefully! I cannot believe it!"

"I assure you I can!" Katherine grimaced. "But I am overjoyed. I never thought, at my age, to be so blessed. I have long prayed to be a mother, and now the good Lord has seen fit to answer my prayers."

"And mine too," Tom added. "I have prayed for a son."

"It might be a girl," Katherine reminded him.

"Whatever it is, I shall be the proudest father alive! So long as you are safely delivered, Kate, and the babe is healthy. We must take good care of you. You must rest and eat well, and not worry about anything."

"I see I shall not need a midwife, with you to look after me, my lord!" she laughed. Then her smile faded. "If I were honest, I am a little fearful. I am thirty-six, and that is old to be having my first baby."

"Never fear, my darling, we will engage the best midwives and doctors to be found," Tom promised. "I will make the announcement immediately, and send letters to all our friends."

"Whatever you wish." Katherine smiled, quelling her fears. "But there is one thing else—something that troubles me."

"What is it, my love?" Tom was eager to reassure her.

She swallowed.

"All *is* well between us, isn't it, Tom? I have feared of late that we might be growing apart."

"Nonsense!" he declared. "I sense no distancing. It is but the fancy of a breeding woman, I'll warrant."

"Of course," she agreed, relieved beyond measure. She had imagined it. There was nothing wrong. Her fears were groundless. No philandering husband could react as lovingly as Tom just had to the news that they were to become parents.

"You rest here," he told her. "I will go and make the announcement." Then he added gaily, "What will we call him?"

"Thomas, of course!" Katherine smiled mischievously. "Or Katherine!"

The sickness continued unabated for the next month, and so the Queen lay abed late every morning, recovering from its onslaughts.

Thus the Admiral was free to wreak mischief. Careless of the consequences, for he was consumed with lust and longing, and confident of his charm and his powers of persuasion, he waxed now so hot in the pursuit of his nubile stepdaughter that, always a man to court risks, he believed he would have what he wanted and get away with it.

And so it was that, one early-spring day, just after dawn, Elizabeth was sliding out of bed when she heard his key in her lock. Kat had not yet appeared, and Thomas's face when he saw that she was alone was jubilant.

"My lord," she began to protest, pulling on her velvet nightgown.

"Shhh!" he hushed, putting a finger to his lips. "I would speak with you privately."

Elizabeth was both appalled and excited.

"What could you have to say to me that cannot wait?" she challenged, fearing that it was something he had no right to say . . .

In a moment, he had crossed the floor and come to stand in front of her, too close for comfort.

"Elizabeth," he murmured, "I have been longing to speak to you. I meant what I said all those weeks ago. I love you." He put his arms around her, enclosing her tightly, and began to whisper into her hair. "I want you . . . wanting you is torturing me."

"Sir!" she protested weakly, knowing that she should push him away but finding that his nearness was too wonderful to resist. "I beg of you . . ."

She could feel her body, her treacherous body, responding. A tremor ran through her. Feeling it, Thomas bent her head back and kissed her gently on her mouth. The touch of his lips was sensual, irresistible . . .

"Ah, so you want it too," he chuckled. Then he kissed her harder, pushing his tongue against her teeth and forcing them apart. Elizabeth felt a deep warmth flooding through her, a beautiful lassitude that left her incapable of resistance. The Admiral's hands were trembling down her back, playing at her waist, and moving daringly over her hips. His touch through the velvet robe and the thin lawn of her chemise was both shocking and glorious. The small voice of wisdom cried out that she should put a stop to this now, but it was drowned out by the swell of great waves of feelings. She responded to the kiss, and let the Admiral's tongue move insistently in her mouth.

"Are you up, my lady?" It was Kat's voice from the inner chamber, calling Elizabeth to her senses. Abruptly, the Admiral let her go and stood panting softly, regarding her admiringly.

"I must leave," he mouthed, "but I will be back, never fear."

No sooner had he silently closed the door than Kat came bustling into the chamber with Elizabeth's clothes. Elizabeth hoped her governess had not noticed her flushed face and dazed expression, and quickly turned her back on Kat, busying herself at the washbasin, slapping a cold damp cloth on her hot cheeks.

It was all beginning again, she thought. She had had such good intentions, but she had not bargained for the effect the Admiral was having on her senses and her emotions. She honestly did not know how she would summon the strength to resist him.

"Good morrow, my Lady Elizabeth, Mrs. Astley!"

Kat stared in horror as the Admiral burst into Elizabeth's bedchamber the next morning, just as she had finished dressing.

"Whatever is the matter, Mrs. Astley? You look as if a ghost had just walked over your grave," Thomas teased her.

"My lord, this is most improper!" the governess insisted. "My lady could still have been abed."

"Mrs. Astley, we have thrashed out these arguments before," the Admiral said patiently, noticing that Elizabeth was looking at him with undisguised appreciation.

"Yes, sir, and then you ceased to come here and outrage my lady's modesty with these visits. I cannot understand why you are back here again. It's indecent!"

"Pray tell me what is wrong with a stepfather come to bid his step-daughter good morrow?" the Admiral asked loftily.

"With respect, sir, does the Queen know you are here?" Kat asked boldly.

"Of course she does," he said, but the furtive look in his eyes gave the lie to it.

"Well, I will speak to her," Kat replied. The Admiral groaned inwardly.

"Nay, do not trouble her, for she is unwell," he urged.

"I will see her this afternoon. She is always better in the afternoons," Kat said defiantly. "If she is content that you come here in the mornings, then I am too. But I must insist that I be present."

The Admiral gave her a filthy look and turned on his heel, leaving Elizabeth aching with loss.

"Yes, I did know," said Katherine sharply. She had been enjoying a peaceful nap in the parlor, and was not pleased to see Kat standing there before her, asking if she was aware that the Admiral had taken once more to visiting the Lady Elizabeth of a morning.

But she had *not* known anything about it, and the news both alarmed and grieved her, although she was not going to reveal that to the governess.

"Then am I to understand that these visits have Your Grace's approval?" Kat persisted.

"They do, Mrs. Astley," answered Katherine irritably. "Although I think it would be wise, for the sake of the proprieties, if you yourself were present. My lord himself would wish that."

"Very well, madam," Kat said. "I will make sure I am always there."

Elizabeth had wandered down to the banks of the Thames, where the water lapped gently at the low stone wall by the landing stage. The Admiral's barge was tied up at the jetty; he had not long returned from London. The days were really drawing out now, she noticed, watching the sun setting in a pink-and-gold sky. She must return to the palace for supper shortly, but not yet. She was savoring these stolen moments of solitude. The atmosphere in the house was tense. There was a coolness between the Admiral and the Queen, who was still suffering the discomforts of early pregnancy; Katherine was, if anything, chillier in her manner toward Elizabeth; Kat was being as vigilant as a mother hawk; and Elizabeth was all too aware of the Admiral's smoldering eyes upon her, and of the excitement that welled up in her whenever he came to bid her good morning.

Kat would probably be looking for her now: She seemed afraid to let Elizabeth out of her sight these days. But Elizabeth did not think that Kat would walk as far as this; Kat had grown plumper of late, and often got out of puff. And besides, the shoreline was concealed by a high privet hedge; she could be private here for a short while.

And it was there on the riverbank that the Admiral found her, and again took her in his arms, she melting against him as if it were the most right and natural thing in the world. She could not help herself.

"Elizabeth!" he breathed, between kisses. "I am in torment!"

"This is wrong," she murmured brokenly, but the response of her body belied her words.

"True love can never be wrong," he said softly.

"But the Queen . . . ," she protested feebly.

"The Queen will never know," he vowed. "I would not hurt her, especially at this time."

His allusion to Katherine's condition drove a spike of jealousy into Elizabeth's breast. In her mind, she saw him making love to his wife, impregnating her . . . The image made her catch her breath. How she, Elizabeth, craved to share that forbidden joy with him. If only she had accepted his proposal of marriage in the first place, she would not be in this sorry situation today. It was not fair.

The Admiral was kissing her neck, his hands holding her waist in a vise.

"I must see you alone," he muttered thickly.

"It cannot be," Elizabeth heard herself answering. But it *must* be, her heart cried. She could bear her need for him no longer.

"Sunday," he said low. "I rarely go to the chapel for morning service, so the Queen will not mark my absence. Plead illness—say your courses have come and your belly aches. Then none will suspect us. And get rid of that dragon that guards you. Then I will come to you, and we will not be disturbed."

Elizabeth felt a fearful thrill at his words. Surely she was not going to agree to this? She knew it was wrong. But her body was afire with longing and she could not help herself.

"Say I may come!" he demanded, gripping her tighter, his dark eyes boring into her.

"You may come," she whispered, and breaking away from him, she began running back toward the palace, her long hair flying behind her in a coppery stream.

She would not do it. She would, she could not deny herself. No, she could not. She was in turmoil, her tender conscience warring with her burning desire. Her inborn good sense seemed to have flown out of the window: She could no longer reason with herself. She knew in her heart that she would have the thing she wanted.

"I think I will lie here awhile today," Elizabeth said from the depths of her bed. "I do not feel well."

"What's the matter?" Kat inquired, poking her head between the curtains.

"I have a vile headache," Elizabeth said. She had thought better of pleading her courses: Kat would soon find her out, for there would be no bloody clouts to dispose of.

Kat felt her forehead.

"At least you have no fever."

"No, it's just a megrim." Elizabeth grimaced, hoping she looked convincing.

"Do you want me to sit with you?" the governess asked.

"No, I just want to sleep. Don't miss the service on my account," Elizabeth told her.

"Very well, then; you get some rest," Kat said soothingly, drawing the curtains together. She busied herself for a bit, laying out Elizabeth's attire; then the door clicked shut and she was gone. Elizabeth let out a long sigh of relief, counted to ten, then jumped out of bed, splashed some rosewater on her face, and brushed her hair. She dared not change her plain lawn chemise for one with embroidery, for Kat would surely ask why she had done so, and nothing must be allowed to rekindle her suspicions.

When the Admiral tapped on the door, she was ready, seated in her chair, her black velvet gown on over the thin chemise. She looked striking, he thought, with her flame-colored, wavy hair spread out on her shoulders. True, she was not conventionally beautiful, with her narrow mouth and undeniably hooked nose, but her eyes, so like her mother's, were knowing and inviting, and her tall, slender body utterly desirable. To add piquancy, she was a King's daughter into the bargain, and that lent a fillip to Thomas's lust for her.

She watched him standing there, looking down on her, his dark eyes brooding and intense. Then suddenly he was kneeling beside her, gathering her into his arms and gently pressing his lips against hers. She was all but lost, still unclear in her mind as to how far she intended to let him go.

"Sweetheart," he murmured, nuzzling her ear, then seeking her lips again. "Oh, I have wanted you."

She could not answer. If this feeling was love, she did not know how to give it voice. Nor did she resist when he scooped her up in his arms, as if she were as light as feathers, and carried her to the bed, laying her down tenderly among the tumbled sheets. Then he was beside her, his face close to hers, his hands thrusting insistently beneath the velvet gown and stroking her body through the filmy material of her chemise. The feeling was delicious; it made her entwine her arms around his neck ever more tightly.

The first alarum sounded when he suddenly ripped open her chemise, exposing her small, pointed breasts, and began to kiss and fondle them vigorously before sliding his hands farther down her body, venturing more daring caresses. The sensations his fingers aroused in her were glorious, but suddenly, they ceased, leaving her desperate for more. He was going too fast for her, fumbling with the points of his codpiece, all the while breathing heavily against her face and whispering words she could barely make out. Then hastily he pulled up her chemise, baring her thighs and buttocks to the shock of the cool morning air. Distracted, and suddenly belatedly aware that she was well on the way to committing not only a sin but also high treason, Elizabeth tried to fend him off, but found her young girl's strength no proof against his aroused masculinity. Blind to her struggles, Thomas was already on top of her, his knees holding her legs apart, then he was forcing himself hugely within her, thrusting backward and forward with increasing vigor. The pain was very great, and she could not stop herself from emitting a series of sharp cries. But the Admiral seemed oblivious, and labored on, his passion ever more urgent. Suddenly he tensed, panting, before the rhythm resumed its urgent pace, faster now, harder, until he climaxed in a series of spasms before suddenly subsiding in a wet, slippery rush, leaving Elizabeth shattered and sore, horrified at the knowledge of what had been done to her—and what she had been a party to.

When the Admiral slumped over her, having seemingly expired from his efforts, she feared he was ill, and wondered frantically what she should do if that indeed proved to be the case. They could not be discovered here like this! Imagine the furor that would provoke! Yet she could not shift him—his weight lay heavy upon her.

"My lord!" she whispered in a panicked voice. "Wake up! Oh, please wake up!" For answer he opened his eyes and winked lasciviously at her.

"Well, my princess, did you enjoy that?" he asked lazily.

Elizabeth had not enjoyed it at all. In fact, it had left her feeling raw, both physically and emotionally. Were women *meant* to enjoy such intercourse? How could they, when it was both undignified and messy, and had left her strangely unsatisfied and completely unmoved? In short, she felt used—used to gratify a man's illicit lust. There had been no uplifting feelings of love to sanctify the act.

Instead, there was only a horrifying awareness of the enormity of what had just transpired. Guilt flooded her; this had been an unforgivable betrayal of her kind stepmother. As soon as the Admiral had rolled over onto his back, she quickly pulled down her torn chemise, with trembling fingers. She was trying to cover her breasts with its tattered remnants when he raised himself onto one elbow, wrapped the other arm around her, and began nuzzling her neck.

It was then that the door opened, revealing a shocked Queen Katherine standing on the threshold.

Elizabeth had never seen a man move so fast. The Admiral leapt off the bed, threw a blanket over her, and began fumbling with the laces of his codpiece. She was mortified, more embarrassed than she had ever been in her life, and she dared not look the Queen in the eye. No words were spoken; there was just a terrible, prolonged silence. Then suddenly Katherine was gone, and the Admiral after her, shouting her name.

"Her Majesty would be obliged, Mrs. Astley, if Your Grace would attend her urgently," the lady-in-waiting said, her face impassive.

Kat, just returned from the chapel, was putting away her prayer book. She looked at Elizabeth, who was sitting reading in the chair by the fire.

"Now whatever can that be about?" she asked.

Elizabeth, before whose eyes the words were dancing up and down, just shook her head, feigning ignorance. She knew, with a sinking heart, that her misconduct would shortly be uncovered, but she could not bring herself to confide in her governess for she feared the storm it would provoke, and was resolved to delay it for as long as possible.

Kat hastened to the royal apartments, wondering all the while, and was admitted at once to the Queen's privy chamber. She found Katherine alone, pacing up and down, her face drawn, her eyes shadowed.

"Your Majesty." Kat curtsied.

The Queen did not ask her to sit down, as she customarily did. Instead, she kept her standing; nor did she herself sit. Clearly she was very agitated.

"Mrs. Astley, when I asked you to head the Lady Elizabeth's household here, I had every confidence in you and trusted implicitly in your integrity," Katherine began, her anger barely suppressed. "But now I find that confidence and trust to have been utterly misplaced."

"Madam, whatever—"

"You will hear me out, Mrs. Astley," the Queen cut in. "Not half an hour ago, I found my husband in bed with the Lady Elizabeth in her chamber. Both were in an unseemly state of undress."

Kat's hands flew to her mouth to suppress the moan of dismay.

"I have spoken with my lord, who is all contrition of course, and he has sworn that nothing of moment took place, which is one small mercy for which we can thank God, I suppose. Yet his betrayal and my displeasure apart, think on the gravity of this matter." Her voice grew urgent. "Elizabeth is second in line to the throne, and a minor under my protection. Her marriage will be a matter of state, and you know very well it is high treason for any man to marry her without the council's permission, let alone take liberties with her. If I make a public show of my anger— which I have every right to do—the scandal would probably ruin us all."

Her ravaged gaze came to rest on Kat; she seemed to be barely holding herself together.

"It is you whom I hold accountable, Mrs. Astley. True, Elizabeth has behaved disgracefully, and in so doing has shown marked ingratitude for the kindness that I have shown her these many years. To say I am most displeased with her is an understatement. But you, Mrs. Astley—you had the responsibility for the virtuous upbringing of her, and you have clearly failed in your duty, both to Elizabeth and to me!"

Kat burst into tears; she could not help herself. She was horrified by what the Queen had told her, furious with Elizabeth, and deeply hurt that the girl should have let this happen after all that had been said. And that she should have kept it a secret and put Kat herself in danger . . .

"Believe me, madam, I tried to stop the Admiral's visits, and I did warn you, you must remember," she protested vehemently. "But you made little account of them. Even so, I made sure I was present whenever he came to my lady's chamber of a morning. As for today, she told me she was ill, and she did seem so, so I left her in bed. *I* cannot be held to blame for her misconduct. Rather it is my Lord Admiral's behavior that is inexcusable, for Elizabeth is but an innocent girl of fourteen, while he is a man of the world."

"That is enough!" the Queen cried, her face flaming. "Maybe we are all to blame. The question is, what to do about it? Clearly Elizabeth cannot stay here. I do not want her in my house any longer than is necessary. But where to send her? Whom can we trust?"

Kat's mind was racing ahead, turning cartwheels. Hurt and resentful as she was, she yet saw the need to remove her charge to a place of safety. The Queen was right: Elizabeth could not stay here. The Admiral was too dangerous, Katherine too hostile. Elizabeth must not remain one moment more than necessary under their roof.

"My sister Joan is married to Sir Anthony Denny," Kat said at length. The Queen would know him well—he had been the head of King Henry's Privy Chamber, and present at his deathbed. "They have a country house at Cheshunt. I know my sister would be glad to welcome me and my Lady Elizabeth, and that we can rely upon her discretion."

Katherine ceased her pacing and sat down at last. She thought for a moment.

"In truth, that sounds a sensible solution, if the Dennys are willing to help. I will write to them now and ask if Elizabeth may go to stay with them."

"Very good, madam," Kat muttered, still smarting from the Queen's harsh criticisms, and grieving at their unfairness.

"You may go now, Mrs. Astley," Katherine said tersely. No sooner had Kat departed than the Queen ran, retching, to the basin, her tears mingling with the vomit, then sank to her knees, sobbing her heart out.

"Tell me the truth!" Kat cried in fury, banging the door shut behind her. "What happened between you and the Admiral?"

Elizabeth started shaking. Never had she seen Kat so moved to anger.

"Nothing of any moment," she faltered. Well, that was the truth: It had been nothing of any moment to her. Yet she knew that was not the answer to Kat's question.

"How far did he go?" Kat demanded.

Elizabeth hesitated.

"Not very far," she answered. Kat's eyes narrowed.

"What did he do?" she persisted.

"He just cuddled me, and kissed me," Elizabeth murmured.

"I was told that his codpiece was unlaced," Kat said, grim. "Did he expose himself to you?"

"No," Elizabeth replied, blushing hotly. Her voice was almost inaudible.

"Do you expect me to believe that you were both there, half undressed on the bed, and nothing happened beyond kissing and cuddling?"

"Nothing else happened, I promise you," Elizabeth lied.

"Well, I hope that *is* the truth," Kat said, half disbelieving.

"It is," Elizabeth said, a little more firmly.

"You do understand what I am talking about, don't you?" Kat asked anxiously. She still had the feeling that her charge was hiding something . . .

"I do," the girl said, unable to meet her gaze.

"Then you have had a lucky escape," Kat told her. "And a narrow escape too, mark me. Whatever possessed you to let the Admiral into your room, without me being there, is beyond me. It was the height of folly—virtually an open invitation. If this got out, your reputation would be in ruins. Do you hear me?"

"I hear you," Elizabeth muttered. "But the Admiral was quite insistent—I found it hard to resist him. If the Queen hadn't come in . . ." Her voice trailed off; she could lie no more.

"Then thank goodness the Queen did come in," declared Kat devoutly. "I have a feeling you will not be seeing the Admiral here again."

"*That* would be a relief," Elizabeth said, and meant it. Handsome and charming he might be, this stepfather of hers, and persuasive with it, yet he had stolen her virginity, the one thing she could never have back. She had not yet quite come to terms with it. Her *stepfather,* the man who should have made it his business to protect her from such things, had not only taken her maidenhead but had also made her a partner in his adultery. And to him it had appeared such a little thing . . .

Well, the deed was done. It was no use wasting regretful tears on it. Somehow, she would find the strength to put it behind her. Already she could sense that she had had a lucky escape. He was just not worth it . . .

The Queen and the Admiral had gone up to London. Neither of them wished to be at Chelsea at this time, and Katherine knew she needed some time alone with her husband to attempt to bridge the rift between them and reclaim him. They were away for some days, and on their return, Elizabeth received a summons to the Queen's presence.

She hardly knew how she would face her stepmother, knowing how treacherously she had behaved toward her. But Katherine Parr was brisk and matter-of-fact in her manner, having persuaded herself that a fourteen-year-old girl was pretty powerless against the strength and charm of a forty-year-old man. In fact, she reasoned, Elizabeth was as much a victim of Tom's lust as she herself was.

"You are to leave this household," she told the red-faced girl standing before her. "You will go to stay with Sir Anthony and Lady Denny, who have written to say that you are very welcome. Lady Denny is Mrs. Astley's sister, as you know, and I hear that Cheshunt is a pleasant house. I am sure you will be much happier there. Master Ascham will go with you."

"Yes, madam," Elizabeth said meekly.

"I am sure I need not remind you that you were foolish indeed to court scandal. I am not sending you away to punish you for it, though, but for your own protection." Her eyes were dark with pain: How she hated having to admit, even indirectly, that her once beloved husband had betrayed her.

"Madam, I do fear for my reputation," Elizabeth said anxiously. "I beg of you, pray tell me if you have heard any gossip about me."

"I have heard none," Katherine assured her, softening in the face of the girl's genuine concern. "Nor will there be, I think, because the matter has been handled so discreetly. If I do hear anything, though, I will inform you or Mrs. Astley."

"You have been more than kind to me, madam," Elizabeth said. "Believe me, I am deeply sorry to have offended you. May I write to you from Cheshunt?"

"You may," Katherine agreed, not trusting herself to say more. She had loved Elizabeth like a daughter, and her feelings toward her were now very confused. Watching the girl curtsy and leave the room, she felt strangely bereft.

The litter was drawn up outside the house. Grooms and porters were loading Elizabeth's baggage and effects onto the carts and sumpter mules, and Kat was arranging the cushions in the chariot and stowing away a hamper of food so that their journey should not lack comforts.

Queen Katherine, attended by her ladies, stood on the steps of the great porch; her pregnancy was just beginning to show, and she had in the last few days taken to loosening the laces on her gown. Beside her stood a forlorn-looking Lady Jane Grey, who was clearly sad to be saying farewell to Elizabeth, whom she so much admired.

"Why do you have to leave, Cousin?" the child asked.

"We have been invited to stay with Mrs. Astley's sister," Elizabeth told her evasively.

"When will I see you again?" Jane asked yearningly.

"Soon, soon, doubtless," Elizabeth interrupted. She was too grief-stricken at the thought of leaving this place where she had once, not long ago, been so happy to think much on her little cousin.

She was relieved that the Admiral was nowhere to be seen: She could not have faced him, she was sure, without betraying, by a chance look or gesture, what had taken place between them.

The Queen regarded the forlorn figure in a green riding habit and jaunty feathered cap, and felt sad. Sad at having failed in her duty to this royal stepdaughter, sad at the prospect of losing one to whom she had been as a mother. Yet it was hard to forgive the girl for what she had done.

Nevertheless, she must be just. Elizabeth was, after all, little more than a child. Impulsively she stepped forward, clasped her stepdaughter's hands lightly, and kissed her on both cheeks.

"God has given you great qualities," she said. "Cultivate them always and labor to improve them. May God go with you."

"And with you, madam," Elizabeth replied, tears welling in her eyes. "And I pray that He will send you a happy hour when the time comes."

"Write to me," Katherine said.

"I will," Elizabeth promised.

"And Elizabeth," the Queen added, "I will warn you if I hear anyone speaking evil of you."

"I thank you, madam," her stepdaughter replied, too choked to express her indebtedness more fully. Then she climbed into the litter beside Kat, and it was drawn relentlessly away, northward on the road toward Hertfordshire.

Cheshunt was a large, imposing moated house built around a spacious courtyard. Sir Anthony Denny and his wife Joan were waiting just across the drawbridge to greet Elizabeth when her litter drew up. Sir Anthony was tall and dark, with a long bristly beard, heavy-lidded, intelligent eyes, and a lugubrious expression; his wife, the former Joan Champernowne, was a younger and prettier version of her sister Kat, dark and amiable-looking.

"My Lady Elizabeth, you are most welcome," said Sir Anthony, bowing deeply. In no way did his face betray his awareness of the reason she had come.

"I thank you for your hospitality, Sir Anthony," Elizabeth said, trying to conceal her embarrassment. How much had Queen Katherine told them of her situation? She could only guess. She smiled as graciously as she could as Lady Denny curtsied to her and then greeted her sister Kat with a warm hug.

"Master Ascham, you are most welcome too!" declared Sir Anthony, shaking the tutor's hand vigorously. "We have a great love of learning in this house."

"Your reputation goes before you, Sir Anthony," Ascham complimented him. "In truth, my Lady Elizabeth, you could not have chosen a better place to lodge—this erudite gentleman is passionate about the new learning and a great lover of God's word to boot."

Their host smiled modestly.

"Pray come within," he invited, and led the way into a fine timberraftered hall of elegant proportions. Behind the dais, a door led to the private apartments, and Elizabeth was escorted up a spiral stair to a suite of rooms overlooking the woods beyond the moat. There was a parlor with a wide stone fireplace, carved chairs and benches, and a large table covered with a Turkey carpet; a bedchamber with a big four-poster bed made up with inviting white sheets, plumped downy pillows, and a rich velvet counterpane; and rooms beyond for Mr. and Mrs. Astley, Master Ascham, and Elizabeth's other personal servants.

"This is most pleasant, I thank you," Elizabeth said to her hosts, but inwardly, she was already pining for Chelsea and her light, airy rooms overlooking those enchanting gardens. Oh, how she ached to be back there . . . They would be seated at the board for supper right now. She could not bear to think that she was no longer a part of that world, and probably never would be again. It would be impossible to return to the old easy relationship with the Admiral after what had been between them, and she was too full of guilt to sit at table with the Queen, knowing that she had sinned with the Queen's husband . . .

That first supper at Cheshunt was the occasion for stimulating conversation and simple but well-cooked fare. Sir Anthony and Master Ascham, increasingly aware of Elizabeth's low spirits, did their best to engage her in their discourse on learned topics, and Kat and her sister were very lively, catching up on all their news. In any other circumstances, Elizabeth would have enjoyed the meal, but she was relieved when the cloth was lifted and the final grace was said. After that, she could plead weariness from the journey and flee to her rooms.

Later that evening, as she was unpacking her books and stowing them away on a shelf, Master Ascham came into the parlor.

"It grows dark," he said, placing another lighted candle on the table. "I'm glad to see you're getting everything arranged, my lady. We can begin lessons tomorrow."

"I shall be glad of that," Elizabeth replied.

"You *will* get used to it here," Ascham said gently.

"Is my homesickness so obvious?" Elizabeth asked.

"Desperately," he said, smiling ruefully.

"Do you know why I am here, Master Ascham?" She had to ask this, had to know. After all, she would be in his company nearly every day.

"The Queen did explain something of it," he revealed. "She was at pains to tell me that you were more sinned against than sinning."

His gentleness seemed to invite her confidences.

"I acted very unwisely," Elizabeth confessed. "I cannot believe it of myself."

"We all have our weaknesses," Ascham told her. "We are but human. And many a young girl has acted unwisely in the presence of a handsome rogue."

"You dare to speak thus of the Admiral?" she asked, surprised.

"I dare to speak the truth. After all, it's what most people think. He *is* a rogue, and he bears far more blame than you for this affair." Ascham was clearly trying to conceal his anger. "He deliberately put you in that situation and took advantage of you. No decent man would do such a thing."

Elizabeth wondered why she felt compelled to stand up for the Admiral. She hated hearing him spoken of thus, even though she knew that Ascham meant well, and was right. Did that mean she still loved Thomas, after what he had done? She could not forget her own complicity in the matter; whatever her tutor said, she knew herself partly to blame. And knowing that, she could still think kindly of her seducer.

"I too did wrong," she said, "and my conscience still troubles me when I think of how badly I behaved toward the Queen. I do realize that, in sending me away, she was acting for the best. And although I would give anything to be back there, I know I am here through my own fault."

"You must stop punishing yourself for it, and face life anew," Ascham counseled her. "Mrs. Astley would say the same to you, I make no doubt."

"I will try," Elizabeth promised. "I have asked God's forgiveness, now I must hope for human forgiveness. I will write to the Queen as I promised her."

"I have had a letter from the Lady Elizabeth," Katherine said, easing her thickening body into the cushioned chair.

"Have you, my love?" the Admiral said, his tone light. Elizabeth's name had hardly been mentioned since her departure.

"Yes. She thanks me for my kindness on the day she left, and says she was replete with sorrow at leaving, knowing I was unwell with my pregnancy. She thanks me also for offering to warn her if I heard any evil spoken of her—not that there should be any cause for it, mind you—" The Admiral winced at her sharp tone.

"Then she says hopefully that if I had not had a good opinion of her, I would not have made such a friendly gesture." She broke off and reflected for a moment. "It was not made so much in friendship as in the knowledge that forewarned is forearmed. Because if any scandal comes of this . . ." She did not finish. Her voice was bitter.

"I am very sorry for it, Kate," the Admiral said, for what seemed like the thousandth time. Would she never cease reminding him of his fall from grace?

His wife had turned back to the letter.

"She ends by saying that she thanks God for providing her with such friends, and desires Him to enrich me with a long life. She signs herself *Your Highness's humble daughter.*" She laid the letter on the table. "There, you can read it for yourself."

She rose to her feet and slowly and wearily walked to the door.

"Kate!" he called after her. "I want us to remove to Sudeley Castle. We have never been there, and I thought it fitting that our child should be born in the principal seat of my baronage."

Katherine turned and looked at him. Her face was guarded, remote.

"I should like that," she said. "There are too many bad memories here."

"We could make a fresh start," he said tentatively, watching for her reaction.

"Mayhap," she said, and walked out of the room.

Elizabeth tore open the first letter. It was a brief note from the Queen, thanking her stepdaughter for her kind words and assuring her of her friendship. Her heart leapt—she had not looked for or expected such generosity of spirit on Katherine's part.

Now she opened the second letter. The Admiral had written to her too! Eagerly, she scanned the single page. He had been brief. He asked after her health, and told her that the Queen was enjoying being at Sudeley very much and eagerly anticipating the birth of her child in August, which was only weeks away now. Elizabeth caught her breath when she read the passage in which he told her that he was resolved to take upon himself all the blame for what had happened, and she was heartened to learn that he would swear to her innocence if necessary. Pray God it would never come to that! He ended by saying that he was determined to be a good lord to her, and that if there was any service he could do for her, she had only to ask.

Was this a covert attempt to rekindle their relationship? Or had he come to his senses and decided, as she had, to put the whole sorry episode behind him and behave honorably toward her? Even now, despite everything, Elizabeth could not suppress a *frisson* of excitement at the possibility that it might be the former, although she was painfully aware that what he had written was certainly no love letter. Even so, she was determined to give him no encouragement.

She wrote back, a courteous note that would bear scrutiny by anyone, thanking him for his letter and the good news of the Queen, and asking him to perform the small service of dispatching to her a book she had left behind at Chelsea.

Weeks passed with no reponse from him, weeks in which she became certain she had misread his overture; then a note arrived with his profuse apologies for having been unable to find the book she had wanted, and his assurance that his failure to do so had not proceeded from a want of goodwill or friendship. That was a bit excessive, she thought, but it was typical of the man, so she wrote back telling him he needed not to have excused his behavior so profusely. *I am a friend not won with trifles, nor lost with the like,* she concluded. Then, wishing to maintain the distance between them and make it clear that any familiarity was well and truly over, she added, *I pray you to make my humble commendations to the Queen's Highness. I commit you and your affairs into God's hand.*

She was relieved they were in touch again. It suggested to her that things had settled down somewhat and that the whole sorry episode was receding into the past. She dared to hope that the Queen had forgiven her, and that one day they would be reconciled. As for the Admiral, she was resolved to forget him entirely, and never betray by a word or gesture that he had ever meant anything to her. In the meantime, her life at Cheshunt would go on, a daily round of lessons, walks, meals, and intelligent conversation with her kindly hosts. All in all, she reflected, she had gotten off rather lightly.

—

In fact, she had not gotten off lightly at all. She had been at Cheshunt for just a month when she awoke one morning in June feeling very nauseous. Retching into her close stool, she wondered whether she had eaten something that disagreed with her.

When the same thing happened the following morning, she still believed that she was suffering from food poisoning. But when, after having felt better in the afternoon, she vomited for the third morning running, she began to wonder, with sinking spirits, if there was a more alarming cause for it. By the fourth day, she had begun to fear that God might indeed be punishing her for her great sin, and on the fifth morning it happened, she knew in her heart, with deadly certainty, that her fears were well grounded. After all, she had seen Katherine Parr in the same condition not four months before. There was no escaping the fact, she told herself, trying to ignore the icy chill that shivered down her spine each time she thought of it, which was more or less constantly: She was pregnant with the Admiral's child.

Her monthly courses, which had only commenced the previous year, had never been regular. She might go two months or more without seeing any show of blood. So she had not thought it odd that she had not bled since April. She had in recent months suffered bad headaches and megrims, so there had been nothing unusual in the fact that the megrims had grown worse lately. She had put that down to the stress of all that had happened recently.

Nor had she laid any significance on the fact that her breasts were now straining against the tight corset she wore: She had been eating better lately and had gained a little weight—or so she had thought.

What should she do? She would rather die than tell anyone her secret. And yet, her common sense told her, someone would have to be told. She did not live in a corner, and people would soon notice her condition. The consequences of that were unthinkable; again that cold shiver. No, she could not cope with this alone. She had to have help.

Terror engulfed her. She could not face Kat's reaction, let alone that of the Dennys. Would they inform the Admiral? Worse still, would they tell the Queen? And could she rely still on Katherine's discretion? If this got out, the scandal would ruin her. She knew she was not permitted to marry without the council's consent. Whatever would they do if they found out she was expecting the Admiral's bastard? It would mean the

Tower for him, or worse. And for her? Would their illicit coupling be seen as high treason? She could already sense the confining walls of the Tower, feel the iron blade of the ax slicing into her neck, see the flames crackling voraciously at her feet . . .

The room seemed to spin crazily; she seemed to be viewing it through a dark tunnel. There was a frightening jarring in her head, and her heart was pounding violently, her knees trembling, her hands sweating. She was going to die, right now, she knew it.

"Oh!" she cried in panic. "Help me!"

Kat came running, saw her standing there, white-faced and shaking, the telltale basin of vomit on the windowsill. Then she too was nearly overcome with panic. She had had her suspicions: There had been no bloody clouts to dispose of for weeks, but she had reasoned—God forgive her—that that might signify nothing. After all, Elizabeth had given her word that nothing of any moment had happened between her and the Admiral. But now, with certainty, she could see the truth staring her in the face. And she, too, saw the Tower, the dungeon, the rope, and—horror of horrors—the flaming faggots.

"What have you done?" Her voice was shrill. "You gave me your word!"

Elizabeth tried to speak but couldn't, so potent was her own fear. The panic was receding, but it had left her drained and shivering.

"Answer me!" Kat hissed urgently. "Are you with child?"

The girl could only nod mutely, her eyes dark pools of terror.

"When was your last course?" Kat demanded.

Elizabeth gulped.

"Just after Easter, I think," she whispered.

"The beginning of April," Kat recalled, "and we are now in late June. When did you . . . When did the Admiral . . . ?" She could not utter the words: They only compounded her own guilt.

"Once, at the beginning of May," Elizabeth said, beginning to weep. "I tried to stop him—he was insistent. I loved him too well!" She was sobbing bitterly now.

"Never mind that. You must be nearly two months' gone," Kat calculated, seeking refuge in briskness. "Are there any other signs? Are you passing water more often? Are your breasts tender?"

"Yes." Elizabeth sniffed.

"Then God help us, you must be with child," Kat said, feeling near to tears herself. "Whatever possessed you to let him get near you? You were warned never to see him alone."

"I loved him!" Elizabeth burst out. "I could not resist him. Oh, what am I to do?"

"God knows," Kat replied. "Let me think." She stood there for a moment breathing heavily. "I shall have to tell my sister. I have no choice."

"What did she say?" Elizabeth asked anxiously, the moment Kat stepped back into the room.

Kat sighed and sat down heavily on a bench.

"She was shocked—rightly, of course. And she would do nothing without her lord's sanction. She called Sir Anthony and told him everything."

Elizabeth hung her head. She liked the Dennys, who had been kind, generous hosts to her, and she valued their good opinions. But now they would, quite justifiably, despise her . . .

"I was mortified," Kat was saying. "The way Sir Anthony looked at me . . ." She felt like howling. "He wants to see you—now."

Elizabeth entered the Dennys's parlor in trepidation. Lady Denny, seated by the hearth, rose and curtsied, then seated herself primly in her chair. Sir Anthony, standing with his back to the fire with a pained look on his face, bowed, then fixed his gaze at a point above Elizabeth's head, as if he could not bear to look at her.

"My Lady Elizabeth," he said stiffly, "I am exceedingly distressed to learn of your condition. If a serving wench in this house were in such trouble, I would dismiss her at once. But I have a long-standing loyalty to the Crown, and to the memory of your late father, King Henry. For his sake, I will succor you in your trouble."

"I thank you," Elizabeth faltered, dismayed at his cold manner. "I do not deserve such kindness."

"It is no more than my duty," he replied, his tone still chilly. "You will stay here until the child is born. For as long as your condition can be concealed, you may join us at meals and go for walks in the gardens and park, although I should prefer it if you would keep within a mile of the house. Later, of course, you must keep to your rooms. We shall give out that you are sick, and keep the details as vague as possible. Kat alone will attend you. No one else must know the truth."

"I am so grateful," Elizabeth whispered. "But what of the child?"

"It will be put out to nurse on one of my Norfolk manors, and then placed with a reliable family. We will say that it was a foundling, left in the church porch. None shall ever discover its identity."

"And *you* must needs forget about it, my lady," his wife added.

"I will," Elizabeth promised. She felt faint, and the nausea was threatening again. But at least she was safe—for the moment, anyway, and if everything went according to plan.

She would never have believed she could feel so sick. Every morning she awoke nauseous, and had literally to run to the basin. The only thing that helped was eating meat or fish, but she could hardly send Kat to the kitchens demanding those things at eight o'clock in the morning, for people might become suspicious. So she suffered.

"Try an apple," Kat would urge. "Joan said it helped her." But Elizabeth could not face an apple. She took one bite and spat it out.

Mealtimes were purgatory. She would be ravenous, but after tasting the food, the desire to gorge deserted her, so she sat there pushing the morsels around her plate until everyone else had finished. Wine tasted oddly metallic, and she could only drink a few sips.

Then there was the tiredness—it was overwhelming. Sometimes she could have slept standing up. She might have the freedom of the house and grounds for the time being, but she spent most of her time resting on her bed, drained by exhaustion. And she lived in fear of the birth pangs to come, recalling every tale of childbed horror she had overheard. She had never realized what gravid women went through, and constantly vowed to herself that, even in happier circumstances, she would never ever again risk a pregnancy.

In the high summer, news came that the Queen was ill; in her advanced stage of pregnancy, the heat was affecting her badly, and she was troubled by severe headaches. Elizabeth read the Admiral's latest letter with a heavy heart.

"Poor lady, I do pray for her relief," she told Kat. "She has taken to her bed with fainting fits."

Kat was still angry with Elizabeth, but she was thawing bit by bit.

"I must confess, I had my misgivings as soon as I heard she was expecting," she said, shaking her head. "Thirty-six is late to be having a first baby."

"I hope she will be all right," Elizabeth said worriedly, thinking of her own ordeal to come.

"That is in the hands of God," Kat stated, "and all we can do is beseech Him to vouchsafe her a safe delivery."

"I do daily so beseech Him," Elizabeth said fervently. Pregnant herself, she was now painfully aware of how deeply she had hurt and wronged the Queen, her kind benefactress, and wanted to make it up to her in any way she could.

Roger Ascham came to her. He did not know she was pregnant.

"With Your Grace's permission, I should like to visit my friends in Cambridge," he said.

Elizabeth was dismayed. The plan was that, when her condition was in danger of becoming evident and she took to her chamber, feigning illness—*feigning?* Elizabeth thought incredulously—Master Ascham should be sent back to Cambridge to pursue his studies there; she had made such progress with him that he had been planning to return to university for good in the autumn anyway. So it would not make much difference if he went a month or so earlier.

Suddenly, though, she wanted him to stay with her. He was kind, and he was ignorant of her situation, so he still treated her with respect and deference—unlike Kat and the Dennys, who were uncomfortably aware of her fall from grace; Kat was brisk with her, her host and hostess distant and unforgiving.

"Do not go," she said plaintively. Ascham looked at her, surprised.

"Whatever is wrong, my lady?" he asked.

"The Queen is ill, and I fear for her," Elizabeth told him, near weeping. "I need the comfort of your presence."

The tutor was taken aback. He had until now accounted the Lady Elizabeth a strong, self-contained person. But she was crying now, and fumbling for a nonexistent kerchief. He gave her his own, then ventured tentatively to place an arm around her thin shoulders as she dabbed at her eyes. Inwardly he sighed.

"Of course I will not go," he told her, albeit reluctantly. "But you know my work here is nearly completed. You know you will not need my services for very much longer, and that I have work to do at Cambridge."

"I know," Elizabeth said. "Yet despite all that, I had hoped you would stay on as my tutor and friend, for I depend on you utterly."

Ascham's heart sank. Admire and like her he did, but Cambridge was calling to him, and he was beginning to fear she would never give him leave to go back there.

He said gently, "I have studies of my own that I wish to pursue, studies I interrupted when I entered your service, my lady. But never fear. I will tarry awhile and put off my departure."

"You are a true friend to me," Elizabeth told him.

Early August, and she was feeling so much better. The only problem was that her belly was beginning to swell. The pointed stomacher, which she must wear for as long as possible, became tighter and more uncomfortable with each day. Soon she must go into seclusion, for she could not keep up this pretense very much longer. It did not seem fair that she should have to live in such a covert fashion when her partner in crime, all unwitting of her plight, was free to come and go as he pleased.

But at least the Admiral's next letter brought heartening news.

"She is better! The Queen is better!" Elizabeth cried, almost dancing into the bedchamber where Kat was laying away sheets in the chest beneath the window.

"Praised be God!" the governess said, ignoring the old familiar dart of jealousy. "I am pleased to hear that."

"And," Elizabeth added triumphantly, "my lord says she is missing my company. Oh, Kat, do you think this means we might one day be summoned to Sudeley? Not yet, of course," she added hastily.

"I would not look for it," Kat warned. "Besides, Her Grace will have much on her mind just now. She will shortly be taking to her chamber, and then she will have a child to care for."

"Yes, she will," said Elizabeth wistfully, but her excitement at the news that the Queen was missing her soon resurfaced, an unlooked-for joy in her shattered world. She turned back to the letter and read it again, just to make sure she had not dreamed it. "The Admiral writes that the babe is very lusty and kicks so often that the Queen cannot sleep at night. I shall write back and ask him to keep me informed as to how his busy child is doing! Do you know, Kat, I'll warrant that, were we to be at his birth, we might see him beaten for all the trouble he has put the Queen to!" She was quite beside herself with elation. Everything would come right in the end, as she had prayed it would—she knew it!

"Lord save us, the Duchess of Somerset is here!" Kat whimpered, bursting into the bedchamber.

"Am I discovered, then?" Elizabeth whispered, thinking the worst.

"I think not, mercifully," Kat replied, "but my fine lady has gotten wind of some scandal and is no doubt come to satisfy her curiosity." Her tone was tart. "She wants to see you."

"She cannot . . . I dare not . . ." Elizabeth was terrified. She feared that her condition stood little chance of escaping the eagle-eyed Duchess's gaze.

"You have no choice," Kat told her. "Get up and dress." She surveyed her charge's slightly swollen body as Elizabeth reluctantly pulled her nightgown over her head. "There's nothing for it, I'll have to lace you tightly," she told her, fetching a clean shift.

When Elizabeth appeared in the great parlor, she looked as slender as ever in her pink damask gown, its stiff stomacher flattening her bulge. She was in misery with the constraint, and light-headed with the effort to breathe shallowly and maintain an erect posture, keeping her shoulders high and her stomach in.

The Duchess Anne came toward her and made her curtsy.

"My Lady Elizabeth, I rejoice to see you in health," she said stridently. "My Lord the Protector sends his greetings."

"Welcome, madam," Elizabeth said distantly, seating herself gingerly in the fireside chair that Sir Anthony had just vacated. "What brings you to Cheshunt?"

"I came to see my old gossip, Lady Denny here, and to inquire after your health, my lady. Rumor has it that you have been indisposed."

"A summer chill," Elizabeth said airily, noticing that her hosts appeared distinctly uncomfortable. "I am better now, I thank Your Grace."

"Better in more ways than one, I wist," the Duchess agreed. "You are far better out of the Queen's household."

"Begging your pardon, madam," Elizabeth bridled, "but Her Majesty was very good to me."

"It was not Her Majesty of whom I spoke," Lady Somerset said, her tone implying that Her Majesty was no doubt responsible for the laxity at which rumor had hinted. Their quarrel over which of them should take precedence at court and wear the Queen's jewels was notorious.

"I know not to what Your Grace refers," Elizabeth said innocently.

"I think you do, my lady," the Duchess replied firmly. "And I say that you were very wise to come here. Or were you constrained to it?"

The atmosphere in the room grew tense. Elizabeth was furious at the woman's temerity. Furious, and at the same time frightened. What rumors had the Duchess heard?

"I invited my sister, Mrs. Astley, to visit, and my Lady Elizabeth was happy to honor us with her presence," Lady Denny said, a touch too hastily.

"I have been made most welcome," Elizabeth added. "Cheshunt is a beautiful house."

"Hardly as beautiful as Chelsea or Sudeley," her ladyship retorted sharply.

"Ah, but the Queen was tiring easily with the child on the way, and I did not wish to weary her at this time," Elizabeth said, feeling as if she was engaging in armed combat. "Her Majesty writes to me regularly, and I expect to see her after she has been delivered."

Knowing herself bested, the Duchess retreated. Short of embarrassing her hosts by openly insulting their royal guest, she forbore to say more, and the talk reverted to gossip of the court and the splendors of Somerset House.

For all the breeze blowing through the open windows, Elizabeth felt hot. Her hands were clammy, and rivulets of sweat were trickling down her neck. The cruelly laced corset was all but unbearable, and she longed to cast it aside and lie untrammeled on her bed. The room darkened, and it seemed that the polite chatter was coming from farther and farther away . . . She swayed in her seat.

"My lady!" It was Kat, stepping forward and shaking her. "Are you all right?"

Elizabeth came to, uncertain what had happened, and stared at her governess, uncomprehending. The blood was pounding in her temples, and she could barely breathe.

"I'm hot," she whispered, and suddenly crumpled to the floor in a dead faint. Kat swooped, falling to her knees beside her, grateful that her ample skirts were shielding any telltale signs of pregnancy in the prone body from the hawk-like view of the Duchess, who was all feigned concern.

"Some wine, Sir Anthony!" she commanded, taking charge of the situation.

Sir Anthony jumped to do her bidding, and his wife carried the goblet to Kat. Kat, meanwhile, had pulled Elizabeth to a sitting position and was relieved to see her coming around.

"Sip this," she murmured, holding the vessel to the girl's lips. "There, feeling better?"

"It's her age," Lady Denny offered helpfully. "I used to faint a lot when I was about fifteen. Here, let me assist you." She helped Kat to get Elizabeth to her feet.

"With your permission, Your Grace, I will help her to bed," Kat said, and she steered her charge through the door, emerging with a sigh of heartfelt relief. Watching them go with narrowed eyes, the Duchess inwardly deplored the lack of backbone in young girls these days . . .

That month, Elizabeth received a letter from a Mr. William Cecil, secretary to Protector Somerset. He wrote that he had been appointed her surveyor, to help administer the lands her father had left for her dowry. His tone was gratifyingly courteous and deferential.

She went to Sir Anthony and showed him the letter.

"Have you heard of this William Cecil?" she asked, hoping that her host would unbend a little toward her. He was still unfailingly civil, but cool in his manner, as if he was barely able to suppress his disapproval.

Sir Anthony took the letter and read it.

"I know him," he said. "He is a clever young man, one of the rising stars at court. You are fortunate, madam, in having him for your surveyor. His intelligence and his wit are impressive."

He handed her back the letter, bowed formally, and walked out. Elizabeth sighed—would he never unbend or forgive her?—then looked again at William Cecil's letter.

"If there is ever any service I can do for you, do not hesitate to command me," he had written. One day, Elizabeth thought, she might just take him at his word. In the meantime, she wrote back, warmly and appreciatively. *I hope one day to thank you in person for your diligence in my affairs,* she told him.

Before long, they were in friendly correspondence with each other, quickly establishing a lasting rapport. It was true what Sir Anthony had said, she discovered: Cecil's wit *was* formidable, and he had a talent for driving to the heart of a problem and finding the best, or at any rate, the most pragmatic, solution. Yet beyond his undoubted abilities, she could sense an affection for, and staunch loyalty to, herself, and that cheered her immeasurably at this time.

The first week in September was warm. Elizabeth was now confined to her rooms, and the days dragged heavily, for she had been persuaded to let Master Ascham return to Cambridge and was already growing weary of having just Kat for company. She wanted to be out of doors and active, but that was just not possible. So she sat about, reading, doing the odd translation here and there, and generally driving Kat to distraction with her complaints.

"I am so bored," she grumbled one evening.

"Then find something to do," a provoked Kat snapped. "The devil makes work for idle hands, you know."

"What shall I do?" Elizabeth moaned.

"How about finishing that little smock you were embroidering for the Queen's baby?" Kat suggested.

Elizabeth thought about it.

"Very well," she sighed. "But first, I must go to the stool chamber."

Alone, lifting up her skirts, she was puzzled to see spots of blood on her white petticoats and stockings. A little alarmed, she grabbed a clout and dabbed at her female parts with it. It came away bloody. Elizabeth caught her breath. What could this portend?

Stuffing another clout between her legs, she hobbled out of the stool chamber and cried, "Kat—help, I'm bleeding!"

"Bleeding?" echoed her governess. "Oh, dear Lord! Look, child, don't fret. Go and lie down. I'll get my sister."

By the time Lady Denny had arrived, the cramping pains had begun, a dull, relentless, recurring ache in Elizabeth's belly and lower back. She lay there rubbing herself, groaning a little.

"I fear it is a miscarriage threatening," Lady Denny said.

Elizabeth did not know whether to rejoice or cry.

"We must get help," Kat said. "She is second in line to the throne. We cannot risk any injury to her. She is four months gone, and it may not go easy for her."

Elizabeth groaned again, louder this time. In a matter of minutes the pain had become dragging, acute, and she was thoroughly frightened.

"We dare not risk her condition being made public," Lady Denny reminded her sister. "Wait—I have an idea."

The woman who was led into the bedchamber at midnight was blindfolded, but by then, Elizabeth was too far gone to notice. The pains were sharp now, knifing through her lower body, searing through her back, her abdomen, her buttocks, and her privy parts, and there was a lot of blood now, seeping from her womb. She was exhausted, feverish, nauseated, and confused.

After Sir Anthony had removed the blindfold, averted his eyes from the bed, and slipped out the door, reminding them to ring the bell for him when he was to return, the midwife squinted in the firelight, realized that she was in a fine mansion—although goodness only knew which one—and allowed herself to be ushered toward the bed by a finely dressed lady who was clearly in charge. There lay a young girl, very fair of face, obviously in the final stages of a premature delivery. A middle-aged woman with anxious eyes sat beside her.

The midwife did not waste time; she prided herself on her reputation, although she doubted anyone would ever give her any credit for tonight's work. Pulling down the bloodied sheet, she prised apart the girl's thighs and took a good long look at what lay between them.

"Has she miscarried?" the older woman asked quietly. The girl was panting, oblivious.

"Yes." The midwife nodded. "Do you have a cloth?"

Kat handed her one. The midwife used it to scoop up the blood clots and the pathetic little scrap of dead humanity that had been born too soon. Then she called for water and towels and tended to the young mother, who had now sunk into an exhausted stupor.

When she was tidied and sleeping peacefully, they rang the bell, and Sir Anthony returned.

"Where is it?" he asked.

"It is dead," Kat said flatly. She handed him the tiny cloth-wrapped bundle. He pulled the wrapping aside and gazed for a moment at the crumpled, purpling face.

"Was it born dead?" he inquired, his face impassive.

Kat nodded.

"Then it has no need of our prayers," he said grimly, and without another word, he threw King Henry's lost grandchild onto the fire. The women all gasped in horror and protest, but Sir Anthony ignored them. He blindfolded the outraged midwife once again and hustled her out of the room, leaving his wife and Kat standing there, hands clamped to their mouths in dismay, watching the flames destroying the evidence of Elizabeth's sin as the girl herself slumbered on and the room filled briefly with the ghastly stench of roasted meat.

The sense of relief was overpowering. She could cope with the dull ache and the bleeding, which was subsiding with each day that passed; that was nothing to what she had gone through. There were some darts of sadness too, but they were fleeting. All that mattered was that she had been reprieved. God had seen fit to punish her, but had then miraculously relented. Rashly, she now realized, she had risked her life in every way. She could have died losing that child. She might well have ended up in the Tower, or worse . . .

Never again, she vowed, would she risk her reputation, let alone allow any man to come near enough to get her with child. The whole experience had been appalling, in every respect, and she could not offer sufficient thanks for her deliverance.

"You don't know how lucky you are," Kat had said, shaking her head, looking down at her as she lay there, wan and exhausted after her ordeal.

Oh, yes I do, Elizabeth had thought. "I can never thank God sufficiently for it," she said. She did not grieve for her dead baby, did not even think to ask what had become of its sad little corpse.

"We are telling everyone it was a sudden fever," Kat explained, spooning her some heartening broth. "Soon you will be up and about again."

That day was fast approaching. Elizabeth was getting out of bed for the afternoons now, and sitting in a chair by the window. Her normal high spirits had begun to revive. Life would soon resume its normal course, and no one would be any the wiser.

Naturally, she had plenty of time on her hands in which to think and reflect on her situation.

"I was right to begin with," she told Kat. "I will never marry. I could not go through that again."

"Nonsense!" Kat retorted. "Lots of women go through it, and live to bear a brace of healthy children. It is unnatural for a girl to remain unwed. You'll get over this, mark my words."

"I *will* get over it," Elizabeth said determinedly, "but I am now more than ever convinced of the benefits of staying single."

Kat sighed. "You say that now, but you may change your mind when another handsome man comes along."

"I think not." Elizabeth's face was set. "I will never again allow love to blind me to all good sense and reason. I must have been mad."

"They say love is a form of madness," Kat mused, "and in your case that was probably apposite."

"I will be circumspect in future," Elizabeth assured her. "I will continue to wear sober clothes and be a virtuous Protestant maiden."

Kat's eyebrows shot up. "A maiden you can never be again," she said, tart.

"Nay, but the world must think it," Elizabeth said, wincing inwardly. "*I* will never give anyone cause to doubt it. I have been given a second chance, and I will not squander it. I will flaunt my virginity as others flaunt their charms, and lead a godly life from now on. None will ever have reason to cast any slur on my reputation."

"Well, you *have* come to your senses," Kat said with admiration. "I am heartily relieved to hear it. But what of the Admiral and your feelings for him?"

"I loved the Admiral," Elizabeth admitted, "I was mad for him, and utterly foolish, and I did the Queen a great wrong, God forgive me. I daresay I love him still—I cannot help that—but not in the same way. My love is now tempered with caution and reason. With God's help, I may forget him."

She rose slowly, steadying herself on the arms of the chair; her legs were still unused to walking.

"I think I will rest for a while," she said, but then a sudden commotion in the courtyard below drew her eye to the window and, looking down, she saw a travel-stained horseman dismounting and hastening into the house.

"He wears the Queen's livery! Do you think he comes with happy news for us?" Elizabeth asked of Kat, who was peering over her shoulder.

"I'll go down and find out," Kat said, hastening to the door. "You lie down."

Elizabeth lay there, contrasting her own experience with the Queen's, and wondering how it would feel to give birth to a much-wanted and loved baby. Then suddenly, Kat burst back into the room, her face grave.

"It is ill news, I fear, my lady. Tragic news. The Queen was brought to bed of a daughter, but took the fever afterward. She is dead, God rest her."

"Dead?" Elizabeth's forlorn cry echoed woefully in the chamber. She could not believe it. Poor Queen Katherine, who had been as dear as a mother to her. She did not think she could bear this new grief, on top of the guilt and everything else that had happened lately. Feeling utterly bereft, she burst into noisy sobbing.

Kat was there at once, cradling her.

"Hush, hush, sweeting. Kat's here. Kat will always be here for you, God willing." Shocked as she was at the tragedy, she could not suppress the treacherous feeling of triumph that had been bubbling up inside her since she had learned of the death of the woman whom she had always regarded as a rival for Elizabeth's affections. Now Katherine was gone, and Kat would never again suffer that sinking sense of jealousy and betrayal that the Queen's love for her stepdaughter had engendered in the governess.

"She did not suffer," Kat said. "She died a most Christian death, and was buried in the chapel at Sudeley. Lady Jane Grey was chief mourner."

Elizabeth did not heed her. Kat let her weep, stroking the damp red tresses from her temples.

"Poor Jane," Elizabeth, calmer now, said later. "I'd forgotten her. What will happen to her?"

"Well, she cannot remain under the Admiral's roof," Kat observed. "It would not be seemly. I expect she will be sent home."

"I am sorry for that," Elizabeth said. "She was happy with the Queen—as was I." The tears were threatening again.

"There is something else," Kat said quickly. "I think you should know that the Admiral himself sent that messenger specially, to break this news to you, my lady." She took a deep breath. "Has it occurred to you, Elizabeth, that his lordship, who wanted to be your husband after the late King died, and loves and admires you, is free again?"

Elizabeth looked up, startled. Her expression was unreadable.

"You may have him now if you will," Kat said, smiling encouragingly. "After a decent time of mourning has passed, naturally. He would have married *you,* if he had had the chance, rather than the Queen. And given what has happened, perhaps he *should* marry you. Having taken your maidenhead, it would set matters right if he made an honest woman of you."

The girl on the bed did not speak. The silence lengthened. Kat saw that a flush had spread over her neck and face.

"No," said Elizabeth.

"Yes!" cried Kat excitedly. "Yes, my lady. You will not deny that you want this, especially if my Lord Protector and the council were to approve it. In a sense, you are married to the Admiral already, and when the King sees that it is what you want, he will approve it, I'm sure. All this nonsense about not wanting to marry! You love the Admiral, you have admitted it! He has been a very naughty man, but he would make you a very proper husband." She could just see the two of them together, such a handsome couple, walking merrily down the aisle, making good sport together in bed, and presiding over the board with their growing family of cherubic children around them. And she, Kat, there to enjoy it all, running the household, feasting her eyes from afar on the Admiral . . .

"Marry, he is a charming man, and handsome to boot!" she went on. "You and he accord well together—you know that in your heart. And he is an important man in the kingdom, destined for great things. He would make a marvelous husband—a fit match for you." She knew in her bones that this was what Elizabeth wanted—even if the girl did not know it herself—and that it was what she herself wanted for her.

"I cannot countenance it, or even think about it. It is not only that the Queen is so recently dead—my mind is made up," Elizabeth declared firmly.

"I understand that," Kat conceded, reining herself in. "But after a suitable interval has passed, and if the Admiral were to show his interest, I'll wager you'll be thinking very differently."

"No," said Elizabeth again.

Kat changed tactics.

"The messenger said that my lord is the heaviest and most doleful man in the world just now," she revealed. "It would be a kindness to write him a letter of condolence."

"I hardly think that the Queen's demise could have occasioned him that much grief," Elizabeth sniffed, her voice heavy with sarcasm. "I cannot believe he loved her that deeply. No, I will not write words of comfort, for he needs them not. And I should hate him to think that I was chasing him. That is the last thing I would do."

"So you do not look to marry him?" Kat persisted.

"No," Elizabeth said for the third time.

But Kat still doubted she meant it.

By October, Elizabeth had fully recovered from her miscarriage, and plans were made for her to leave Cheshunt.

"The King has placed Hatfield House at your disposal, madam," Sir Anthony informed her, a little less stiffly than was his custom, because he was relieved to be getting rid of his unwanted guest at last. Elizabeth's presence in his house had caused nothing but trouble, and she had long outstayed her welcome. Nevertheless, he had not once failed in his courtesy toward her.

Elizabeth too was relieved that her stay at Cheshunt had come to an end—in fact she never wanted to see the house again, nor be reminded of the ordeal she had endured there. And it would be good to be back in her old, familiar childhood home, mistress of her own household, and free to come and go as she pleased. Her step was light as she hurried about her rooms, humming and gathering her possessions for Kat to pack in the big traveling chests. Kat was naturally sad to be bidding her sister farewell, but she too had had enough of Cheshunt and blessed the day they departed, trundling away in the litter as Sir Anthony and Lady Denny stood waving a shade too enthusiastically on the porch.

"I am pleased to be reunited with you all again," Elizabeth told her reassembled household, now gathered in the great hall to receive her. She had taken only a few servants to Cheshunt; the rest had remained for a time at Chelsea, and had then come here to Hatfield to make all ready. "I trust you were well looked after by the Admiral and the late Queen."

Was she mistaken, or did she detect a few furtive smiles, whispered exchanges, and an undercurrent of mirth among her people? She could not be sure, but it bothered her a little. Surely word had not gotten out of what had happened between her and the Admiral?

Word had. Her women, those who had been at Chelsea, kept glancing at her in a knowing, unsettling way, making her cheeks burn. Of course, they would remember the morning romps in her bedchamber; her maids had been witnesses to that on several occasions, and servants loved nothing better than to discuss the private business of their betters. Well, she must trust upon their loyalty not to turn idle gossip into something more malicious. At least only a handful of trusted people knew about her pregnancy, and they could be relied upon never to talk.

Kat, bustling into the kitchens later that day, was herself disconcerted to come upon some young scullions gossiping.

"And they do say that the Admiral was alone with her in her bedchamber on more than one occasion!" one was saying.

"I'll wager I know what they were up to!" the other smirked. "Making the beast with two backs!"

"And what exactly are you talking about?" Kat barked, descending on them like an avenging angel. Both the boys looked scared.

"Well, out with it!" she insisted.

"It were just gossip, missus. No offense meant," the first lad excused himself.

"Gossip about the Lady Elizabeth?" Kat demanded to know.

The youths looked embarrassed. Just then, one of the cooks intervened.

"You may as well know, Mrs. Astley, that the gossip has been of nothing else for a long time, I'm sorry to say."

"Then we must put a stop to it!" Kat cried, horrified. "I will speak to the Chamberlain and the Steward. Such idle talk undeservedly disparages my lady's reputation, and could get those who spread it into serious trouble."

The Chamberlain and the Steward were duly summoned to the parlor to speak with the governess. Elizabeth, Kat had decided, was better left out of this.

"As well command the tide to go back," the Steward observed unhelpfully. "I'm not surprised the servants are gossiping, given what I have heard."

"It was the women of Lady Elizabeth's bedchamber that started it," the Chamberlain explained. "Apparently they had been quite scandalized by what they had witnessed—although I don't pretend to know if there was any truth in it. Women, of course, just can't keep quiet—and now the whole household is abuzz with it."

"You must command them to stop," ordered an affronted Kat. "Threaten them with dismissal or whatever punishment you like, but still their tongues."

"Very well, Mrs. Astley," the Chamberlain said. He departed with the Steward, shaking his head.

Elizabeth saw her servants going about looking subdued, and guessed why. She could sense that people were still whispering about her, and she caught the odd salacious grin in her direction. Going about the house, she was aware that all eyes were on her, and that she was the object of much covert speculation. It made her resolved not to give people any further cause for gossip. She took to dressing more severely than ever, in high-collared black gowns unadorned by any jewelry save her mother's initial pendant at her neck and a miniature prayer book clasped at her waist; she affected plain hoods with modest black veils, and walked about with her eyes discreetly downcast and her hands folded virtuously across her stomacher. She spent a lot of time on her knees in the chapel.

"I know one way in which you can put a stop to the gossip," Kat said one evening as they sat by the roaring fire. "Marry the Admiral."

"No," Elizabeth said.

"I'll warrant you'll change your tune when you see him." Kat smiled archly. "He'll be coming a-courting soon, mark my words."

"I sincerely hope not," Elizabeth said, shocked. "That would be far too soon."

"Remember, he did not waste time in pursuing the Queen," Kat reminded her.

"He will find that I am made of sterner mettle," Elizabeth said, frowning.

"Listen, my lady, I beg of you," Kat urged, resorting to desperate measures. "Your late father, King Henry of blessed memory, wanted you to marry the Admiral."

Elizabeth stared at her.

"My father wanted it? But he had no good opinion of him—I have heard people say that."

Kat was beginning to regret the lie. "Only because the Admiral was a rival for Katherine Parr," she said.

"There was more to it than that, surely," Elizabeth answered. "I heard that my father refused to let him serve on the regency council. That he did not trust him." And he was right, she thought.

"Well, maybe my information is wrong," Kat blustered, "although I know what I was told. He was good enough for a Queen, so why not for you? Why should you quibble at marrying him? It would be a good match for you, especially now. With the Queen dead, God rest her, you lack a powerful protector. As your husband, the Admiral would fill that role perfectly."

"No!" repeated Elizabeth, more sharply this time, and turned away, making it very clear that the matter was to be spoken of no more.

Kat would not give up so easily. At every opportunity, she extolled the Admiral's charms and pressed Elizabeth to accept him as a suitor.

"But he has as yet made no approach to me," the girl pointed out.

"Oh, he will, given the chance," Kat assured her, indulging in the anticipated delights of life in the wedded couple's establishment, with herself ordering all, delighting in their love for each other, rearing the children, weaving her secret fantasies about the Admiral, and growing old respected, honored, and needed.

Elizabeth wished there were someone else in the household to whom she could turn for advice, but there was no one. She wondered if she could confide in William Cecil, but then thought better of it, for as the Lord Protector's secretary, he might consider it his duty to inform his master of what might be afoot. Kat was right: She did need a protector, as armor against all the gossip and her deep-seated fear that the truth about her might come out. And she *had* accorded well with the Admiral—too well, she thought with an unwanted tremor of remembered pleasure—but that was firmly in the past now. She had found him compellingly attractive, and amusing company to boot. Given her bastard status, it would be a good match, perhaps the best she could hope for, since all past negotiations for a princely marriage for her had fallen down on account of her illegitimacy. On the other hand, she was now second in line to the throne, and greater than the Admiral might yet ask for her hand. Then, of course, she ran the risk that any other husband might discover that she was no virgin, and expose her sin to all the world. But then again, if she married Thomas Seymour, she would lay herself open once more to the dangers and miseries of pregnancy and childbirth, and that prospect terrified her.

What to do? She found herself agonizing over it, day and night.

"I *have* thought about the Admiral," she said one evening to Kat as they sat at supper. In fact, she had thought of little else these past weeks.

"And what have you thought?" Kat asked, not quite as nonchalantly as she had intended, for she was barely able to suppress her excitement.

"That I might marry him, if he asks," Elizabeth said carefully. "*Might,* I said. It would depend on several things. For a start, he has given no indication that he has any desire to wed me."

"Oh, he will," Kat chimed in, spearing a piece of roast pork on her knife. "He loves you but too well, I know it. And he is the noblest unmarried man in this land."

"You may speak truth," Elizabeth replied, considering. "But though he himself would perhaps have me, yet I think the council would not consent to it, for the council is ruled by my Lord Protector, and he is ruled by his wife, who hates my Lord Admiral for marrying the Queen. They will not let him marry the King's sister and make himself even greater thereby."

Kat looked crestfallen. She had not thought of that.

"You may be right," she said reluctantly.

"And it would be too dangerous to marry without the council's permission, as the Admiral and the Queen did," Elizabeth pointed out. "The Queen was not of royal blood. I am."

"You could wait until the King is declared of age, and then ask his permission," Kat suggested optimistically.

Elizabeth laid down her napkin and drained her goblet.

"Kat, he is eleven. We would have to wait at least four years. Can you see the Admiral doing that? No, he needs sons to succeed him, and he will need to start breeding them soon."

She sighed. "Even were he to ask for me, I do not see that a marriage between us could ever be possible."

"There must be a way," Kat said determinedly. She was not going to see her bright future blotted out.

Elizabeth stood shaking, gazing down at the sealed letter in her hand. There was no mistaking that handwriting.

"Well, aren't you going to open it?" Kat urged. They were alone in Elizabeth's bedchamber, and unlikely to be disturbed.

With trembling fingers, the girl broke the seal and unfolded the paper. The words, scripted in black ink in spidery handwriting, danced before her eyes, and it was a moment before she could make sense of them.

There were no words of love, just a formal salutation. *It is convenient for princesses to marry,* he had written, *and better it were that they are married within the realm than in any foreign place. So why might not I, a man made by the King your father, marry you? If you were to honor me with your hand, I should be the happiest man alive. I await your answer with impatience.* There was a flourishing signature at the end.

"He has asked me to marry him," Elizabeth said at length, breathing evenly to steady her pounding heart.

"What did I tell you?" Kat cried jubilantly. "You must send him your answer with all speed."

Elizabeth looked at her aghast.

"Answer? Are you mad?" she replied. "There will be no answer. I have no wish to appear too eager, and besides, he should have approached the council before proposing marriage to me."

"How do we know he has not?" Kat asked.

"We would be fools to assume he has!" Elizabeth retorted.

"But what will you do?" Kat cried, panicking lest her cherished plans fall through.

"Nothing," Elizabeth said. "Dear Kat, I know you want this for me, and to speak plain, I think I want it for myself, but if my Lord Admiral is keen enough, he will not be deterred by my silence. Mark my words, he will not go away!"

Elizabeth lay tossing in her bed, wrestling again with her impossible dilemma. She remembered still the sweet pleasure and the excitement that the Admiral's presence had aroused in her, and she yearned to feel it again, but fresher in her mind was the memory of fear and pain, the bloody miscarriage, and the specter of the Tower and the block.

Marriage to the Admiral, however—a properly sanctioned marriage—*might* make her think differently. But would even *that* have the power to banish from her mind the terrors that were now associated with wedlock and childbearing? Dare she take the risk?

William Cecil had written from the court. There was much in his letter about politics and social gossip, but Elizabeth's eye was drawn immediately to his mention of the Lord Admiral.

His ambition is plain for all to see, Cecil had written, apparently in passing. *To my mind, he is an intemperate fellow who will meet a bad end.*

Was this some kind of warning? Elizabeth wondered. But how could Cecil know what had been going on? Unless, of course—Heaven forbid!—the Admiral had been indiscreet and rumors had spread. She shivered, then hastened to take up her pen.

As to the Admiral, she wrote, after several lines deliberately devoted to responding to the other points in Cecil's letter, *I have ever thought him rash and given to foolish fancies.*

There, she thought. That should counter any speculative gossip.

"We are to visit the court at Christmas!" Elizabeth announced excitedly. "The King my brother has summoned us. In truth, I feared His Majesty had forgotten me, for I had not had word from him in many weeks."

"That's wonderful news, my lady!" Kat enthused.

"But we are not to be lodged at Whitehall, for that would not be seemly, he writes. He is not married, so there are no ladies staying at court. We are to stay at Durham House on the Strand—my father left it to me, you remember." Elizabeth was nearly bouncing with excitement. "Oh, it will be good to go to London again! I do hope my sister Mary will be at court too, for I have missed her sorely of late."

"But Durham House has been standing empty for ages," Kat pointed out. "It will need cleaning and airing at the very least."

"Then let's send Master Parry ahead with some of the servants to ensure that all is made ready," Elizabeth suggested.

"A good idea," Kat agreed. She wondered if the Admiral would also be at court for Christmas.

"I am sorry, my lady, but the Lord Protector has established a mint in Durham House," Thomas Parry said dolefully, looking distressed. Elizabeth knew him to be an honest, decent man, even if he was a bit of a busybody, and although he could be hot-tempered with lesser folk, he was also a timid one. She doubted very much that he had made any protest about the appropriation of her property.

"Did his lordship know that Durham House is mine?" she inquired.

"Oh, no, my lady," Parry said, twisting his bonnet in his hands. "He had no idea. He was most apologetic and asks Your Grace's pardon. He regrets, however, that he must crave your indulgence for a while longer, because the mint cannot easily be moved, and certainly not in time for Christmas."

"It is no matter," Elizabeth said. "I will find a lodging elsewhere." But where? she wondered. Immediately, her thoughts strayed—as they often did these days—to the Admiral, and then it came to her . . .

"We will ask my good stepfather the Admiral if he can help us!" she declared mischievously.

Kat, sitting sewing by the fire, looked up in delighted surprise.

"Master Parry, I pray you, go back to court, and ask the Admiral if he knows of any house that I can use during my visit to London," Elizabeth went on.

"Very good, madam," muttered Parry, not relishing the prospect of another cold and rain-mired journey to London in the depths of December.

"Master Parry!" cried the Admiral, clapping the Welshman on the back and steering him toward the warmth of the hearth. "You are most welcome. Take off that damp coat. Fowler! A towel for Master Parry, and hurry!" His man disappeared into the inner chamber.

Parry was looking at his surroundings. The courtier lodging occupied by the Admiral overlooked the iron-gray Thames. It was one of the better ones, naturally, for my lord was the Protector's brother and the King's uncle, and it had its own privy. There was a buffet displaying silver plate and a portrait of the late Queen Jane, the Admiral's sister, resplendent in gold damask. Parry thought her no beauty—too pale for his taste.

The Admiral gave him a cup of wine and invited him to sit down.

"What can I do for you, Master Parry?" he asked.

"I come from the Lady Elizabeth," Parry stated.

"Ah." The white teeth flashed in a grin. "I have been waiting to hear from her. I trust she is well."

"Much restored," Parry said. "She wasn't well for a long time. Fevers, you know."

"I was sorry to hear it," the Admiral said, growing slightly impatient. When would Parry come the point?

"Her Grace would visit the court for Christmas," the Welshman told him. "Durham House, where she was to lodge, is taken by the Lord Protector for a mint. My lady has sent me to ask if your lordship knows any place she could lodge in London."

The clever little minx, thought Seymour. So this is her reply to my letter: a request for help. She commits herself to nothing, and keeps me guessing. He had to admire her cunning.

"Master Parry," he said expansively, "my own house, Seymour Place, with all my furnishings and household stuff, is at my Lady Elizabeth's disposal whenever she needs it."

"That is a *most* generous offer, my lord," Parry declared, impressed.

"I have ever had a special affection for my Lady Elizabeth," the Admiral said. "The late Queen, God rest her, thought very highly of her." He sighed.

Parry frowned slightly. If rumor spoke truth, his genial host had indeed had a special affection for Elizabeth—too special by far.

"I should very much like to see her again," Seymour said. "Perhaps, when she is next at Ashridge, I could visit her, since I have estates nearby."

"I am sure that Her Grace would be pleased to receive Your Lordship," Parry told him.

"When she comes to court," the Admiral went on, "may I suggest that she asks my Lord Protector's wife to help her recover her London house. That was left to her by the late King, was it not?"

"Oh, aye," Parry confirmed.

"What other lands were assigned to her?" the Admiral wanted to know.

Parry briefly listed them.

"Has King Edward confirmed her title to them?" his host persisted.

"Not as yet," Parry answered, wondering what all this was leading to.

"Well, a word of advice," said the Admiral confidentially. "Her Grace might also ask the Duchess of Somerset to assist her in exchanging those lands for estates in the West Country, near to my castle of Sudeley. I myself will put in a good word on her behalf. Now how many servants does she have?"

This was beginning to feel like an interrogation, Parry felt, doing a quick reckoning in his head.

"Ten," he said.

"And how much does she spend on household expenses?"

"Her Grace is careful with money, my lord. I myself keep her accounts." He mentioned a few figures.

"Ah, I think I can improve on those," said the Admiral confidently. "I make various economies in my own household, and I should be happy to pass on the benefit of my experience, if it would help."

"I am flattered that your lordship should condescend to assist me," Parry said sincerely.

"Perhaps I should say that I am thinking ahead to a time when our two households may become one," divulged the Admiral with a wink. Immediately, Parry understood and approved. To his mind, his young lady could not do better than match herself with the Admiral, a true gentleman to be sure, whatever people might say about him.

As Parry's horse trotted toward the gatehouse archway at Hatfield, he espied the Lady Elizabeth, wrapped in a fur-lined cloak, walking through the park with her dogs.

"My lady!" he cried, pulling up and dismounting. Elizabeth waved and quickened her pace toward him, the dogs yapping about her skirts.

"Well met, Master Parry! Did you see my Lord Admiral?" she called.

"Aye, and he has been most accommodating. He says that Seymour House is at your disposal whenever you need it."

"That is uncommonly kind of him!" Elizabeth cried, clapping her hands. Her cheeks were flushed, and not just with cold or exertion. "I will write to thank him."

"His lordship spoke of more than lodgings," Parry said.

Elizabeth stared at him, a little breathless.

"He did?" she asked.

"He asked about your estates and your expenditure—I will explain all later. But he said this was against a time when your two households would be one. Do you take his meaning, madam?"

"I know that the Admiral wants to marry me," she said, happy to confide in Parry, whose loyalty and devotion were unquestionable.

"In truth, my lady, you could not have a better offer," the Welshman assured her. "He is a most kind and thoughtful gentleman, and has your true interests at heart. In my humble opinion, this would be a good marriage for you, if the council is agreeable, of course."

Elizabeth's manner changed subtly.

"*If* the council is agreeable," she said coolly. "When that comes to pass, I will do as God shall put into my mind."

She turned and walked a little way off, rubbing her hands to keep them warm. She knew she was wavering in her resolve, and she could not understand herself. She loved the Admiral, did she not? She certainly basked in his admiration and enjoyed flirting with him. And she had been flattered as well as disturbed by his proposal of marriage. Yet when it came to committing herself, she found she could not do it. She blew hot, then cold. It made no sense to her. Mayhap the disastrous consequences of their one coupling had had a more damaging effect on her than she realized. Or was it that she knew in her bones that this marriage would never be allowed to take place—that she was courting danger even in contemplating it?

She had been eager to hear of the Admiral's response to her request. Yet as soon as Parry had pointed out the advantages of their marriage, her excitement had vanished and been replaced by fear—yes, that was it, fear. And a touch of anger too, for she was beginning to suspect that the Admiral had put Parry up to urging her to accept his suit.

Parry was still standing where she had left him, huddled in his cloak. She made her way back to him.

"Who bade you tell me to accept the Admiral's offer of marriage?" she demanded to know.

"Why, no one, my lady," Parry answered. "I merely gained the impression that my lord would make you a good husband. He *is* in earnest, you know. He even suggested that you exchange your dower lands for others that lie near his in the West Country."

"Did he indeed!" Elizabeth cried, outraged. "What does he mean by such a suggestion? Does he ask for my hand just to get his own on my property?"

"I know not, my lady," protested Parry, flustered, "but I am sure he looks to have you above all else."

"What else did he say?" Elizabeth asked suspiciously.

"He suggested you make suit to the Protector's wife for help in exchanging your lands and in recovering Durham House," Parry ventured unwillingly.

"I will not be a suitor to that insufferable woman for favors," Elizabeth fumed. "When next you see the Admiral, you may tell him I will have nothing to do with her. And now I think you should go and tell Mrs. Astley all that transpired when you met the Admiral, for I wish to know nothing that she does not know. I cannot be at peace until you have told it all to her."

No one, she thought, as a chastened Parry remounted and rode off, must ever have cause to accuse her of secretly conspiring with the Admiral through her cofferer.

Elizabeth returned to the house to find William Cecil waiting for her with some documents to sign.

"I could not resist the opportunity of bringing them in person, my lady," he said, bowing. "I have long wished to meet you."

Elizabeth was impressed with this fair-haired, fork-bearded gentleman with sharp, intense eyes and a large hooked nose. He exuded integrity and strength. Instinctively, she felt she could trust him. And that was proved later that day when, shortly before he left, she ventured to broach with him the subject of the Admiral.

"I need your advice, Master Cecil," she said as they strolled together in the long gallery admiring the portraits that hung there. He waited for her to go on. "You will remember that, in our letters, we mentioned my Lord Admiral in passing. Lately, he has offered his help in exchanging my dower estates for others." She did not mention that those other lands were to be near Sudeley. "And he has offered to help Master Parry make economies in the running of my household."

Cecil, who had heard much that he did not like about the Admiral, and scurrilous rumors linking the rogue's name to Elizabeth's, immediately smelled a rat. The Protector had dismissed the rumors as mere gossip, but Cecil himself privately suspected that Elizabeth had indeed been compromised in some way, and was determined to protect her. Should anything happen to King Edward—God forfend—then Elizabeth was the Protestant hope for the future, and because of that, he, Cecil, was prepared to lay down his life for her if need be.

"May I offer you some advice, my lady?" he asked. "Do not allow the Admiral to interfere in your financial affairs. It would not be wise. I do not judge him the most reliable of men."

Elizabeth was silent for a moment.

"Why do you say that?" she inquired.

"I work for his brother." Cecil smiled. "He knows him better than any other, and he has not as yet entrusted him with any political office. Neither did your esteemed father, King Henry. Who am I to question the wisdom of two such eminent statesmen?"

Elizabeth said carefully, "Yet the Admiral is at the center of affairs, it would seem."

"He likes to think he is," Cecil replied, "but his greatness is largely in his own mind. It would not be wise to become too embroiled with him, my lady. I assure you, I speak purely for your own good."

"I thank you for your advice," Elizabeth said, relieved, yet a little downcast all the same.

When William Cecil had gone, she pleaded a headache and went to bed early, needing to think. She felt weary of it all, weary of her seesawing emotions, weary of thinking up strategies to ensure that the marriage could go ahead, weary of all the intrigue and furtiveness. And now it appeared that the Admiral was not all that he seemed.

Leave it, she thought. Leave it to God—and the council. She could only marry the Admiral with the latter's consent, she saw that clearly now. So let the Admiral approach the council and let *them* decide her fate.

If they said no, she would not defy them. Having escaped danger once, so recently, she had no mind to court it again.

In the middle of December, Kat arrived in London to oversee the ordering of Seymour House for Elizabeth's stay. There, she found in residence Lady Tyrwhit, a distant cousin of Queen Katherine. Kat took an instant dislike to the woman, a sour-faced, middle-aged matron who looked as if she had a permanent smell under her nose—and an insufferable snob too.

"Who are *you*?" she inquired haughtily after Kat had been announced.

"I am the Lady Elizabeth's governess," Kat bristled, "and I am come to make all ready for her."

"Oh, yes, I remember you now. Well, I shall be gone soon. My husband being at court, I am invited to spend Christmas at Somerset House with the Duchess." She eyed Kat closely, her light blue eyes narrowing.

"You do know what they are saying about the Lady Elizabeth and the Admiral?" she asked.

Kat was instantly on her guard. "*What* are they saying?" she barked.

"That a marriage is in the air," Lady Tyrwhit told her. "He has kept on the late Queen's maids-of-honor in his household, and people are concluding that it is for my Lady Elizabeth's benefit. There is much talk that he will soon be paying court to her."

"It's mere nonsense, this idle gossip," Kat declared firmly, although inwardly she was rejoicing at this welcome evidence of the Admiral's intentions. "She cannot marry without the council's consent."

"Exactly," Lady Tyrwhit emphasized. "But there is talk of clandestine arrangements . . . it's probably just a rumor, as you say. But I thought that, as her governess, you should know what is being bruited, so that you can be on your guard."

"I thank you," muttered Kat through gritted teeth.

She was heartily relieved when Lady Tyrwhit packed her bags and left two days later, then dismayed, only hours after that, to receive a summons to Somerset House. There, in a palatial room with carved pillars and a battened ceiling picked out in gold, the Duchess Anne awaited her, granite-faced, imperious, and extremely angry.

"I am hearing things that concern me greatly," she began in her overbearing way, keeping Kat standing before her. "There is unsavory gossip at court *and* in the City about my Lady Elizabeth and the Admiral."

Kat felt a chill of fear. Who had talked? More crucially, what had they said?

"What gossip?" she asked.

"That he was overfamiliar with her when she was in the Queen's household. That *you* encouraged it—"

"That is not true, madam!" Kat interrupted, indignant.

"Silence!" thundered the Duchess. "I have not yet finished speaking. I am told that you encouraged this familiarity simply by not doing enough to put a stop to it. Do you deny that?"

"I was worried. I went to the Queen and asked for her help," Kat protested. "But she did not take it seriously, and neither should you, madam, for it was all innocent." And may God forgive me the lie, she prayed.

"Mrs. Astley," hissed the Duchess, "I may as well tell you that a lot of people *are* taking it seriously. Servants have talked, and as a result, the Lady Elizabeth—the King's own sister—has become the subject of common gossip. It is said that you left her and the Admiral alone together in her bedchamber."

"There *were* one or two occasions when he came early, and I was not aware he was there, but he would not heed me when I begged him to desist," Kat explained defensively. "That was when I spoke to the Queen." But the Duchess was implacable.

"I heard rather differently. It strikes me, Mrs. Astley, that you are not worthy to have the governance of a king's daughter!" she hissed. "I have decided that another shall have your place. Now go, for the sight of you offends me."

Kat turned, her eyes blurred with tears of anger and shame, and almost ran from the Duchess's presence, knowing that this terrible woman, being the Lord Protector's wife, did indeed have the power to remove her from her post. She was shaking with the unjustness of it, and with dread in case the Duchess carried out her threat. She could not bear the thought of being torn apart from Elizabeth, who was as flesh and blood to her, and the very focus of her existence.

Worse than that prospect, though, was the realization that they were all in danger. If any hint of what had really gone on ever got out, their enemies—and to be sure, the Duchess was one—would pounce. Then it would be the Tower, and the block, and no mercy shown.

Back at Seymour House, Kat brushed aside the servants who came asking her for instructions. She was too agitated to listen to them, being consumed with an overwhelming need to get back to Hatfield. If she could entrench herself there, she thought irrationally, she could preempt disaster. Elizabeth, she knew, would never consent to being deprived of the woman who had been like a mother to her since early childhood.

Grabbing a few things, she stuffed them into a bag and shouted for the grooms to harness the horses to a litter. Then she hastened out of the house.

On the journey north, she had time to reflect. She saw that she had been wrong in urging Elizabeth to marry the Admiral. She should never have meddled in such a dangerous matter. It was true, she should have been firmer at Chelsea, but she had had her reasons for dithering—shocking as they seemed to her now, for she was painfully aware that she had allowed her jealousy of the Queen and her infatuation with the Admiral to color her judgment. And then when she *had* tried to put a stop to the frolics, it had been too late. Maybe she was even indirectly responsible for Elizabeth's fall from grace.

The Duchess was right, she wasn't fit to have the care of a king's daughter—but the Duchess, of course, didn't know the half of it. No one should ever know that, Kat vowed. But what of the Dennys? Would they talk? And that midwife? Yet why should they? If no one suspected anything, no one would ask any questions. And even if they were tempted to reveal anything, they risked censure or worse for having concealed the truth. Elizabeth's secret was safe, quite safe, she was sure.

"You are back early," Elizabeth said, embracing Kat. Then she saw her governess's face. It looked . . . haggard, haunted. "What is wrong, dear Kat?"

"There is gossip in London, about you and the Admiral," Kat blurted out.

Elizabeth paled. "What gossip?"

"There is talk of your marriage," Kat told her. "He has rashly kept the Queen's maids in his household—to wait on you, when you are his wife, it is said. I fear he has been most indiscreet."

"Did you hear anything else?" Elizabeth asked. Her frightened eyes met Kat's.

"No, nothing more," Kat said briskly. "But what I *have* heard has convinced me that now is not the time for you to think of marriage with the Admiral. Without doubt, such a thing will not be possible until the King comes of age. It is clear as day that the Lord Protector and the council would never suffer you to marry my lord. Therefore, child, it would be better if you did not set your mind on this marriage, seeing the unlikelihood of it."

Elizabeth relaxed a little.

"Fear not, Kat," she said. "I had already come to that opinion myself. I have thought long and hard on it, and I am well aware of what is at stake."

"I thank God for your good sense," Kat told her, feeling somewhat calmer.

"Do not worry, I will stick to my resolve," the girl assured her.

Yes, but will I? Kat asked herself. I had so wanted this for her. For us all.

"Maybe it would be prudent not to go to London after all," Elizabeth said. "Give the rumors time to die down. If I stay here at Hatfield, unwed and living a virtuous existence, that should give the lie to them."

"I think that might be for the best," Kat agreed.

"So are you feeling better now that we have agreed on that, my dear governess?" Elizabeth asked.

"Somewhat amended," Kat lied. Any minute, any day, the order for her dismissal might come. She did not have it in her heart to tell Elizabeth that. And anyway, she was hoping and praying she would never have to, that the Duchess would relent and spare her the agony of being parted from her beloved charge.

CHAPTER 15

1549

On the eve of Twelfth Night, Kat Astley and Thomas Parry sat by the fire sharing a pitcher of mead.

"I wonder when the Admiral will press his suit," Parry said. "I have noticed that there is much goodwill between him and Her Grace."

"I know that well enough," Kat replied, "but I dare not speak of it anymore." Haltingly, painfully, she explained about the Duchess's threat. "All the same," she added, "I have a great affection for the Admiral, who has ever been very good to me, and is the most magnificent lord, you must agree; and I was so pleased when I learned he wanted my lady for his wife." Her eyes brimmed with tears. "I wish her his wife of all men living!" she sobbed, burying her face in her hands. "I am sure he might persuade the council if he tried."

Parry awkwardly reached over and patted her hand. "You're too taken with a handsome face, Kat," he said, not unkindly. "No, let me finish. I'm not so sure about the Admiral now. He has tarried too long in this matter, and that is why people are talking. Thanks to his tardiness, the Lady Elizabeth's reputation is blotted. And only the other day, I heard someone saying that he had treated his poor wife cruelly and dishonestly."

"Tush! Tush!" Kat cried. "I know him better than you do, or those that speak evil of him. I know he is eager to marry my Lady Elizabeth, and *she* knows that well enough. He loves her well, and has done for a long time. I *must* tell you that the Queen was jealous of the Admiral's affection for my lady. She confided to me that she found them together in an embrace. *That's* why Elizabeth was sent to Cheshunt."

Parry's jaw dropped.

"So the rumors are true?" he asked, visibly shocked. "There *was* some undue familiarity between them?"

Seeing his reaction, Kat was horrified at herself for having said too much. She wished she had bitten her tongue out; it would be her downfall, she knew.

"I cannot say any more," she said fretfully. "I will enlarge on this another time. Thomas, you must promise never to repeat to anyone what I have told you."

"I won't," Parry said. "You know that."

"Promise me!" Kat urged.

"I won't say anything," he repeated.

"Say 'I promise,' *do*," she begged.

"Very well, I promise I won't repeat what you told me," he declared.

"That is as well," she told him, "for if this got out, Her Grace would be dishonored forever, and utterly undone."

"I would rather be torn apart by wild horses," Parry assured her.

The Admiral stood before his brother, simmering with anger. How dare Ned summon him here like an errant schoolboy?

The Protector was brief and to the point.

"I am told that you have spoken of visiting the Lady Elizabeth at Ashridge," he said accusingly.

"Is it now illegal to visit one's stepdaughter?" the Admiral sneered.

"The word is that you hope to marry her," Ned said coolly.

Seymour laughed mirthlessly. "I? Marry Old Harry's daughter? You must take me for a fool."

"A fool who retains his late wife's maids so that they may serve a new bride. A fool who has made inquiries as to the Lady Elizabeth's fortune. A fool who, if rumor speaks truth, chased after her when the Queen was alive. Shall I go on?"

"It ill becomes you, the Lord Protector of England, to heed common gossip," the Admiral retorted. "And that's all it is, gossip."

"Often, little brother, there is no smoke without fire," Somerset reminded him. Then his manner turned glacial. "I warn you, Tom, if you go anywhere near her, I will send you to the Tower."

"I'd like to see you try," Tom flung at him, then stamped out of the room. "I'll see you in Hell first!"

"Lord save us! The Admiral is in the Tower!" cried Kat, running through Elizabeth's apartments as if the devil were at her heels.

"No!" faltered Elizabeth, rising to her feet, pale with shock. She had been working on a translation with Master Ascham, recently returned from Cambridge at her request to further her studies, and he too looked shaken by the news.

"Where did you hear this?" he asked Kat.

"John, my husband," she said, breathlessly. "He went to London on estate business, and he heard it bruited there. People are talking about nothing else. As soon as he had the story, he raced back here as fast as he could. Oh, what is to become of us?" She could not contain her distress.

"What happened?" Ascham pressed her.

"It seems the Admiral was involved in a plot to overthrow the Lord Protector, a very dangerous and foolish enterprise, from what I hear. But that was not all. Three nights ago, he broke into the King's bedchamber at Hampton Court, intending God knows what mischief."

"But how did he get past the guards?" Ascham interrupted.

"It is said he had a forged key to the door from the privy garden. But the King's dog, a good guard dog, barked loudly, and before the Yeomen of the Guard came running, the Admiral shot the dog dead with his pistol. They arrested him on a charge of attempting to murder the King."

"That's preposterous," Ascham commented. "If he wanted to usurp his brother's place as Lord Protector, he would wish to preserve the King's life, surely. Unless, of course, he was plotting to marry the Lady Mary and seize the throne. But she is a Catholic, so that is unlikely."

While they talked, Elizabeth had sat there silently, desperately trying to take in the news and calculating how it might affect her. At the same time, she was aware of a great void where her grief for the Admiral should be. For if these charges were to be proved true, he was a dead man, this man who was to have been her husband. Surely she should be in terror for him, beating her breast and weeping her heart out. But no. Suddenly, in the light of what had just happened, she saw him as a rash, shallow fellow who cared for nothing and no one but himself, and who had brought her nothing but troubles. Suddenly, she recognized her feelings for him as mere infatuation.

Her terror now was all for herself, for if they interrogated the Admiral, as they surely would—not to mention those who had had dealings with him—her own name might well be dragged into the mire with his. And it was clear there was far more to his schemes than she had ever suspected.

"He did not intend to marry the Lady Mary," she said. "He meant to have me. I thought it was because he loved me." Her voice broke. "And now I see he might have compassed a greater treason through that marriage."

Kat wrapped loving arms around her, but Elizabeth would not be comforted.

"They will question us," she said bleakly. "We must be prepared."

"It may not come to that," Ascham said, without much conviction.

"I fear it will," Elizabeth insisted. "We must all stay firm and admit nothing."

The next day, Elizabeth and Kat were passing through the great hall when they heard the clatter of many hooves approaching. Seconds later, to their astonishment, Thomas Parry crashed through the main door, his face puce, his bonnet askew.

"I would I had never been born, for we are all undone!" he cried, wringing his hands. "You may have these back, my lady!" And so saying, he tore his chain of office from his neck, pulled the signet ring from his finger, then threw them on the floor and dashed toward the stairs that led to the chamber he shared with his wife. Elizabeth stared after him gaping; Kat clapped her hand over her mouth and whimpered.

Almost immediately, in the open doorway, there appeared a group of finely dressed gentlemen. Elizabeth, collecting her wits, recognized them as members of the council. At their head was William Paulet, Lord St.

John, Great Master of the King's Household, and behind him there was . . . Oh, no, she thought. Her face visibly fell when she saw Sir Anthony Denny, stiff-faced in his somber black; he, more than anyone, she feared. With him was Sir Robert Tyrwhit, husband to the late Queen's cousin, of whom Kat had spoken so disparagingly—Kat, who was now gazing at their visitors in mute horror.

Remembering her rank, Elizabeth drew herself up to her full height and clasped her hands composedly at her waist. Belatedly, the councillors bowed.

"Gentlemen, greetings," she said, trying to keep her voice steady. "To what do I owe the pleasure of your visit?"

"Your Grace, I fear we can take little pleasure in the task before us," Lord Paulet told her, watching her closely. "You will have heard, I expect, that the Admiral is in the Tower on a charge of high treason. It is our sorry duty to question all those who have had dealings with him. We must crave your cooperation, for some are members of Your Grace's household."

"My house is at your disposal," Elizabeth told him. "Will you sup before you begin?"

"I thank you, madam, but we stopped at an inn on the road. We must proceed as soon as possible, and begin with Your Grace. Is there somewhere Sir Robert and Sir Anthony can talk with you in private?"

"The schoolroom is empty," Elizabeth told him, her spirits plummeting further. "Mrs. Astley here will see that we are not disturbed."

"I wish to question Mrs. Astley myself in the meantime," Paulet told her. "There are guards with us who will ensure we are not interrupted."

Elizabeth's heart began thumping. Guards? She looked hard at Kat, as if steeling the governess to discretion, but Kat seemed frozen with fear.

"Please use the parlor," she told Paulet.

"My lady," said Sir Anthony, indicating that she should precede him and Sir Robert to the schoolroom. "Please lead the way." Elizabeth turned toward the stairs, marveling that her legs could still carry her.

Seated at the table before the mullioned window, she hoped she looked the picture of youthful innocence in her demure blue velvet gown, blue being the color of virginity, and unbound copper tresses, her loose hair betokening not only royal rank but the maiden state. Denny and Tyrwhit—a thin-faced, unsmiling ferret of a man, huddled in his furs—took the chairs opposite. How much did Tyrwhit know? she wondered. Had Denny betrayed her already? If so, why go through this charade?

"Tell us about your relationship with the Admiral," said Denny without preamble.

"He was a kindly stepfather to me while I was in the Queen's household," she said.

"Too kindly, if rumor speaks truth," Sir Anthony replied, gazing at her fixedly. "I am told that he led you to indulge in unseemly behavior." Elizabeth made herself smile.

"The Admiral has a wicked sense of humor," she said. "He was always jesting. I was but a child, and he played silly games with me."

"It is said that these games got out of hand," Denny said.

"Yes, that was what Mrs. Astley thought, mistakenly, of course, but you see, she has always been overprotective of me." She smiled wryly. "She even complained to the Queen, but Her Grace wisely made little of it. She knew these games were but harmless sport, with nothing evil intended. She used to join in herself sometimes."

"I see," said Sir Anthony, who saw a lot more but forbore to say anything compromising. Changing tack, he asked, "Has the Admiral ever proposed marriage to you?"

"He wrote to me suggesting it, late last year. I did not reply. I was waiting for him to approach the council. For my part, I was resolved to be guided by the council in all things."

"Did he ever speak to you of overthrowing the Lord Protector?" Denny inquired.

"Never," said Elizabeth.

"When he proposed marriage"—this was Tyrwhit—"did he ever hint that he proposed to make you Queen?"

Elizabeth looked suitably startled. "No," she said.

"I think you know more than you are willing to tell us," Tyrwhit persisted.

"You are mistaken, sir," Elizabeth protested. "I have told you what I know, and will answer any other questions you have to the best of my ability."

"Robert, I pray you allow me to continue this initial investigation," Denny said. "Time presses, and there is Master Parry to be interrogated."

Sir Robert rose, his chair scraping the floor. "Of course," he said. "My lady." He sketched a bow and left the room. The door clicked shut.

"Now, madam," said Sir Anthony, turning to Elizabeth, "you and I have matters to discuss."

Elizabeth said nothing. The silence was punctuated by a log crackling on the hearth.

"I promise you that I have not betrayed you," he told her, shifting in his seat. "If anyone reveals what really happened at Cheshunt, I will say that I was there and that all you suffered was an intermittent fever. The only other people who know the truth are my wife, Mrs. Astley, and the midwife who attended. I do not think the midwife poses a risk—she was brought blindfolded to the house. My wife will say as I instruct her. That leaves Mrs. Astley. If she admits anything, I will dismiss it as nonsense, and suggest that she has cracked under questioning and is making it up. I was at Cheshunt at the time, after all, and my testimony will carry greater weight than hers."

"Why are you covering up for me, Sir Anthony?" Elizabeth asked, astounded. He looked gravely at her.

"My lady, although I cannot but deplore your fall from grace, I served your father and I serve your brother. I am loyal to the House of Tudor, and I am a devout Protestant, like yourself. You are King Henry's daughter, and should any evil hap befall King Edward, those who follow God's word will look to you as the preserver and defender of true religion within this realm. So I will say nothing to place you in jeopardy. For my brethren on the council, I cannot speak. Some would bring you down— they are not very farsighted, I fear. So it is up to you now. You must shift for yourself as best you can."

Gratitude welled up in Elizabeth's heart. She would never have expected to find such a staunch ally in this correct and unbending lawyer.

"I can never thank you sufficiently," she said, weak with relief. "And I hope you do not think too unkindly of me. I was but fourteen, and inexperienced in the ways of the world."

"It is those who have had the care of you that are to blame," said Sir Anthony sternly. "And now, I must return to London. Make no mistake, you are not out of danger yet. Use your mother wit to escape it. I wish you well."

He rose and bowed, still stiff and awkward in her presence, then was gone before she could utter further words of thanks.

—

When Elizabeth returned to her privy apartments, she found them deserted apart from two maids who were standing there looking rather frightened, and Blanche Parry.

"I've been looking for you, my lady," she said, in her lilting Welsh voice. "Everyone is summoned to the great hall."

"Then we had best go down," Elizabeth told her.

Sir Robert Tyrwhit had gathered the whole household together. Striving to stay calm, Elizabeth took her seat on the dais, and when the last stragglers had come scurrying in, he stood beside her and addressed them all.

"I am to tell you that the Lord Admiral has been committed to the Tower on a charge of high treason," he began in his reedy voice. "He has plotted to overthrow the Lord Protector, his brother; he intrigued to marry his ward, the Lady Jane Grey, to the King; and most heinous of all, he schemed to take the Lady Elizabeth here to wife, and purposed to rule the kingdom himself."

There were gasps and murmurs of shock and disapproval. Sir Robert held up his hand. "All here will be questioned. If you know nothing of these high matters, you have nothing to fear. But there are some among you who have acted rashly. Mrs. Astley and Master Parry have been arrested and taken to London by Sir Anthony Denny for interrogation." Elizabeth flinched, aghast at this news, then forced herself to look impassive, even though she was near to tears.

"In their absence," Tyrwhit continued, "the council has deputed me, Sir Robert Tyrwhit, to take charge of the Lady Elizabeth's household. You will take your orders from me now. That is all. You may disperse to your tasks."

As the servants scattered in their several directions, murmuring fearfully of what they had heard, Sir Robert turned to Elizabeth.

"I regret to inform you, madam, that Mrs. Astley and Master Parry are being committed to the Tower," he told her in a low voice. Elizabeth found she could not speak. She buried her face in her hands and let the tears run through her fingers, staying there weeping silently for a long time, with Sir Robert standing impassively by.

"I beg of you, set them free, they are as innocent as I am," she sobbed at length.

"I'm afraid I cannot do that," he replied. "And their innocence, like yours, is yet to be proved."

"I was under the impression that it was guilt that had to be proved," Elizabeth said sharply, dabbing at her eyes. "Have they confessed anything?"

"I think you should rest, madam," Tyrwhit said, ignoring her question. "I will talk with you again when you have composed yourself."

Reluctantly, Elizabeth rose.

"Attend to your mistress," he instructed Blanche Parry, who was hovering at the edge of the dais.

"I go now," said Lord Paulet, pulling on his gloves. "Are you content to remain here in charge of this investigation?"

"Yes, my lord." Tyrwhit nodded.

"Do your best to obtain more evidence of treason; I make no doubt you will find it here. The Protector wants a watertight case before he sees his brother executed."

"How far am I to press my Lady Elizabeth?" Tyrwhit wanted to know.

"As far as you like. Let her stew for a while," Paulet advised. "Leave her be for a day or so, give her time to consider. I am sure she has much to tell us."

"And if she incriminates herself? She is His Majesty's sister, after all."

"That will depend. If she admits to the alleged immorality, or even to compassing marriage, then persuade her to lay the blame on her servants, Astley and Parry. But if you uncover evidence that she was a party to the Admiral's treason, then the law must take its course. The council would have no alternative but to enforce it, if justice is to be served."

Sir Robert pulled at his beard, frowning. "And the penalty?"

"Death by beheading or burning," replied Paulet with a grim look.

Elizabeth tried desperately to concentrate on her books, but she was aware that not far off, her people were being interrogated, one by one. Those servants who attended her were subdued, nervous, and clearly frightened to enter into conversation with her. Only Blanche Parry, dear, faithful Blanche, seemed happy to keep her company. Blanche had stayed with her throughout the past two days, sleeping on a pallet in her chamber, serving her meals and acting as her tire-woman. Of course, Blanche was not Kat—no one could ever replace Kat, whom she was missing and fretting about dreadfully—but her presence was a calming one.

It was strange that Sir Robert had not summoned her back for questioning. Since they had spoken in the great hall, she had not seen him. She had remained in her apartments, going through the motions of daily life and expecting any minute to be called to his presence, but he had sent no word. That worried her. Only by talking to him could she divine any sense of what people were saying about her—and this she was desperate to know. Surely, if anyone had said anything against her, he would have asked her about it. Surely he would. It was the not knowing what was happening that was eating at her.

In the end, she could bear the suspense no longer.

"Go to Sir Robert," she ordered Blanche, "and tell him that I have remembered certain matters that I forgot to tell Sir Anthony Denny. Hurry now."

An hour later, there was a knock on her door, and Sir Robert entered. Elizabeth remained seated and bestowed on him a regal nod.

"Madam, you have something to tell me?" he inquired.

"Yes," she said. "I recalled that I wrote several letters to the Admiral about everyday matters. One was to ask for his help in recovering Durham House from the Lord Protector. And then I remembered that, when Mrs. Astley went to London, she heard gossip that the Admiral hoped to marry me, so she wrote to him asking him not to visit me for fear of suspicion."

"Is that all, my lady?" Tyrwhit asked, a touch irritably. "I think you must have more to tell me."

"In truth, sir, I cannot think of anything else," Elizabeth said innocently.

"Madam, think of your honor, and the peril that might ensue from your failure to disclose pertinent facts. You are but a subject, and bound by the laws of this realm. We know that the Admiral behaved dishonorably toward you and that Mrs. Astley did little to prevent him—rather, she seems to have encouraged him. What a meddlesome woman she is. Look, madam, if you will be open with us about what happened, no blame will attach to you. All evil and shame will be imputed to Mrs. Astley and Master Parry. His Majesty and the council will take into account your youth, and be merciful."

"Mrs. Astley and Master Parry did nothing evil or shameful," Elizabeth replied firmly, determined to protect her servants. "I will not accuse them falsely just to please you."

"Madam, I do see in your face that you bear some guilt," Tyrwhit challenged.

"Then you must have something wrong with your eyesight, sir," Elizabeth retorted spiritedly. "I have nothing to confess to you, for there *is* nothing to confess."

"But there was some secret understanding between you and the Admiral that you would marry?" Sir Robert persisted, ignoring the jibe.

"There was never any such understanding," Elizabeth stated.

"Did Mrs. Astley suggest that you consider such a marriage seriously?"

"No," she lied. "And *I* would never consider marrying anyone without the express consent of His Majesty and his council; nor would Mrs. Astley or Master Parry have expected me to marry the Admiral without such consent."

Sir Robert looked at her, sitting there so self-possessed and calm. Oh, you are a clever one, he thought. Yet you will not best me in the end.

"Well, we shall talk of this more anon," he said, preparing to leave her. "Astley and Parry are being questioned in the Tower, even as we speak, so no doubt we shall have a great deal to discuss at our next meeting."

"I doubt that very much, sir," Elizabeth declared defiantly.

The next day, Sir Robert was back. Maddeningly, he did not say if he had had word from the Tower. Elizabeth was in an agony of suspense, wondering what was happening in that fortress of ill repute. She had never visited the Tower, so she could only imagine it, but knowing what had happened to her mother there, and to Katherine Howard, she always thought of it as a horrible place where lives were snuffed out and dreadful tortures applied. The Admiral was languishing there now, and she had lain awake all last night wondering what was happening to her dear Kat and good Master Parry . . . She feared that their interrogators would not be so nice in their methods of questioning. And was poor Kat shivering in a dank dungeon? She could not bear to think of it. It was all she could do to keep her own head in the face of this danger.

Sir Robert sat down at the table, uninvited. Elizabeth closed her book slowly.

"Come on now, madam, let's have the truth," he said. "Confess that you agreed to marry the Admiral."

"I cannot confess to something I never did," she pointed out.

"He seems to think you were willing," Tyrwhit offered.

"He was ever in hope," she said. "I did not encourage him."

"But you did consider the matter."

"I talked about it with Master Parry and Mrs. Astley after Parry had visited the Admiral in London, but as a possibility only."

"Yet you approached the Admiral and asked him to lend you his London house."

"He is my stepfather," Elizabeth said. "My own house was taken by his brother, my Lord Protector. I did not know who else to ask for help with finding accommodation. I but wanted to be able to visit my brother the King at Christmas."

"Hmm," murmured Tyrwhit. "You have a good wit."

"I have need of it, when you twist everything I say," she retorted.

"I am trying to help you," he said. "You are young. No one will blame you for behaving rashly. It is the Admiral whose guilt we seek to prove."

"Then you must ask elsewhere, for I was not a party to it," Elizabeth declared.

It had been going on for a week now, and she had not broken under the pressure of questioning, or betrayed her servants. Still she did not know what was being said about her in the Tower, but the fact that Sir Robert kept going over the same ground with her gave her hope that neither Kat nor Parry had revealed too much.

Sir Robert was becoming increasingly irritated; it was clear that he really believed she was concealing something. Today he looked haggard and peeved.

"Do you know what people are saying about you?" he asked. "They are saying that you also are in the Tower because you are with child by the Admiral."

"How dare they!" Elizabeth cried, shocked into an outburst. This was far too close to home for comfort. "These are shameful slanders!" It grieved her that the people should think ill of her.

"Well, unless you tell us the truth, men will come to all manner of rash conclusions," Tyrwhit said.

"I *have* told you the truth," Elizabeth stormed.

For answer, he took a letter from his pocket. "The Protector sent this for you. In it, he urges you, as your earnest friend, to disclose everything you know."

"Which I have done," she retorted. "But thank my lord anyway for his consideration. To be truthful, I am more concerned about the slurs on my honor that are bruited about, for they are shameful slanders. I will write to his lordship, desiring him to declare publicly that these tales are but lies, wicked lies about His Majesty's own sister! I beg of you, Sir Robert, ask the Protector if I may appear at court, so that I may show the world that I am not with child."

"I will relay your request to the Protector," Tyrwhit said, "but he will look more favorably on it if you were to admit that you and Mrs. Astley agreed that you should marry the Admiral."

Elizabeth sighed. "How can I do that? We never agreed any such thing, and Mrs. Astley would never have had me marry anyone without the consent of the King's Majesty and the council. Sir Robert, I say this on my conscience, which I would not put in jeopardy, for I have a soul to save."

Tyrwhit, impressed despite himself, gave up for the moment. But he was to return, day after day, and try every tactic he knew of—persuasion, bullying, threats—to make Elizabeth confess. And every day, he found himself getting nowhere.

Until the day came when a large scroll of depositions arrived from the Tower. Then his fortunes changed.

When next Sir Robert came to her chamber, he had a triumphant look about him.

"Read these, my lady," he said, almost pleasantly, laying the parchments before her.

Elizabeth read them. They were depositions made by Kat and Master Parry, and bore their signatures—in straggling handwriting that betrayed their turmoil and fear. Her heart began thudding, and she felt faint. They had revealed everything that had happened—the morning romps, in increasingly shameful detail, the Admiral's shameless pursuit of Elizabeth, the cutting of her gown, the Queen finding them both in a compromising situation, Elizabeth's banishment, and—more recently—the Admiral's scheming to marry her. Mercifully, there was no mention of her lost child, but there was more than enough to ruin her reputation. Her cheeks burned with shame. She wished she could dissolve into a void. She could not catch her breath.

"Sordid reading, my lady, is it not?" Sir Robert observed. He had been watching her closely.

Elizabeth found her voice. "As you said, my lord, I was young, and swayed by a practiced rogue."

"Even so, you should have been mindful of your honor," he rapped at her. "You are a princess of the blood."

"That I know, sir, and I *was* mindful, to my limited power. It was the Admiral's conduct that was sordid, not mine. I committed no treason. There is nothing here that can incriminate me, for I never plotted or consented to marry the Admiral. Nor has Mrs. Astley committed any crime. She may have been foolish and indiscreet, but that was all."

"Oh, you are clever, madam," Tyrwhit declared, maddened at her evasiveness. "But I will tell you this: I am still of the opinion that you and Mrs. Astley have more to tell us, that you have not revealed all you know. As for Master Parry, he is a worthless sort, a spineless man of straw. We shall certainly be hearing more from him."

A man of straw indeed, Elizabeth reflected bitterly, recalling how Parry had sworn he would rather be torn apart by wild horses than betray her. Yet she could not find it in her heart to condemn him. She knew it would matter much to him, making such a promise and then breaking it through fear.

"How dare you malign him!" Elizabeth retorted, furious. "I dread to think how they extracted that confession from him."

"I assure you that very little pressure was required," Tyrwhit revealed. "He and Mrs. Astley suffered a short spell in the Tower's dungeons, then they were brought face-to-face. Oh, they talked! And they will talk again, mark my words. You all sing the same song, but you had obviously decided on the note beforehand. You will change your tune soon enough."

Elizabeth shot him a withering look. She could not rid her mind of her faithful servants, incarcerated in freezing, dark dungeons.

"I shall require you to make your own deposition," Sir Robert told her. "I will return tomorrow."

Elizabeth read over what she had written. Most of it merely confirmed what Astley and Parry had said. All she would admit to was knowing that the Admiral had desired to marry her, and that there was gossip about them. She declared that the rumor of her being with child was false, and asked for it to be publicly refuted. There! There was nothing here that could incriminate anyone. With her customary flourish, she signed her name, looked up at Sir Robert, and smiled sweetly, knowing that, despite everything, she had bested him.

When he had gone, glowering, she wrote again to the Lord Protector, begging him to do all in his power to salvage her reputation and her good name. "I beseech you, my lord, to have my innocence publicly proclaimed," she urged.

It took no fewer than four letters in this vein before Somerset replied with an assurance that he would issue a proclamation declaring that the rumors were lies. And it was at this point that the relentless questioning ceased.

"Is your investigation completed, Sir Robert?" Elizabeth asked mischievously, coming upon her tormentor and his disdainful wife in the gardens. It was a crisp, sunny morning, and she was taking her customary brisk walk.

"My instructions are to proceed no further, since the Lord Protector is satisfied of your innocence," he replied stiffly. His expression said that, even though the Lord Protector was satisfied, he was certainly not, but he forbore to say anything more.

Elizabeth was filled with an overwhelming sense of relief. She was safe. Her secret was safe. But the relief was tinged with anxiety.

"What of my servants? Are they not innocent too?" she asked sharply.

"They are to remain in the Tower for now," Sir Robert informed her, raising a hand to still her protests. "Do not fret, they are comfortably lodged. But to be plain with you, neither is fit to return to your service. Instead, on the council's orders, my lady wife here is to act as your governess."

Elizabeth stared in dismay at the high-nosed woman beside him, who was now belatedly curtsying to her. She remembered Lady Tyrwhit from Katherine Parr's household, and knew she had never liked her. Lady Tyrwhit had been one of those who, as the Admiral's amorous interest in Elizabeth escalated, had grown increasingly disapproving of the girl. And Lady Tyrwhit had no doubt witnessed the Queen's grief over the affair. Thus she was not likely to look kindly upon Elizabeth now. Nor did her glacial stare betray any warmth of character. Instead, there was overt hostility.

"Saving your pardon, madam, but Husband, I have no desire to serve this young lady," Lady Tyrwhit said boldly.

"I am sorry, Beth, but the council has ordered it." Sir Robert turned to Elizabeth. "I hope you will thankfully accept her, my lady."

Elizabeth was distraught. "Mrs. Astley is my governess," she cried, "and neither she nor I has so demeaned ourself that the council should seek to replace her."

Outraged, Lady Tyrwhit retorted tartly, "Seeing you had Mrs. Astley for a governess, you need not be ashamed to have an honest woman put in her place!"

"I want no other governess!" wailed Elizabeth, bursting into tears and running back toward the house. Once there, she locked herself in her bedchamber, threw herself on her bed, and gave way at last to a passion of weeping. And so she stayed, all day and all night, refusing food and drink, mourning the loss of her dear Kat.

On the morrow, she emerged pale and red-eyed, and sought out Sir Robert.

"I must tell you, sir," she said shakily, "that I fully hope to recover my old governess."

"The love you bear her is to be wondered at," Tyrwhit sneered. "In truth, if it were left to me, you would have *two* new governesses, for it looks as if you need them."

"I do not care what you think," Elizabeth told him. "I have written to the Protector to express my dismay at your wife being appointed my governess, because people will say that I deserved to have such a one because of my lewd behavior, which is most unfair." Her eyes brimmed with tears again. "And I have asked him, once more, to proclaim my innocence to the world, for he has not yet done so."

"I wish you joy of your requests," Tyrwhit said with finality, and bent to his papers.

He had accused her of being pert with him! The Protector had apparently lost all sympathy for her, and insisted that she have Lady Tyrwhit as her governess. And here the woman was, transferring her things into Kat's chests, making Kat's chamber her own, while poor Master Astley desolately removed his wife's belongings to a meaner room in the north wing.

Elizabeth now found that the only time she could be alone was at night, and even then Lady Tyrwhit locked her door and slept in the outer chamber, forbearing to join her husband in their marital bed. Not, Elizabeth told herself, that she could ever imagine them paying the marriage debt!

Lady Tyrwhit's supervision was relentless, and Elizabeth chafed under the oppressive new regime she devised, being confined to the schoolroom for hours on end, and being made to sew through the long evenings. How she hated that! Playing her lute or virginals was forbidden, as were dancing and riding out in the park. Elizabeth thought she would suffocate with the tedium. Even Master Ascham grew resentful at Lady Tyrwhit's constant presence during lessons.

"I have my orders," she would say whenever he protested that there was no need for her to stay.

Lady Tyrwhit's presence in her life was bad enough, but Elizabeth was also worrying constantly about Kat, and missing her dreadfully. No one would tell her anything of what was happening in the outside world, and she was anxious Kat was being ill treated or pressed to reveal more. Already, she had cracked under pressure. Worst of all, Elizabeth had no one in whom she could confide. Master Ascham was constantly watched, so closely that she dared not even pass a note to him, and she was unable to write to Sir William Cecil, for it was impossible to smuggle out a letter, so vigilant were her guardians.

Again and again she begged Sir Robert to petition on her behalf for Kat's release, but he repeatedly refused. She began to wonder how long she could bear this existence. Her courses had dried up, she had begun to suffer appalling headaches, and there were days when she felt so nervy that she could not rise from her bed.

Then there came the day—early in March it was, and the buds green

on the trees—when Sir Robert summoned Elizabeth and her household
to the great hall once more.

"The former Admiral," he announced, "has been attainted for treason
by Parliament, and his life and all his goods are forfeit."

Elizabeth sat still in her high seat, breathing deeply, trying to master
her pounding heart. Attainder, she knew, was the preamble to execution.
The Admiral would die, as surely as night followed day. The man who
had first stirred her senses, who had romped with her, kissed her, and
briefly joined in the most intimate of all embraces with her, would soon
be carrion for worms. She wished she could weep for him, but all eyes
were upon her, and she must not betray by any gesture that she was affected by the news. Nor did she think she *could* weep; indeed, she wished
she could feel more. There was only a dreadful sense of shock, and regret . . . and most of the regret was for herself. What a fool she had been.

They were all dispersing now, and Lady Tyrwhit was there, as ever, at
her back as Elizabeth rose to return to her apartments, her shoulders and
her spirits drooping.

"Well, he had it coming to him," that lady opined as they reached the
schoolroom. "It's no more than he deserves."

"Perhaps if his abilities had been recognized and put to good use, he
would not have needed to resort to treason to achieve his desires," Elizabeth challenged her. "It was not just or fair that one brother had all the
power, and the other none."

"Each to his desserts," Lady Tyrwhit observed. "He was a scoundrel
all his life. Especially to his poor wife." There was no mistaking the
venom in her tone.

"He was ever kind to me," Elizabeth pointed out, wondering why she
felt impelled to defend the Admiral. Was it that she needed to defend her
own conduct?

"Yes, we know all about that!" retorted the governess.

"You mistake my meaning deliberately," Elizabeth accused her.

"There is no excuse you can make for him," Lady Tyrwhit said dismissively. And it was true, Elizabeth realized reluctantly.

That night, she could not sleep, but kept tossing and turning, her mind in
torment. To begin with, her fears were for Kat, for if the Admiral was
now judged guilty of treason, might not Kat be convicted as an accom-

plice? And what would happen to her then? She was not of high rank, so beheading might be seen as too good for her. That left burning, which was the fate of female traitors. Elizabeth howled when she thought of that, pressing her face into her pillow so that no one should hear her.

Eventually, she did drift off to sleep, but then she was troubled by a ghastly nightmare in which there floated before her, out of the mouth of Hell, bodies writhing in agony, lapped with flames of fire. Three had grinning, severed heads, suspended above bloody, ragged necks. Two were women, and to her horror Elizabeth beheld Katherine Howard, her pretty face livid with intolerable heat; the other she dared not look at, but she knew it for her mother. And the third—in her dream she was forced to open her eyes, and then she beheld the handsome visage of the Admiral, mouthing wordlessly at her, reaching out charred hands . . .

She woke screaming, then stuffed the sheet in her mouth. Coming back to reality was almost as bad as the nightmare she had just experienced. She lay there listening—all she could hear was Lady Tyrwhit snoring in the next room. She relaxed a little. The woman had not heard her. Then she found herself weeping, weeping for the Admiral who had loved her with his body and set her afire with his kisses; for little Queen Katherine, who had sinned carnally and betrayed her marriage vows; and for her mother, of whose love she had been cruelly deprived, and who had been accused of the vilest crimes.

All condemned to death for indulging in stolen love, for enjoying the sweetest of life's pleasures. Living beings, full of vitality and life, capable of arousal and passion—yet all had found that it was such a small step from the warm tumbled bed to the cold ax and the grave. Elizabeth suspected that she would never again surrender to desire without fearing that it might have fatal consequences; would never again give herself to a man without remembering the fate of these three.

"I have some tidings for you, madam," Sir Robert said, a few days later. "Astley and Parry have been released from the Tower."

"Oh, that is good news!" Elizabeth cried. At least there was some light in this present darkness. "When will I see them again? Are they returning here?"

Sir Robert looked uncomfortable.

"I fear not, madam. The council will not allow it."

"I will write to the Protector," Elizabeth said defiantly.

"It will do you no good," he warned her.

"We shall see," she replied.

When she saw the horseman through her window, she hoped that he had brought a reply from the Duke of Somerset. But when Sir Robert entered her chamber and she saw his grave mien, she realized that he brought news of far greater import.

His eyes never left her face as he delivered it, with Lady Tyrwhit and Master Ascham standing by, watching her too.

"Madam, it is my heavy duty to inform you that yesterday, the Admiral died on Tower Hill." There was a brief silence.

"God rest him," Elizabeth said simply, betraying neither by word nor expression her inner turmoil.

"I trust he did not suffer too much," Ascham said quietly.

"Bishop Latimer reported that he died badly—dangerously and horribly, he said. God had obviously forsaken him." Elizabeth sensed that Tyrwhit was saying this in the hope of provoking her into uttering something rash and indiscreet.

"Did he say aught of my Lady Elizabeth?" Lady Tyrwhit asked. He has briefed her, Elizabeth thought.

"He did write a final message, scratched with the point of a lace on his shoe, but it was considered treasonable, and was destroyed," her husband said. "It was a foolish thing to do when he was about to face divine judgment." He shook his head. "His fate I leave to God, but he was surely a wicked man, and the realm is well rid of him."

Elizabeth turned her back on them and stared out the window at the snowbound gardens below.

"He was a man of much wit and very little judgment," she said quietly, knowing they were all waiting on her every word. Well, she would say no more, however traumatized and confused she felt. One thing she had learned from this whole sad and dangerous business, and that was that she must in future keep her own counsel and never betray her true feelings. It was a harsh lesson for one who was just fifteen years old.

PART THREE

THE QUEEN'S SISTER

CHAPTER 16

1553

As the tall young woman pulled back the curtains and opened her window, the sun streamed in, burnishing her waist-length wavy hair. Her face was pale, her posture dignified. The severely cut black gown set off her slender figure to advantage, but its high-standing collar lined with fine white lawn and its lack of adornment suggested modesty and purity. There was a gravity about her that made her seem older than her nineteen years, and yet there was something of the coquette too. One only had to look at the way she moved her delicate hands with their long white fingers, vainly displaying them to advantage against the black stuff of her gown.

She moved to the table and picked up a letter, and her intelligent face registered a frown as she reread it for the third time. She certainly could not go hunting until she had dealt with this, or decided how to deal with it. But what should she do?

It had been some years since she had been in such a difficult dilemma. She thought back to that earlier time when she had faced danger. She had been lucky to escape so lightly, she knew, but it had been a close thing.

She shuddered to think how her reputation had been all but ruined. Even after she had thought herself safe, that midwife had come forward with her lurid tale, and Elizabeth had thought herself discovered. Fortunately, most people had dismissed the woman's story as far-fetched, and of course, she couldn't be sure that it *was* the Lady Elizabeth whom she had attended. It all sounded most contrived.

Elizabeth had suffered, though, and not only from grueling anxiety. Her courses had returned, but they were much more painful than before. She was cursed with megrims, stomach pains, and jaundice. Often, her many ailments had obliged her to take to her bed; things had gotten so bad that at length, the Lord Protector himself had sent the King's physician to her. Thanks to his kindly ministrations, she had slowly recovered, although she doubted she would ever be as well as she had been before.

In the end, the shameful gossip and the odious whispering had died down, and Elizabeth had firmly put the whole terrible business behind her, resolved to give lie to the rumors and to conduct herself in such a manner that no scandal should ever again attach itself to her name. And this she had accomplished—witness the somber clothes, as became a virtuous Protestant maiden, the laying away of her jewels, the pious observances in chapel, the frugality with which she lived, and the esteem in which she was now held at court and in the kingdom at large. The King her brother loved her; again she was his sweet sister Temperance. He corresponded with her regularly and looked forward to her visits, even though he still insisted on the strictest formality on the rare occasions when they were permitted to be together; and whenever he summoned her, she went to court splendidly attended, as the great magnate she was. Her only indulgence was her music, something she could not live without, and she never let a day go by without playing for hours on her instruments or welcoming musicians to her house.

Kat bustled in, an older Kat, a touch stiffer in the joints since her sojourn in the Tower, but very firmly in charge of the household again. After promising the council never again to speak of any marriage plans for her charge, Kat had been restored to Elizabeth at the end of that terrible summer, although by then Elizabeth and Lady Tyrwhit had developed a grudging respect for each other. It was Lady Tyrwhit who, fond of collecting proverbs, had reminded Elizabeth of Cicero's saying *Semper eadem,* which she now took for her motto, remembering that long-ago conversation with her father, whose memory she so revered. But Lady Tyrwhit could never have replaced Kat. Elizabeth had not forgotten their blessed and joyful reunion, both of them weeping on each other's shoulders, mindless of rank and etiquette . . .

"Is something wrong?" Kat asked, clearing away plates and cutlery from the table. Although the letter had arrived the night before, Elizabeth had told no one about it.

"I think I have one of my headaches coming on," Elizabeth said, folding up the paper and putting it in her pocket. Her headaches—often so bad that she could not see to read—were a legacy of that other time. But this time she was feigning.

"Can I get you anything?" Kat was all concern. "A brew of feverfew?"

"No, thank you. I think I will rest awhile." Elizabeth went into her bedchamber and lay down on her bed. Then she remembered that she always had to have the curtains closed when she suffered a megrim, so she got up and drew them before lying down and taking out the letter again. At this rate, her head would be aching for real.

The letter was from John Dudley, Duke of Northumberland and Lord President of the Council, the man who now ruled England in the name of the fifteen-year-old King. Northumberland had overthrown Somerset four years before, and sent him to the block some two years later.

"There's a kind of justice to it," Kat had said. "After all, Somerset had his own brother executed. The mills of God grind slowly, but they grind exceeding small."

Kat rarely mentioned the Admiral, and when she did, it was with sadness. She had been smitten with the man, that much had become clear, but Elizabeth did not blame her. He had had a talent for making women respond to his charm. Her own feelings about him were still confused. She was sure now she had never truly loved him. Probably she had been merely infatuated, beguiled by the attentions of an older, attractive, and experienced seducer. Even now, remembering his dark good looks, she could still feel a thrill in her heart—a thrill that was tempered by sorrow and, yes, resentment, for Thomas Seymour had, through his foolish scheming, brought her nothing but trouble and pain. She had almost been brought down in his dramatic fall, her youthful folly threatening to implicate her in his rash grab for power. But he had paid for that, dearly, and she hoped he was at peace now.

She still shuddered when she thought of the precariousness of her situation back then. But now, it seemed, she might again be in peril. She did not like or trust Northumberland, a cold, ruthless man, unscrupulous and greedy for power. His dismissive manner toward her, on the rare occasions she visited the court, had led her to suspect that he held her to be of very little account. He controlled the young King, and through him the country; he had no time for the King's bastard sisters. The only thing she could admire about Northumberland was his staunch Protestant faith. There was no doubt that he would defend it to the death.

The King her brother was another such. "The new Josiah," they called him, and it was true. He was zealous in his faith, and he had been harsh to their sister Mary, constantly wrangling with her over her illegal celebration of the Mass in her household. Mary, it was rumored, had even tried to flee the realm. Were it not for the threats of her cousin the Emperor, the most powerful prince in Christendom, she would stand in the greatest peril indeed. Elizabeth had always taken care never to get involved in this interminable quarrel.

Yet Edward let Mary largely alone these days. He was ill now, this strange, wise-beyond-his-years boy. It had begun last year with a fever that many attributed to measles or a mild attack of smallpox, but since then the King's health had inexorably declined. He had not been seen in public for months now, and it was rumored that he was suffering from a fatal consumption.

Elizabeth had begged, again and again, these past weeks, to be allowed to visit him, but Northumberland had steadfastly refused to allow it, ignoring her outraged protests.

"I wouldn't mind, but he allowed Mary to visit the King," she had complained to Kat, and then dashed off another angry letter to Northumberland, demanding to see her brother. Again, the Duke put her off with excuses, much to her mounting chagrin. At length, she had ridden out determinedly from Hatfield, making for London, but the Duke's men had met her on the road and ordered her to go back. Frustrated and angry, she had sent Edward letter after letter, but had received no reply.

Her suspicions had mounted. If rumor spoke truth, and the King were indeed dying, why the secrecy? It was as if Northumberland were plotting something, she thought perceptively. Then, in May, had come the news that the Duke had married his son Guildford to Lady Jane Grey, and alarm bells began ringing inside Elizabeth's shrewd head.

"So he allies the Dudleys with the blood royal," she fumed to Kat. "I mistrust his intentions. She was betrothed to Somerset's son."

"I don't understand why it bothers you," Kat said perplexedly, thinking that Elizabeth was worrying over trifles. "Surely the Duke can marry his son to whomever he pleases?"

Elizabeth shook her head at Kat in exasperation and sighed.

"It has pleased him to marry Lord Guildford to a girl who is in line to the throne," she explained.

"But the Lady Mary is next in line, then yourself," Kat said. "Your father passed an Act of Parliament decreeing it, *and* he made provision for it in his will."

"Yes, and who comes after us? The heirs of my father's sister Mary. That means the Duchess of Suffolk and her daughter, Lady Jane."

"But the Lady Mary and yourself both come before her," Kat pointed out, looking puzzled.

"And we are both bastards, and in law, strictly speaking, we cannot inherit. Only that Act of Parliament, the work of our father, stands between us and the House of Suffolk." Elizabeth got up and began pacing up and down. "A king's will has no force in law. An Act of Parliament can be repealed. I hope I am mistaken, but I fear that the Duke has some sinister design up his sleeve."

Kat's jaw dropped. "He wouldn't dare?"

"We shall see," Elizabeth said grimly. "I would put nothing past him."

The letter had confirmed her worst suspicions. Northumberland had invited her to court, saying that the King was unwell and wished to see his dearest sister. How strange, she thought. He has been ill for months and I have been forcibly kept from seeing him. Why this summons now?

Was Edward really dying? Had he asked for her, hoping she would reach his side in time to say a last farewell? If that were the case, she must go to him, her poor brother. Truly, her heart grieved for him; she was consumed with sorrow. To have shown so much promise, then been brought to this, so young—it did not bear thinking about.

But supposing this was a trap set by Northumberland to snare her? She still thought it very odd that after months of preventing her from seeing the ailing King, the Duke was now summoning her to his bedside. And in that she smelled danger. Oh, what should she do?

Kat came in, and seeing her wakeful, padded softly over and sat down, resting her cool hand against Elizabeth's brow.

"No fever, thank goodness. How are you feeling now, my lamb?"

"Not good," Elizabeth murmured, holding Northumberland's missive beneath her skirts, crumpled in her hand.

"Has it affected your eyes?" Kat asked. "Only there's a letter come for you. Here."

She held out a folded paper bonded with plain wax. There was no imprint of a seal. Elizabeth raised herself on the bed and opened it. There were just a few words printed across the page: *On no account go to court, if you value your life.* There was no signature, and the handwriting was unfamiliar. Or was it?

"Who is it from?" Kat asked. Elizabeth ignored her.

"Kat, can you bring me my coffer—that one, on the chest," she indicated. Frowning, Kat fetched it and placed it on the bed. Resting on one elbow, Elizabeth went through the papers it held, then extracted a couple and held them side by side with the note she had just received.

"As I thought," she muttered. William Cecil had done a good enough job of disguising his handwriting—good enough to deceive most people, but not her. There were too many similarities, but then perhaps that was intentional.

"Oh, my head," she groaned, stuffing all the papers back into the coffer, locking it and clapping a fist to her brow. "Can you get me some poppy syrup, please. I need to sleep."

"Of course," Kat assured her, then paused. "What was in the letter? And what were you doing?"

"Oh, nothing," Elizabeth sighed. "Just looking up something Master Cecil had written. Boring estate business. All I need just now." For this to succeed, she thought, even Kat—especially garrulous Kat—must be kept safely in ignorance.

When Kat came to look in on her that evening, she was tossing and turning and complaining of severe pain in her stomach and head.

"Summon the physician," she moaned distractedly. When he arrived, brow creased in concern, she put on, she felt, the most convincing performance.

"A summer ague, my lady," he pronounced after testing her urine and feeling her pulse. "A disorder of the humors brought on by the heat."

What a load of nonsense, she thought, and wondered briefly if the man was worth his stipend. But, she reasoned, he *was* helping her, even if he was incompetent.

She sighed a little and flung her arm across her forehead.

"Will you write me a certificate?" she asked peevishly. "You see, I have been summoned to see the King, and I so wanted to go, but . . . ." Her voice trailed off. "I want him to know that there is a good reason for my failure to attend him, especially as he is unwell himself."

"Oh, no, Your Grace must not go near the King," the doctor counseled. "Judging by the reports I have heard of his condition, it would do neither of you any good. I will write a certificate now." He turned and rummaged in his bag.

"And will you kindly dispatch it for me?" Elizabeth wheedled.

"Of course, my lady," he said, scribbling.

Elizabeth lay back on the pillows, satisfied that she had put off the danger for the time being.

On the ninth day of July, Elizabeth received another letter from Northumberland. Kat brought it to her as she lay in her sickbed in her darkened bedchamber.

"What does the Duke say?" she asked weakly.

Kat broke the seal and briefly scanned the page.

"Oh, my God," she said in a choked voice. "The King is dead, God rest him."

"Dead?" echoed Elizabeth, swallowing. "Of what?"

"A consumption of the lungs," Kat whispered. "The rumors were true."

Elizabeth immediately regretted staying away from the court. Her brother had been dying, had needed her, and she had not been there. She saw in her mind's eye fleeting images of a fat toddler imperiously clutching a gold rattle, a solemn child diligent at his books and his prayers, a young ruler sitting like an icon on his throne. Her little brother, the hope of his House. How her father would weep this day.

Tears flooded her pillow as she tried to imagine her brother's sufferings in his last days. Kat sat there stroking her hair from her temples, dabbing at her own eyes with a kerchief.

Eventually, Elizabeth began to wonder what this tragedy would mean for her. Had her sister Mary been proclaimed queen, as was her right in law? And was she herself now the next heir?

Rousing herself from her grief, she reread the Duke's letter.

"There's something I mislike here," she murmured. "He writes in haste, he says, to inform me of the King's passing, which was three days ago, on the sixth. *Three* days ago, Kat." Elizabeth sat up. "Why has it taken him so long to inform me?"

"No doubt he is very busy," Kat said uncertainly. "There will be much to do. And he has to make all ready for the new Queen, your sister."

"Did he delay in informing her as well?" wondered Elizabeth. "He cannot welcome her accession. He has given her much grief and clashed with her over religion many times these past years. I doubt she will be too forgiving. And then we shall see what happens to our fine Duke!"

Kat stared at her. Elizabeth's seemingly irrational fears were beginning to make sense. Suddenly, she understood why her young lady had taken to her bed.

The next news, picked up by Parry in the tavern at Hatfield, was even more alarming. Mary had not gone to London, nor had she been proclaimed queen; instead, she was in Norfolk, raising an army, if rumor were to be believed. Hearing this, Elizabeth immediately staged a relapse, resolved to keep to her bed until she knew more.

Her peace was disturbed by the arrival of a deputation from the council. Alarmed, she refused to receive them.

"I am not well!" she declared.

"But my lady, they are insisting," a frightened Kat pleaded.

Knowing herself bested, Elizabeth shrank down beneath the covers, pinched her cheeks to give them a hectic, fevered appearance, and lay prone. The lords filed in respectfully, acclimatizing their eyes to the gloom. Kat stood by the bedhead, for propriety's sake.

"We are sorry to find you so unwell, my lady," Sir William Petre, the

Secretary of State, said gently, peering at the bed. "I would that our business could wait, but I fear it is pressing."

"I am listening," Elizabeth said listlessly.

"My lord of Northumberland has been concerned about the succession. England does not want a Catholic queen. I speak of your sister, the Lady Mary, you understand. The question of bastardy was raised." Petre gulped nervously. "I am to tell you that it was the late King's will and desire that the Crown be left to his cousin, the Lady Jane Grey, who is trueborn and a stout Protestant."

Elizabeth was outraged. Little Lady Jane to be queen? No one would allow it. The people would not want it. Jane herself would not want it, surely. The King must indeed have been deranged in his last illness—deranged or suborned by Northumberland.

"Parliament has settled the succession first on my sister and then on me," Elizabeth reminded the lords, keeping her voice low for effect, and suppressing her fury. "The Lady Jane comes after us and her mother, my Lady Suffolk."

"With respect, Your Grace," Petre continued, "in law, the Lady Mary and yourself are bastards, and King Edward set aside your claims in a device he signed on his deathbed, which is soon to be enshrined in an Act of Parliament."

"Then it has as yet no force in law," Elizabeth pointed out.

"That is true," chimed in Lord Paulet. "Which is why we are here. My lord Duke offers you a million crowns to renounce your claim."

Elizabeth resisted the urge to sit up and scream at them. *Scurvy knaves!* she wanted to cry. *You'll not deprive King Harry's daughters of their rights!* But she curbed her temper.

"A bribe?" she asked drily.

"An inducement," Paulet amended.

"Call it what you will, I cannot accept," Elizabeth told them. "Has my sister been offered a similar bribe?"

"Not as yet." Petre coughed nervously.

"Then you must first make this agreement with the Lady Mary, during whose lifetime I have no claim or title to resign." Reaching for her kerchief, she made a great show of mopping her brow. The lords looked at one another uncertainly.

"Are you sure we cannot persuade you, madam?" Paulet persisted.

"Very sure," Elizabeth said firmly. "And now, gentlemen, you have exhausted my strength. I must rest. I pray you leave me in peace, and bid you farewell."

Shaking their heads, the lords left the chamber. After seeing them out, Kat returned.

"They've gone," she said in a relieved voice.

"I'll wager they'll be back," Elizabeth predicted. "They'll pester me until I give in."

"I'm not so sure," Kat opined. "They seemed uncertain of their ground. I heard them saying something about dealing with the Lady Mary first. I didn't like the sound of it."

Elizabeth felt a stab of alarm. "Neither do I," she said. "For when they have dealt with the Lady Mary, for certain they needs must deal with me. We must be on our guard. I think, Kat, that it is time for another relapse."

That evening, there was an urgent knocking at Elizabeth's door.

"It's me, Master Parry, with important news!" a voice cried. Kat put down her sewing and hastened to admit him, as Elizabeth, who was sitting up in bed reading, clutched her shawl tighter about her.

"Lady Jane Grey is proclaimed queen in London!" Parry cried, breathless. "I had it from a merchant who stopped at the tavern on his way north. She has gone in state to the Tower to await her coronation."

"How dare they!" cried Elizabeth, fiery with indignation. She found herself feeling fiercely protective of Jane, whom she was certain was an unwilling accomplice in all this. Quiet Jane, who loved nothing better than to be left alone with her books and her studies. "It is quite clear that Northumberland married his son to poor Jane so that he could place them both on the throne as his puppets. He has a taste for power now and doesn't wish to give it up. It is madness! I know the English people—they will not accept it. A monarch cannot be forced upon them."

"Many are muttering against it," Parry told her. "There was some cheering at the Tower, but mostly the people are angry. They do not know the Lady Jane, but they love the Lady Mary."

"Well, that is something," Elizabeth said grimly. "And what news of the Lady Mary?"

"Supposed to be in Norfolk still, madam. She was summoned to court but it appears she was warned off, because she suddenly fled to her estates in the eastern shires."

Had Cecil gotten word to Mary too? Elizabeth wondered. Strange, after what he had said to her all those years ago about supporting a Protestant succession. But perhaps it had been someone else. Or perhaps his admirable principles extended to championing the lawful heir, whatever her faith.

"What shall we do?" Parry was asking plaintively.

"Nothing," said Elizabeth decisively. "We lie low here—I shall lie low literally—and wait upon events. That seems to me the safest course."

There followed several anxious days in which there was no news. Elizabeth was desperate to know what was happening, and sent Parry daily to the tavern in the village to see if he could pick up any gossip, but the locals had nothing to add to what he had already heard.

John Astley was of the opinion that the council had too much on its hands to worry about Elizabeth for the moment.

"You may be right," Elizabeth said cautiously. The Astleys and Master Parry were closeted in her bedchamber; they were the only members of the household who knew her sickness was diplomatic. "And I have no intention of drawing any attention to myself."

"The longer this goes on," Parry said, "the more likely it is that the Lady Mary is managing to elude them. For if they had taken her, we would have heard by now."

"Indeed," Elizabeth said cautiously. "But let us not count our chickens yet."

"There is talk in the village that large numbers are rallying to the Lady Mary's banner," Master Astley reported the next day. "I know not if this is true, but there may be some substance to it."

Elizabeth curbed a surge of optimism.

"Pray for a happy outcome!" she enjoined them all. "This is in God's hands now."

It was just over a week since the Lady Jane had been proclaimed queen when Kat came hastening into Elizabeth's privy chamber with her husband and Master Parry hot on her heels.

"The Lady Mary has been proclaimed queen!" she cried. Elizabeth shot up out of her chair, and a smile spread across her face. There could not have been better news!

"In London?" she asked excitedly.

"Yes, and in all the shires! There was a proclamation made in Hertford this morning."

Elizabeth thrilled to hear this. The right line restored, and herself once more next in the succession. She was suffused with a great warmth toward her sister, who had, through her courage and presence of mind, made this possible. And she was boundlessly grateful too to God, who had shown His hand in the cause of truth and justice.

"The whole country has rallied to Queen Mary!" Parry declared. "Northumberland is taken—he was apprehended in Cambridge after his army deserted him—and his sons too. He is now in the Tower, and his fate all but certain."

"The usurper Jane is there too," John Astley added. "Although whether she will suffer death for her treason is doubtful."

"She is very young," Elizabeth said, recalling the slight, red-haired child she had last seen at Chelsea, and remembering how rashly she herself had behaved when *she* was Jane's age. She felt pity for Jane, that poor innocent tool, who had been led unwillingly into treason and might now pay the price for it.

"I'll wager she had no choice in the matter, and that it was all Northumberland's doing," Kat put in. "*He's* the one who should suffer for it, not that poor girl."

"I know my sister will be merciful," Elizabeth said. "She has a kind heart, especially where children are concerned, and Jane is not much more than a child." She paused for a moment. "Queen Mary. It has a ring to it, yet it seems strange that a woman should rule."

"Strange indeed," Astley commented with feeling, "and unnatural, a woman holding dominion over men."

"In my experience, a lot of wives do that," Parry grumbled drily.

"I am sure she will be guided by her councillors," Astley said. "A woman's role is to obey and serve."

"Not if she can help it," muttered Elizabeth mischievously. The men frowned.

"The Queen will marry, of course," Kat said. "She must marry, because she needs a son to succeed her."

"Isn't it a bit late for that?" her husband queried. "Her Highness is thirty-seven, rather old for bearing children."

"Little you know," retorted his wife. "At least she must try."

"Her marriage will bring one advantage," Parry observed. "Her husband can offer her guidance and make decisions for her."

"That in itself might be fraught with problems," Elizabeth stated thoughtfully. "If she marries a foreign prince, he might interfere too much in the affairs of the realm. Yet if she marries an Englishman, his rule might raise jealousies and factions. And think: As queen, she will wield dominion over her subjects, yet how is she to reconcile that with the obedience that a wife owes to her husband, who is her lord and master? That is a question unanswerable."

"It is indeed," replied Parry, impressed by Elizabeth's acute logic.

"It will take all her wit to solve it," she said. "Yet what is of greater concern, to me and to many, is what will happen to the Protestant Church in this realm. The Queen, as we all know, is a staunch Catholic."

"Is it too much to hope that she might extend tolerance to those of the new religion?" Parry wondered. "After all, she has been under constant threat for practicing her own faith these past years."

"My sister is stiff in her opinions," Elizabeth said. "Still, she has come to the throne on a tide of popular approval. She will surely wish to retain the goodwill of her Protestant subjects."

"Or she might see that approval as a mandate to return England to the old faith," John Astley pointed out.

"You are shrewd, sir," Elizabeth commented. "Well, we will soon know, and we must pray for a happy outcome. For my part, I shall play it cautiously, and I urge you all to do the same. It may be possible to hunt with both hare and hounds in this matter. Now, if you will excuse me, I must write to Her Majesty, congratulating her on her happy accession. And then we must go to London to greet her, without delay, so hurry and make ready! All other considerations aside, this is a joyous day!"

The royal cavalcade had just come into sight, and Elizabeth, waiting on the road to Wanstead, spurred her horse. Behind her rode her close attendants and two hundred mounted men, all clad in the Tudor livery of green and white. She knew she looked impressive in the saddle, straight-backed in her pure white raised-damask gown, her red locks loose about her shoulders.

She had not seen Mary for five years now. Her sister had spent the greater part of Edward's reign immured in the country, fighting her interminable battles with the King and council over religion. Elizabeth had expected her to look older—Mary was, after all, middle-aged now—but she was quite unprepared for the sight of the Queen's prematurely lined face.

At first, the impression she got was one of magnificence. Mary had always had a penchant for lavish dress, but today she looked truly majestic. Her gown was of purple velvet, her mantle of crimson lined with ermine, and she sparkled with jewels. As a virgin and a queen, she wore her red hair loose too, but closer up you could see that it was finely streaked with gray. And her face, with its heavy brow, piercing, wary eyes, blunt nose, and thin, pursed lips, looked haggard and tired in the cruel August sunlight.

But there was no time to reflect on her sister's changed appearance. The Queen must be greeted, and with suitable deference. With a graceful arching movement, Elizabeth dismounted from her horse, then knelt in the dusty road, head bent.

"Sister!" Mary's deep, gruff voice exclaimed as she too dismounted and hastened toward Elizabeth. Grasping her by the hands, she raised her, embraced her, and kissed her, nor would she let go of her hand as she spoke to her.

"It is a great pleasure to see you," she said, smiling with genuine warmth. "I am delighted that you came to meet me."

"I rejoice in Your Majesty's glorious accession and great good fortune," Elizabeth told her, returning the smile. "None is more overjoyed than I to see you triumph over your enemies."

Mary was so elated by the universal acclaim that had greeted her victory that she was willing to forgive all but her most deadly enemies. In this expansive and merciful mood, she was also prepared to overlook Elizabeth's unfortunate religious views and the scandal that had attached itself to her name four years ago—having herself experienced the impact of that rogue's charm, she was inclined to believe that Elizabeth had been more sinned against than sinning—and to suppress her disturbing suspicions about the younger woman's paternity. Nothing must be allowed to mar these heady days of rejoicing. All the same, as she moved on to greet and kiss Mrs. Astley and the other ladies in Elizabeth's train—many of them noblewomen who had joined it en route—she could not but be aware that, next to her radiant, simply garbed, nineteen-year-old sister, she herself looked old, worn, and overdressed. And she did not want her subjects to see her in that light, for she was aware that she must be perceived not only as being equal in health and strength to the great task ahead of her, but also as a great catch in the marriage market, and capable of bearing the heirs that were essential for a Catholic succession.

Side by side—Mary, despite her misgivings, had insisted—the sisters rode into London at the head of the great procession, preceded only by the Earl of Arundel carrying the shining sword of state. At Aldgate, the Lord Mayor came bowing low, offering the mace of the City, with a loyal speech of welcome. Mary returned it to him with grateful thanks for his faithfulness and homage. Then the trumpets sounded and the long cavalcade slowly moved forward, through streets packed with happy, cheering people, waving, clapping, and weeping with joy. Houses had been hung with banners and streamers and bedecked with flowers, and everywhere you could see placards painted with the words, VOX POPULI, VOX DEI—the voice of the people is the voice of God.

"God save the Queen!" the citizens cried. "God save Great Harry's daughter!" "Jesus save Her Grace!" And sometimes, amid the joyful din, Elizabeth heard her own name shouted aloud. Of course, it was but natural: Until the Queen bore a child, she was next in line to the throne, the people's hope for the future. She thrilled to their greetings, basking in their approval—a thing so fickle, she was well aware, but something to be assiduously courted and cherished.

In the distance, the guns on the Tower wharf boomed a salute. On her left, Mary was nodding and graciously raising her hand in acknowledgment of the people's acclaim. Behind rode the Lady Anna of Cleves, grown rather fatter than when Elizabeth had last seen her, waving enthusiastically at the crowds. Then came the great ladies of the realm, the lords and gentlemen, the foreign ambassadors and the officers of the royal household—more than a thousand persons in all.

By and by, they came to the drawbridge that led to the great gate of the Tower, where the Queen was to lodge for the next fortnight. Here, the noise of the guns was quite deafening, drowning out the loyal oration given in the Queen's honor by a hundred well-scrubbed children. Mary smiled in acknowledgment, then proceeded across the bridge and into the fortress, her sister reluctantly following.

As the vast bulk of the mighty Tower loomed above her, Elizabeth knew a moment of panic. She had never been to this place before and did not want to enter it now. Yes, she knew it was a royal palace before all else, but since two queens had been beheaded here, the Tower had acquired a more sinister reputation. She shuddered, thinking of how her mother must have felt when she arrived on that long-ago May afternoon, accused of treason. Of course, Anne had not come in triumph through the main gateway, but by the watergate, where traitors were brought by barge. Kat had told her that.

She must not dwell on Anne's fate now, she told herself. This was a happy, joyful occasion, and it must not be overshadowed by morbid thoughts. Yet she could not stop herself from wondering whether sad little Jane Grey could hear all the cheering from the place where she was being held prisoner. The poor girl must be quaking in her shoes at the thought of what might happen to her, although Elizabeth knew, because Mary had told her, that the Queen was resolved to be merciful.

The inner bailey was packed with spectators, but Elizabeth's eyes were immediately drawn to the four prisoners who knelt on a grass sward near the gateway. She knew them all. Foremost was the Catholic Duke of Norfolk, now eighty, who had been accused of treason by Henry VIII but spared the block because the King had died before he could sign the death warrant; he had spent the whole of Edward's reign in the Tower. There was Stephen Gardiner, Bishop of Winchester, whom Mary had once hated for supporting the annulment of her mother's marriage; but Gardiner, another staunch Catholic, had shown his mettle by resisting the religious reforms of Protector Somerset, and thus ended up in prison. Behind him knelt Somerset's widow, the once proud Duchess Anne, an old friend of the Queen's; she had been shut up here after her husband's execution. And lastly, a young man, Edward Courtenay, in whom flowed the royal blood of the Plantagenet kings of England. He had been a prisoner since childhood, when his family had fallen foul of King Henry.

The four prisoners, still kneeling, lifted their hands and begged for the Queen's mercy. Mary's eyes filled with tears. "These are my prisoners," she declared. "They must be set at liberty." Then she dismounted and walked over to them, raising and embracing each in turn. When they had been joyously reunited with their relations and friends, the Queen and her entourage proceeded to the palace that adjoined the White Tower, where Mary could take her ease for a space before embarking on the monumental task of ruling her kingdom.

As she followed Mary, reining in her frisky white palfrey, Elizabeth's eyes strayed unwillingly to the east, and the chapel of St. Peter ad Vincula. There lay her mother's mortal remains—hurriedly coffined in an arrow chest, Kat had said, since no other provision had been made for them on that terrible day seventeen years ago. And in front of the chapel, a greensward, innocent looking and peaceful in the brilliant sunshine. It had been there that the scaffold had stood . . .

Elizabeth jerked her head around quickly, unable to bear the sight of it anymore. She would avoid this place in future, she promised herself. Mercifully, the royal apartments faced the river, so she had no need to come this way again.

For Elizabeth, expecting the Queen to keep a splendid court like their father's, the ensuing weeks brought some disappointments. The treasury was all but empty, and Mary could not afford to be lavish, but she did insist on ceremony, and she was happy to indulge her love of music, dancing, and drama.

"The people expect it of me," she told Elizabeth. "They like display and magnificence. That was why our father was so popular. But I have not the means to pay for such spectacles as he put on. And as an unmarried lady, I must be circumspect and have a mind to decorum."

"I do miss the masques of my father's day," Elizabeth complained to Kat after having sat through yet another morality play. "But the Queen says she has no money to lavish on such extravaganzas. At least they are staging *Ralph Roister Doister* next week. I saw it performed at my brother's court, and it is well worth seeing. I could not stop laughing, because the characters are constantly at cross purposes."

"The Queen never lacks for money when it comes to dressing sumptuously," Kat observed, starting to brush Elizabeth's hair.

"In my opinion, she overdresses," Elizabeth said. "She changes too often, and she wears too many jewels. Her tastes are Catholic, of course." She was aware that her own plain attire stood out—an overt statement of her supposed virginity and her Protestant faith—among the peacock finery worn by the ladies of the court.

"Well, she looks like the queen she is," Kat said. "It is expected of her."

"The people would love her whatever she looked like," Elizabeth observed, "if only because she is our father's daughter and of the true Tudor line. And she will keep their love because she is determined to be merciful. Tonight, she told me that only Northumberland is to suffer death for the late conspiracy. The Lady Jane is to be spared, although she must stay in the Tower. She is lodged in the Gentleman Gaoler's house with every comfort."

"She's a fortunate young lady," Kat said. "I hope the Queen is not being too merciful for her own good."

"She could hardly have executed the whole council." Elizabeth smiled grimly. "All of them were involved in it. But she needs those experienced statesmen—rascals the lot of them—to help her rule. So she has pardoned them all."

"She is a good lady at heart," Kat said, "and I am glad she seems well disposed to you."

Mary had given much evidence of that. Whenever she appeared in public, which was often during these early weeks of her reign, she insisted that Elizabeth be in the place of honor at her side, and invariably held her hand. Sometimes, it was quite obvious that the cheers were as much for Elizabeth as for the Queen, but if Mary noticed, she gave no sign. All was harmonious between the two sisters—until the third Sunday in August.

The previous Sunday had seen Mass celebrated, by the Queen's decree, in the chapel of St. John the Evangelist in the White Tower for the first time since King Henry's day. Mary had emerged with tears in her eyes, having given thanks that she was now, at last, free to practice her faith openly again, and she had been gratified to see so many courtiers at the service. Yet she was sad not to see her sister among them.

On the following Saturday, as they sat together on the dais sipping wine after a very amusing evening spent watching *Ralph Roister Doister* in the presence chamber, Mary turned to Elizabeth.

"It would make me so happy if you would come to Mass with me in the morning," she said.

Elizabeth looked uncomfortable.

"Your Grace, I fear I cannot. I am of the reformed faith." She fingered the little gold book at her girdle; it contained the fervidly Protestant prayer composed by her brother on his deathbed. Mary had been given a similar gold book, but disdained to wear it. Instead, while permitting Edward to be buried according to the reformed rite, she had ordered a private requiem Mass for his soul, to be celebrated in her own chapel.

Mary frowned. "Sister, I fear you have been brought up in error. I care too much for you to see you given over to heresy. Will you not open your mind a little and join me in worship?"

"I wish I could say yes, madam, truly I do," Elizabeth said, looking distressed. "It grieves me that I cannot be of one mind with Your Majesty on this issue."

"It grieves me too," Mary said. "You are my heir, and it is unthinkable that my heir should be of the reformed faith."

"Might I, with respect, remind Your Majesty that, during our brother's time, you were under great pressure to abjure your faith?" Elizabeth asked. "You followed your conscience and stood firm. Having been through that, can you not appreciate my position?"

"Yes, but mine is the true faith, and I was right to defend it," Mary declared. "It is my dearest wish that my people return to the Catholic fold. It is for this, I believe, that God sent me a victory. I am to be the instrument through which His will is to be accomplished." Her eyes were shining, and Elizabeth recognized the fervency that made it impossible for Mary to brook any views other than her own, a fervency that might make her dangerously intolerant.

"So you see," the Queen was saying, reaching over and squeezing Elizabeth's hand, "it is very important to me that you at least attend Mass. Who knows, you may derive some spiritual benefit from it? And God may turn your heart."

"Alas, madam, what can I say?" Elizabeth replied. "The last thing I wish to do is offend you, but I cannot betray my faith."

Mary's manner chilled. "Will you at least give the matter some thought?" she persisted.

"I will," Elizabeth promised, saddened by the rift that she had opened. "And now, madam, I beg leave to retire. I promise I will pray for guidance."

Mary nodded, unsmiling. "Good night, Sister," she said.

Elizabeth curtsied low and made her way out of the chamber, the lords and ladies bowing as she went.

Simon Renard, the new Spanish ambassador, watched the young woman leave. He had been standing behind the Queen's chair, and when Elizabeth had gone, he leaned forward, sure of Mary's ear. As the representative of her beloved mother's country and a staunch Catholic, the suave and clever Renard—a handsome and experienced diplomat and intriguer—had quickly charmed his way into the Queen's confidence. Already, she had taken to consulting him even before her own councillors.

"Majesty," he said quietly. "Forgive me, but I could not help overhearing your conversation with the Lady Elizabeth."

Mary turned to him, clearly upset by Elizabeth's response to her request.

"I fear for her soul, Simon," she said.

"Do not trust her," he replied. "She is full of enchantments, and knows well how to manipulate people."

"She seems sincere enough in her beliefs," Mary said. "Of course, she has been corrupted from her youth, and her mother was a heretic, but I think that in this matter she is ruled by genuine scruples of conscience."

"Madam," Renard said patiently, "you are goodness itself, too good to see faults in others. Do you know why your sister will not go to Mass? It has nothing to do with scruples, I am sure, but everything to do with her wanting to be seen as the Protestant heir, the hope of those who would obstruct Your Majesty's sacred duty."

"No, my friend, I cannot believe that of her. She has shown herself utterly loyal and supportive these past weeks."

"Think on it," Renard persisted. "Those clothes she wears—are they not the habit of a Protestant? Yes, they are simple, but they are worn for effect, and since all the other ladies are nobly attired, they stand out. Does it not occur to you that that is deliberate? She is very clever, your sister. If

I may offer my humble advice, command her to go to Mass. You are the Queen, and she is bound to obey you."

Mary shook her head. "I am loath to constrain her. This is, after all, a matter of conscience. I should prefer to cozen her gently, so that she comes to the true faith of her own free will."

Renard sighed. "Madam, I will pray that she responds to your kindness. Forgive a hardened cynic if he fears it will be wasted."

"We shall see," Mary told him, sighing. "I will pray for a happy outcome."

The following Saturday, Elizabeth received a summons to the Queen's privy chamber. Knowing what was to be asked of her, and unhappy after a week in which relations between her and Mary had been slightly less warm than hitherto, she approached in trepidation. But Mary smiled and raised her from her curtsy with her former affection.

"I am sorry I have not had much time to spare for you," she began. "I have been with my council for most of the time. There is an overwhelming amount of state business to attend to, and many great matters to discuss."

She moved to the prayer desk that stood near the window and looked up at the ornate crucifix that hung on the wall above it. "There has hardly been time even for my usual devotions, but God will understand, I make no doubt. After all, some of it is His business."

She turned, a regal figure in crimson silk and cloth of gold.

"It is of religion that I wish to speak to you. Have you thought on my request?"

"I have thought of nothing but, madam," Elizabeth told her, with a heavy heart.

"All I ask is that you accompany me to Mass," the Queen said. "Your absence has been noticed. There are those who would have me command you, but I should prefer you to come of your own free will."

"Alas, madam, my conscience cannot permit it," Elizabeth declared, looking genuinely distressed.

"Sister," Mary said sternly, "I know that in our brother's time many were constrained to heresy. You were at an impressionable age, too young to know your error. No, hear me out." She stilled Elizabeth's protest with a raised finger. "I must tell you that I am resolved to restore the Mass and bring England back in penitence to obedience to Rome. However, it is not my intention to compel or constrain my subjects' consciences. What I hope for is that they may be brought to the truth by God working through learned and virtuous preachers. And to this end, if you are in agreement, I will provide some good doctor to give you instruction, so that you may learn the truth about the Catholic faith."

Elizabeth felt trapped. She could not accept. Conscience apart, the people must know her to be a champion of the reformed faith. Yet she was painfully aware that, if she wanted to keep the Queen's love and goodwill, she must agree at least to take instruction. But the thought was anathema to her.

"I cannot," she said at length. "Forgive me, madam."

"I am disappointed in you," Mary told her, and turned away.

That disappointment soon showed itself in public. There was no more standing at the Queen's side on ceremonial occasions, no holding of hands, no affectionate embraces. And those like Renard, who loved Mary and distrusted Elizabeth, made sure that the reason for the rift was soon openly known.

Alone in her chamber with Kat, Elizabeth wept.

"I was so happy," she sobbed. "Happy to be back at court at last, and to have the Queen's favor and the people's love. And now she has placed me in this intolerable position and I am made to seem her enemy, who wished her nothing but good." She blew hard into her kerchief.

"Why not just go to Mass?" Kat suggested. "Go through the motions. The Queen will be delighted, and will receive you back into favor."

"And be a hypocrite?" Elizabeth asked, stung. "Once the pretense is adopted, I shall have to keep it up. And what of those who will not compromise their faith? What will they think of me? Did you hear they were demonstrating in London, and someone threw a dagger at a priest who had been sent to celebrate Mass in Saint Paul's? Many people bitterly resent the changes that are being made. I am their only hope for the future, and if I am seen to be attending Mass, they will be bereft."

There was a tap on the door, and Blanche Parry entered.

"My lady, the French ambassador is without and asks to see you," she said.

Lifting her eyebrows, Elizabeth rose, dabbed at her eyes, and hastened to her mirror. No, he would not see that she had been crying. She straightened her French hood, pinched her cheeks, smoothed her black skirts, and stood back to admire herself. "This is going to be interesting," she murmured, opening the door to the outer chamber.

When she appeared, tall and dignified in her black damask gown, the ambassador, Antoine de Noailles, bowed flamboyantly. Elizabeth had observed him about the court over the past weeks, and had concluded that he was clever, wily, and no friend to her sister. Indeed, he had supported Northumberland's bid to make Lady Jane Grey queen.

"Ambassador, welcome," she said, extending her hand. "To what do I owe the pleasure of this visit?"

"Madame, it is so gracious of such an excellent and beautiful young lady as yourself to receive me," de Noailles declared. His teeth gleamed whitely through his neat beard as his dark, saturnine face creased into a smile. Elizabeth knew flattery for what it was, yet she still thrilled to it, and acknowledged it graciously with a slight upturning of the lips.

"It has come to my knowledge that the question of religion has become a sword between Her Majesty and yourself," the envoy continued smoothly. "That is most regrettable. The problem is that the Queen, while inclined by nature to be tolerant, is under the influence of the Spaniards, and you know how zealous the Spaniards can be when it comes to matters of faith. I need not mention the Inquisition . . ."

Elizabeth hid another smile. It was no secret that the French and the Spanish, those two great European rivals for power, cordially hated each other, and were at pains to play each other off in a bid to secure the friendship of England. Indeed, for decades, for this very reason, the kings of England had played a clever game, one small David between the two great Goliaths of France and Spain, forging alliances and breaking them in order to rein in the power of these mighty Catholic kingdoms. De Noailles's blatant maneuvering was hardly unexpected.

She waited for him to continue.

"My King wishes me to assure you of his friendship," he went on. "There are those in France who would prefer not to see the English throne occupied by a queen whose family connections understandably led her to look kindly upon Spain and all its doings, however repugnant they may be to the rest of us. And I am sure you yourself, madame, find your position very difficult. With France behind you, you will be stronger."

What was the man proposing? That with French backing, she set herself up as a rival to her sister? She would not be such a fool.

"Thank your master for his kindness," Elizabeth said aloud. "If I ever need it, rest assured I shall call on him."

"You may need it sooner than you think, with Monsieur Renard dripping poison into the Queen's ear," de Noailles said. "Madame, you are young and beautiful. The people love you. The love they have for the Queen will soon evaporate when she forces them to accept the Catholic faith. Then France will be ready to champion your cause."

"Is not your King a Catholic too?" Elizabeth asked innocently.

"Yes, but he has no desire to see England allied with Spain," de Noailles stated, revealing the steel beneath his courtly exterior.

"I will remember that, Ambassador," Elizabeth said, extending her hand again to show that the interview was at an end.

"Go carefully," warned Kat, when he had gone. "He is virtually inciting you to commit treason."

"Is he?" Elizabeth asked impishly. "I thought he was assuring me of French support in my quarrel with the Queen over the Mass. And I committed myself to nothing."

"Madam," Renard said urgently, "make no mistake, that villain de Noailles is deliberately cultivating the Lady Elizabeth's friendship with a view to setting her up in opposition to yourself. I have seen them in converse together about the court. They are as thick as thieves."

"I cannot believe that my sister would be disloyal to me," Mary said, dismayed.

"She has been disloyal in this matter of the Mass," Renard pointed out. "She is a heretic and she is intriguing with your enemies. Her popularity is a threat to your security."

"My people love me!" Mary cried, shocked. "That is preposterous."

"Ah, but how long will that love last when this present mood of elation has passed?" Renard asked. "All governments become unpopular at some stage. It is the nature of power—you cannot have the approval of the people in everything you do. But waiting in the wings to make mischief is this sister of yours, who is clever, ambitious, and sly."

Mary slumped in her chair and sighed.

"I have to admit," she confessed wearily, "that despite my loving behavior toward her, and the fact that I have tried to feel for her as a sister should, I cannot love or trust Elizabeth. I can never forget that she is the daughter of the Concubine, the woman who ousted my sainted mother from my father's affections. Every time I look at her, I see Anne Boleyn, and I remember the misery that woman caused me. Is my mistrust and dislike down to my own fantasies, or is Elizabeth really a threat to me?"

"You should trust your instincts, madam," Renard said with conviction.

"I will take your advice, dear friend," the Queen assured him.

They were now at Richmond Palace, and the Queen had made public her determination to restore the old faith, and her resolve not to force her subjects into compliance. Nevertheless, Protestant clergy were forbidden to preach, which prompted many to defy the Queen's decree and then found themselves committed to prison. Archbishop Cranmer, who had pronounced Mary's mother's marriage to King Henry invalid, was among them. There were violent protests in London, and many Protestants deemed it wise to flee abroad.

There was much talk of the Queen's marriage. The word at court was that she was considering Prince Philip of Spain, son of the Emperor Charles V and one of the most ardent champions of Catholicism in Europe.

"The English will never accept it," Elizabeth told an anxious de Noailles as they strolled by the Thames at Richmond. "Not so much because he is a Catholic, but because he is a foreigner."

"Such a marriage would be a perpetual calamity for all Christendom," de Noailles said vehemently. "But fortunately, it is not the only match under consideration. Bishop Gardiner is pushing for the Queen to marry Cardinal Pole."

Elizabeth stared at him.

"But he is to be our new Archbishop of Canterbury. And surely he has taken vows of celibacy?"

The ambassador shrugged.

"The Pope, I am sure, would be most accommodating. The Cardinal would make an excellent choice, for he has the royal blood of your Plantagenet kings in his veins."

"I doubt he is willing," Elizabeth said. "*I* heard that the Cardinal counseled the Queen to stay single. To me, that would seem the safest choice, but I fear she would never agree."

"She wants a Catholic heir," de Noailles reminded her. "As for a husband for her, there is always Edward Courtenay, whom Her Majesty freed from the Tower. He comes from a great Catholic family, and he too is of the old royal blood."

"But he is just twenty-seven!" Elizabeth remarked.

"The same age as the Prince of Spain, I believe," the envoy chimed in.

"And he has been shut up in the Tower for years. It is said he cannot even ride a horse."

"He can learn. He is well educated, extraordinarily handsome, and has a natural civility."

Elizabeth recalled the tall, fair young man whom she had seen about the court. He seemed a trifle weak-faced for her taste, not dark and dashing like . . . She pulled herself up. She had trained herself to forget the Admiral.

"He is too naïve and ignorant of the court and society," she pronounced dismissively.

"Bishop Gardiner likes him well," de Noailles observed.

"That's no recommendation!" Elizabeth laughed, but really, she knew, it was no laughing matter, because the hard-line Catholic bishop now enjoyed great influence with the Queen.

"Of course," de Noailles murmured, lowering his voice, "you yourself could marry Courtenay. It would be a marriage tailor-made for our times: the mingling of Tudor blood with Plantagenet blood, Protestant with Catholic."

Elizabeth looked at him coolly, well aware of what he was hinting at.

"I have no mind to marry," she told him.

The ambassador looked disbelieving. "I think you are jesting with me," he said.

"I was never more in earnest!" Elizabeth retorted and walked on briskly, leaving him astonished.

She sought out William Cecil, on whose advice she had come increasingly to depend, and found him in his lodging, helping his servant to stow away his belongings into a battered old traveling chest.

"You are leaving court, William?" she asked sharply.

Cecil turned a resigned face to her.

"Yes, my lady. There is no place for me here anymore. My Protestant views are too well known, and it is remembered that I served the former government."

"But you will continue to serve *me,* I hope?" Elizabeth replied.

"Of course, madam. It will be my pleasure." Cecil smiled. "In fact, I am off to Hatfield this afternoon to arrange for the chimneys to be repaired."

"I rejoice to hear it," Elizabeth told him. "Some of them are badly cracked."

"I did tell your steward to put the work in hand, madam, but I fear he has been dilatory."

"And I have not been there to prod him!" Elizabeth smiled. "Anyway, William, I have not come here to talk of chimneys. I need your advice. The French ambassador is suggesting that I marry Edward Courtenay."

Cecil raised his eyebrows. "I thought the Queen had plans in that direction."

"She does," said Elizabeth, absentmindedly picking up and folding a shirt. "So why should de Noailles propose him for me?"

Cecil frowned. "I fear there can be only one reason. My lady, this is not just a ploy to get you a husband. It smacks to me of treason!"

"Aye, and to me too," Elizabeth replied. "Yet I do not wish to forfeit the friendship and goodwill of the French King. I simply said I had no wish to marry."

"A clever reply," Cecil approved. "Never commit yourself."

"I don't intend to," she smiled. "Had you heard that Cardinal Pole is also in the running to wed the Queen?"

"Cardinal Pole? They'll suit each other very well." William chuckled. "They could spend all night saying their prayers!"

He turned to her, the smile fading.

"This Edward Courtenay," he said. "He is not for you."

"Do you think I would have him?" Elizabeth retorted with a grimace.

"Not for one moment," Cecil said, grinning. "Just take my advice and go carefully in this matter. You are dicing with treason if you ever give any appearance of approving such a match."

"I will take care, dear friend," Elizabeth assured him.

—

"My Lady Elizabeth!" Courtenay sketched an elegant bow.

They had met on the orchard path, coming from opposite directions. Elizabeth had been enjoying a long walk in the bright sunshine, attended by Kat—now very grand in her new role as lady mistress and companion to the Queen's heir—and the bevy of maids who had been appointed to serve her.

"Lord Edward." Elizabeth smiled. This was not the first time that Courtenay had waylaid her. "I trust I find you well."

"It is Your Grace's health that is more precious," he replied. He was rapidly learning the ways of the courtier after his many years in the Tower.

"I am all the better for seeing your lordship," she told him, returning the compliment. He really was a likable fellow, for all that he seemed so much younger than his years.

"Then, my lady, I hope it will please you to hear that the Queen has graciously consented to restore to me the earldom of Devon." He had clearly been bursting to tell her.

Elizabeth gave him an arch look. "If rumor speaks truth, my lord, she has a mind to advance you much further than that."

Courtenay's expression turned furtive. He offered her his arm and steered her farther along the path, out of earshot of her women.

"May I speak plainly, madam?" he asked.

Elizabeth nodded. "Of course."

"Monsieur de Noailles has told me that the Queen's Grace is set on marrying the Prince of Spain," he confided.

"Monsieur de Noailles is getting a little ahead of himself." Elizabeth smiled. "I do not think anything is certain yet. The Queen blushes every time marriage is mentioned, and it is all her councillors can do to get her to talk about it. I know, for I've heard them grumbling."

"Ah, but we do not know what is discussed in secret," Courtenay persisted. "I believe the ambassador has many spies, and that he knows things we do not."

"That's as may be, my lord," Elizabeth said, a trifle sharply. "All that matters to me is Her Majesty's happiness."

"I think her singular desire is to marry Prince Philip," Courtenay declared. "As for myself—well, my heart is set elsewhere."

"May I know the name of the lady," Elizabeth inquired pleasantly.

"It is yourself," he breathed, looking at her amorously.

Elizabeth pretended to be overcome with maidenly confusion.

"Why, my lord," she said, pressing a hand to her cheek, "I know not how to answer you . . . I am flattered, I assure you, but I need time to take this in. I had no idea, really."

"I hope you do not think me presumptuous," Courtenay asked anxiously.

"No, I—I am just surprised," Elizabeth simpered.

"I do not think the Queen will refuse her permission," he said brightly.

"Permission for what?" Elizabeth asked.

"For us to marry," he said, beaming eagerly. Poor boy, she thought, he must still be a virgin, having been locked up all those years. But marry him?

"Let us not think of that yet," she counseled hastily. "I must ponder on it. I had determined, you see, to live a single life."

"There are many good reasons why we should marry," Courtenay urged. "We are both of royal blood, so we are near equally matched; we are of meet age; and I am in love with you, my lady."

Elizabeth turned away so that he should not see her smile. Poor fool, he had no idea what being in love was. To him, it was mere courtly protocol. But there was something more behind this, she suspected.

"Did Monsieur de Noailles suggest this marriage?" she asked.

"Yes, it was he who encouraged me to press my suit," the naïve young man replied. "He said that our union would have King Henri's backing."

"Indeed it would," Elizabeth said. "However, much as you love me—and I am flattered that you do—I think we should wait awhile and test our feelings for each other."

"I hope you will not be a cruel mistress," Courtenay pleaded.

"I could never be unkind to so ardent a suitor," Elizabeth told him. "And now, my lord, we must adjourn our talk, for the dinner hour approaches and I must make ready. Farewell." She extended her hand, which Courtenay, dropping hastily to one knee, seized and kissed.

"What was all that about," asked Kat, eyeing his retreating back suspiciously.

"Oh, another of my many proposals of marriage!" Elizabeth laughed.

"Unfortunately, this one is in earnest, courtesy of the machinations of the French ambassador."

"I trust you turned him down and sent him off with a flea in his ear!" Kat bridled.

"I played along with his little fantasy," Elizabeth told her, looking mischievous. "I told him I would think on it, and dissuaded him from rushing off to ask for the Queen's blessing. After all, he's supposed to be *her* suitor. Nothing can come of it, I promise you."

Courtenay was clearly the man of the moment. Everyone expected the Queen to marry him.

Elizabeth's friends could talk of little else, and her privy chamber became a forum for gossip.

"The courtiers are flocking to him, greedy for his patronage," Parry said. "They kneel when they address him. Imagine!"

"The nobles are cozening him with rich gifts," John Astley put in. "My lord of Pembroke has just presented him with some fine steeds."

"What use will they be, since he hasn't yet the skill to ride one of them?" Elizabeth smirked.

"He has the skill to ride women, we hear," Kat muttered.

"What did you say?" Elizabeth pulled Kat around to face her. Kat looked at Master Parry, who reddened.

"Saving your pardon, my lady, but it is being bruited about the court that my lord Earl is making up for lost time in the stews of Southwark."

Elizabeth smiled. "I'll warrant the Queen doesn't know *that*," she said.

"I hope he has the wit to be discreet," Astley said. "Really, the man is insufferable, giving himself all these airs and graces. He's already boasting about the splendid suit he will wear for his coronation."

Elizabeth's smile faded. So much for his being in love with me, she thought. Not that she felt anything for Courtenay, but his overt maneuvering to marry the Queen was surely evidence that his protestations by the river had been purely self-seeking. It surprised her but it stung. How insulting to be jilted thus!

"And the Queen has given him a ring that belonged to King Henry," Kat was saying. "It was worth sixteen thousand crowns."

"It sounds as if she is seriously thinking of marrying him," her husband opined.

"My sister could not be such a fool," Elizabeth declared, with a touch of bitterness. "He is shallow and empty, and she will soon see through his flattery."

Alone in her bedchamber that night, still prickling from Courtenay's swift change of heart, Elizabeth looked into her mirror, seeking to salve her wounded vanity. Of course, Mary was the Queen, and a much grander match than one who was just heiress presumptive to the throne. But how could Courtenay compare Mary to her? The face that was gazing back at her so intensely was far more youthful and beautiful than the Queen's, and surely a wonderful prize for any man . . . But not for Courtenay, she thought grimly. She was saving herself for someone far better than he . . . If, that was, she could ever find a man worthy of her rank and her love; a man for whom she would be willing to surrender her freedom; a man who could persuade her that marriage was worth the risks . . .

"My Lady Elizabeth!" Courtenay swept off his hat and bowed low. The courtiers in the gallery stared.

"Well met, my lord, at last," Elizabeth said sharply, pausing to glare at him haughtily. "Tut, tut! I have been hearing disquieting rumors that your love is given to another, whose name I dare not speak."

Courtenay had the grace to look abashed.

"Pay no heed to rumor, madam. My heart is yours and ever shall be."

"Ah, but is mine yours?" she answered softly, smiling mischievously, then continued on her way, leaving him gawping disconcertedly after her.

Queen Mary gazed at the portrait of the young man in elegant black, whose manly pose—hand on hip—showed off to advantage his trim physique and muscular legs in their silken hose. Philip of Spain had dark brown hair, large, soulful eyes, a straight nose, very full red lips beneath a lighter brown mustache, and the prominent Habsburg jaw, which was not quite disguised by his short, neat beard.

What was it that attracted one person to another? Was it purely looks or bodily attributes, or was it something of character that was revealed in a person's face? Why was it that Mary, whose senses had never yet awakened to a man's touch, yet who had cherished romantic dreams of all her many suitors, should have taken one look at Philip and felt her insides melting away? For he was beautiful in her eyes, the very embodiment of all that was desirable in the masculine form. And having taken that look, then drunk her fill, she was lost.

Renard was watching the Queen closely. Her reaction to the portrait was obvious, and more than he could ever have anticipated.

"Madam?" he said gently. Mary collected herself and smiled radiantly. "Yes, Simon, I like what I see," she said.

"He is the finest match in Christendom," Renard pointed out. "He is the heir to a huge empire compassing much of Europe and stretching even to the Americas. He is famed for his wise judgment, his good sense, his sound expertise in government, and his moderation."

"Looking at him leaves me in no doubt of all that," Mary said, "but forgive me, I must ask this. My ambassadors abroad have sent other reports that he is cold and cruel."

Renard shook his head ruefully.

"They have been misled by the Prince's enemies," he declared. "He is not cold. He loved his late wife, and when she died in childbirth, he was grief-stricken." Since then, he had been living with a mistress, but Renard refrained from telling Mary that. Such things were regrettable, but not unusual. It was the way of the world: Great men married for duty and bedded their mistresses for pleasure.

"As for being cruel, madam, I can only think that your ambassador was of the new religion and offended by witnessing what follows upon those great acts of faith over which the Prince has sometimes presided." Mary had heard much of these acts of faith—autos-da-fé, they called them, the long religious ceremonies staged by the Spanish Inquisition, at which large numbers of heretics and lapsed converts were exhorted to recant and perform acts of penitence; those who refused would be sentenced and handed over to the secular authorities to be tortured and burned at the stake immediately afterward.

"As a good daughter of the Church, Your Majesty knows that such punishment is a heretic's last chance of salvation," Renard continued. "Thus, far from being cruel, His Highness has shown himself most merciful in his zeal for the Inquisition."

"Of course," Mary agreed. "And he would be just the helpmeet I need to persuade this godforsaken realm to return to the true faith. Yet I have one other reservation, I fear."

"Tell me," Renard encouraged her.

A slow flush infused the Queen's cheeks. "The Prince is but twenty-six, and I am thirty-seven. He might feel he is too young for me."

Renard laughed dismissively.

"The age gap is a trifle, madam. His Highness is an old married man with a son of seven! And he is as eager for this marriage as you are. You have only to say the word."

"I don't know . . ." Mary sounded doubtful and confused. "Believe me, I *am* inclined to this marriage, but I fear my council's reaction. I am aware that many still cling privately to their heretical beliefs, and there are many too who would resent my taking a foreign prince as my husband. The English are very insular, Simon, and suspicious of foreigners. Some of them even think the French have tails!"

"Now, that I can believe!" he chuckled. "But I would counsel that you broach the matter gently."

"I cannot broach it at all," Mary said, her blush deepening. "I cannot face discussing such a delicate matter with so many gentlemen."

"Then I will ask my master the Emperor to make a written approach to them," Renard said soothingly, wondering how on earth Philip would fare when it came to more intimate matters. "He will be tactful and ac-commodating, rest assured."

"I'm not sure . . . ," Mary said again. "This is all too . . . too—"

"What is it you fear?" Renard asked softly, regarding her sympatheti-cally.

"It is marriage itself," Mary confessed, hardly daring to meet his eyes. "I have never felt that which is called love, nor have I ever harbored voluptuous thoughts. My father King Henry proposed many suitors for me, but nothing came of it, and in truth, I never thought much of mar-rying until God was pleased to raise me to the throne. I assure you, as a private individual, I would not desire it. But . . ." Her eyes strayed to the portrait and lingered there. "That is why I must leave it all to the Em-peror, whom I regard as a father."

"I understand, madam," said Renard avuncularly. "My master will do as you wish."

Elizabeth entered the council chamber white-faced and nervous, know-ing full well why she had been summoned. There they sat, in a line along the far side of the table, these hard-bitten, influential men, with many of whom she was well acquainted. Some were staunch Catholics, some had gladly reverted to the old religion, while others, she knew, paid mere lip service to it, but all were desirous of keeping their places, which was why they were ready to turn on her now.

As she seated herself in the chair facing them, the Lord Chancellor, Bishop Gardiner, frowned at her, bushy eyebrows furrowing above his big nose.

"Madam, you should know that Her Majesty is becoming less tolerant of those who persist in heresy," he began, "and she is particularly angered by your own failure to attend Mass."

"My lords, I had understood that Her Majesty had made it clear she would not compel or constrain men's consciences," Elizabeth stated, determined to hold her ground.

"That is her position until Parliament determines upon the matter," Gardiner conceded. "But is it her hope that her subjects—and above all her heir—will embrace the true faith as fervently as she does."

"We understand that the Queen has several times asked you to attend Mass with her, but that you have refused," the old Duke of Norfolk, her great-uncle, barked at her. Age had not softened his martial manner.

"I refused on the grounds of my conscience," Elizabeth protested, "and if the Queen's Grace insists on constraining her subjects to obedience, then why did she issue proclamations leading them to believe otherwise?"

As soon as she had said it, she wished she could have bitten her tongue out. In her anger, she had allowed her customary caution to desert her and had gone too far, certainly. Yet she had but spoken the truth. What other answer could she have made?

The lords' faces were grim. Some were muttering to one another.

"That is a rude and disrespectful response," Gardiner told her, his expression severe, "and this council censures you for ignoring the Queen's wishes, not only in this matter of the Mass, but also for repeatedly failing to heed her honest requests that you put aside your plain garb and don more suitable attire."

"Is it now a crime to dress soberly and modestly?" Elizabeth retorted tartly. "Forgive me, I did not know."

"You know very well why you wear those clothes, and it has nothing to do with modesty. You do it so that the Protestants know you for their friend, to the despite of the Queen."

Elizabeth took a deep breath. Angry though she felt, it would do her no good to antagonize these ill-disposed men further.

"I should like to see the Queen and explain myself to *her*," she said. "I pray you, ask her to grant me an audience."

Mary kept her waiting for two days before the summons came to attend her in the long gallery at Richmond. During that time, Elizabeth had had leisure to reflect on her situation and discuss it with Kat.

"I fear that a compromise is called for," she said. "Much as I wish to be seen as a friend to the Protestants, I dare not risk incurring the Queen's wrath by openly adhering to my faith."

"There's no point in putting yourself in danger," Kat agreed. "The Queen started out by promising tolerance, but she seems to be changing her tune, and things can only get worse if rumor speaks truth and she does wed Prince Philip. Marry, we live in perilous times."

"We do indeed," Elizabeth replied, her heart sinking at the prospect of the coming confrontation.

"Do not trust her!" Renard warned, his eyes glittering in the flickering candlelight.

Mary was disturbed by the vehemence in his tone.

"She is my sister," she said slowly, "and so far she has shown herself loyal. It is only in this matter of religion that she has fallen short."

"And there lies her treachery!" Renard declared. "That troublemaker, the French ambassador, is stirring up dissidents and heretics in a bid to discountenance my master the Emperor and prevent Your Majesty from marrying Prince Philip. The Lady Elizabeth is in league with him, I am certain. I have even heard it said that the papists are having their turn, but the Lady Elizabeth will remedy all in time."

"I cannot believe it of her," Mary said, twisting her rings anxiously.

"Do not underestimate her, madam," the ambassador warned. "She seems to be clinging to the new religion out of policy to attract and win the support of the heretics."

Mary rose and walked to the latticed window. Below her, the wide, moonlit courtyard was empty. Most people in the palace would be abed by now, but she knew she herself would not sleep well tonight with this vexing matter of her sister on her mind.

"You have evidence that she is intriguing against me?" she asked.

"Not as yet," Renard admitted. "Of course, I may be mistaken in suspecting her, but it is safer to forestall than to be forestalled. She is clever and sly, and possessed of a spirit full of enchantment. In my opinion, madam, she is so dangerous that she should be sent forthwith to the Tower, or at the very least away from court, for her presence here is undoubtedly a threat to Your Majesty's security."

Mary stared at him.

"You truly think she wishes me ill?"

Renard shrugged. "She is ambitious. She might be persuaded to conceive some dangerous design, or others might do so in her name."

"I confess that the same considerations have been in my mind too," Mary said. "I find it hard to believe that *she* would go so far, but I have no doubt there are others who would not scruple to set her up in my place if they could. But without any evidence against my sister, I cannot put her in the Tower. No, I will not."

She began pacing back and forth.

"All would be solved if she consents to convert to the true faith. That is my earnest desire. And it is necessary too, for she is the heiress to the throne."

"Until Your Majesty has a son," Renard said gently.

Mary blushed.

"When that happens, I shall not need to fear my sister anymore," she observed. "But for now, I must do my best to bring her back to the fold and disappoint her heretical followers. I see her tomorrow. She has asked for this audience because she is clearly worried about her position. I, in my turn, shall use it to press home my advantage."

Elizabeth threw herself on her knees before the Queen. She had built up and up to this meeting, and now that the moment had come, she could not stop shaking, and was even near to weeping; the fact that it happened to be her twentieth birthday, and that there would be no merry celebration this year, only made her feel worse. The presence of the Imperial ambassador, a dark, menacing basilisk standing behind Mary's chair, made her even more fearful.

"Well, Sister," Mary said, her face unsmiling, her eyes wary, "we both of us know why I have sent for you."

Elizabeth's heart sank still further. It was not difficult to summon up a tear.

"I see only too clearly that Your Majesty is not well disposed toward me," she faltered, "and I can think of no other cause except religion. Yet I beg Your Majesty to excuse me on this issue, as I have been brought up a Protestant and was never taught the doctrines of the ancient religion."

Play for time, she had told herself.

"I entreat Your Majesty," she went on, "to arrange for me to take instruction from some learned man, and be given books to read, so that I might know if my conscience will allow me to be persuaded that way."

Mary's face had lit up in joyful hope, but Renard was looking askance at Elizabeth, his eyes quizzical. She was in no doubt that he knew her to be insincere.

"I am heartily gratified to hear that," the Queen said. "You shall have your instruction, I promise it."

"I thank you, madam," Elizabeth murmured, head bowed.

"It is my dearest wish that you embrace the true faith," Mary told her. "I assure you, Sister, that if you come to Mass, belief will surely follow. It is my pleasure that you attend the service in celebration of the Nativity of the Blessed Virgin Mary tomorrow."

Elizabeth fell back on a tried-and-tested excuse. She placed her hands on her stomacher and assumed an expression of suffering.

"Alas, madam, I fear I am unwell. I am plagued by the most fearful pains in my belly."

Both Mary and Renard were frowning.

"You are well enough to come here and plead your case," Mary said firmly. "God must not be put off with excuses. I expect to see you there."

As Elizabeth emerged reluctantly from her apartments, with Kat and her ladies in tow, she was dismayed to see curious courtiers lining the gallery that led to the chapel. If it was bad enough having to attend Mass, it was even worse having people knowing about it, and some of those watching her with disappointment and disapproval in their eyes were of the new faith.

"Kat, my stomach is aching so," she said loudly, putting on an air of suffering and staggering a little. "Oh, oh."

She was still sighing when she saw the Queen's procession approaching, and she moaned slightly as she dropped in a curtsy by the door to the chapel.

"Good morning, Sister," Mary said, raising her up. "I trust you are feeling better this morning."

"No, madam," Elizabeth groaned. "I am ill."

Mary looked exasperated.

"You will feel better when you are spiritually refreshed," she said briskly and sailed on into the chapel. Elizabeth clutched desperately at her stomach with one hand and tugged at the sleeve of Susan Clarencieux, the Queen's chief lady-in-waiting, as she passed.

"Pray rub my stomach for me, Susan," she groaned.

Mrs. Clarencieux glared at her, well aware of the game she was playing.

"Madam, we must take our seats, as the Mass is about to begin," she hissed, standing back so that Elizabeth could precede her. Seeing no way of escape, Elizabeth walked slowly to her place, deliberately fiddling with the tiny gold book that she wore at her girdle, the one that contained the prayer of her brother Edward, and she was praying that those of the late king's persuasion would take her gesture as a signal that she remained staunch in her faith.

She had not been to confession, of course, so she could not receive the bread and the wine, and when the Host was elevated, she closed her eyes and bent her head, as if in prayer. But this was enough to satisfy the Queen, who embraced her warmly afterward and presented her with a costly diamond, a ruby brooch, and a rosary of coral. Elizabeth put that last object away in a drawer, determined never to wear it. Nor did she turn up for Mass the following Sunday.

"She is dissembling, madam, the better to play her own game!" Lord Chancellor Gardiner thundered.

"Now she shows herself in her true colors," Renard chimed in. "Madam, you are harboring a serpent in your bosom, as I have warned you before!"

Mary sent for Elizabeth.

"I beg you, Sister, speak freely," she urged. "You must say if you firmly believe what Catholics have always believed concerning the Holy

Sacrament, that it becomes the actual body and blood of Our Lord at the moment of consecration."

Elizabeth paled. She swallowed, aware that Gardiner and Renard were watching her like hawks about to swoop, and sensing the danger in which she would stand if she gave the wrong answer. She must retain Mary's sympathy at all costs, for there was much at stake.

"Madam, I *have* seen the error of my ways," she said, low, "and I have been planning to make a public declaration that I attended Mass because my conscience moved me to it, and that I went of my own free will."

Mary smiled and embraced her impulsively.

"You gladden my heart with your words," she told her. "Why, you are trembling! There is no need, Sister. All is well."

"I feared I had displeased Your Majesty," Elizabeth said.

"Not anymore," Mary said warmly.

Renard, watching Elizabeth depart, could barely contain his exasperation.

"She is deceiving us all," he told the Queen. "She failed to give a direct answer to your question."

"She is lying about her conversion," growled Gardiner.

Mary looked distressed.

"You still think that, dear friends?" she asked.

"I fear so, madam," Renard answered. "She is a hypocrite. One day she knows nothing about the Catholic faith, the next she realizes she has been in error. She is clever, but not that clever. And Your Majesty, forgive me, is too trusting, and too ready to believe the best of everyone."

Bishop Gardiner hummed agreement.

"It troubles me to think that, if I died before bearing a son, my throne would pass to one whose beliefs are so suspect," Mary said slowly, twisting her rings again. "Indeed, it would burden my conscience too heavily to allow Elizabeth to succeed me, if you are right and she only goes to Mass out of hypocrisy. It would be a disgrace to my kingdom."

She sank down in her chair of estate, older doubts about Elizabeth surfacing in her troubled mind.

"She is, after all, the daughter of one of whose good fame you might have heard," she observed with irony. "One who received her just punishment."

"She has inherited too much of that lady's character to make a good queen," Gardiner observed. "I admit I was once taken in by her mother's superficial charm, but I saw the light in time."

But Mary was not listening. She was wrestling with a particular worry that had festered in her breast for many a long year, and had lately been the cause of many sleepless nights. Now, with her other pressing concerns about Elizabeth, she could contain herself no longer.

"I must tell you that I doubt she is my father's child," she blurted out, surprised at herself, for she had never voiced this to anyone in her life.

Gardiner and Renard stared at her in astonishment.

"Hear me out," she said, a little breathless at her own candor. "I heard it said, many years ago, soon after the Concubine's fall, that Elizabeth bore a resemblance to Mark Smeaton, the lute player who was accused of criminal relations with that woman. More than one person remarked that the child bore his face and countenance. And if that is true, then she is not my sister at all, still less the lawful heir to my throne."

"I heard those bruits too, but I fear they were mere malicious gossip, more's the pity," the bishop said. "I saw that fool Smeaton, and I couldn't detect any resemblance. And she does have a look of Your Majesty's late father, do you not agree?"

"I wish I could see it," Mary said.

"It is impossible to prove or disprove paternity, so I counsel you not to go down that road, madam," Renard put in. "I never saw King Henry or Smeaton, so I cannot comment, but these doubts are based only on rumors. There is no evidence, nothing solid on which to base any case for disinheriting her."

"That is what bothers me," Mary said. "It does not allay my doubts, though."

"The best solution," Gardiner said, business-like and practical, "is for Your Majesty to marry as soon as possible and produce an heir of your body. Courtenay is ready and willing, so what, madam, are you waiting for?"

Mary winced at his bluntness, her blush deepening. She was remembering secret reports she had received concerning Courtenay's expeditions to the brothels of London.

"He is too young," she said dismissively.

"And he is in league with the French ambassador, who is plotting to marry him to the Lady Elizabeth," Renard added. "And in this respect, as well as the other, *she* is greatly to be feared, for she has her eye on Courtenay, make no doubt. I fear too that, if you turn Courtenay down, madam, his friends might hatch some design to menace you and set up Elizabeth on the throne with Courtenay as her husband."

"I think you wrong Courtenay," Gardiner protested. "He has not the wits to devise such a plot."

"That is what worries me," Renard said. "He will be easily led by others. You are overfond of the boy, my Lord Bishop."

"We were many years in the Tower together," Gardiner said stiffly.

"I fear that has clouded your judgment," Renard retorted dismissively. "No, madam," he continued decisively, not giving the outraged bishop a chance to respond, "you must marry, and the Prince of Spain eagerly awaits your answer."

"The English people will never accept him as their master," Gardiner blustered, determined to reassert his view. "Courtenay is the better candidate."

"No," said Mary. "Enough, gentlemen. The matter is too delicate. I must go and pray for guidance."

As soon as the door had closed, Gardiner turned to Renard.

"The Queen is a woman, and these matters are beyond her," he said despairingly.

"That is why she must marry, and soon, so that she can benefit from her husband's wisdom and guidance," Renard pointed out.

"And bear children," Gardiner added. "That will put my Lady Elizabeth's nose out of joint! Her Majesty should marry Courtenay."

"Prince Philip would be the greater match," Renard countered.

Elizabeth had a megrim on the day of Mary's coronation. It came on as she sat with a smiling and bowing Anna of Cleves in the chariot immediately following the Queen's, so that she found herself waving at the crowds through a blinding blur of zigzag lines, and by the time she was seated in her place of honor in Westminster Abbey, one side of her head was gripped in a raging agony, and all she longed for was to lie down in a darkened room and have her forehead bathed in cold water. The soaring music, the Latin chants, and the blaring of trumpets were torture to her, as was the glare from hundreds of lighted candles. She had to keep her head down and her eyes closed, so that almost all she saw of the great ceremony was an occasional peep at her white damask skirts spread out upon the blue carpet that had been laid in the church, and the richly shod feet of those who passed in procession near her. Only once did she lift her aching eyes, and that was to see the crown placed on her sister's brow. She was struck by the rapture in Mary's face . . .

Afterward, she had to sit with the Queen and the Princess Anna at the high table in Westminster Hall, where a magnificent coronation banquet was served. She winced as the Queen's Champion clattered noisily into the hall on his charger and, as was his custom, challenged any man to dispute Her Majesty's title. The sight of the food made her feel nauseous, and all she could get down herself were sips of wine.

Hours later, after the cloths had been lifted and the tables removed, hippocras and wafers were served, and the Queen began to circulate around the hall, receiving the congratulations of her guests. Elizabeth leaned her aching head against the cool stone of a doorway, then suddenly de Noailles was beside her, his smile ingratiating.

"I trust I find your ladyship in good health," he said, bowing.

"In faith, my coronet is too heavy," Elizabeth complained, rubbing her hot brow. Renard, a faintly sinister figure in his customary black, was hovering nearby, she noticed.

"Have patience, madam," de Noailles counseled. "This small crown will soon bring you a bigger one."

"I do not understand," she replied loudly, but Renard had gone. What will he report of me now? she wondered.

William Cecil came rarely to visit her these days, for he was no longer popular at court and feared to compromise her, but one day, as she was riding in Richmond Park, she espied a familiar figure approaching on horseback.

"I thought I would find you in the vicinity, my lady," he called in greeting. "I came in haste to warn you. You'll have heard the news of Parliament."

"I know that England is officially returned to Catholicism," Elizabeth said, reining in her mount and looking behind her. Her attendants were a long way off.

"Aye," he said grimly. "And it is now forbidden to criticize the Mass or own the Book of Common Prayer. There are uprisings in London, and do you wonder? They are vandalizing the churches and attacking priests."

"Soon it will be too dangerous to practice our faith." Elizabeth shivered.

"Many are fleeing abroad," Cecil told her. "They are probably the wise ones."

Something more was troubling him. She could read it in his face.

"What bothers you, old friend?" she challenged. He liked her directness.

"Something I have to tell you," he sighed. "You should know that your father's marriage to Queen Katherine, Her Majesty's mother, has been declared valid by Parliament; that Act makes the Queen legitimate . . ."

"And myself still a bastard." Elizabeth laughed bitterly. "Am I to be disinherited then?"

Cecil did not answer immediately.

"No, Parliament would not agree, but the Queen had asked if it were possible," he revealed. "I thought you should be aware of that. Know thine enemy—it's prudent to do so."

"So she still distrusts me," Elizabeth said, shaken by this news. Did Mary hate her that much? She had not realized it.

"You can hardly blame her," Cecil commented. "She knows as well as you do that you go to Mass on sufferance, and that in your heart you adhere to your faith. She wants a Catholic succession—that's why she would disinherit you."

"What can I do?" Elizabeth asked him.

"Bide your time," Cecil counseled. "Put not a foot wrong. Keep going to Mass. God will understand."

That evening, as they sat at supper in the presence chamber, Mary leaned over to Elizabeth and pressed a small package wrapped in silk into her hand.

"For you," she said, her eyes glinting.

"I thank you, madam," Elizabeth replied, surprised and pleased at this apparent mark of favor. "That is most kind of Your Majesty."

Her smile faded when she opened the tiny gold diptych and saw inside the miniatures of King Henry and Queen Katherine.

"It has an eye and chain so that you may wear it at your girdle," Mary said, eyeing her closely.

"I am humbly grateful," Elizabeth forced herself to say. Had Mary shouted her triumph from the rooftops, she could not have made her meaning plainer. For if Katherine's marriage to their father had been a true one, then Anne Boleyn's had been no marriage at all. That was the message this gift brought. A message confirming and underlining Elizabeth's bastardy. And she was expected to wear it, and proclaim thereby to the world her flawed status.

Never! she thought. It would go in the drawer with the coral rosary.

Renard took the proffered stool and seated himself gratefully by the brazier in Mary's linenfold-paneled closet. It was late evening and the Queen looked weary, he thought, sagging almost in her carved oak chair.

"My master the Emperor would know your answer to his son's proposal," he said gently. "He has written to Your Majesty's council but received no reply. He grows impatient, I fear."

Mary did not speak for a while. She was thinking of the handsome man in the portrait, the man who made her heart flutter in her maiden breast, the man who was to assist her in her great task of returning England to Rome, and fretting because she knew he could never love an aging virgin such as she was.

"I thank the Emperor for suggesting a greater match than I deserve," she said at length. "However, I am not sure that my subjects will accept a foreign prince as their king, and I do not yet know if my council will give assent to the marriage. Then I fear that, with all his cares and responsibilities abroad, the Prince will have little time to spend in England, and I can hardly leave my realm for long periods. And I know there are fears that he will involve us in his own wars. Then—and I know we have talked of this before—he is only twenty-six years of age. A man of twenty-six," she pressed on, blushing, but determined to make her point, "is likely disposed to be amorous, and such is not my desire, not at my time of life. I have never harbored thoughts of love. So you see, I cannot possibly make up my mind quickly."

Renard bestowed on her his most avuncular smile.

"Madam, hear me out. Prince Philip is so admirable, so virtuous, prudent, and modest as to appear too wonderful to be human," he declared extravagantly. "Far from being young and amorous, His Highness is a prince of stable and settled character. If Your Majesty accepts his proposal, he will relieve you of the pains and labors that are rather men's work than the concerns of ladies. His Highness is a great prince to whom your kingdom could turn for protection and succor. Your Majesty would do well to remember that you have enemies: the heretics and malcontents in your realm, the French, and the Lady Elizabeth. All would rise against you if they had the means."

Mary seized upon this opportunity to deftly change the subject.

"I am happy to report that the Lady Elizabeth no longer has the means, at least in one respect," she informed Renard. "I spoke with Courtenay last week, and he confided to me that he has never had any wish to marry her, as she is too great a heretic. I told him he could never look to have me, which I fear somewhat offended him, so I offered to find him a suitable Catholic bride, but he declined. I am hoping he will go abroad, and I have made that clear to him. He just makes mischief in this realm, and now that I have turned him down, he may make more. Look." She handed Renard a sheaf of pamphlets.

"This is outrageous!" he exclaimed, looking them over rapidly and reading scurrilous and obscene assertions about Philip's morals that were in part too close to reality for comfort, and were doubtless based on information obligingly provided by that rat of a French ambassador.

Renard collected himself hastily. "These are intended purely to blacken Prince Philip's name, which would be to Courtenay's advantage. Make no matter of them, madam, for none of these calumnies is true." He stroked his beard. "What concerns me more is Courtenay's claim that he does not wish to marry the Lady Elizabeth. I do not believe it. She has shown him marked favor and is often in his company. I see their friendship as a threat to Your Majesty."

"I have thought of a solution," Mary said suddenly. "Elizabeth shall be found a Catholic husband abroad. That will curb her ambitions."

The day was crisp and clear, and Elizabeth was exhilarated by the wind gusting past and fanning out her long hair as she spurred her horse in the hunt. Ahead, the Queen was forging forward in the midst of her favored courtiers, the ever-present Renard galloping at her side. There were wild shouts as the quarry was sighted and cornered, then everyone reined in their steeds as Mary dismounted for the kill.

Elizabeth sat in her saddle watching impassively as blood spurted from the throat of the terrified deer. As its pounding heart stilled, and the courtiers cheered, she was suddenly conscious that the horseman next to her was Courtenay. He seemed unaware she was there, so she tapped him lightly on the arm.

"Madam." He nodded, his manner correct and formal, then turned away.

Elizabeth cared not a fig for Courtenay; in fact, she despised the posturing fool, but she had enjoyed flirting with him and had also been mischievously willing to fuel the rumors about them, if only to discountenance the Imperial ambassador. But she was damned if she was going to let her once ardent suitor treat her so discourteously.

"Why so distant, my lord?" she challenged.

"I should not be seen with you, madam. We are watched," he said stiffly, looking at Renard.

"We have been watched for weeks," she retorted. "It never bothered you before, even when wagging tongues had us married!"

"I would not now presume so far," he muttered.

"Rumor has it that you presumed farther and were spurned," she said softly. "Really, my lord, you are too fickle, and cruel to one whom you were supposed to love."

The visage he turned to her was ugly; he was looking at her as if he despised her.

"Did I say I loved you, madam? I forget. Maybe it is your fantasy, for I am of no mind to mate with a heretic, nor one who has fallen so far from the Queen's favor. I value my place in the world. Now, if you will excuse me."

His words came like a slap in the face. She was speechless as she watched him riding off. Suddenly she wanted to be away from it all, away from the intrigue, the backbiting, the rumors, the suspicion, and the ever-present sense of impending peril. Her position at court was becoming increasingly dangerous, she realized, but it was also blindingly clear that she was no longer held in esteem in high places. Had she been, Courtenay would never have dared to behave toward her in such an insulting fashion.

Out of the blue, she found herself longing for the peace and tranquillity of Hatfield, longed to be back there with Kat and Ascham and Parry, to immerse herself once more in that familiar domestic existence. As they rode back toward the palace, on an impulse, she steered her horse alongside the Queen's.

"Your Majesty, may I have leave to retire from court?" she asked plaintively.

Mary frowned.

"Why?" she demanded.

"I am weary of the court, madam, and wish to be in my own house."

"No," said the Queen. "I cannot allow it."

"But madam—"

"I said no!" Mary barked. "Let that be an end to it."

Dispirited, Elizabeth fell back.

"What was that about, madam?" Renard inquired, leaning sideways in his saddle toward the Queen.

"She wants leave to retire to Hatfield," Mary told him, her lips pursed. "Does she really think I could let her go? Once there, she would be free to scheme against me. No, I want her here, where I can keep an eye on her."

"Very wise, madam," Renard observed. "I saw her in conversation with Courtenay earlier. I am convinced she is plotting with him and Monsieur de Noailles against Your Majesty. Again, madam, I urge you to send her to the Tower, where she can make no more mischief."

"No," Mary said, looking obstinate. "I prefer to keep her here. And if Courtenay is intriguing with her, he will soon tell his mother about it, for he now confides everything to her. And his mother will then tell me, for we have been good friends for years. We have only to sit and wait."

"The Queen is betrothed!" Kat said, coming upon Elizabeth as she sat desolately embroidering a bookbinding in her bedchamber. "She is to marry the Prince of Spain! It's all over the court."

Elizabeth rose to her feet, the binding forgotten.

"She's made up her mind at last. I had hoped she would turn him down." She had no doubt that Mary was making a calamitous mistake.

"So had a lot of people, if you keep your ears open and listen to what many are muttering," Kat said.

"In truth, I fear for this realm," Elizabeth said with conviction. "This prince will bring the Inquisition to England. He is no friend to Protestants. And he may drag this impoverished land into his ruinous Habsburg wars. Surely the people will not stand it."

The people would not. There were riots and violent protests. They would not have a Spaniard for their king, nor see England become a minor possession of the Empire. This Philip, they feared, would rule harshly and ruthlessly, for were not all Spaniards like that? Who had not heard the dread tales of his cruelties and his bloody way with heretics? The Queen must be mad even to consider such a marriage.

But, her word once given—hesitantly, almost painfully—the Queen was deeply committed.

"I will wholly love and obey the Prince," she vowed to Renard. "I will do nothing against his will, and if he wishes to take upon himself the government of my realm, I will not prevent it."

"Nothing must stand in the way of this great alliance," Renard insisted. "But there is still Lady Elizabeth. I fear she poses the greatest threat. She is your heir, her heretical views are known, and those who oppose this marriage may seek to set her up in your place. Madam, you must neutralize her, either by committing her to the Tower, or by deferring to her as the heir to the throne, with courtesy and favors. That way you might just ensure her loyalty and support—but I doubt it." He shook his head. "I would prefer the Tower."

"I cannot imprison her," Mary declared. "That would be unjust, as I have no grounds. But it is becoming increasingly difficult for me to show friendship to her. I cannot trust her, nor can I forget the injuries her mother inflicted upon mine, God rest her. Yet I prefer to let things stay as they are for the present, with the added proviso that anyone seeking to visit her at court first obtains my permission. That should put paid to Monsieur de Noailles's mischief."

Hating herself, Elizabeth walked along the gallery to the chapel. It was Sunday again, and she was on her unwilling way to Mass. At the doorway, the Queen waited, her ladies standing behind her. As Elizabeth approached, Mary ignored her. Instead, she turned to her cousins, the Duchess of Suffolk and the Countess of Lennox, and signaled to them to follow immediately behind her to the royal pew.

Elizabeth stood rigid as a statue, aghast and humiliated. The Queen had publicly snubbed her. She, the heir to the throne and second lady in the land, alone had the right to follow Her Majesty into chapel, taking precedence over everyone else. But Mary had, in one devastating gesture, thrown doubt on her status and shamed Elizabeth before the watching courtiers. There they stood, smirking behind their hands, whispering and staring. It was not to be borne.

All Elizabeth's instincts told her, once more, that she was in danger and should leave court as soon as she could. After Mass, she sought out her sister and knelt before her. Again, she begged leave to retire to her estates. Again Mary refused.

When Elizabeth saw a grave-faced William Cecil waiting in her great chamber one morning in November, she knew he brought bad news.

"I obtained leave to see you on the pretext of estate business," he explained. "But I really came to tell you that Lady Jane Grey and her husband have been tried and condemned."

"But she is only sixteen!" Elizabeth cried, shocked. "She is younger than I. And I had thought the Queen was ready to be merciful."

"Oh, I think she is," Cecil assured her, "but she cannot be seen to be in public. The word from my contacts here at court is that the trial was but a formality to please the Spanish ambassador, who wants Jane executed, and is no friend to you, madam, as I am sure you know."

Elizabeth felt faint and panicky. Her heart was pounding, her palms sweating. "They do not really mean to execute Jane, then?"

"I doubt it," Cecil replied. "My information is that the Queen intends to leave her in the Tower until such time as she herself has an heir. Master Renard is not too happy about that, but they say the Queen is determined to spare the girl. After all, she didn't want the crown; it was forced on her. So she is no traitor. No, it's not the Lady Jane that Her Majesty has to fear. It is others plotting on her behalf, because that foolish young lady, unlike yourself, madam, is showing herself to be still a staunch Protestant. So she may yet be the focus of another plot to make her queen. So many people are angry at the prospect of the Spanish marriage, there's sure to be more than one hothead who will risk his neck to declare for her."

"So she is not yet safe," Elizabeth said, her heart thumping in her breast. "And neither am I, William! I too might be the focus of a Protestant plot. I have not been overzealous in embracing the Roman faith, and

I have made it clear I go to Mass under duress. So if the Queen can condemn a girl of sixteen, who is her own flesh and blood, to death, then she can condemn me. And something tells me that, if Renard had his way, she would."

"Calm yourself, madam," soothed Cecil, putting a tentative arm around her shaking shoulders. "It is believed by most people that Jane will not die. Her life is safe. Even though some are pressing for her death, the Queen is a merciful princess, and just."

"I pray that you are right," Elizabeth told him, her eyes clouded with fear. She knew that she herself could no longer count on the Queen's affections and merciful nature. Suddenly, the world seemed an even more dangerous place to be in.

As soon as Elizabeth entered her lodging at court, she saw the letter that had been pushed under the door. Warily, she stooped to pick it up.

"What is that?" asked Kat, coming in behind her, her face lively with curiosity.

"I don't know," Elizabeth replied, her heart heavy with foreboding. Warily, as if the letter were contaminated with poison, she broke the unstamped wax seal.

The signature at the bottom of the brief note—which was followed by the words *Burn this, for the love of God*—was unfamiliar to her.

"It is from a Sir Thomas Wyatt," she said. "He claims he writes to me out of love for the Queen and this realm of England. He desires to prevent the Spanish marriage, for he has traveled in Spain and seen what the Inquisition has done there."

"Sir Thomas Wyatt?" Kat interrupted. "There was a poet called Sir Thomas Wyatt. His family was close to your lady mother's; his sister attended her on the scaffold. There was talk that this poet was at one time in love with your mother, and a rival with King Henry for her love."

"I have read some of his poems," Elizabeth said. "He wrote much of love. Were they written for my mother?"

"Some of them were, I believe," Kat told her. "They must have been, as they were no longer circulated at court after she died. This must be his son."

"It's a pity he did not inherit his father's eloquence," Elizabeth observed. "This is clumsily written." Her eyes scanned the letter. "He says he has friends in high places who are committed to using force, if necessary, to prevent the Queen from marrying Prince Philip. He names Courtenay, Monsieur de Noailles . . ."

"That wouldn't surprise me," Kat put in.

"He says he intends no harm to the Queen, that he and his friends are all devout Catholics but also patriotic Englishmen. He asks for my support."

"Don't give it!" Kat cried.

"Do you think me a fool?" Elizabeth retorted. "I'm in enough trouble as it is, and these are dangerous times. I shall burn this and forget I ever received it. In fact," she added, beginning to pace up and down while wringing her hands in agitation, "I foresee much mischief brewing. I think I will fare far more safely away from court. I *must* get away. I am going now to the Queen, to ask once more for leave to go to one of my own houses."

Mary eyed her kneeling sister with suspicion.

"Why do you wish to leave court?" she asked sharply.

"I long for the peace of the country, Your Majesty," Elizabeth replied steadily. "I weary of being constantly in the public eye here. I would resume my studies in quiet and contentment. In truth, I look for no more in life."

Mary sat silently, deliberating with herself. Should she let Elizabeth go? Was the girl truly a danger to her, as Renard insisted? Or was she sincere in her desire to lead a more private life? In truth, Mary would be happy to see the back of her, to be spared the sight of this constant thorn in her side, whose vibrant youth was such a contrast to her own fading looks and whose questionable paternity was a subject that occasioned Mary much concern.

Suddenly, she could bear the sight of Elizabeth no longer. Her sister had caused nothing but trouble, and she would be happy to be rid of her.

"Very well," she said coldly. "You may go to Ashridge, as you desire. But I warn you, your present game is known. If you refuse to follow the path of duty and persist in seeking the friendship of the French and the heretics—no, I will not be gainsaid, I know what you have been up to— you will bitterly repent it."

"Madam," cried Elizabeth, shocked, "I have never sought the friendship of the French nor allied myself with heretics. I am Your Grace's true and loving subject. I would never conspire against you, never. I am a devout Catholic and will be taking priests with me to Ashridge so that I can enjoy the consolation of the Mass."

"I am told you have had secret meetings with Monsieur de Noailles," Mary accused her.

"Whoever told Your Majesty that wishes me ill," Elizabeth protested. "It is not true. I have only ever discoursed with him where all the world may see us."

Mary looked unconvinced.

"Madam," Elizabeth continued, "I am most humbly grateful that you are permitting me to retire from court. I assure you that, while I am at Ashridge, I will do all in my power to please you and earn your favor."

"Hmm," said the Queen. "You may go. I wish you a safe journey."

As soon as Elizabeth had risen from her knees and curtsied her way out of the room, Mary drew aside the curtain concealing the doorway to the inner closet, behind which Renard had hidden himself. He looked worried.

"Your Majesty, I fear you have been overlenient with the Lady Elizabeth. You should keep her here, under your eye."

"I do not want her here," Mary said firmly.

"Surely you were not taken in by her playacting?" Renard frowned.

"I was not," Mary assured him. "Like you, dear friend, I believe she will bring about some great evil unless she is dealt with. But there is no proof, and my conscience will not let me proceed against her without any evidence."

"You will have her watched?" the ambassador urged, his face full of concern.

"Naturally. I will have spies placed in her household," the Queen said. "You need not fear."

"An excellent plan, madam," Renard approved, relaxing a little. "And so that she does not suspect anything, may I suggest that Your Majesty takes leave of her in sisterly fashion?"

Mary sighed.

"I suppose I must," she said. "Yet I can scarcely believe that she is my sister. She is no longer the sweet, winning child whom I so loved when my father was alive. I fear that vanity, heresy, and ambition have changed her. I can no longer think of her as my dear sister, but as a viper in my bosom."

"Holy Mother, give me the strength to go through with this marriage," Mary prayed. "Make me a good wife, as you were, and intercede with your Son to grant me the blessing of children." A tear came to her eye as she imagined herself—at long last—holding her own baby in her arms.

She was alone in her closet, kneeling at her prayer desk, and so deep in prayer that she did not notice the door behind her opening slowly, or the soft patter of feet retreating. She heard the thud, though, and she smelled the dead dog before she swung around and saw it, lying there obscenely on the rush matting, its jaw slack, its eyes staring.

Her hand flew to her mouth to stifle the scream, but when she saw how evilly the wretched cur had been mutilated, she began to whimper in fear. Its head had been tonsured, like a priest's, its ears slit, while the rope pulled tightly around its neck was evidence enough that it had been suffocated.

It was a warning, no less, a harbinger, perhaps, of more violence to come. Mary was in no doubt that the dog had been flung at her in protest of her impending marriage. She ran to the door and looked out—moments too late. There was no one there. In all her large household, there would be no hope of tracing the culprit.

Sobbing, she hastened to seek out Renard.

Elizabeth noticed that the Queen looked pale and drawn—nothing like a happy bride who was soon to be married. Her manner, however, belied her appearance, for it was warmer than it had been in weeks.

"Rise, Sister," she said. "God keep you on your journey."

Elizabeth remained kneeling. Encouraged by Mary's kinder demeanor, she felt emboldened to make an appeal to her.

"Your Majesty," she said, "I beg of you not to believe anyone who spreads evil reports of me in my absence; and if you do hear such false and malicious reports, I pray you will do me the honor of letting me know, so that I can have a chance of proving them slanders."

There was such sincerity in her face and her voice that Mary was momentarily nonplussed.

"I will do as you ask," she said briskly, despising herself for being suborned by this clever sister of hers. "And before you go, I have New Year gifts for you." From a lady-in-waiting, she took a warm sable hood and two fine ropes of glowing pearls, and presented them to Elizabeth. For a moment, their eyes met, then Mary looked away.

"I thank Your Majesty most humbly for these beautiful gifts," Elizabeth said, genuinely touched.

Mary bent forward and quickly embraced her.

"Go with God," she said.

The December wind was icy, and the journey northward arduous, but as she sat in the jolting litter, Elizabeth felt a little warmed by her sister's affectionate farewell and the unexpected gifts. She must build on this, she decided, with increasing certainty of success, and as they neared Ashridge, she summoned a courier and ordered him to ride back to Whitehall.

"She asks for copes, chasubles, chalices, and other ornaments for her chapel," Mary told Renard thoughtfully.

"Madam," he urged, "do not be deceived. She but thinks to lull you into a sense of false security. I know her tricks."

"You still think her a hypocrite, then?" Mary asked. "I was rather hoping that she had indeed come to the truth."

"Your Majesty is too full of goodness to believe evil of others," Renard purred, "but you cannot afford to relax your vigilance. She is devious, and thinks nothing of making a mockery of God."

"Nevertheless, if there is the tiniest chance that she is sincere, I must send what she asks for," Mary declared. "It is for God's service, after all."

Despite the freezing weather, and Kat's protests, Elizabeth was taking her usual morning walk. Wrapped in a thick cloak and her new sable hood, and booted and gloved against the chill, she strode forth through the park, her feet kicking up a sludge of decayed leaves and dirty snow. Kat, puffing and blowing, was struggling to keep up.

"In faith, my lady, let us go back," she begged. "I cannot feel my fingers, they are so cold."

"Soon," Elizabeth promised. "But there is something I must show you first." She was making for the shelter of the trees that lay ahead.

"Can't it wait till we're back at the house?" Kat asked plaintively.

"No. We are watched," Elizabeth said in a low voice.

"Watched?" Kat echoed.

"Aye. Did you think the Queen would leave me here unsupervised to plot—as she fears—against her?"

"But you would never do that!" Kat exclaimed.

"No, I would not," Elizabeth affirmed stoutly. "But others might do it for me. Look."

She thrust into Kat's gloved hands a piece of paper.

"Another letter from our friend Wyatt," she muttered. They were now shielded from the house by the solid trunks of ancient oaks.

Kat read it.

"This is treason!" she gasped, her face draining of color.

"I know," said Elizabeth. "They want to marry me to Courtenay, and to what purpose? To unite the royal blood of Plantagenet and Tudor and place us on the throne. So much for Wyatt protesting he meant no harm to my sister."

"But four armies, ready to march on London?" Kat cried, appalled.

"Shhh!" Elizabeth hissed, looking around her nervously. There was nothing, no one—just frost-shrouded woodland and the bare skeletons of trees.

"The Queen must be warned!" Kat urged.

"By whom?" Elizabeth asked. "By me? And how do I explain how I came by my information? I should have to produce this letter, in which Wyatt asks if I will act as their leader, with Courtenay. It will look as if I have encouraged them up till now, and it will give that fox Renard a pretext for urging the Queen to deal with me as a traitor. No, Kat, I have been here before, remember, with . . . with . . ."

She could not say the Admiral's name. He had been dead nigh on five years, and yet the memory of him, and the danger in which she had stood, still scarred her soul. Kat stared at her compassionately. She remembered all too well. She herself had been in the Tower.

"No," Elizabeth said, recovering herself, "I will not involve myself in any way. I will destroy this letter and keep my own counsel. There are hideous consequences when one intrigues against princes. My enemies would rejoice to see me condemned for treason. I have no intention of giving them that satisfaction."

She strode onward, leaving Kat struggling to keep up with her.

"No, they can prove nothing against me," she was saying, "yet still there is danger. These conspirators that Wyatt names—there is Sir James Pickering, whom I thought to be a true friend to me. Not two months ago, he came privily to me and asked for my views on the proposed marriage with Spain. Most pressing he was. But I would not be drawn, Kat. Then there is Sir James Crofts, another who has shown himself friendly of late."

They were heading deeper into the woods now.

"I am going to need all my wits about me in the coming weeks," Elizabeth went on. "I shall summon some of my tenants to the house, to come discreetly armed for my protection."

"Against whom?" Kat asked.

"Against fate!" Elizabeth told her smartly, then halted suddenly and looked at the older woman.

"You look cold, dear Kat," she observed. "We should go back now."

"I thought you would never notice," Kat muttered gratefully. "I am freezing, and I am all of a tremor too when I think of this conspiracy."

"You know nothing about it," Elizabeth told her firmly. "And neither do I. In our silence is our safety."

They were nearing open ground now. Elizabeth stopped suddenly, placing a finger to her mouth.

"Listen!" she whispered.

Kat strained her ears. All she could hear was the wind stirring the branches above them, and the occasional cry of a bird. Then it came, a sound like a stealthy footfall on bracken, not far off. Her terrified eyes met Elizabeth's alert ones.

"Is someone spying on us?" Kat mouthed.

"Assuredly," Elizabeth replied, smiling grimly. "Hark, there it is again. But they would not have heard anything. We were over there. Our invisible stalker is coming from the opposite direction. Too late, I fear!" She laughed mirthlessly.

"Eavesdroppers hear no good of themselves," she said in a loud voice. "Fancy, Kat, spying on a lady and her companion! Are fashions and furbelows now matters of state interest?"

With a look of devilment in her eyes, Elizabeth tossed back her hood and went striding home, her long red hair blowing behind her. A long way behind her, the watcher in the trees stood stamping his feet.

CHAPTER 17

✤

1554

The Yuletide decorations had been down for nearly three weeks when Sir James Crofts arrived at Ashridge.

"I cannot see him," Elizabeth said. "I am not well."

She was not lying. For several days now, she had suffered from bloating and feverishness, and her joints were aching fearfully. Her physician had diagnosed an inflammation of the kidneys and prescribed rest, so here she was, lying on her bed, fretfully bemoaning her condition and listlessly trying to read a book. The last thing she needed now was to be embroiled in the wild and wicked schemes of Wyatt and his friends.

Isolated as they were, both by the bitter weather and by the Queen's determination that her sister should have no opportunity to plot mischief with the enemies of the Crown, Elizabeth and Kat had been growing increasingly anxious for word of what was happening at court and in the outside world. There was no news of any date being set for the Queen's marriage, and none—thankfully—of any uprisings or conspiracies; Elizabeth was beginning to wonder whether the whole plot had been just a fantasy on Wyatt's part. But now here was one of the named conspirators, waiting for her in the great parlor.

"He says it is urgent, my lady," Kat said anxiously.

"Tell him I am ill," Elizabeth snapped. "No, wait. I need to know what is going on. Tell him I will be down as soon as I have tidied myself." So saying, she heaved herself unsteadily off the bed, then sat down quickly, her head spinning. It was minutes before she could rise and make herself ready.

"Come with me," she said to Kat. "I want a witness."

One glance at her visitor's disheveled appearance warned her that this was no social call.

"Greetings, Sir James," she said, and looked at him questioningly.

"Madam, I have little time," he said urgently. "The marriage treaty with Spain is signed, and the people are rising against it. The council has sent troops to put down a revolt in Exeter. Our scheme is still to go ahead, but Courtenay has betrayed us, and the Queen knows about our plans."

"*Our* plans?" Elizabeth echoed coldly.

"Sir Thomas Wyatt has told us that you are privy to them, madam."

"I am privy to nothing, sir!" Elizabeth snapped. She knew that she must at all costs stay out of this conspiracy, or it could cost her head.

"Forgive me, madam, but I was given to understand that you were with us." Crofts looked frightened and embarrassed.

"And who gave you to understand that?" Elizabeth demanded to know.

"Wyatt himself, Madam. He is even now raising the men of Kent, for we have had to bring forward the date of our uprising. The Duke of Suffolk is with us, and I am now on my way to the Welsh border to raise support there. Indeed, I must hurry, because time is not on our side."

Elizabeth stared at him, her anger erupting. The presumption of the man!

"Do you realize that what you are planning is high treason?" she asked him, looking dauntingly like her father in a rage. "Did it occur to you that, by coming here like this, you compromise my safety as well as your own? Your foolhardiness beggars belief!"

"I came in all loyalty to warn you," Crofts protested. "Courtenay has told them that you are with us."

"He has *what?*" Elizabeth cried, horrified, noticing that Kat's face was a mask of terror.

"He has confessed that he planned to marry you and that Your Grace was—er, not unwilling," Crofts told her, shamefaced.

"I was never willing!" she declared hotly. "He had no right to implicate me, for I have never said I would marry him. And your loyalty, Sir James, should be to your Queen, not to me."

"My lady," he protested, "I have your interests at heart, truly. Wyatt has sent me to urge you to go to your house at Donnington, which is securely fortified. You will be safer there. Believe me, madam, your safety is precious to all true Englishmen."

"I am going nowhere," Elizabeth stated flatly. "I am ill. No, do not try to persuade me," she said, lifting her hand to still his dissent. "I am the Queen's loyal subject. I command you to leave this minute. I will not house a traitor under my roof."

Swallowing, Crofts bowed sketchily and fled. Minutes later, she heard his horse's hooves thudding away into the distance. Exhausted, physically and mentally, she sank to the floor and rested her throbbing head against the cool plaster of the wall. Her thoughts were teeming, her emotions in turmoil. It would be known—Mary's spies would see to it—that Crofts had visited her. Yet would her response also be known? Would Kat be seen as an impartial witness? And should she not, this very minute, write a report to her sister of what had taken place?

But no, she dared not. Always, it was best to do nothing. The very fact that Sir James Crofts had visited her was compromising in itself. And anyway, the Queen already knew what was afoot.

Wyatt—the absolute cheek of the man!—had sent a messenger, Sir William Saintlow, with a communication for Elizabeth.

"He pleads with me to get myself as far from London as I can, for my safety," she told Kat. "My safety! He should have thought of that when he embroiled me in his schemes. Well, he shall have his answer."

She returned to the parlor, where Sir William was waiting. He looked up hopefully.

"I pray you thank Sir Thomas for his goodwill," Elizabeth said, "but tell him from me that I will do as I think fit."

Looking crestfallen, Sir William left hurriedly.

—

There followed three days of waiting, wondering, and worrying. The strain told on Elizabeth, who again took to her bed.

"You have a letter from the Queen," Kat said nervously, rousing her from a fitful sleep on the fourth morning. Elizabeth struggled to sit up.

"What does it say?" she murmured, striving to pull it open.

It was a command to hold herself in readiness to return to court as soon as she was summoned. It was, Mary told her, for the surety of her person.

"At least she says that my presence there will be heartily welcome to her," Elizabeth said. "And if she truly suspected me of treason, she would not have sent this at all. But her meaning is clear. She does not trust me, and she wants me under her eye. And she desires an immediate answer."

She slumped back in the bed.

"In truth, Kat, I feel so ill that I cannot go anywhere," she moaned, raising her arm to shield her eyes from the light and thus ease her aching head. "In fact, on top of everything else, I think I have a cold coming on. My throat is sore and I feel shivery all over."

Kat pressed a cool, plump hand to Elizabeth's forehead.

"You're burning up, my lady," she pronounced. "It would be folly to get out of bed, let alone travel, in this weather. It'd be the death of you."

"But the Queen will think I am feigning illness," Elizabeth groaned.

"You would only be speaking the truth," Kat told her. "Let her send her physicians if she will—they will corroborate it."

"Indeed, I have no choice," Elizabeth replied. "Will you write for me?"

"I don't believe her," Mary said, handing the letter to Renard. "It is clear that she is involved in this conspiracy. I am disgusted at her conduct."

"Bishop Gardiner believes she has been intriguing with the French too," Renard said.

"That would not surprise me," Mary commented tartly. "In faith, I cannot believe she is truly my sister. No trueborn sister would be so false."

She moved farther down the gallery, wringing her hands. Suddenly, she found herself face-to-face with a portrait of Elizabeth in a pink gown, done a few years earlier. The young face stared out warily at her.

"Take it down!" she said abruptly. "I cannot bear to look on her anymore."

"There is news from London!" Parry announced. Spurred on by an anxious Kat, he had ridden some miles to the nearest tavern and managed to return unchallenged.

"Tell me!" Kat demanded before he had even shaken the snow from his cloak.

"Wyatt and his friends have been proclaimed traitors. The Duke of Suffolk is among them—he declared for his daughter, as Queen Jane."

"The crass fool!" Kat cried. "He was lucky to escape with his head last time."

"It's not *his* head I'm worried about," Parry said, "but that poor girl's. Shut up in the Tower, she has nothing to do with this."

"She cannot be other than innocent," Kat pointed out. "The Queen must know that."

"Innocent or not, she has royal blood, and there will always be those who would raise her up as a Protestant rival to the Queen. As events have lately proved." Parry was shaking his head.

"The Queen is merciful," Kat insisted. "She would not harm an innocent girl."

"Others might force her to it," Parry warned. "That's what people are saying. And there's more. The Duke of Norfolk has been sent into Kent with an army to deal with Wyatt and his men. This is serious, Mrs. Astley."

"I will tell my lady," Kat said, trembling. "Oh, what grievous tidings. I fear we are in terrible danger."

As more worrisome days passed, ominous with a dearth of news, Elizabeth's condition did not improve; however, the malaise in her body was as nothing to the fever of anxiety in her heart. Her bed had become a sanctuary, a refuge from the perilous outside world. Cocooned between her sheets, she could believe she was safe from the Queen and the traitors alike. But early in February, a party of riders were seen approaching Ashridge.

"Oh, my God!" Kat cried, hand to her mouth, as she peered from the window and recognized three privy councillors and two of the royal physicians. In a frenzy of fear, she hurried to Elizabeth's bedside and roused her.

"A deputation from the council . . . here, my lady. God have mercy on us!" she panted.

Elizabeth blinked at her, uncomprehending at first. Then she was instantly awake, her head swimming, her heart pounding. The room swung violently and did not right itself for several seconds; blood pounded in her temples.

"My nightgown," she ordered weakly. "Help me put it on."

Kat fetched the black velvet robe and eased Elizabeth into it. Then she tidied the sheets around her and brushed her hair over her thin shoulders before smoothing her own skirts and walking slowly downstairs, bracing herself.

The Steward had brought wine, which Elizabeth's Chamberlain was serving to the visitors. The three councillors looked grim and purposeful, Kat saw; the doctors' faces were grave.

Lord William Howard, Elizabeth's cousin, spoke first.

"Mrs. Astley, we are come to see the Lady Elizabeth, to ascertain if she is well enough to travel to London."

"Why?" cried Kat, unable to stop herself.

"The Queen's Majesty has commanded it," Lord William informed her. "Pray take us to her."

"She is abed and very ill," Kat told him, her heart fluttering.

"Nonetheless, we are commanded to see her," he insisted.

"Very well," Kat said, pursing her lips, realizing that further argument would be futile. "This way, please."

Elizabeth appeared to be dozing when they entered her bedchamber, and she affected surprise at being awoken by her visitors.

"My lords," she murmured weakly. "Forgive me . . . This is an unexpected honor."

Ignoring her words, Lord William stared straight above her, fixing his eyes on her coat of arms, which was embroidered on the tester.

"Madam, we are commanded by the Queen to determine if Your Grace is as sick as we had been led to believe," he told her.

"You may see for yourself," she murmured. Her pallor looked genuine enough, Lord William thought, but of course much could be feigned by the clever use of cosmetics.

"It is Her Majesty's pleasure that you come with us to London," Sir Edward Hastings informed her. "She has sent Dr. Wendy here, and Dr. Owen, to decide if you are well enough to travel."

Elizabeth began to tremble.

"As you can see, I am ill," she said. "I would know why Her Majesty has commanded me to London."

"It is in connection with the late rebellion," Howard told her. "She would have you safe with her."

"Rebellion?" Elizabeth repeated. "What rebellion?"

"Have you not heard? The traitor Wyatt, with seven thousand men, marched into London just a week ago, and would have taken the city had it not been for the courage of the Queen's Majesty, who went to the Guildhall and, in a brave address, which I myself heard, rallied the Londoners to her cause."

"It was inspiring," added Sir Edward. "It was as if King Harry had come among us again. Her Majesty was never more her father's daughter."

"Thus, but with difficulty, the rebellion was suppressed," Howard continued. "God be praised, the Queen is safe, and all her council with her, and the traitor Wyatt is in the Tower, along with the other conspirators."

"And the Lady Jane, who was proclaimed Queen by the rebels, is sentenced to death." This was the third councillor, the stern-faced Sir George Cornwallis.

"Sentenced to death?" Elizabeth's whisper came out as a croak. An ice-cold tremor was rippling down her spine. She thought she would faint. There was no question in her mind but that she was being summoned to London to meet a fate similar to poor Lady Jane's—nor in Kat's either, evidently, for that good woman had just burst into noisy tears.

"The Emperor has demanded it," Lord William said. "He warned Her Majesty that Prince Philip would never set foot in England while the Lady Jane lived, for he would fear too much for his safety and for the security of Her Majesty's throne."

"But the Queen was disposed to be merciful to the Lady Jane," Elizabeth said tremulously.

"In the wake of recent events, she cannot afford to be," Lord William replied. He had no intention of telling the suspect young woman before him how her sister had agonized over signing the death warrant; how, indeed, she was doing everything she could to avoid having it put into effect. Even now, he knew, she was trying to persuade Jane to convert to the Catholic faith to save her life.

Elizabeth was so consumed with terror that she was unable to speak further.

"Our orders are to escort you back to London, if you are fit to travel, even if it means carrying you to court in the Queen's own litter, which she has sent for the purpose," Howard told her.

"My lady is not fit to leave her bed, let alone travel," Kat protested, her eyes red with tears.

"That is for us to decide, mistress," Dr. Owen said. "The Queen has appointed us to examine the Lady Elizabeth to determine the nature of her illness. Now, if you would leave us, gentlemen, I am sure that Mrs. Astley will prepare my lady."

Throughout it all, Elizabeth lay limp and listless. Mary, she was certain, was only having her examined in order to forestall her dying on the way to London; for if that happened, the Queen might be accused of having her sister's blood on her hands. But once Elizabeth was in the capital, securely immured in the Tower and tried and condemned in a court of law, Mary could safely do what she liked with her, and the world could only applaud her for having rid herself of a traitor.

So struck by fear was Elizabeth at this dreadful prospect that she was barely aware of the doctors' hands on her body, prodding her gently through the thin lawn of her chemise; of pissing into a basin so that they could examine her urine, which they had poured into a tall glass bottle; of them taking a pulse, commenting on her pallor, and discussing which of the four humors was imbalanced in her body.

"She is shivering, but her temperature is little raised," Dr. Owen said.

"She has watery humors, would you agree?" diagnosed Dr. Wendy.

"Indeed. But between you and I . . ." He drew his colleague away from the bed and lowered his voice. "Most of her symptoms stem from a fear of just punishment. Yes, she is a little unwell, but she is shamming too. There is no reason why she should not return with us to London."

Kat was watching their faces anxiously. She did not like what she saw.

"Well now," said Dr. Owen, approaching the bed. "You have had a touch of the watery humors, my lady, affecting your kidneys, but nothing to worry about. In our opinion, if you use the litter that Her Majesty has so kindly provided, you are certainly fit to travel."

Elizabeth stared at him, horrified.

"*No!*" she cried piteously. "I am not well enough." Then she checked herself. "Of course I wish to obey the Queen's Grace, as in all things, and be conformable to her commands. I am very willing to travel too, but not just yet. I fear my weakness to be so great that I will not be able to endure the journey without imperiling my life. I beg of you, sirs, grant me a few days' grace until I have better recovered my strength."

Dr. Owen frowned.

"There is nothing seriously wrong with you, madam," he said.

"Then why do I feel so ill?" she asked.

"Might I venture to suggest that your malady is not of the body but of the mind?" he replied gently.

"The aches and pains are real enough," she retorted. "And I cannot stop shivering." The shivering was only partly due to her condition, she knew, but in some irrational way, she felt that, by delaying her departure from the safety of Ashridge, she was preserving her life. Who knew, in a few days' time, more of the truth might have come to light—they questioned prisoners in the Tower, didn't they?—and her innocence made plain to the Queen.

"I will confer with the lords," said Dr. Owen, and he and Dr. Wendy went out. As soon as the door closed, Kat hastened to Elizabeth's side and rocked her in her arms.

"I will not let them take you!" she declared vehemently.

"I fear you will not be able to prevent them," sniffed Elizabeth. Her head was aching fit to burst.

They remained in a close embrace, comforting each other as best they could, until Lord William returned.

"We have heard the opinion of the doctors, madam," he said stiffly, averting his eyes once more. "All excuses must be set aside. You must be ready to travel in three days' time."

When they brought Mary news that Lady Jane's head had fallen, the bitter bile rose in her throat, and she staggered into her closet, falling to her knees before the statue of the smiling Madonna.

"What am I become?" she moaned, burying her head in her hands. "That I, who set out promising to be a merciful princess, should have shed the blood of an innocent—and my own blood at that! Oh, God, have pity on me, poor, miserable sinner that I am!"

A hand touched her gently on the shoulder, and she turned a tearstained face to see the sympathetic eyes of Renard looking down on her.

"Forgive the intrusion, madam," he said. "I saw how painfully you took it. But it was a necessity. Yet, even so, still you are not safe on your throne. Two more heads must fall before you can know true peace of mind. Your Majesty knows to whom I am referring."

"Courtenay," Mary said, swallowing, "and . . ."

"The Lady Elizabeth," he said softly. "These are the two people most likely to cause trouble in your realm. You have been strong in eliminating the Lady Jane. Now be strong again. Deal with this threat once and for all. And when these traitors have been removed, you need have no fear for your crown."

Bishop Gardiner was standing in the doorway, listening.

"His Excellency speaks sense, madam," he added. "By cutting off its hurtful members, you would be showing mercy to the whole common-wealth."

Mary looked anguished. It was one thing to execute her cousin, she thought—quite another to order the death of her sister. If, of course, Elizabeth really was her sister. I wish I could believe she wasn't, she thought bitterly.

"Wyatt must be questioned rigorously," Gardiner was saying. "I feel sure he has much to reveal about the Lady Elizabeth's involvement in his conspiracy."

"I will give the order," Mary said queasily, knowing what it would mean for Wyatt. "What of Courtenay? Has he talked?"

"He has been examined several times, but says nothing," Gardiner told her. "I think he knows little. He has not the wits to conceal it, poor fool."

"What of the other rebels?" Renard asked. "The rank and file, I mean?"

"Madam, you must not show weakness at this crucial juncture," Gardiner urged, his beak-like face frowning in concern.

"Some will be hanged, in London and in Kent, as a deterrent to anyone else who looks to conspire against us," the Queen said resolutely, aware that if she showed any inclination to mercy, her advisers would put it down to womanly weakness. "The rest will be allowed to return to their homes." She looked hard at Gardiner and Renard. "I trust that the result of all this bloodshed will be to establish my rule more firmly than ever and enable the alliance with Prince Philip to be concluded."

"God has willed it so, madam," Gardiner said.

"His Highness is even now making preparations to come to England," Renard assured her.

"Then these harsh measures have been justified," Mary said slowly. "God indeed works in mysterious ways, gentlemen, but in the end I feel sure we shall see His church properly reestablished in England and the true faith fully restored."

"Amen to that," said Gardiner.

Wrapped up in her great cloak and sable hood, and leaning heavily on Kat's arm, Elizabeth made her shaky way downstairs to the great hall, shivering in the face of the blast of cold air that enveloped her as she approached the open porch. She felt faint and weak, and could not control the involuntary shudders that kept threading through her body every time she thought, with dread in her heart, of what surely lay ahead for her.

The councillors, somber in their black garb, waited by the litter, their faces set and stern. As Elizabeth descended the steps, her knees buckled, and it was all that Kat could do to keep her upright. To begin with, not one of the men moved to help her—they just stood watching. At length, Sir George stepped reluctantly forward to assist Elizabeth into the litter. She virtually fell, half swooning, onto the velvet cushions. As the leather curtains were drawn tight, to obscure her from public view, and the little procession began to move off, she was gripped by terror, with blood racing through her head, her heart thudding, her palms sweating, her bowels turning to water. She was going to die, here and now, she knew it, and the prospect made her panic all the more.

Kat watched in horror as Elizabeth's body suddenly convulsed in a mighty spasm and doubled up into a fetal position. There were no tears: It was clear that the girl could hardly speak.

"My lady is ill!" she cried.

The litter slowed to a halt and an irritated Lord William peered through the curtains. But he could see at once that Elizabeth was in a poor case, and hastened to confer with his fellow councillors.

"I do not want her dying while she is in our custody," he muttered. "When all is said and done, she is still the heir to the throne and King Henry's daughter. And if the Queen were to die tomorrow . . ."

"It is treason to speak of the death of the Queen," Cornwallis reminded him.

"It is indeed, but we have to face facts. If that young lady becomes queen—which is possible, as Her Majesty is no longer young and not in the best of health—then she can hardly be expected to look with favor upon those who did not treat her kindly. And clearly, she is not feigning this. Go and see for yourself."

"We'll take your word for it," Sir Edward said. "And I agree, we should treat her with care. Let us aim for just six or seven miles a day. That shouldn't tax her strength too much."

"I blame the doctors," Howard said, frowning. "Telling us she was well enough to travel, then scurrying off back to court. Now look at what we have to cope with." He nodded toward the litter. Elizabeth had thrust her head out between the curtains and she was being violently sick, with that dragon of a nurse holding her shoulders and clucking in sympathy. Vomit dribbled down the side of the carriage. The men turned away in distaste.

Their progress was slow. Elizabeth lay in a trance-like stupor, her face bloated and drained of color, her hands working in distress, and every few miles, Kat would shriek for the procession to halt because her young lady was about to throw up again. At the places where they sought shelter for the night—discreet inns, or the houses of men of proven loyalty to the Queen—the councillors had to carry Elizabeth to her bed, so weak was she. Terror had prostrated her, terror and genuine bodily suffering, so that she could barely keep down sips of wine or boiled water. She grew thinner daily, her dull, heavy-lidded eyes staring out over high, gaunt cheekbones, her shoulder blades painfully outlined above the low square bodice of her gown.

Mercifully, they were nearing London by then.

"Not long now," the councillors nervously assured themselves.

"Pray God she gets there alive," Howard said fervently.

"In faith, I fear for her life," Sir Edward confessed. "She is so ill."

"I have never relished an official duty less," Cornwallis commented.

"Is there any news of the Lady Jane, I wonder?" Elizabeth murmured to Kat as they sat in the private chamber of an inn on the Great North Road, eating their dinner—or rather toying with it, for Elizabeth could eat nothing, and was in fact finding it hard to maintain an upright posture at the table. Kat looked stricken. She had hoped that Elizabeth would not ask that question.

Elizabeth took one look at her face and felt faint again. Terror pierced her like a knife.

"She is dead," she said. "You do not need to tell me."

"I overheard the councillors talking," Kat told her. "In your weak state, I thought it best not to tell you just yet."

"I cannot believe that my sister went so far as to order her death," Elizabeth whispered, trembling. "She had promised mercy." She thought of her poor little cousin, whose only crime had been to be born with Tudor blood in her veins. It was terrible to think that that bright young girl was dead, that she had been done to death in so brutal a manner, and she not yet eighteen.

"Events conspired against the Queen's good intentions, I fear," Kat observed mournfully.

"And against me too," Elizabeth added, her voice full of fear. "Am I to be next?"

"You have committed no treason," Kat pointed out.

"Neither had Jane," Elizabeth said. "She was the tool of ruthless fools who rose in her name. As they rose in mine too. I am as much of a danger to Mary as Jane was, and that is why I fear for my neck."

She was becoming agitated once more. Kat seized her hand.

"Calm yourself," she urged. "Jane had been proclaimed Queen; she accepted the crown, knowing it was not hers by right. Your cases are different. Do not give in to your fears. There was evidence enough against her. There is none against you. Hold fast to that."

"I shall have to," said Elizabeth, trembling.

Presently, they came to Highgate, a village on the northern heights overlooking the City of London. As their destination grew nearer, Elizabeth somehow found the strength to confront what lay ahead, and the determination to outwit her enemies. She felt a little better. That night, snug in a comfortable bedroom in the house of a Mr. Cholmley, a man zealous in the service of the Queen yet chivalrous to his unfortunate guest, she even managed to partake of a little broth.

The next morning, she was better still. The color was returning to her cheeks, and she did not wobble so much when she walked the few steps to the privy. When she looked in her mirror, however, she could see that her face was still somewhat swollen, her stomach yet a little bloated. But those things, she reasoned, might play to her advantage. With the beginnings of returning physical strength there had come a resurgence of hope. At heart, she felt stronger: She was girding herself for battle.

It was advisable, she felt—and it would not be difficult, considering that her recovery was by no means complete—to maintain the semblance of illness. Today, they would enter London, and she knew that if she could win the people's sympathy, her position would be more secure. She was, after all, the heir to the throne, the young, Protestant heir who might well stir the imaginations of all those citizens who had rioted and demonstrated against Mary's Catholic reforms. And she had done nothing wrong, had committed no treason. No one could prove anything against her.

"I'll wear the white damask gown," she told Kat. "No jewels. And some of the borax and egg-white paste, to whiten my skin. I want the people to see me looking wasted and ill."

Supported by Kat, she looked like a ghost as she made her painful way toward the waiting litter.

"Leave the curtains open," she commanded. "I am feverish and need some air."

"Is that not unwise?" Lord William queried. "Your Grace should keep warm."

"I want them open," Elizabeth said firmly, and there was a look on her face that brooked no argument. She was determined that the people should see her.

"Very well, madam," Howard agreed. "To Whitehall!" he cried, and the procession set off down Highgate Hill.

Elizabeth's heart was thumping with relief. She had feared she would be taken straight to the Tower, and had not known how she would face it. Instead, she was going to Whitehall, where she might have a chance of pleading her case personally with the Queen. All was not yet lost. And as she was borne through the narrow streets of Westminster, and saw recognition, admiration, hope, and sympathy in the many inquisitive faces that peered into the litter, she felt heartened. She would survive this, as she had survived the scandal of the Admiral: She felt sure of it.

The lodging assigned to her was isolated from the rest of the court, and outside it stood two stalwart Yeomen of the Guard, who crossed their pikes behind her as soon as she had proceeded through the doorway.

"So I am to be held prisoner?" she asked of Lord William, her frightened eyes belying her haughty tone.

"You are to remain in your rooms," he told her.

"I have done nothing to merit such treatment," she protested. "I wish to see my sister the Queen. I pray you, Lord William, to request an audience for me."

"I regret that will not be possible," he said stiffly. "Her Majesty will not see you until you have been examined by the council in regard to your recent conduct."

Elizabeth was beginning to feel faint again. The long journey, the trek through the palace, the shocks following upon her arrival, and her own weakness had exhausted her. As soon as Lord William had gratefully departed, she sank down onto a settle and wept.

"Come now, my lady, these rooms are not so bad," Kat said, trying to achieve some semblance of normality in the midst of impending tragedy.

It was true: They were hung with two small but fine tapestries and a few paintings, and in the inner chamber there was a handsome oak bed adorned with a rich coverlet and velvet curtains. There were pallet beds for Kat and Blanche, and a prayer desk stood in one corner, adorned with a silver crucifix, while in the outer chamber, cold chicken and wine had been set out on the table. The apartment had its own privy, in a curtained recess in the wall, and its mullioned windows overlooked a garden.

Blanche Parry was already unpacking the chest that contained Elizabeth's clothes.

"Why don't you lie down for a bit, my lady?" she suggested.

"I think I will," Elizabeth agreed wearily, taking a sip of the wine. There was nothing more she could do now until the council summoned her, so she might as well make herself as comfortable as possible.

Yet she had not been lying on her bed for ten minutes when there came a sudden clatter and banging from above her head.

"Good God, what's that?" she grumbled. "I want to sleep."

Kat, sewing in the chair by the fire, looked up. The noises persisted, then after a time the room gradually began to fill with the strong aroma of fish.

"God's blood!" Elizabeth swore. "What *is* going on up there?"

Kat frowned.

"Shall I go and find out?" she asked. "I could ask the guards."

She went to the outer door and opened it. The two men standing there looked at her suspiciously.

"Don't worry, we're not trying to escape!" Kat said tartly. "I merely wish to know who occupies the rooms above us."

One man looked puzzled and pulled at his beard. The other thought for a moment, then said, "It's the Countess of Lennox, mistress."

Kat knew the Countess of Lennox, the former Lady Margaret Douglas, who was King Henry's niece and the Queen's own cousin. A spirited, ambitious woman, she had caused much trouble in the past with her illicit love affairs and constant intriguing. She was close to Queen Mary, a staunch Catholic, and consequently no friend to Elizabeth.

"Has the Countess taken up cooking?" Kat asked wryly. "It seems as if she has her own kitchen up there."

"Yes, one of the rooms was converted only last week," the guard told her, warming to this amiable-looking woman with the droll sense of humor. "She's that important, is my lady, that she gets her own kitchen and cooks. The rumor is"—he thumbed his nose—"that she's to be named the Queen's heir." His fellow guard frowned, and suddenly the man realized just who he was talking to.

"But the Lady Elizabeth is the Queen's heir," Kat declared.

"I'm only repeating what I heard," the guard excused. Then he straightened up, aligned his pike, and stared straight ahead.

Kat hurried back to Elizabeth and reported what she had heard about the Countess having a kitchen installed. She said nothing of the rumor that the guard had mentioned: Elizabeth already had enough to contend with. Kat was praying there was no truth in it.

"The Countess hates me," Elizabeth commented. "I'll wager she knew I was coming and has done this on purpose, to annoy me. God only knows how we'll get any sleep."

"They can't cook all night!" Kat assured her. But they did: It seemed that the Countess had an insatiable appetite for food and desired to eat more or less constantly. After three days of noise and smells, Elizabeth knew for a certainty that she had wagered correctly, and that it was all for the purpose of discomposing her. What with her malady, her fears, and the disturbances upstairs, she did not think she could feel much worse.

But she was wrong.

"Madam," sighed an exasperated Renard. "What more proof of her complicity in the rebellion does Your Majesty need? The traitor Wyatt has admitted that she responded to his messages; copies of letters she sent to you have been found in the French ambassador's postbag, and it is certain that the whole enterprise was undertaken to set her on the throne. If you do not seize this opportunity of punishing her, you will never be safe!"

Mary ceased her pacing and regarded him unhappily.

"She has committed no overt act of treason," she said, "and our law does not provide for those who have merely consented to treason to be put to death. All the same, I cannot but agree with you. As long as my sister lives, I have no hope of seeing the kingdom at peace. As time has proved, her character is just what I have always believed it to be." Her voice was bitter.

"Then have her indicted for treason, madam!" Renard urged.

"No." Mary was adamant. "It would be inadvisable to proceed against her at this stage. My councillors fear that to do so might provoke another rebellion. She is popular, you know." She sniffed contemptuously. "But I for one am convinced of her guilt. All that is needed is proof, and to that end, I have ordered the council to question her."

"A wise decision, madam." Renard beamed approvingly. "And one, I make no doubt, that will provide a solution to the problem."

Elizabeth stood stony-faced in front of the fireplace as Lord Chancellor Gardiner and eighteen other privy councillors filed into her chamber.

"Madam," Gardiner, black-browed and severe, began, "we are credibly informed that you were a party to the late rebellion, and the Queen's Majesty has commanded us to uncover the truth."

Elizabeth faced him steadily.

"I am innocent of that charge," she declared. "I have done nothing against the Queen. I am Her Majesty's loyal subject and sister."

"The traitor Wyatt, under questioning in the Tower, has told us that you sent him messages," said Sir William Paget.

Elizabeth permitted herself a wry smile. "I can well imagine what form that questioning took," she said, "for otherwise he would not have invented such falsehoods."

"Do you deny that you sent copies of your letters to the French ambassador?" Sir George Cornwallis barked.

"I do. But what has that to do with the rebellion?" Elizabeth asked, genuinely puzzled.

"It shows you to be in collusion with him. He was helping to plot your marriage to Courtenay. The rebels would have overthrown Her Majesty and set you and Courtenay up in her place."

Elizabeth flared.

"I have *never* said I would marry Courtenay," she snarled. "As for the rest, I had no involvement in any such plot, even though I was supposed to be so nearly concerned."

"You lie," Gardiner accused her. "Do not imagine that we are cozened by your dissembling. I warn you, madam, if you do not admit your guilt and throw yourself upon the Queen's mercy, you will incur the severest penalties."

Frightened though she was, Elizabeth held her ground.

"I have done nothing worthy of reproach," she insisted. "I cannot ask mercy for a fault that I have not committed. Is that what you would have me do?"

The councillors looked at each other doubtfully. Some of them were there on sufferance; they were thinking that the Queen might not long outlive her coming marriage, and that Elizabeth would soon be their sovereign lady. Thus they were reluctant to offend her.

"I need only to come face-to-face with the Queen my sister to convince her of my innocence," Elizabeth declared. "I pray you, once more, to crave an audience on my behalf."

"That is out of the question," Gardiner said briskly, knowing how Mary would react to such a request. "The Queen is soon to depart for Oxford, and it is her pleasure that you be taken to the Tower while the matter is further tried and examined."

His words came like a slap in the face. The Tower . . . She was to go to the Tower, the place she had always dreaded, as a prisoner suspected of treason. Just as her mother had, all those years ago. And Anne Boleyn had not left it alive, had instead suffered the agonies of confinement and faced a terrible death. What else could her own imprisonment portend but a similar fate? For in Mary's refusal to see her and removal to Oxford, she divined something ominous. Her fate had already been decided, she was certain. These interrogations were but to provide them with pretexts. Look at what had happened to Lady Jane Grey. Had Jane's execution been but a prelude to her own?

The fear that consumed her left her near speechless, but she battled desperately to control, it, knowing that she must defend herself. She had to do something to escape the terrible fate that was in store for her. Shaking, she found her voice.

"As God is my witness," she swore to the lords, "I deny any involvement with the traitor Wyatt. I am altogether guiltless, I swear it, and I trust that the Queen's Majesty will be a more gracious lady to me than to send me to so notorious and doleful a place." Her words ended on a sob.

"Those are the Queen's orders," Gardiner said grimly, backing toward the door, and the other councillors hastily bowed themselves out after him. Some, she noticed, had kept their caps and bonnets low over their eyes. Are they so shamefaced? she wondered. Or do they not wish me to know who they are? How insolent not to remain uncovered in my presence, the presence of the heir to the throne!

But then it occurred to her that she might not remain heir to the throne for very much longer, might soon be nothing but a convicted traitor whose life, titles, and goods were forfeit. At that, her courage deserted her, and she sank weakly to the floor.

She was still there four hours later, sobbing piteously, with a distraught Kat powerless to console her, when four of the lords returned.

"Our orders are to dismiss all Your Grace's servants except for Mrs. Astley and Mistress Parry," Cornwallis informed her.

"So I am expected to shift for myself?" Elizabeth cried woefully.

"No, madam, they will be replaced by such as are proven to be faithful to the Queen's Majesty," he informed her. At his words, six dour-faced, soberly attired men and women entered the room. "They will accompany you to the Tower in the morning."

Elizabeth could not answer him.

It grew late, and very dark. Kat, who could not still her own trembling, offered to light candles, but Elizabeth, still crouched on the floor, shook her head. Then, around midnight, flickering lights outside lit up the gloomy chamber. Fearfully, Elizabeth rose, uncurling her numb limbs, and limped to the window, peering out at the gardens below. There were drawn up rank upon rank of white-coated soldiers. All detailed to guard one defenseless girl, she thought bitterly.

"Come to bed," Kat pleaded. "You will need all your strength for tomorrow." She alone understood the dread in Elizabeth's heart. Strong men had quailed when committed to the Tower; this girl's mother had died violently there. It had been an ordeal for Elizabeth to visit the place at the time of her sister's joyous reception. How much worse would it be for her on the morrow?

"Think you I can sleep?" Elizabeth asked, her eyes haunted.

"Just rest, I beg of you," Kat beseeched her.

She lay there, wide awake, willing sleep to come, but it proved elusive, as she had feared it would. She could not stop her mind wandering in perilous directions, conjuring up images of scaffolds, blocks, axes . . . would they behead her with a sword, as they had her mother? She imagined what it would feel like, walking those last few steps to death, knowing that in minutes she would be facing eternity. She had always feared that if she once crossed the threshold of the Tower as a prisoner, she would never emerge alive. Tonight, she must pray for her soul, for she was almost certainly going to be taken there on the morrow.

When they came for her in the morning, she was hollow-eyed and disoriented, a wraith in her severe black gown and hood. She had disdained to put on the finery that was her usual garb these days, thinking it made her seem vain and worldly; simple clothes would emphasize her youth, her innocence, her purity—and of course, none knew that she had no right to sympathy on that last count.

There were two of them this morning: my lords the Marquess of

Winchester and the Earl of Sussex, important nobles both, and her friends in happier times. Now they had assumed grave, business-like countenances, but she thought she could detect a certain reluctance in their manner.

"Madam, we are come to conduct you to the Tower," Winchester said. His words, expected though they were, chilled her.

"The barge is waiting," Sussex told her, "and you must come without delay, my lady, for the tide tarries for nobody."

"May I know what is charged against me?" Elizabeth asked.

The two lords exchanged glances. Winchester swallowed.

"There are no charges against you, madam," he informed her. "You are being taken for questioning."

"I am innocent!" Elizabeth cried, her distress shocking to see. The men blenched, embarrassed and awkward in the face of womanly tears. "I beg of you, my good lords, wait for the next tide. I am ill prepared . . ."

"Madam, we cannot," Sussex said miserably.

"Then let me see the Queen and plead my case," she begged.

"The Queen will not see you, you have been told that," Winchester reminded her.

"Then at least let me write to her," Elizabeth beseeched them, desperate to delay the inevitable moment of departure. If only she could contrive to miss the tide, that would ensure her another blessed day of freedom.

"I cannot permit that," Winchester said.

"A word," Sussex murmured, tugging at the Marquess's sleeve, and the two men retired to the inner chamber, leaving Elizabeth breathless with hope.

"Maybe we should agree to what she asks," Sussex was saying.

"It will probably do her more harm than good," Winchester opined.

"My lord," Sussex reminded him, "remember that we are in the presence of a lady who might one day become our queen. Dare we refuse her request? It might rebound on us in the long run."

Winchester thought for a moment.

"You may have the sow by the right ear," he agreed. "Let her write."

When they returned to the outer room, Sussex fell to his knees before an astonished Elizabeth. "You shall have liberty to write your mind," he told her, "and as I am a true man, I will deliver your letter to the Queen and beg an answer, whatever comes of it."

Elizabeth could not sufficiently express her gratitude. It was a blessed relief to know that she had at least one friend on the council, and it afforded her a glimmer of hope.

"If ever I am in a position to do you favor, my lords, do not hesitate to ask it of me," she assured them, and then sat down to compose the most important letter she had ever written.

Knowing that she was pleading for her very life, she poured out her heart. She reminded Mary of her promise never to condemn her without first having heard what she had to say in her defense. She remonstrated against being sent to the Tower without just cause, for she deserved it not. She protested before God that she had never plotted, counseled, nor abetted anything injurious to the Queen. She begged that she might plead her case in person with Mary before she was committed to the Tower.

Do not condemn me in all men's sight before the truth be known, she begged, her handwriting becoming more sprawling as her quill flew over the page and her desperation increased. She even referred to the Admiral, claiming that he would not have suffered death if he had been allowed to speak in his defense before his brother the Protector. *I pray God that evil persuasion will not set one sister against the other,* she declared. Kneeling in humility, as she put it, she craved but one audience with Mary. "I am innocent of any treason," she insisted, "and to this my truth, I will stand in to my death," she concluded.

At last, the letter was finished. It wasn't very tidy, for she had crossed out phrases and added words here and there in her frenzied determination to ward off a terrible fate. Then something struck her. The last sentence ended at the top of a fresh page. Once the letter was out of her hands, her enemies could forge her handwriting and add anything they liked in the space that was left. But she would not give them the chance. Taking up her pen again, she drew bold lines, diagonally, across the blank part of the paper. At the very bottom, she wrote: *I humbly crave but one word of answer from yourself. Your Highness's most faithful subject that has been from the beginning, and will be to mine end.* After this, she signed her name, with its customary elegant flourishes, and sat up straight, laying down the quill. She had done her very best; the matter was in God's hands now.

"Have you finished, madam?" Winchester and Sussex had been waiting somewhat impatiently.

"Yes, my lords," she told them.

"Well, we have missed the tide." Winchester sighed. "The river will now be so low that it would be dangerous to attempt getting past London Bridge. Those piers are perilously close together."

"The next favorable tide will be around midnight," Sussex informed them.

"I do not think that we should take the Lady Elizabeth under cover of darkness," Winchester considered. "Some fools might take it into their heads to attempt a rescue. Better to wait until tomorrow morning."

"That would be much wiser," Sussex agreed. "It is Palm Sunday and we can make the journey while everyone is in church. That way we avoid any likelihood of demonstrations on my lady's behalf." He turned to Elizabeth, whose face was registering the deepest dismay. She wanted the people to see her taken to the Tower; she wanted them to voice their displeasure. Her plight must be known, so that protests could be made.

"I will take your letter to the Queen now," Sussex said.

Sussex quailed before Mary's anger. She would not look at him.

"You delayed carrying out my orders for *this*?" she cried. "You allowed yourselves to be suborned by that cunning and devious girl?"

"Your Majesty, she pleaded with us most piteously," he told her. "It would have taken a heart of stone to refuse her." Too late, he realized what he had said: that Mary herself must have such a heart. The Queen was frowning darkly.

"Such a thing would never have been tolerated in my father's time," she snapped. "I wish he could come back, if only for a month, and give you, who are supposed to be my councillors, the rebuke you deserve! Now go, and see to it that there is no further delay."

Elizabeth looked out her window. The dismal Sunday morning, with its leaden skies and teeming rain, mirrored her despondent mood. There could be no more delaying tactics. Very soon, they would come for her. How had her mother conducted herself on that fateful day they had taken her to the Tower? Kat had spoken of her courage, but also of her wild veering from tears to laughter. Elizabeth knew herself to be perilously near to such hysteria. She must be brave, and remember that she was a king's daughter—and that she was innocent.

"Madam, it is time," Winchester said, opening the door to her chamber. "We must make haste."

Elizabeth straightened her shoulders and took a deep breath.

"The Lord's will be done," she said. "If there is no remedy, I must be content with that."

Surrounded by guards, they led her, with Kat and the royal servants following, down the stairs and out into the gardens. The rain was lashing down so heavily that Elizabeth's velvet cloak and black gown and hood were soon soaked through. As they hastened between formal flower beds and along the water gallery that led to the river, she kept looking up at the palace windows, desperately hoping to catch a glimpse of the Queen and attract her attention. But Mary, it seemed, had no inclination to watch her prisoner being taken away. The unfairness of it all struck Elizabeth deeply.

"I marvel much at the nobility of this realm," she declared, looking accusingly at Winchester and Sussex, "who meekly suffer me to be led into captivity, and to Lord knows what else, for I do not."

Sussex bent his head to her.

"Not a few members of the council are sorry for your trouble, my lady," he murmured in a low voice. "I am myself sorry that I have lived to see this day."

Elizabeth stared at him, her eyebrows raised in surprise, but there was no time to answer, for they had reached the jetty and the barge was waiting. She was directed to sit in the cabin, along with the lords and her attendants, and as soon as they had settled themselves on the cushioned benches and the curtains had been drawn, the rain-drenched oarsmen pushed off, and they were on their way downstream. The Thames was turbulent, and Kat looked distinctly queasy. Elizabeth normally enjoyed the unpredictability of river craft and the motion of the tides, but today, on this dreadful day, she too felt sick as the barge rocked and bucked on the strong currents.

Suddenly, the swell of the waves increased, and the boat began to rear and plunge. There were frantic shouts from outside.

"We must be nearing the bridge," Winchester said uneasily. He rose, staggered, and made his unsteady way out of the cabin. As he disappeared, the boat seemed to rise up of a sudden, hover in the air, and then crash down. In the cabin, they could hear the slap of water across the prow of the barge, and the curses of the oarsmen as the master shouted orders. Kat was whimpering in fright. Even Elizabeth began to fear that they would sink. They were being tossed helplessly in the tempest, and might at any moment crash against the massive piers that supported London Bridge.

"Turn back!" she heard Sussex yell.

"No, make for the shore," Winchester ordered.

"Too late!" roared the master. "Sit down!"

Unable to bear the suspense and the fear any longer, Elizabeth thrust her head through the curtains. Gusts of rain spattered in her face. Above her loomed the bridge, dark and menacing; below her, the remorseless waves. The boat was perilously near to the piers, it was going to founder on them, they would all drown . . . but no. There was a sudden rush as the current violently and suddenly swept them through, and within seconds their vessel emerged on the other side of the bridge, where the water, although choppy, was calmer. There were cries of relief and the odd invocation of thanks to Our Lady, and then the oarsmen recommenced their steady rhythm.

But ahead loomed the great threatening bulk of the Tower. Elizabeth watched in mounting dread as they drew nearer to the forbidding stone fortress and could see the cannons on the wharf—those same cannons that had announced her mother's death. There was the White Tower rising beyond the huge curtain walls, and below those walls, the watergate, the massive, barred wooden doors of which were gradually grinding open to admit the Tower's newest prisoner. Herself.

This way her mother had come. And she was still here, her bones rotting under the chapel floor.

The barge was slowly turning toward the gate. In panic, and still shaking from the ordeal of shooting the bridge, Elizabeth suddenly got up and threw open the door to the cabin. The lords stared at her wild eyes and trembling lips.

"I beg of you, my lords, allow me to enter this place through any gate other than this," she cried desperately. "For I know that many have passed through it and never come out again."

Winchester and Sussex looked at her with compassion, knowing that they could not help her in her distress. She tried once more.

"Such a gate is not fit for a princess to enter," she protested. "I will not use it!"

"You do not have a choice, madam," Winchester told her.

Elizabeth stood there glowering, clutching at the door handles to steady herself, the rain running in rivulets down her face. She looked the image of misery, with her damp hair plastered about her temples, the defeated slump of her shoulders and her clothes soaked through. The Marquess, a chivalrous man, took pity on her.

"Here, Madam, take my cloak," he offered, unclasping it and handing it to her, but she pushed it away.

"No!" she sobbed. "Leave me alone."

They had almost reached the watergate. There, on the privy stairs, stood the Lieutenant of the Tower, Sir John Bridges, a well-set man with a broad face and an avuncular manner, waiting to receive his prisoner. Behind him, solid and impassive, were drawn up six Yeomen Warders.

The boat bumped against the landing stage, the oars were raised, and the securing rope was thrown over the bollard on the jetty. Winchester and Sussex leapt ashore, their feet splashing in the water that had pooled on the paving stones.

"Come, my lady," Sussex beckoned.

Elizabeth stood defiantly by the cabin door. She had decided that she was not going anywhere, that nothing would make her move from this last bastion of safety.

"Nay, my lords," she said, shivering. "I do not intend to get my shoes wet." She glared at the Lieutenant and his men.

"Madam, in the Queen's name, I command you to come ashore!" Winchester shouted above the wind. "You must obey."

Slowly, reluctantly, Elizabeth balanced herself along the passageway between the oarsmen and placed a tentative foot on the landing stage.

"Here lands as true a subject, being prisoner, as ever landed at these stairs!" she announced in a loud but shaking voice. "Before Thee, O God, do I say this, having no other friend but Thee alone. O Lord, I never thought to come in here as a prisoner."

Her voice broke again as she crept nearer to the steps. She looked at the waiting men, willing them to take pity on her. "I pray you all, good friends and fellows, bear me witness that I come in as no traitor, but as true a woman to the Queen's Majesty as any as is now living; and thereon will I take my death!"

She was near to collapsing now, and tears were mingling with the raindrops on her hectic cheeks. Some of the warders moved forward impulsively and threw themselves on their knees before her. "God preserve Your Grace!" they cried. The Lieutenant frowned and barked an order, at which those who had broken ranks quickly rose and returned to their places shamefacedly.

"Madam, you must come with me," Sir John Bridges said.

Now Elizabeth's courage did fail her. She was going to die in this place, she knew it. The prospect was so terrible that she was unable to take a step farther. Her legs would support her no longer, and she sank down on the wet stairs, great shudders racking her body.

"You had best come out of the rain, madam," Sir John said gently, reaching a hand down to her.

"It is better sitting here than in a worse place!" she wailed, ignoring it. "For God knows where you will take me!"

"You may have no fear on that count," he assured her. "You are to lodge in the palace, where rooms have been prepared for you."

"Is that where my mother lodged?" she sobbed.

"I believe so, madam," he told her.

"I cannot go there," she told him. "It would be torture to me."

"They are the most comfortable rooms available, and meet for Your Grace's high estate," Bridges said patiently.

"Comfortable they may be," she flung at him, "but for my mother they were an antechamber to the scaffold!"

Her attendants were climbing out of the barge now. Kat moved to go to her, her face working in distress, but Sir John stayed her with a gesture. One of Elizabeth's grooms burst into tears. She looked up sullenly, accusingly. The youth flushed and wiped his eyes on his sleeve.

"I thank God I know my truth to be such that no man can have cause to weep for me," Elizabeth declared.

"Then you must take comfort from that, madam," said Sir John, once more offering her his arm. "Come now, let us go into the warm. A fire has been lit for you."

She looked at him, summoning the courage to go with him, then slowly rose to her feet. Skilled in dealing with men and women facing imprisonment, torture, or death—not a month ago he had attended Lady Jane Grey on the scaffold, much to his distress—the Lieutenant tucked her hand under his arm and led her slowly up the stairs.

The little procession wended its way through the outer bailey to the royal palace, a complex of ancient buildings that lay between the White Tower and the River Thames. There, Sir John escorted his prisoner through seemingly endless chambers and galleries until they came to the Queen's lodgings and the rooms that had been prepared for Elizabeth—a great chamber, bedchamber, and privy.

Elizabeth was startled at their splendor, although clearly they had not been used for many years: There was a closed-up, musty atmosphere, as if dust had been left to gather, and here and there patches of damp. But the friezes of classical motifs were beautiful, as were the intricately patterned floor tiles and the gilded battened ceilings. The furniture was sparse, and obviously not that which had once graced these rooms, but it was well polished and adequate for its purpose.

"Mrs. Astley and Mistress Parry may remain with you, madam," Sir John said. "Your other servants will be housed downstairs. The warders will admit them as necessary."

"I thank you, sir," Elizabeth whispered, watching him select a key from the heavy ring he held in his hand. The lords bowed and followed him out. As that key turned in the lock, with awful finality, Sussex suddenly began to weep.

"Let us take heed, my lords, that we go not beyond our commission," he warned. "For she is the King our late master's daughter, as well as the Queen's sister. Let us deal with her in such a way that we will be able to answer for it in future, for just dealing is always the best course."

"My lord speaks truth," Bridges said softly.

"Aye," Winchester agreed. "Perform your office lightly, my Lord Lieutenant."

Left alone with Kat and Blanche, Elizabeth listlessly explored her rooms. The first thing she did was try the door at the far end of her bedchamber, but of course it was locked. Where did it lead? she wondered. If these two rooms had been Anne Boleyn's presence chamber and state bedchamber, as seemed likely, would she not have had other privy apartments? Were they behind the door? Her mind conjured up images of dusty, bare rooms, faded splendor, adorned now only by cobwebs and patches of mold.

"My mother was lodged here," she whispered to Kat.

Kat put an arm around her, visibly upset by the events of the day.

"She was, my lamb—at least, before her trial. Lady Lee, that was with her in the Tower, told me that after it she was moved to the Lieutenant's lodging. So she could not have been here for long."

"The decoration is very fine," Elizabeth commented.

"It would be," Kat said. "These rooms were done up for her coronation, three years earlier. When she came here as a prisoner, she said they were too good for her."

"They are good enough for me," Elizabeth retorted with something of her old spirit. She moved to the mullioned window. The casements had been secured. The window looked down upon a courtyard surrounded by walls, with the river beyond.

"Did they think I would try to escape by the window?" Elizabeth asked, trying in vain to undo one of the catches. "It's a long drop."

"Obviously they are taking no chances," Kat observed. "Prisoners have escaped before. There are lots of tales."

"I'm more concerned about having no fresh air," Elizabeth muttered. "These rooms are stuffy—they need airing. I shall complain to Sir John."

She looked around her again, at the walls, bare plaster beneath the blue-and-gold frieze, the fire crackling in the stone hearth, the serviceable oak table and benches, and tried to imagine how the room would have looked at the time of her mother's triumph.

This place made her shiver. It was like having a ghost standing just behind her. It had been surprisingly easy seeking out memories of her mother in the lush, leafy paradise at Hever, Anne's former home; but here, where she had met her fate, the very stones spoke of tragedy and doom.

"I don't like it here," she told Kat. "Did the Queen think to add to my miseries by shutting me up in this, of all places?"

"I don't like it much either," Kat agreed, "but just remember that it could be much worse. You could have been shut in a dungeon."

The first night was terrible, at least to begin with. Lying in the dark, horribly aware of where she was, Elizabeth's imagination kept invoking the most terrifying images of her likely fate, and when she did sleep fitfully, her dreams were of pain and blood and death, so real that she awoke with a jolt, sweating and panting in fright. It was a blessed relief to hear the gentle snoring of Kat and the even breathing of Blanche as they slumbered on their pallets on the floor.

It was then that she became aware that there was another presence in the room, a presence barely perceptible in the dim glow of the dying embers of the fire. There it stood, dark and still at the foot of her bed, a woman, by the shape of it, a woman in a French hood like a halo, her face shadowed in the gloom.

It was strange that she did not feel frightened, even when she realized that the figure before her was not of this world. Indeed, she recognized it, as her thoughts went winging back to Hever, to that visit to the Princess Anna, all those years ago, when—she was sure of it—this same figure had appeared to her in a similar manner. She had felt comforted then, and she did now, and to her dying day she would believe that this was her mother Anne come to give her comfort and strength in her ordeal. Anne, the one person who would understand what Elizabeth was suffering now. The bonds of love, she reflected, as she willed Anne's shade to linger some while longer, must be stronger than death.

"My lady mother?" she whispered. The words felt strange on her tongue. The figure did not move, but there was a kind of recognition, she felt—or, rather, hoped; and then the apparition began to fade, until she could see it no more and began wondering if she had dreamed the whole thing. But the sense of having been comforted and fortified with renewed courage was strong in her. She knew it would give her the wherewithal to face what lay ahead.

Sir John proved accommodating about the windows, sending men at once to free the casements. He was unfailingly courteous and respectful. And he wasted no time in inviting Elizabeth to dine with him each evening in his lodging. Grateful as she was to be escorted every night through the palace precincts to his comfortable half-timbered house, her visits were something of an ordeal, for it faced Tower Green, where there still stood—ominous and sinister—the scaffold that had been erected for Lady Jane Grey's execution.

Why had it not been taken down? Elizabeth wondered, with great trepidation. Was it because they expected it to be used again? And was she to be the next victim? Were they so certain that they could prove her guilty?

On the second evening, over the roast partridge and stewed plums, she could not stop herself from asking Sir John about it.

"I have received no orders," he said. "With her marriage to the Prince of Spain fast approaching, I am sure Her Majesty has more important things on her mind than ordering the dismantling of that scaffold."

Elizabeth hoped he was right. Nevertheless, she could not rid herself of the dread conviction that the scaffold had been kept in place for her, and every time she saw it, the horrible thing, she began to tremble.

The Lieutenant's lodging itself was a place of sadness and doom for her. She never forgot, as she supped on good, wholesome fare and exchanged intelligent conversation with Sir John and Lady Bridges, that the last acts in her mother's tragedy had been played out in the rooms above her head. She could see their latticed windows whenever she approached the house, and was painfully aware that those windows looked out directly onto Tower Green. If she had braced herself to look out, Anne could have watched her scaffold being built.

"Lady Lee said that the carpenters who built it kept them awake all through those last nights with their hammering and banging," Kat told her. Since their arrival in the Tower, Kat had not been exactly forthcoming with confidences about Anne, for she did not wish to add to Elizabeth's present distress: They had to be coerced out of her. Yet Elizabeth felt she had to know the truth about her mother's fate, that in some way it would give her courage to deal with what was happening to her now.

Very little *was* happening, in fact. There had been no interrogation, no visits from the council. Elizabeth wondered if they were trying to wear her down with the agony of suspense. Well, she thought tartly, that will get them nowhere. I am as innocent now as I was on the day I came here.

But was she truly innocent? she asked herself as she paced along the wall-walk, a privilege that had been accorded her for her recreation. It was almost as much of an ordeal as her visits to the Lieutenant's lodging, for from the walls she could see the river, busy with its craft, and people unheedingly enjoying their freedom. Looking away, and pacing ahead of the five attendants on whom Sir John had insisted, she asked herself if it had been treason not to inform the Queen of the letters she had received from Wyatt. Had it been right to ignore them? Yet what could she have done? They would only have accused her of conspiring with the man: The fact that he had written to her at all would have been all the evidence they needed to bring her down. So yes, she had done the best thing. Whether it was the right thing was another matter.

She was calmer now. She had wept and stormed a lot those first few days in the Tower, but as it gradually became clear that her enemies were in no hurry to hasten her to her death, she began to feel stronger. She was eating better too. Her servants were permitted to go out and buy food for her, and to prepare it themselves.

"There is less risk of poison that way!" she told Kat with grim humor; but seriously, she did not think that any would attempt to get rid of her by underhanded means. In fact, apart from the lack of freedom and the ever-present fear of what might happen to her, her existence was fairly comfortable.

Until Sir John Gage, Constable of the Tower, arrived.

"You have allowed her to go out on the walls?" the Constable repeated, clearly alarmed.

Sir John Bridges eyed his superior with disfavor. Gage had ever been one for sticking rigorously to the rules.

"It was so that she might take the air, sir," he explained.

"I cannot allow it," Gage declared. "The practice must stop. And I noticed that her windows were open. Who permitted that?"

"I did," Bridges said, a touch defiantly. "She has been very ill. She says she needs fresh air."

"Nonsense!" the Constable averred stoutly. "All this pandering to her must cease. She is a prisoner like any other."

"Prisoners of rank are usually allowed some privileges," the Lieutenant persisted.

"She is no ordinary prisoner!" rapped Gage. "She is the Queen's sister, and my orders are to keep her straitly. She is not to communicate with anyone, do you hear me? No walking on the walls or leaning out of windows to attract attention."

"She does not—" Bridges began.

"And she is not to write any letters," interrupted Gage. "I trust you have not given her writing materials?"

"I saw no harm in it," the Lieutenant replied, bristling.

"For God's sake, man! She is suspected of treason. If she plots mischief from here, *our* necks will be at risk. You must take them away. See to it!"

Elizabeth felt quite sorry for Sir John as he stood before her, embarrassed and clearly unhappy, and told her that she was to lose her privileges.

"The Constable has his orders, I fear," he told her. "I cannot gainsay them, much as I would."

"I understand," she said evenly, but inside her heart was sinking. She could not believe that this new severity emanated solely from Sir John Gage's fussiness and determination to interpret the rules as strictly as possible. She was convinced that there was a more sinister reason for it. Others would have been questioned by now, she was sure. What of Courtenay, that spineless fool? Had he said something against her? Was this withdrawal of privileges but a prelude to something far worse?

She watched Sir John collecting her paper and pens.

"Now I am truly a prisoner," she said.

"I will do what I can for you, madam," he assured her.

When he had gone, she fought back tears. How was she to occupy the long, dragging days with no walks, no means of studying? And she would stifle here with the windows shut.

A key turned in the door and Kat was let in, puffing and blowing.

"The cheek of it!" she fumed, her face puce. "The soldiers at the gate made us hand over the food we bought in the market. For security reasons, they said. Security reasons my eye! Those common rascal soldiers have taken it for themselves, I'll warrant."

Elizabeth rose, fear channeled into anger. How dare they!

"Go now, to Sir John Gage, and say that I sent you," she commanded, "and make a complaint to him on my behalf."

"I'll tell him!" Kat warned.

Bravely, she clung to her resolve when faced with the stern stare of the Constable.

"Don't you frown at me, woman," he rapped.

Kat shrugged. "It's your men who are doing this," she said boldly.

"By God, for your impertinence, I could put you where you will see neither sun nor moon!" he threatened.

"May I appeal to your chivalry then, as a knight?" Kat asked craftily, suppressing her fury at being spoken to thus. "The Lady Elizabeth fears that someone will poison her. That is why we, her servants, go out to buy food and prepare it for her. She needs to eat well in order to build up her health. Will you deny her even this?"

The Constable thought for a while.

"Very well," he said at length. "But if anyone tries to smuggle any messages in with the food, it will go harshly with them."

"Do you take us for fools?" Kat retorted. "We wish to preserve our mistress, not add to her danger. But I thank you anyway for this small kindness."

So they continued to buy food as usual, only Elizabeth could not eat it, so full of dread was she.

"Take it away," she would say as Kat brought dish after dish of savory-smelling delicacies to tempt her.

"You must eat, for the sake of your health!" Kat remonstrated with her, but Elizabeth waved her away.

"What point in preserving my health when I am to be sent to the scaffold soon?" she moaned. Being treated more harshly had crushed her spirits.

"You don't know that!" Kat cried. "Do not even think about it. If they were going to proceed against you to that end, they would have done it by now."

"They are gathering evidence," Elizabeth said flatly. "They are looking for the means to convict me. Lady Jane's scaffold is still there. I shall be next, I tell you." Her voice rose with hysteria.

"Pull yourself together!" Kat commanded. But Elizabeth could not. Some days she could barely drag herself from her bed, so dispirited and scared was she.

What will happen to me? she kept asking herself. When will they come for me? Every tap on the door had her shaking in terror. Daily, she expected to hear the dread summons to the block. Despairing, she could think of nothing but how she would feel walking those few short steps, kneeling down in the straw, being blindfolded . . . And then the blow, the cold steel slicing into her neck. Would there be much pain? Or would it be over before she knew anything about it?

The ax featured large in her nightmares, waking and sleeping. She had heard awful tales of bungled executions, which now came back to haunt her. In her father's reign, old Lady Salisbury had gone to the block for treason and been butchered by an inexperienced headsman. There were stories of people suffering several chops of the ax before their heads were severed. She could imagine the blood bubbling in her throat, the incomprehensible agony, the awareness of being mortally wounded, like an animal laid low.

But wait! Her mother had been spared the ax, hadn't she? Her father had sent to France for a skilled swordsman. Even in death, Anne had had the best. The kinder, quicker death. That was it. She would beg the Queen to let her die by the sword. It was all she could think about.

She grew thinner and paler. Her eyes were shadowed, tormented. Kat and Blanche looked at her anxiously, fearing that she was slipping away before their eyes. Sir John Bridges too noticed the state she was in when he came daily to inquire after her health. He knew she was taking little sustenance, because for days now she had made excuses not to join him for dinner.

"She is suffering from being cooped up in those rooms without fresh air," he warned the Constable. "Sir, I fear she will become very ill if you do not help her."

Sir John Gage frowned.

"I have my orders," he stated.

"Yes, but will the Queen thank you if she dies in your care?" Bridges pointed out.

Gage had to admit that she would not. "Very well, then. She may walk around in the old Queen's apartments. You may open them up. But the windows must be kept closed, mind you."

Sir John shook his head. It was not enough, he knew, but it was something.

Elizabeth watched, light-headed from lack of food and sleep, as the Lieutenant unlocked the door in the bedchamber. As she had expected, the rooms beyond were layered in dust and shrouded with cobwebs. The air was heavy, stale; it made her cough a little.

Surely her mother had not been here? No one had refurbished these gloomy rooms for decades. They boasted no friezes, no fresh paintwork, no gilded ceilings. Instead, there were faded and cracked wall paintings, in blue and vermilion, depicting ancient kings and angels, and the cracked, faded tiles on the floor bore imprints of leopards and fleurs-de-lis. Here and there lay a broken stool, a battered old chest, but otherwise the rooms were bare. The windows were caked in grime, so there was no point in trying to see out. Kat wrinkled her nose; this place smelled of dead things.

"It was fresh air I wanted, not must and decay," Elizabeth said bitterly to the Lieutenant. "I can hardly breathe in here. Let us go back, I pray you."

As the door shut on the deserted chambers, she threw herself on her bed.

"If I don't have some fresh air, I will die," she wept.

"I will do what I can," Bridges told her.

"There is a walled garden at the side of my house," he told her when he returned not half an hour later. "Sir John Gage has given permission for you to use it whenever convenient, on condition that the gate remains locked and an armed warder is in attendance."

Elizabeth felt somewhat heartened at this news. Would they really be looking to her health and comfort in this way if the Queen was seeking her death?

It was pleasure enough just to sit in the garden and bask in the weak sunlight of approaching spring. Simple pleasures . . . they were the best; she had never appreciated them so much as now. The vivid hues of early flowers, the green buds on the trees, growing things pushing their way up through the dark soil. New life burgeoning, and with it a gleam of hope.

A little face appeared above the wicket gate. The warder, a family man who was secretly sympathetic to the unfortunate princess in his custody, grinned.

"It's you, young imp!" he said. The little boy, about five years old, laughed, then resumed his scrutiny of the garden's other occupant. Elizabeth ventured a smile.

"He's the Keeper of the Wardrobe's boy," the warder told her. "Aren't you, Adam? And here's his sister. Good day, Susanna."

A second chubby face, framed by blond curls, peered through the bars. It smiled, and Elizabeth caught a glimpse of gaps between milk teeth. She smiled back and waved. The child disappeared. Minutes later, she was back, and a pudgy hand grasping some newly picked flowers thrust itself through the gate.

"May I?" Elizabeth asked the warder. At his nod, she moved swiftly across the grass and graciously accepted the offering.

"What's your name?" the boy asked.

"Elizabeth," she told him.

"The Lady Elizabeth?" he asked in wonder.

"You know who I am?" she inquired, startled.

"You're the poor lady who has been locked up," he said. "My father and mother say you should be let to go free."

The warder smiled ruefully.

"I wouldn't go around saying that, young man," he told the boy. He turned to Elizabeth. "Little pitchers have big ears."

"Indeed they do," she agreed. Her heart felt lighter than it had done in weeks. It was cheering to know that some folk believed in her innocence and sympathized with her plight.

"What are the common people saying about me?" she dared to ask the man.

"Well—" He looked about him to check that no one was within earshot. "I shouldn't tell you this, my lady, but I've heard many say it's a shame that King Harry's daughter is locked up in the Tower. Not one has said they believe you to be guilty. The people love you, and there's a lot of murmuring against those who have put you here."

"I thank you," whispered Elizabeth, tears springing to her eyes. "You have brought me much comfort." Surely, the Queen would not contemplate flying in the face of popular opinion and putting her to death. No monarch would be so rash . . .

The next day she sat out, the children were there again, two pairs of eyes peeping over the gate.

"Lady!" piped up a little voice. "For you!"

Susanna was thrusting her hand through the bars, holding out an object. It was a miniature bunch of keys. Elizabeth had to laugh.

"I trust Sir John Gage has no objection to my receiving these." She smiled at the amused warder and bent to pat the child's head.

"The child gave her keys?" Gage was furious.

"Toy keys, sir," the warder said, regretting he had ever mentioned the gift to the Lieutenant—who had, of course, felt duty-bound to report it to his superior.

"And entirely harmless," Bridges added.

"This time, perhaps," Gage muttered. "But these children could be used to smuggle messages to the Lady Elizabeth. My orders are to prevent her from communicating with anyone in case she plots further treason."

"Just keep an eye on the children," Bridges said evenly to the warder.

"And if they attempt to give her anything, you will answer for it to me!" the eagle-eyed Constable commanded.

It was a pretty posy, made up of delicate spring flowers and clumsily tied with a ribbon. Young Adam bowed as he presented it to Elizabeth, who was about to curtsy in return when the warder snatched it from her.

"Orders, madam," he said, his manner far less friendly than hitherto. "You there!"

His fellow guard, who was keeping watch on the other side of the garden wall, responded to his summons.

"Yes?"

"Take this boy to the Constable, and give him this." He handed over the bouquet. Instantly, the children started wailing, and Elizabeth looked on horrified as the terrified Adam was borne off, struggling and protesting.

"Do you enjoy tormenting innocent women and children?" she raged at the warders, her blood up. But they ignored her, leaving her shaking with fury. The one who had shown himself friendly just stood there impassively by the gate, staring straight ahead.

Hauled before Sir John Gage, the boy stood speechless with fright.

"Who gave you these flowers?" Gage barked.

"N-no one, sir. We picked them," Adam whispered.

"Has anyone asked you to hide a secret message in them?"

"No," answered Adam, surprised.

"I mean the prisoner Courtenay? Did he give you a message for the Lady Elizabeth?"

"No, sir, I promise, sir." The child looked totally bewildered.

Sir John looked at him darkly.

"You have been very naughty, giving that lady gifts. It is not allowed.

I warn you, boy, that if you dare to speak to her again, you will be soundly whipped. Is that clear?"

"Yes," squeaked the cowering miscreant.

The next day being fine, Elizabeth returned to the garden. Lying under a tree, engrossed in her book, she was interrupted by a movement at the gate and looked up. The warder was munching his noon-piece, a hunk of bread wrapped around a slab of cheese, and was bending down to pick up a flagon of ale.

Adam stood a few paces beyond the gate.

"Mistress, I am sorry, but I can bring you no more flowers now," he called softly, then ran off, to her dismay. She did not see the children again.

"Madam, you are summoned before the council," the Lieutenant told her. "They await you in the lower chamber."

Elizabeth began to tremble. The long days of silence had led her to dare hope that nothing had been found against her. Now those hopes were shattered. The time had come for her to use her wits to save her skin. She had never felt more alone.

The councillors were seated along an oak trestle table. Bishop Gardiner, the Lord Chancellor, was at the center. All stared at her unsmiling as she entered, head high, hands clasped demurely over her stomacher, and made her way to the chair that had been set for her facing her interrogators.

Gardiner rustled his papers importantly and rested his hawk-like gaze on her.

"My Lady Elizabeth, we are here to examine you regarding the talk that you had at Ashridge with Sir James Crofts, who asked you to remove to your house at Donnington. Why did he require this of you?"

"My house at Donnington?" Elizabeth repeated, playing for time. "I have so many houses, my lord, I cannot call this one to mind, so sure it is I never went there."

"Sir James Crofts told you it was better fortified than Ashridge. You seemed to know of its existence then," Gardiner retorted.

Elizabeth pretended to consider. "Ah, yes, *that* house. You must forgive me, sirs, I have never been to it, and I had forgotten about Sir James advising me to go there."

The councillors exchanged exasperated glances.

"Bring in Crofts," Gardiner said wearily.

Elizabeth stared as the prisoner was escorted into the chamber by Yeomen Warders. When last she had seen him, Sir James had been a handsome man, but now his fine features were scored with lines of anxiety and his hands were trembling. Prompted by his jailers, he recounted what had happened at Ashridge, omitting no detail. Elizabeth gathered her wits.

"I only understood that you were concerned for my safety," she protested. "And clearly I did not take your advice." She turned to the councillors.

"Gentlemen, nothing more passed between myself and this man. This is a waste of your time and mine, as I have little to tell you of him, or indeed of anyone else who is imprisoned here for this cause." She stood up.

"My lords, do you mean to examine every common prisoner in order to trap me? Because if so, methinks you do me a great injury. If they have done evil and offended the Queen's Majesty, then let them answer for it accordingly. But I beseech you, do not join *me* in this sort with such men. I am no traitor, as you should well know!"

Gardiner took no notice.

"So you do remember Sir James suggesting you move to Donnington?" he persisted.

"I do now," she agreed. "But what harm is there in that? Might I not, my lords, go to my own houses at all times?"

Some councillors shifted uncomfortably. Others exchanged uneasy glances.

"My Lord Bishop, we seem to be here on a wild goose chase," Sussex said. "Remember, this lady is the heir to the throne . . ." The warning in his voice was unmistakable.

The Earl of Arundel got up, walked around the table, and fell to his knees before a startled Elizabeth.

"Madam, we are certainly very sorry that we have so troubled you about vain matters," he told her.

"My lords, you do sift me very narrowly," she said, "but I feel well assured that you will not do more to me than is consistent with God's will, and I pray that He will forgive you all."

Gardiner stared at her, marveling at how cleverly she had succeeded in turning the interrogation to her own advantage. The Queen, he knew, would not be pleased.

"There is nothing further to be gained here," he told his colleagues brusquely. "You may return to your lodgings, madam."

"My prison, you mean," Elizabeth said spiritedly, elated at the way the interview had ended. Then she turned, chin held high, and swept past the bowing lords.

"I had been expecting, madam, to hear that the Lady Elizabeth and Courtenay were to be put to death," Renard said, his face grave.

"There is, as yet, nothing that can be proved against them." Mary's voice betrayed her agitation.

"Then I am sorry for it, and so is my master the Emperor," he told her. "He knows, as does Your Majesty, that while those two traitors are alive, there will always be plots to raise them to the throne, and that it would be just to punish them, for it is publicly known that they are guilty and deserve death."

"But not publicly proved!" Mary interrupted.

"Which is very regrettable, madam—for you, and for your kingdom." Mary heard the ominous note in his voice.

"You know how hard I have worked for this marriage," Renard went on. "So you will understand that it grieves me sorely to tell you that the Emperor is of the opinion that, while the Lady Elizabeth lives, it will be very difficult to guarantee Prince Philip's safety in this land. In the circumstances, therefore, I cannot recommend His Highness crossing to England until every necessary step has been taken to ensure that he is in no danger."

Faced with the unbearable prospect of her cherished dreams evaporating, Mary could not stop herself from bursting into tears. She was heaving with distress, mortifyingly aware that this was not the conduct that ambassadors expected from a sovereign Queen.

"I would rather never been have born than that any harm should come to His Highness!" she sobbed. "I assure you, evidence will be found, and that those two will be tried before he comes."

"My master will be relieved to hear that," Renard said coolly.

The council members were debating, brows furrowed, tempers fraught.

"But what is to be done with the Lady Elizabeth?" Winchester was saying. "Her guilt is by no means established, and there is no case against her."

"Aye," chorused some voices, among them Sussex's and Arundel's.

"Not so fast, my lords," Gardiner interrupted. "We have the Queen's security, and that of this realm, to consider, and in order to safeguard those things, the Lady Elizabeth should be sent to the block."

There was an uproar of disapproval.

"She is the heir to the throne!"

"She is innocent!"

"There is no evidence against her!"

"Look to the future," Sussex urged. "She may yet be our queen. Her Majesty is in poor health, she is marrying late in life, and childbirth is perilous at the best of times. Think of what might happen if, the Lady Elizabeth having been executed, the Queen were to die? We should be engulfed in a civil war between rival claimants for the throne."

"The French would press the claim of their Dauphine, the Queen of Scots," Arundel warned. "By force, if necessary, I'll warrant. And what would that make us? A subject state of France and Scotland."

"Not to be borne!" Sussex cried, echoing a chorus of outrage. "But the only alternative would be Lady Jane Grey's sisters, untried unknowns. No, I say free the Lady Elizabeth, for nothing has been proven against her, even after the most rigorous examinations of the rebels."

"You are fools, all of you," Gardiner growled. "She has outwitted us all. I have no doubt she was up to the ears in the late rebellion, but she has cleverly covered all her traces. I say execute her."

Sir William Paget frowned.

"My lord, you may not be aware that the Queen, who shares your opinion, has just consulted the chief judges of the land on this matter, and they told her that there was no evidence to justify a condemnation. *No* evidence, mark you, my lords, not just *insufficient* evidence. She should be set at liberty and restored to her former estate."

"No," Gardiner said. "That would leave her free to plot treason again. If you must have her freed, at least consent to her being disinherited."

"And that will bring us back to the problem of the succession," Paget argued.

"The Queen may well bear a healthy son and heir," Gardiner opined.

"Yes, or she may die in childbed, which is more likely."

The other councillors murmured their agreement.

"The best course," Paget declared, "would be for the Lady Elizabeth to be released, and then married abroad to some friendly Catholic prince. That way we may satisfy the Queen and the Emperor, for it will assure a Catholic succession."

The lords nodded their agreement.

"Aye, aye," they chorused.

"I will inform the Queen of our decision," Gardiner said sourly. "But I doubt she will like it!"

Elizabeth looked up from the stone bench in the garden to see a tall dark figure blotting out the sunlight. There was a young man standing on the short length of the wall-walk that led to the Garden Tower. A very handsome young man, and he was gazing down admiringly at her.

"My Lady Elizabeth," he said, making a courtly bow. "Lord Robert Dudley at your service. Your Highness has no doubt forgotten me. We once played childish games and shared lessons."

"I remember it well, Lord Robert." Elizabeth smiled, delighted to see a friendly face and thrilled that it belonged to such a charming gallant. "I beat you at fencing!"

Lord Robert grinned. "I blush to be reminded of it," he said ruefully.

"What are you doing up there?" she asked.

"I am allowed up here sometimes for my recreation," he told her. Again that devastating smile. It was hard to believe that the strutting boy had grown into the dark Adonis standing above her, silhouetted against the sky. He had moved and the sunlight was shining on his face, accentuating his debonair features and proud mien. He looked like a gypsy; she had always found dark, swarthy men more attractive than those insipid blond fellows like Courtenay, who looked like they had milk in their veins instead of blood. The Admiral had been dark too . . .

"I am sorry for your plight, my lady," he called down to her. "I too am in ward here. I understand how you must feel."

Of course, he had been here months, she realized. He had supported his father Northumberland in putting the Lady Jane on the throne, and he was now paying the price of his treason. She had heard he had been sentenced to death, as his father had been. He must still be mourning the loss of that father, and wondering whether he too would be sent to the block.

Yet his manner was cheerful. Cheerful and rather bold. She admired boldness in men. His spirit, as well as his looks, reminded her of the Admiral, whose manner had also been bold—overbold . . . the Admiral who now lay moldering headless in a grave in the chapel not many yards from here. She hoped that the handsome Lord Robert would not meet a similar fate. Maybe it was the engaging and bone-melting way he was smiling at her . . . She returned the bold smile, investing it with an unconscious seductiveness.

Robert was thinking that he could like this lady very much indeed. She was not beautiful, to be sure, but there was about her an obvious allure, a suppressed dynamism. She was spirited and sexy, and she represented a challenge. He was a young man who relished challenges, and he sensed they would be evenly matched in that respect.

She glanced at her warder, who was watching them and frowning.

"I may not talk to you, my lord," she said.

"Of course, my lady, I understand that," he said. "But if you ever have need of me, and it is within my power to help you, you have only to ask." He swept another bow and moved out of sight.

A rash promise, she thought, smiling, considering that he was a convicted traitor. And yet somehow it did not seem so impossible that he could fulfill it. There was about him an air of determination, of tenacity, of ambition. He had been here so long that there must be some hope of him escaping the ax. The Tower surely could not hold such a one forever.

"I am sorry, Simon, but my council will by no means consent to the execution of the Lady Elizabeth," Mary told Renard, hardly daring to look him in the eye. "Nothing has been proved against her, nor is it likely that any further evidence will come to light. And in view of what the traitor Wyatt said on the scaffold this morning, I dare not proceed further against her."

"Your Majesty is better informed than I am," Renard said. "What did Wyatt say?"

"He declared that neither Elizabeth nor Courtenay was privy to his rising," Mary told him. "Most people would agree that a man facing divine judgment would not lie, but I am not of their number. I cannot believe that the rebels would have contacted my sister unless they were certain of her support."

"I agree, madam," Renard said, "but despite the lack of evidence, we must be pragmatic. You cannot allow her to go free."

"Nor do I wish to," Mary said quickly. "Yet I cannot be seen to be keeping an innocent person in the Tower. My councillors wish to marry her abroad, but given that she is still under suspicion of treason, that would be too dangerous a course, I fear. No, I shall consult them again. But one thing I must know, Simon. Will the Emperor consent to the Prince coming here now?"

"The Emperor will understand your difficult position, madam, and accept that Your Majesty cannot resort to tyranny to achieve your ends. He has decided to take a practical view, and has written that the alliance between our two kingdoms is so important that nothing must be allowed to stand in its way. I am to tell you that the Prince is even now preparing for his departure. He will soon be here."

Mary's eyes lit up with joy.

"Praised be God! My prayers have been answered!" she cried.

"You know that there have been demonstrations against the marriage in London?" Renard asked gently.

"They have been dealt with," Mary said sharply, the smile vanishing. "Some of my subjects do not know what is good for them, I fear. The rest, I am glad to say, rejoice for me, and for England."

"As do I, madam"—Renard smiled—"and His Highness too. I hear he is an eager bridegroom." He hoped that sounded convincing.

Mary blushed deeply.

"I trust he will not find me wanting," she said humbly. Looking at her faded, tired face and thin, flat-chested body, Renard could have wept for her.

CHAPTER 18

1554

There is no justification for keeping the Lady Elizabeth in the Tower!" Sussex said, barely concealing his anger. "Let her return to court, madam."

Mary, seated in her cushioned chair at the head of the council table, quelled him—and those who were about to support him vociferously—with a look.

"It would not be honorable, safe, or reasonable to receive my sister at court," she said. "My pleasure is that she be held under house arrest at some secure place in the country where she can be kept under surveillance."

The councillors did not risk arguing with this, for it was clear that Mary had made up her mind. Only Gardiner looked satisfied.

"Has Your Majesty considered where?" Arundel asked.

"I was going to ask among you, my lords, if any man here is willing to be her custodian," the Queen said hopefully.

There was a prolonged and deathly silence. Then Sir Henry Bedingfield stood up.

"I will take on the honor of this responsibility, madam," he announced.

Mary looked at him gratefully. She knew him to be a loyal man, conscientious and reliable, and with a rigid sense of duty. Unimaginative, though, and a bit of a plodder. She would hardly have noticed him but for one thing: His father had been her mother's jailer during the last years of her life, and he too had been a stickler for the rules. With this proven example behind him, Sir Henry was an ideal and obvious choice.

"It would seem that a readiness to ensure the safekeeping of royal ladies runs in your family, Sir Henry," she said with a smile. The little man puffed out his chest with pride and bowed chivalrously to her.

"It will be my privilege to serve you thus, madam," he replied in his high, fretful voice.

"I make no doubt that my sister will get no satisfaction if she tries her mischievous tricks on you, sir," the Queen told him. "You will not be swayed by her caprices, I am sure."

"Never!" he agreed fervently. "Although I fear that mine will not be an easy task."

No, it will not, the other councillors thought, looking at him thankfully, glad to have been spared this unwelcome responsibility.

"I have decided that the Lady Elizabeth will be lodged at the old palace of Woodstock in Oxfordshire," Mary said. "You will escort her there as soon as is convenient."

Hearing the tramp of scores of marching feet approaching, Elizabeth sped to her window. There, in the courtyard below, she saw rank upon rank of soldiers falling into line, and before them, mounted on horses, Sir John Bridges and Sir Henry Bedingfield, whom she knew slightly by sight; he was a member of the council, she was certain.

Terror filled her soul. She could not breathe. This was it: They had come for her. Her death was imminent!

"Kat!" she cried in panic. Kat came running.

"Have they taken down the Lady Jane's scaffold?"

"I know not," Kat replied.

"Yes, they have," Blanche, overhearing, chimed in. "It was dismantled yesterday."

Elizabeth caught her breath. "Why didn't you tell me?" she gasped.

Then the threatening possibilities of her situation struck home again.

"Look!" she pointed. Kat and Blanche looked down at the ranks of soldiers.

"They have come for me," Elizabeth wailed, nearly hysterical, and icy fingers of fear gripped Kat's heart. When Sir Henry Bedingfield was finally announced, she was cradling Elizabeth in her arms, determined to protect her from whatever lay ahead.

Sir Henry bowed. Elizabeth could barely breathe.

"My lady," he declared loftily, "I am come to escort you to a more comfortable place of confinement, to the royal palace of Woodstock. There, I am to be your guardian, by order of the Queen's Grace."

So it was not to be the scaffold, Elizabeth thought feverishly. They were planning to hide her in the country and do away with her by stealth. She must beware the poisoned cup, the suffocating pillow . . . If they could not get rid of her by fair means, they would do it by foul. Which was why they had chosen this insignificant—and therefore disposable— fellow to be her keeper.

"If the murdering of me were secretly committed to your charge too, would you see to it that those orders were carried out?" Elizabeth challenged him, with a desperation born of panic.

Sir Henry's jaw dropped; he was clearly shocked.

"I would most certainly not," he declared, bristling. "I am a man of honor. And the Queen's Majesty, you may be assured, would never stoop so low. She is an upright lady. She has even provided an escort of soldiers so that you may be protected from attacks by Catholics. I should warn you that feelings are still running high in the wake of the late rebellion."

"Don't delude yourself, Sir Henry," Elizabeth snapped. "Those soldiers are there to prevent any Protestants from rescuing me."

"That is also true," he conceded, unruffled. "Now have your women make ready, madam. I do not wish to delay our departure. I have my orders."

That was a phrase that Elizabeth was to hear repeated many times over the coming months, until she was fit to scream whenever Sir Henry uttered it. For the moment, however, she had not his measure, nor he hers, and so they confined themselves to gentle sparring. That theirs was never going to be an easy relationship became apparent as soon as the barge that would convey them to Richmond, the first stop on their journey, pulled away from the Tower and the watching Lieutenant and assembled warders. Sir John had bowed low at her departure, and assured her of his friendship. Mercifully, that tyrant of a constable was nowhere in sight, the craven bully!

Bedingfield, who had intended to carry out the transfer of his prisoner as discreetly as possible, was horrified to see crowds lining the riverbanks.

"What are they all doing there?" he asked incredulously. "Who told them of your coming today?"

"How should I know?" Elizabeth replied, nodding graciously in either direction and basking in the cheering shouts of the waving onlookers.

"Someone must have talked," Sir Henry fretted. "Close the curtains!"

"I cannot, I need air!" Elizabeth protested. "I feel faint!"

"It *is* quite warm today," Kat added helpfully. Indeed, it was unseasonably hot for April.

Sir Henry knew when he was defeated.

"Very well, then," he conceded, "but you must not acknowledge the people."

Elizabeth meekly concurred and just sat there, inclining her head and smiling. Sir Henry looked at her suspiciously.

"You should keep your eyes modestly downcast," he told her.

"Are those the Queen's orders?" she asked provocatively, leaving him at a loss for words and desperate to wipe the smug smile from her face.

Suddenly, there were deafening reports of cannon fire.

"Oh, my God, what is that?" Bedingfield leapt to his feet with such urgency that the barge rocked alarmingly.

Elizabeth laughed.

"It is coming from the Steelyard," she told him. "I think the German merchants there are letting off a salute in my honor."

Sir Henry was outraged.

"Good God, how dare they? Bloody Protestants, the lot of them, I should imagine. This is not supposed to be a triumphal progress, madam. Remember that you are still a prisoner."

"I doubt that you will let me forget it," Elizabeth answered wryly.

"There will be repercussions from this, I am sure," he told her fretfully. "The Queen will be angry."

Elizabeth's merry mood dissipated in an instant. She saw with clarity what might happen: Mary, convinced by these demonstrations, that she, Elizabeth, was even more of a threat to her throne than she had envisaged, deciding that enough was enough. Mary, signing her death warrant . . .

"Close the curtains," she said abruptly to Kat.

It felt strange to be in Richmond Palace, where once she had delighted in being at court, in happy ignorance of what the future held. Of course, it was pleasant, after two months in the Tower, to stay in more congenial surroundings, but Elizabeth was still full of fear when she thought of what might happen to her. For all Sir Henry's protestations, they might yet send an assassin secretly to do away with her. It might even be tonight, especially after what had happened this day . . .

When the genial Lord Williams, who was traveling with them as second-in-command to Sir Henry, bade her good night after supper, she clutched at his sleeve.

"Pray for me," she begged him, her eyes wild, "for this night I think to die."

He looked at her compassionately. Poor girl, she had endured much, and undeservedly so, he believed.

"You need have no such fears, my lady," he soothed, his sincerity shining forth. "You are safe with me."

But still she could not sleep. Despite the assurances of Bedingfield and Williams—decent men, she was certain—her life might still be in danger. Look at what had happened to those poor Princes in the Tower, back in wicked King Richard's reign. They had disappeared, never to be seen again, and rumor had it that they had been suffocated as they slept, the poor innocent children. She too might disappear, if her enemies had their way; and if they were determined enough, neither Bedingfield's vigilance nor Williams's would serve to protect her.

So it was with a heavy heart that she climbed into the waiting litter the next morning.

"This is a bit dilapidated," Kat complained crossly. "Couldn't you find any better for my lady, Sir Henry?"

"I regret not," he told her, swinging himself into the saddle. "Come, make haste. Onward!"

—

It was the same story in every town and village that they passed through. Word of her coming had winged ahead, and everywhere, to Sir Henry's distress, the people were waiting for her, calling down blessings on her name, throwing flowers at her litter and clapping enthusiastically as she was carried by.

"God bless Elizabeth!" they cried. "Long live our princess!"

The soldier riding beside her litter leaned down in his saddle.

"They love you, my lady!" he declared delightedly. She looked at him quizzically; it had been her experience that friends could be found unexpectedly anywhere, even among her jailers.

It occurred to her now that the people's love and loyalty might help her to escape her doom. Never before had the power of public opinion been brought home so forcibly to her, and she realized, with a great lifting of her spirits, that this popular acclaim could prove to be one of her most powerful weapons. She would use it to her advantage, she promised herself.

"Tell them I am being drawn like a sheep to the slaughter," she said, and the soldier discreetly relayed the message to a group of people standing outside an inn. As word spread, there were cries of "Shame!" and loudly voiced protests. Sir Henry, hearing them, could not understand why the people were so angry, and spurred his horse on so that they could get away quickly, but Elizabeth felt heartened and a little reassured.

At Windsor, they stayed in the comfort of the Dean's house, where Elizabeth was treated with every courtesy. In the morning, crowds were lining the streets as she made her departure, and as they rode through Eton, the scholars threw their caps into the air and cried, "*Vivat Elizabetha! Vivat! Vivat!* Long live Elizabeth!" Tears came to her eyes when she heard it. She had not realized she was held in such devotion.

Sir Henry was deeply unhappy and worried. In every village now, they were ringing the church bells in Elizabeth's honor, and the good country folk would come bearing gifts—cakes, fruit, or flowers, usually.

"Any who ring bells will be sentenced to the stocks!" the harassed Bedingfield proclaimed, but as soon as he had gone on his way, the offenders were released. "And madam, you are not to accept any of the gifts." He was concerned in case there were messages concealed in them. One never knew what the French ambassador would get up to next!

But the people ignored Sir Henry's strictures. They tossed their offerings into the litter, or thrust them into the hands of servants, until Elizabeth was surrounded by an abundance of gifts.

"God save Your Grace!" the villagers cried.

"These people are clearly remiss in matters of religion," Bedingfield fumed to Lord Williams.

"You cannot punish everyone who demonstrates affection for the Lady Elizabeth," Williams told him, secretly delighted by the demonstrations.

"No, but I should dearly like to," Sir Henry muttered.

Lord Williams was also somewhat disturbed in his mind. If the people were so devoted to Elizabeth, it was best to treat her well and with deference. So when, on the third night, they came to his mansion at Rycote, he held a great banquet in her honor, having secretly sent ahead to summon his neighbors to attend.

"Isn't this going rather too far?" Bedingfield said sniffily as he regarded the laden table, the seat of honor placed next to the host's, and the waiting guests. "Have you forgotten that the Lady Elizabeth is the Queen's prisoner?"

"She is also the Queen's heir," Williams replied, "and we would do well to remember that."

At that, Sir Henry forbore to complain further; he simply sat stiffly through the meal, a specter at the feast, unable to enjoy the delicious food or the sparkling conversation. But Elizabeth made the most of the occasion, talking merrily with the guests and wolfing down the fancy fare. It was an all-too-brief escape from the frightening reality of her situation.

"I have been marvelously well entertained," she told Lord Williams at the end of the evening. "I thank you, and I am sorry that you are coming with us no farther." They were to press on without him to Woodstock on the morrow.

Williams caught the note of fear in her voice.

"I am certain that all will go well with Your Grace in the end," he told her, "and that you fret needlessly. Remember, if I can do you any service, I will be happy to perform it."

"It is comforting to know that you will not be far off," she answered.

—

There were even crowds at the gates of Woodstock, Sir Henry noted with irritation. Thank God they were nearly at their destination.

Elizabeth peered out of the litter as the gates closed behind them and craned her neck to see ahead. She had never been to Woodstock, for it had fallen into disuse early in her father's reign. Looking ahead, she could see why, for the old medieval palace, which lay north of the remains of the moat, was grim and decayed. As they drew closer, she could see crumbling and cracked masonry, broken windows, weeds, and encroaching creepers. It looked the ideal setting for a murder.

"Am I to lodge *here*?" she cried in dismay.

Sir Henry slowed his horse until her litter drew level with him.

"No, madam, the palace is uninhabitable. Lodgings have been prepared for you in the gatehouse."

So horribly fascinated had Elizabeth been with the palace that she had failed to notice the gatehouse. It looked as old as the house, but was clearly in better repair.

"It seems far too small," she observed petulantly, and indeed it was. There were just four rooms, two up, two down. She had never lived in so cramped a place.

"Where are my servants to lodge?" she demanded to know.

"They must shift to find accommodation in the village," Bedingfield told her, himself dismayed at the prospect of living in such close proximity to his difficult and unpredictable prisoner.

"That is not at all convenient," she informed him.

"Those are my orders," he said heavily. "Mistress Parry may lodge with you to look after your personal needs."

"What of Mrs. Astley?" Elizabeth cried, the dismay on her face mirroring that on Kat's.

"She is forbidden to stay here," he told her. Both women gasped in dismay.

"I cannot be parted from her," Elizabeth insisted.

"I have my orders," Bedingfield replied. "Mistress Parry alone is to attend you. Mrs. Astley must find lodgings elsewhere."

"May she visit me?" Elizabeth asked sharply.

"I fear not, madam. I have my—"

"I shall write to the Queen!" Elizabeth interrupted him.

"I regret that will not be possible," Bedingfield revealed. "My orders are that you are not to write or receive any letters. However, I myself will inform the council of your complaint. Now, Mrs. Astley, I must ask you to leave."

Kat threw her arms around Elizabeth and bade her a tearful farewell.

"Words fail me," she wept. "We have gone through so much together . . . We have survived the Tower . . . And now we are to be cruelly parted!"

Elizabeth disengaged Kat, grasped her hands, and held her gaze.

"Hold fast!" she counseled, blinking back her own tears. "Find somewhere to stay in the village, and then I shall have the comfort of knowing that you are nearby. With God's help, I shall soon be cleared of these false charges, and then we will be reunited. Be brave!"

Kat nodded, sniffed, and dried her eyes. Elizabeth watched her go, weeping silently, then allowed Sir Henry to lead her to the upper floor, where she was to be kept in captivity. Her critical eye roved over her new surroundings. An obvious effort had been made to provide some of the comforts due to one of her rank. In her bedchamber, there was a tapestry, so ancient that it could have been salvaged from the old palace, but fine; an oak buffet on which a few items of plate were displayed; and a great tester bed. At least the furniture was good: She recognized pieces from Hatfield, and even some stuff that must have been provided by the Queen.

"Look at that ceiling, my lady," exclaimed Blanche Parry, trailing behind. "Lord knows when that was done."

The vaulted ceiling of the outer chamber was painted blue and adorned with gold stars, much in the fashion of the previous century. The walls had been hung with painted cloths to hide the bare plaster, but for all the fire burning in the grate and May sunshine, the room was chill, for the windows were narrow and set deep into the thick stone walls. The only advantage of this dismal place, as far as Elizabeth was concerned, was that there was virtually nowhere an assassin could hide.

As Blanche began their unpacking, Sir Henry was fussing around, rattling keys in doors and becoming very agitated.

"Three of these locks don't work," he complained to the two guards who were accompanying him. "See if *you* can get the keys to turn."

"It's useless," they told him after much jangling and cursing.

"Have a locksmith summoned," he ordered testily. "And get two more men to keep watch."

"I am not going to run away, Sir Henry," Elizabeth told him sharply, having watched the exchange.

"I have my orders," he told her. "And perhaps I ought to make everything quite clear now, madam, if you would be so good as to sit down for a moment." Indicating that she should take the only chair in the room, he elected to stand before her, feeling that it gave him greater authority. He was annoyed to find himself slightly in awe of this slender, naughty—nay, dangerous—girl.

"The Queen has stipulated that you are to be treated in such good and honorable sort as may be agreeable to her honor and her royal estate," he announced, a trifle pompously. "Mistress Parry apart, you are to converse with no one out of my hearing. You may walk in the gardens or the orchard, but only with myself in attendance. Thomas Parry will continue to look after your finances; I am informed that he arrived earlier but has gone off to seek a lodging in the Bull Inn, although I fear that might prove a marvelous place to make mischief in, tut tut."

"Mischief?" echoed Elizabeth.

"Gossip!" fretted Sir Henry. "And the possibility that traitors might seek him out. You never know who might be lurking around the corner. I shall have to keep an eye on him."

"Parry is trustworthy," she said.

"So trustworthy that he and the woman Astley ended up in the Tower not many years back, I recall," Bedingfield reminded her. "No, I see the need to be vigilant. And your other servants will be watched and searched, in case they attempt to carry messages, so do not think, madam, to attempt any contact with your *friends*." His tone was disparaging.

"Now, as to domestic arrangements. You are forbidden to have any canopy of estate above you when you dine."

That is the least of my concerns in this godforsaken place, Elizabeth thought.

"Your laundry will be searched for hidden messages," Sir Henry continued. "Any book that you read will first be subject to my approval. And if you have any requests, they must be forwarded to the council."

"May I breathe?" Elizabeth asked defiantly.

Bedingfield ignored her.

"Supper will be ready soon," he said. "I hope you will honor me with your company."

"I am rather weary," she said, "and not very hungry. I think I will have an early night." After all, what else was there to do?

"I want some of my books," she said. "Cicero, my English Bible, and my Latin Psalms."

Sir Henry looked alarmed, wondering what pernicious influences such books might contain. He supposed that the Psalms were all right, but he knew nothing of Cicero, whoever he was, and as for an *English* Bible . . .

"I doubt Her Majesty would approve of an English Bible," he told her. "You may have the Psalms."

Elizabeth flounced off, fuming.

"I need more maids about me," she demanded.

"That is not permitted. One should be sufficient. I have my orders."

"I want a tutor, so that I can practice conversing in foreign tongues," was her next request. "I fear my skill at languages has grown rusty of late."

"The council will never agree," Sir Henry said.

"Could you not engage one yourself?" she asked mischievously.

"That would be out of the question," he told her. "All persons coming into contact with you must be vetted. I have my orders."

"I should like a pen and some ink," she said. "I wish to write to the council."

"I will pass on your request," Bedingfield answered.

"No need to wait for that," she told him. "You can read what I write before it is sent."

"Madam, I am marvelously perplexed by your constant demands," he confessed, looking distressed. "I fear I cannot agree to this."

"Don't tell me—you have your orders!" she said, making a face.

"That is unfair. Would you have me gainsay them?" he challenged.

"I would have you use your own good sense!" she retorted. "At least let me send a message to the Queen my sister. Just a short message. Please."

"I have my orders," he repeated.

"You are like a parrot!" she cried, irritated beyond courtesy.

"Madam, bear with me, I beg of you. I am myself unable to grant your desire or say nay. Everything must be referred to the council. Believe me, I shall do for Your Grace what I am able to do."

After the first few weeks, her sense of being in danger dissipated. There were no terrors for her here, just endless boredom and monotony. Nor was there any news from court; Bedingfield would not discuss what was going on in the outside world, so she had no means of knowing if a date had been set for the Queen's wedding, or even if it had already taken place. Nor were there any letters, for she was not permitted to send or receive any; she particularly missed Cecil's witty missives, and his wise insights into affairs.

Her worst enemy was frustration, and her sole pleasure lay in baiting Bedingfield. As her fears for her life faded, she grew indignant that she was being kept in confinement when nothing had been proved against her. And as she could not remonstrate about this with the Queen or the council, she took out her vexation on their instrument, the luckless Sir Henry. He, for his part, was determined to obey his orders to the letter, and remained impervious to her whims and her tantrums.

Even her customary fondness for walks in the garden had palled, although they at least provided some respite from the tedium of her days, but the security measures upon which Sir Henry insisted drove her to desperation. One day, after watching him patiently unlock and lock six pairs of gates in turn, she lost her temper and screamed at him.

"You jailer! You do this only to taunt me!" Of course, it was an unfair accusation, but she was too angry to care. Sir Henry, stung by her outburst, fell to his knees before her.

"Madam, I am your officer, appointed by the Queen to take care of you and protect you from any injury. I hope you will agree that I have been a kindly guardian, and that I have accorded you the proper courtesies."

Elizabeth's anger cooled in the face of his earnestness.

"Be at peace, good man," she said wearily. "I grow tired of being a prisoner. I am young, I want to be out in the world, enjoying its pleasures, not shut up here with so many rules and restrictions. Can you not understand that? Or have you forgotten what it is like to be bursting with energy and zeal for life?"

Sir Henry had never felt the way she described, so he was at a loss for what to say to her.

"I counsel you to have patience," he begged.

Patience? How could one be patient when one was unjustly incarcerated?

Idly, she gazed out of her window, willing the hours to pass, willing her captivity to end. The worst thing about it was that its continuance proclaimed her guilty in some way, as plainly as if it had been cried in every market square. She realized, of course, why Mary distrusted her so, but there were laws in England, and they were there to protect the innocent. Or so she would have thought. If only she could have five minutes—just five minutes—with Mary, to plead her case.

Struck for the hundredth time by the unjustness of her confinement, she took from her finger a ring and, using the sharp edge of the diamond, began carving words in a spidery hand on the thick glass of the window.

"Much suspected of me, nothing proved can be," she wrote, and then added, "Quoth Elizabeth, prisoner." Sir Henry frowned when he saw it, but said nothing.

With the summer came a return of her old sickness. Her face and body swelled up, and she felt feverish. Worst of all was the black depression that lay like a pall over her normal feisty spirit.

Sir Henry, summoned, looked down on her with some sympathy as she lay in her bed.

"I wish to be bled," she said weakly. "The evil humors must be released from my body. I pray you, send for the Queen's physicians, Dr. Owen and Dr. Wendy. They have treated me in the past, and I trust them."

"I will pass on your request to the council," Sir Henry said, embarrassed to be in her presence when she was in bed clad in nothing but a shift, and anxious to leave the room.

"While I lie here suffering?" she whimpered, enraged that he was putting his infernal orders before her health, but she had not the strength to protest further. Besides, Sir Henry had fled.

A week later, back came the council's unfavorable reply, and following soon upon it, a local doctor whom Sir Henry had summoned.

"I would rather die than see him!" she declared, her fury belying her obvious weakness. "I am not minded to make a stranger privy to my body. I see I shall just have to commit it to God!" And so saying, she folded her hands on her breast, as if in prayer, and lay there in the attitude of a tomb effigy.

Driven near to despair, Bedingfield hastened away to write yet another of his seemingly endless succession of letters to the council. By the time Dr. Wendy and Dr. Owen arrived, Elizabeth was very poorly indeed.

"She must be bled immediately," they pronounced, alarm in their faces. Sir Henry stood by while it was done, averting his eyes when Elizabeth pulled up the bedclothes and exposed a slim foot and ankle to the barber surgeon; yet he had not missed the look of triumph on her face when the royal doctors appeared, a look that proclaimed her the winner of this round in their endless sparring match.

This was not her only victory.

"The council has approved your many requests to write to Her Majesty," Bedingfield announced tightly, coming to pay his daily respects one morning toward the end of the month. "Writing materials will be brought to you."

"Good," said Elizabeth, much recovered now, and determined to stress to Mary how unfairly she had been treated. When paper, pen, and ink were set before her, her words flowed passionately across the pages, pouring out her grievances in detail and giving voice to her anger and frustration. When the letter was finished, Sir Henry took one glance and flung it on the table.

"You cannot send this, madam!" he protested. "The Queen is certain to be offended."

"*I* am offended," she cried, "at being treated like a traitor, without trial or condemnation!"

"Nevertheless, you cannot send this as it is. I insist you tone it down."

He was implacable, so she had no choice but to rewrite the letter. Sir Henry read it and nodded approvingly.

"That is much better," he said, and went off to find his sealing wax. As soon as he had gone, Elizabeth quickly substituted her earlier version, folded in exactly the same way. When Sir Henry returned, he sealed and stamped it without another thought.

—

Bedingfield stood before her, his face tragic.

"I cannot understand it," he said plaintively. "I have received a reprimand from the council for allowing you to send such a disrespectful and rude letter to the Queen. I cannot understand it. I read your letter . . ."

"You did, Sir Henry," Elizabeth said sweetly. "And I had rewritten it at your behest."

"Now, if it had been your earlier version," he said, "I could have understood it. But there we are. You are forbidden to write to Her Majesty again."

"I am very sorry for it," Elizabeth said, not minding too much, for she had said what she wanted to say to Mary, and felt better for it; surely it was Mary's pricking conscience that had goaded her to anger? "I suppose I may write still to the council?"

"Oh, no," said Sir Henry hurriedly. "I'm sure they mean that you are forbidden to write to the Queen *and* the council."

"Does it say that?" Elizabeth asked, nodding at the missive in his hands.

Bedingfield hurriedly scanned it. "No, it only mentions the Queen, but, of course, it must apply to the council too."

"That is just your assumption!" she accused him angrily. "You cannot prevent me from writing to the council without specific instructions. I will be cut off from the world if you do that. Why, it would leave me in a worse case than the lowest prisoner in Newgate!"

"I am sorry, madam, but I must keep to the spirit, rather than the letter, of my orders," Sir Henry insisted.

"Then I see I must continue in this life without all worldly hope, wholly resting in the truth of my cause!" Elizabeth stormed, bursting into passionate weeping. Incapable of dealing with her when she was in such a state, Sir Henry made a hasty exit, leaving Blanche Parry to comfort her mistress.

"I have some good news, madam," Bedingfield said meekly four days later. "The Queen herself has clarified matters. You may write to the council whenever you wish."

"I am glad of it. I knew you were mistaken," Elizabeth told him. She hoped her outburst had done some good. The Queen *must* be convinced of her innocence; otherwise, she would have kept her in the Tower. Or was Mary *still* keeping her confined in the hope that some new evidence against her would come to light? If that were so, she might be here forever . . . she *had* to plead her cause!

She wrote to the council that morning, begging for an audience with the Queen. She dared to hope that this time her request would be granted. But days went by with no response.

"The council is busy just now," Bedingfield told her. "There are but days to go until the Queen's wedding. They have much to occupy them."

"Is the Prince of Spain here in England?" Elizabeth asked curiously. Half of her was pleased for Mary, that she had at last found a husband; the other, less loyal, part of her feared that Philip would quickly sire an heir on her sister, and so deprive her, Elizabeth, of her place in the succession. She did not know how she would bear that.

"He is expected any day," Sir Henry told her. "He might even have arrived by now."

More time went by. Still no answer. Elizabeth began to fret.

"They have all gone to Winchester for the wedding," Bedingfield informed her. "I daresay you will receive a reply when they return to London."

"Don't tell me that the council will transact no business in Winchester!" Elizabeth countered. "Or are they all busy making floral garlands for the bridemaids?"

What she really wanted was a chance to speak to Mary while the Queen was still in a euphoric mood over her marriage; that way, she might be more tenderly inclined to lenience and compassion. But the twenty-fifth of July, the date appointed for the royal wedding, came and went, and still, days later, there was no letter from the council.

Elizabeth grew sullen and resentful in her anxiety. She came to believe that this Philip, this Catholic Spaniard, this known friend to the dreaded Inquisition, had further poisoned Mary's mind against her. What else was she to think?

She went to Mass. She had long taken care to attend regularly, hoping that it would go well for her with the Queen as a result, but now, when prayers were asked by the chaplain for Queen Mary and King Philip, she could not bring her lips to form the words. Bedingfield saw it and reported her omission to the council. Another black mark against her.

Mary lay in bed, watching the summer moonlight streaming through the open casement. Beside her, Philip—her Philip, her darling, her joy—was

breathing evenly. This marriage had certainly brought its manifold political advantages, but to her personally, privately, more than she had ever
dreamed of. Her young, personable husband was courtesy itself, in bed
and out of it, and paid her the most considerate attentions. He had been
gentle with her on their wedding night, endlessly patient with her inex-
perience and maidenly modesty. The pain had been great, but she had
borne it with queenly fortitude, and now, after several weeks, she found
that paying the marriage debt was much easier. She was even beginning to
enjoy it a little, although of course she could not tell Philip that; what
happened in the marriage bed was never referred to by either of them.
Her part, as she understood it, was to lie still, submit to his attentions, and
pray for an heir. She was managing, she thought, rather well. Just let her
get pregnant, and then that constant thorn in her side, her sister Elizabeth—if she was her sister, of course—could go hang herself.

Next to her, Philip was pretending to be asleep. He was praying that
his dried-up spinster of a wife would soon be with child, so that he could
in conscience abstain from her bed and perhaps, if he could contrive it,
get back to Spain for a while. He hated it here in England, and he knew he
was hated in return. As for his bride, he had done everything his father
had exhorted him to, had shown every attention, even though he had had
to shut his eyes and gird his unwilling loins when it came to storming that
virginal fortress; he had gotten through it by thinking of his beautiful
mistress in faraway Madrid.

Well, the thing was done now; he had gotten used to his innocent, loving, submissive wife. One woman was much the same in bed as another,
after all—except that this one thought it proper to lie rigid and unmoving
while he was laboring away at his duty. Fortunately there were ladies
aplenty at the English court, many of them willing . . . It had not taken him
long to stray from the marriage bed. Still, he was there most nights, doing
his best to get an heir, swallowing his distaste. This marriage might be made
in Heaven as far as the future of the English Church and other political considerations went, but the price he was paying personally was dear in the extreme. To be frank, he thought, it would take God Himself to drink this
cup. Dear Lord, I beseech You, let her conceive soon, he prayed fervently.

"I shall write to the council again," Elizabeth declared in August, when
the Queen had been married for a month.

"Wait awhile longer," Bedingfield counseled.

"No, this waiting is intolerable to me," she defied him.

"I cannot permit it," he told her.

"God's blood!" she flared. "Their lordships would smile in their sleeves if they learned how scrupulous you are! I beg of you, please, write to the council for me. Make suit to their honors to be a means to the Queen's Majesty for me and to consider my woeful case, for I have not received the comforting reply to my request that I had hoped for."

"Very well, I will write," Bedingfield groaned, capitulating.

"And while you are about it," Elizabeth said, quickly recovering her composure, "ask them to make suit to the Queen, for very pity, to consider my long imprisonment—it is five months now, mark you—and either to have me charged with my supposed offense, so that I can answer for my conduct, or grant me liberty to come into her presence. Believe me, Sir Henry, I would not ask those things unless I knew myself to be clear before God."

Sir Henry was used by now to Elizabeth's extravagant declarations, but the honest man in him had come to suspect that they were the fruit of frustrated innocence rather than the bravado of a villainess. To be plain, he wished she *could* convince the Queen of her innocence, for he was heartily weary of his responsibilities and would be happy to see the back of his troublesome charge.

"If the Queen will not consent to see me," Elizabeth was saying, "then I ask that a deputation of councillors be allowed to visit me, so that I can protest my innocence to them, and not think myself utterly desolate of all refuge in the world."

"I think I can remember all that," said Sir Henry resignedly. "I'll write to them now."

It was nigh on September before Elizabeth received a response, in the form of a letter from Mary herself to Bedingfield.

"The Queen has spoken at last," Sir Henry informed her. "An audience is out of the question. To be plain, she feels your complaints are somewhat strange. You may make of that what you will, of course, but she says you need not fear you have been forgotten, and that she is not unmindful of your cause."

"I know what game she is playing," Elizabeth said slowly. "She is waiting until she is with child before she decides what to do with me. I will be less of a threat to her then."

"Remember that it is the Queen's Highness of whom you speak," Sir Henry reproved. "You should show more respect. To my poor understanding, this is a hopeful letter, and may presage better things for you."

"I wish I could believe you," Elizabeth said doubtfully. "All I know is that I am cooped up here interminably, with no end to it in sight, no hope of liberty. My only pleasure is in my books, and many of those you have banned." She glared at him. "Perhaps if I could have a copy of Saint Paul's Epistles—even if you won't allow me my English Bible?"

"The Epistles you may have," he told her, "but the English Bible never. The government is now proceeding more harshly against the reformed religion than ever before. Not only would possession of such a book be wrong, it would be mightily dangerous. If I were you, my lady, I should forget I ever owned a copy."

True to his word, he soon afterward brought her a copy of St. Paul's Epistles in Latin. Reading them brought her some comfort, and she spent many hours making translations into various languages, then laid down her pen, wondering why she was doing this. Her life—nay, her youth itself—was being wasted; she could be enjoying herself, living it to the full, adorning courts and charming young gentlemen. Instead, she was immured here at Woodstock, shut up like St. Barbara in her tower.

Dejectedly, she turned back to her book, seeking comfort from it, and after a time, wrote in the flyleaf: *August. I walk many times into the pleasant fields of the Holy Scriptures, where I pluck up the goodly herbs of sentences, so that, having tasted their sweetness, I may the less perceive the bitterness of this miserable life.* Then she lay down her head on her arms and wept hot tears of self-pity.

"Great news, my lady!" Sir Henry announced one morning late in September. "The Queen's Majesty is with child! England is to have an heir."

Elizabeth was aghast. She had not for a moment seriously envisaged Mary becoming pregnant. She was too old, too ailing, was she not? She herself had thought her place in the succession sure, unassailable; she had taken it for granted and looked forward to the day when she might, by God's will, be crowned Queen and given the safekeeping of her realm and all her people—for already, she thought of them as hers. But she had been wrong on both counts. Was this not God's will too, this promise of an heir born of the Queen's body? And if He in His mercy saw fit to send Mary a son, what future was there for her, Elizabeth? A life in confinement, or lived under constant suspicion? Marriage to some safe gentleman or minor prince, followed by a yearly succession of children? She was utterly dismayed at either prospect. She saw, suddenly and very clearly, that the only safe place for her in the future was on the throne.

For all her inner dread, outwardly she appeared calm. She was making a conscious effort to please Mary: She was going to Mass regularly, she had ceased bombarding the council with requests, and she had even curbed her relentless demands to Sir Henry.

"That is wonderful news," she said aloud. "I will pray God to vouchsafe Her Majesty a safe delivery and a healthy son."

"Amen to that," replied Sir Henry, impressed by her reply. "And methinks that, when she has a son, the Queen will look more favorably upon you, my lady."

"*When* she has a son." Elizabeth sighed. "That will be months away!"

"In May, I believe," Bedingfield told her. "Not too long to wait." He did not tell her of another possible escape route: that the council and Parliament were discussing various prospective foreign bridegrooms for her. All too often, such proposals came to nothing, so why disturb her with them?

Christmas was nigh. Sir Henry had ordered various delicacies, and the servants had been given permission to festoon the gatehouse with evergreens, but Elizabeth feared it would be a poor affair compared with the festive seasons she had enjoyed in the past. What would they do for revelry? Read St. Paul? The thought of the stately Bedingfield casting aside his dignity and romping around as the Lord of Misrule almost made her laugh out loud, although her mood was bitter.

But there was further gloom yet to be cast over this Yuletide. Only days before Christmas Eve, Sir Henry came to her, his face grim.

"Madam, I bring news of great import, which may affect you if you are not careful," he told her. Elizabeth laid down her pen and looked at him warily, shivers of her old fears shooting down her spine.

"Last month, as I informed you, Cardinal Pole was made Archbishop of Canterbury, and England was received back into obedience to Rome," he reminded her. "Now Parliament has reinstated the law against heretics, which means that those suspected of heresy may be examined and, if found guilty, burned at the stake."

Elizabeth frowned, giving a little shudder as the blood seemed to freeze in her veins.

"But the Queen began her reign promising tolerance!" she cried, forgetting her resolve to hold her peace.

"Times have changed," Sir Henry said dolefully. "Her Majesty, I know well, hoped then that her subjects would of their own accord revert to the Catholic religion. Many did, but there were also many who did not, and who demonstrated and made riots against the new laws. Now the Queen is in hope of a son, England is reconciled with Rome, and she and King Philip are zealous to see the true faith established in this kingdom. My lady, I hold to that faith, and I am a true Englishman, but I do fear that this new law will unleash in this realm a persecution such as has been seen in Spain, and that it will also herald the arrival of the Inquisition here."

"Those are my fears exactly," Elizabeth said, amazed that she and Sir Henry should for once be of one accord. "Believe me, I do not fear for myself—why should I, for I too am reconciled to the Roman faith and attend Mass regularly? But I fear for those who cannot in their consciences embrace that faith. Who should make windows into men's souls? When it comes down to it, there is only one Jesus Christ. The rest is a dispute over trifles."

"I doubt that the Queen and Cardinal Pole would agree with you, madam," Sir Henry said. "They might even construe such words as heresy. But fret not—I shall not repeat them. I have seen that you are faithful in your attendance at Mass."

"I am relieved to hear it," Elizabeth told him, swallowing her fear.

"I but wish to warn you to keep your own counsel on matters of religion," Sir Henry went on. "I know you were brought up largely in the reformed faith, and I feared you might, through force of habit and custom, betray some affiliation with it that might be misconstrued, were the wrong ears to hear it."

"I thank you for your care of my safety," Elizabeth said gratefully, then could not resist adding, "For once, it is welcome to me!"

Even Sir Henry had to smile at that.

CHAPTER 19

T he burnings have begun," Blanche Parry whispered, a look of distress on her face. "I heard Sir Henry saying that a man was burned in Smithfield, and that soon afterward Bishop Hooper went to the stake in Gloucester. It sounded as if his sufferings were dreadful—I could not bear to listen. Oh, my lady, how could anyone do such a cruel thing to another human being?"

Elizabeth made Blanche sit down on the settle beside her and took her hands.

"They do it because, in giving the poor wretches a taste of Hellfire on earth, they think to make them recant at the last minute and so save their souls," she explained gravely. "They do not think they are being cruel; they think they are doing a kindness. What is a short time in earthly flames compared with an eternity spent roasting in Hell? That is their logic. Yet it seems to me that those who order this—and I do not name names—have put mercy behind them. It is this new allegiance to Spain that has brought these cruelties."

"I do not understand such matters," Blanche said sadly. "All I know is that I cannot rid my mind of what I just heard. It was *horrible!*"

"Spare me the details," Elizabeth said quickly. "I can well imagine."

Echoes of the public outcry against the burnings soon reached Woodstock.

"The people are angry," Sir Henry said. "There have been widespread protests, and seditious writings against the Queen and the council. Many offenders have been caught and put in the pillory."

With the country in ferment, and increasing numbers being sent to the stake, news and rumors flew fast. There were terrible stories of the sufferings of Protestant martyrs—for such they were now being called.

"There's no doubt that a lot of them are foolish, ignorant folk," Sir Henry observed as he sat at dinner with his prisoner. "One couldn't recite the Lord's Prayer, another couldn't name all the Sacraments, or so I heard."

"They need educating, not persecuting," Elizabeth said. "Did no one think to give them instruction?"

"The bishops and the Queen's officers are zealous in their duty, and wish to be seen to be," he told her. "They don't ask too many questions. There was an awful case in Guernsey—I can hardly bear to tell you."

"Tell me," Elizabeth commanded. She had to know. Forewarned was forearmed, especially as many people were aware of her own former open adherence to Protestantism, and doubtless there were many who suspected where her true convictions still lay.

"It was a woman," Sir Henry related, "and she was with child. Her labor had already begun when she was chained to the stake, and her babe was born as the flames were lit. The executioner threw it back into the fire."

"Oh, my God," Elizabeth said. Behind her, Blanche, who was waiting at table, stifled a horrified sob.

"Often the faggots are damp," Sir Henry went on relentlessly, "and the burnings are prolonged. Far from condemning the suffering wretches, the crowds are angry on their behalf, and they do all they can to comfort and aid the heretics. It has gotten so bad that the council has ordered extra guards to be present at each execution to prevent this from happening."

"It seems to me that, far from stamping out heresy, these burnings may well be encouraging it," Elizabeth commented. "Some people might conclude that the reformed faith must be worth dying for."

"I heard a rumor," Sir Henry said confidentially, "—although whether local gossip can be relied on is another matter, for these tales often get quite garbled by the time they reach us here—that Bishop Gardiner is also horrified by the scale of the persecution, and has urged the Queen to use a kinder form of punishment, but she will not agree. It may not be true."

And it may well be, Elizabeth thought, recalling the fanatical gleam in Mary's eyes whenever she spoke of her faith, and her single-mindedness. Yet surely the influence of her husband, King Philip, must be in part responsible for the burnings. It sounded as if the Queen was deeply in thrall to him—or besotted. Had she lost her wits so far as to risk losing the love of her people, which Elizabeth knew to be the most precious thing a sovereign can have?

Later that evening, after Sir Henry had gone and the table was cleared, Blanche returned to help Elizabeth prepare for bed.

"I could not speak earlier, my lady," she said, "but when I went to the village today, the guard wanted us to stop for a drink at the Bull, and there, when he had gone outside to piss, I had a quick word with Master Parry. He said to tell you that there is now great hatred throughout the land for the Queen, that many are praying that her pregnancy will have a calamitous end, and that the people are looking to you, my lady, as their deliverer."

Elizabeth was deeply moved by this, and gratified; indeed, it offered a glimmer of hope that the love of the people, now forfeited by Mary, would turn to herself and somehow prove her salvation, despite the expected birth of a Catholic heir. But her natural caution quickly asserted itself.

"That was unwise talk," she said reprovingly. "I hope that none overheard it."

"Oh, no, my lady," Blanche assured her. "We were alone in the porch. Master Parry had followed me out when I was waiting for the guard."

"That is as well," Elizabeth said. "If such a thing were repeated openly, we would all suffer for it. I know I can rely on you to hold your tongue."

"I promise I will," Blanche said, and took up the hairbrush.

"My lord and dear husband," Mary said tenderly, rising awkwardly from her chair as Philip entered her chamber. "It is a pleasure to see you here."

The King bowed, thinking that his wife was looking drained and pale; doubtless she was suffering the strain of her pregnancy and was distressed at the tumult that had erupted in the wake of the burnings.

"I trust I find you well, madam," he said, taking her hand and kissing it.

"All the better for seeing you, my lord," she told him, gazing at him in adoration.

"I came to tell you that I have made my decision," he said.

"You have?" Mary replied nervously. He recalled her terrible distress when he had first told her of his plans to leave England for the Low Countries to fight the French now that she was with child. How she had begged and pleaded with him to stay. The sight of her abasing herself thus had aroused only distaste in him; it had not in any way touched his cold heart. What *had* swayed him had been the council's fears that, without him at her side, the Queen would pine away and die.

"I have decided to remain in England until our son is born," he told her.

"Oh, that *is* joyful news!" Mary cried, her eyes shining. "You cannot know how much of a comfort to me your presence is. You have made me the happiest woman alive!"

Philip suffered her grateful, cloying embrace, then disengaged himself and took the chair on the opposite side of the hearth.

"I wanted to talk to you about your sister and Courtenay also," he said. "This latest French plot to bring about their marriage . . . It worried me, even though it could not have succeeded. This kingdom will never be at peace till the matter of these two seditious persons is settled."

"What can I do?" Mary asked, reluctant to be discussing matters of state when she and Philip could be talking of love.

"Send them into exile, to places where they can be kept under supervision," Philip advised. "Send Elizabeth to Brussels, where my father's agents can keep watch on her, and Courtenay to Rome, where His Holiness the Pope can be relied upon to be vigilant."

"I like that proposal," Mary said, considering. "But exiling Elizabeth now, at such a sensitive time, could provoke another rebellion. My spies tell of discontent across the land." Her brow furrowed. She had heard of the upsurge in Elizabeth's popularity, heard and deplored it, but reality had to be faced.

"Gardiner wants you to disinherit her," Philip said, "but I told him that, in that case, should any terrible chance befall Your Majesty, the King of France would press the claim of his daughter-in-law, the Queen of Scots, and the last thing I want to see is an England ruled by the French. My father and I would lose all the advantages we have gained through this marriage."

"If I died there would be civil war, make no doubt of it," Mary said bleakly. "The heretics would espouse the cause of the Lady Elizabeth. The only remedy is to marry her to a Catholic prince faithful to Your Highness. There was some talk of the Duke of Savoy."

"Steady as a rock, and an excellent choice," Philip replied thoughtfully, pulling at his golden beard. "But before any decision is made, I would meet with this sister of yours. I must confess, I am curious to meet a lady who has been the subject of so much controversy."

"Meet Elizabeth?" Mary echoed, mortified. She could not bear the thought of Philip contrasting her own faded looks with the youth and vigor of her sister; could envisage Elizabeth working her wiles on Philip—whose susceptibility to attractive women she had heard of, much to her distress—and him bending his ear to her cause.

"No," she said, instinctively and abruptly, so that he looked at her in surprise.

"Why not?" he asked. "We will make no decision as to her future until after your confinement, but I do feel she should be brought back to court so that I can keep an eye on her until then." And, he thought to himself, it would be wise to establish a good working relationship with Elizabeth just in case she ever does become queen. Her grateful goodwill for his rescuing her from prison would surely prove the basis for such a rapport.

"I don't want her here," Mary said, becoming agitated. "She makes trouble wherever she goes."

"According to her jailer's reports, her conduct has been impeccable lately," Philip reminded her. "She goes to Mass regularly and behaves like a good Catholic. With our son due to be born soon, she cannot pose any threat to you now, madam."

"Her conversion was mere expediency," Mary sneered. "I do not believe it was sincere for one minute."

Philip was thinking that, even as a furtive Protestant, Elizabeth would be preferable to Mary, Queen of Scots, any day. "Bedingfield's reports would suggest otherwise," he said aloud. "Come now, let her be brought to court. I will see that she has no opportunity to make trouble. You need not concern yourself overmuch with her."

"Very well," Mary agreed reluctantly, her heart plummeting. All her instincts screamed that bringing Elizabeth back would cause her nothing *but* trouble; yet she was unable to refuse Philip anything.

"And Courtenay: He shall go into exile," Philip decided, glancing at her for approval.

"That too," she conceded, resting her head on the back of her chair and closing her eyes. Let Philip deal with it all. He was right. She should not bother herself. But Elizabeth, back at court? She could not bear the thought.

It was April again, and the buds green on the trees; Elizabeth had now been incarcerated at Woodstock for nearly a year, and the arrival of spring had left her in an agony of restlessness. She was aching to be free, to be gone from this hateful place.

And then, quite suddenly, her prayers were answered.

"I am commanded by the Queen to escort Your Highness to court," Bedingfield informed her. She squealed with delight, clapping her hands for joy.

"At last! At last!" she cried. "This is what I have beseeched God for."

Then she noticed Sir Henry's face, which remained grave.

"You are to remain under guard, madam," he warned her.

"No matter," she sang, her spirits soaring. "I will have a chance to prove my innocence at last, once and for all!"

She was barely aware of the gusting winds that rocked the litter alarmingly as they proceeded toward London, leaving Woodstock behind. She was overjoyed to be out in the world, to be breathing different air. She took enormous pleasure in seeing houses and villages and people, the colors of the spring flowers, the young lambs grazing in the fields.

But then the blasts became so savage that even Elizabeth grew fearful. Unable to bear the violent flapping of the litter's curtains, she tied them back, but then had to endure the wind buffeting her face.

"Can we not seek refuge in some manor house?" she yelled at Bedingfield, who was struggling to keep his horse from rearing.

"No, madam!" he shouted. "My orders are to stop only at the places that have been arranged. We must press on regardless."

A sudden gust swept Elizabeth's hood out the window, leaving her hair streaming, its pins askew. A groom brought the hood back to her, but it was impossible to set herself to rights in the litter, so the procession halted briefly while she alighted, crouched in the shelter of a hedge, hastily plaited and bundled up her hair, and pinned the hood firmly into place.

"I daresay I look like a scarecrow!" she fumed as she returned to the litter. "What *would* the Queen think if she could see me? Really, Sir Henry, you could have more care for me and find us a decent shelter from this tempest!"

"I have my orders, madam," he repeated miserably.

Word of Elizabeth's coming had gone before her, and as had happened a year earlier, the people, defying the wind, came flocking to the roadside to welcome and cheer her. On the last morning, as they left the George Inn at Colnbrook, she was delighted to see a large company of her own gentlemen and yeomen waiting to salute her, and would have gone over to greet them and express her thanks had not Sir Henry hurried her into the litter and made her draw the curtains.

By and by, they approached Hampton Court. Elizabeth was thrilled to see once again the familiar red-brick palace rising majestically on the banks of the Thames. How she had longed to be back at court—and now she was really here, ready to take up her proper place in the world once more.

She had thought that they would process through the base court to the grand processional stair that led to the royal apartments, so she was discomfited to find that they were being directed to a privy entrance at the rear of the sprawling palace. The guards uncrossed their pikes, and she was conducted through the arched door and up winding steps to the royal apartments.

Here, the Lord Chamberlain was waiting to receive her. He bowed and explained that she had been assigned an apartment near to those of King Philip and Cardinal Pole.

"The servants you have brought may stay with you, madam," he explained, "but you are not free to leave your rooms until the Queen's pleasure be further known." That much was evident from another pair of guards who stood, halberds raised, outside the door.

Elizabeth turned to the waiting Sir Henry, whose responsibility for her was now at an end.

"Farewell, Jailer," she said impishly. "I hold no grudge against you. You were but doing your duty. I make no doubt that you are glad to be relieved of your responsibilities."

"God Almighty knows that it was the most joyful news that I had ever heard," he told her fervently. "Believe me, I wish you well, madam."

Elizabeth bent forward and whispered in his ear. "If ever I have the power to have any prisoner sharply and straitly kept, Sir Henry, I will send for you!"

She smiled wickedly and watched him depart, escaping with heartfelt relief, no doubt, to the council chamber. Then she turned and went into her lodging, and was pleasantly surprised to discover that she was to be housed in a degree of splendor.

Blanche, who was allowed to come and go as she pleased, soon put paid to Elizabeth's hopes of pleading her cause to Mary.

"The Queen has gone into seclusion to await the birth of her child, my lady," she informed her disgruntled mistress.

"Then why am I here?" Elizabeth asked. "Surely it was the Queen who wished to question me. Had it been the council, they would have sent a deputation."

Such a deputation arrived the following afternoon, much to her surprise and concern.

"Madam," Bishop Gardiner said, bowing, "the Queen has taken to her chamber and cannot see you just now, but she is convinced that you have much to confess to her. If you would have an audience with her, you must tell all to us first. I assure you that, if you do confess, Her Majesty will be good to you." The old man suddenly fell to his knees. "I beg you, submit to the Queen!"

This was not what Elizabeth had been hoping to hear. She had returned in high hopes of a successful meeting with her sister. Was she still suspected of treason? Had she really only been brought back to court as a prelude to being consigned once more to the shadowy grasp of the

Tower? That was unthinkable. She must stay strong and not betray such fears.

"I am innocent and therefore have nothing to confess," she declared firmly. "Better for me to lie in prison for the truth, than to be abroad and suspected by my prince. In yielding, I should confess myself an offender toward Her Majesty, which I never was, and the Queen and the King would thereby ever afterward conceive an evil opinion of me."

She stood indignant and proud. The lords began murmuring among themselves, wary of angering her further.

"I will convey your words to Her Majesty," Gardiner said, rising to his feet.

"I tell you, madam," the Bishop said, "nothing further is likely to be obtained from the Lady Elizabeth."

Mary, resting on her bed, hands crossed over the huge mound of her belly, grimaced and tried to raise herself. Her ladies came hurrying to help her.

"I marvel that she should so stoutly stand by her innocence," she said bitterly. "Well, she shall not be set at liberty until she has told the truth. She will remain here under house arrest."

King Philip, who had been standing by the window, looking out over the privy garden, came over to her bedside.

"Let me talk to her," he said. "I should very much like to meet her."

"It would do no good, my lord," Mary told him jealously.

"Nevertheless I insist," he said, adamant.

"The decision is mine," she faltered. "I am the Queen, and she is my sister."

"And I am your husband," Philip said challengingly. "I command it." His blue eyes were icy, beautiful but cold.

"Very well," Mary capitulated, with great reluctance. "I see I cannot dissuade you."

"My finest robes, Blanche," Elizabeth ordered. "That is what the Lord Chamberlain said. The Queen has commanded me to put on my finest robes and prepare to receive the King. And I too would look my very best, for much depends on this meeting."

He was married to her sister, but Philip, she knew, was an experienced

and handsome man of twenty-eight, and he must be not only curious
about her but also susceptible to feminine charm, if rumor spoke truth.
She must dress to advantage, and present herself at her most beguiling . . .

She had few outfits with her—much of her wardrobe had been left at
Ashridge—but she had brought one court dress, packed in the hope that
she would one day have occasion to wear it. It was of white damask
beaded with pearls and had a low, square neck, cut wide on the shoulders;
it showed off her small breasts and slim waist to perfection. She would
wear her red hair loose, as a royal virgin.

Thus attired, she sank into the deepest of curtsies when the door
opened late that evening and the King was announced. A well-set,
brown-haired man with a pointed gold beard strode into the room. He
was much shorter than she had expected; he owned the famous jutting
chin of the Habsburgs, and his eyes were chilly, but he greeted her courteously, nonetheless, and himself raised her to her feet. She smiled at him,
and in that moment, the cold eyes took fire and began regarding her appreciatively, raking up and down her person . . .

King and princess they might be, but in that moment they were both
aware of being first and foremost a young man and a young woman alone
together. Elizabeth had been deprived for so long of male admiration that
she responded involuntarily to the King's admiring scrutiny. The shock
of lust that coursed through her loins was as unexpected as it was delightful. She was careful, though, to remain outwardly calm, and bent her
head demurely so that Philip should not see the triumph in her eyes and
the flush in her cheeks.

"So you are the lady who has been causing such an uproar," he said, in
heavily accented Latin.

"It was never my intention, Your Majesty," she replied in her own
eloquent and fluent Latin. "I assure you, I have been greatly slandered by
my enemies. I am innocent of the things that were alleged against me."

He stood unspeaking, regarding her closely. She ventured a peek from
under her eyelashes, then, seeing that some dramatic affirmation was
called for, threw herself to her knees in front of him, taking care to lean
forward sufficiently to expose as much of her bosom as was seemly above
the low-cut gown.

"As God is my witness, I never intended any harm to the Queen my
sister," she cried, shaking her head so that the burnished red tresses swung

about her shoulders. "But no one believes me, and for well above a year now I have lived in the awful knowledge that everyone thinks ill of me, and it is *so* unjust." The tears that now welled up were genuine, but she arrested their flow. No man was at ease with a weeping woman, though a hint of distress might melt the hardest heart.

Looking at her, and marveling at how different from her sister she was, Philip could now understand why Mary had not wanted him to see Elizabeth. For the young female kneeling before him was slender and charming, and if she was not conventionally beautiful with her thin face and hooked nose, she had an undefinable allure about her that inspired the most erotic thoughts in him. What would it be like to take this girl to bed and do with her as his fantasy led him? Nothing like the ordeals he had had to endure on the matrimonial couch, that was certain!

Was she as innocent as she claimed? He did not know and, frankly, no longer cared, but he wanted her friendship at the very least.

"I believe you, Princess," he said at length. "Do not distress yourself further." Suddenly, his strong hands were grasping her forearms and he was pulling her to her feet. In her relief that it was going to be all right—after hearing his words, she could not but assure herself that all would now be well—she felt light-headed; swaying slightly, she nearly lost her balance and, righting herself, fell gracefully against his chest.

Instantly, there was that *frisson* between them, a *frisson* she had known once before, all those years ago, with the Admiral. A feeling of recognition, of her bones melting, of desire fueled by physical closeness—and there was no feeling like it. She felt alive again in that instant, gloriously alive, and desired.

Yet it was she who pulled away. He was the King, and married to her sister. There was no question of anything ever being between them, and the rational part of her mind bade her be glad of it. For in the course of her long seclusion, she had discovered that the most important thing to her in life was freedom: the freedom to come and go as she pleased, to make her own choices, and not constantly to have to submit to the will of others. Such freedoms did not come with marriage—indeed, *any* close entanglements with the opposite sex. Better by far to be satisfied with the sweet, heady pleasures of flirtation and courtship than to commit herself further to any man. What she loved was being admired, being wanted, being pursued—but she did not think she wanted ever to be caught.

"I beg your pardon, sir," she apologized, standing back.

"I would be a friend to you," he said.

"Your Majesty does me too great a kindness," she replied. "Forgive me if I am overwhelmed. I am not used these days to being listened to and heeded."

"One day, I hope, you may have the chance to repay me with a similar friendship," Philip said softly. The edge to his voice told her that there was more to his meaning than mere politics.

"If I can ever be of service to Your Highness, I shall not hesitate," Elizabeth replied and swept another low obeisance, feeling that she had played a good hand by winning Philip over.

The Queen's child was due any day now. Early May, the doctors had said, but when the middle of May arrived without any sign of a birth, they tugged at their beards and said that, yes, they had miscalculated, and that the babe would surely come later than expected.

Mary remained in strict seclusion, and in another part of the palace, Elizabeth too was confined to her rooms, for she was still under guard. Yet isolated as she was, she could sense the undercurrents of tension that were pervading Hampton Court. Thanks to Blanche, an avid listener to gossip, she was aware of the foreign ambassadors, waiting to send news of the birth to their respective governments; of the courtiers, laying bets as to the sex of the infant and speculating as to why the Queen had been so wrong about her dates; and of the King, anxious to see his son safely born and to be away to war. For him, a single hour's delay seemed like a thousand years.

But the days turned into weeks, and it was now nearly June. Looking at his wife, Philip was certain that her belly had shrunk a little, and a terrible suspicion came upon him, which he dared not voice, for she was by now so dejected that she spent much of her time sitting on cushions on the floor with her knees drawn up to her chin, staring at the wall. He wondered that a gravid woman at her stage could manage such a position, but again he kept his fears to himself. He was beginning to doubt that this pregnancy would have a happy outcome, and was even starting to speculate that his wife was not pregnant at all but suffering from some female malady. In which case, it was of the utmost importance that her rift with her sister Elizabeth was immediately healed, and that he be recognized as the one who had brought about a reconciliation and the restoration of Elizabeth to her proper place in the succession.

Yet he had to go carefully with Mary. There must be no suggestion that all was not well.

"Why not send for Elizabeth?" he said gently. "I assure you that your fears about her are unfounded, and that she wishes you nothing but well. Receive her back into favor. She could be a support to you at this time, and her company could help to relieve the tedium of waiting."

Elizabeth's company was the last thing Mary wanted just now, and she suspected that Elizabeth had used her wiles on Philip to bring him to this glowing opinion of her, but she was anxious to please him, for—much to her grief—he was going away as soon as this tardy infant was born, and she wanted to make sure that he had reason to come back to her.

"If it pleases you, my husband, I will send for her," she agreed, suppressing her forebodings.

"I will have her summoned," Philip said with one of his rare smiles.

Elizabeth was astonished and afraid when, at ten o'clock that evening, the door to her lodging opened and there stood Susan Clarencieux, Mary's chief lady-in-waiting. What could this betoken? she wondered. Had the Queen been delivered, and had Clarencieux, who had never been a friend to her, come to inform her and gloat over her displacement?

"I am here to escort you to Her Majesty's apartments," Clarencieux said coolly. "She wishes to see you and hear you make answer for yourself."

Elizabeth turned pale. So Philip's assurance had been premature. Mary still suspected her. And if she did not give a good account of herself, all unprepared as she was, it might go ill with her this night.

Trembling, she turned to Blanche Parry.

"Pray for me," she muttered, "for I have no idea whether I will ever see you again." Blanche looked at her tragically with tear-filled eyes.

The lady-in-waiting was brisk.

"There is nothing to fear, I am sure. The Queen is disposed to be merciful. I suggest you put on your finest clothes for the audience."

When Elizabeth was ready—she had laid aside the seductive white gown in favor of a high-necked crimson velvet one—Clarencieux held her torch aloft and led her down the stairs and across the moonlit garden to the Queen's lodging. There, they ascended to the privy chamber, and when they were admitted, there was Mary, alone in the room, seated in her chair of estate, her graying red hair straggling over the shoulders of the loose robe she was wearing. There was little sign of any high stomach beneath it, and she looked older and very drawn, with deep lines dragging her mouth downward.

Unsmiling, she extended her hand to be kissed, but Elizabeth, overcome with emotion at being in Mary's presence at last, and seeing her sister so ravaged, threw herself on her knees, weeping uncontrollably. This was the Mary who had been a second mother to her in childhood, her Queen to whom she owed loyalty and fealty, whose mind Elizabeth's enemies had poisoned. Things *must* be put right between them while there was still time, for Mary looked old and ill, and not only were there ties of kinship and allegiance to be mended, but there was also a pressing need for the older woman to look with kindness upon the girl who might yet be her successor.

"God preserve Your Majesty!" she cried, tears streaming down her face. "Whatever people have reported of me, you will find me as true a subject of Your Majesty as any!"

Mary turned away, breathing heavily. She waved Clarencieux out of the room, leaving only the two of them in the flickering candlelight. When she did speak, her voice was heavy with sarcasm.

"You will not confess your offense, will you? You stand stoutly in your truth. Well, I pray God it may so fall out."

Elizabeth was stung. "If it does not," she answered vehemently, "I desire neither favor nor pardon at your hands."

"Well," Mary said, disappointed that Elizabeth had not denied her guilt more categorically, "since you so stiffly persevere in your truth, and will not confess any wrongdoing, are you saying that you have been wrongly punished?"

"I must not say so, if it please Your Majesty, to you," Elizabeth replied meekly.

"But you will to others?" Mary pursued.

"No, if it please Your Majesty!" Elizabeth protested. "I have borne the burden and I must bear it yet. All I humbly beseech is for Your Majesty to have a good opinion of me, and to think me your true subject, not only from the beginning, but forever, as long as life lasts."

The Queen said nothing. Instead, she rose stiffly and went over to the window. The casement was open to let in the balmy night air, and a soft breeze stirred the tapestry that hung nearby.

"God knows if you are speaking the truth," she murmured, turning to gaze fixedly at her sister.

"I take Him for my witness," Elizabeth said firmly. In that moment, her face was lit up in the glow from the candles and Mary could clearly see the outline of their father King Henry's profile. There was no doubt of it, no doubt at all: It was him to the life. Good, honest woman that she was, she realized that she had deeply wronged Elizabeth with her baseless suspicions. Now, God be praised, it would be easier for her to do as Philip wished.

Elizabeth was wondering why Mary kept staring at her, but suddenly she saw something that disturbed her. The Queen's robe was gaping slightly, revealing the fine chemise beneath; yet for all that she was at full term, the swelling of her belly was hardly visible. Elizabeth was puzzled, but there was no time to speculate further, for Mary had moved swiftly toward her, holding out her hands and grasping Elizabeth's in a claw-like grip.

"I want to believe you, Sister," she said, her eyes moist. "For the sake of the kinship between us."

"Then believe it, madam, for you have no cause to doubt it!" Elizabeth urged her. "I would never betray you nor wish you harm, I assure you."

"Then we are perfect friends again," said Mary, attempting a smile. "And you shall be set at liberty forthwith, and take your place at court."

Elizabeth fell to her knees again and kissed the Queen's hand most fervently.

"You shall have no cause to doubt me, I swear it!" she vowed.

When she had gone, her heart singing, away into the night, Philip stepped out from behind the tapestry.

"A touching scene," he observed. "You have her on your side now. There is no more need to fear her." He walked to the table and poured himself a goblet of wine.

"Think you not I can dissemble with the best of my race?" Mary retorted. "Yes, I have taken her back into favor. Yes, I may have wronged her. Maybe she was not as culpable as we suspected. But as for fearing her?

I shall fear her to my dying day!" And she burst out in copious, noisy tears.

"All the better then that you keep her under your eye," Philip said coolly, sipping his drink. "But mind that you treat her with respect, if not affection."

Mary looked at him miserably. She was not a fool: She was in no doubt that Elizabeth was now under Philip's protection, and that in some ways, she might be more important to him than Mary herself. Small wonder, she thought bitterly, for Elizabeth represented the future.

Dear God, she prayed, when will my son be born?

Elizabeth was not sure what to do next. The guards had been removed and the Chamberlain had told her that she might receive visitors, but few came, and she deemed it wise to keep to her rooms for the present. It was as well, because, due to the Queen's prolonged confinement, the court had sojourned overlong at Hampton Court, and the palace was now fetid with the stink of overflowing privies and hundreds of sweaty bodies. On her few forays from her lodgings, Elizabeth witnessed scuffles and scraps between courtiers frustrated at being cooped up in such an atmosphere.

Everything was in suspense, waiting on the Queen's delivery. The business of the kingdom was at a standstill, the mood of the people ugly. The King rarely appeared in public, so embarrassed was he at the interminable delay and the whispers to which it was giving rise.

June came and went; July—and the doctors said again that they had muddled the dates. The expressions worn by the courtiers were deeply skeptical, Elizabeth noticed. Faces turned to her in expectation and hope. Inwardly elated, she ignored them; she dared do no else.

One day, she looked out of her window and glimpsed the Queen in the privy garden. Mary appeared to be her normal slender self; there was obviously no babe inside her. Yet still the pretense was maintained that the birth was imminent.

"It would take a miracle!" Elizabeth observed privately to Blanche, who, in the absence of her beloved Kat, had become her confidante. She knew she could trust Blanche, who was utterly devoted to her.

"It is the judgment of God," whispered the Welshwoman.

"That's as may be," Elizabeth replied, ever practical, "but the continuance of this charade, to my mind, is a ploy to keep the people in hope, and thus in check."

"It cannot go on forever," Blanche said.

"No, it cannot," Elizabeth agreed. "The Queen has been pregnant for eleven and a half months now."

"Is she ill?" Blanche asked.

"I think not," Elizabeth considered. "My belief is that she desired a child so much that she believed she was pregnant. Unless it was all a pretense, but that I cannot accept. My sister is too honest a lady."

"Whatever the case, I hope we can move from here soon," Blanche said. "The palace is unbearable, what with the heat and the stink."

"I think there will be an announcement soon," Elizabeth opined. "This cannot go on for much longer." She was striving to suppress her inner excitement, for the abandonment of Mary's hopes would mean the restoration of her own.

There was no announcement, just the Lord Chamberlain telling her that the King and Queen had removed to the royal hunting lodge at Oatlands with their attendants.

"Her Majesty desires me to tell you that you are absolutely free and may go where you will," he informed her. His manner was far more deferential than hitherto, for it was now almost certain that the Queen would have no child, and the courtiers, who had reacted to this realization with pity or scorn, were according Elizabeth a new respect as the likely successor to the throne.

She could go where she pleased? Her heart leapt in elation, for on hearing those words, she realized that she was, indeed, free at last.

In August, the Queen summoned her to Greenwich to be present when Philip departed for the Low Countries. Elizabeth was gratified that Mary wanted her there, but put out when the Queen insisted that she travel by water rather than by road.

She does not want the people showing their affection for me, she thought. And she wants me under her supervision, for she does not trust me.

She was even more offended when she saw the ramshackle old barge that the Queen had sent to collect her. It had been patched up and painted, but it was still a sorry sight, and there were cries of "Shame!" from the riverbank, where hordes of common folk had gathered, as if in defiance of the Queen's command, as soon as word of her coming spread.

At Greenwich, she found her sister too busy to see her. In fact, Mary was making the most of her final hours with Philip. All too soon, the time passed, and when the moment came for his departure, she said her agonizing, tearful farewells in private, then stood stony-faced at the top of the great staircase, helplessly watching him descend and walk away from her and through the great doorway, bound for the waiting ship that would take him to Flanders. Until he was out of sight, she held on to herself, then when she could bear it no longer, she withdrew into her apartments and hastened to a window in the gallery, desperate for one last glimpse of her beloved. Following with the other ladies, Elizabeth watched her sister break into anguished sobs as she waved her kerchief at the distant figure on the departing ship.

It did not do to give your heart to a man so entirely, she thought. Men did not value what they came by easily. Once you loved, you laid yourself open to pain. She would not make the same mistake as her sister, that much was sure.

With Philip gone, the court was a gloomy place. It was as if it had gone into mourning. As if in reflection of the Queen's desolation at being deprived of both her expected baby and her husband, its inhabitants had taken to wearing dark colors.

"I suppose I must go about looking like a crow in these weeds," Elizabeth grumbled, holding up her black velvet gown. "You would think the King had died."

"I mind there was a time when Your Grace liked to dress in black," Blanche reminded her archly.

"That was in my brother's reign," Elizabeth said dismissively. "We are all good Catholics now, and must dress the part. But I must say I do not relish looking like a nun."

"I do not think Your Grace would make a very good nun!" Blanche giggled.

"I would be a very rebellious nun!" Elizabeth laughed. "I should certainly eat too much!"

There was not much occasion for laughter these days. Occasionally,

Mary would send for her, although clearly she did not delight in Elizabeth's presence. She made it quite clear that she was extending her favor only because it was Philip's desire that she should do so.

"His Majesty has written again of you," she would say. "He constantly commends you to my care, and requests that I be a gracious prince to you." Her tone always implied that, but for Philip's exhortations, relations between them would be far less cordial.

And indeed, as Mary had feared, Elizabeth was proving a constant thorn in her side. Her youth and barely restrained vitality were in themselves enough to arouse the older woman's resentment, but above all Mary could not bring herself to trust her sister, and must always think the worst of her. Then she would despise herself for it, and remind herself that Elizabeth was truly her own flesh and blood, to be loved as such. But she found that so hard, so very hard.

"She hates me," Elizabeth told Blanche. "When we meet, we exchange mere courtesies and discuss the weather. I know she is jealous of me, if only because I enjoy the favor of the King. And because I am her heir. I can understand it, of course: What man loves his own winding sheet?"

"But Your Grace goes with her to Mass daily," Blanche said. "That must please Her Majesty."

"Oh, yes, and I even fasted for three days for the sake of saving my soul," Elizabeth reminded her, wincing at the memory of how ravenous she had been at the end of it. "Yet it avails me little. The Queen remains suspicious, Cardinal Pole is unfriendly, and the courtiers shun my company. But I have one friend at court. Master Ascham was recently appointed Latin Secretary to the Queen, and she has agreed that he may spend some time each week in study with me. I have so longed for some intellectual stimulation!"

It was wonderful to see Master Ascham again, and it was clear, from the broad smile on his face when he rose from his bow, that he too was delighted at the prospect of resuming his tutelage of Elizabeth. But all too soon it became evident that their abilities were now evenly matched and that he could teach her little.

"I marvel at your learning!" he told her. "Your mind is so well stocked."

"That is a miracle," she told him, "since I was more than a year without the means to pursue my studies."

"Your understanding of Greek is better than mine," he enthused warmly. "And I am struck with astonishment at how you grasp the political conflicts in Demosthenes. I never understood them so well. I might teach you words, my lady, but you teach me things!"

Elizabeth beamed at him, drinking in his praise.

Their sessions together were not always so lighthearted.

"They have burned Bishops Latimer and Ridley," Ascham told her in October, his face heavy with grief. "Two of the finest minds in the kingdom."

"Take care, Roger," Elizabeth warned. "Even the walls have ears here. Your sympathy might be misconstrued for heresy."

He bent forward.

"That would not be far from the truth," he murmured. "I conform outwardly, but my heart is still wedded to the reformed faith. And yours too, I'll wager, madam."

"Shhh!" Elizabeth hissed. "You'll have us both fried! I am the Queen's loyal subject, and I will not gainsay her on any matter."

"An answer answerless," he observed.

"I like your turn of phrase," she smiled. "I will remember it for future use."

Her smile faded.

"Did they suffer much? The bishops, I mean."

"Latimer died quickly," he told her. "I had it from one who was there. But Ridley—his agony was terrible. It took him three-quarters of an hour to burn."

Elizabeth shuddered.

"Cranmer will be next," she said. Cranmer, that zealous Protestant, who had helped her father to break with Rome, who had declared Mary's mother's marriage null and void and her daughter a bastard. There would be no mercy for Cranmer.

"In truth, I long to get away from the court," Elizabeth confided nervously. "It is so treacherous and full of menace. The intrigue, the backbiting, I weary of it all. I feel too that I am here on sufferance, and I fear that, with an ill-chosen word or deed, I might quickly find myself in disgrace once more, or worse . . ." She was thinking, he knew, of the martyrs, the scores of brave men and women who had chosen a fiery death rather than recant their faith.

"Take heart," he murmured. "The people love you. Openly they speak of you as their savior, the one who will call a halt to this brutal persecution and pack the Spaniards off home."

"Me, with my little power?" Elizabeth asked with a sad smile.

"One day," he mouthed.

Days later, with the Queen's blessing—given with more alacrity than was flattering, for it was obvious that Mary was glad to see the back of her—Elizabeth was on her way to Hatfield, happy to be riding northward to her own house. How the people came running to see her, crying her name and cheering from the roadside! So rapturous was their acclaim that she feared it would give great offense to the Queen and rebound on herself, so she sent her gentlemen among the crowds, with instructions to quiet and restrain them. Yet still the bells rang out in every parish to proclaim her coming, and she could not hide her delight.

"This is some hope of comfort to me—as if appearing out of a dark cloud," she told Roger Ascham, who had been given leave to accompany her to Hatfield and was riding by her side.

But there were a few in her retinue who were not smiling. She knew who they were: servants who had been appointed by the council—spies, no less. She noted their set faces and leaned closer to Ascham.

"Rest assured, Roger, we need to be on our best behavior even in the privacy of Hatfield. No one will come or go, and nothing will be spoken or done, without the Queen's knowledge."

"You think so?" He frowned.

"I know it!" She smiled grimly, bending to receive a posy from a little girl who had darted out from the crowd. "I will be watched, so we had best make sure we attend confession and Mass regularly. Is that not so, William?" She looked at faithful Cecil, her surveyor, who had come to meet her on the road and was riding on her other side. She was glad to see him again, this trusted friend of hers, who had always given her such wise advice as well as unstinting loyalty.

"I should always counsel Your Grace to conform to the Queen's wishes," he said. "My constant prayer is for the preservation of Your Grace."

"Mine too!" Elizabeth added, grinning and lightening the mood, and both men laughed.

—

Waiting for her at Hatfield was Kat, dear Kat, whom the Queen had now restored to her service. She flung herself into Kat's waiting arms with scant regard for ceremony, and both women had tears on their cheeks when they drew apart. And Thomas Parry, brought back to his duties as her treasurer, was waiting also, bowing low until she raised him up and kissed him. There was so much to talk about—eighteen months of their lives to catch up on—and supper that night, which was served in the small parlor, was a private, merry occasion, attended only by Elizabeth and her closest friends. They were still there in the small hours, when the embers of the fire were dying and the room growing chill, although they were laughing so much that they did not notice.

That night, Blanche Parry willingly relinquished her customary duties to Kat, who had performed them for so many years.

"It is *so* good to have you back," Elizabeth said for the hundredth time as Kat began brushing out her long hair. Kat had grown noticeably older and a little stouter. "I cannot tell you how much I missed you, and how I feared for you," Kat confided. "There was a time . . ."

"I know," Elizabeth interrupted with a shiver. "Don't let's speak of that. It is over and done with. All I have to do now is keep my wits about me and stay alive. God will take care of the rest. The future is in His hands."

Elizabeth had not been at Hatfield three weeks when Thomas Parry came hastening to her, his face betraying fear.

"I am just returned from the market, my lady," he panted. "There is talk . . . talk of a plot to assassinate the Queen and set Your Grace on the throne."

"A plot?" Elizabeth went cold.

"Aye. More than one, if rumor is to be believed. But all has been uncovered by the council."

Elizabeth started trembling. If she were to be implicated in these plots, she would not be given another chance, of that she was certain.

"The craven fools!" she cried. "How dare these traitors conspire in my name? Do they not realize that they place me in the most terrible danger?"

Any moment now, she realized, the Queen's officers might come for her. She must preempt them: She must write and protest her innocence. She flew to her desk.

I am Your Majesty's most loyal subject, she protested passionately. *I had nothing to do with these treasonable conspiracies.*

There was no reply. And after several agonized weeks of waiting, she realized there would never be. All she could conclude was that there was no evidence against her, or that no councillor was prepared to move against her.

CHAPTER 20

1556

Elizabeth stared at the letter with its royal seal dangling.

"She cannot mean it!" she cried.

"What does Her Majesty say?" Cecil asked, looking up from his papers. He was rarely away from her these days—almost constantly in attendance as not only her surveyor but also her unofficial secretary and counselor.

"She wishes me to marry King Philip's son, Don Carlos," she told him, her face registering distaste. "He's ten years old, for God's sake, a hunchback, and mad to boot!"

"He is a good Catholic," Cecil said wryly.

"Such a good Catholic that he tortures children, servants, and animals!" Elizabeth retorted. "I heard he had bitten the testicles off a dog."

She began pacing up and down, so great was her indignation.

"This is the Queen's revenge! She has been plotting this for a long time. She wants me out of the country and safely married in Spain, as she thinks that I will then pose no further threat to her. Well, I will not consent to it, and I shall write and tell her so. She cannot force me to marry a madman!"

"Well said!" Ascham smiled from the end of the table.

"She will not marry him," Mary told Cardinal Pole. "She alleges he is mad."

Pole considered awhile, deliberating, while the Queen waited. Good man that he was, his understanding of political affairs was not as acute as Gardiner's had been. She missed Gardiner, dead these six months, and she missed Philip even more. He had been gone for far too long, and she ached for his presence. *He* would know what to do with Elizabeth, and whether to take her alleged involvement in these recent plots seriously. But Philip's letters had become fewer and fewer, and at Christmas he had summoned the last members of his household from England. Mary saw that as ominous, but she dared not voice her fears in case they became reality. What if she never saw him again? She would pine away and die, she knew it.

"Your Majesty is set on this marriage?" Pole was saying.

"Indeed I am," she told him. "By removing my sister bodily from this realm, I will rid myself of the chief cause of all these recent disturbances."

"Has Your Majesty considered that any plan to send the Lady Elizabeth out of the kingdom might provoke insurrections on her behalf?" Pole asked. Really, this problem of the princess had to be resolved, he knew, for it was proving a distraction from the great work of restoring the faith in England. "She is popular, and has given no cause for offense."

"Her very existence offends me!" Mary cried shrilly. "How do I know she is not plotting against me? Her name has been at the center of all those half-baked plots. And there is that traitor, Sir Henry Dudley, skulking in France and raising a force with a view to overthrowing me, and the French are backing him. Their aim, I have no doubt, is to put my sister on the throne."

"Again, we have no proof that she is involved," the Cardinal pointed out. "Her past experiences will have taught her that it would be foolish in the extreme—indeed, fatal—to involve herself in any treasonable conspiracy."

"Nevertheless, this protest against the marriage with Don Carlos— could it be that she disdains to go to Spain because she has hopes of my throne?"

"That is mere speculation, madam, and again, there is no proof." Pole was growing weary of Mary's obsessive suspicions.

"She was at Somerset House until February, and that was when we first heard of the traitor Dudley's activities," Mary recalled. "I want that house searched, and any papers found there examined. We may yet find something to incriminate her."

"Very well, madam." Pole sighed. "I will give the order. But I warn you that you may end up looking rather foolish."

"I will risk that," Mary snapped.

In May, the Queen's officers arrived at Hatfield.

"We have orders to arrest Katherine Astley," they informed an aghast Elizabeth.

"No," she whispered. This was as unexpected as it was awful. What did it herald? The beginning of some new calamity? Would the Queen never trust her, nor those she loved?

"No!" wailed Kat.

"Where are you taking her? What has she done?" Elizabeth demanded.

"Our orders are to convey her to the Tower for questioning," the Captain said.

"But why?" Elizabeth persisted, wrapping her arm tightly around the weeping Kat.

"The council wish her to be examined about certain papers that were found in Somerset House," he informed her.

"Papers?" Elizabeth echoed.

"I know nothing of any papers!" Kat cried. "I have done nothing wrong!"

"No, but they think to use you to trap *me*," Elizabeth muttered. "They dare not move against me because I have the King's protection, but they would if they found aught against me. Be careful what you say in case it is misconstrued and twisted into treason. They remember that you talked once before under questioning. They think to make you do it again."

"Come now!" the Captain commanded, and Kat was hustled out to the waiting litter, looking back desperately over her shoulder.

The papers, it seemed, were merely a pretext. As far as Kat could tell, there was nothing in them to incriminate herself or anyone else. But she was so distressed that she could not think straight, and her interrogators were relentless in their questioning.

"Tell us again. Did you or the Lady Elizabeth know anything about Sir Henry Dudley's conspiracy?"

"No!" Kat protested for what seemed like the thousandth time.

"Has either of you had any contact with the traitor Dudley?"

"Never. We are both loyal to the Queen, and the Lady Elizabeth's love and truth is great in regard to Her Highness. If she thought me lacking in my allegiance, I am sure she would never see me again."

She was not believed—she had protested their innocence too loudly, it was felt—and after several days, she found herself cast into the Fleet Prison, with only rats and mice for company in her damp, fetid cell. There she gave way to despair. If they could treat an aging woman thus, how far might they proceed against her beloved Lady Elizabeth?

Back at Hatfield, Elizabeth endured an agony of suspense, wondering what they were doing to Kat and praying for her return.

Her hopes were raised when, in June, Lord Hastings and Sir Francis Englefield, loyal councillors both, came to see her.

"Madam, we are come to extend the Queen's apologies for the removal of your servant Mrs. Astley," Sir Francis said. "However, her arrest was necessary because her conduct might have exposed Your Grace to the manifest risk of infamy and ruin."

"My lords, what are you talking about?" Elizabeth demanded. "Mrs. Astley is as loyal to the Queen as I am myself, and she loves me so well that I know she would do nothing to my injury."

"That is yet to be established, madam," Hastings said, "but in token of Her Majesty's goodwill, she has sent you this diamond ring, saying she knows you to be so wise and prudent that you would never wish to undertake anything to her prejudice."

"Indeed I would never," Elizabeth said firmly. "But I am concerned about my servant. I trust she is well housed and fed?"

The men exchanged uneasy glances.

"Don't tell me—she is in a dungeon!" Elizabeth snapped. "Well, that will be remedied at once. I will give you money to pay for a better lodging for her, and for food to be sent in. Until, of course, she is released,

which should be forthwith, for she has done nothing worthy of reproach."

"Let us hope that she proves herself an honest woman," Englefield said
piously.

"It is for the State to prove that she is not," Elizabeth reminded him.

"They can get nothing out of the woman Astley," Cardinal Pole said.

Mary frowned. "I had hoped she might be of use," she confessed. "Of
course, it is really my sister whom I would like questioned, but that is not
possible." Not without Philip's approval, Philip, who was clearly susceptible to Elizabeth's wiles. Mary would do nothing without his sanction.

"I would have had *her* consigned to the Tower, but for the fear of
reprisals," she said aloud. "I have sent a fast courier to the King asking for
his advice."

No need to wonder what that will be, Pole thought. And he was right.

"His Majesty wills that I send a kind message to my sister," Mary told
him just days later. "He urges that I use loving and gracious expressions to
show her that she is neither neglected nor hated, but loved and esteemed
by me." Her voice was bitter. If only Philip had so great a care for her
own feelings. "And he says I should invite her to court."

"A sound suggestion," Pole commented. "His Majesty shows great
wisdom. Better to have the Lady Elizabeth here, under your eye, than free
to plot sedition at Hatfield."

"I thank Her Majesty for her kind invitation, but regret that my domestic
duties here preclude me from accepting," Elizabeth told the royal messenger. "Perhaps I may reconsider when my servant, Mrs. Astley, returns."

It was a bold message, and afterward she sought out Cecil and told him
what she had said.

"I wonder if I should have been so provocative," she murmured.

"Having done nothing wrong, you have every right to express indignation," Cecil told her. "They will prove nothing against Mrs. Astley, of
course. They have only proceeded against her because they dare not proceed against you, madam. That is transparently clear. So calm yourself,
for you are in no danger, and neither is your good Mrs. Astley."

"You speak sense," Elizabeth said. "If it were not for your wise counsel, I do not know what I should do."

—

The next thing was the arrival of the elderly Sir Thomas Pope, a genial Catholic gentleman, whom the Queen had appointed governor to her sister.

"I am not so stupid that I do not realize he is here to keep an eye on me," Elizabeth told Cecil. "Since when have I needed a governor?"

"He is here for your protection too," Cecil advised her. "His vigilance will prevent your enemies from accusing you of any subversion. If I were you, madam, I would make him welcome."

"I will take your advice, old friend," Elizabeth promised.

With Sir Thomas Pope came a widowed gentlewoman, Mrs. Cox, sent by the Queen to replace Kat. She was the image of moral rectitude, pious, sober, and chaste, yet amiable and willing, but Elizabeth refused to allow her to perform Kat's duties.

"Blanche Parry will undertake them," she informed Mrs. Cox. "We are used to each other, and she served me well when Mrs. Astley was absent before."

Mrs. Cox nodded meekly and dipped her curtsy, but she saw to it that she was a constant presence in Elizabeth's life; there she would be, at mealtimes, in the gardens, in the gallery, and in the parlor of an evening. Elizabeth bore her presence with fortitude, remembering that what Cecil had said of Sir Thomas Pope also applied to Mrs. Cox.

Sir Thomas she liked. He was a learned man, a man of law who had founded a college at Oxford, and his intellect was lively. He made an entertaining dinner companion, and when Master Ascham was present, the conversation was stimulating and witty.

"Did you know I used to be a friend of Sir Thomas More?" he asked her.

"I did not," Elizabeth replied. "I know there was a great stir when my father, King Henry, sent him to the block."

Sir Thomas sighed. "That were a pity, whatever the right of it. He was a marvelously learned man, with a merry spirit, and a great one for educating girls, too."

"Ah, then I cannot but approve of him!" Elizabeth smiled.

They talked some while of Sir Thomas's plans for his new college, at which he became very animated.

"Shall you admit ladies?" Elizabeth provoked him.

"The very idea!" He chuckled.

"Ah, but if you did, my lady here should be first in line!" Ascham put in admiringly.

"Then I must eternally regret that our rules prevent me from having the pleasure of enrolling you, madam," Pope said chivalrously.

On another occasion, the talk turned to entertainments.

"I hear you enjoy drama," Sir Thomas said to Elizabeth.

"I love nothing better than a good masque or play," she told him.

"Then with your permission, we shall stage one here!" he promised, and thus it was that she and her household came to enjoy rousing performances of that old favorite, *Fulgens and Lucrece,* and the poet Skelton's famous old-fashioned interlude *Magnificence*.

"My father used to speak of this play," an appreciative Elizabeth told Pope. "He loved the way the political evils pitted their wits against the political virtues." Sir Thomas smiled approvingly.

"Next week, we shall put on a masque," he announced. "Will Your Grace do us the honor of dancing in it?"

"I should love nothing better!" she declared, recalling the heady days of her childhood, when she had thrilled to the masques at court. The only thing to mar her pleasure was her continuing worry over the absent Kat.

In July, there were graver matters than masques to discuss.

"I am instructed by the council to inform Your Grace of a most disturbing incident," Sir Thomas said, looking distressed.

Elizabeth seated herself. "Tell me," she said sharply, wondering what new trouble was afoot.

"A schoolmaster called Cleobury, from Suffolk, recently took it upon himself to impersonate Edward Courtenay, Earl of Devon," Pope related. "And he made a priest in Huntingdonshire proclaim from his churchyard that Queen Mary was dead, and that Your Grace and your—forgive me, I am only quoting what is written here—beloved bedfellow, *Edmund* Courtenay—heavens, he couldn't even get the Earl's name right—were now Queen and King of this realm."

"That is outrageous!" Elizabeth cried angrily. "How dare this fellow presume to name me in this calumny!"

"Indeed, indeed," Sir Thomas agreed. "You will be gratified to learn that he and the priest were arrested, and that under questioning it became clear that they were acting entirely of their own accord."

"So why did the council see fit to acquaint *me* with this wickedness?" Elizabeth asked. "It is nothing to do with me!"

"They say that they but wish you to know the whole circumstance, so that it might appear how far these men abused Your Grace's name."

"In truth," she replied, "how will the Queen ever trust me if foolish men bandy it about so wantonly and treacherously? I must write to her and let her know that I am sensible of her position."

For she did fully understand now why Mary saw her as a threat. Even if she herself was loyal and true, there would always be those who would seek to conspire in her name—that much was becoming clear. Yet was this not, in part, Mary's fault? If her rule had been popular, and there had been none of these terrible burnings, or the enforcement of her religion, there would have been no need for any man to rebel or rise against her. The only way to keep the throne safe was through the hearts of the people. Of course, Elizabeth could not say as much to the Queen, but she did attempt to reassure her as eloquently as she could of her own loyalty.

Whatever others suggest or compass by malice, she wrote, *I know well that Your Majesty should rest in the sure knowledge that I am true; so that the more misty clouds obfuscate the light of that truth, the more my honest thoughts should glisten and dim their hidden malice.*

All she could hope for was that, as she now understood and sympathized with Mary's position, Mary would understand and sympathize with hers.

Elizabeth was ill that August, laid low with jaundice and attacks of breathlessness. Missing Kat's homely ministrations, she suffered miserably in the heat, unable to read or concentrate on anything for very long, and wishing she were well again so that she could go out riding or for the long walks she so much loved.

She was convalescent, and still chafing against her inactivity, when Sir Thomas came to her in September and informed her that Courtenay was dead.

"He died in Padua," he related.

"Of what cause?" Elizabeth asked curiously.

"Of a fever, following a fall," Pope said.

"There was perhaps more to it than that," Cecil revealed later when they had a few moments alone together. "More of human help than divine, or so they say. There is talk of poison and assassins. His death stood to benefit both England and Spain, and certainly it has removed the threat of a Plantagenet claimant making a bid for the throne."

"And scheming to marry me," Elizabeth added. "Think you the rumors are well founded?" Her eyes were anxious. "Because, if so, I fear I will be next."

"They would never dare," Cecil declared. "Not while King Philip is your protector. He has no desire to see the Queen of Scots on the throne. That would not suit Spain at all. So calm your fears."

"Courtenay was a frivolous young man of little substance," Elizabeth recalled, breathing deeply to ward off the breathless attack that fear had provoked. "I cannot pretend I am not relieved that he is dead, may the Lord forgive me. I have grown weary of my name being linked to his. God has once again shown His justice."

And God again showed His justice the next month, when Mary was moved to free Kat from prison. Again, Elizabeth welcomed her faithful servant with open and loving arms, again they wept on each other's shoulders, bitterly regretting the wasted months of separation and anxiety.

Clearly, the tide had begun to turn again, and evil had once more been averted. That the Queen was of the opinion that Elizabeth no longer needed to be kept under surveillance was made plain when Sir Thomas Pope announced his imminent departure.

"I shall be sorry to lose such a good friend," she told him sincerely.

"And I, madam, am loath to leave. I have enjoyed my time here," he replied, bowing low. Then, mounting his horse, he was off, cantering down the road back to London.

Watching him go, Elizabeth wondered if she was free at last of the intrigues and perils that had surrounded and threatened her these past few difficult years. Somehow, she could not quite believe it.

"The Queen has summoned me to London," she told Kat that November. "I am to come in some state, for she has an important matter to discuss with me."

"I wonder what that can be?" Kat looked suspicious.

"Mayhap she wishes to talk of the succession," Elizabeth opined. "With the King gone so long, and her health so uncertain, she cannot be in hope of an heir of her body."

"Let us pray she has come to her senses at last," Kat said fervently. "You deserve to be honored as her successor. And I shall see to it that you go to court looking every inch the part."

Soon, the bed was heaped with gorgeous fabrics and rich gowns, and Elizabeth was raking through her jewel chest searching out her finest pieces.

"I shall summon my tenants," she declared. "I shall have two hundred gentlemen to attend me, and all shall wear new velvet coats."

And so, regally attired in dark green velvet furred with squirrel, which set off her burnished red tresses to perfection, she rode through London, bowing to left and right to acknowledge the joyous welcome of the people. At Whitehall, the Queen received her graciously, raising and kissing her, and led her into her privy closet, where delicious sweetmeats and hippocras had been left ready.

Elizabeth was struck by how prematurely aged and melancholy Mary had become. Certainly she had been overburdened by the cares of state and plagued by ceaseless plots, yet Elizabeth was sure that the King's absence had more to do with it than anything else. Mary was pining, that much was clear, had been pining for fifteen months now, and there was no end to it in sight.

As soon as the pleasantries had been exchanged, the Queen came to the point.

"His Majesty has found a husband for you," she said.

Elizabeth stared at her, shocked.

"In view of the recent conspiracies—none of which, we know, were your fault—both he and I feel that it would be best for you to be married to some trusty Catholic prince who can be relied upon to be loyal to both England and Spain. Such a prince is the Duke of Savoy."

Elizabeth was appalled.

"Madam, I have little inclination to marry at all," she said quickly.

Mary smiled faintly. "Neither did I, Sister. I too experienced the same maidenly reluctance, yet when it came to it, I discovered that all my fears were unfounded."

If only you knew, Elizabeth thought. Aloud, she replied, "I do not fear marriage, madam. Rather, I am resolved to live out my life in the state of virginity, as a single woman."

"But that is unnatural," Mary demurred. "All women need the fulfill-ment that marriage can bring. You cannot live like a nun! And besides, princesses like us must marry for reasons of state. The King and I have been very happy . . ." Her voice trailed off, and she looked anything but happy.

Elizabeth was desperate. The idea of marriage was distasteful to her for pressing reasons. When she came to the throne—and now, in her mind, it had become *when,* not *if*—she had no mind to share power with any husband; she would have but one mistress in her realm—herself—and no master. She had seen the unhappy consequences of her sister's marriage, and did not want any repetition of them. Moreover, how could she, as queen, rescue England out of the clutches of Rome if she were married to one of the greatest Catholic princes in Christendom? Then there was the thing she had vowed she would never submit to again, the bed thing, with its terrible risks of pregnancy and death. She prided her-self now that she was above wanting it. Once bitten . . .

She could not marry Savoy; she *would* not!

"I cannot consider it! I would rather die!" she burst out, finding, to her dismay, that she was weeping. "I am not a well person," she protested. "Your Majesty does not know all of it, but I assure you that the afflictions suffered by me are such that they have ridded me of any desire for a hus-band." There! She had gone as far as she dared.

Mary looked at her robust, healthy sister sitting opposite and was at a loss for words.

"Afflictions?" she repeated. "What afflictions?"

"Female afflictions," Elizabeth said shortly.

Mary reached across tentatively and touched her hand.

"I am your sister as well as your Queen," she said. "You can tell me, woman-to-woman."

"I cannot, for shame," Elizabeth replied, hanging her head so that Mary would think she was blushing. "Suffice it to say, I know for sure that I am not capable of congress with any man. So I beg you, madam, do not force me to this marriage."

Again, Mary was nonplussed. Was this yet another of Elizabeth's tricks? Could she believe it?

"I am sorry to hear that," she said gently. "It may be that this is a problem that can be remedied. Have you consulted a physician about it?"

"I need no physician to diagnose what I know to be true!" Elizabeth declared. "I beg of you, madam, do not press me further. The matter is too painful to me."

She sounded genuinely upset, and so Mary deemed it wise to leave all discussion of the marriage for the time being.

"I am sorry to see you so distressed. We will talk further of this another day," she said. "Now if you wish to retire, I have had Somerset House made ready for you."

"I thank Your Majesty for your kindness," Elizabeth said, dabbing at her eyes with her kerchief. Then, making her obeisance, she thankfully withdrew, relieved to have deferred the matter of Savoy for the present. For one terrible moment, she wondered if she had gambled too far—and that Mary might insist that she be examined by the royal doctors or a panel of matrons, who would surely find that she was no virgin at all, and might even discover evidence of her pregnancy, for all she knew. Yet she reasoned that the danger of that was slight, counting on Mary's innate prudery and reticence regarding such matters. And Mary had been sympathetic, had not pressed the matter. At the very least, Elizabeth had bought herself some precious time in which to figure out what to do next in order to wriggle out of consenting to this marriage. But how much time?

It was clear how the wind was blowing by the number of lords and ladies who came to pay their respects to her at Somerset House over the next few days, Elizabeth noticed. Among them was Frances Sidney, Countess of Sussex, whose husband had ever been a friend to Elizabeth, especially in the dark days when she had been a prisoner in the Tower. Frances was a striking redhead and so like Elizabeth in looks, they could almost have been taken for twins. Elizabeth warmed to her so readily that the pair of them were soon bosom companions, and the Countess's visits frequent and prolonged.

Elizabeth wondered whether she might confide in this new friend. She had told the trusted members of her household—Kat, Ascham, Parry, Cecil, and Blanche—how fearful she was that the Queen would force her into marriage with the Duke of Savoy, and their reaction had at once heartened and dismayed her.

"You must resist it!" Cecil had enjoined her. "The Queen's health is poor; it cannot be long now. The good people of this country have put their trust in you, and look to you to deliver them from this persecution. Marrying the Duke would be a recipe for disaster. If all excuses fail, you must escape abroad, and hold yourself in readiness to return when the time comes."

"Abroad?" Elizabeth exclaimed.

"William speaks truth," Ascham said. "It is wise advice, and you would do well to heed it."

"But how?" she had asked.

"The French ambassador would be only too happy to help." Cecil smiled. "His master would do anything to discountenance this pro-Spanish government."

"But I cannot approach him directly," Elizabeth pointed out. "My every move is watched."

"And I carry no weight," Cecil added glumly. "I am persona non grata with the Queen and council, and an unknown as far as foreign courts are concerned."

"I could write a letter to Monsieur de Noailles," Elizabeth suggested.

"Too risky," Cecil said.

"What is needed, madam, is some loyal person of consequence who could approach the ambassador for you," Roger Ascham deduced.

"Alas, there is no one," she replied. "And anyway, I must think on the matter. It would be a drastic step, leaving this kingdom."

This morning, however, she had received a personal note from the Queen, saying it was her pleasure that Elizabeth give her an answer without delay with regard to marrying the Duke. There was no doubt about it: She was being pressed into agreeing to the match.

And now, sitting opposite her in the great chamber, was the young Countess. Dare Elizabeth ask her to be an intermediary to the French ambassador?

"I would do anything in my power to assist you!" the Countess declared when Elizabeth said she craved a favor, one of great import.

"You must first swear to keep this matter secret," Elizabeth said gravely. "It is a high matter of policy, involving the Queen herself, and your involvement would incur some risk to yourself. If that is unacceptable to you, then we will say no more of it."

"Dear madam, I have said I would serve you, in any matter, and I stand firm in that!" Frances declared passionately.

Elizabeth relaxed.

"Then this is what I want you to do," she said.

"I cannot agree to it," de Noailles said. "The Lady Elizabeth's place is here, and she should not be contemplating such a desperate step. She should remember what is at stake."

"But she is being forced into this marriage!" the Countess protested, her face white and agitated beneath the dark hood of the cloak she had worn to conceal herself on this late-night expedition to the French embassy.

"On no account must she leave England!" the ambassador said with finality. "She must tell the Queen that she does not consent to this marriage."

"She has done that, but the Queen is putting pressure on her."

"Then she must resist. She cannot be forced into it."

"I do not think you understand, monsieur. It would be dangerous for her to displease the Queen."

"And even more dangerous for her to attempt an escape. Even if she succeeds, she will put her chances of attaining the throne in jeopardy." De Noailles was adamant.

"I am disappointed in you, sir," retorted the Countess with spirit. "I had thought to find you ready to assist a lady in distress. But if you will not help me, then I must make shift for myself. I am sure the King your master will heed my request if I lay it before him in person. He will grant her a refuge."

The ambassador looked at her, astonished.

"I beg of you, madam, do not do this," he pleaded.

"My mind is made up. You will not dissuade me," she answered. Gathering her cloak about her, she swept out of the room, passed furtively through the door of the embassy, looking from left to right in case she was seen, and disappeared into the night.

"Does anyone know why the Countess of Sussex took it upon herself to go to France?" the Queen asked her councillors. Most of them looked blank.

"Our intelligence is that she has lately returned from that land," Cardinal Pole supplied. "It seems strange that she went there without first seeking a safe conduct from Her Majesty here. Nor does she have any connections in France, nor any reason to go there, which seems odd."

"I am credibly informed that she had visited the Lady Elizabeth frequently before her departure," Mary said. "Which is why I smell a rat."

"Shall we have her questioned?" Lord Hastings suggested.

"She has been questioned already," Pole told him. "She insists her trip was made purely for private purposes, but when asked what they were, she seemed unable to say for certain."

"My advice is to keep an eye on her, madam," Paget said. "It may be that her journey was innocent. But since the Lady Elizabeth may be concerned, you never know."

Elizabeth stood before Mary. The privy closet was chilly despite the burning brazier, the weak December light fading.

"I have summoned you here to have your answer as to whether or not you will marry the Duke of Savoy." The Queen, swathed in furs, opened the conversation.

Elizabeth fell to her knees. Resist, they had said; resist with all your might. That was her only alternative now, after the French ambassador and the King of France had insisted she remain in England.

"Madam, I crave your indulgence, but I cannot marry him," she declared. "Your Majesty knows why."

The Queen blushed faintly. "Such matters may be remedied," she said decidedly. "I will send my physicians to you."

"Madam, I beg of you, no!" cried Elizabeth, panic mounting.

Mary's anger flared.

"Why do you thwart me at every turn?" she shrilled. "You are my heir, God help me, yet at times it seems you are more my enemy."

"I am Your Majesty's most assured friend," Elizabeth protested hotly. "My feelings about marriage have no bearing on that."

"Your marriage is an affair of state, negotiated to the advantage of this kingdom—*my* kingdom!" Mary pointed out. "Do not defy me in this most important regard."

"But madam—"

"Enough!" Mary snapped. "You know that I have the power to disinherit you? Or put you in the Tower, or even send you to the block?"

Gathering all her courage, Elizabeth outfaced her.

"I think we both know, madam, that neither the King nor Parliament would sanction any of those punishments," she said softly, quivering at her own daring.

Mary stared at her.

"You grow too insolent!" she cried. "May I remind you that it is the King who desires this marriage? He will not take kindly to being thwarted. I warn you, Sister, there will be repercussions from this, and if it is in my power, I will choose someone else to succeed me!"

"Then, madam, I make no doubt that the Duke will no longer find me as desirable a bride!" Elizabeth retorted.

"You will leave court!" Mary exploded. "Without delay! I cannot bear the sight of you."

"I will go to Hatfield then, with your permission," Elizabeth said evenly. She had begun to feel her power.

"You may go to Hell for all I care," Mary flung at her. "And you may rest assured that I will never name you my successor."

"Name me or not, that is what I am!" Elizabeth countered, then rose to her feet and curtsied herself out of the room, leaving the Queen speechless with fury.

Philip was coming back to England!

Mary's heart was bursting with jubilation and thankfulness as she sank to her knees in the chapel before the statue of the Virgin and Child. He was returning to her; his household was on its way ahead of him. Soon, they would be reunited, and once again they would enjoy that blessed union that God had ordained for all married couples. And if He was willing, there might yet be some chance of a child, a Catholic heir to succeed her . . .

In her joy, she was unable to feel any more rancor toward Elizabeth, had put their quarrel firmly behind her, and was indeed happy to comply with Philip's request that her sister be summoned to Greenwich for the Christmas festivities, there to await his coming.

Elizabeth looked up with surprise when Mary, having summoned her back from Hatfield, greeted her graciously and presented her with a fine gift of plate.

"I am not worthy," she murmured, astonished at the Queen's change of heart.

"You may thank the King's Majesty," Mary replied, but there was no real sarcasm in her voice. She was a woman in love, and her beloved was coming, very soon . . .

CHAPTER 21

1557

Ruy Gomez, Philip's great friend and close adviser—but lately arrived in England—stood before the Queen.

"Your Majesty will have heard that the French have broken their truce with us and attacked Douai," he said gravely.

"Indeed I have," she replied, "and I have demanded of my council that England go to war to support Spain."

"Yes, madam, but we have received reports that your councillors have refused their consent," Gomez said accusingly, almost glaring at her in his stiff, Castilian manner.

"That is true." She sighed. "They say that England cannot afford a war, that this war does not concern us, and that we are not bound by treaty to support the King in his wars. I have, of course, declared to them my pleasure."

"May I remind Your Majesty that declaring war is the sovereign's own prerogative?" Gomez asked coldly.

"I fear to do that without my council's support," Mary demurred.

"Perhaps Your Majesty will act when I say that the King has commanded me to tell you that his coming to England will be dependent on your promise to declare war on France," Gomez said smoothly.

Mary's sharp intake of breath was audible. It was cruel, cruel . . . but even now, she would not blame Philip. I am on the eve of bankrupting my kingdom or my heart! she thought. But there was no choice.

"Tell the King that I promise to persuade my council to agree to the war," she said faintly. "And I pray you, beg him not to be afraid to come here!"

The bells were pealing and the court en fête for Philip's arrival at Greenwich. Elizabeth, alighting from her flower-bedecked barge, saw that her sister's tired face was radiant with expectation, observed her agitation as they waited for the King to disembark, and watched as Mary clung tightly to him, unable to restrain her tears. He, in turn, maintained his usual correct composure, but when he came to raise Elizabeth from her curtsy, he muttered, "Think not that I am come just to persuade this people to war. I am come to conclude your marriage with Savoy, so think not to defy me."

Elizabeth bent her head, her cheeks flaming. Did he think to suborn her, with the throne so nearly in her sights? Well, he would find that he had met his match. She was resolved not to marry with Savoy or any other.

She rode with the King and Queen to Whitehall, through streets packed with cheering citizens, but their shouts were not for Mary and Philip. Sensing the royal couple's displeasure and resentment, Elizabeth dared not acknowledge the people's acclaim. She stood fuming at a court reception for the King's kinswomen, the Duchesses of Parma and Lorraine, who had come to England, it was rumored, to escort Elizabeth to Savoy and her wedding to its Duke.

When presented to the Duchess of Lorraine, the former Christina of Denmark, whose famed beauty was still apparent, Elizabeth could not resist reminding her of a youthful indiscretion.

"I am sure Your Grace recalls that you might have been my stepmother," she said with a smile. "You will remember that my father King Henry asked for your hand."

The Duchess's cheeks flushed pink.

"I was very young at the time, Highness," she said.

"Am I right in saying you told him that if you had two heads, one would be at his disposal?" Elizabeth asked wickedly. The courtiers laughed.

"I may have done," the Duchess replied, looking embarrassed and put out.

"Instead, he married that lady there," Elizabeth said, pointing across the room to Anna of Cleves, now grown very fat. Anna was not at all well, she had heard; there was talk of a canker in her breast. Suppressing a shiver of concern, Elizabeth bent forward suddenly so that only the Duchess could hear her.

"I would rather die than submit to this marriage," she said low.

The Duchess looked confused, but the King came to her rescue, lifting her hand and kissing it.

"I trust you are being made welcome, dear cousin," he said, his eyes locking with the Duchess's. In that instant, Elizabeth knew that there was more than a bond of kinship between them.

Mary, watching across the room, had come to the same—for her, sickening—conclusion. Rumors had preceded Philip's arrival. How could he bring his mistress to England and flaunt her like this? And this marriage they were all clamoring for—could de Noailles be right when he warned that the Duke of Savoy, for all his standing, was poor and effectively stripped of his wealth?

Jealousy got the better of her. She would not pander to Philip's schemes, not when he was brazenly flaunting his mistress.

The next morning, Mary summoned Elizabeth and suggested she return to Hatfield. It was best, she said, that her sister was away from these political intrigues; privately, she did not want Elizabeth witnessing Philip flirting with that hussy his cousin. That Elizabeth should see her betrayed was not to be borne!

"But this matter of my marriage?" Elizabeth asked. "I had been given to believe that the Duchesses had come to conduct me to Savoy. In truth, madam, I had not realized that matters had progressed so far. I beg Your Majesty—"

"Have no fear," Mary interrupted. "Remove yourself from court. Do not return until I summon you. You will not be troubled."

Utterly relieved at finding Mary an unexpected ally, Elizabeth departed, her heart lighter, her mind freed for once from anxiety.

—

Philip regarded Mary with unconcealed distaste, seeing the wrinkles that had been graven by worry and melancholy, the thin body, the flat chest.

"I tell you, madam, she must come to court!" he commanded, ignoring her protests. "If I have to force her to take Savoy, then so be it."

Mary looked at him sorrowfully.

"You know my council is against the match," she reminded him. "And she herself is unwilling."

"Then offer to acknowledge her as your successor in return for her consent to the marriage," he suggested.

"Even if she agreed, which I doubt, the council would not approve it, of that I am certain. And she cannot marry without the council's permission."

"Am I to understand that you yourself are in agreement with them?" Philip demanded of her, his eyes narrowing.

"I have heard that the Duke is poor and thus not so great a match as we would wish."

"He is willing to come and live in England," Philip said quickly.

"What can he offer her, then?" Mary asked.

"He is a good Catholic and loyal to me," Philip answered.

"It is not enough," Mary said flatly. "Not enough to make me defy my council and override my sister's objections."

"Then you are failing in your duty of obedience to me, your husband," he accused her.

"And what of your duty to me as your queen?" Mary reminded him. "You are my consort."

"And you are my wife!" he objected hotly. "And as such, subject to my rule."

"You forget yourself," Mary cried, perilously close to weeping. "I am sovereign of this realm, and hold dominion over *all* my subjects. God knows I have tried to please you in all things, but sometimes the interests of my kingdom must come first. I cannot make Elizabeth marry against her will, nor against the will of my people."

"Bah!" sneered Philip. "You must make her do as she is bid. As you value my love."

The threat was all too clear. With a breaking heart, Mary summoned Elizabeth from Hatfield.

"No, madam, I cannot consent to it," Elizabeth said sorrowfully but resolutely.

"If you could but see your way . . . ," Mary cajoled, much against her better instincts.

"Madam," Elizabeth cried vehemently, "I assure you, upon my truth and fidelity, that I am not at this time minded to do other than I have declared to you—no, not even were the greatest prince in Europe to offer for me!"

"Then I must tell the King that you are adamant in your refusal," Mary said defeatedly. "Although, in truth, I do not blame you for it."

"I pray you do that, madam," Elizabeth begged her.

"Go back to Hatfield," the Queen said. "I do not know what the King will do, but it will go better with you if you are not here."

Elizabeth needed no second bidding. Later that month, when Mary paid an unexpected visit to Hatfield and the Savoy marriage—along with other contentious subjects—was not mentioned, Elizabeth concluded that the Queen had overruled her husband and that the matter had been quietly dropped.

During those brief days of the visit, the sisters were for once in harmony. Elizabeth received Mary with all honor, and went to considerable trouble to entertain her. There was a Latin play, a bear baiting, dancing, hawking, a recital given by herself on the virginals, and many other delights. The choicest food was served, and the finest wines. Mary's enjoyment was unfeigned. It was good to be away from the court and enjoy a peaceful sojourn in the country.

Elizabeth was hoping that Mary would say something about acknowledging her as her successor, but the Queen did not raise the subject. She was too preoccupied with the war in France.

"I have at last persuaded the council to send troops," she said. "I could do no less for my husband's cause."

It is not *our* cause, Elizabeth thought angrily.

"The King himself is to take the field." Mary's voice was anxious.

"He is leaving England again?" Elizabeth asked, surprised, then wished she could have bitten out her tongue: Her sister looked so tragic.

"He is needed on the Continent," Mary said. "He is waiting for the Spanish fleet to come for him." She turned anguished eyes to Elizabeth. "Pray for him, I beg of you," she enjoined. "And for me too. I cannot bear it when he is away."

Elizabeth promised to do so. They had little opportunity for further private talk, since so many entertainments had been planned, but relations between them remained cordial, if not warm, and all too soon the visit came to an end.

The sisters embraced that last morning in the courtyard.

"God go with you, madam," Elizabeth said as the horses were led over to the mounting blocks.

"I thank you again for your excellent hospitality," Mary called down from the saddle. "Farewell!" As she turned to ride away, Elizabeth and her entire household sank to their knees. The visit had passed off far better than she could ever have expected, Elizabeth thought.

There was a knock on the door of the royal bedchamber. Philip climbed out of bed, donned a velvet robe over his nakedness, and answered it. There was a brief exchange of muffled conversation; then he returned to his wife.

"The fleet has been sighted!" he cried, his face lighting up in the glow of the candles. "I must make ready!"

"Need you go so soon?" Mary whispered, dread in her heart. She had cherished these past nights, had given herself to him without reserve, and had almost managed to convince herself that, when it came to it, he would not leave her.

"My army is waiting," he told her, splashing his face with water from the golden basin that stood on the oak chest. She could see that he had gone from her already.

"I will leave my confessor with you," he said, "in the hope that he will be able to persuade you how vital it is that Elizabeth marries Savoy."

"I thought we had discussed that," Mary said, dismayed.

"Well, think again," he ordered her. "And think what might happen to our alliance if she takes a husband of her own choosing, who might plunge this kingdom into confusion!"

Mary said nothing. Speech was beyond her. All she could think of was that he was going from her.

"I must impress upon you the need for haste," Philip went on, relentless. "If necessary, the marriage can take place in my absence. And there is another thing."

Mary looked up miserably. He turned to face her, lacing his hose.

"It is desirable, nay, imperative, that you name Elizabeth your heir." If Mary died, he wanted a friend on the English throne to preserve the alliance, and with Elizabeth so beholden to him, he was convinced that he held her in the palm of his hand. Of course, there was also the highly desirable possibility that she might become more than a friend . . .

"No," Mary said, finding her voice and bitterly regretting that her last words to Philip would be words of defiance. "She may be my sister, and mayhap she *is* loyal to me these days, but she was born of an infamous woman who greatly outraged the Queen my mother and myself."

"You must forget that," Philip told her dismissively. "You must settle this matter of the succession."

"God may yet settle it for me," Mary said, blushing slightly. Anything to give him reason to return to her . . .

"You cannot count on that," Philip replied, losing patience a little. He was convinced that, for all his recent efforts in the marital bed—and a great trial they had been—Mary was too old to conceive. Look what had happened the last time!

Mary lay back on the pillows, deeply hurt.

"I am distressed that I cannot please you by naming Elizabeth my heir," she confessed, "but I have examined my conscience on the matter, and considered your arguments with a true and sincere heart, and still I know I am in the right, for that which my conscience holds it has held these many years. She is a heretic at heart, and I will not leave my throne to her."

"Then I am extremely displeased," Philip told her, his face thunderous.

He was still angry when, two days later, he bade her farewell on the quayside at Dover. Stony-faced, he dropped a dutiful kiss on her cheek, then strode away to the gangplank and bounded on board his ship. As she watched it being borne away on the waves, Mary bravely fought back tears, convinced she had looked her last on him.

The letter bore a plain seal. There was no crest. Elizabeth slit it open and was pleasantly surprised when she saw the signature. Lord Robert Dudley. So they had released him from the Tower at last.

He had written offering to serve her. He had sold land, he said, and was sending her money by separate courier, as proof of his loyalty. And lest there should be any doubt, he was prepared to die for her if need be.

Now, there's a man with an eye to the future, she said to herself, smiling. A man whose mettle matches my own, I shouldn't wonder. She called to mind his dark Italianate looks—my Gypsy, she thought—the proud bearing and strong, manly physique—and felt the stirring of desire, quickly suppressed. It would not do to cherish carnal thoughts of any man, in her situation. She might appreciate Lord Robert's admiration and zeal for her and her cause, but that was all, she told herself. She wanted no more from him; she was done with all that, and he was, after all, a married man. She herself had attended his wedding, back in her brother's time.

"What do you know of Robert Dudley?" she asked Cecil idly.

Cecil looked at her suspiciously.

"A rogue," he said impishly. "A brave man, but impetuous, and a good Protestant—or was—but a born intriguer. And since his release from prison, a favorite with the ladies too, I hear. Why do you ask?"

"I have had a letter from him." She handed it to Cecil.

"Well, well." He smiled. "It is good to have friends."

"I think I shall like having Lord Robert as a friend," Elizabeth opined coquettishly, unconsciously holding the letter to her breast. Cecil was thoughtful.

"I hear he has made a point of befriending members of the King's household," he told her. "He could prove useful to you in more ways than one. Cultivate him. A man who sells off land in your cause is one you may surely trust."

"I thought you said he was a rogue," Elizabeth taunted him.

"Perhaps I misjudge him," Cecil conceded. "His treason was long ago, after all. Methinks he has grown less hotheaded after that spell in the Tower!"

Elizabeth wrote to Dudley, thanking him for his gift and his desire to do her service. Her letter was the first of many. Soon, they were in regular correspondence, he lavish with his compliments and protestations of loyalty, she more reticent yet promising much, building bridges that she might, one day, wish to cross. She came to look for his letters, to thrill to his extravagant compliments, and to enjoy composing replies that he might take which way he would. There was no harm in it, she told herself. A mild flirtation—it added spice to her often dreary days.

M ay God help us, Calais is lost!" Cecil cried in a rare passion, bursting into the closet where Elizabeth was checking over Parry's accounts.

"Lost?" she echoed, shocked.

"It fell to the French at the beginning of January, after they mounted a surprise attack," he told her.

"I cannot believe it," she whispered, crestfallen. "Calais has been in English hands these two hundred years and more."

"Aye, and it was the last bastion of our territories in France," Cecil added. "Its loss must be a terrible blow to the Queen."

"But it is her fault!" Elizabeth declared. "It was she who embroiled us in this war, just to please her husband the King."

"Yes, she must bear the blame," he agreed. "She has to live with that. And I'll wager the King lifted no finger to save Calais."

"Surely Her Majesty will send troops to retake it?" Parry asked.

"Alas, my friend, I doubt this realm can bear the cost," Cecil answered. "By all accounts, the treasury is bankrupt. The country has never been weaker in strength, money, men, and riches. It makes me ashamed to be an Englishman."

"And the burnings go on apace," Elizabeth added. "The priests rule all. The realm is exhausted, our people out of order."

"I've even heard the Queen accused of being a traitor to her own country," Cecil revealed.

"And now we have a plague of influenza," Parry added. "Just to add to our troubles. I'll warrant it's been sent by God to punish the Queen for her sins."

"What remedy is there?" Elizabeth asked rhetorically.

"The people are looking to Your Grace," Parry told her.

"That's as may be," Cecil said hastily, "but there is further news, and you will not like it, my lady. The Queen again believes herself to be with child."

Elizabeth stared at him, horrified, then did a rapid calculation.

"But the King has been gone six months!"

"My contacts at court tell me that Her Majesty wished to be sure before making any announcement."

Elizabeth was incredulous.

"Can it really be true? Or is she misled yet again?"

"Maybe it is time for a visit to court, madam," Cecil suggested.

The needle flew in and out with speedy precision. At last, at last, thought Elizabeth with satisfaction as she snipped the thread and held up the tiny garment, which completed the layette she had hurriedly made as a gift for the Queen. It was her pretext for visiting court.

She arrived in February, attended by a great train of lords and ladies, and Mary received her graciously once more. Her belly was clearly distended beneath the unlaced stomacher, but she looked ill, drained, and hollow-cheeked.

"I trust that Your Majesty is in good health?" The conventional courtesy sounded all wrong.

"I am a little tired," Mary replied, "but that is to be expected in my condition. It will not be long now. Soon, I will be taking to my chamber to await the birth."

"I shall pray for a happy outcome for Your Majesty," Elizabeth promised.

She showed Mary the layette, the minute white garments, beautifully stitched and embroidered. The Queen was touched, impressed by the delicate workmanship.

"I thank you from my heart," she said warmly, "especially as I know how much you hate sewing!" They exchanged mutual smiles, Elizabeth trying not to stare at her sister's ravaged face.

"You will stay for the birth?" Mary pressed her.

"That is what I have come for, madam," Elizabeth told her. And to see if there really *is* a birth, she thought.

Days later, at the beginning of March, Mary went into seclusion, attended only by her waiting women and midwives, and the whole court held its breath and waited to see what would happen next.

There was no child. Inwardly triumphant, Elizabeth could not bear to face the Queen and witness her grief. Two months they had waited, two long months, until the Queen had finally given up hope. Now, sunk in a black depression, ill and feverish, she rarely emerged from her apartments.

"What they thought was a child is in fact a dropsy," the Countess of Sussex confided to Elizabeth.

"I fear for Her Majesty," Elizabeth said. "She has lost everything that mattered to her. And now it is whispered that she cannot live long."

"She has made her will," Frances confided. "My lord my husband told me."

"Did she name me her successor?" Elizabeth asked, instantly alert.

"No, madam, she did not. She was still expecting to be delivered, so she bequeathed the kingdom to the heirs of her body."

Elizabeth sighed. "She must resolve this sooner or later—especially now, with her being so unwell."

"She is not so ill that she cannot interest herself in the fate of the wretched heretics," Lady Sussex muttered. "Seven were burned in one fire at Smithfield this week. And it goes on, and on, with no end in sight."

"We can only live in hope," Elizabeth said, her meaning deliberately ambiguous.

She presented herself before the Queen, who looked beaten and ill. Elizabeth commiserated with her. Then she begged for leave to retire to her own house.

"Go with God," Mary said, kissing her.

"I hope to find Your Majesty much amended when next we meet," Elizabeth replied, and would have bent in her curtsy but for the Queen sister stopping her with a hand on hers.

"I know we have had our differences, Sister," she said, "and that there are some between us that can never be mended. Yet I have valued your support at this most difficult time"—she struggled to stem the ever-ready tears—"and I pray most sincerely that we may be better friends from now on."

"That is my earnest desire too, madam," Elizabeth said. They embraced, sisters and rivals, against whom the stars had conspired from the first, for the last time.

Elizabeth now knew that nothing but the Queen's life stood between her and the throne. She was therefore resolved to use this quiet time at Hatfield to prepare for her great destiny. She spent many hours closeted with Cecil, making plans, compiling lists of the people who would serve her, and drawing on all the lessons she had learned from her studies, her books, and her experiences to make ready for the formidable task that lay ahead of her.

The Duke of Feria came to Hatfield to see her, sent especially for the purpose from Spain by Philip.

"The King my master presents his compliments, Your Highness, and wishes me to express his goodwill," the Duke said, bowing low.

What, Elizabeth thought, no browbeating of me to marry Savoy, or anyone else for that matter? I was being buried alive with pressure to take a husband! What a change of tune!

Then suddenly it became clear. Philip knows that Mary is not long for this world, she realized. He is extending his friendship to me, sovereign-to-sovereign. For Philip, like she herself, had expectations of a crown: His father the Emperor was known to be dying, and he would soon be King of Spain.

"My master wishes you to know that he is a friend to you," Feria continued, "and hopes that he might in time become more."

Elizabeth raised her eyebrows. What could the ambassador be saying? Surely Philip was not proposing himself as a husband for her when his wife was still alive and reigning? Yet what else could she construe that remark to mean? It would certainly explain why the dreaded name of Savoy had not been mentioned. But marry Philip? Never!

"Tell your master the King from me that I am much pleased to see Your Excellency and gratified by his kindness and favor to me," she said aloud. "I am ready and willing to do his pleasure if it is at all in my power."

Feria was not done yet.

"There is a rather delicate matter I must broach, Highness. If, by happy chance, you ever find yourself in a position of power, my master seeks an assurance that you will remain true to the Catholic faith."

Elizabeth was on her guard. "Were it not for the fact that I know he means well, I should reprove your master for raising such a prospect," she said lightly. "The Queen still lives—may she long do so; it is treason for a subject to predict her death, therefore I may not discuss it."

Feria was impressed despite himself. Bowing himself out, he was struck by how deftly Elizabeth had handled that. To be sure, his master would have his work cut out dealing with that lady, and all Europe too, to boot!

As autumn drew in, Cecil grew worried. There was no doubt that the Queen was dying, yet by all reports, she had still refused to name her successor.

"You may yet have to fight for your throne!" he warned Elizabeth.

From his estate in Norfolk, Lord Robert wrote urgently, saying much the same thing, and offering to raise his tenantry if need be. Already, he was in correspondence with his friends at Philip's court. "The King wishes this kingdom kept in the hands of a person in His Majesty's confidence," he told Elizabeth. "That person is yourself. You may be sure of his support."

"The moment approaches, Your Grace," Cecil said. "Prepare yourself. It cannot be long now." Elizabeth thrilled to his words. She would be ready when the moment came.

Not knowing how much time they had, Cecil and Thomas Parry wrote urgently to the commander of the northern garrison at Berwick, who in turn appealed to the northern lords and gentry to support Elizabeth.

Ten thousand men stand ready to maintain her royal state, title, and dignity! the commander wrote back only days later.

As news of the Queen's illness spread, letters began arriving at Hatfield, letters from all over the land, from lords, knights, gentlemen, even yeomen, assuring Elizabeth of their staunch support, which they offered to back up by force if need be.

"I will never forget such kindness," she told Cecil and Kat and the others, tears in her eyes. "And I will repay it whensoever time and power may serve."

Then the courtiers began arriving at Hatfield, like rats deserting a foundering ship. All were come to pay court to the rising star and obtain her favor. When, having thanked them for their goodwill, she bade them return to St. James's Palace to attend the Queen, they begged to stay. Soon, the house was bursting at the seams with visitors, and newcomers had to be sent to find lodgings in the village. Yet still they came, a steady stream of well-wishers and self-seekers.

They were followed, in November, by the Master of the Rolls and the Controller of the Royal Household, sent to Elizabeth by the Queen herself. These two gentlemen bowed very low and looked grave. For a moment, Elizabeth thought they had come to tell her she was queen. But no.

"Her Majesty's condition is deteriorating rapidly, Your Grace," the Master of the Rolls informed her. "The Counsil is praying daily for her recovery, but to little avail. Indeed, it is obvious to all that she cannot last long, and this being so, my lords have persuaded her to make certain declarations concerning the succession. Madam, she has named you her heir, asking only that you will maintain the true religion and pay her debts."

Elizabeth walked over to the window, staring out unseeing across the park. It was coming, and soon, the moment for which she had long been preparing. In a matter of days, she would be queen. Her great battle for survival was almost over. She could not quite believe it.

Then she recalled Mary's condition requiring her to maintain the true religion. Well, she would do that! She would accept that condition, and even swear to it if need be. For Mary had not specified which religion. For now, it would be wise to dissemble. Another answer answerless was called for!

"I am humbled by Her Majesty's favor," she said, bowing her head. "Pray my lords, convey to her my assurance that, when God calls me, I will do all that is needful for the salvation of this kingdom."

"We will," the Controller promised. "And now all that is needed, madam, is for the council to confirm your right. I am sure there will be no difficulty."

"In the meantime, I shall pray for the Queen's Grace's restoration to health," Elizabeth said.

"That would take a miracle, madam," he replied, with the Master sadly nodding his assent.

Sir Nicholas Throckmorton, one of her faithful friends at court, sent her a brief message. *You shall know, when you receive from me a sacred token, that your hour has come,* it read. The promise in his words brought home to her just how near the throne was, and she blessed him for his forethought.

When I see it, I shall know, she thought. I shall know beyond a doubt that I am queen.

The Duke of Feria, finding no reason to stay at court, and mindful of his master's orders to cultivate Mary's successor, wended his way once more to Hatfield, where Elizabeth entertained him to dinner. He was struck by the new air of authority about her, yet dismayed to see the palace alive with young folk, courtiers and many whose religious views were suspect.

"Heretics and traitors," he muttered to himself. "Blatant self-seekers! Could they not have waited until the breath had left the poor Queen's body?"

Was he imagining it, or was Elizabeth a little less friendly than she had been before? He hoped he was mistaken, for her behavior was faultless. She congratulated Philip on his long-awaited accession to the Spanish throne. She sparkled enough at dinner, and kept Feria laughing with her witty conversation—but there was a brittle edge to her mirth. Then, when the hippocras and spices had been brought, and the cloth drawn, she grew serious.

"I should like you to express to King Philip my appreciation for all he has done for me," she said to the Duke, "and tell him that I look forward to being his friend in future. Tell him too that while the French hold Calais, they will never have my friendship."

Was she sincere? To Feria, her words sounded too glib, too rehearsed. He sensed that there was a deep intelligence at work here, an intelligence that even the wisest of men might not be able to divine. She might promise much on the surface, but she should never be trusted.

"His Majesty will be overjoyed to hear that, madam," he said formally, then added, so that there should be no mistake about it, "After all, Your Grace will owe your crown to him, for it was his persuasions that led to the Queen naming you her heir."

"Not so, my lord!" Elizabeth exclaimed with some passion. "I will owe my crown not to Philip, but to the attachment of the people of England, to whom I am much devoted, and the Queen herself knows that in her heart. *Vox populi, vox Dei,* remember: The voice of the people is the voice of God!" Seeing that he was offended, she added, "But I am grateful to the King for his efforts on my behalf, naturally."

Feria was determined to press his point. "His Majesty has also made your marriage his concern, madam."

Elizabeth smiled, tossing back long hair into which threads of diamonds had been laced, and pressed her elegant fingers against her cheeks.

"I know he wanted me to marry the Duke of Savoy, but to be candid with you, I have seen how my sister has lost the affection of her people as a result of making a foreign marriage—and I mean no disrespect here, for you must yourself be aware of that and will appreciate that I myself do not wish to make the same mistake."

Seeing his crestfallen face—had he really been about to broach the subject of her marrying Philip?—she leaned forward and gave him an arch look. "I might," she giggled, "marry the Earl of Arundel. He keeps mooning about here, making sheep's faces at me!"

Feria was a little shocked at her levity. Seeing his expression, Elizabeth's smile faded.

"Take no offense, my Lord Duke—it does me good to enjoy a little jest, and Heaven knows, there have been few opportunities for jesting in recent years."

"I am aware of that, Highness," he said quietly. There was a pause.

"Mine has not been an easy path to the throne," Elizabeth reflected, "and I am not there yet. I do not count my blessings before time. But when I think of what has been done to me during this reign, I feel highly indignant, for I have been under suspicion for most of it—for no cause, mind you—and even in danger of death. No, it has not been easy." Her eyes were flashing.

"But I have been fortunate in my friends. Cecil, for instance—I presented him to you earlier. I have already appointed him my secretary, for his wisdom and his fidelity."

"A wise choice," Feria conceded. Heretics and traitors all, he was thinking as Elizabeth enumerated the men whom she had chosen to serve her. At the same time, he could not help but admire her perspicacity and her incisive cleverness. She knew exactly what she was doing and what she wanted; he could not doubt that she would be a strong ruler. And she had the Tudor charm too, as well as the Tudor duplicity. She is her father all over again, he reflected.

When Mary woke briefly from her long stupor, Susan Clarencieux was there, watching by the bed. The faithful woman's eyes were brimming.

"Do not weep for me," the Queen murmured. "I will not need tears where I am going. And my dreams—so vivid they are—seem to offer me a foretaste of Paradise. There are little children, like angels, playing sweet music for me, giving me more than earthly comfort." In her drifting consciousness, they were the children she had longed for but never had, the children her empty arms had ached to cradle.

The priests came to celebrate Mass by her bedside.

"This is my greatest comfort," she told them, joyfully receiving the Host.

But later, as she lay listless on her pillows, the tears did come.

"She weeps for King Philip," the ladies said.

"No," came the weak voice from the bed. "Not only that. I weep for my greatest failure. When I am dead, you shall find the word *Calais* lying in my heart." Mary's face was twisted in pain.

Throughout the long November night, she felt her life ebbing away.

"Send to my sister Elizabeth," she urged, with all her failing strength. "Exhort her to preserve the Roman faith!"

"We will, dear madam," her attendants promised. Then they saw that she had faded into slumber again.

And still they came to Hatfield. The Great North Road was congested for miles with horses, litters, and sumpter mules as the courtiers and other notables flocked to the heir to the throne. And Elizabeth, for all her gratification at their coming, was shocked to see it.

The Queen still lives, she thought. Their first duty is to her. But no, they have seemingly forgotten that: In the race to seek favor with their future sovereign, they have abandoned their mistress to die alone. Well, it is a lesson well learned, she told herself. When it comes to the succession, I shall *never* reveal my hand. I shall keep them guessing!

As soon as the dawn had risen, Mass had been celebrated again, and Mary had made her responses in a clear voice. At the elevation of the Host, those with her saw her tremble as she bent her weary head in devotion.

Afterward, as her women bustled around the bedchamber, making all tidy, she fell asleep. But later, when they looked again, they saw that sleep had deepened into death, and that, gentle as a lamb, she had made her passage.

It was a crisp November day with a chilly breeze, but that had never stopped Elizabeth before. Soon after breaking her fast, she was out in the fresh air, pacing across the park at Hatfield, exhilarated at being by herself for once, and relieved to have left behind her the teeming, expectant household.

Some while later, she was seated under a great oak tree, wrapped in her heavy cloak, and reading her New Testament in Greek, when she heard the distant sound of galloping horses' hooves. Nearer and nearer they approached until she could see three riders making their way through the park toward the house. She shrugged and went back to her book. More place-seekers arriving, she thought dismissively. But then it became obvious that the riders had espied her, for they were turning their steeds and advancing in her direction. As they came nearer, she recognized the Earls of Arundel and Pembroke, sitting importantly in their saddles, and Throckmorton—yes, Throckmorton!—between them.

Her heart began to pound as she rose to her feet. Her hour was upon her, she was certain, and it seemed to her, as she endured those endless final moments of waiting, that Destiny and Providence had been preparing her all her life for it, and keeping her safe and secure. All the troubles, terrors, and obstacles that had beset her—her bastardy, her mother's execution, her precarious childhood, the scandal of the Admiral, the perils of religion and of being too close to the throne, her imprisonment in the Tower and subsequent house arrest, Mary's mistrust and the unwelcome schemes to marry her off against her will . . . She had survived them all, and to this purpose. What else could this be but God's will?

The lords were dismounting, falling to their knees on the damp grass before her.

"The Queen is dead. Long live the Queen!" they cried jubilantly. Then Throckmorton rose and pressed into her hand the token he had promised to bring her—Mary's coronation ring.

Elizabeth wanted to shout her triumph and gratitude to the skies, but the words would not come—she could not speak, so overwhelmed was she with emotion. Breathlessly, she sank to the ground, her heart bursting with thankfulness.

"This is the Lord's doing," she declared, finding her voice at last. "It is marvelous in our eyes!"

Then, collecting herself, she rose and gave the kneeling men—her subjects now—her hand to kiss, and bade them attend her back to the house, striding through the park, her chin high, her shoulders proud, looking every inch the queen. This is *my* kingdom, she thought, looking about her at the vast sweeps of grassland, the tall stately trees, the distant cottages and the great house before her—*my* England! And thus—the lords following behind leading their horses—she arrived at Hatfield to receive the acclaim of her people. And there, waiting in the courtyard, magnificent on his white charger, was Lord Robert Dudley, doffing his plumed cap and bowing low in the saddle, his eyes warm and twinkling.

Author's Note

In telling this story of Elizabeth I's early life, I have endeavored to keep as far as possible to the known facts. Most of the characters and events in this book are a matter of historical record, and much of the dialogue—although slightly modernized in places—is based on the actual words of people who lived at the time (sometimes transposed to another character for the purpose of putting across a point of view). However, I have nevertheless taken some dramatic license, and telescoped events here and there, particularly in the latter sections of the book. For example, I have dealt with certain issues in just one conversation when there might have been two or three that were relevant, and I have omitted one or two unimportant episodes in the interests of avoiding repetition, since they merely echo what has gone before.

I make no apology for the fact that, for dramatic purposes, I have woven into my story a tale that goes against all my instincts as a historian! Indeed, I have argued many times in the past, in print, in lectures, and on radio and television, why I firmly believe that Elizabeth I was the Virgin Queen she claimed to be, since the historical evidence would appear to support that.

Yet we can never know for certain what happens in a person's private life. There were rumors and there were legends, and upon them I have based the highly controversial aspect of this novel, Elizabeth's pregnancy. I am not, as a historian, saying that it could have happened; but as a novelist, I enjoy the heady freedom to ask: What if it had?

It is on record that in 1548 there were rumors about Elizabeth miscarrying Seymour's child. It was noted that she "was first sick about midsummer," about a month after arriving at Cheshunt, and the illness lasted until late autumn; during it, according to Mrs. Astley, Elizabeth had not gone more than a mile from the house. The very paucity of information about this illness could have been the result of a cover-up on the part of those who were anxious to avoid scandal.

The gossip about Elizabeth and the Admiral continued well into 1549. Jane Dormer, Duchess of Feria—a friend of Mary Tudor and therefore not unbiased—recalled many years later how a country midwife was visited by a mysterious gentleman in the middle of the night. He made her ride blindfolded with him, and took her to a mansion she had never seen before, to attend to "a very fair young lady" who was in labor. As soon as her child had been born, the man brutally had it "miserably destroyed." The midwife talked, and word soon got about that the young lady had been Elizabeth, no less, although the woman had not been sure about that. These are the original sources on which I have based this part of the novel, although, as a historian, I should like to stress that there is no reliable evidence that Elizabeth had a miscarriage, and that the theory rests on rumor and supposition alone.

The accounts of Admiral Seymour's morning romps with Elizabeth, and the shocking episode when her dress was cut to ribbons, are all based on fact. But it occurred to me during the course of writing this book that the traditional view of Elizabeth's governess, Kat Astley, as simply a loving and protective mother figure just does not fit in with what is known of her behavior with regard to the Thomas Seymour affair. Hence I have spun a subplot about her motives, which explains what possibly drove her to act as she did. It is on record that, immediately after Queen Katherine's death, Kat began pressing Elizabeth to marry Seymour.

Mary's suspicions as to Elizabeth's paternity are a matter of historical record—and unlike this story, they were never resolved—as are her increasingly difficult relations with Elizabeth. Modern readers may find the child Elizabeth unduly precocious; I make no apology for that, because she was exceptionally advanced for her years, as well as being formidably intelligent and sharp, and in this novel her precocity is based largely on that famous quote made to her governor when she was not yet three—"Why, governor, how hath it, yesterday Lady Princess, and today but Lady Elizabeth?"—and on her early letters, such as the one on page 68, as well as my own experiences as both mother and teacher of children.

Elizabeth's admiration for her father and reverence for his memory are also well attested. However, we have virtually no evidence for her feelings about her mother, and no means of knowing if she believed Anne Boleyn to be innocent or guilty. I suspect that the grim details of her mother's fate were too terrible to be disclosed in full to so young a child, and that she would only have found them out gradually. Nor do we know why Henry VIII banished Elizabeth from court in 1544; I have offered my own imagined version of events here. The supernatural scenes are fictional, but they are based on something that my mother experienced many years ago.

I have referred to Traitors' Gate as the watergate throughout, for it was not known as Traitors' Gate until the seventeenth century. There is no historical evidence to support the long-standing tradition that Elizabeth and Robert Dudley met, and perhaps were first attracted to each other, while they were prisoners in the Tower, but I have contrived one encounter!

Elizabeth's story has all the elements of high drama: suspense, tragedy, intrigue, and the dynamics that exist between strong and vivid characters. The sources I have consulted would be too numerous to mention here, and I would do better to refer any interested reader to the extensive bibliographies in my books *The Six Wives of Henry VIII*, *The Children of Henry VIII*, and *The Life of Elizabeth I*.

Above all, I have tried to remain true to Elizabeth, the greatest of all queens, and to portray her in character, from early childhood onward. She was a truly remarkable woman, and it has been sheer joy being able to write about her once more.

Acknowledgments

First, I wish to acknowledge my huge debt of gratitude to Anthony Whittome, my commissioning editor at Hutchinson, for suggesting this project and inspiring me to write with renewed enthusiasm about Elizabeth. I should also like to thank him for his expert and sensitive editorial suggestions, and to express my gratitude also to my line editor, the author Kirsty Crawford, whose own books I have so greatly enjoyed, and to the editorial teams at Hutchinson, Arrow, and Ballantine, in particular Kate Elton, James Nightingale, Mandy Greenfield, and Shona McCarthy.

I want to say a special thank-you to my agent, Julian Alexander, who has been tremendously supportive throughout, as ever, and whose invaluable creative suggestions have informed this novel. And I should like to thank Susanna Porter, my editor at Ballantine in the United States, for her enthusiastic and very helpful contributions, and Lisa Barnes, my American publicist.

I wish to convey my gratitude to Jeff Cottenden and Richard Ogle for producing another stunning jacket. I should also like to thank all the publishing teams in marketing, publicity, and sales for the excellent, but often unacknowledged, work that they do.

I cannot sufficiently express my appreciation to the historian Sarah Gristwood, author of *Elizabeth and Leicester,* for taking time out from a busy schedule to read my manuscript and offer her professional and much-valued observations. I wish also to say a huge thank-you to all the other kind people who have helped and supported me in various ways throughout the writing of this book, notably the historian Tracy Borman, who is herself currently researching a book on Elizabeth I; and also, in no particular order, my mother, Doreen Cullen; my son, John Weir; my daughter, Kate Weir; my cousin, Christine Armour; John and Jo Marston; Peter and Karen Marston; David and Catherine Marston; Samantha Brown at Historic Royal Palaces; Siobhan Clarke, Ann Morrice, Leza Mitchell, Lesley Ronaldson, Sarah Levine, and Kathleen Carroll at Hampton Court; David Crothers and Richard Stubbings at Kultureshock; Alison Montgomerie and Roger England; Jean and Nick Hubbard; Richard Foreman; Ian Franklin; Kerry Gill-Pryde; Father Luke at Holy Cross, Carshalton; Laurel Joseph at Whitehall, Cheam; Roger Katz and Karin Scherer at Hatchards; Gary and Barbara Leeds; Patricia Macleod and Anita Myatt at Sutton Library; Heather Macleod; Ian Robinson, for web design and management; Shelley and Burnell Tucker; Jane Robins; Jessie Childs; Nicola Tallis; Martha Whittome; Christopher Warwick; Kate Williams; Pete Taylor; Jo Young; Richard McPaul; Linda Collins.

Last, as always, my loving thanks go to Rankin, my husband. Without your constant devoted support, this book wouldn't exist!

ABOUT THE AUTHOR

ALISON WEIR published her first book, *Britain's Royal Families*, in 1989, and has since written many other historical works, among them *The Six Wives of Henry VIII, The Life of Elizabeth I, Eleanor of Aquitaine, Henry VIII: The King and His Court,* and *The Princes in the Tower,* as well as two novels, *Innocent Traitor: A Novel of Lady Jane Grey* and *The Lady Elizabeth.* She lives in Surrey, England, with her husband.

ABOUT THE TYPE

This book was set in Bembo, a typeface based on an old-style
Roman face that was used for Cardinal Bembo's tract *De Aetna*
in 1495. Bembo was cut by Francisco Griffo in the early six-
teenth century. The Lanston Monotype Company of Philadel-
phia brought the well-proportioned letterforms of Bembo to
the United States in the 1930s.